The Limited Edition Bicentennial Cadillac Convertible Joy Ride

ADVANCED PRAISE FOR MICHAEL JAI GRANT

"Michael Grant is a natural storyteller, literally setting the wheels in motion from the start. He has an eye for detail and obvious compassion for his characters, equally attuned to both teenage Eve and her octogenarian fellow runaway, Muriel. This is a road trip story unlike any you've read before, so jump into the back seat and enjoy the ride."

—Jennifer Armstrong, author of over 50 books including **'Shipwreck at the Bottom of the World'**. Many of her books have been designated as Notable Books by the American Library Association and the International Reading Association.

"This is a capacious page-turner of a novel, old-fashioned in all the best ways. Grant engages the imagination and lifts the spirits as he draws on a singular mix of delightful influences: Imagine Thelma, Louise, and Herbie the Love Bug eating fried green tomatoes at the Whistlestop Café. With its poignant plotting, nimble prose and winking humor, Joy Ride is a joyful read."

— Jim Gladstone, writer and cultural journalist, author of **'The Big Book of Misunderstanding.'**

ADVANCED PRAISE FOR MICHAEL JAI GRANT

"Michael Grant has written a thoroughly entertaining road trip bildungsroman whose principal characters consider their lives from opposite ends of existential crisis — the youthful angst of the as-yet-unknown, and a fading wisdom of how to accept the ultimately unknowable. With pathos and subversive humor, Grant constructs an intelligent framework for the plot, with a clever choice for narrator. All the elements of good storytelling are on display, told through prose with velocity and wit. It's a novel worthy of your consideration."

—Chris Millis, author, screenwriter

"Michael Grant's novel is a unique exploration of generational relationships and captures the truth that human connection supersedes age or circumstance. Michael Grant does a brilliant job of weaving his characters' many back stories into an entertaining page turner. Joy Ride illustrates that age has no limit on friendship, understanding, forgiveness and hope. Redemption is a beautiful thing especially when it involves a Cadillac! Bravo Michael Grant!"

—Candice Rosen, author

ADVANCED PRAISE FOR MICHAEL JAI GRANT

"Joy Ride is indeed an excursion, immersing the reader in a journey that highlights generational priorities and pitfalls. Grant deftly captures the essences of a teen girl and an aging woman, putting their nuances into a delightful interplay as the two fumble through life on the lam. From the scent of a car that's out of its era to the physical repercussions of aging, the book hits all the senses. Joy Ride drives the reader through the intersections of family, religion, and identity, carefully considering their complexities. Grant gives his readers a front row in the backseat of the book's titular Cadillac to an engrossing story whose truths echo through all of our lives."

—Julie Casper Roth, Filmmaker-Educator

The Limited Edition Bicentennial Cadillac Convertible Joy Ride

MICHAEL JAI GRANT

Wordbinders Publishing
Commerce City, Colorado

Wordbinders Publishing
An imprint of Journey Institute Press,
a division of 50 in 52 Journey, Inc.
journeyinstitutepress.org

Copyright © 2023 Michael Jai Grant
All rights reserved.

Journey Institute Press supports copyright. Copyright allows artistic creativity, encourages diverse voices, and promotes free speech. Thank you for purchasing an authorized edition of this work and for complying with copyright laws by not reproducing, scanning, or distributing any part of this work in any form without permission.

Library of Congress Control Number: 2023942915

Names: Grant, Michael Jai
Title: The Limited Edition Bicentennial Cadillac Convertible Joy Ride
Description: Colorado: Wordbinders Publishing, 2023
Identifiers: ISBN 978-1-7373591-7-3 (hardcover)
Subjects: BISAC: FICTION / Action & Adventure |
FICTION / Family Life / General |
FICTION / Sagas

First Edition

Printed in the United States of America

1 2 3 4 5 6 7 8 9 10

This book was typeset in Garamond, Anko / Visia Pro
Cover text in Century / Garamond

For Eleanor M. Zimmerman

Contents

MONDAY — 11
- Chapter 1 — 13
- Chapter 2 — 27
- Chapter 3 — 35
- Chapter 4 — 49
- Chapter 5 — 65
- Chapter 6 — 81
- Chapter 7 — 105
- Chapter 8 — 117

TUESDAY — 129
- Chapter 9 — 131
- Chapter 10 — 171
- Chapter 11 — 191

WEDNESDAY — 215
- Chapter 12 — 217
- Chapter 13 — 241
- Chapter 14 — 275
- Chapter 15 — 295

THURSDAY — 317
- Chapter 16 — 319
- Chapter 17 — 337
- Chapter 18 — 359

FRIDAY — 389
- Chapter 19 — 391
- Chapter 20 — 409

THANKSGIVING — 431
- Chapter 21 — 433

Acknowledgements — 465

MONDAY

12 | The Limited Edition Bicentennial Cadillac Convertible Joy Ride

Chapter 1

Eve stormed across The Deerwood parking lot to fetch her paycheck, the magenta stripe in her dark hair twisting with the pounding fury of every step. She was sick of work, of sweeping gray and white remnants from the floor of the noxious salon. She was sick of the residents there, so old, so many demented. She was sick of school, all commotion and petty dramas. She was sick of the lingering Florida heat ignoring summer's turn to autumn. Eve was even tired of her own stomping—when was she finally going to get a car? This angry energy propelled her across the pavement as she lamented her life: everything was annoying, everything was difficult, and everything she thought she understood about the world was wrong.

Her mother was a liar.

I was about two miles away when Eve stopped for a moment to tie her shoe and catch her breath. In ten more minutes we would enter each other's worlds and become instantly and forever entwined, but first I had to wait for Lucy and Muriel to return with the groceries.

It falls on me to tell Eve's story, which is equally Muriel's story, and my own. I cannot fully explain how I am able to tap into others' minds to share the parts where I wasn't physically present. I have theories, and we'll get to that, but at the risk of taxing your patience in the opening moments of this drama, suffice it to say that Yes, I am a car, and No, I do not talk or fly or have absurd magical powers. I cannot drive myself or even pop my trunk without a human turning the key, and before we go any further with your sensible questions about my unusual omniscience, it's far more important that you learn more about Eve before she finishes tying her shoe.

Almost a full day had passed since Eve's best friend, Laura, had confided that Liam was going to ask Eve to homecoming. Laura said Liam told Christian at swim practice, and Christian, Laura's brother, had no reason to lie. It was a sure thing, and Eve spent her Sunday evening shuffling between her trigonometry assignment and her closet.

Which ironic T-shirt to wear? *Tammy is riding vertically in a hot air balloon, directly over a point P on the ground.* Jeans, leggings, or shorts? *Tammy spots a* parked car on the ground at an angle of depression of 30°. Maybe a skirt? *The balloon rises 50 meters and the angle of depression to the car is 35°.* But then sneakers? Or boots? Is it still too hot for boots? *How far is the car from point P?*

Eve was unable to find an easy answer in either realm, and every time she thought something was solved, she circled back and reconsidered, literally spiraling on the sculpted beige carpet in her bedroom. While seeking fashion advice from the internet, a rabbit hole led her to the accidental epiphany that would keep her up until dawn and change . . . everything.

With her new information, she achieved less than an hour of anxious sleep. She showered in a fugue until the hot water ran out, then reworked her hair and dark eye makeup a half-dozen times before attempting another round against her wardrobe. The milky morning evaporated against the rising sun as Eve perfected the studs and loops in her ears—seven in all. She finally clomped her way to school, giving Liam at least eight minutes before homeroom to ask her, but the foreground task of securing her first real boyfriend seemed minor in light of her unfathomable revelation.

Nothing else mattered. Not even a first date. Sorta . . .

Eve pulled her morning books together and trekked down the industrial soap–scented corridor to Liam's far-end locker, the one decorated with little alligator magnets and a *Class of '19* sticker. He didn't show up before the bell, so she made her way to homeroom on the other side of the building, where Laura eagerly prodded: "Did he ask yet?"

"No, but hey, I have to tell you someth----"

"He will. I promise."

"All right." Eve shrugged, poorly feigning a cool indifference they both knew she didn't feel. Eve had to tell Laura what she had discovered on her laptop, but it was the wrong time for a serious talk.

"Hang in there," Laura said. She slugged Eve's arm gently, fully misreading the source of her closest friend's visible angst. "He'll ask."

Liam Walsh was a year older and a senior, which felt significant, but he and Eve were in the same Spanish class because she tested ahead in most subjects. She went through her typical day, bored but attentive, while her stomach churned. She thought she would see Liam in the halls or at lunch, long before Mrs. Lanza forced them to converse *en Español*. She pictured his large white teeth and the slight overbite his plush lips struggled to contain. His thick and perfectly proportioned eyebrows arching over Irish green eyes. His beautiful swimmer's build. Thick legs. Wet muscles.

Her mother was a liar.

Liam wasn't at lunch, which was normal. He and Christian often went off campus to enjoy burritos with other seniors who had cars, while Eve and Laura remained caged in the cafeteria with an anguishing choice between pepperoni pizza or the slightly purple thing the school labeled meatloaf. Both meals came with limp green beans and micro-cubes of carrot.

"Have you seen him?" Eve asked as she pressed paper napkins to her pizza, soaking up the yellow grease.

"Yeah, didn't you?" Laura reassured. "He was hanging out before fourth."

Eve brightened. They were just missing each other! But they normally crossed paths a few times a day, and she hadn't seen him in the halls, despite her many walks to the other side of the building between classes and a mad dash to arrive before the bell. She couldn't shake the feeling he was avoiding her.

Not that it mattered. What mattered was her discovery.

"Hey listen, last night----"

"Can you believe Durand gave us double homework?" Laura interrupted. "And we're supposed to read half of *The Stranger* in one night?"

"I read it again on Friday," Eve admitted. "It's not long."

Laura glared at her.

"We had the whole weekend," Eve explained. "And it was on the list."

"The summer list? No . . ."

Eve raised one eyebrow.

"You're such a dork!" Laura declared loudly for the benefit of all the students who didn't have friends with cars. She used any excuse to garner attention, typically at her best friend's expense.

"Whatever, hey listen----" Eve said, looking around to see who might overhear as she prepared to reveal the big news, but Laura was already packing her bag.

"I have to get Jenny's physics before next period or Mr. Benson'll kill me." Laura laughed. "Twenty bucks and the bitch won't even text it, can you believe?"

Spanish 3. Last period. Mrs. Lanza delighted in wearing colorful Latin American attire, and she was as oblivious to the cultural appropriation as she was to the snickering behind her back. The classroom was set in a broad semicircle so Mrs. Lanza could stand in the center and twirl in her embroidered rebozos while rolling her r's.

"*¡Hola estudiantes!*" she sang. "*¿Como estas, Eva?*"

"It's Eve," she muttered.

"*Mi nombrrre es Eve*," Mrs. Lanza corrected. She was unbearable. And Eve was pretty sure she was from Sweden.

The bell rang, and Mrs. Lanza was about to shut the door when Liam burst in. "Sorry!" he said. "Coach Hays needed me."

"*Está bien, Liam. Toma asiento.*"

He looked at her quizzically. She pointed toward his seat.

He found his place, directly across the room from Eve. She watched him put his bag down, unzip his hoodie, check his phone, click off the sound, stash it deep in his pocket, take off his hoodie and stretch it against the back of his chair, grab a pen, grab a notebook, flip the page, set it on his desk, shuffle his feet, take the cap off his pen and place it on the bottom of the pen, turn the page again, test the pen on the corner of the page, smile at his little doodle, scratch his ankle, and then look up at Mrs. Lanza, who was spinning Spanish phrases in all directions from the center of the room. Finally, Liam looked across at Eve and smiled.

She smiled back and then waved a small wave.

She instantly felt stupid and wished she hadn't waved at all. What was she thinking? She was acting like a freshman, not a junior! Laura was right: she *was* a dork! She was—

Liam waved a small wave back, and then he winked at her.

Eve was momentarily restored. He was there, smiling and waving and winking. And he was going to ask her to homecoming! If nothing else, at least she had this gorgeous, perfect guy, so friendly and kind, charming and thoughtful, smart and popular . . . and he had a car. She needed a car. After what she had discovered in the middle of the night, she *really* needed a car.

Class ended, and he bolted before Eve had a chance to collect her books.

He was gone. And he hadn't asked.

Laura caught up with Eve at her locker a few minutes later. Eve thumbed through her textbooks slowly, deciding what was needed for homework, eminently distracted.

"So . . . ?"

"So what?"

"So what, what? What did he say?"

Laura could see moisture forming a glaze beneath her friend's dark lashes.

"Oh honey, he'll ask. I promise. Christian said so."

"That's not it. I need to tell you some----" Eve stopped herself. The hall was screaming with slamming lockers and chatter, and Laura was scrolling through something on her phone. Eve asked, "So why didn't he?"

Laura didn't know, but she swore to find out.

"No!!" Eve begged. "Everyone will think I'm desperate or something. Promise me you won't talk to anyone."

"Okay, I won't," Laura said, subdued.

"Promise."

Laura sighed. "Okay, I promise, but *you have to calm down*!"

Eve couldn't calm down, and she didn't have any more time to explain it to Laura. Liam was important, but he was also a small problem. She had a bigger problem. Much bigger.

Her mother was a liar.

Eve slammed the books she didn't need back into the locker and spun the dial with unthrottled hostility. She threw her bag over her shoulder with such force that her body lurched forward on impact. "I have to get my check."

"You gonna walk?"

"You have a car?" Eve snarled.

"Hey, I'm on your side!" Laura growled back. "But I'm not gonna wait around for Christian's practice, so I guess I'm on the fucking bus."

"That's bullshit. We're juniors," Eve whined.

"I gotta find a new best friend. Someone with a car."

"Me too," Eve smirked. "Hey, nice knowin' ya."

"Or maybe your mom could ask *GOD* to get us a car!" Laura jibed.

"Grow some balls and ask your rich dad again," Eve said, exasperated.

"Love you, bitch." Laura smiled.

"K."

They hugged, and Eve felt a little better. "And you are desperate," Laura whispered in her ear. Laura took off for the bus, and Eve walked away from the cinderblock campus, crossed the park, went up the busy road past a few strip malls, and turned into The Deerwood. With each step, her frustrations amplified. Liam had every opportunity to ask her. He could have stayed after Spanish. He could have taken her to lunch instead of going off with his buddies. He could have texted or called or DMed. Did he change his mind? Was it her shirt? The earrings? Her stringy hair? Maybe he hated her shoes. She knew she should have worn her boots, but she was right about it being too hot, and they gave her blisters if she walked too far, and she had no idea if she was going to get a ride from her new boyfriend *who didn't freakin' ask!*

Something crawled up her throat, and she spat on the hot pavement.

Liam didn't even matter; her mother was a liar.

Eve finished tying her other shoelace and looked up. Fifty parking spaces of The Deerwood loomed ahead, and she took a deep breath. At least she didn't have to work—Monday was just a payday!

Mrs. Rubinow sat at an oversized melamine desk to the left of the vestibule. The automatic doors were calibrated for the pace of elderly residents and remained open much longer than was required for Eve's brisk entrance. The air conditioning mixed with the muggy afternoon, resulting in a slightly salty mist that stained the glass.

Eve stood over the paycheck-pickup clipboard and tried to draw ink from a pen. "This one's dead," she said, returning it before pulling her long hair into a tie. Her bangs were matted from the sweaty walk, and the ends had yielded to the humidity and frizzed. She hated Florida.

Mrs. Rubinow sighed and opened a drawer filled with dozens of pens.

"We try not to say that word around here," she quipped. "Try this . . ."

Eve accepted the replacement and watched as Mrs. Rubinow returned the inept pen to the same loaded drawer. Eve scrawled her signature and traded the clipboard for her check. While she waited for Mrs. Rubinow to retrieve her earnings from a thick, rubber-banded stack, she casually suggested that sorting through the pens to find the good ones would be a worthwhile undertaking. Mrs. Rubinow offered her a silent scowl.

Mrs. Rubinow was an obese sixty-year-old woman with shocking red hair and lips to match. She wore red floral prints and took off her red shoes every day before settling in to manage the reception desk. She once told Eve that she liked the feeling of the cold tiles on her tired feet. Eve wasn't sure how her feet got tired if she was always sitting down, but she knew enough to keep that thought to herself.

Eve looked around the lobby while Mrs. Rubinow continued her search. The Deerwood's salmon wallpaper had mismatched hues and visible seams. An aging grand piano sat in the corner of the room behind a heavy barricade of flaccid velvet ropes. Mrs. Rubinow had once complained that music distracted her from doing her job, so the piano remained locked. Multiple mismatched club chairs flanked a sagging floral sofa, and everything was covered in polyester fabrics that were easy to clean in case of bladder accidents, or worse. There were empty oversized pots beneath large windows that framed the central open-air courtyard beyond. Eve assumed the plants had committed suicide to avoid living in such an ugly and depressing lobby.

"Eve Harvick, here we go."

Eve reached for the check, but Mrs. Rubinow pulled it back slightly with her red nails.

"Hold on. I ate a tomato from the salad bar," said Mrs. Rubinow. Eve raised her eyebrow, wondering what that had to do with her check, and Mrs. Rubinow mistook it as a request for more detail. "One of those little cherry tomatoes. It tasted funny."

The red clothes, hair, and makeup made Eve begin to wonder if Mrs. Rubinow only ate red foods as well. Beets, apples, red velvet cake, cherry pie filling straight from the can . . .

"That's too bad," Eve replied, reaching again for her check.

"I need you to watch the desk so I can go to the ladies' room." Though her voice was low and calm, Eve could see the perspiration forming on Mrs. Rubinow's brow. It wasn't a request.

"I'm just here for my----"

"You know what to do, right? Sign them in and out and if you have any problems, call Maria," Mrs. Rubinow replied as she tossed Eve's check on her keyboard, just out of reach, and quickly gathered her skirt.

"How long will----"

"Oh Christ, Eve, I don't know. Think of this as your opportunity to organize the pens."

Eve dropped her front teeth to her bottom lip and maneuvered to the back of the mauve desk as Mrs. Rubinow shuffled past her, smelling like a watermelon air freshener. *Must have been one mean little tomato to take her down*, Eve thought. Before Mrs. Rubinow slipped around the corner, Eve noticed she was still barefoot. *Gross.*

Eve sat at the desk and ripped into the envelope: $292.40. Six afternoons and two full Saturdays spent sweeping the floor and washing and cleaning the used barrettes and pins, minus the government deductions. At this rate, it was going to take her half a year before she could afford a down payment on something ancient and probably missing a windshield—and that was assuming her mother didn't ask her for help fixing the car they already had, a tired Toyota that spent half its life in the shop. Eve looked into her immediate future and saw endless bags of smelly cut hair and dirty smocks.

She shoved the check into her backpack and opened the pen drawer. She pulled out three pens and tried them. None of them worked. She thought about Liam and his pen in Spanish class. She wondered what he drew. She wondered if he had excellent penmanship or if it was sloppy, like a future doctor's. She noticed his pen was often in the corner of his mouth, and she watched him press his lips around it to pull off the lingering spit when he took it out to write. She wondered what his pen tasted like. She wondered what *he* tasted like. Was he really going to ask her? Would they kiss? Would she get to enjoy those lips as much as his stupid pen did?

Eve returned her new collection of assorted bad pens to the drawer and slammed it shut. She clicked on the computer and saw that Mrs. Rubinow was in the middle of a game of solitaire. Eve ended the game prematurely and put the computer back to sleep.

She pulled out her phone and checked her texts. Nothing. There was a voicemail from her mother, but Eve flicked off the screen without listening to it.

She wondered how long it would take for Mrs. Rubinow to clear the tomato, and then she realized Laura was right—she *did* need to calm down. But Laura didn't know what was really going on. Laura didn't know what Eve had discovered on her computer in the middle of the night.

Eve was wrestling with the idea of pulling out her new trig assignment

20 | The Limited Edition Bicentennial Cadillac Convertible Joy Ride

when I finally pulled into the building's porte cochere. Eve could see from her position at the desk that Lucy was driving and Muriel was my front-seat passenger. They talked for a moment before Lucy got out, slammed the door, and shredded a path toward the front desk.

"Oh hey, Eve! Where's Mrs. R.?" she blurted as she suddenly gripped the edge of the desk, compelled by an invisible force.

"Bathroom break," Eve replied. "Sign in?"

"Can you do it? I've gotta----" Lucy leaned in, and Eve could see that a slippery sheen had formed on the large woman's forehead as Lucy shout-whispered, "I've *really* gotta pee."

"TMI," Eve muttered.

"Yep, it's a UTI," Lucy replied, mishearing her. "And prob'ly too much cranberry juice and----"

"Mrs. R's already in there." Eve cut her off.

"Damn." Lucy did a quick visual scan for the closest private alternative—people *had* been known to urinate in all sorts of places at The Deerwood. Lucy weighed her roiling bladder against the distance to Muriel's apartment, two floors up on the other end of the building, and decided she could make it. "I'll be right back. Mrs. W.'s a little out of it today, and I left the air on. She's good for a few." She said all of this over her shoulder, huffing toward the elevator.

"Which room again?" Eve called out, reopening the pen drawer.

"Three twelve!" Lucy lobbed back, her hips and arms visibly dancing while her legs remained glued to each other. The elevator doors closed at the teasing pace of a snail.

"Three twelve," Eve repeated, discarding two bad pens back into the drawer before she found a good one and transferred *Mrs. Worth and Lucy/ Caregiver – 312 – 3:50 p.m.* to the chart.

Such drama! Eve thought as she spun the clipboard back to its starting position and returned her eyes to me. *Drama,* she thought again, describing and admiring my long, bold lines. She'd seen me before, but always from a distance, like this. Eve had once asked Lucy in the salon what it was like "to drive such an amazing car!" (her words, not mine).

"Oh, that old thing?" Lucy laughed in reply while someone lathered Muriel's hair in the warm sink on the other side of the room. Lucy got real quiet and serious, and Eve stopped sweeping to learn her secret. "That car is the best part of my job. Every week we go out shopping or down to the beach, and just driving her around, she's happy as a bee on flowers." Eve wasn't sure if she meant Muriel or me. "I think it helps her head, too," Lucy continued. "She gets real talky and clear . . . and then she tells me stuff." Lucy raised an eyebrow. "Mmmhmm. And of course, everybody's lookin' at us and honkin' their horns and we get all sorts of questions in parking lots and gas stations. I tell you, it's a hoot driving that smooth old beast, but don't go telling Laura any of that or her daddy will be all over me. He wanted to sell it the moment Mrs. W. moved in here, but somehow she won that round. He hates that car."

"That's crazy! It's so beautiful!"

"He doesn't like competing for attentions—it's like he's got a sibling rivalry with that Caddy!" Lucy laughed hard, releasing a small snort.

Eve delivered a small laugh in solidarity. Eve would have loved to have a sibling rivalry, but that required a sibling. I saw, even back then, how it made Lucy happy to see Eve laugh, even if it was clearly forced. Eve's eyes used to sparkle before she started working in The Deerwood's salon, and Lucy had watched their luster fade under the reality of her workplace. It went beyond the monotony and buzzing fluorescent lights; if the salon clientele failed to keep an appointment, it could easily mean a stroke, heart attack, cancer, pneumonia, or any of a thousand lurking perils. Eve always maintained she was "fine," but Lucy knew it was a practiced response.

The lobby was empty again. "I'll be here," Eve said to no one while she looked at me and imagined what it would be like to be anywhere else. Eve was visibly transfixed by my lines and immaculate sheen as she observed how my two doors and extended length made Muriel's white head seem comically small. Eve understood Muriel's desire to stay rooted on my cool seats instead of rushing back to her nondescript quarters. Muriel maintained her perpetual gaze past the windshield as she slowly moved her head from side to side, presumably listening to music. Laura told Eve a lot of stories about her Grams—how smart and pretty she used to be, how everything had slipped away virtually overnight. Eve wondered what it was like to live in the present with no memory of the past, or to live in the past, unable to recognize the present, or to constantly bobble between the two with no footing in either realm.

The lobby doors closed, but through the glass, even from a distance, Eve thought she could see Muriel's lips moving. Eve wondered if she was singing, or talking to someone who wasn't there, the way most of the residents with dementia or Alzheimer's did. More minutes passed while Lucy and Mrs. Rubinow continued to address their independent urgencies. Eve knew it could take a while for Lucy to weave through the corridors and summon the "Slowevator," as Laura called it, and Mrs. Rubinow remained inexplicably busy in the bathroom. Perhaps she ate two tomatoes.

Eve kept an eye on Muriel while becoming aware that the lobby was remarkably empty. Typically, someone would be napping on the couch or reading a four-year-old magazine near the clunky mermaid mosaic on the far wall. Usually, a janitor would glide through with a mop, a case manager would pass by clutching thick files stuffed with maladies and solutions, or a sales associate would energetically lead a tour touting The Deerwood's amenities. But Eve was alone at the desk and Muriel was outside with me, singing her songs or talking to ghosts in my air conditioning.

The never-used stairway door by the elevator flung open, and Lucy burst through and ran toward Eve in a panic.

"You have your license, right?" she squawked between hard breaths.

"Yeah?"

"I need you to park the Caddy in the basement and bring Muriel up to her room. Here's the key."

"What?"

"It's spot number ten, straight in front of you when you go down the ramp. The card on the keychain opens the gate. Just pull in all the way until the tires hit the curb so it doesn't stick out. It won't scrape. You can take the elevator from there and go right up to her room, three twelve. Just park the car and bring her up, okay?"

"Where are you----"

"My Albi had a heart attack." Lucy stopped spewing information for half a second and sucked in more air before continuing, while Eve tried to process everything she said. "They found him on the floor----"

"Oh my god, okay go. I've got this," Eve said, rising.

"They called the ambulance, but I have to go. Just get Mrs. W. settled in her room. She naps after our rides, and Viv will be here soon to get her to dinner. You don't even have to stay," she said, using the small towel that lived on her shoulder to blot her falling tears.

"It's okay, I'll stay."

"Just get the car and Mrs. W. and----"

"I've got it," Eve interrupted, taking the keys. "Go. We'll be fine."

"Albi had a heart attack. Oh my lord, Albi had a heart attack. What that man puts me through . . ." Lucy continued talking to herself as she left the building in a half run, her phone in one hand and her personal car keys extended in the other. Eve took my keys and headed outside. She heard Lucy's tires peeling out of the parking lot as she reached for the handle on my driver's side door. She clutched it, and in that moment, like a spark of static transferring the collected energy of a carpeted floor through a fingertip, I learned everything.

"Hi," she said cautiously, climbing into the driver's seat.

"Laura? Is that you? What are you doing here, sweetheart?"

"Uh, no," Eve said, pulling her bangs back. "Lucy asked me to park the car and bring you up. She had an emergency."

"An emergency?"

"A heart attack."

"Lucy had a heart attack?!" Muriel cried out, turning white. "But I just saw her!"

"No, no! Sorry! Lucy's fine, *Albi* had a heart attack."

"Albi?"

"That's what she said."

"Albi?" Muriel pronounced again, slowly, studying Eve's face. Eve seemed familiar, but Muriel couldn't place her. A cashier at the supermarket, perhaps, or someone's granddaughter who visited from time to time.

"Anyway, she had to run, so I guess we should get you upstairs."

Eve closed my door and faced forward to assess my cockpit. She was surprised by my simplicity: my upper dashboard has two tiers of controls with four vents and the speedometer. The lower portion, to the left of my steering wheel, handles the lights and temperature, and my radio sits to the right of the driver. Everything is set in a highly polished wood veneer. A ballad was playing softly through my radio, and I felt Muriel relax as she resumed her head-swaying and her muted karaoke, in perfect tune.

". . . because liiife is what you maaake it and this chaaance I'm gonna taaake it . . ."

Eve turned up the volume and continued to take in my spotless white seats, red-carpeted floor, and the famous Cadillac insignia impressed into the wooden center of my three-pronged steering wheel. Muriel and I didn't allow so much as a speck of dust anywhere. Eve spotted the gold, engraved plaque fastened slightly above my glove box:

This 1976 Fleetwood Eldorado
is one of the last 200 identical
U.S. production convertibles.

Eve gulped. She'd never been in a vehicle quite like me. In the fifth grade, she'd secretly climbed into a black Mercedes parked in the garage at a classmate's birthday party. That car was saturated with a crazy assortment of sleek and perplexing buttons. She made up functions for the mysterious switches and giggled uncontrollably, pretending the car might fly right out of the garage and into the clouds if she pressed the right button—or blow up if she touched the wrong one. Eve remembered the heavy scent of leather and cigars, cologne and perfume, and the overwhelming feeling of not belonging in such an opulent environment.

But I was different. I held Muriel's hint of lavender fragrance in my leather, and it had a calming effect. Eve felt cradled and comfortable as I naturally conformed to her strong body. I saw her imagining herself as the rightful and distinguished driver of such a rare and fine automobile, and for a brief moment, all her problems felt very far away.

Eve checked the mirrors, pressed the brakes, fastened her seatbelt, and prepared herself to drive around the building and into the underground garage. She didn't pay attention to Muriel's continued scrutiny until Muriel finally declared: "You wash my hair."

"Sometimes," Eve admitted. "Usually I just sweep up and take care of the smocks."

"You're Eve."

Eve was amazed that Muriel knew that; after nearly a year of collecting and bagging boatloads of their shorn locks, she still didn't think any of the residents knew she existed. Most of them seemed to be under a dull spell, and those who weren't chatted so relentlessly about themselves that there wasn't room for Eve between their words.

"Laura talks about you," Muriel explained.

"Oh?"

"She loves you."

Eve nodded in agreement and smiled, which prompted Muriel to smile, too. Eve noticed her teeth were the originals, a little crowded on the bottom with a little silver on the sides. Eve turned her focus back to my dashboard and checked the mirrors again. She wanted to get Muriel settled. I could feel her anxiety growing over the prospect of Mrs. Rubinow's return to an empty desk and the subsequent face she would make, screaming red. Eve drove about fifteen feet with a confidence that I found inspiring. Then she turned my tires toward the parking garage.

"No, no, don't turn right," Muriel injected.

We stopped.

"Go left," Muriel urged, gesturing faintly with a thin arm.

Eve felt her adrenaline beginning to rise. "What do you mean?" she asked cautiously.

"Go!" Muriel repeated, pointing toward the exit with both hands raised. "Let's get out of here!"

"You mean, like . . . *drive away*?"

Muriel's luminous blue eyes met Eve's with a startling clear focus as she coolly and quietly commanded the young girl: "Yes, Eve. Let's drive away."

As the words reverberated and the concept took solid shape, I felt Eve slip out of her temporal reality. She saw herself waiting by the alligator magnets, Liam's wet lips sucking on a pen, Laura smiling by the pool, spilled coffee on the kitchen counter, her laptop and the photo, crucifixes in the stairwell, Mrs. Lanza spinning, piles of shorn hair, Tammy and the hot air balloon, computer solitaire, the mosaic mermaid, the prayer group gasping up the stairs, Lucy running out of The Deerwood, a moldy tomato, her mother sorting markers at the craft store, her father with his warm beard pressed against her cheek.

Her father.

Eve's eyes vibrated as she flipped through the disjointed echoes like playing cards. Finally, she began to focus on the present thoughts that mattered: Eve wanted a car. She *needed* a car. She had worked endlessly for a car. And now she was in a car, a perfect car, and her senior passenger wanted her to drive away.

Could she?

Eve's backpack was still at the front desk.

She swallowed hard, realizing if she went inside to retrieve it she might be stopped before we could leave. Mrs. Rubinow didn't see us arrive, so it was possible she was none the wiser, but if she was already back at the desk, she would no doubt summon another adult to park me, or she might even dare to do it herself. But Eve needed her phone, wallet, laptop, books, and other necessities. She needed her license. Her life was in her bag, and she had to get it.

Eve put me back in Park and told Muriel to stay put. In one swift motion, she opened the door and made a beeline for the desk. Mrs. Rubinow wasn't back, and the lobby remained eerily silent. Eve grabbed her bag and immediately heard an aggressive double flush from the nearby restroom. Then the elevator dinged, indicating someone else was about to arrive on the ground floor. She had mere seconds before there was a crowd.

She ran, but her mind moved faster than her legs. It didn't seem possible that they could actually drive away—in the space of only six minutes, she had gone from an angry salon-girl student picking up her paycheck to . . . what was this? Chauffeur? Criminal? Was it possible to leave? To *really* leave? Or, it dawned on her in a flash, did Muriel think she was going back to the beach or the supermarket? Eve couldn't catch her breath. Someone had replaced the air with glue.

She flew back to us and seemed to toss her bag in my back seat, close the door, and click her seatbelt simultaneously. She quickly checked that Muriel was also secure, grazing her blue cardigan and noting its softness. The two women looked at each other and made immediate assessments. Muriel saw a shoddily dressed, harried young woman with too much eye makeup, five-too-many ear piercings, and long bangs partially obscuring her face. But she also found a reassuring familiarity and sensed the innate kindness in Eve's gray-green eyes. Eve saw a dignified old woman with willowy arms folded neatly in her lap, a tan leather purse that perfectly matched her shoes, and impeccably tailored slacks. Muriel's gentle white curls were already a touch overgrown, and Eve wondered if she was on the schedule for another cut later that week. Would she be back for that haircut? Would we all be back in an hour? Or a week? Or never?

Muriel touched her hand to Eve's quivering knee. In one remarkable second, Eve's knotted thoughts vaporized as she gazed into the clear pools of Muriel's calm eyes.

"Let's go," Muriel urged again, but gently.

Eve found one more playing card: her mother blocking the doorway, wearing a pea-green sweatshirt emblazoned with *WWJD?* in massive white letters.

What Would Jesus Do? Eve thought as she clutched my steering wheel, shifted into Drive, and carefully slid her foot off the broad brake pedal and to the right.

Her mother was a liar, and Eve didn't care about Jesus.

Jesus didn't have a car.

She pressed her full weight down on my slender gas pedal, and I roared.

Chapter 2

Technically, I started my life in a factory in Detroit. Actually, there's some confusion about my origin certificate and it's possible I came to be in Linden, New Jersey, but the factories in both locales were similar, and in truth, it doesn't matter. I have fourteen thousand fraternal siblings, most of whom are gone now, but two hundred of us were created special and identical. To my knowledge, we notables are still alive and well and presumably in our protective garages. Somewhere there's a list.

I remember everything from the moment they installed my radio. The battery, the windshield, and my 238-horsepower engine were already in place, and they added to my powers of sight and drive, but it was the radio that connected me to the world beyond myself, past the unwavering glow of factory lights and the steady rumbling of overworked conveyor belts that carried me from nothingness into being. The radio was my education; I could listen without illuminating its display and I could hear beyond the scope of its registered dial. I was always listening: the news programs taught me language and the history of struggle, the endless chatter schooled me on pathos and the malleable lines between truth and manipulation, and it was through the music channels that I found emotion and empathy, connectivity and love.

I remember when they inserted the key and fired me up for the first time. I was ready to transport up to six adults in comfort and style, and I quickly realized I could feel my passengers beyond their physicality through my hand-stitched white leather seats and elegant red piping. When someone touched my #11 Cotillion White body, I could somehow see into that life—not the future, that would be ridiculous—but I could see their past and feel their present state of being. I cannot explain this power of perception any more than I can explain my own consciousness. It may not make sense, but that's the way it is.

Life is often like that.

As my travelers confided in me, I listened patiently and conformed to the contours of their needs. I believe most vehicles do this innately, but through my powers of comprehension, I could share their emotional language. I nurtured and provided solace, and sometimes, if they were willing to listen, I imparted solutions to their problems—though most seemed to believe they came up with the answers on their own.

And there were so many problems!

My first passenger wore a white, lint-free bodysuit and shoes with synthetic felt on the soles to repel debris. He was clean shaven and his wild hair was contained within a net. He compulsively checked himself for grease or dirt nearly a dozen times before he sat down. He drove me from the last doorway of the assembly line to my first parking lot, maybe a quarter mile away. In the few moments we spent together, I learned his wife was about to give birth to their fourth child and he needed more money to support his expanding family. He told me someone was going to spend more dough to acquire me than he earned in a year, but because I was one of the last, one of the Limited Editions, I was bound to live, as he sang it, "a sweeet life."

I held his torso in place, supported his legs and backside firmly, and told him he should ask for a raise. He was a loyal and reliable contributor in the effort of producing us beauties, and he deserved a respite from his financial stress. I wordlessly told him to quit smoking and that four children were probably enough, but, like most ambitious young men, he discounted what he assumed to be his own thoughts, and I felt him reject the advice. He winked at me when we parted, however, and offered me good luck. He gently closed my door and rubbed away his lingering fingerprints with a special cloth while I returned his good favor. We never saw each other again. Maybe everything turned out fine, but if not, I did my part.

I waited for a few weeks under a snug plastic sheet and listened. During the day, motors tore through the air overhead, whistled along the tracks edging the factory, and hummed by the street near my fence. Everything seemed to be in motion, with an endless parade of materials shifting through the ether and uniting for new purposes. When the mechanical sounds finally came to rest, the crickets took over, working in tandem with frogs and other critters to keep the night air from settling too deep. Before the first blip of orange cracked an indigo horizon, small birds resumed the conversation, interrupted by an occasional rooster and freshly energized dogs.

One night was different. A piercing cacophony split the humid dusk with thousands of pops, cracks, rattles, and whistles. Some were so strong that even in Park, I rocked against the booms. I was still so young and naive that I thought I might lose my grip on this earth and bounce right off the pavement! I could see the colors in broad strokes from beneath my sheet, a reflective glow against my glass. Somehow, that violent celestial dance soothed me as the splashes of ignited chemicals gave their performance and then floated away from their elevated stage. Every clap silenced the crickets, reactivated the dogs, and thrilled the human populace nearby. It was a momentous and magnificent night out there in Detroit, or possibly Linden, on Sunday, July 4th, 1976.

Nine weeks later to the day, I met Muriel Worth at the Great New York State Fair, outside Syracuse. I was the biggest prize in the Grand Prix Bicentennial Raffle, and a single chance to win me set the contenders back ten dollars.

Back then, my original list price was a little over $13,000 and you could buy a decent one-bedroom apartment in New York City for that. The average annual wage was a little over $9,000 and most cars cost less than $4,000, so taking a ten-buck chance on a vision like me was a no-brainer.

Muriel once confided that she had no prior intention of buying that ticket, and even the trip to the state fair had been a fluke. Ira had business in Rochester the week before Labor Day, so the family took a late-summer road trip to the Finger Lakes region and discovered the fair as an enjoyable diversion. Muriel quickly bought the kids pink cotton candy and a string of ride tickets, and told them to meet up by the quilting booths in three hours. People didn't monitor their kids back then like they do now—they set them free to explore on their own, and the freedom worked both ways, allowing Muriel and Ira to enjoy a few hours to themselves.

They strolled past the butter sculpture and the stockades. They petted the heads of sedated goats and other livestock. They looked at the tractors. They looked at the combines. They looked at the latest color televisions in the Modern Electronics booths, including a striking 25" RCA ColorTrak with Dynamic Fleshtone Correction. They lamented having missed Bob Hope and Neil Sedaka's performances on the main stage, but they were happy to catch Bobby Vinton.

And they kept circling back to me.

I was in the center of the action, surveying the crowds as I slowly spun around on a large motorized disc. A white chain on red posts forced the envious to keep their distance, and there were four guards posted should anyone dare to touch me. Next to my right-hand door was a large, clear, ball-shaped barrel filled with ticket stubs. Each stub represented a chance at winning me or one of the consolation prizes, including a Sony BetaMax player, a Marantz audio receiver, and a Speed Queen washer/dryer set in the popular almond color. Almost half a million people attended the fair that year, and there were no less than thirty thousand numbered stubs in that barrel.

I saw Muriel lightly clutch Ira's arm the first time she saw me. Her nails were the color of a robin's egg and she lifted her gold-framed sunglasses to get an unobstructed view. She was perspiring lightly beneath a blond curl that bounced against her forehead as she looked at Ira, then back at me, then back at Ira, and then down as she dug ten dollars out of her purse.

"I have to try," she said. He couldn't object, equally mesmerized by my glitzy length, as she purchased one of the last tickets sold.

Like everyone, Muriel was seduced by my svelte body and exquisite paint job. I'm a unique shade of white and I sport gorgeous matching hubcaps. Other Cadillacs had the standard #19 Sable Black hubcaps, which were also pretty sexy, but not matchy-matchy like mine. I was given an exclusive thick–thin and thin–thick red-and-blue pinstripe on my hood, and people went crazy for it. I was a sought-after symbol of American pride and achievement. Major movie producers, Long Island millionaires, and even the royal family of Saudi Arabia snatched all of us up in less than a month. As far as I know, only two of us have ever passed one hundred thousand miles on the odometer, and most of us have averaged less than twenty thousand miles in our entire lives. We were only driven in small doses to keep our white paint glistening and our admirers in awe.

Muriel and Ira left to collect their children as I continued to spin, projecting my beauty on all sides. A short while later, a small army surrounded me. The disc stopped spinning, and I was driven down a ramp, along a guarded road, and up another ramp to the stage at the end of the infield amusement area.

I remember seeing Muriel near the front of the crowd, which quickly grew into a buzzing mob of thousands. Out of all those people, I saw her. Somehow... we both knew.

A sweaty announcer suffocating in a shiny white suit with a red-white-and-blue necktie clutched the microphone. "How about that performance?!" he cried out. "Bobby Vinton, ladies and gentlemen!" The microphone squealed with feedback as thousands of mothers reflexively covered their children's ears. "Whoa-aaa ... Sorry 'bout that ... Ben?"

A man in a brown jumpsuit with armpit stains and audio-technic superpowers appeared from nowhere, tapped the microphone into submission, and disappeared again. The emcee continued, rambling on about sponsors and America and greatness and farms and other important topics. Prominent men arrived in star-spangled ties to bow at appropriate moments. There was some polite clapping now and then, but most of the spectators were united in their boredom as they shifted and waited for the real fun to begin.

Finally, it was time to give things away.

You didn't have to be present to win, and every ticket had a corresponding phone number and address somewhere in a ledger, but it was also entirely possible that the winner was there. The winner could be anyone.

Muriel got excited when she saw the paper-filled globe arrive on stage. Her number was in there, somewhere near the top. She looked to Ira for encouragement and received a wink and a squeeze on the shoulder, but her expression fell when nine more globes arrived, each and every one of them filled three-quarters to the brim with little torn stubs, each promising someone else a fabulous future with me at the helm.

The emcee reached into a separate master globe that contained ten dinner-plate-sized red plastic discs, each with a magic number hidden inside. He opened the first disc and revealed a glitzy, glittering "7" as the crowd oohed and ahhed. He made his way to globe number seven, and Ben appeared, again out of nowhere, to spin it around and around and upside down, exhaustively mixing the tickets. The emcee enjoyed drawing out the fevered anticipation for about as long as it could be justified, bringing the crowd near to the brink of rioting. Then he grabbed a stack from deep inside the globe, shook them out, and produced one small piece of thick paper in his extended hand, which was dripping with sweat. "Dang, it's hot tonight," he chuckled, "Hard to believe it'll be snowing in a few weeks."

"Get on with it!" people screamed.

"Okay, okay . . . heh heh, here we go folks. Four Two Nine Five Six Three Eight," he called, enunciating with care.

From my elevated perch, I noticed a bald eagle soaring above the crowd, skimming the evening breezes. I saw him witness the tens of thousands of contenders as they suddenly looked down at their tickets and simultaneously hushed. Assuming they were responding to an influx of voles, the eagle dropped down to find his meal amongst them, but he was quickly scared off by an emphatic woman near the side who shouted, "That's me! That's me!!" A mix of cheers and a few boos accompanied her as she made her way up to the stage, took a bow, and was directed to sit on a cloth director's chair next to her fabulous new television.

"That's right, honey, stay right there, yeah, right there," smiled the sweltering emcee as Ben positioned her for the newspaper photograph.

The process was repeated a few more times as the prizewinners celebrated and more and more people streamed into the arena. As the sun neared the horizon, the fairground lights were illuminated to replace its glow. A few wild screams could be heard beyond the massive field as disinterested teenagers continued to enjoy the twisting and spinning rides.

Finally: "This is it, folks."

The emcee reached in and pulled out the final red disc: globe number ten.

He pranced over to the last globe, touching the happy prizewinners on the shoulders as he passed, anointing them with significance.

"Are you ready?" he snickered into the microphone.

"Do it already!" People cried and cheered. It was simply too exciting, and emotions were impossible to contain. I was a legendary offering and they all wanted me. They could picture themselves arriving at fancy restaurants, basking in the envy of their friends and neighbors, even earning applause at gas stations. "That's my car . . ." they all thought.

"Are you suuure you're ready?"

Ben shook the globe for at least thirty seconds.

"C'mon!" the crowd screamed.

He shook it some more.

"Are you surely sure you're surely reaaaddddyyy . . . ?"

"Pick already!"

"Do it!"

"You're a jerk!"

"I want my car!"

His hairy hand pushed into the wad like a fist into their guts, and everyone fell silent. His stocky arm swam for a moment before he delicately pinched the solitary sliver with its seven printed numbers. This was the ticket. This was the moment. Ninety thousand people held their breath in the arena, and another million watched from home on the live news broadcasts. Some mothers covered their children's mouths with their palms as the emcee cleared his throat.

"Six Eight Seven . . ."

"Fuck!" yelled a guy near the side.

"Four Three. . ."

"Goddammit!" a woman uttered next to Muriel, but she didn't hear it. Her focus was intense, every muscle taut, her tongue pressing hard against the back of her teeth.

"Five . . ."

Muriel slid her hand deep into her pocket and touched her ticket as he called out the last number. She closed her eyes and inhaled.

"One."

She lifted her smooth hand into the evening light and read the saturated black ink printed on her stub as the announcer called it again, confirming.

Muriel whispered to Ira and clutched his hand. Then she called out, "I've got it!" and instantly found herself in a blurred frenzy as a sea of human iron filings discovered the central magnet. Muriel and Ira were swiftly joined by a half-dozen burly farmers who truly made my heart sing with patriotism as they formed a ring to protect her from the sudden onslaught. Everyone wanted to see the woman who won the car. The farmers carried her up as the crowd whooped and hollered. Muriel gave the emcee the ticket, and he confirmed the number and handed her the long key. My key.

If you had told Muriel that morning that she would drive the family home in a brand-new 1976 Limited-Edition Bicentennial Cadillac Eldorado Convertible, she would have laughed in your face and offered you a second lemonade with a double shot of whiskey.

Fireworks again, but this time I got to see them from the front and center of the stage as my new friend and owner leaned solidly against me. And as she leaned, I learned.

I may have been constructed by a thousand men earlier that year in Detroit, or Linden, and I may have been perceptive before we ever met, but on that steamy, energized night, somewhere on the outskirts of Syracuse, in the electric moment when Muriel's fingers first brushed across my side, when she found the door handle and slipped into the driver's seat—I like to consider that the night I was born.

Chapter 3

Eve needed a plan. She had walked across The Deerwood parking lot hundreds of times but had never actually driven through it by herself. She was well practiced with small and modern cars, but I'm a king-sized boat-on-wheels with a massive trunk and hood. Very few teenagers today have experienced anything like me from the driver's seat. To add to the pressure, Eve suspected I was worth the price of a college education—maybe more. She had to be careful. Extremely careful.

She thought about money. She didn't have enough for the trip that quickly formed in her mind as we pulled onto West Hillsboro and headed east.

"Oh good," said Muriel. "That's very good."

Eve didn't know if Muriel was complimenting her driving or appreciating the departure itself as we traveled two blocks and successfully negotiated our first intersection together. Eve wondered if Muriel was also thinking about a destination, but she decided it was best not to broach the subject prematurely. She stole a quick glance while stopped at a red light and confirmed that Muriel was content; she wore a closed-lip smile and continued humming to my old radio. The destination talk would come later. First, we needed to get some distance and some money.

Eve looked down and saw Muriel's purse. Did Muriel carry cash? Did Lucy use Muriel's credit cards when they went shopping, or did Lucy pay for everything with a designated card from her own wallet? Would Muriel even know? What else was in her purse?

Eve had about $250 in the bank, her new paycheck in hand, and a $10 bill in her wallet. She contributed to the house and car expenses, and she also paid for her own clothes, entertainment, and lunch. She tried to save what she could, but money got swallowed like rain down a gutter, and Eve knew the fresh earth of her plans would need as much liquid as possible to remain viable. Her bank apps and cards could be tracked or cut off at any moment, and she had to get to the bank counter with her latest paycheck before they closed. Eve suddenly wished she had a job that paid cash: Laura babysat and always had loads of tens and twenties, plus she didn't lose any of it to taxes. But Laura also had to deal with sticky, whiny, smelly children, and Eve felt certain that sweeping up elderly hair scraps was a better option.

Eve turned into the bank parking lot, remembering to signal first, and then crossed my steering wheel hand over hand, as taught. I was proud of her for immediately recognizing that expert driving skills were essential; there would be no running yellow lights, driving on the shoulder, texting of any sort, or speeding up to pass slower cars. These immature shenanigans were for Laura's brother and his reckless friends, not her. Eve even debated turning off the stereo, thinking the music might be detrimental to her concentration, but she also feared it would upset Muriel, who tapped her thumbs to the beat and occasionally thumped her right foot.

"Quick stop," Eve said as she carefully positioned us on the far side of the lot, away from all the other vehicles. She feared she would misgauge my width if she tried to park between other cars, and she might clip my mirrors or scrape a bumper. She was also terrified of discovering a door-ding or scratch from someone less careful. I was amused that *these* were her paramount fears in those early moments, but I appreciated her caution.

"Fine," Muriel said, between the beats of a new song.

Eve debated for a moment whether she should leave Muriel behind and keep me running, or give me a rest. It was the same predicament Lucy had encountered only a few minutes before, but heightened: leaving an old woman in a cool car under the front shade of her managed care institution was one thing, but it was fully another to leave the same woman baking in a public parking lot near a busy strip mall. Eve pressed a button to lower a window. It was uncomfortably warm, but not nearly hot enough to boil a brain. Eve lowered Muriel's window with the driver's side controls, and as Muriel turned to the right to see what was happening, Eve quickly snatched her leather purse from the floor and popped out of the car, shutting the door behind her. She leaned against my frame while holding Muriel's purse just below her line of sight.

"I'll be right back. You okay?"

"Fine," Muriel said again with a nod.

"Do you need anything?"

"I'm fine," she said again.

Eve glanced at her phone. She had three minutes.

"Okay, don't go anywhere."

"I'm fine," Muriel said for the third time.

Eve cocked her head, a little unsure if Muriel was actually responding to her questions or parroting herself, but it didn't matter. It couldn't matter—time was running out. Eve raced across the parking lot and tore through the bank to the teller's window, where she exhaled a casual comment expressing her relief for the short line at the end of the long day.

"Why do you want this?" the teller asked plainly.

The teller actually said *"How* do you want this," but Eve's mind struggled to answer what she had misheard. Why was she emptying most of her account? To buy a computer from a stranger on Craigslist? To get a tattoo? How big was a $500 tattoo?

It was the end of the day, and the teller decided not to wait for a reply from the hectic teen. She counted out a stack of twenties. "Need an envelope?"

"Sure?" Eve replied, still a bit confused. She looked around to see if anyone was witnessing the girl with the stripe in her hair who was about to walk away with a massive wad of cash. Even though it was her own hard-earned money, she felt obvious and illicit, like spilled ink on white silk. A few people were performing transactions with other tellers, and a woman with a haircut similar to Eve's mother's was blocking the view of a banker in a glass-walled office near the back, but no one accosted her. No one demanded to know the reason for her withdrawal. No one asked if she was about to abscond with an elderly woman in a fancy car and flee the state.

The teller handed Eve her cash with the requisite "Have a nice day."

Feigning normalcy, Eve casually walked out of the bank and entered the separated front vestibule with the ATM. She took Muriel's purse from her shoulder and found a matching wallet inside. There were two FloridaTrust credit cards, one with the familiar blue and orange logo and another that was entirely gold. Eve probed deeper and found Muriel's driver's license. *They don't take licenses away from the elderly in Florida*, she considered. *They prefer to let their grown children take away their cars.* Eve briefly wondered how Muriel managed to keep me, her glorious Cadillac, despite Laura's dad.

When Eve popped the first of Muriel's cards into the ATM, it asked her for the PIN. Eve whispered to Siri for the most common PIN numbers and then held her breath as she entered *1234*. The ATM aggressively declared her attempt *INVALID*. Eve pushed the button that allowed her to try again and entered *0802*, Muriel's birthday, according to her license. *INVALID* blazed again.

Stop shouting at me, she thought, knowing she had one more chance before the machine would either spit out the card or gobble it up into its mechanical bowels and freeze the account. Either way, the bank would be alerted to her attempted fraud and the gig would be up. Eve looked at Muriel's driver's license again and tried to figure it out. Was Muriel sentimental? Was it her anniversary? Was it a completely arbitrary combination of numbers that Muriel always used? Was it part of her phone number? Or her phone number in reverse? Did Lucy program the card with her own PIN since she was likely the one who took out cash? Was the PIN from an old address? Or part of an old zip code? Or a dog's birthday? Had the bank programmed the PIN randomly when it was set up, and Muriel continued to use it instead of creating her own? There were nearly one hundred million possible combinations of four-digit PINs, and Eve had already squandered two of her three chances to get it right.

The teller came by and locked the door to the branch. It was after 4:30 p.m., the last customer was gone, and the main bank area was closed. Eve searched Muriel's purse for a clue, a slip of paper, an envelope with scribbles on the back—anything that could help her figure out the magic numbers. If a criminal stole her purse and wanted to take out money, what would he do? Eve realized he would probably hold a gun to Muriel's head and simply ask for it.

Eve hit *CANCEL* to eject the card and hustled back to the car to ask for the number. She didn't know what her gun would be until she approached from the passenger side and Muriel called out, "Laura?! What are you doing here?"

Eve realized this was her play. "Hi Grams!" she immediately sang back, adopting Laura's endearing moniker for Muriel. "How are you?" She tried to match Laura's higher voice and general enthusiasm.

"You look different," Muriel noted, squinting into the sun despite a feeble attempt to shield her eyes with her palm.

"I just got a haircut." Eve spun around, pointing at the salon in the strip mall. She quickly tucked her lengthy locks behind her ears, stuffed the bulk of it down her back collar, and pulled her bangs to the side, approximating Laura's style. She also bent her knees slightly in an awkward attempt to make herself look shorter.

"Oh. It looks nice."

"Thanks! Hey listen, you gave me your card to pay for the haircut, but they only take cash, and I forgot the code for the ATM. Do you remember it, Grams?" Eve looked back at the salon and held up her index finger, signaling to no one that she would be back momentarily with their imagined fee.

Muriel looked down and rubbed the edges of her eyebrows in small circles.

"The code?" She looked at her legs and wondered why she was wearing pants—*we usually stopped by her apartment to change before we went to the beach. It was very hot, and very unlike her not to put on a bathing suit and a sundress instead of pants.*

"The code," Eve prompted again.

"What?" Muriel snapped, studying the fabric.

"Do you remember the code for the card? We need some money."

Money for pants? Muriel couldn't remember what Laura had said until she looked up again, into the bright corona surrounding the eclipse of

Laura's head. Laura's head with a fresh haircut. She looked different.

"Of course I know the code," Muriel said, slightly miffed at the insinuation that she might have forgotten her own PIN. "It's Ira. I-R-A."

Eve tried to mask her growing exasperation while continuing to play the part of her best friend and holding the imagined strip-mall barbers at bay. "Isn't it four numbers?" she probed. She struggled to maintain a partial smile despite the premonition that our trip was going to end before it really started. We had enough cash to start, but Eve didn't want to risk getting stranded somewhere, or caught, if we couldn't make it all the way.

"Four numbers?"

Eve dug her teeth into her lips. Without the code she would have to bring me back to The Deerwood, apologize to everyone, probably lose her job, face Laura's wrath, and return to school the next day with an incomplete trig assignment. Liam would never ask her out, she'd never get another car, and, worst of all, she would have to explain everything to her mother. This would require talking to her mother—and her mother was a liar.

"I-R-A?" Muriel said again, genuinely perplexed.

"Try to think, Grams."

Muriel tried to think. She visually scanned my dashboard, hoping I could provide the answer. She looked up at Eve with mounting confusion. "Did you do something with your hair?"

Eve turned around, shut her eyes, and let out a tight and silent scream. This wasn't happening. She was so close . . . so close . . . She emptied her lungs a few more times and let it all go. Her breath was a frothy wave returning itself to the vast ocean, carrying broken seaweed and crumbling sand castles, smoothing the muck. She slowly opened her refreshed eyes, and the answer glistened like flat, smooth sand: there was no reason to lie. She brought her hair out again and kneeled beside Muriel's door with her face at my window height so Muriel didn't have to look into the sun.

"What's going on here?" Muriel croaked. She was nearly as pale as my paint.

"I'm not Laura, I'm Eve. Do you remember me? I work in the salon?" Muriel paid attention and appeared to comprehend, so Eve went on. "You asked me to take you for a drive, but we need some money to keep going and I don't know the code on your card. If you know the code, we can keep going, but if you don't know it, then we'll have to go back."

"Go back?"

"To The Deerwood."

"Oh, no," Muriel said, flat and defiant. "No, we're not going back there."

Muriel studied Eve's face and got lost in it. She seemed to know this girl. She definitely wasn't Laura, but she was curiously familiar. Muriel thought she might be one of Sandra's girls: Abby? Or Nancy? But the girl crouching in front of her had given her name, and it was something else. She wasn't Abby or Nancy. Or Laura. She had just said her name and already it was lost. It was so hot at the far end of the parking lot. So hot and bright and tiring.

"I beg your pardon, but I've forgotten your name," Muriel said. She was formal and polite. She felt as if she was being introduced to someone she'd already had a nice time with in the past, but not in a definitive way—like an assigned dining partner on the second night of a cruise.

"I'm Eve," Eve repeated as she tried to keep another wave from breaking.

Eve was a very familiar name. Eve was someone Muriel knew and trusted. She once took a trip with Eve—she remembered that. She could even picture Eve driving her around. Did they go shopping? Were they shopping now? Muriel looked out the window and saw her FloridaTrust branch in the background. That was Lem's business! Did Eve work with Lem? It seemed unlikely—Lem didn't hire teenagers, and Eve was wearing ripped jeans instead of a smart suit. Plus, she looked about Laura's age, but she wasn't Laura. Laura didn't have a colorful stripe in her hair or all that stuff on her ears. Was this Nancy?

Muriel's brilliant eyes moved back and forth like a metronome set to vivace. Eve could see her companion physically struggling to organize her thoughts, and she regretted confusing her. All she needed was the code, which Muriel had stated was I-R-A. But what did that mean? How could it only be three letters?

"Muriel, who's Ira?" Eve asked gently.

"My Ira?" Her darting eyes stopped suddenly and turned wet.

Eve felt rotten. She'd made a big mistake. Muriel was in no condition to partner with her on a road trip. She was lost in her dementia or whatever it was, and she didn't even know that she didn't know. She was too fragile. Eve sighed with the heavy knowledge that she would have to bring Muriel back and face the consequences. We weren't leaving Florida. And Liam hadn't asked her out. And her mother was never going to change. But her father...

"He's dead," Muriel said, and suddenly it was Eve's turn to face confusion. How did Muriel know about her father? What else did she know? "He died," Muriel elaborated, "but that's still my code: I-R-A."

"Oh," Eve uttered, recognizing the mistake.

During her year in the salon, Eve had witnessed many of the memory-challenged residents regain cogency for a few moments before sliding back into their murk. It was possible that with the fleeting return of Muriel's memory, her PIN was somehow accurate. While Eve wrangled with these thoughts, Muriel continued without hesitation: "So where exactly are we going?"

Eve wasn't sure how to answer. She knew the distance from Google Maps, but she didn't know how long it would take to accomplish the drive. Definitely days, possibly a week—there were too many factors involved, including Muriel's coherence. Eve also knew traveling so far could wear me down, and she wanted extra money in case I needed a new muffler or something. But she was worried that if she revealed the destination, Muriel would back out, and without Muriel's help, Eve would lose her chance. Her mother's car would never make the trip, and she couldn't afford to leave on her own meager resources.

We had to go. This was it.

"It's pretty far," Eve cautiously admitted, without admitting anything.

Muriel closed her eyes and put her fist under her chin. The same action in a movie would have seemed fake and overacted, but with Muriel the gesture was genuine, and striking this pose seemed to magically cure her perplexity. A moment later, Muriel relaxed her arm and responded to Eve with a renewed and rigid mind: "Okay, kid. Pretty far sounds pretty good to me."

Eve exhaled again.

"But you listen to me now." Muriel's voice rose. "Don't you ever pretend you're Laura with me again. I love that girl and that was a nasty little trick." Muriel's cut was sharp and deep.

"I'm sorry." Eve winced.

"We can fool all the other assholes, but not each other, okay?"

"I'm really sorry." Eve blushed as the cold slime she felt inside leaked from her eyes.

"All right, it's okay. Okay, Eve. Save your tears for when we really need them." Muriel reached over and squeezed Eve's shoulder. Eve released a stifled laugh and wiped her cheek. She instantly understood why Laura loved her Grams so much. She suddenly wished she had one or two of her own.

"So, what are we still doing here?" Muriel bleated. "It's too hot to sit around!"

"Uh, I still need your code to get some money," Eve reminded her.

"The code? It's Ira. I-R-A."

The circle was drawn again and Eve was unsure what to do. She didn't remember seeing letters on the ATM keys, but maybe Muriel had given her the correct code all along and she had been too arrogant to accept it. Maybe FloridaTrust offered PINs with only three characters for their elderly customers. All Eve could do was try. "I'll be right back."

"That's fine," Muriel said, quietly reflecting that she was frequently left in cars while people ran their errands around her.

Eve put the blue-and-orange card back in the ATM and was again prompted for the code. She was delighted to discover that there were, in fact, both numbers and letters on the keypad, and I-R-A corresponded to *472*. Eve typed them in, but a digital *X* remained on the screen, prompting her for the final number.

There were four required digits, of course, and her chances of hitting that last number were still only one in ten. *Shitty odds*, she thought. The ATM beeped, requesting the last digit. *Fuck!* Eve looked back at us across the parking lot, the aggravation rising in her chest. From her angle, she could see my front bumper, and for the first time, she noticed my license plate. I had a vanity plate depicting a cluster of sweet oranges hanging over the Florida state map. The top read *MYFLORIDA.COM,* and the bottom proclaimed I was registered in the Sunshine State. Sandwiched between them and pillow-embossed in vivid green letters, Eve read my distinctive moniker: IRA1. Eve slapped the wall with her left hand in an exuberant high five as her right hand flew to the "1" key and pressed it.

A moment later, the screen switched to the familiar blue background and she was given full access to the account. Her heart continued to pound as she requested a balance. The machine showed $2,121.96. Eve was delighted and withdrew $1,000, the bank's daily limit. Then she put in Muriel's other card, the gold one. She pressed *4721* and was once again granted access. She requested the balance and gasped when $238,098.12 appeared on the screen.

Eve had never seen so many numbers following a dollar sign. She could hardly fathom it. Who was this woman with her incredible car and so much money? Eve looked at the purse she was holding and felt its soft and creamy leather as if for the first time. The zippers were gold and embossed with the letters YSL. Eve knew it was expensive and figured it cost about $200, misvaluing the rare Yves Saint Laurent item by over a thousand. The machine prompted her for more instructions, and Eve decided to try something bold. She pressed *1* and then *0-0-0-0* . . . maybe . . .

The ATM replied that $2,000 was the daily limit for the gold card account. Eve took it and put all the money in the envelope from before. She was tucking it inside the purse when a loud knocking erupted from the locked-up banking side of the ATM vestibule.

It was Lemuel Worth. Laura's dad. Muriel's son.

"Hi, Eve. How's it going?" he called cheerfully through the glass.

Eve wondered if Muriel's mental issues were contagious when she grasped the lunacy of her decision to perform her felonious transactions at her best friend's father's bank, her own mother's bank, and probably the bank of a dozen other people she wished to avoid.

Lem, as he was ubiquitously known, was the branch manager and principal loan officer at FloridaTrust, and he had opened Eve's account with her first paycheck shortly after he'd recommended her to the job at The Deerwood. He practically owned the bank, according to Laura, and was a pillar of the local banking community. Eve realized it would be like going to Disney World and thinking you *wouldn't* see the castle. Her stomach fell three feet, landing somewhere near her quivering knees. How could she be *so* stupid?

Despite his perpetual presence in her life, Lem existed in an orbit that rarely attracted her direct attention, like a moon exerting a mild influence from a great distance. Laura always appeared embarrassed when her father was around her friends, so Lem pretty much left them alone in Laura's room, or in the family room, or swimming in his pool. On the rare occasions when he appeared like Haley's Comet at a birthday party or a family event, Cindy Worth, his wife, typically outshone him with her own meteoric sparkle.

"Hi." Eve responded so meekly that Lem wasn't sure if she had spoken at all. She did her best to summon a smile, praying she wouldn't vomit on the putty-colored floors.

"Is Laura with you?" he asked.

"No . . ." came her chalky response. Her mouth hung open for a moment. She wasn't sure if it was more incriminating to say anything else, or nothing at all.

"Oh okay. Your Mom just left."

Her mother?

"I guess you missed her?"

Her mother?!

"I can give you a lift home if you want. You took the bus, right?"

Eve had to escape. She had to escape at that very moment. She had to get in the stolen car with the stolen lady and the stolen cash and run run run as far far far as she possibly could. But she also couldn't appear suspicious. She had to give him an answer. She had to give him an intelligent answer. Something that made sense. Something he would accept without hesitation. She had to think. She couldn't think. She couldn't be stupid again. *Her mother was at the bank?*

"Umm—Mom and I are meeting at Chuck's Deli. She's probably in line already and wondering where I am," Eve said, finding the answer. "I should get over there."

"Chicken salad?"

"What?"

"Get their chicken salad on a croissant. It's really the best."

"Yeah? Oh, okay, thanks," she said, trying to laugh and appear loose and look normal with $3,000 of Lem's mother's money in the purse behind her hip.

"I also love their cookies," he continued with a chuckle, giving his round belly a little pat. "The peanut butter ones are incredible. They're not dry at all." Accurately sensing that his daughter's friend didn't want to discuss his skilled navigation of the deli's menu, he gave up and said through the glass, "Well, have a nice afternoon."

He turned to walk away. Eve shut her mouth, but before relief could find its way back into her taut body, he turned back again and lingered with his mouth slightly open as if he had more to say. As he stared into her, Eve discovered Mr. Worth's eyes were as richly blue and hypnotic as Muriel's. Somehow she'd never really noticed them, or him, but as he stood by the ATM vestibule, he quickly filled her view like a large planet with a thousand-mile storm resembling a glaring eye. The longer he hovered in the doorway, the lower her organs sank and pooled. Lem's continued non-exit had Eve's innards approaching her ankles.

Lem dropped his gaze to Eve's feet, and it looked like he was studying her shoes. Then he abruptly twisted his mouth into a crooked smile, spun around sharply on his own shiny black heels, and sprinted off into the deeper recesses of the recently closed bank.

Eve never saw the gold SUV that stopped briefly in front of the glass doors during their exchange. The SUV was behind her, and it blocked Lem's view of the parking lot. Without the SUV, Lem would have seen me in the distance, gleaming like a white brick on the black pavement. He would have seen his mother's white hair reflecting a patch of sunlight through the opened window. By concentrating on the SUV, he also failed to discern that it was his mother's expensive YSL TopZip Tote partially hiding beneath Eve's trembling arm.

Cindy bought the purse for Muriel the previous Christmas, using Muriel's credit card. Muriel rarely purchased things for herself, so Lem and Cindy reasoned it was their job to balance his mother's self-neglect by purchasing extravagant presents for her (with her money), knowing that in the end these possessions would be passed down to Cindy or Laura. Lem and Cindy had a brief discussion about karma as Cindy cut off the tags and wrapped Muriel's purse, Cindy's future purse that she had picked out for herself, in the renovated craft room of the house that Muriel had also unknowingly paid for. Together, Lem and Cindy decided they didn't believe in karma.

The gold SUV had provided a handy distraction, but Lem's intense focus on the afternoon's closing procedures didn't hurt, either. He visited the ATM vestibule to check on supplies and exchanged his hello with Eve while visually assessing the remaining quantities of deposit slips, envelopes, and pens. But when he was about to leave, it was the gold SUV that glued him. It pulled up when he arrived, but no one got out to perform a transaction and he couldn't make out the driver through its tinted windows. It made him nervous. He wanted to make sure Eve wasn't left alone in the vestibule with the mysterious driver, but when it slowly began to pull away, he knew she was safe, and he went to the next task thinking of nothing beyond the slips, envelopes, and pens. Eve never saw the SUV, and she didn't hear it drive off over the sound of her own hammering heart.

    She returned to us and slipped the purse onto the floor unnoticed, as she distracted Muriel once again by closing the passenger window with the master control on the driver's side.

    Eve was worried about how much time we had squandered at the bank as she drove us to her house quickly, but still with great care. While waiting for a green light en route, she prayed her mother had returned to the craft store when she finished whatever she had been doing at the bank. She also hoped Muriel's absence remained undetected at The Deerwood. Mrs. Rubinow hadn't seen Lucy drive up, so it was logical to assume that Mrs. Rubinow thought Eve was an irresponsible brat for leaving the desk and nothing more. It appeared Lucy had been too frantic to call Mr. Worth about her predicament—if she had called, then Eve would have been detained at the ATM. I could feel Eve trying to put together a possible timeline for the impending discoveries, but I could also feel ten other thoughts squeezing the relatively useless ones out.

    "One more errand," Eve said as we arrived.

    Muriel returned another "fine" with a placid nod.

    Eve ran inside her house, grabbed three large garbage bags from the kitchen drawer, and stuffed a week's worth of clothes into them. She didn't own a suitcase. She snagged random items from each of her drawers and made a point to include her limited collection of sweaters and sweatshirts before moving on to the bathroom. She emptied her sundries into reusable shopping bags and stuffed two pairs of shoes and a few paperback books on top. Her laptop was already secure in her backpack on my back seat, but she grabbed the charger. She grabbed a small sewing kit. She grabbed her book-clip reading light.

    Eve flew to the kitchen again, and grabbed fruit, cereal, and a plastic carton of orange juice. She grabbed a box of crackers and an unopened block of cheese. She grabbed a dish towel and wrapped it around two forks, two spoons, and two knives. She crammed in everything she could think of and tottered outside, overcome by the weight of her belongings. She opened my trunk and shuddered to discover I was still holding onto two bags of groceries from Lucy and Muriel's afternoon trip. The refrigerated items were still cool because everything had happened so fast.

    Eve didn't have time to look through the grocery bags. She shoved them to the side and threw everything else in the back. She pushed down on my colossal trunk lid and was surprised when I took over the final inch with my electric pull-down feature. I secured her important possessions with a quiet little clink, like the sound of champagne glasses in a toast.

Muriel dozed in my passenger seat with her mouth open, emitting a sweet little snore. Eve decided Muriel should have a few things, too, and wiping the sweat off her brow, she charged back into the house, decelerating hard when she got to her mother's room. No matter how many times she was in there, she always shuddered at the expanding preponderance of her mother's religious decor. Eve pulled a few sweaters from the closet, hoping her mother wouldn't miss them. She bypassed the pants but grabbed a few skirts, hoping Muriel's hips approximated her mother's physique. Muriel could wear Eve's shirts and socks, and Eve would buy some new underwear, somewhere, once we were finally on our way.

Before she left the room, a familiar photo caught Eve's eye: Judith on a staircase in her wedding dress, holding a bouquet of yellow roses. Eve thought the smile looked strained, like someone bracing for a car crash. She also thought it was odd her father wasn't in the photo and, considering her newfound knowledge, that the photo was displayed at all. Eve stepped on a creaky floorboard and mistakenly attributed the sound to the massive, hand-carved, painted maple cross suspended over her mother's headboard. Jesus was slumped and emaciated, his mouth forming a distorted oval as he cried out in perpetual pain. Painted blood streamed down his wooden, knotted body.

She had to get out of there.

Eve went to the emergency-fund ceramic jar with the slotted top in the kitchen pantry. They had both resolved to contribute twenty dollars from every paycheck. Eve had been diligent and was dismayed to discover that her mother had apparently forgotten all about their pact. Eve took $200, leaving something for the next car repair or high utility bill, both of which seemed to occur monthly. Even now, angry as she was, she wouldn't leave her mother stranded.

Then Eve reconsidered and took the rest. Her mother was a liar, and this *was* an emergency! She noted the clock on the microwave and cursed herself for wasting even more time listening to the creaking Jesus and worrying about her mother's shitty car.

When Eve finally plopped herself in my driver's seat and readied herself for the trip, she discovered Muriel was awake—and she wasn't wearing any pants. The trousers were wadded up in a ball on my floor. Muriel's milk-white legs were a shining, fertile field with random sprouts of short white hair. A vast and complicated system of purplish varicose veins surrounded her knees and crawled up her outer thighs. She wasn't unfit, like many of The Deerwood's sedentary residents, but even with her thin frame, her legs seemed oddly thick in the thighs, with loose flesh hanging down. Muriel was wearing an adult diaper.

"Hi, sweetheart," Muriel said warmly. "We should get going, we don't want to miss dinner."

Eve didn't know how to respond or what to do next. She wasn't sure if she should drive off immediately or spend a few minutes getting Muriel back into her pants, and reality. She tried to manufacture a full reply, but only another enervated "Oh?" escaped. Eve continued to look at Muriel's legs while her fingers trembled on my ignition. Eve again confronted the notion that what she was considering was *a really bad idea,* and she should take Muriel back to The Deerwood and keep me for herself to accomplish her mission. But in that scenario, Eve would become a car thief and likely spend the rest of her teenage years either on the run or locked behind bars.

In Florida.

No, she and Muriel had to go together, she decided. It was the only way it would work. And it had to work.

"He's waiting!" Muriel wailed. "Let's go!"

Eve looked at Muriel cautiously as her fingers continued to hover. *It's a fifty-one forty-nine decision,* she could hear her father saying. It was one of his favorite expressions.

Her father.

Eve obliged Muriel, sparked my ignition, and pulled away. After a few blocks, she thought to check my fuel gauge, and based on her limited experience with the old Corolla, she incorrectly calculated that I had approximately two hundred miles worth of fuel remaining. Rush hour had already started and traffic was dense. Eve wanted to look at the map on her phone, but she also wanted to achieve some distance before she planned our actual route. She knew I-95 would be our main line, but she had to consider the side-road options. The turnpike was the fastest way out, but she didn't want to risk electronic toll cameras screaming our whereabouts. There were so many tiny yet comprehensive decisions to make, and though we drove in a straight line, her head swam in a multitude of directions.

Eve's phone rang.

Muriel was startled, possibly thinking it was a doorbell, and she instantly reached down, found her pants, and placed them over her legs. She looked at Eve with her head down, like a dog caught eating chicken bones out of the garbage. Eve touched Muriel's shoulder lightly and said, "You were hot, no big deal." Muriel relaxed and looked at her pants. She was unsure if it was necessary to put them back on. Eve's phone continued to ring. It was Laura. Eve pressed *DECLINE* and sent her best friend to voicemail.

Not now.

The phone rang again. It was her mother.
DECLINE, DECLINE, DECLINE.
Definitely not now, and maybe not ever . . .

Within seconds, a text arrived from Laura and then another from her mother. Eve ignored them both and shut off the sound without taking her eyes off the road. Muriel managed to wrest her pants up to her thighs, but she couldn't negotiate the seatbelt and the diaper simultaneously. She gave up and focused her gaze out the side window. It was impossible for Eve to know that Muriel was trying to spot the beachside restaurant where Ira and all the grandchildren were waiting, fifteen hundred miles up the coast and twenty years in the past.

She navigated me carefully through the choked evening traffic, eventually reaching an on-ramp and crawling north. The screen of the silenced phone continued to glow and throb as more messages piled into its memory banks. Eve's tensed shoulders didn't descend for a full hour until she looked into my rearview mirror and saw the scores of shimmering headlights urging us on into an amethyst dusk.

Chapter 4

Earlier that day, about the same time Eve arrived at The Deerwood to collect her paycheck, Judith Harvick entered her local branch of FloridaTrust to meet with Lemuel Worth. I learned about the details of this meeting later on, as well as many other encounters I will come to share, but for clarity's sake I think it is best to provide a mostly chronological accounting of what happened, back in that messy October.

Lem was meditating when she arrived, a common occurrence on slower days when all the pens were stocked, all the loans were in the pipeline, and the tellers were performing without the need for supervision. Lem had about an hour with absolutely nothing to do. He couldn't leave—someone might fill out a loan application or require a large-bill cash conversion at any moment—but he'd already read the news, played a few online games, and watched a few videos on YouTube. He used his private iPad to do this while connected to the free Wi-Fi graciously provided by the family-run drugstore on the other side of his wall. The bank tracked every keystroke, but in five years of abuse, the drugstore still didn't have a password or even seem to notice.

Lem wasn't practicing a spiritual meditation or even a stress-reducing time-out. Lem put himself into a heightened state of concentration by repeating his mantras about money.

I am a money magnet. Money flows freely to me. I am worthy of all the richness I desire.

It was always about money. Where was the money, was there enough money, how could he get more money. He made a repeated effort to convince himself that he had made all the right choices for his mother, who was finally settled and safe, and that her money—the family's money—was secure. Occasionally, a subversive thought would rise up like a worm poking through the dirt, reminding him of the lines he had crossed when he rearranged Muriel's estate.

I am financially free. I permit myself to rise.

Then, in his mind, he rose like a bird and flew to that slimy anti-money worm, clawed it from the earth and swallowed its negativity whole, banishing any notions that he may have sidestepped anyone's version of morality.

I deserve all the money I have, and all the money I will always have.

"Is this a bad time?" Judith asked with a knock at his open office door. Unbeknownst to Lem, it was her second attempt at getting his attention. He looked up and saw that the pleasant-looking, somewhat mousy woman was back. He wondered how long she had been standing there while he stared blankly toward the distant corner of his desk thinking about money-birds and worms.

"You were totally lost there," she said quietly, belying her amazement that he didn't see her.

"Ha, sorry about that." He straightened his tie, cleared his throat, and shifted to stand up. He struggled with the rotating chair on wheels as his heavy frame sought leverage.

"Don't get up," she said, taking her own seat on the other side of the desk. His feet found the floor and he resumed a balanced, bankerly posture.

"How are you, Mrs. Harvick? Nice to see you again."

"I'm well, thank you. I'm here about the car loan?"

"Of course." Lem entered the last four digits of her social and her birthday to unlock the system. "Let's see. Okay. Okay."

About two seconds later, Lem learned her loan had been denied, but he stalled in the hopes of providing a pleasing and friendly atmosphere for what was about to become a gloomy experience. Customers didn't like being denied loans.

"Let's see. Um, it's coming up. The computers are slow today."

Judith waited patiently, understanding that the excuse was socially acceptable but likely untrue. Computers were rarely slow—it was the users who were incompetent. She sat with her legs uncrossed but pressed together tightly, her back straight, her hands folded neatly on the black faux-leather purse in her lap. Her hair was pulled back, and she had taken extra time to put on a touch of neutral lipstick. She wore a white blouse and a khaki blazer that matched her shin-length khaki skirt. She felt extremely professional and businesslike in her black hosiery and one-inch heels. The simple gold cross resting on her neck was polished and unadorned.

The cross was four inches tall and looked weighty. It was all Lem could see when he looked at her.

"I think we've finally got it," Lem said, continuing to stall. He started playing with the mouse and manipulating the screen, which was turned away from Judith. He clicked and repeatedly scrolled up and down. "Would you like some water or anything?"

"No thank you."

"Coffee?"

She shook her head.

"We have pretty good coffee here. It's really no problem."

"No, I'm fine. Thank you."

"Okay," he said flatly. Playtime was over. He put the mouse to the side and clasped his hands together gently. He looked directly into Judith's brown eyes, which were like a solid wall of mahogany, and said, "I'm very sorry, but it looks like your loan was denied."

Here it comes, Lem thought. Many customers went through the stages of grief when they found out the bank wasn't going to lend them money by expressing anger, denial, bargaining, depression, and acceptance in one shot: "What the hell do you mean?! That can't be right, did you use the right numbers? Well, is there anything I can do? I really need this loan to get back on my feet . . . Oh well." Sometimes the stages were self-resolved in a quick monologue, but more typically it was a lengthy back-and-forth process. He hated the pleas, the petitions, the indignation. He had heard about a loan officer at another bank who was stabbed by a disappointed customer. A week later, Lem had encountered a wrath so threatening that the bank assigned him a bodyguard for three days. Delivering tough news was the most stressful part of Lem's job, aside from the ever-present possibility of a robbery or a hostage situation, though Lem felt confident he could survive by hiding under his thick desk and using his iPad as a shield.

Lem didn't know why people assumed the loan decisions were up to him. He wasn't the bank and it wasn't his money. There were algorithms and computer models and a thousand factors involved in the decision that went far beyond the scope of his "final approval." He was simply the messenger, and people shouldn't shoot the messenger.

Lem hoped Mrs. Harvick would go through the stages of her loan-denial grief quickly so he could get back to the important business of thinking about money. He also wanted to shop online for some deeply padded dress shoes with more room in the toe.

"Okay," she said. She picked up her purse, stood, and stretched out her hand to shake his.

Lem was confused. She had skipped all the steps! And Judith Harvick didn't look like someone who skipped steps. She was in her early forties, not wealthy, not destitute, not pretty, not ugly, not fat, not thin, not short, and not tall. She had brown hair that was neither straight nor curly. She didn't wear nail polish or any form of eye makeup. There were two pinprick piercings in her small earlobes, but no earrings. She was devoid of all accouterments except for some flesh-toned lipstick and her concerningly large cross. She wore no rings. Judith was as nondescript as a sheet of blank paper. It didn't help that she also showed no emotion. *She would be perfect for government work,* he thought as he glanced at the loan application on his screen and reconfirmed that she was the assistant manager at the local arts and crafts store. Judith earned $19.35 an hour and worked thirty-five hours a week. She lived in a late 1970s duplex townhouse and paid about $1,500 a month.

"Has something changed?"

He looked up. Judith's hand was still extended.

"Uh, no. I was just looking through your application to see if there was anything else I could do."

"So I wasn't denied?"

"No, you were. Again, I'm sorry."

"Okay," she said again, as complacent as the first time, no anger, no pretense. Lem listened to her say "Okay" like she actually believed it. It was too strange. Judith had decided she wanted a car loan and had gone through the process of investigating products from various sources, filling out the requisite paperwork, and collecting her financial documents. Because she feared a hacker might compromise her identity, she had driven to the bank to meet with him and personally submit her request. Then she had waited patiently for the bank to enter her data (which went online anyway), and she had taken time off from work to meet with him a second time. Despite all this effort, somehow it was completely "Okay" that she was denied? Her calm acceptance was unnerving and illogical.

"Are you sure?" Lem asked.

Judith lowered her hand. "Am I sure about what? You said I was denied."

"Yes, that's true. But, I mean, do you want an explanation? I don't want you to think of FloridaTrust as the bad guy."

"I don't think of you as a bad guy, Mr. Worth. I know how these things work."

"Sure," he blurted, "but if you're going for a loan somewhere else, I'd be careful. There are a lot of sharks out there with rubber interest rates and balloon payments and----"

"Thank you. I'm not exactly sure what we're going to do, but it will be fine." She took a long moment and swallowed before she felt compelled to add, "My car is on its last breath and it would make life a lot easier if Eve also had a car, but if I don't have what it takes, then I'll have to work with what I have, and Eve will have to earn it for herself, too. The challenge will be fortifying."

The challenge will be fortifying?

She continued, "We may not have all the answers, Mr. Worth, but we always have the answers we need. And your answer is 'No' and I accept your answer, so I'll be on my way."

"Wait----" Lem said, indicating she should sit.

"I have to get back to work," she replied.

"This won't take long, I promise. There may be a way... Please..."

Judith reluctantly sat down again.

Lem pulled his chair in and straightened himself. He studied the computer, hoping her numbers were right on the edge so he might tip the scales in her favor. If he could help Judith and Eve with their automotive needs, it would relieve him of the burden of having to purchase another car for his own kids. Christian had friends with cars, but Lem was tired of Laura's constant complaints that she was too old for the bus and could never get around. Cindy had added that she didn't want her life to revolve around Laura's needs and that it was too dangerous for an attractive sixteen-year-old to rideshare with strangers in Florida. But if Eve had a car . . .

Judith was silent as Lem analyzed her expenses.

"It looks like your food bill is pretty high. Higher than most," he said, wondering with some jealousy how she could eat so much and maintain her lithe structure.

"I use Quicken to keep track of all of my receipts," she replied. "It's to the penny, and it includes the cash I use at the farmers' market."

Of course it does, he thought. *She tracks her cash.*

"The IRS must love you." He laughed.

Judith didn't laugh.

"But, see, it's a lot higher than the average for two people, and you don't look, uh . . ." He stopped himself. "Do you eat out a lot?"

"No, Eve and I both cook. Most of the food is organic—maybe that's it? And I also donate weekly to the church's food pantry," she said.

"Oh?" he replied.

"They need all the help they can get."

"Right. Well, hey, I think that's great," Lem said. He hoped he sounded sincere because internally he believed she was being manipulated. The church had plenty of money. They had immaculate, air-conditioned, multi-thousand-square-foot buildings with new paint and perfect lawns and no tax bills, yet she bought *extra* food for them and reported the expense as part of her own consumption? Without considering the write-offs? Lem continued, "It also shows here that you donate quite a bit to charity."

"At least ten percent, but I'll give more if I take on extra hours or if Eve can grab another shift."

"How is Eve?" he asked. "Still at The Deerwood?" He remembered seeing her in the salon a few weeks earlier, combing out Mrs. Pratt's wiry hair.

"She's a teenager," Judith said coolly.

Lem chuckled knowingly.

"She's not certified to cut hair, but they let her assist with the coloring and blowouts. Mostly she sweeps the scraps."

"Does she get tips?"

"I don't know," Judith said, suddenly wondering how much Eve earned.

"I didn't see Eve's income on the application."

"No, I only put the money I make on the form. Her money is her money."

"But you said her money contributes to the household expenses."

"Well, yes, that's true, but I don't want to involve her in this."

"Mrs. Harvick," Lem pushed the computer screen to the side to focus on her. "Mrs. Harvick, the loan is for Eve to have a car, so wouldn't you say she's kind of involved anyway?"

Judith began to feel as though she were on a witness stand. An uncomfortable wetness spread quickly through her armpits.

Lem continued, "I also think the food you donate can be counted as part of the ten percent you give. We don't have to record it as a ten percent donation, *plus* all the food, do we?"

Judith shifted in her seat, which was also growing warm.

"And is it a rule, this ten percent? Or is it more like . . . a guideline?"

It was an inquisition. Judith had already been denied the loan, but he continued to challenge her, to question her decisions. Her authority. She flapped her arms once to release some heat and replied, "It is a Biblical commandment, Mr. Worth. Numbers 18:26, 'You must present a tenth of that tithe as the Lord's offering.'"

Lem rolled himself back slowly, away from her and the computer.

"I didn't mean to upset you," he said carefully.

"I'm not upset."

They paused and looked into each other's eyes, her dark brown meeting his cool blue. After a long moment, he blinked and resumed speaking. "The thing is, looking this over, I think I can legitimately change some of these numbers to more accurately reflect your situation . . . and that might make the difference on your loan."

Judith realized she was clenching her toes. She flexed them to release the pressure. She was embarrassed about her rising anxiety, and she silently prayed for God to protect her and give her the strength to remain true under Mr. Worth's scrutiny. She knew the bank would make money if the loan was accepted, but she also really wanted a reliable car, and maybe one for Eve, if she started behaving. And if she apologized.

"Would you be willing to let me try?" he pressed.

"I won't lie," Judith said.

"Of course not!" Lem laughed. He had to remind himself that Judith didn't know anything about his financial prowess. "No one's going to lie, Mrs. Harvick! But the food you donate shouldn't be in your personal food budget, and the money you so generously give, well, that can go into a different category that doesn't register as an ongoing expense. You aren't *legally* obligated to make these donations. What you're doing is great, but it's voluntary."

She glared.

"It's *considered* voluntary by FloridaTrust," he amended. "Also, I think a reasonable portion of Eve's earnings could be added into your household's sources of income and, I'm just spitballing here, maybe if we classify Eve's contributions as an ongoing *gift*, then we won't have to include her W-2s in the application. Your statements already show when she gives you money, and that, that, *that* can come from anywhere. You're allowed to accept gifts, Mrs. Harvick. Even from your daughter." He was getting excited. "Basically, uh, if we rework the same numbers into different categories and drop a bit of what you donate—just a bit—it might, it might, it *might* tip the scales in your favor. You didn't pick a car yet, so I think I can put this through as a personal loan instead of a preapproval for a car loan, and since you're already a valued customer with FloridaTrust, that could get you a little more money, or possibly a better rate."

Lem clicked a few keys and blinked his bright blue eyes.

"You might just get everything you want, Mrs. Harvick." He beamed.

Judith thought about it. Perhaps God had provided this bulbous man to help her. Both Lem and God obviously knew more about finances than she did, and after Richard, she had learned that numbers were not immutable. She remained wary, but decided to see where the river might take her. If it went too far, she could always paddle to the side and rescind her application. And if it worked, she might reach the open ocean and have reliable vehicles by the end of the week! Then maybe Eve would stop hating her for five minutes. Judith stopped sweating.

"Go for it," she said, leaning back and pulling on the lapels of her blazer as she adjusted to his ideas.

Lem exaggerated Eve's approximate income and added unverifiable tips. He cut their food expenditure in half, discarding the food bank extras and their predilection for organics. He eliminated the expense of the straight donations and, in less than a dozen keystrokes, he increased Judith's total income by $17,400 a year. He printed a paper reflecting the change and gently placed it in front of her with a pen, seeking a signature.

Judith looked at the distilled, two-dimensional profile of her multidimensional life. It held the power to propel her forward, constrain her to the present, or consign her to an unknown freefall through its implied deceit.

Mr. Worth appeared to be a good, honest, hardworking, fair-minded individual who genuinely wanted to help her achieve her goals. But the paper he wanted her to sign professed she earned nearly thirty-five percent more than she did. Even with Eve's income, it seemed outrageous. If Judith stopped donating and helping—stopped being who she was—it would still be a huge stretch to imagine that she could manifest that kind of money. She didn't know exactly how much Eve earned, but was it enough to make them a full one-third richer? Could she put her trust in FloridaTrust? Judith had related her financial story, and like a perverse game of telephone, Lem had changed the entire synopsis when he read it back to her. He was the manager and the loan officer and this was what he did, day in and day out. People everywhere seemed to get loans all the time, and people everywhere also drove beautiful cars. Maybe this was how the world worked, but to Judith, it didn't *feel* right. It didn't *feel* honest. Maybe Mr. Worth wasn't sent by God to help her. Maybe it was a test. The pen remained on the paper, and Judith's hands remained clasped in her lap.

"Can I get in trouble for this?" Judith whispered.

"Trouble? What do you mean?" Lem responded, genuinely perplexed.

"The IRS? Will they . . . find out? Will my taxes go up if they find out?"

"They can't find out anything," he said, a little too quickly. "What I mean is, there's nothing *to* find out that can't be explained if someone wanted more details. This isn't a lie, Mrs. Harvick. This is a legitimate representation of your income and expenses. I assume your daughter is paid legally?"

"What do you mean?"

"She doesn't get anything under the table?"

"What?! No! No, I would never allow that. She gets a normal paycheck."

"Okay, well that's an additional income to your household that you didn't report on your first application. And you *do* donate food and you *do* give to charity, but those expenses aren't fixed. You can change your mind at any time about those things, so they don't belong on the application."

"But I won't," Judith insisted.

"I understand that, but from a legal perspective, you don't have to give ten percent to the church. You choose to, but you don't have to, and the bank is more concerned with your obligations than your choices. You could choose to go to Disney World every day of the week or buy a thousand doughnuts for your friends, but you wouldn't report any of that as an expense on your loan application, would you? Do you understand? If you didn't give away that money, then you would more than qualify for the loan based on your total household income, including Eve's share."

She took this in and replied, "Let's say I qualify for this, but somewhere down the road I can't make the payments. You're saying if I stop donating, then I *will* have the money I need for the loan? Is that what these new numbers mean?"

"Exactly!" Lem said, relieved that she understood the concept.

Judith stood up and extended her hand once more.

"Thank you, Mr. Worth. I really appreciate your time and effort on this."

Lem was dumbfounded. "You're going?"

"Yes. I can't sign these papers."

"I don't understand----"

"I think you do. It's pretty clear that I can't afford the loan, so it's better if I don't take it."

"But you *can* afford the loan."

"I can only afford the loan if I stop doing God's work, and I can't do that. I *won't* do that to God."

Lem was both baffled and bemused. Even in southern Florida, he didn't encounter many people who talked like her or believed in their religion so . . . painfully. Not when it came to money. Not when it came to getting a car or a home or a boat. Judith seemed to be a perfectly normal woman who wanted a loan that he could get for her, but she was willing to give it up for a bunch of strangers who took from the church, and from her. They didn't care if it held her back. The church certainly didn't care. Yet Judith was happy to give it all away—even at the literal expense of her daughter.

Lem thought about Laura and how she babysat when it suited her, but she didn't rely on the money. He quickly considered how different her life was from her best friend's. He pictured Eve at The Deerwood, sweeping hair, maybe even his mother's hair. Those sliding glass doors were really rolling iron bars. He couldn't imagine what Eve must think when she compared her life to Laura's. She had so little, and they all had so much.

"You think Eve will understand?" he pried.

Judith smiled broadly, clutched her purse, and buttoned her blazer.

"She doesn't know I'm here, so she won't be disappointed. I'm sure one day she'll get a car, but today is not that day. Thank you again, Mr. Worth. It was nice seeing you. God bless."

Judith turned and left as quietly as she had arrived, while Lem remained seated and slowly rolled his chair back. He couldn't decide if Judith Harvick was a smart woman or a fool, but he knew Laura would have thrown a fit if he could get her a car but didn't because of . . . because of . . . was it a *principle*? Judith was brainwashed. Who were these people who demanded ten percent of a person's income? Ten percent was a lot of money! Especially for a woman with such limited means! Lem could never trust any invisible godly force that demanded such a price. He respected the nobility of living in a lower income bracket and helping others, but to what end? What was the point? Why couldn't those people feed themselves? If the food she provided stopped coming, then maybe they would feel a touch of *incentive* to find some work, he thought. Everyone should work for what they have, just like he did. Every damned day. How did it help God, or anyone else, if Judith Harvick was on the brink of needing charity herself because she gave so much away?

He took back the paper and pen. He shredded the printed document but saved Judith's revised application on his computer. *She'll come to her senses*, he thought. *If Eve is anything like Cindy or Laura, she'll find out what happened and they'll have a big fight. Judith will come back with her long mouse-tail between her skirted mouse-legs and Lemuel Worth will be happy to provide her a wonderful loan on behalf of FloridaTrust.*

It was the end of the day and Lem had to run the closing chores. He stood too quickly and a splash of dizziness doused him. As he flattened his palms on the desk to steady himself, a strong and painful pressure in his right big toe overwhelmed the vertigo. He would have to tell Cindy that the southernmost tip of his right foot was sore again. The Keys, he liked to call it. She'd make him feel better. She always made him feel better. He might even get sex on a Monday!

Lem left his office without realizing he never shook Judith's hand.

***

Judith returned to work. She traded her skirt for a pair of beige jeans and her blazer for a smock in the craft store's oversized restroom. She sniffed her armpits and was relieved her flush of sweat had been temporary, noting that the overwhelming scent of cinnamon in the store would likely supersede any of her body's odors. She tucked her flexible measuring tape, pen, pencil, sharpie, and calculator into her outside pockets. She checked her phone before she went to the main floor to see if Eve had responded to her voicemail suggestions for dinner. Eve still wasn't talking to her, and Judith decided to eat a salad alone. Eve could take care of herself.

Judith saw a new message from Kathy that must have arrived when she had silenced the phone at the bank. Kathy confirmed that they had made a unanimous decision: the prayer group would now meet on Wednesdays at Paul's house instead of Judith's on Tuesdays. Kathy knew Judith worked until 9:00 p.m. on Wednesdays and wouldn't be able to attend anymore. Kathy's message began with a shaky and apologetic overture, but over the course of twenty seconds she became forcibly pragmatic and stern. She concluded by saying they would see her for church on Sundays, and they would all continue to pray for her, and especially for Eve.

It was the correct course of action, and Judith appreciated their consideration in taking nearly a week to make the decision—or at least to announce it. That was a small kindness. Still, losing her group was a major blow, and Judith swallowed hard. She would continue to pray for Eve, like always.

She closed her eyes, knowing the incident would replay itself in her mind again, no matter how hard she fought to repress it. Was it really only a week ago? Six days. It had been six long days of mutual silence since Judith put out her typical spread of baked goods and candy and Eve thundered through the front door, late from work and drenched in sweat.

"You'd better hop in the shower—they'll be here in ten minutes."

"Then you should have picked me up," Eve hollered from the upstairs hall leading to her room.

"The car's in the shop again. I texted you. You couldn't get a ride?"

"From who?"

"Dorie?"

"Dorie lives in the exact opposite direction, and I'm not going to ask my *boss* for a stupid ride home."

"Well, that's silly, I'm sure she wouldn't mind. What about Laura?" Judith called up the stairs, straining her voice over Eve's loud music. "Or her brother?"

Eve didn't answer, and Judith heard the shower start up. A few moments later, various congregants began to arrive and mingle. Judith served up the cookie platter and then called for Eve to turn down the music, but Eve was still in the shower and didn't hear her. Judith excused herself and went into Eve's room to find the stereo.

"What are you doing?" Eve asked from the doorway, wrapped loosely in a well-worn bath towel. "We both agreed you wouldn't come in here."

"I'm turning it down," Judith whispered, spinning the knob. "People are already here."

"I don't care, this is my room! You're not allowed in my room!"

"Calm down, I'm leaving," Judith said. As she turned to exit, she noticed a photograph on Eve's dresser. It was unframed and casually leaning against a Disney World snow globe. The five-by-seven showed Eve and her father on a beach near Miami. Eve was six years old and sitting on Richard's shoulders, her arms outstretched as if embracing the entire world in a gleeful hug. Her smile was luminous despite the dark gap from a missing front tooth. Richard beamed in the sunlight, and Judith could almost feel his thick beard and mustache through the flat image.

"Where did you get that?" Judith demanded, pointing across the room.

"Get out!" Eve yelled.

"Where did you get that picture? It was in *my* photo album in the back of *my* closet! If I'm not allowed in your room, then you're *certainly* not allowed in mine!"

"It's me and Dad, it's not yours!"

"You had no right to take it!" Judith lashed out, surprised by her own raised voice.

"Well, you have no right to keep it locked up in your ugly room," Eve spat back. "You're not even in it!!"

"Who do you think *took* the picture, Eve? Who?"

"I dunno, *Judith*. Fucking GOD?!"

Judith could hear a collective gasp from the seventeen souls gathered for prayer in her living room below. Eve and Judith stood frozen on either side of the bedroom, neither daring to budge.

"I pray for you," Judith whispered.

"Get out!" Eve seethed. Judith made a motion toward the dresser to retrieve the photo, but Eve blocked her, slapping Judith's hand away and losing her damp towel in the process.

"We have guests!" Judith recoiled, assessing her hand.

"I don't care!" Eve wailed. "I don't care about your fucking prayer group or any of that bullshit! I'm sick of it! It's not like it's making any of you better people, it's all just stupid crap!"

"Oh no, Eve. Oh no . . ." Judith cried out as she quickly ran to the hall and down the stairs to escape the outburst and find comfort with her friends. Judith wailed, "She's possessed!" as Eve continued her rant against religion. She chased Judith until she reached the landing of the open stairwell and saw Kathy and Earl staring up at her. Their faces seemed contorted, as if something was pulling rigorously at their guts, and Eve heard the slow tick of the Berlin clock on the wall before it fully dawned on her that she was stark naked in front of everyone. Kathy's sister was also there with her husband, and Larry, their teenaged son with the brain injury, along with another kid Eve knew from school, the neighbor from two doors down . . . everyone. A lingering drop of water slid off the end of Eve's magenta stripe and hit the floor. She screamed, ran back to her room, slammed the door, and turned the music as high as it would go. Iced tea glasses on the coffee table downstairs clinked from the heavy bass.

So the meetings were moved to Wednesdays and away from the Harvick household, although Judith was still welcome to attend if she could find a way to change her inflexible work schedule. Eve would be graciously allowed back if she wrote a formal apology to each member of the group, including Larry, who clapped when he saw her naked. She would also have to agree to attend the church for weekly services as well as volunteer for an assortment of other functions through the end of the calendar year.

Eve expressed no interest.

Judith wiped her eyes and put her phone deep in the pocket of her smock before settling in to work the rest of her shift. She continued her progress on reorganizing the framing section and helped a young customer and her father find the newest selection of paint-by-number beach scenes.

***

Four hours later, Judith hit a speed bump a little too quickly, and her car resumed the bup-bup-bup sound she had spent nearly $800 to eradicate only two weeks prior.

She rounded the corner into her townhome development and followed the winding streets until she found her driveway, distinguished only by a small black metal cross perched over the garage.

Someone was standing at the front door and her lawn appeared to be on fire.

Judith reached behind her seat and clutched the metal bat she kept for such occasions—this being the first. She was surprised by its warmth and how comfortable it felt in her grip. She feared having to use it and hoped Jesus would protect her, but in case He was busy with someone more in need, she was happy to have it by her side. As she cautiously approached the lawn, she discovered that the flickering glow was the result of nearly a hundred illuminated paper bags. One bag had caught on fire from within, but it was nearly consumed by the time she arrived. She used her shoe to smother the paltry embers into the bag's sandy base and the green grass of her shared lawn. The figure at the door was unaware of her presence, focused solely on ringing the bell. He appeared in silhouette against her porch light.

"Hello?" she called out from a relatively safe distance.

Liam had expected someone to open the door from within and was startled when Judith's voice came from the opposite direction. He spun around. "Oh hey! Is Eve home?"

"Who are you?" she asked, peering at him. Her trepidation lifted somewhat when she saw that her visitor was a clean-cut high school kid with oversized teeth and flowing bangs to match. He was young and slender, and holding a bouquet of sunflowers. He didn't appear to have any wayward piercings, visible tattoos, or leather tendrils hanging from ripped clothing. Kids in letterman jackets seemed increasingly rare, and she didn't want to scare this one off. At the same time, she remained visibly annoyed about Eve and their fight, her cranky car, the shenanigans at the bank, and now the dozens of little fires burning in bags on her front lawn.

"I'm Liam."

"Am I supposed to know you, Liam?"

"I go to West Hills? I'm Christian's friend?"

"What are you doing here, on a school night?"

"Is Eve home?" he said, stroking the door. "I was kinda . . . I was hoping I could talk to Eve."

"She didn't answer?" Judith assumed Eve was home and had no idea why she wouldn't be. Drama club didn't meet on Mondays. "Did you hear the bell inside? It's a little touchy."

"Yeah, I hear it," he said, pressing it again. "Maybe she's, like, taking a shower or something?"

Judith didn't want to envision Liam imagining her daughter taking a shower, and she quickly sputtered, "No, she's probably just wearing her headphones. I'm sure she's home. Hold on."

Instead of doing the simple thing and going inside, Judith took out her phone and called Eve. She wanted to keep her eye on Liam. He seemed nice enough, maybe a little simple, but every day there was another report on the news of someone being accosted by a friendly stranger, and Judith wasn't about to unlock her doors for someone strong enough to earn a letterman jacket. She continued to hold the bat by her side. Eve didn't answer. Judith texted. No answer. She called again, surveying the glowing luminaria while she paced.

"I don't understand this," she said, referring to the lack of communication from Eve, but Liam thought she was talking about his expansive display. He replied, "It says 'HOME' with a question mark."

"Home?"

"Yeah." He shrugged but still managed to look proud.

"What does that mean?"

"Oh, you know, it's like 'PROM?' but for homecoming."

Judith's face was blank.

"I wanna ask Eve to homecoming. Is she here?"

Judith could now see how the bags would form the word when viewed from Eve's bedroom window, which overlooked her front lawn. It concerned her that Liam had considered the view and knew which window was Eve's. Judith was uncomfortable with this boy and his effusive gesture, but she was more enraged by the idea that Eve had somehow attracted him. She thought about Eve's accidental nudity in front of the prayer group; it had been the first time Judith had seen her daughter's fully developed breasts, and it appeared Eve attended to the pubic hair beneath her hourglass hips. She was beautiful, and the boys were already buzzing around her. Judith realized it was going to take a lot more than prayer to protect Eve. She texted her daughter again, and then again, while Liam waited patiently on the porch with his hands in his pockets, paying no attention to the bat in Judith's hand.

Chapter 5

I could feel Eve's angst rising with each vibration of her phone; every notification was a mini-earthquake in her pocket. Eve knew she had to communicate with someone before the police were summoned, or she would be forever trapped in Broward County. She had to assume that everyone knew we were gone, everyone was worried, everyone wanted answers. They all wanted to return me and Muriel to our respective cages, and Eve figured they were building a new one just for her. She wondered which member of Team Muriel would call the police first, and whether Mr. Worth was the type of man to shoot first and then ask questions—why wouldn't he be, where his rich mother was concerned? Eve also wondered who would call Judith to explain her dastardly stunt. How would her mother react? Would Judith try to talk Lem out of involving law enforcement, or would she sign the arrest warrant herself? Eve hoped Judith's religious convictions might instill a desire to protect her daughter, but Judith also believed in higher powers of justice, and Eve could see her praying that a little jail time would straighten out her irreverent child. Judith's predilection for higher concepts of religion over the nitty-gritty concerns of their daily life was one of the million reasons Eve needed to get out of there. Judith was the only one who appeared to understand God's Will in their townhouse, and Eve found it suspicious that He always favored her mother's notions—especially since her mother was a liar.

We were nearly an hour north of Deerfield Beach in congested evening traffic, edging past the signs for West Palm Beach. The sun was losing power as it skipped along the horizon and threatened to drop into the city lights to the west. As the last of its orange light strobed between distant homes and trees, Muriel felt as though the long shadows were tugging against her cheek, drawing her reluctantly back into full consciousness. Too often she preferred the comfortable and familiar blanket of her dreams with its rolling waves of memory—grandchildren playing happily in the sand, in the snow, in the pool. She was reluctant to open her eyes, but once reality began to accelerate, she fully perceived the terrain beyond my windows.

"Eve?" she asked, both awake and aware.

We waded through the traffic under Eve's remarkable guidance while the other half of her mind was busy reassessing each one of the afternoon's decisions. Her hair still smelled like coconuts from the morning shower and she was wearing the same underwear she'd put on at 6:45 a.m., but the gulf of hours between the thick sunrise and the thinning sunset felt, bewilderingly, both compressed and expansive. She remembered chatting with Laura by Liam's locker and watching his pen dart in and out of his mouth in Spanish class. *Was that really today?*

"Eve?"

Eve glanced over at Muriel. She looked different. She seemed . . . stirred. She wasn't merely awake, she was *vivid*.

"Hey," Eve said gently, unsure if more words were required. She wanted to stay focused on the road and redirected her attention straight ahead.

Muriel sat up and soon noticed that her pants weren't entirely up to her waist and that part of the padding showed. She quickly unbuckled her seatbelt, extended her legs, and pulled the fine linen of her pants up and over her buttocks. "That's better," she said. "I hate wearing them, but . . . I guess sometimes . . ." Muriel looked out at the buildings as the clouds above them turned purple. "Why are we in West Palm?"

Eve had spent so much time drawing up a mental blueprint for the trip that she had completely discounted Muriel's relevance to the project. She thought Muriel might sleep through most of the journey, but only an hour into it she was already unusually cogent and seeking answers.

Despite the drama in the bank parking lot and a few quiet sessions in the salon, Eve really only knew Muriel through Laura. Most of what she knew seemed pretty mundane and typical of most grandparents. Eve didn't know Muriel well enough to reveal her full plan, and she feared it could prematurely send Muriel over some unknown edge. Muriel clearly wanted to leave The Deerwood, but if she knew the scope of Eve's intentions . . . At this point, too much information was simply too much information. We were still only thirty miles from The Deerwood's lobby.

"We're taking a trip," Eve decided to respond, keeping her voice cheerful.

"A trip?" I knew Muriel liked trips. I knew Muriel liked *planned* trips.

"Yeah."

Muriel raised her eyebrows, sensing that Eve's itinerary was more of a tumbleweed in the wind than the rooted-oak programming she preferred.

"Well, that sounds fun," Muriel hedged. "Where are we going?"

Eve stalled by putting on my blinker and repeatedly checking the adjacent lane.

"Where are we going with my car?" Muriel pressed.

Eve turned off the blinker and found Muriel's eyes reflecting the last ember of sunlight. "We're going home."

Muriel perked up as the word snuggled against her deeper mind. *Home* was a beautiful word; perhaps the most beautiful of them all, next to *Love*. Upon hearing it, Muriel instantly conjured a pink Victorian structure with a roaring fireplace and the mingling, sweet aromas of ginger cookies, morning coffee, and wood polish. Home was populated by the people she cared for, both the living and those captured in the photographs that preserved their joy. Home was warm and safe and familiar, and Muriel was delighted that Eve was so intent on driving there.

We were all going home, and Eve quickly returned her focus to the front. Muriel was delighted until she began to sort through the details Eve had purposefully concealed, and as the sun finally fell beyond our reach, Muriel's eyes darkened. We were in West Palm Beach, which meant the pink Victorian was far, far away. Eve had told her we were taking a trip, and Muriel considered that people typically took trips *away* from their homes, not *to* them. Muriel had begun to unravel these small paradoxes when we passed a sign alerting us to the exit for Blue Heron Boulevard. Muriel bolted upright and nearly scraped her head on my fabric roof.

"Oh, you're bringing me back to *my place*?! It's finally fixed? You little fox!" Muriel poked Eve's leg with her finger. "This is great!" she gushed with unconstrained excitement as she tapped her hands rhythmically against my dashboard. "You're bringing me home!" she sang. "Now I get it! *Finally!!*" Eve didn't know what Muriel was referring to, but the woman suddenly looked bright and energized, as if she were made of lightning. "This is so wonderful, what a true surprise!" she went on.

Eve's confusion increased when Muriel rambled, "Is Lem already there with my things? And the children? I knew that was him in the truck you let pass and you're just driving the car to throw me off. Ha. What a sweet little plan you all made behind my back! You think you can pull one over on the old lady? How delicious! Hey, turn here."

Eve followed Muriel's curious enthusiasm and we exited for Blue Heron. She wanted to know why Muriel was so fired up. She also saw that I was getting hungry for more gas.

"That's it, follow the signs. You know where it is."

"Uh, actually they didn't give me *exact* directions. From here, I mean," Eve said, feebly playing into Muriel's reverie. "And I think I lost them in traffic. Good thing you woke up when you did."

"Yes," Muriel said with a strange certainty. "Yes, good thing. Take this over the bridge and we'll be on the island soon enough, but follow the curve slowly or we'll end up in the water."

"Got it."

Muriel's excitement began to seep into Eve. Holding the leather purse, seeing the bank balance, and even driving me around had made Eve profoundly curious about Muriel's life before The Deerwood—and now she believed she was about to see it. She didn't know what Muriel meant when she said it was fixed, which was concerning, but she accepted that she didn't really know anything about Muriel's circumstances at all. Laura had never explained why her Grams was at The Deerwood or how long she had been there. Eve also didn't know if Lucy had been with her before she moved into managed care.

Eve also knew nothing about Muriel's medications.

There was an invisible and uncrossable chasm that existed between Eve and the residents who came to the salon. The gulf of seventy, eighty, or even ninety years, imprinted by life experiences in the very texture of their flesh, was a murky abyss that neither side seemed to have the tools, or desire, to navigate. When Eve washed their hair and massaged their scalps, she learned a little about their lives through subdued queries, but sifting through the mud of their stories rarely yielded more than a few flecks of gold. She'd come to believe that at one time, all her customers had possessed cared-for homes and experienced remarkable friendships, lengthy careers, drunken escapades, familial feuds, ardent conquests, magnificent vacations, and rebellious children—and perhaps even participated in some insurrections of their own. They'd lived fully in their time, but now the suds were sliding down the drain and taking these shining nuggets with them—or they were already too deeply buried amidst their tired, failing abilities. Sometimes Eve was privy to glints of their shimmering histories before they disappeared through cheesecloth memories—dribbles about a secret relative, tales of building their empires or surviving a war—but mostly she heard surface-level talk about body aches, feelings of abandonment, and what it was like, both physically and metaphorically, to shrink.

On a good day, and with the right patron, Eve could occasionally steer the subject to geography. It wasn't exactly gold, but it was still a precious metal to Eve, who had never left the state. Only a small handful of the residents had spent their whole lives in Florida—the majority were snowbirds. They came to escape the harsh winters and eventually clipped their own wings to avoid the hassles of flying between two places. Conceptually, they enjoyed living in Florida permanently, but Eve had discovered that most of them dealt with the oppressive southern summers the same way they had once endured their overbearing northern winters: by staying indoors and wishing for a respite, however short, and a return to their sorely missed favorite season.

Eve particularly enjoyed hearing stories about twelve-foot piles of snow and the colorful glow of ice over buried Christmas lights. She reveled in descriptions of crowded skating rinks in Central Park or the seclusion of a frozen mountain lake—so cold you could literally drive a truck on it and so thoroughly thickened you had to use a crazy-long drill to get to the fish, who magically survived! She longed for details on every subject so she could insert herself into their recollections, but the elements often dissolved as quickly as they appeared, like snowflakes on a warm tongue.

But here, at last, was a small bridge; a connection to a life that existed before the jaws of The Deerwood closed and chewed and swallowed. Eve was about to drive me on the very same streets that Muriel and I had once traveled and she was going to get a glimpse of Muriel's former Floridian life! Muriel became very real to Eve in that moment—she was no longer just another old woman who occasionally needed a haircut.

The last four miles of Blue Heron Boulevard contained an unremitting series of motley strip malls, fast-food outlets, drugstores, and pawnshops. Eve saw tightened bands of low, flat homes with bars on every window cowering between the retail buildings. We passed a police department near Old Dixie Highway, and Eve tensed when three cars pulled out behind us with their lights and sirens blaring. They turned quickly in the opposite direction, but her nervous system remained on edge. The further we drove away from I-95, the more Eve questioned our detour. *Muriel used to live here?* she pondered anxiously. She wondered if Muriel had confused Blue Heron Boulevard with something else, since so many Floridian streets were named after colors and birds.

Her fears subsided when we crossed a mile-long bridge over Lake Worth Lagoon and Muriel let forth a squeal like a toddler catching air on a swing set. "We're almost there!" Muriel expelled through a toothy smile. The road curved at the bottom of the bridge, just as Muriel had predicted. A moment later, we were parallel with the ocean and heading north on North Ocean Drive.

This was Singer Island, a five-mile slip of elevated land that stretched from Palm Beach Shores to Juno Beach. A two-lane road bisected the vulnerable ridge, with a serene inner-coastal waterway lapping against the west side while the rambunctious Atlantic pummeled the east. Nearly everyone who resided on Singer Island was treated to the spectacular panorama of the infinite ocean on one side or cinematic sunsets on the other. Eve tried to peer into the expensive-looking array of neighborhoods bordering the waterway to our left, but she settled for ogling the buildings on the right, which competed for occupants by promising the best views and finest amenities. She saw hundreds of wraparound terraces that boldly projected into the flawless vistas. She saw cut-glass chandeliers reflected in floor-to-ceiling mirrors, with additional layers of glass capturing the city lights and evening colors beyond. She tried to imagine the fortunate souls who lived amongst these skyrise crystalian homes.

"We're up on the right in about a minute," came the directive.

Muriel was happy and animated, but I could sense Eve's uneasiness mounting. The bypass was glittery fun, but Eve felt she was nearing the vicinity of a dangerous truth: Muriel had left this paradise for an inland assisted living facility, and Eve didn't know if that was actually Muriel's choice. If the move was temporary, as Muriel claimed, then when was she scheduled to move back? Or if it was as permanent as it appeared, had someone lied to Muriel? Eve didn't know whether she was liberating Muriel or about to crush her hopes. The minute passed quickly for Muriel, but for Eve it was eternal.

"Here! Turn here!"

We turned into a driveway, drove up the small hill, and stopped at the gatehouse. Eve was certain the show was over and the curtain was falling. An attendant slid his window open as Eve's came down, pulling a salty breeze into my interior.

"I'd know that car anywhere, my gooodness, Mrs. Worth, is that you?"

Muriel leaned over Eve and looked up at the thin man with the long drawl, and they both beamed.

"My gooodness, we haven't seen you in a looong time!"

"I know it, Ernie. How is everyone? How's Mitzi?"

"Ah, uh, okay, yeah—sure. We're fine here, doin' just fine." He cleared his throat. "And Laura? That you driving now? Well my gooodness, that means we all got old." He laughed. Eve waved but didn't admit to anything.

Muriel continued to talk across Eve and asked, "Is Lemmy here yet?"

The guard shot Eve a look of pure puzzlement. She motioned for him to come closer as she whispered, "She thinks she's moving back in. I don't know what Mr. Wor—my dad told her, but that's what she thinks."

As his face fell, Eve turned and remarked brightly to Muriel, "I guess that wasn't them on the highway. I'm sure they'll be here soon."

"You were driving too fast," Muriel countered with a cluck.

The man shifted on his feet, indicating his clear discomfort with the situation. He whispered back, "You know they sold her apartment a long time ago." Then, loud and clear, he said, "So they're letting you drive this beast, huh? You must be extra special because *nobody* drives Mrs. Worth's car but Mrs. Worth, isn't that right?"

"She won't even let Christian drive it. Just me!" Eve maintained the charade.

He laughed again and said, "How *is* your brother? Still swimming?"

"Yeah, he's great. Graduating this year."

"Which—?"

"We're not sure, maybe Syracuse. He'll probably get a scholarship," she said preemptively and in the precise manner Laura used when she answered the frequent question.

"Well my gooodness, time flies," he said with a sigh.

"Yeah . . ." she agreed, though at that moment it was crawling.

Muriel unbuckled her seatbelt and slid over to join in the conversation, but Eve politely asked her to put it back on. Muriel obliged, but called out from the passenger side that Ernie should let us in already.

The guard took a deep breath and lowered his voice, so only Eve was in earshot.

"So what's the plan?" he whispered.

"I don't know. They're not really behind us. I thought we were going for ice cream, but then she insisted I drive her all the way here. Do you think maybe she could come in for a few----"

"No," he said, flat and quick, and then he whistled a long exhale over the impossible ask, as if she'd come expecting him to sell her a diamond for a dime. "You drove all this way, but you should've called first."

Eve raised her eyes pleadingly, indicating Muriel, "It's been . . . rough. We're improvising."

His face scrunched. Muriel was no longer a resident, or even a guest, and only residents and pre-approved guests and workers were allowed through the gates. But Muriel *was* a resident once, and even a friend, for over a decade. She had always given him a nice bottle of wine and a generous envelope of cash every Christmas. She baked his favorite brownies with walnuts for his birthday. Then Ira died and she sold her stake and moved away, but the condo rules remained in place. All forty-three pages of them. Double-sided.

Eve watched his slight and expressive face hollow as she prepared to turn us around. She was going to have to come clean with Muriel about her entire plan. She needed Muriel's approval and support or we'd never make it—the detour to Singer Island was proof of our vulnerability. Plus, Eve had sworn she wouldn't impersonate Laura but less than two hours later she was already doing it again. She began to wonder if maybe her mother was right and maybe she *was* out of control. Maybe she did need an army of people praying for her. Or time behind bars.

"My mom's sick, too," the man whispered.

Eve removed her hand from my gear lever.

Then, clear and loud, he said, "Pull straight in and park up by the tennis court in the visitor's lot—you know where it is. Don't go in the garage, use the visitor's lot."

He reached into a deep drawer filled with paperwork. Eve wondered how there could be so much paperwork for a gate guard; it seemed like such an easy job. Ernie handed her a set of keys.

"Penthouse C is empty, but people are interested. Do you get me?" Eve didn't know what he meant, but she didn't want to show her ignorance. Sensing her confusion, he spoke slowly: "People are interested and want to see it with their *realtors*. Sometimes the *realtors* come around sunset time to get an evening feel." He winked. She got it. Then he added a few caveats: "Thirty minutes. No pool, no beach, no rec room. Tell her whatever you need to, but then . . . that's it."

Eve was stunned, but she readily accepted the key.

"Enjoy your tour, Mrs. Worth."

"Thank you, Ernie," came Muriel's response from the passenger seat.

Eve mouthed a huge *Thank You* as the gates opened, and we parked. They left me behind as they walked through the immaculate tower's double-height glass doors, but I learned everything I'm about to tell you when they returned.

The lobby was the antithesis of The Deerwood's decor, with beautiful white leather furniture and a polished marble floor. The paint was fresh, and there were enormous flowers and tropical plants tastefully placed on polished concrete coffee tables. Eve and Muriel took the elevator to the penthouse, turned the key, and flicked on the lights.

Eve gasped. The space was enormous and the glass went on forever. Muriel darted past Eve and went directly to her left, into a bathroom, and shut the door hard.

"Are you okay?" Eve asked.

"I need a minute. It was a long ride."

And we're just getting started, Eve thought.

Eve shut the main door and explored the rest of the apartment in utter silence, practically on her tiptoes. She feared her footsteps might draw attention from the tenants below, who would come up and question them, or worse, start to socialize. All she could hear was a low whistle as the wind whipped through micro-seams beneath the balcony's sliding glass doors. The wraparound balconies were alluring, but Eve didn't dare broach the massive sheets of glass—the last thing she needed was Muriel flying off a windy balcony while under her care.

The penthouse was empty, save a few sculptural light fixtures the previous owners had left behind. From the window in the main bedroom, Eve could see the pool area twenty stories below, along with interlaced octagonal planting beds and private terraces for sunbathing. Turquoise-painted steps led to a thatch-roofed tiki hut over the Jacuzzi, and from there she could see an illuminated, manicured boardwalk stretching down to the soft-sand beach. From their great height, she could already see the early stars piercing the deep indigo of the horizon, and when she turned her head, she encountered a vast plane of twinkling city lights fighting for equal attention.

Eve opened a smaller window and listened to the crashing surf.

This is what it's like to be rich, she thought. *Rich people exist in glass palaces between the oceans and the stars.*

Eve used the main bathroom quickly, noting that it was the size of her bedroom. The only time she'd seen so much marble in one place was at the mall. She returned to the penthouse foyer just as Muriel reappeared, and they spoke simultaneously.

"You first," Eve said, politely.

"I'm all set," Muriel repeated sweetly, running her thumb along her waistband.

Eve was perplexed. "We have a few minutes if you want."

"Thank you, but I'm good."

"Don't you want to see the rest of your place?"

Muriel remained planted and indulged Eve by slowly and carefully surveying the apartment. When her eyes reached a particular section of the living room, she trembled a little and sighed. "You know, I lived here for a long time, a long time ago. Well, downstairs two flights, but we used to come up and play cards with Sylvia and Bernie, right over there in that corner." Muriel pointed as if she could still see them, laughing at the bridge table and Sylvia's green floral chairs. "I guess they're gone now, too. Let's go."

Eve didn't understand. Muriel had been so excited to return to her condo, but she didn't want to take three minutes to walk around or take in the view? Eve remembered when Laura had joked about her Grams having "silly putty brains," but Muriel seemed completely together and totally in control. She wasn't fully in the fog like so many others at The Deerwood, yet something critical was . . . off. Muriel had asked for one thing, and got it, and then she didn't seem to want it. Was she playing a game? As they rode down in the elevator, Eve wondered if Muriel still believed Lem was following them with a truck full of furniture, or if she had ever believed it at all.

They climbed back into my cabin, and I absorbed their short experience as they buckled themselves in. My seats were still warm from their traveling bodies and my engine had barely cooled in the temperate air. We stopped at the gatehouse on the way out.

"My gooodness, that was fast."

"Hi Ernie. Yeah, I guess, uh . . . I guess she's not interested in . . . making the purchase? At least not right now?" Eve didn't know if she needed to continue the ruse, but she wanted to protect Ernie in case the gatehouse conversations were recorded. As she spoke, she gave him a look that he correctly read: *I don't know what's going on either, but this is pretty much how it is these days.*

He leaned down. "You take care, Mrs. Worth. Nice to see you again."

Muriel leaned over and blew him a kiss with both hands. Then he turned back to Eve and she dangled the key over his waiting palm. Instead of grasping it, he pressed his other hand over hers and formed a bony sandwich with her hand as the filling.

"*You* know I'm not Ernie, right?"

Eve froze. She, as Laura, was supposed to know this guard from her many years of visits with her grandparents. She could explain how Muriel might have forgotten his name, but Laura would definitely know it. Eve looked for a nametag on his white-collared shirt. She looked past him for a placard on the booth. Something. Anything. He still held her hand, which she fought to keep from trembling.

"I----I----" she stammered.

"Ernie and I switched our shifts back when my Mom got sick."

"Oh?"

He didn't say anything for a moment and Eve's mind raced. If she only knew his name! She would say, "Of course, Joe, I was just playing along," but without the name, she was stuck. He looked into her multicolored irises, and Eve was terrified he was about to remember that Laura's eyes were pure brown.

"Maybe you forgot, too," he sighed. "That's okay, you were pretty young when she left." Then he whispered, "You didn't correct her, though. Most people try to correct them and that drives them nuts. You're a good kid. She's lucky to have you." He took the key and let her hand go after a tender shake. "I won't tell Mitzi you were here. I didn't log you in and I'm not going to mention it, but next time make an appointment with the office first. It's easy enough, okay?"

She nodded. "I will. And I . . . I hope your mom gets better."

The man who wasn't Ernie shrugged. Eve lifted her foot off my brake pedal when he was about to open the exit gate, but then he abruptly called out, "Wait!!"

I didn't squeak—that sound came from Eve's throat as she slammed the pedal to stop my roll.

"Did you turn off the lights?" he asked.

"Yeah, I think so. We did, didn't we?" Eve turned to Muriel.

"Let's go," Muriel replied.

"I'm sure we did," Eve told the guard, not remembering.

"Okay, great," he nodded, but the painted steel bar preventing our exit remained down. "So are you still going for ice cream?" he said, stalling. It dawned on Eve that this nameless man wasn't used to working the night shift with its lack of stimulation. Human contact was a luxury not often afforded to gatekeepers in the later hours.

"I . . . we'll find something on Blue Heron," Eve said.

He furrowed his brow into a sudden cringe. She'd said something wrong. His eyes narrowed as he peered at her—everyone knew there was better ice cream up near PGA Boulevard. His gaze now probed the length of my body—no one would make a deliberate stop on Blue Heron after sunset in such an expensive automobile. And what managed care facility allowed teenagers to take their compromised grandmothers out for a ride, at night, alone? And on a school night? At his own mother's home, the visiting hours ended at 4:30 p.m. Something wasn't—

"We're going to the River House," Muriel called out, interrupting his thoughts. "With the family. They're meeting us there after work."

The nebulous thought bubble popped, and he relaxed. "Well, my gooodness, the River House is a great choice."

"Thank you," Muriel said.

"Don't fill up on the salad bar! Save room for dessert."

"Thank you," she said again, this time waving her hand with the attitude of a resident looking to leave the premises quickly and without further interference.

"Tell your dad I said hello!" he called to them as the gate lifted.

"We will!" Eve assured him, and we swiftly exited. When we reached the end of the stone-block driveway, she pressed my signaling wand down and turned my wheels to the left, preparing for our return to the highway via Blue Heron. She realized she was panting a little.

"No, no, Eve. We want to go right."

"But the highway is left."

"And the River House is right," Muriel insisted.

"Are we really going there? I thought----"

"No, we're not going there, but we want *him* to *think* we are." She said these words with a shrewdness that caught Eve like a bear trap. Eve looked squarely at Muriel.

"But we have to get back to the highway."

"Trust me, turn right and head north. It's faster."

Eve took off the blinker, and I continued to idle at the T-junction while she studied Muriel's face.

"Are you sure?"

Muriel raised one eyebrow crisply.

"Can I ask you something?" Eve pursued.

"You may."

"Do you know what's happening right now?"

Muriel's face caught the lights of a passing car and she spontaneously brightened. As the car sped past and she returned to shadow, Eve could still see her afterimage pulsing, like a ghost.

"What do you mean?" Muriel said quietly.

"I mean . . . What *was* that? What did we just do?" Eve's face was contorted, pleading. "Why are we here? You had me pull off the highway and scam our way into your old apartment, but then you didn't even wanna see it?"

But Eve was wrong; Muriel was desperate to see Singer Island again. Muriel needed to confirm what Lem had done to her when he removed her from her private balconies and ocean views and sent her to The Deerwood, that locked crypt of lethargy in a wasteland of underused parking lots. Muriel once shared her vibrant stories with a multitude of friends, but Lem had exchanged that audience for a population fixated on the details of their arthritis and constipation. He had shoved her into a meat grinder of forced aging that shredded her sovereignty and mashed her into a loaf of geriatric numbness. When he took her condo from her, it was more than a forfeiture of her location; it was a foreclosure on her potential.

Lucy was forbidden from taking Muriel to Singer Island, or even hinting that it might still exist. As part of her job requirements, she was mandated to support Lem's fabricated story to Muriel about the seawall collapse. But when we drove up the elegant ramp and Muriel saw her proud building standing firm, she realized she was as strong as any buttress and the waves wouldn't take her, either. She wanted her life back and Eve was the only one who could help her get it, so she would help Eve as well. She would give Eve money. She would provide guidance. Whatever Eve wanted, she would have, because Lem's Laws no longer applied and no consequence could be worse than the exile and isolation of those last, lost years. But Muriel had to go to Singer Island and prove it was still there, to evince his deceit, and to justify whatever she might do or say going forward to secure her freedom. She would explain it all to Eve, but in that moment, her immediate goal was to get us moving again and beyond the range of the curious guard.

"I had to pee," Muriel said. Another set of headlights from the opposite direction illuminated Eve's face as it shifted from white confusion to red panic. "And you did, too, so I figured we may as well go somewhere nice instead of some crummy gas station."

Eve crumpled. She covered her mouth with her fingertips, feeling her lips as they struggled to find any words that might describe the unnecessary and strange anger bouncing between her ears. She couldn't determine whether Muriel was sick or not. She began to wonder if Muriel had plied Lucy with too much cranberry juice and feigned her sleepiness, just to get her out of the car. Eve's mind felt tangled. *Did Muriel plan all of this?* Muriel was the one who told Eve to drive away, after all, but somehow, Eve still felt like she was in control. Or at least in charge. Sort of.

Eve resented being manipulated—it was one of her mother's expert skills. A few weeks before, Judith had offered to take Eve bowling and then dropped her off with an annoying church youth group who sang prayers before every frame.

Eve tried to reassess: Muriel had been completely incoherent at Eve's townhouse! She'd had her pants off! And her memory was also spotty at the bank, but was any of that real, or was Muriel . . . acting? Did she know when she didn't know? So how was Eve supposed to know? Eve realized she had never learned how to drive in the fog . . .

We turned right and drove about a mile up the A1A until Eve found a turnoff where she could think without worrying about "Ernie" chasing after us. The two women remained quiet for a long moment as they processed their separate thoughts and I continued to run my steady engine.

Eve seemed upset and possibly angry, and Muriel couldn't figure out why. Muriel tried to work the afternoon backward and got stuck on how Eve had ended up driving her car. She remembered the moment Lucy got out and Eve climbed in, but why had that happened? And then something else happened at Lem's bank—was Laura there? An image flashed of Eve stuffing garbage bags in the trunk, but then a strange film seemed to smother her memory until Muriel woke up from her nap and the sunset dissolved it. Muriel's apartment at The Deerwood faced north, and this was her first sunset in years. As she basked in its familiar warmth, she also felt grief, for losing the sunset was yet another forgotten indignity. Finding it again provoked her, and those beaming rays restored her awareness, to a point. At first, she had genuinely thought Lem was following in a truck with all of her furniture. She didn't know why, but that seemed right. She was obviously moving back home, she'd thought, until she had a chance to really think it through. While waiting at all those long lights on Blue Heron Boulevard, it had dawned on her that if she were truly moving home, then Lucy or Lem would be driving me, not Eve, and it would be morning and not evening because moving anything after 3 p.m. was against the condo rules.

"Eve?"

Eve looked at her, the magenta stripe quivering slightly with her visible agitation.

"Eve, Lemmy kept telling me it wasn't there anymore, and Lucy wouldn't drive me, either, but with you behind the wheel . . . I had to see it for myself. I had to know. And I needed you to see it, too, so if I ask about it, when I get . . . you can tell me the truth because my mind these days—I don't know."

Eve struggled to understand. "Mr. Worth said the building was gone and you couldn't go back?" Muriel nodded. "The whole thing—your apartment and everything, just gone?" Muriel nodded again and her head hung low. Eve continued. "My mother lied to me, too." They looked at each other, and I could feel the seeds of a deep, mutual respect being planted as they comprehended that both of their lives were a misery because of the people who professed to care the most.

"Can I ask you something?"

"You may," Muriel replied.

"So . . . like . . . how am I supposed to know when you're okay?"

When Muriel had lived on the ocean, she could see the entire horizon line from her balcony. From one edge to the other, two clean shades of blue were divided on a sharp and distinctive line. As her illness progressed, the water and sky had slowly merged into a soupy beryl mist.

"At this particular moment I'm feeling pretty good," Muriel finally answered, sensing that the colors were beginning to separate and the line had the potential to return. "Except I have a rotten son and you have a rotten mother."

Eve swallowed the news, which wasn't news at all.

"But we also have my car and whatever you put in the trunk and grabbed from the bank!"

Eve blinked three times rapidly.

"So shall we continue with the kidnapping?" Muriel tittered.

"It's not really . . . kidnapping . . ." Eve sniffled as she wiped her wet eyes with her sleeve, and Muriel gave her a small cackle. They both agreed to find a better word to describe their situation as Eve put me in gear and we headed back up the road.

"We need gas," Muriel said. "There's a station a few miles up, but the bathroom is smelly. I'm glad Frank finally gave us that key." Eve snapped her neck to the right.

"You knew his name was Frank." She groaned.

A few moments later, Eve filled me up and grabbed two hot dogs, two sodas, and a bag of strawberry licorice. She paid cash for everything. Muriel's enervated palate was reawakened by the tasty junk food, and she hoped her years of steamed-to-mush vegetables and bland fish were behind her.

"Soda tastes different now," Muriel said, slurping audibly through a straw as Eve passed her a napkin. They consumed their snack on the bench in front of me, on a laughable patch of grass by the gas station. Beyond the gritty fuel pumps and cinder block cashier's hut, on the other side of the street, Eve saw a polished stone wall protecting an expensive glass and steel home. The disparity was as jarring as the sight of Muriel enjoying a cheese-smothered hot dog in her cashmere cardigan, or the sixteen-year-old holding the keys to a vintage Cadillac.

"They're calling you," Muriel said, putting the soda down. She was close enough to Eve to feel the vibration through her pocket.

"They probably called the police. I don't know what to say."

"I can help with that," Muriel mused.

"How?"

"I can help with a lot of things," Muriel said. She was about to take another bite and then added, "but only if you tell me what's really going on." She paused for a moment to consider the responsibility she had just assumed before continuing with the hot dog.

Eve still wanted to talk to Laura about what she had discovered on the computer, but she was afraid using the phone would announce her location. She also thought about confiding in Liam, but he had failed to ask her out, so that firework was dud. She was so angry with her mother that she wasn't sure if they would ever talk again. There was no one in Eve's small universe—no one except for this intelligent, offbeat, mysterious, wealthy woman with glowing blue eyes, a long white car, and a straw that was bubbling up with purple grape soda. Eve took a prolonged sip of her own and then told Muriel everything.

Chapter 6

A few hours earlier, Lemuel Worth closed the bank and opened the windows of his black Jaguar to let the heat escape. He took off his suit jacket and silk tie and placed them neatly on the light-gray leather seat before rolling up his sleeves and fanning the air, which made little difference. He removed the reflective sunshade and folded it into its sleeve. The car felt August-hot, not October-hot, which prompted the idea of taking a swim, but Lem readily rejected the notion in favor of a simpler plan: plop into shorts and find a beer. Or an old-fashioned, if there was any bourbon left. Television and alcohol were more refreshing at the end of the day than the inground pool that Lem enjoyed looking at but rarely used.

He knew he should exercise, but he wasn't in the mood; the thought of gasping on a sweaty treadmill for half an hour was both daunting and ludicrous. Lem had once thought it was better to exercise in the morning hours, but an article touting the health benefits of extra sleep had convinced him to favor his pillow over any sunrise exertions.

And his toe hurt.

The Jaguar's polished side panel reflected a misshapen yet wholly accurate version of his expanding frame. He had been fit throughout high school and college, and beach photos from when the kids were little depicted a robust and muscular physique, but somehow, slowly, the inches arrived, his pecs softened, and his biceps jellied. As Christian gained strength in his teenagerdom, he appropriated his dad's former figure like some sinister doppelgänger from a horror film. Christian could eat anything without consequence, while Lem seemed to thicken from a gumdrop. This didn't stop Lem from eating gumdrops, however.

He decided he *would* swim. Christian swam and his body was spectacular, plus Lem liked to swim because it was the only physical activity that didn't seem to hurt his toe. Swimming was good. He would swim. It was decided. As more hot air left the oven of his car, Lem pictured himself swimming, back and forth and back and forth. There was too much back and forth. Lem preferred the lengthy laps of an Olympic-size pool; his own pool was far too short for cardio exercise—it was more suited for margarita parties. He remembered scanning a shopping catalog on an airplane and finding a harness system that kept a person tethered in place while swimming away from the wall. He had toyed with the idea of getting it half a dozen times, and now he thought again about buying the contraption when he got home. It was decided. But Lem also wished he could test it out first to make sure it was both comfortable and strong enough for his vigorous strokes. None of the neighbors had one, and Lem figured if it were a good product, then everyone would be talking about it. It didn't make sense to buy a novelty item that wasn't proven with five-star reviews and bona fide local testimonials, so Lem ruled out the harness purchase and swimming altogether, and opted instead for a round of sit-ups to combat his soft middle—after he changed his clothes and decided whether it was to be a beer or bourbon Monday.

Seven minutes passed before Lem's car was sufficiently cooled. Twelve minutes later he pulled into the left bay of his three-car garage, the closest to the kitchen door, and five minutes later he was in his underwear on the bed, applying deep pressure with his thumbs to the tender middles of his aching feet while avoiding his rowdy toe. He was prone to ingrown toenails, and if he didn't cut them completely flat at the tops, they would dig into the fleshy sides and collect debris, causing small infections that would sometimes bleed right through his shoes. When the stabbing pain of each step was too much to bear, he rolled around in his chair at the bank and stood on his other foot to offer awkward, forward-leaning handshakes to his customers. Most of them probably assumed he was battling hemorrhoids when he performed this maneuver.

Several years ago, a doctor friend had shown him a painless technique whereby Lem could carefully shave down the center of his broad toenail by scraping it gently with a small metal blade or a piece of glass. The toenail was thicker in the middle than on the sides, which produced the curve and kept pressure on the edges. Reducing the curve alleviated the pressure and, thus, the pain. It was brilliant, but Lem had been aggressive and shaved off too much of the nail. It had cracked down the middle with his first step, which landed him in the emergency room, writhing in pain. He stayed in his walking cast for nearly a month and told everyone he broke his foot slipping on the wet pool deck after an hour of laps. It was a far nobler explanation.

Lem wore his socks with half an inch of extra material inside his one-size-too-large shoes so his toes would never reach the edge, but the larger shoes forced his feet to clench for a grip, and their spaciousness only added to his misery. He couldn't win.

Lem finished changing, forgot all about the sit-ups, and shuffled over to Laura's room on his way to his drink. Like Laura herself, the room was cheerful and filled with sunshine. With Cindy's exacting guidance, Laura had chosen light-pink walls and white, textured fabrics bordered by deep-purple trims. All her stuffed animals sat on a white shelf that completely encircled the room, like fuzzy spectators in a colosseum. Above her immaculate desk, a massive corkboard showcased Laura's personality with magazine clippings, yearbook ideas, silly notes, photos of friends and family and travel, concert tickets, the floor plan of Brad Pitt's house, and a small, clear bag of jelly beans that Eve had given her, though neither could remember why.

"Hi Daddy," Laura said, looking up from her book.

"Hey, whatcha reading?"

"*The Stranger.*"

"That's the one where the guy kills his mother?"

"She's dead at the beginning, but I don't think he killed her. Wait, did he? Dad!!"

"Maybe I'm thinking of something else. How is it?"

"Weird. He doesn't really care about anything. He just, like, goes to the funeral and smokes and drinks coffee and stuff. I don't really get it."

"Yeah, well if you smoke at Gram's funeral she'll climb right out of that coffin and kick your butt!"

Laura blinked rapidly.

"I mean, you know. She hates smoking."

Another blink.

"Heh." He cleared his throat and smiled at her. It was forced and unnerving. Somewhere after her thirteenth birthday, his ability to communicate with her eroded quicker than a mudslide, and this sixteen-year-old version of his daughter made him feel like a total high school dork, which had never actually been the case.

"Are you okay?" Laura asked cautiously.

"Fine," he said. He flexed his feet, which sparked a slight grimace. He didn't want to admit he was also feeling a little light-headed. His typically pinkish skin assumed a slight and sweaty sheen under Laura's continued stare. Her look reminded him of his mother's. "You know your Grams caught me smoking once," he said, feeling the need to explain. "Then she gave me *The Look* and I never smoked again."

Laura knew The Look—Muriel once gave it to her when she wore her favorite ripped jeans to a restaurant—but Laura didn't understand why her father was talking about smoking or The Look at all. She continued to stare at her father, reproducing The Look unknowingly and renewing the typical feeling of discomposure on both sides. "Smoking's gross," she finally said, shaking it all off. She had to read seventy-five pages of *The Stranger* and she couldn't pay someone else to do it, so it was time for her father to leave her alone.

The phone rang. She didn't recognize the number, but it was local. Laura raised her "one moment" finger to her father while she answered.

"Hello?"

"Laura? It's Vivette at The Deerwood. Is your friend Eve there, by any chance?"

"No, why?"

"Oh, I thought . . . It's okay. Okay, bye." She hung up.

Laura put the phone down, and Lem could see a little crinkle between her eyebrows.

"Who was that?"

"Viv."

"Viv----Vivette? From----"

"Yeah," Laura answered.

"Why is she calling you?" Lem asked, his eyes narrowing.

"I don't know, she said she's looking for Eve," Laura said, instantly regretting it. Lem was always pleasant when Eve came over, but then he would disparage her after she left. He overshared about his disapproval for her piercings, her "Nazi boots," as he liked to call them, and the purple in her hair, which was sometimes blue or green. Laura argued that the boots were awesome, and Cindy colored her hair all the time, so who cared, but Lem said it was different because Cindy was trying to look like a fashionable person and Eve was trying to look like a punk criminal. Sometimes her dad was so old.

"Eve was at the bank when we closed up," Lem said.

"Probably cashing her check. She said she was going to pick it up—I'll tell Viv," she said, scrolling to retrieve the callback number.

"*I'll* tell her," he said, holding out his hand for the phone as Laura dialed.

"Hello?" Vivette replied quickly. Her voice was strained.

"Viv? It's Lem. What's going on?"

As he pressed his ear to the phone, Laura watched as her father's shoulders shot up and then came down, way down, his back hunching into a curve. He seemed to melt as the tiny voice filled his ear. He sat on the edge of Laura's bed, lifted his sore foot, and started rubbing it again. Something was wrong. Very wrong. Laura went over to her laptop, opened the Messages app, and quickly texted Eve: [U ok?]

"No," Lem said into the phone. "I'll call her . . . yes, now . . . yeah, okay, bye." He hung up. "Were you with Eve after school? When she got her check?"

"No," Laura said, indicating she had a book to read, and whatever this was it had nothing to do with her and she wouldn't be blamed. But she also had to know more, so she added, "She said she was walking over. Why? What happened?"

"And then I saw her at the bank . . ." he muttered, calculating.

"What happened?!" Laura bleated a second time.

Lem was forming a silent timeline in his head until Laura pushed against his thigh with her book. "What!" he blurted. "Oh—Viv said Albi had a heart attack and Lucy left early, but no one's seen Grams. She isn't in her room and I guess she didn't go to dinner. Vivette can't find her."

"What does that mean? Who's Albi?"

"I don't know, but they're looking everywhere for Grams," he said, trying to think. "I have to call Lucy." He looked at Laura's phone like it was an unknowable alien device.

"But why is Viv looking for Eve? What does she have to do with it?"

"I'm not entirely sure, but Vivette said Eve was at the desk when Lucy and Grams got back because that woman with the red hair----"

"Mrs. Rubinow?"

"Yeah, she didn't see them come in, but it's on the clipboard."

Laura couldn't make sense of the flying bits of information—it was like someone took the top off a blender mid-blend. "Why was Eve at the desk?" she asked. "She just went to get her check and that's, like, not even her job."

"I don't know," Lem said, equally confused. "But Viv said Eve might know where Lucy went, and if Grams went with her."

"I just texted her," Laura said.

"*Call*," he said, annoyed, as he handed her the phone. He couldn't understand why everybody was always texting when it was so much easier to have a real conversation. Lem got up to retrieve his own phone to call Lucy, but first he had to talk to Cindy to see if she knew anything—people often called upon his wife long before they thought to reach out to him. He stopped at the doorway and spun around, "Eve doesn't wear those Nazi boots at work, does she? There are Jews there, ya know."

"She wears a smock, Dad, and she's the furthest thing from a Nazi," Laura said, infuriated that he had taken yet another opportunity to put Eve down. "Hey, Grams is probably eating cookies again. Did they check Mrs. Thorpe's? That was only, like, a few months ago," she reminded him, hoping to deflect some heat from Eve.

"Oh. Right." Lem vaguely remembered when they had found Muriel hiding in her neighbor's closet, polishing off a box of Thin Mints. He didn't pay much attention to the reports of her odd behaviors. He paid other people to do that now.

"She also likes the courtyard," Laura ventured. "She likes to sit on the ground next to the trees and she's easy to miss. You have to actually go in there to see her."

"Really?" Lem said with mild jealousy. Laura seemed to know so much more about his mother's current life than he did—but then again, he also didn't want to know every detail. He started to feel calmer. Other people could handle this. It wasn't like Muriel could wander off—all the exterior doors had security codes, and the front desk was manned twenty-four seven. "I'll call your mother and Lucy, and you tell Viv what you just told me. Did Eve text you back?"

"No, but she might be DND." He looked puzzled and she elaborated, "Do Not Disturb? We both have a lot of homework . . ." She pointed to the book again and Lem finally left her room. She wasn't too worried about her Grams, either, figuring they would find her asleep next to the courtyard palms or eating a stolen treat in some remote corner. Laura checked her messages again—she *was* worried about Eve. Eve was *never* DND, and she had seemed so stressed out about Liam at school . . .

Early evening shadows crossed the polished Italian-ceramic floors as Lem made his way back to the kitchen on sore feet, bracing his steps by shifting the weight to his heels and the sides. It was slow going and he was tired. Anything that had to do with The Deerwood or his mother instantly drained him. Muriel had seemed to be doing fine with assisted living and her medications, but Lem began to wonder if it was finally time to ramp up to twenty-four-hour care. He was reluctant because of the massive cost. Christian and Laura's college funds were set and wouldn't be affected, the mortgage and car loans were paid, the credit cards were current, and the bank accounts were flush, but it would still cost far more than he made at the bank to afford the upgrade, and they'd have to cut deeper into Muriel's own resources—his inheritance—to manage it.

Lucy was already an additional expense. She stayed with Muriel an hour before lunch through dinner, six days a week, and typically we went for our drives on Mondays and Thursdays to break the monotony. Either Lem or Laura visited every weekend, often independent of each other, and Christian or Cindy joined one or the other about once a month. Vivette and other staff at The Deerwood checked on Muriel regularly and took care of her needs at night and in the morning until Lucy arrived. Muriel slept on a rubber-lined mattress in a bed with rails that she could raise and lower herself with a button. A sensor in the bathroom and another by the front door triggered a light in the unassuming attendant's station down the hall, so Muriel always had someone to help at a moment's notice, if needed. There were activities and movies throughout the day to keep the residents occupied, regularly scheduled field trips for those who were capable, and a social room well-stocked with crafts and games, with an unlocked spinet piano that no one played. The salon was the primary time-filling hub, and it was nearly always booked.

Shifting to twenty-four hours would require moving Muriel to another standard of care. She would need at least two people to work in twelve-hour shifts, seven days a week. She would need a more expensive unit on a code-locked floor, with a separate bedroom and bath to accommodate the caregivers. It would add no less than $10,000 a month to the already sizable bill. It would eat her fortune—especially if Muriel lived a long time—and to mitigate the loss, Lem would sell his mother's remaining assets, including her fine art, her jewelry, and, before any of that, me. If her status required twenty-four-hour care, there could be no plausible argument for keeping an old Cadillac around, and my value would afford her at least a year of extra help.

Lem made it to the kitchen and retrieved his phone from the island. Cindy didn't answer, and he didn't leave a message. Lucy also didn't answer, and he left two voicemails and a text.

Then he texted Vivette again to see if she'd had any luck, ignoring his own pique about texting versus calling.

Vivette responded: [Still looking]

[She likes cookies. Check Thorpe]

[I remember]

He didn't have Eve's number, but he also didn't want to bother her, even if she were "disturbable" again. Laura would let him know when she called. It dawned on him that perhaps Laura was right and maybe he was a little too harsh when it came to Eve. He outwardly blamed her wild look, but internally he knew he was apprehensive because she was poor and Laura was well-off and he didn't want Eve taking advantage of them. But Laura didn't seem compromised, and they could certainly afford to give Eve some pizza now and then. He remembered his daughter telling him that Eve was the smartest person she knew. He was intrigued: Was she book-smart or artist-smart? Was she college-bound smart or drug-pushing, shoplifting, street-savvy smart? He could easily picture Eve singing whiny folk songs under a spotlight against a brick wall in a coffee shop, but he could also picture her tackling something technical, like architecture, or writing code for Google.

The more he thought about her, the more he realized how little he actually knew. He wondered if Eve had a boyfriend. Or a girlfriend. He wondered if she had any other friends, beyond Laura. All he really knew was that Eve was kind of pretty under all the pretense, she had a positive reputation at The Deerwood, and she had a weird and complicated mother. He vowed to get to know her better, a little for Laura's sake, but more to satisfy his own growing curiosity.

As he opened his first beer and looked at his phone, his thoughts turned to Lucy. She had failed him. He felt bad that he was going to have to fire her, especially when she'd had such a rough day, but Albi's heart attack wasn't his problem; his mother's care was the only concern. Lucy just took off, and that was unacceptable. He paid for her to be there and she wasn't—she may as well have stolen money straight from his gray leather wallet.

Lem felt pleasure as the beer made its way down, but the first burp rose with a gassy indignation as he reflected that Vivette had called Laura instead of him. If she wanted Eve's number, then perhaps Laura was the fastest route, but it was Muriel who was missing—why call a kid for an adult problem? If Lem hadn't happened to be in Laura's room when Vivette called, would he know anything at all? He began to suspect that maybe this type of activity happened more often than he knew. Maybe his mother was always getting lost or hiding out with fattening goodies. Maybe The Deerwood wasn't as reputable as he thought. Maybe the online reviews were rigged. He'd thought Lucy was nearly perfect, but he was clearly wrong about that. Maybe it was time to look for another place.

Lem took a long sip. He was pissed. The Deerwood had no problem taking his money every month, but the residents could disappear for hours on end without the families being informed? "Fuck," he muttered as he considered all the work it had taken to move her there in the first place. He looked at his phone again, saw nothing, and considered having a second beer. He glanced at the refrigerator door. Held under a magnet from Aspen, Colorado, a photograph showcased his family in their forest-green ski outfits, holding each other in a tight line like a centipede. It was a portrait of prosperity and unity, and Lem remembered being happy halfway across the country, on a mountaintop between the sea and the sky. But he also remembered feeling the shadows of potential trauma. Skiing was dangerous and people were always breaking bones and hitting their heads on trees, getting frostbite and pulling muscles. He felt like it was only a matter of time before his luck would run out and his blood would stain the snow. Then he drank in the idea (with more beer) that he might be a negative person, like Cindy said, but how could he avoid it? Hurt was everywhere. Pain was ubiquitous. People were constantly plotting and scheming and lying to further their own agendas. Even those harsh mountains were rocky proof that life was primarily about friction, and nature's intent was to push, contradict, rip, counter, and destroy whatever was in its path. Was he supposed to be above nature?!

Lem exhaled. The picture on the mountain was beautiful. It was a sunny day and they were warm. The mountain wasn't aggressive; it was peaceful and serene. And they didn't see anyone get hurt the entire week they were there. The Deerwood wasn't the enemy; it was the answer. It was good. People were good. Everything was fine. The beer was delicious. Laura had a good friend in Eve and a special and enviable relationship with her Grams. All nice. Muriel may have been hard on him, but she was soft with his kids. Good for them.

Lem grabbed a second beer and continued his strenuous efforts to see light instead of dark. Whoever the hell Albi was, he'd had a heart attack, and Lucy's quick departure probably made all the difference between life and death for the poor fellow. Muriel was playing hide-and-seek, but Vivette was on it, making calls and searching from room to room, exceeding the duties in her job description. And for poor Eve, who punched a clock for her meager earnings, life was difficult, but she was working her way through it with strength and resilience.

Lem fell into the soft white leather couch in the family room with his brown glass bottle. He elevated his feet on the pillows and looked through his French doors at the inviting light-blue pool edged with slate. There was no way he could swim now. Not until his mother was found.

As he relaxed even further, his mind reversed again.

Animals ate people in those mountains, and sometimes lost people ate each other. Lucy was irresponsible. The Deerwood was negligent. Vivette was incompetent if she couldn't locate his mother—his mother who told her granddaughter things she wouldn't tell her son. And on the subject of mothers, Eve was completely unaware that Judith was giving away her car money (and likely her college tuition) for homeless pancake breakfasts and AA meetings at some church. Eve had to walk to The Deerwood after school to collect her check because she couldn't even get a ride, and then she'd been inexplicably commanded to fill in for the woman at the front desk, only to go home to some nutty prayer group before she could even start her homework. Oh, Cindy was naïve! Lem knew in his heart that people were conniving, malicious, and sloppy.

Lem scratched his ear and took another sip.

Something was up.

Laura had promised she would tell him the moment she reached Eve, but her door on the other side of the house remained closed. Maybe Eve was eating dinner and her mom had a rule against using the phone at mealtime, or maybe they were already praying—both DND actions, to be sure. But it didn't feel likely.

Eve wasn't writing or calling.

Lucy wasn't calling.

Vivette had called Laura, not Lem.

His mother was missing and everyone was avoiding him.

Lucy knew something, and that witch at the desk knew something, too. If Eve knew something, then Laura *had* to know something. Laura said Eve walked to The Deerwood from school, but how did Eve get to the bank? Why would her mother meet her at Chuck's Deli instead of giving her a ride over there?

Lem remembered his original plan and reached for his phone to call

Cindy. Then he realized he had brought the nearly empty beer out with the new one, and the twin beers didn't leave room for his phone, which had stayed quietly behind in the kitchen. He surveyed his heavy body, willing it to stand.

Around the corner and down the long hall, Laura's concern was slowly evolving into fear—not specifically for her Grams or Eve or Lucy or Vivette, but for all of them when they faced Cindy's inevitable reaction. Laura believed her mother had the power to summon the police, the FBI, and the entire world's armies, and she could command them all to disassemble The Deerwood brick by brick until Muriel was found. Laura didn't know what Eve was doing, but she knew they had to connect before Cindy returned from the stores and unleashed herself upon them all.

Lem banged suddenly on Laura's door and burst into the room before she had a chance to grant him permission. He was visibly agitated, and Laura felt violated, shrinking into the farthest curve of her papasan chair.

"Where's Eve?!" he demanded, his chest heaving.

"I don't know!" she wailed.

He glared at her, wishing he could summon knowledge from another human's brain, but she claimed she didn't know anything, and he wanted to believe her.

"She didn't text back and it goes straight to voicemail," Laura whined.

He sat on the edge of the bed again. He wasn't sure what was happening, except that everything *felt* wrong. The pieces didn't fit, like two jigsaw puzzles tossed together on the same table.

"Do you have Eve's mom in your phone?"

"No."

"Really?" He raised his eyebrows.

"No, Dad, and Eve doesn't have your number, either." She peppered her words with ire.

"Cut the sass. What about her brother?"

"You know it's just Eve and her mom!" Her voice pitched higher.

"All right! I'm worried!" he replied, his intonation matching hers.

Laura's phone rang. It was Vivette. Laura quickly put the phone on speaker.

"Hey, we looked in all the rooms, closets, bathrooms . . . then someone said check the garage because, you know, she likes to sit in her car."

Laura watched the relief cross her father's face as he said, "Oh jeez, of course!! I should've said go check there first! Stupid, stupid. Was she napping in the back?"

Vivette didn't reply. They could hear her sharp breathing.

"Well??" he asked again. Laura tensed.

"Mr. Worth, the car isn't down there," came the quiet reply.

"Goddammit," he seethed, "I put the sign right there by the goddamn keys: *Never Park the Caddy Outside*. The sun is too strong and it'll ruin the leather, and it has to be hand-washed with cloth diapers because of the pinstripe. Lucy *knows this!*"

"No, Mr. Worth, you don't understand. The car isn't outside, neither. We checked all over the parking lots and even up the street."

"What are you saying?"

"Mr. Worth, the Caddy's gone."

Laura belched and tasted remnants of pepperoni. Lem felt the familiar pin-like stabbing in his swollen toe as freshly heated blood coursed through his extremities.

"Mrs. Worth must have gotten the key from somewhere and taken it for a drive."

Laura's bright room assumed a strange and sudden darkness. Lem's chest tightened. Cindy had asked him to shave it a few days earlier, and he could feel the reemerging yellow-white hairs itching against his shirt.

"But that's impossible! She can't drive anymore!" His mind raced. With her inadequate reflexes and mushy memory, it was easy for him to imagine us sailing through an intersection into a multi-car collision, or driving into the ocean, or getting lost in a forty-acre parking lot at the mall. Lem didn't want to be negative, but he could only assume that we were doomed. "What the fuck, Vivette?!"

Lem couldn't see that Vivette was hunched over Muriel's little kitchen table, already leaking tears, sweat, and snot before hearing his reprimand. "Oh god, Mr. Worth, oh god, I am so sorry, but I don't know what's happened! I got here to take her to dinner like always and that's all I know! I called Lucy a thousand times, but she won't answer. Mr. Worth, we looked everywhere and----"

"Okay, okay, shush . . ."

Vivette's eyeliner was running, and she smeared her lipstick up her cheek as she wiped away some saliva. "We checked the courtyard and the office and Mrs. Thorpe's closets----"

"*Please* stop," Lem repeated. He couldn't control his pounding heart and thumping toe. "I need a minute."

"We looked in all of the bathrooms and even under the cars----"

"Please stop talking for just one second."

"The salon supply room----"

"*Shut up!!* Shut up shut up shut up!!"

Vivette stopped. Laura looked down and realized she had ripped the first thirty pages clean off her book. She was also in tears, mirroring Vivette. Lem rarely raised his voice, leaving most of the discipline and all of the hysterics to Cindy, and his own eruption surprised him. Every pore in his body was open, and he was glazed with sweat and looking a little like a pink doughnut.

"*Call* Eve again. *Now!!*" he commanded as he hung up on Vivette.

Laura wiped her face and texted Eve: [CALL ME]

Four seconds later Laura's phone rang, and she answered it without looking.

"Hey bitch!" she cried out, "Oh thank god!!"

"Excuse me?" came the reply.

"Eve?"

"No, this is Judith Harvick, her mother."

"Oh! I'm—I'm so sorry, Mrs. Harvick!" Laura said, flushing red.

"Do you always answer the phone like that, young lady?"

"No, I didn't—I thought . . . is Eve there?"

"Funny enough, that's why I'm calling you," Judith said sternly.

"You're . . . wait, what?" Laura's red face went pale with confusion.

"There's a young man standing here on my porch who says he knows you. Liam something? He gave me your number."

"Really?" Laura said, excitedly. "Liam's there? Like, right now?"

"Yes, like right now," Judith said coolly. "He wants to talk to Eve, but she's not home yet and . . . I'm sensing she's not there, either."

"No, she got her check after school and then," she looked at her father, "then she went to the bank. My dad saw her there."

Silence.

"Mrs. Harvick?" Laura continued.

"I also saw your father at the bank today. How strange."

"What is she saying?" Lem asked.

"You saw Eve's mom? I thought you saw Eve?"

Lem snapped his fingers quickly and took the phone from Laura.

"Mrs. Harvick, it's Lem. So Eve isn't with you?"

"Well, no, I figured she was having dinner at your house. I tried to make a plan, but she's not talking to—she's on her own for dinner tonight."

"She told me she was meeting you at Chuck's Deli before your big meeting?"

"What meeting?"

"She said it was your prayer group."

Silence again.

"Mrs. Harvick?"

Judith muttered something barely intelligible about "Wednesdays, not Mondays."

"Mrs. Harvick, what's going on? Where's Eve?"

"I have no idea, but I had a long day at work, and I guess this is Eve's *boyfriend* burning bags of candles and making a mess of my lawn, and your daughter just called me a 'b,' and I haven't even parked the car yet," she said, exasperated. "Look, Eve and I had a fight last week, and she's been, well, let's just say she's been sparse about returning my texts."

And that's when Lem fully understood exactly what had happened. He separated the facts from his emotions, extracted Vivette's words from her tears, saw through Laura's subtext, and waded past Judith's confusion and into her confessions. There was only one puzzle on the table after all, and all the pieces fell neatly into place. The picture was clear, and deeply disturbing.

"Mrs. Harvick, I think your daughter took my mother for a joyride in our family car."

"What?!" Judith laughed. "That's ridiculous! How would that even happen?" Her laugh was airy, but substantial.

"My mother is missing from The Deerwood and Eve was there today to pick up her check. Our caregiver had some sort of emergency and I think there was a mix-up or something. Anyway, my mother and the car are both gone, and she can't drive herself anymore. You said Eve lied about your dinner plans, and she isn't texting you or Liam or even Laura. I'm pretty sure----"

"She's not talking to Laura, either?" Judith's concern, and ability to think, suddenly thickened like cold tar. "That's . . . not . . ." She was trying to follow.

Lem started to say, "I think, we think----"

"I'm coming over," Judith interrupted. "Give me a few minutes, I have to get rid of this boy."

Lem hung up and looked at Laura. Her best friend, Eve Harvick, was a liar, a thief, and a kidnapper, and it was now his fatherly duty to ban her from his property and forbid Laura from talking to her ever again. Eve was a wicked influence, with that stripe in her hair and the metal in her ears and those disgusting, racist, worn-out, death-grabber boots. She was a bad person, and he knew it all along.

But Laura looked delighted, her face both bright and pure.

"Liam's really asking her to homecoming?" she said with unrestrained excitement streaming from her eyes. "Like, really??"

***

Judith's car clacked as she drove through Lem and Cindy Worth's manicured development with its large grassy plots and illuminated palm trees. She'd told Liam he could take a picture of his luminarias and text it to Eve, then pack it all up because she had to go. He complained about the angle and how it was meant to be seen from her bedroom window. Then he lifted his arms to snap the picture, revealing the ridges of his cement-like abs. Judith quickly looked away, then secretly looked back. *Eve could do a lot worse*, she thought. He sent the text, and they both started blowing out the candles while they waited for the reply that never came. She dismissed Liam when he collected the last bag, with strict instructions to contact Judith the moment Eve replied. Spending time with Judith while dismantling his romantic gesture was probably not the evening he'd envisioned, and moving all of those bags of sand was no easy task, either. Judith saw him wipe away the sweat from his cheeks as he hopped into his jeep—without even considering they were really tears.

Meanwhile, Lem couldn't imagine why it was taking Judith so long to arrive. Left to his thoughts, and a third beer, he suddenly considered that Eve and Muriel could *both* have been kidnapped by *someone else*. Someone who wanted me. Or a ransom for Lem's wealthy mother. Or a teenage girl to violate and discard—or all of it in one tidy package. It was a miserable thought, but it seemed to hold together better than the idea of Eve and Muriel absconding on their own—especially if Eve had homecoming plans with her new boyfriend.

A third thought entered Lem's mind: it was also possible that *both* situations had occurred! What if Eve and Muriel took off for a while, and *then* they were carjacked?

He pictured Eve at the ATM. Was she under duress? Was someone lurking outside the ATM lobby? Only David Copperfield could hide a nineteen-foot-long white classic car like me in plain sight. Lem tried to replay the scene in his mind, but his frantic memory couldn't bring it back clearly. He had opened and closed the bank a thousand times, and all he could recall was that Eve had been there and nothing had seemed out of the ordinary. She had performed a standard ATM transaction without appearing scared, troubled or working against her will. She hadn't tried to catch his attention with a covert signal, and he certainly would have noticed any signs of fear or a visible bruise—he was a banking professional who was trained to look for such things, after all. Eve had looked normal. Weird as usual, but still normal for her. So he'd been friendly, as always, and then carried on.

Lem was confident that no matter the outcome, he wouldn't be blamed. He was already replaying the encounter with an eye toward the statement he might give to the police, or his expert testimony at the trial. To me, it all seemed preemptively corrupt, the mark of a man with a guilty conscience, to think such irrational thoughts before any malfeasance could even be defined.

Lucy would fall, regardless. Whether prison or a civil suit were in the cards would be up to the police and his attorney, but Lem would ensure that Lucy would never be a caregiver again. She was practically a part of the family, though, and he thought about the nasty period when Muriel had started her new Alzheimer's medication and cried for weeks about her burning limbs, the nightmares and hallucinations, and her hypersensitivity to noise and light. Lucy got her through all of that, soothing her, massaging her hands and feet, staying late into the night, and quietly singing her back to sleep after the wicked dreams. Lucy wore the badge of Family Hero, but Lem had paid the bills for all of her overtime (with his mother's money). Once the dosage had been regulated and Muriel was finally subdued, Lucy's job became pretty easy. She found the time to complete intensive needlepoints while caring for his mother, and he suspected she'd used the gas card for her own tank once or twice. She had to go.

Judith finally arrived and parked on the street where she typically dropped off Eve, fearing her old tires might leave a mark on the Worths' pristine white driveway. Framed through her car window she saw their broad three-car garage and the oversized, cut-glass double front door with its matching sidelights. As Judith walked up the slight hill on a smooth path, she realized she had never taken a step in this neighborhood, despite Laura and Eve's years of friendship. She approached a deep front porch with a trickling water feature made of copper, and black wicker furniture perfectly aligned beneath a row of skylights. She snapped a red rubber band on her left wrist for forgetting the Tenth Commandment and further reminded herself that this . . . this wasn't a social call.

Lem answered the door, and for an awkward moment, neither was sure if a handshake was appropriate.

"Did Eve text Laura yet?" Judith said.

"Laura!!" he yelled toward the back of the house, and she bounded out.

"Hi Mrs. Harvick," Laura said with a buoyancy that belied the quiet terror she so often felt when in the presence of Judith's bony clavicle. It seemed strengthened beyond reason from supporting the crucifix. It was also one of Judith's softest features.

"Did you reach Eve?" Judith asked again.

"No."

"Dammit," Lem said, and Judith flinched. "Oh god, sorry," he added as she recoiled a second time, like a cat rubbed backward. He thought she might bare her fangs and hiss, but she calmly expressed that she'd prefer if he didn't use the Lord's name in vain. Lem said, "I can promise you I'll try, but I can't promise to keep that promise." He offered this with a slight laugh that rose with a burp from all the beer. Judith was silent.

"Awkward . . ." Laura whispered, and Judith nodded in agreement.

"Drink?" Lem asked.

"No."

They made their way to the formal living room and sat in an angular collection of white leather furniture that surrounded a thick glass coffee table on polished chrome legs.

"Let's start at the beginning," Lem began. "First, Eve took my mother and the car----"

"Are we sure of that?" Judith interrupted.

"Well, I saw Eve at the bank," he said.

"And she was with your mother?"

"Well, no, I didn't *see* Mom, but, uh . . . I've been racking my brain about that."

"Oh," Judith nodded, processing. She looked around at the high ceilings and the art and wondered if there was ever an occasion to use the gray marble fireplace in Florida. "Is it a nice car?"

"It's a Cadillac," Laura chimed in. "Vintage."

Lem thought it was weird that Judith was acting like a detective instead of a worried mother. It was even stranger when she snapped the rubber band that was around her wrist and casually suggested, "Maybe they were carjacked and someone took Eve's phone?"

"Jesus!" Laura called out. "Daddy?"

"The language?" Judith called in her direction before returning to Lem. "I'm just saying, let's not *assume* my daughter did anything wrong here. You didn't see your mom or the car, so we don't really know what's going on."

"I suppose," he admitted.

"Thank you," she replied, displaying a weird grin as if she had won a contest that none of them had entered.

Lem wondered if Judith preferred a more violent scenario over the decidedly genteel and likelier notion that Muriel and Eve drove to the beach or the mall. Her composure was unnerving, and it aggravated his fears. "Shit, we have to call the police," he said, reaching for his phone. "We've already lost a lot of time."

"No!!" Judith blurted, launching forward like a bullet, confounding even herself with the immediacy of her conviction. "No, please wait----" she repeated with a touch more control. In the same moment that had reinforced Lem's hypothesis about an alternate felon, she had reversed her own position and decided it was more likely that Eve and Muriel did, in fact, simply go to dinner somewhere. A carjacking at The Deerwood was preposterous, and if they were accosted at the bank, it would be on the security cameras. She also knew that God would protect them. If Eve was responsible for this mess, then it was Judith's job, as her mother, to safeguard her child first and then punish her, but ultimately the outcome was up to God.

"So now you think she did it?" Lem confirmed.

Judith nodded. "I don't know why you didn't see your mom and the car, but Eve usually deposits her checks on her phone. I just remembered she showed me how to do it—but you said you saw her in person?"

"At the ATM."

"She only goes there to get cash, and she lied about our dinner plans," Judith told Lem. "And she isn't texting you?" she glanced at Laura. "Still nothing?"

"I'm not going to press charges, I just want them back home safe," Lem reassured Judith, knowing Cindy would hound him into pressing charges the moment Eve returned. "But we *have* to call the police or we'll be negligent."

"For what?"

"For not reporting them as missing."

"They're not missing," Laura interjected. "It takes twenty-four hours before someone is officially missing, and the police won't do anything for forty-eight hours because most people come back on their own." She spoke glumly, as if she knew from experience.

"How do you know that?" Judith asked.

Laura flashed her phone, revealing Google's answer.

"Twenty-four hours?" Judith repeated. It seemed excessive. Judith assumed Eve was completely unaware that she was risking her otherwise bright future with this stupid stunt, and if the Worths got the police involved, the situation would likely escape Judith's control. If Eve was actually in danger, however, and her own mother didn't call the police . . . was that worse? Judith scoured her memory of scripture for a relevant parable describing the moment where inaction translated into sin. She also knew there was a very specific word to describe the action of making a choice based on random possibilities: gambling. She snapped the rubber band and texted Eve again. It was all she could think to do.

Lem wished he'd given Muriel a cell phone for emergencies. She wouldn't know what to do with it, or even how to answer it, but he would feel better knowing she had it. At least it would ring and his name would come up so she'd know he was thinking about her. Or looking for her. And she would have her own line to freedom if someone forced her to drive away against her will.

"I can't wait twenty-four hours to find my mother," he said.

"You're right, that's too long," Judith agreed.

They sat in silence for a long moment, unsure how to proceed. Judith prayed.

Lem wanted Cindy to come home and tell them all what to do. He got the automatic text reply, [I'm driving and will contact you soon], and knew she wouldn't be long. He was also hungry and wanted lasagna, but if it took too long, they could also go out. Or order a pizza. Or Chinese. He didn't want to grill, but he sensed that Cindy might drop a bag of steaks on his lap when she arrived, even though it was a Monday.

Laura wondered if she'd have to go to school the next day.

"I couldn't get a car loan and it seems God provided another set of wheels," Judith half-joked to no one, breaking the silence.

"The loan is still yours if you want it," Lem scoffed.

Judith snapped her rubber band again for entertaining the temptation. The sound was in sync with the second hand on the modern black-lacquer clock in the adjacent dining room. Judith had failed to notice it at first, but in the vague quiet she began to notice everything, including Lem. His face seemed lost in the pillows of flesh that surrounded his primary features, but he might pass for handsome with a better haircut and a hundred fewer pounds. No matter his age or weight, his magnetism was secured by his beautiful, oceanic eyes.

Tick. Tick.

Lem studied Judith. Her posture was perfect and her hair had a nice shine. It was a pretty reddish brown that seemed to match what little he could see of her narrow eyes. He thought she would benefit greatly from some simple highlights and basic makeup. He wondered if her gold crucifix was as heavy as it looked.

Tick. Tick.

Laura browsed her Instagram after paying five dollars for a detailed synopsis of *The Stranger* and a series of key study questions with the answers. It was lost on her that the package contained more words than the actual book.

Tick. Tick.

"Let's call the police," Lem reiterated.

"You're not sending my daughter to juvie for taking your mother to the beach! We have to wait!"

"Twenty-four hours, people," Laura said again, curling her legs. Lem clenched his teeth.

"They went to the beach and they'll be back any minute," Judith said calmly. "Or they went somewhere else and they'll call soon. I *know* they will. It's only been a few hours and Eve is a *good girl*."

Laura affirmed the sentiment in the direction of her father, who relented with another "Fine, we'll wait." He got up to fetch another beer. "You sure you don't want anything?"

"I'd like some water, please, since you're offering."

Laura jumped up and ran to the kitchen to retrieve a blue glass bottle of Saratoga water and another beer for Lem, who never fully stood. Judith sipped it like a rare wine, appreciating the expense. Suddenly, Laura and

Judith's phones chimed in unison like church bells after a wedding, and they both swiped their screens with rocketing hope.

[Hello. We needed a little break, so we're taking a drive. Please don't worry. We are safe and everything is fine. We will be back soon.]

Laura showed her dad the text, and Judith relaxed with her water and exhaled, "See?"

"What the hell, you think this is good?" Lem bellowed.

"I asked you not to use----"

"Hey lady, you're not at the bank, this is *my* fucking house and I'll say whatever the *hell* I want. And this is *far* from *fine*."

"Why?"

"Because your goddamned daughter stole my fucking car!!"

Judith stood and prepared herself to leave. Laura stayed cross-legged in her chair on the far side of the room, watching the adults. She remembered seeing her father turn the same shade of scarlet a few years prior, when his toenail split.

"Where are you going?" Lem demanded, taking a stumbling step in her direction.

"I'm not required to listen to your cussing, Mr. Worth. As you said, it's your house and you may choose whatever words you like, but I choose not to hear them. Thank you for the water, Laura." She reached to place her bottle on the coffee table, but she couldn't find a coaster amidst the piles of carefully chosen art books. "They said not to worry and they'll be back soon."

"And what do you think 'soon' means? An hour? Midnight? Next week?" Lem's anger blazed.

"As soon as they need," she replied. Her calm words spread like thick oil toward his fiery rage.

"You're insane! That text means shit! My mother might be locked in the trunk or ditched on the side of the road for all we know!"

"Don't be ridiculous!" Judith cried out, "Eve's not a monster!" She remained deeply afraid of leaving her condensation-covered bottle near the expensive books, or on the spotless glass, or on the floor of the Worths' fancy house.

"Eve didn't write that text," Laura said quietly, ignoring their escalating tones. Lem glared at her, mistakenly thinking she wasn't on his side. "She shortcuts everything. 'Are' would be the letter 'r,' and she'd say something like 'driving, back soon, car ok,' not 'we are taking a little drive' and all the rest."

Judith looked at Lem and shrugged in agreement.

"So who wrote that? Grams??" Lem asked. "Now she's driving around and texting? Is it *Freaky Friday*?" he huffed. He knew the words were in

Muriel's voice and style. It was possible Eve had pressed the microphone icon and activated the speech-to-text feature, but it would be grossly inconvenient if Muriel were even partially culpable. If Muriel wrote the text, then his kidnapping theory was debunked, and it also indicated that she might have orchestrated the drive in the first place. He knew his mother was desperate to leave The Deerwood, and it was possible she might have lured Eve along with the promise of some sort of reward.

[We are taking a little drive.]

Where were they going?

[We both need a break.]

A break from what? His mother didn't do anything.

[We'll be back soon.]

When was soon? Where were they? When when when? Where where where?

Lem noticed Judith's uneasiness as she continued to look around the room for an appropriate place to leave her wet bottle. He couldn't bear her and she had only been in the house for thirty minutes. *No wonder Eve split*, he thought. It was Judith's insistence on waiting that had halted his impulse to summon the authorities, and once the text arrived, she'd seemed satisfied. For Lem, however, the text signaled that an ambiguous third party might still be involved. Maybe Eve didn't write it, but could his mother really craft such a text? Lem believed there was a strong possibility that their loved ones could be hostages or rape victims, and Judith seemed absurdly dismissive of that plausible reality. *Something's wrong with her. She's off.*

"So no police?" Judith asked, heading toward the door with her bottle.

"We'll see."

"Why 'we'll see'?" she said, turning back. "They said they'll be home soon."

"Maybe you're not comprehending what's happening here—or maybe you get it and just don't care—but my mother is on a special medication that she's not getting right now, and it could affect her in some pretty terrible ways. And if Eve's driving the Caddy? What does she know about driving a big car like that? They could both get seriously hurt, and I know if one of *my* kids did something like this----" He glanced at Laura. "I'd be *flipping the fuck out*! But you're acting like it's five o'clock on a Friday!" His face assumed the same shade of red that Mrs. Rubinow used on her fingernails.

Judith didn't cower under his tirade, but it was a struggle. After Richard, and excepting a few rough patches with Eve, she had enjoyed an emotional stillness for nearly a decade. Now Lem was a howling ocean wind and she couldn't seem to keep his savage froth away. She decided it was never going to end until she spoke her piece.

"Of course I care about Eve. She's my baby."

"Well your baby has taken----"

"Please don't interrupt me," she countered. Her words slid across the room as if on ice, and Lem froze. "Mr. Worth, I have faith. I have faith that your mother and my daughter are going to be fine, no matter what, and I'm allowing my faith to guide whatever situation they've gotten themselves into. They sent us a message, and I received that message through my faith. Now I'm happy to share this faith with you, and your family, and all of God's children, but I *will not allow* your fears and skepticism to be our guide."

Lem recalled their conversation at the bank and realized he was powerless against her rigid ideologies. Judith brought everything back to her personal understanding of God, and she processed every decision through that filter. Again, he felt Eve's misery. Maybe she did need a little break, but it was a bad choice to take that break with his mother and his property.

"As for acting like it's five o'clock on a Friday?" Judith continued, "I'm not the one who's drinking."

"We should text them back," Laura said, cutting her off.

"Fine. Tell them they have until nine," Lem said, studying his Rolex. "And when they get here, we'll ground them both: yours until she's thirty and mine until she's dead. Agreed?"

Judith shook her head from side to side, responding to his feral temperament with open sadness. Laura translated the Lem-speak into [Come home now] and inserted an emoji of a worried face.

Two minutes later, the chimes responded with a smiley face wearing sunglasses.

"There you go," Laura said, believing that the whole incident was done and she would have to go back to school on Tuesday. Lem didn't understand the meaning of the yellow cartoon.

"Why is your mother on medication?" Judith asked.

"She has Alzheimer's."

"Oh, I'm so sorry."

"Yeah . . ." he sighed. "She's lucid maybe half the time, maybe less. She asks me the same questions over and over, mostly about her old condo. When she's clearheaded she gets very angry and depressed. She told me it's like sleepwalking and being awake at the same time. After Dad died, she couldn't live on her own, so we moved her there and she hates me for it." He looked at Laura, and she nodded in sad agreement.

"Eve will take care of her," Judith said, trying to sound supportive.

"You really don't get it." He sighed. Judith didn't know what they went through when Muriel was living alone on Singer Island. Judith hadn't seen the moldy plants, the laundry room insanity, the spoiled milk cartons in the guest shower. She didn't know about the piles of cooked spaghetti that had laced the gardens sixteen floors beneath Muriel's balcony. She hadn't dealt with the neighbors' complaints when Muriel wandered topless through the lobby to fetch her mail. Someone had even defecated in the condo's oceanside Jacuzzi, though it was never proven that Muriel was the culprit. And Judith didn't hear Muriel's rants when Lem attempted to modulate any of her behaviors.

What if Eve got tired and Muriel decided to drive? What if Muriel fell asleep in the passenger seat and had a nightmare and started scratching at Eve's face while they were on the road? What if Muriel wandered off while Eve was pumping gas? Did Eve know how to change an adult diaper, or have the wherewithal to tell Muriel to use a few sheets of toilet paper instead of throwing the entire roll in the bowl?

Faith and belief are distinctive concepts: Judith's faith, based on her trust in a higher power, stipulated we would all be fine, but Lem's belief, based on experience, indicated that Muriel was both capable and incapable of anything, and, apparently, so was Eve. Even though I have been meticulously cared for, I'm also over forty years old, and being primarily mechanical, I can be a little unpredictable, too.

Judith went to the door, her empty blue bottle still in hand. She now had confirmation from the source that we were safe, so she concluded that whatever journey her daughter was on was God's Will, and all she could do was go with it. She didn't have to support it, and there would certainly be repercussions, but she wasn't going to get upset like this poor man, who was unwilling to accept that his mother might even benefit from an evening jaunt. Judith knew she couldn't change whatever it was that Eve and Muriel wanted for themselves because that might be what God wanted, too. She didn't know if Muriel had tempted Eve or if it was the other way around, but she quietly admired both of them for their moxie.

Judith wasn't going to sit around pining for Eve's return, and she was keenly aware that Eve knew that. They were becoming increasingly distant and even on their best days, spoke little more than a few courteous words. College wasn't far off, and soon Judith would have the unlimited peace she desired. She loved her daughter, but she was also tired. She was tired of the fights. She was tired of the embarrassment. She didn't know how to parent Eve anymore, nor how to be her friend. Judith also knew she couldn't be honest with Eve about Richard while continuing to protect her—it was a paradox that had forced a cut that wouldn't heal, and Eve felt the wound without knowing its source.

This little blip was another test, and Judith pressed the cross against her chest, resolving to maintain her decision not to worry, not to get upset. Eve and Muriel would come back soon, and they had the means to easily contact anyone if they truly got into trouble. "If we threaten them, they'll probably stay out longer," she finally said. Lem wanted to disagree, but he couldn't form an argument. Judith said, "I'm going home. God bless."

Before she reached the front door, Cindy and Christian came in through the garage. Cindy plunked three bags of groceries and two bags from the mall on the counter while Christian took off for his room, his head buried in his phone, oblivious to the visitor clutching her blue bottle at the front door.

"You're Eve's mom, right?" Cindy asked as she approached. "Janice?"

"Judith."

"Laura, you gotta let me know when we have company! Lem, go start the grill!"

Chapter 7

Welcome
We're Glad Georgia's On Your Mind
Georgia—Site Of The 1996 Olympic Games

Eve barely had time to read the entire sign before we crossed the invisible boundary that confirmed Florida was behind us, once and for all. She exhaled the lingering sweetness of licorice against my steering wheel. *This is happiness,* she decided. She wished she could hold on to the feeling and wear it like a ring or bracelet—something that could be touched and turned whenever she felt down. The simple joy she derived from that singular road sign confirmed that her decision to leave was the right one.

We had been together only a few hours, but it already felt like the events leading up to the trip had occurred in some far distant past. Long strips of repetitive roadways often have that effect. After Muriel and Eve had shared their heart-to-heart and fueled me up, we rejoined the waning evening traffic heading north on I-95. The first exit Eve became conscious of was #83, north of Palm Beach. The numbers were going up, but she didn't know where they would end. The goal was to get out of Florida before finishing the day—it was a psychological brass ring that Eve was willing to stretch herself beyond reason to snag. But after five hours of steady driving, we still hadn't crossed the boundary of the Sunshine State, and I was growing increasingly hungry for gas, yet again.

I remember passing the signs for Daytona Beach at Exit #261. Eve perked up then, assuming we were near the border, but cruel white letters appeared on a reflective green sign to announce that Jacksonville was still another hundred miles away. *How fucking big is Florida?* Eve's tired mind wondered. Eventually we traversed Jacksonville, and again she thought we were close to the edge, but the exit numbers continued to climb. It was nearly twenty minutes later when #380 finally appeared with a small yellow notice: *Last Exit in Florida.* Eve was on the verge of collapse. She had barely slept the night before, and it was nearing eleven when she gently guided me down Exit #3 into Kingsland, Georgia. We parked in front of the Comfort Inn on Edenfield Drive where the marquee boasted clean rooms were available for only fifty-five dollars.

"Muriel?" Eve said quietly as she turned me off and unbuckled her seat belt. When I released my grip on her waist, she felt a twinge as some digested hot dog matter shifted.

Muriel had fallen off her sugar spike shortly after the Singer Island gas station and enjoyed a deep sleep for most of the drive. She had dreamed about Ira and the beaches of Cape Cod and blurted out occasional non sequiturs about trees and the Taj Mahal. She had woken up under the brighter lights of Daytona and Jacksonville, but neither woman felt compelled to talk, and Muriel had slipped gently back into her slumber when the darker roads resumed. I played soft music at a low volume, and occasionally Eve turned my dial to find a new station when we went out of range, quickly dodging the umpteenth religious broadcast.

"Muriel, are you awake?" Eve repeated.

"Yes," she said, rubbing her eyes as she looked around. "Where are we?"

"Georgia."

"Oh?"

"I'm going to get a room for the night, okay?"

Muriel seemed to think about it for a moment.

"We're in Georgia," Eve repeated. "We just crossed the border."

"Are you going to get a . . . a . . ."

"I'm going to get a room."

"Okay, good. Let's get a room."

Eve hesitated. "Do you want to come with me?"

"What? Oh, no. No, I'll stay here and rest a little. You might have to move the . . . the thing. I'll stay here," she said, rubbing her eyes some more.

"Okay," Eve said, feeling a little wary of Muriel's sleepy speech. She didn't want to leave her, but she had to get a room, so she took my keys and locked Muriel in before heading off to secure lodging.

Muriel opened her eyes fully when Eve shut the door. She felt the same fatigue that typically accompanies international travel, with its jolting time changes and debilitating postures. Humans have learned how to transport themselves across vast distances in short amounts of time, but their fragile circadian rhythms continue to lag and often take days to recalibrate. I'm fortunate I don't experience this problem, but I've seen it enough to know. Even though we remained in the same time zone, Muriel's experience of this common languor fueled a fresh confusion. She looked through the windshield and saw Eve enter the building, but she couldn't understand why we were at a hotel, or why I was outside at night. She wondered if Lucy got lost and quickly remembered it wasn't Lucy driving; it was the girl. The girl. She couldn't remember the girl's name. Part of the long day returned in scraps, the images hovering and spinning around her head, visible yet inaccessible, like a mobile suspended over an infant's crib. She looked down to find her purse, and the darkness swallowed her legs. She looked to her left and saw that the driver's seat was empty. Maybe Lucy was inside getting snacks, or maybe directions. No, not Lucy. The girl. Her granddaughter? No . . .

Muriel closed her eyes again, and I could feel her struggling to trust that someone would come to take care of her. She once again found herself succumbing to the eerie feeling that the world was frantically outpacing her. The sensation would occasionally trigger outrage during the day, but late at night, and especially in the darker nights when she couldn't even see her own legs, she forced herself to surrender to the befuddlement until that wet thicket of black paste was simply too much to bear. Then she would cry. People so often require a release from their thoughts and bodies; so much of our chaotic universe exists within their small and fragile frames, and it seems impossible to contain.

But Muriel also knew she was a survivor. She survived her mother, she survived Ira's death, and she survived the unexpected challenges of raising her children. Lemuel had always been difficult; always scheming or taking whatever shortcut he could find. She didn't seem to have any authority over him, and she could never understand why he was so crafty and manipulative when he got everything he ever wanted anyway. And the way he'd twist her words! She would send him to his room for acting up, and an hour later she'd find him standing in the hallway in front of his door. "You sent me *to* my room, but not *in* it," he would argue. She had hoped he'd become a lawyer with such talents, but he also took shortcuts in school and failed to develop the aptitude. Muriel had to begrudgingly apply the old adage: a cheat will cheat himself. She wasn't surprised when he ended up with a career in corporate banking.

Sandra wasn't the best in school, either. She was smart, but she used her heart more than her mind—and her libido was stronger than both. She gave up her virginity when she was barely thirteen, "by accident," and Muriel had cried for weeks. Sandra was honest, which had made her an easier child than Lem in most ways, but her effervescent and seemingly perpetual youth made Muriel feel stale. Sandra was eight years younger than Lem, and when she finally left for college, she asked her parents if they were going to sell the house and move into a retirement village. "We're barely fifty!" Muriel had snorted with resentment. "We can't even get a discount at the movies!"

Sandra flipped her hair and shrugged. "Well, it's something to think about."

Muriel looked into my side-view mirror and thought she saw Grace smiling back. She gasped and threw her hands up reflexively—Grace!! Grace was always in her heart, but also fully out of reach. When Muriel blinked and looked again, the mirror showed her normal reflection, scowling from the fright. She pulled on my handle, but my door remained locked, and my seatbelt was tight. Unable to move in the confining dark and surrounded by her disappointments, another old memory loosened...

Years before, when the children were especially unruly, Muriel would exile herself to the attic. It was an unfinished space adorned with random wires and meaty cobwebs, and though the center of the room was tall enough to stand in, the entire ceiling was overrun with thousands of prickly nail ends that could bloody one's scalp if one stood in the eaves. This was, of course, learned through experience, and the children were banned from the topmost floor. Attic access was achieved by entering the far guest bedroom at the end of the hall. The room had two identical doors: one for a closet and the other hiding the stairs. The locked attic was used for seasonal clothing, lesser-used kitchen paraphernalia, outdated textbooks, forgotten Christmas decorations, and family heirlooms that failed to find a place in the rest of the large home. One such item was an Astrakhan lambswool cap with silk-lined earflaps that nobody could wear because it had belonged to Muriel's grandmother, who had an especially tiny head. Some things were impossible to let go.

Muriel liked to meditate in the quiet attic on her circular lavender rug in the center of the room. She would close her eyes and face the large window, feeling the bright squares of diffuse light passing through undulating oak leaves on the other side of the old glass. She breathed deeply and in a rhythm with the rustling leaves and felt her frustrations begin to dissolve.

During one particularly ferocious argument with Lem, she had fled to the attic to calm down and accidentally slammed the door with such force that the doorknob popped clean out. Lem, equally enraged, fled with little Sandra to get ice cream using the loose change he had swiped from Ira's dresser.

It took ten minutes to control her breathing and another fifteen to release the tension in her back and neck and chin. When she felt that her equilibrium was adequately restored, she tiptoed down the attic stairs and discovered she was trapped. The sun was disappearing, and she flipped the switch at the bottom of the stairs, releasing a brilliant blue flash that streaked through the room and kissed every nail-end as the loud pop of the spent bulb was absorbed by the attic's deepest eaves. There was another bulb on the far side of the room, but it had burned out months before and Muriel had forgotten to replace it.

Muriel spent nearly two hours alone in the dark worrying about the safety of her petulant son and innocent toddler. She thought about kicking through the door but resisted, knowing it would be impossible to match a replacement with the closet door—the darkness was preferable to desecrating their symmetry. She wasn't afraid, at first, but as the evening stretched on, it brought her mind to strange places. A slight draft from the window blew across her neck, convincing the triggered hairs that spiders were poised to bite her. She poked the swelling bump on her knee, derived from her scramble up the stairs after the lightbulb burst. A set of old stuffed animals sat in a bin without its top, and when the streetlamp sensors cast a hazy orange light outside the window, it reflected in the plastic eyes of those fuzzy creatures. As Muriel moved her head from side to side, the light made the animals look like they were moving along with her, both mirroring and mocking her shaking head. A strong wind passed over the roof and she could hear the oak branches creaking from the force. She couldn't remember if she had turned off the oven. Or unplugged the iron. Or shut the back door. Each of these elements was fairly innocuous, but in combination, they overpowered her earlier Zen and allowed a cold dread to manifest and fester. Eventually, her husband and the children came home together (Lem and Sandra walked to Ira's office), and they released her from her petrifying isolation. Under his father's instruction, Lem hugged Muriel and meekly apologized. She wanted to slap him, but instead she accepted his apology and kissed his cheek, tasting the remnants of peppermint ice cream.

Back in Georgia, with her legs lost in the darkness, the driver missing, and an unrecognizable hotel in the forefront, Muriel relived all of her trapped-in-the-attic feelings. She knew the spider was lurking, the stuffed animals were watching, and the creaking tree branches might fall.

Eve popped back in and started me up. She was buzzing with energy from her second wind, or at that point, her tenth. She drove to the far side of the building, and we carefully backed into a spot so my trunk could provide easy access to the walkway by their room. Eve glanced quickly at Muriel but didn't fully see her until after turning me off for the night. Muriel was trembling. Her face was white and the veins in her eyes looked like thin, burning vines.

"Oh my god, what's wrong?" Eve asked her. She quickly took off Muriel's seatbelt and clasped a warm hand on her companion's shoulder. "Are you hurt?"

"Where were you?" Muriel cried.

It was impossible for Eve to believe that her seven-minute absence could trigger such a reaction. "I told you I was getting us a room. Did something happen? Did someone try to break in?" she said, looking around quickly.

"The doorknob fell out and it's very very dark in the dark in the dark it's so dark . . ."

Eve saw that my handle was intact. She didn't understand. It wasn't *that* dark, and my cabin lights worked perfectly when Eve opened the door. Eve surmised that Muriel's eyesight was probably weak—the old people in the salon were always complaining they couldn't see at night anymore. Eve cracked the door open and my light stayed on. She didn't move her hand from Muriel's shoulder.

Muriel calmed instantly. It was as simple as that. She located her purse and gathered herself. "That's much better." She wiped her nose. "Thank you. Now it's gone."

"What's gone?"

"The animals," Muriel whispered, pursing her lips. "And the spider."

"You saw a spider?"

"In the attic."

Muriel's confusion transferred to Eve, who felt her own version of bizarre panic. She didn't know what else she could have done differently, other than turning on the overhead light before she went inside. She reconsidered the decision to leave Muriel in the car, but concluded it was still better than Muriel being confused in a public space. "I'm sorry," she said. Eve felt as if she had pushed a young child down a bumpy slide before the kid was ready, and even though the kid was totally fine, she harbored a quiet guilt. Muriel continued to scrutinize Eve. Then, suddenly, she recognized her.

"Eve?"

Eve swallowed.

"Eve? Are we still traveling?"

Eve smiled. "We made it to Georgia!" She glanced over her shoulder at the beautiful highway that had facilitated our escape. "We're gonna spend the night here, okay?"

"Okay." Muriel replied. "Did you pack a sandwich?"

"No, are you hungry?"

"No, but we should make some sandwiches before we leave. Give me a few minutes, I'll be ready soon."

Eve knew the sooner she got Muriel into a comfortable bed, the sooner they could both recover from the long day's craziness. She opened my trunk and grabbed the bag with her toothbrush and a spare, thankful that her mother insisted they keep one for the overnight guests they never had. They didn't have a guest room, or even a pull-out bed, but if someone suddenly visited the Harvick household for an impromptu overnight, he or she would at the very least be treated to a clean toothbrush. Eve decided she would deal with finding fresh clothes and reorganizing her rampant packing in the light of day.

"Did you find the sandwich?" Muriel asked again.

Eve closed my trunk and took Muriel's arm in hers without answering. Muriel had no problem walking, but Eve didn't want to take any chances. She knew people in Florida were always breaking their hips, and even though we were finally in Georgia, that didn't automatically render Muriel immune. Eve got the furthest room from the lobby on the ground floor. It was an exterior corridor motel with dark-beige stucco and light-tan doors. Within minutes, they settled into a clean and simple room with two double beds. The beds were wrapped in green comforters with little pink flowers, and Eve wondered if people took them off before they had sex or if couples did the deed on one bed and then slept in the other. She tried to figure out which bed might be grosser. She couldn't remember the last time she had been in a hotel, but she did recall a news report about invisible hotel germs.

Muriel used the bathroom first, with the door slightly ajar. About ten seconds in she called out, "Eve, I need you."

These four small words pounced on Eve like a starved tiger, and she prepared herself for imminent carnage.

"Ummm . . ."

"I need a sleeve."

"I don't know what you mean. A sleeve?"

"No, a *thing*. I'm wet."

They didn't have any adult diapers. Eve also didn't know what brand she wore, or her size. It was going to be a problem.

"Can you go without it for one night? We'll get some in the morning."

"There should be one under the sink but I can't reach it. Please help me."

Muriel thought she was home. The tiger was hungrier than Eve had thought.

"You want me to come in there?"

"I can't reach."

"I'm pretty sure we're out."

"No, Lucy just got more."

Eve counted to ten in her head, knowing she had to go in and not wanting to see what she knew she would see. She knocked on the door and opened it slowly, averting her eyes from the old woman on the toilet with her pants around her ankles.

"You don't have to be shy," Muriel said pleasantly. "Everybody goes to the toilet."

"I know," Eve said, ducking down and opening the cabinet under the sink.

"Ira and I were comfortable with each other. It's hard not to be after all those years, I suppose."

"Yeah, okay sure," Eve replied, "There's nothing in here."

"Really?"

"Sorry."

"Shoot," Muriel said.

"So I'll go? Or do you need . . . help?"

"I'm fine," Muriel replied as Eve scampered out quickly, again averting her eyes. She flipped on the television and wiped her hands vigorously on her pants after touching the remote. A few moments later Muriel flushed, washed her hands, and opened the door. Her slacks were draped over her arm and she wore the same diaper as before. Eve jerked her head away reflexively.

"You put them back on?"

Muriel stared at her blankly.

"You . . . you said you were wet."

Muriel looked around the room and then walked over to the far bed. Eve popped into the bathroom and rubbed her temples in small circles while she peed. As she stroked away the tension, she tried to comprehend Muriel's mindset, as well as her own responsibilities. She knew Muriel shouldn't be sleeping in a wet diaper, but what could they do? It would be worse if she pissed all over the bed without it, but could she get an infection overnight? Or a rash? Eve decided a morning shower would take care of everything and she'd deal with it tomorrow.

She'd deal with everything tomorrow.

Eve returned to the room. Muriel had taken off her sweater, shirt, and bra and lay propped up against the pillows with her naked chest above the covers.

"Oh!" Eve gasped, but this time she couldn't stop herself from looking. Muriel's breasts were surprisingly full, with barely a sag and no visible wrinkles. She had little shell-pink nipples that Eve imagined could belong to a woman a quarter her age. "Sorry," she muttered, finally turning her head away.

"You say that a lot," Muriel replied.

A late-night comedian was on a talk show, making jokes about a celebrity. It was insipid and Eve couldn't imagine why anyone cared, but Muriel seemed captivated.

"Hey, do you want a T-shirt?" Eve asked, cautiously.

Muriel didn't reply. Eve quickly returned to the bathroom to brush her teeth. When she was done, she opened the new guest toothbrush and, trying to keep her gaze above Muriel's neckline, she handed it to her.

"You should brush your teeth," Eve said.

Muriel stared at the wand in her hand.

"Brush your teeth?" Eve gestured in semicircles around her mouth as Muriel held the toothbrush like it was a foreign object that had fallen from the sky. Eve sat next to her and held her hand with the toothbrush, gently. She brought it to Muriel's face, repeating the brushing motion, but Eve could see her blue eyes had dimmed, like the sky behind a dull cloud.

"That's okay, we'll do it in the morning," Eve said. She took the toothbrush from Muriel's hand and put it on the nightstand between the beds. The comedian continued to ramble, and within minutes, Eve heard a quiet snore settling in the dips between the audience's laughter. She lowered the volume on the television so it was barely audible, but left it on. She checked the door and made sure the chain was in place and the latch was fully secure.

Eve stripped down to her underwear, put on a fresh T-shirt, and crawled under the sheets. The coolness was refreshing, but as her body warmed the cloth, it became even more comfortable and conforming. Eve closed her eyes. Her mind raced despite her fatigue. She was in Georgia. This was the first time in her life she'd been anywhere other than Florida, and even within Florida she never went to the exotic places, like Naples or The Keys.

She remembered the time her parents took her to Disney World, but they didn't want to spend money on a hotel, so they left at six in the morning and drove over three hours to get there. There were long lines to get in, with even more lines limiting the number of rides they could enjoy. The trip was supposed to be a treat and she didn't want to complain, but it had tried her young and unpracticed patience. She was nearing the breaking point when she turned around and saw Snow White smiling down at her, wearing a blue puffy top, a long yellow skirt, and a high white collar. Snow White kneeled down, gave Eve a hug, and told her a secret that Eve failed to remember. She also told the dazzled little girl to look for her in the Main Street Electrical Parade.

It was a thrilling invitation, but Judith was afraid of getting home too late, and they left the park before sunset. Eve peered out the rear window the entire ride home, hoping to catch the glow of the parade or a glimpse of the fireworks, but the sky didn't turn to glitter until they were too far away to see it. Eve had been told throughout the day how special she was and how good she was, but all she could think about was standing up Snow White. Was Snow White disappointed? Would they see each other again? Did Snow White ever go on road trips?

Eve opened her eyes and stared at the ceiling. The television cast a flickering blue glow across the popcorn stucco. A smoke alarm by the bathroom door flashed a small green dot every few seconds, confirming their safety.

Eve thought about the journey ahead and started to make a shopping list, mentally writing the items on the ceiling. Maps. She wasn't sure if she should use her phone for directions because someone might be able to track it. She disabled all the location services, but she wasn't sure if that was enough—she didn't know how the Maps app actually worked. She knew I-95 ran straight from Florida all the way up, but she needed to know where to get off so they wouldn't end up in Boston or Bangor. Plus, they might be forced to take an unexpected detour, so they needed printed maps. Were there still printed maps in the world? And diapers. But what kind? She would have to look at what Muriel was wearing and pray for a descriptive label. She cringed at the thought. She didn't smell anything, yet, but . . . still. She hoped Muriel might recognize her brand on the shelf at the store; otherwise, there was going to be some trial and error. It could get mucky.

Eve tossed for a few more minutes, then got up. She went to the window and pulled back the drape. She saw the highway beyond the parking lot; a vast, sloping ramp joined it high above the hotel. Trucks and cars tore through the night, their orange sidelights streaking past, but the sound was muted behind the heavy glass and broke like waves against a sand barrier hundreds of yards from the shoreline.

I watched her through the window as she wondered if she should leave Muriel behind. So far, all her choices had been based on impulse, but now she had some time to think it through. If she slipped out of the room before Muriel got up, she wouldn't have to deal with diapers or toothbrushes or memory lapses. She could drive me straight through to the end in one shot.

Another dark thought loomed: if she also took Muriel's wallet, it might take days until they figured out who the old woman was, how she got there, or where she belonged. That could buy Eve even more time.

But Muriel was also Eve's insurance policy. If we had taken off from The Deerwood without Muriel, Eve would probably be spending the night in a Floridian jail instead of a Georgian hotel. Muriel made everything possible.

And Muriel was her friend.

Eve also considered that if it came down to it, she could tell the police that Muriel had kidnapped *her*. "I'm the victim," she would say. "I was getting my check when Muriel asked me to help her with the groceries. I reached in the trunk to grab a bag, and next thing I know I'm locked in there and my head's bleeding and this crazy old lady's driving me around . . . and then she forgot about me! *For days*!" Eve wondered if she had the guts to smack her own forehead with my tire iron.

In yet another vision, Eve saw herself screaming to the police, "Let us go or I'll drive off this bridge! I can swim, but can she?"

I watched the poor exhausted girl as she laughed at her own malevolent thoughts. We both knew it was all rubbish, movie plots playing themselves out in an overly tired mind. In real life, Eve would never do anything that might hurt Muriel in even the smallest way. She was even concerned about Muriel spending twelve hours in the same diaper. Eve had accepted her role as Muriel's caregiver and knew it was going to be a tough job, but it was a promotion from sweeping hair and, so far, she was enjoying the commute.

And Muriel knew how to deal with Lem. Those formal texts that Eve worked out with Muriel had probably bought them at least a day, but Eve silently wondered why her mother hadn't called the police. Why wasn't her name flashing on the bottom of the television screen? Why didn't *White Cadillac Plate IRA1 Two Adult Women* appear on the Amber Alert signs? The lack of a manhunt verified for Eve that Judith didn't care. So be it. Muriel didn't make Eve feel like an obligation. Muriel listened to her. She trusted her. With Muriel, Eve felt . . . nurtured.

And Muriel had money, something Judith couldn't seem to figure out. Eve remembered living in a large house with a pool and a jungle gym in the yard. When she turned five or six, she was treated to a big birthday party with lots of friends, and she thought she even remembered a pony. Her father put her on his shoulders, and they walked to the driveway where a pink bicycle greeted her, with gleaming chrome spokes and her name spelled out in sparkles on the license plate. But then her father was gone and before long, the house, the birthday parties, and even the bike disappeared. Her mother lost whatever money they had, and now she was working for Jesus even more than herself. With Laura's help, Eve had found a definition that fit: Judith was a spiritual narcissist. She wouldn't even upgrade their ancient coffee maker, the one that routinely vomited all over the counter, because God *wanted* her to have that problem. But Muriel would never allow an old machine to rule her life. Muriel didn't apologize for her prosperity. She didn't consider her success to be a sin, and she didn't have to wear a massive cross on her chest to get everyone's attention. Eve thought Muriel was a much better role model. She was an inspiration. She had a Cadillac.

What Muriel didn't have was full control over her bladder. Or her mind. Sitting in the dark for five minutes caused immediate trauma. Still, there was no way Eve could take the trip without her. Not when she had confided in Muriel over hot dogs and licorice.

"There's no turning back," she whispered to me through the window. Then she winked at me and closed the drapes, leaving a small slit for the parking lot lights to shine through in case Muriel woke up in the middle of the night.

Eve returned to the bed and discovered wonderful geometric patterns dancing along the ceiling's bumpy surface as she gently lost the fight against her heavy eyelids. The television's sleep timer tripped, and the comedian disappeared into a rectangular void. The longest day was finally over.

Tomorrow, Eve thought.
Tomorrow it starts again.
Tomorrow we'll get maps and diapers.

Chapter 8

"Because she's *my* mother!" Lem hollered, but Cindy had already slammed the bathroom door, flipped the fan to high, and turned on both faucets full blast in an attempt to create an aural barrier between his words and her ego. It didn't work, and she could still hear him whining, "The next time *your* mother goes missing, you can handle it any damned way *you* want!"

He wasn't sure why he was yelling at her because they were actually in full agreement that summoning the police was the best course of action, but Lem was mad at himself for overriding his own internal logic and agreeing to honor Judith's wishes to wait. He needed Cindy's support, but she was too upset with him to oblige.

Cindy Worth sat on the closed toilet and tried to think. Only a few hours earlier, she had been enjoying a pleasant afternoon shopping for shoes and envisioning her grand entrance at the Southern Florida Bankers Convention in Key Largo. Then Christian had texted that he needed a ride from swim practice because his good friend Liam was attending to some other project. She abandoned the shoes and rushed to scoop up her son, who complained she was late instead of being thankful. Then she suffered through food shopping with him. Christian moaned there was never anything to eat, yet she dropped over $250 a week at the store and he ate nearly half of it.

"What do you want?" she asked, and he pointed to pizzas, burritos, Pop-Tarts, and the like, but Cindy refused to stock the house with processed garbage while she and Lem were trying to lose weight. She stuck to the outer aisles and filled her green basket with fresh fruit, veggies, fish, and meat while Christian rolled his eyes, disappeared, and reemerged with boxes of cookies and crackers and a heavy block of cheese.

"You can use your own allowance for that crap," she said, though they both knew she was going to pay for everything at checkout.

By the time she pulled into the garage, they were both "hangry," even though Christian ate a full box of crackers and a quarter of the cheddar on the short ride home. He immediately sulked off to his room, barely noticing Judith, and Cindy was instantly annoyed that no one had bothered to inform her they had a dinner guest. Despite the ambush, she had ingratiated herself, as one does, and then Judith left! It was an appalling slight against Cindy's hostessing prowess and Lem's masterful grillwork.

Cindy had already shifted from "Happy Shopping" mode to the role of "Servile Spouse & Mother" when Lem dropped the news that Albi had a heart attack and Eve drove me off into the sunset with Muriel. Cindy didn't know who Albi was or what one event had to do with the other, but when Judith vanished, Cindy reflexively pulled out her phone and dialed the police. That's when Lem snatched the phone out of her hand and canceled the call before she could press send. It was shocking and invasive and the first time Lem had ever done anything so blatantly insulting. Then Laura shared the text from the runaways, and her explanatory jabbering made everything seem increasingly surreal. Where was Lucy? Where was Vivette? Where was Muriel? How did Eve steal the Caddy?

Cindy sat on the closed toilet while Lem's voice came through the locked door and bounced along the marble floor with a pronounced echo. She was deciding whether she should correct Lem and Judith's mistake and continue her call to the police. The scale was evenly balanced between her level of responsibility toward Muriel and Eve and the effect her perceived negligence might have on her public reputation. She was also perturbed about me and whether I would maintain my value in the hands of an out-of-control teenager.

She stripped down, put on her black silk robe with the gold monogram, and wiped off her shopping makeup. Illogically dismayed by her completely normal pores, she hurriedly smeared on a face mask. The drying green clay covered her brewing rage as it sucked up negligible traces of oily grit. She opened the door a few inches and hissed, "You never called."

"You didn't answer."

That part seemed irrelevant to her. "How long was she here, Lem? How long did it take her to get here? How long were you all in my living room making decisions that affect my life without even bothering to call?" Cindy's voice rose as she talked, and she fought to keep her lips pursed to avoid cracking the mask.

"This isn't about you—that freaky brat abducted my mother!"

"But *you* let Janet leave!" she snapped her fingers at him. "Just like that, like I don't even exist!" Snap snap.

"Judith," he corrected.

"And you grabbed *my* phone . . ." She scowled under the mask and quickly put her hands to her cheeks to see if it had fractured.

"Because you weren't listening to me!" Lem thought about apologizing but decided against it. He had nothing to be sorry for. "And yeah, she was here for a while, but the whole time, we were waiting for you to get home from your little shopping spree."

"I was shopping for your birthday, you asshole," she lied, her pace accelerating, "and I had to get Christian from school and food for the week."

"Okay, all right. Calm down before you tear your face," Lem said as a jagged fissure appeared near her ear.

"Don't you tell me to calm down. There was an emergency, and that woman was here 'for a while' and you didn't think to call your wife. That's what happened."

"Because we were waiting for you to get home! Didn't I just say that? You wanted me to tell you everything on the phone while you're squeezing the avocados?"

"How did Janelle even find out? Did you call *her first?*" Cindy pressed.

"For god's sake, it's Judith, and no, Judith called Laura looking for Eve, and----"

"So the phones *are working.* And everyone's calling everyone but me."

"You're taking this too far," Lem stammered. "I called you, you didn't answer, and then, yeah, we didn't call you because we figured out what to do."

"Which is nothing. You *decided* nothing." Her hissing resumed.

"No, we decided to wait. After we got that text, we figured it was best to let them . . . you know . . . do their thing. Once we knew they were okay."

"Are they okay?" she implored, raising an eyebrow into the creases on her forehead. "You got a random text from an abducted and impaired woman who asked you politely to back the fuck off? And you listened to it?"

"She's not totally impaired," Lem insisted. "And it wasn't random."

"Oh, please don't be blind *and* stupid, I can't handle both!" she squealed.

"We all thou—we *all* thought the text was pretty clear."

"But you know your mother didn't write that text, right?"

"Laura says she did."

"Bullshit."

"Laura said she did!" he hollered. "Mom texted!"

"Bullshit, Lem. It's all bullshit and you know it."

The clay crumbled.

"Crap!" Cindy said, looking in the mirror. She hurriedly sought more goop to repair her disintegrating face.

"It's not crap. We talked the whole thing through," Lem said, trying to hold it together. "We didn't call the police because technically no one's missing for twenty-four hours. If we thought someone else took them we'd call, but then we got the text."

Cindy stood in the bathroom doorway.

"What's twenty-four hours got to do with it?" she asked. "Who said twenty-four hours?"

"Laura read it on Google."

"Umm, shouldn't *the police* be saying that? Lem, did you even think about how far they could get in twenty-four hours? That's like Arizona or Minnesota. Or fucking Mexico."

"Shit."

"Yeah, shit." She returned her attention to the mirror. "Grams can't text anybody, so if Laura's saying Eve didn't write it, then they're probably not alone."

"We should call the police . . ." Lem said tentatively.

Cindy's "Gee, ya think?" was delivered as if from a slingshot. "I don't know, Lem, you and your good friend Miss Crossy-Cross already made the decision and it's pretty clear you don't want me involved, so do whatever the fuck you want." Cindy tapped her cheeks lightly, checking the density of the resurfaced mask. "You know what, I think you're right. She's your mother and it's none of my business. We don't even have to talk about it. We're done here, good luck, pal."

"Don't be like that----"

"No, no, it's fine. Go ahead and live your life without me, if that's what you want. You're absolutely free to go ahead and make big decisions with relative strangers, what do I care? I'm just the wife who gets your son from swim practice and buys and makes all the food." She downshifted into her favorite ditzy-Marilyn-Monroe voice. "I can't really help with something *this* important."

She looked at him through the mirror as he stared.

"This is your crisis, Lem. Not mine," she finished in her own angry voice.

"Mexico," he muttered to himself. He was looking past her, fixated on the nagging question of how far we could go with whatever cash Eve had managed to extract from the ATM. Twenty-four hours was also Colorado. Or Connecticut. Or even parts of Canada. And what if they sold me and bought plane tickets with the cash? France! Japan! Siberia!

Cindy returned to the bedroom and calmly sat on the edge of the bed next to her husband of twenty-three years. She dropped her hand on his knee and felt his emotions coursing like an electric current. He was destabilized and on the verge of tears. He was upset with her, but she knew it was misdirected. He was angry with Eve and Muriel for forcing him into an unfamiliar situation. He was outside of his comfortable, normative box.

He was disturbed by Judith and wanted to believe that everything was likely her fault. He wanted to watch TV with a beer and eat lasagna. He didn't want to grill. He laid back on the bed and groaned.

"Hey, wife. Are you going to make dinner or what?"

Cindy flung around and straddled him, her black robe billowing, expanding her frame into a dark tower. Lem couldn't avoid her scary, green mud–masked face. He thought she might say, *"We'll get them, my pretty, and your precious car, too!"* but instead, she cackled: "You know you're screwed, right?"

"What do you mean? Why?" he asked, trapped under her heft but not averse to it.

"They're not coming back tonight. Why would they? You think Eve wants to live with what's-her-name? Or that your mother wants to go back to The Deerwood? Forget it. Even if they didn't plan on it before, by now I'm sure they've figured out they can go wherever they want—and it's going to be on you because you didn't call the police. No, dear, you're totally screwed. I tried to help, but you left your balls on the floor back there, buddy. Don't expect me to come around and stick them back on."

"You weren't even here!" Lem maintained, hating that she was right. "It was the right call!"

"Yep." Cindy climbed off him and retreated to the bathroom.

"Ask your daughter!"

"Yep," she repeated.

Lem sat up, practically whistling from the hot steam building in his voice. "Hey! Listen to me! We hashed it out and gave them a curfew, but Judith said if we try to force something, then Eve might go crazy and leave Mom behind somewhere! We have to play their game!"

"Why are you screaming?" she called from the bathroom.

"I'm not screaming," he yelped, "but I don't want you to think I'm some sort of pushover for doing exactly what anyone else would do!"

"Ah, no you didn't, babe." As she removed the mask, her voice found a new boisterous level. "You're not helping Eve or your mom, you're just protecting Julia----"

"Her name is Judith!!"

Cindy paused. "Hey, what's your deal with her anyway?"

"I barely know her."

"Well, she took off pretty fast when your wife came home, I'm just sayin'."

"Get real," he said, shuddering at the insinuation.

"Hey, maybe she's relieved that Eve's gone. It doesn't seem like they have a lot in common," Cindy noted, comparing Judith's prim appearance to Eve's fashionably reckless style.

"I don't know."

"Isn't it weird we barely know her? I don't remember talking to her at any of the bake sales or seeing her after the school play."

"My parents didn't really know Alan's parents. Did your parents know Becky's?" He couldn't see Cindy shaking her head behind the bathroom door.

"God, we knew so many parents when the kids were little, but I guess everyone kinda disappears when they grow up," she said. They both took a protracted moment to quietly ponder the nature of their adult relationships. "I bet Eve's a holy terror," Cindy concluded to her fully cleansed face in the mirror.

Lem lifted his head. "You think?"

"To her mom? Sure. She's sixteen, Lem. All sixteen-year-old girls are terrors."

"Laura's not bad to you."

"She has her moments."

"Really?" He couldn't recall a single incidence of rebellion and suddenly wondered if there was another entity living down the hall, a young woman with a completely separate existence that he wasn't permitted to see. Lem knew anyone who challenged Cindy was in for a rough time, but he was hard-pressed to regard Cindy and Laura as a contentious pair. He thought of them as a happy mother–daughter team, especially when they were shopping.

"The thing is, you never know their true motivations," Cindy continued.

"Laura or Eve?"

"Religious people." Cindy returned from the bathroom, her face glowing with a golden aura, freed of all mud and makeup. Lem loved when she was natural, and he rarely got to see it. His wife's pure face was magical.

"Oh," he said, enjoying the view of Cindy's clean-shaven legs poking out from her slightly opened robe. She untied the belt to give him a little view before she sat on the bed and began to rub his shoulders. "Thank you." He exhaled.

"Maybe it's not your fault you made a bad decision," she cooed matter-of-factly.

"Shut up," he sighed, trying to relax as she worked her knuckles into his knots.

"Although sometimes you are pretty stupid," she said.

"Fuck you."

"Aww . . ." As she stretched his meaty shoulders, he felt his strongest sentiments on the subject draining away. Her nimble fingers were firm and precise, and she maneuvered them with experience to dissolve his tensions. He loved that she was a powerful woman and he was the beneficiary of her skills. When she was in charge, his life seemed easy, and he wished he had been more persistent in his attempts to reach her so she could decide exactly what to do.

On the other side of the exchange, Cindy, in her heart, trusted Lem implicitly. She could see the point of waiting for Muriel and Eve to return on their own, especially after seeing the text, but she wasn't about to give Lem any easy satisfaction. He didn't call her enough, and he should have kept at it, even if the result would have been the same.

"You're seducing me, aren't you . . . ." His voice was soft.

"Maybe a little," she whispered.

"What about dinner? The kids . . .?"

"You've got a lot of tension here, Mr. Worth. That sort of negative energy isn't good for anyone," she said as her persistent kneading traveled to the base of his thick back.

"A few minutes ago you called me a fucking idiot and now you wanna play?"

"I believe I used the words 'pretty stupid,'" she clarified.

She lifted his shirt off in a fluid motion and continued her work on his overflowing love handles. Her knuckles were hard yet filled with warmth, like dark stones left in the sun.

"I'm really upset," he said.

"I know, baby."

"My mother's gone."

"I know, but it'll work out. Just breathe . . . let it out . . ." She moved around him and slid her tongue around his left nipple a few times before leaving it with a tender kiss and stretching to the other side.

"She might not come back. I'll never see her again."

"Don't be ridiculous." She removed her robe and pressed her breasts against his abdomen. She held his neck and continued pulsing her hands, pressing them into the freckled flesh below his collarbone.

"It's already dark out."

"They're safe."

"I'll check the credit cards. Maybe they charged for gas and we can find them."

"That's very smart. You're a very smart man." She kissed his mouth deeply, hoping he would stop talking, but also fully aware of his patterns. After years of making love, she knew it took him time to calm his mind and mouth before his energies shifted into his body, the body she suddenly craved.

Lem loved kissing her. Her face smelled like mint and earth, and she tasted like cherry candy. He had one more thought he needed to express before he could abandon his disquietude and focus on the more exciting task of generating some mutual pleasures.

"I didn't do anything wrong," Lem heard himself say.

Cindy stopped moving. She held his head in her hands and looked into his swimming-pool-blue eyes. She wanted to understand this man, to penetrate his thoughts, to fully realize the nature of his psyche. *What did your mother do to you?* she wondered. Who was responsible for this timidity, the constant second-guessing and desperate need for approval? His eyes were clear but revealed no answers as they aligned with her own, pupil to pupil. In a flash, her need for a sexual release overwhelmed her.

He felt her sudden flush of warmth and watched her relent as the sarcastic response she was attempting to formulate evaporated against a hard desire for deeper touching, longer kissing, more flesh.

I didn't do anything wrong, he thought to himself, extending his conviction. *It's right to wait. Waiting is the best plan.* He pictured us driving down the highway in my elongated frame as a sizzling sunset reflected against my white panels and chrome. Lem's mind entered me and moved into the back seat, where he had spent many enjoyable sessions with Cindy in their early years. Sex was still new, back then, and he remembered fumbling in the soft space, terrified of leaving a stain on my leather. It took practice and diligence before they found the ideal position, his knees on my red carpet as he faced backward while Cindy elevated her muscular legs and held them firm against my front headrests with her ankles. In between his thrusts, he would look out the back window to see if someone was coming to interrupt them, but it never took long for my windows to fog.

Lem chuckled to himself, and Cindy knew this was the sign that he had fully escaped his mind. She moved down his soft body until she found where he was firm, and they coalesced.

***

Laura listened to her parents fighting behind the closed bedroom door and knew they would end up screwing each other. She hated that she knew this. Her mother was overwhelming, superficial, and rigid, and her father was shapeless and malleable. Mom crippled Dad's spirit and Dad nurtured Mom's despotism, but somehow their marriage worked, most likely because they fought without losing love, and they were always having sex. It was annoying. Laura was a ferociously curious virgin, and she was naturally disgusted by the idea that her podgy parents were the paradigm of a healthy physical relationship. She longed for the day when she could stop surfing the web and start learning for herself, hands-on and more-so. She'd seen enough online, and she wanted to know what a penis actually *felt* like.

But first she absorbed every word of their argument to see if there was new information. She needed to hear from Eve. Did she really teach her Grams how to text? Laura had tried once, but it was like giving a TED Talk on quantum physics to children who still ate crayons.

When the first energized groan behind her parents' door sounded, Laura escaped to the kitchen. She applauded the architect of their house for putting the primary bedroom far enough away that she didn't have to hear their wails and grunts. She thought it was odd that everyone had forgotten about dinner as she reheated some leftover pasta. Christian walked in with headphones on, grabbed a box of cereal and a carton of milk, and returned to his room. Laura noted he didn't grab a spoon or a bowl, confirming her belief that boys were pigs.

Laura picked up the phone to call Eve again, but quickly put it down. She'd sent dozens of texts earlier, but it was clear her friend wasn't ready to communicate. Suddenly, Laura felt very lonely and bored.

She finished eating, then found her torn book and tried to read it, already forgetting she had bought the notes. It was impossible to concentrate, and her eyes wandered over the same paragraphs three times. At one point she heard her mother cry *Yaaah!* from the other side of the house, so she put on her headphones, too. She tried to picture her dad at the bank instead of thrusting with her mother. It was difficult. She scanned her social media accounts, liked a dozen posts, and then turned to her trigonometry textbook. She looked at one problem and closed the book; it wasn't going to happen. There were plenty of viable excuses to avoid homework and possibly school altogether. It wasn't every day that your grandmother and best friend disappeared.

Time passed and her worry grew. Laura flossed and brushed her teeth. She feared she was spitting up chunks of blood from the stress until she recognized the residual tomato sauce from her lukewarm dinner. She checked her complexion carefully and dabbed an expensive salicylic cream on a forming blotch. *You have to calm down! Your skin!* She despised her little outbreaks and was militant in her regimen. She never pressed her skin or popped a zit, opting to apply the expensive creams her mother provided, even if they took at least a day to work. She knew the lunchroom pizza didn't help, but it couldn't be avoided. The alternatives weren't even food. Laura looked forward to the end of her acne era, though she was already showing marked improvement over prior years. Laura kept her headphones blasting while she performed her nightly routine. She wasn't remotely tired, but she crawled into her soft bed anyway. She wasn't interested in watching TV without someone to share it with, and her homework was all but forgotten. Even Instagram and TikTok seemed pointless and tedious.

All that mattered was getting a text from Eve and Grams.

Laura forced herself to relax. She put on a YouTube guided meditation that led her from a bubbling stream to a waterfall, then a pond, a lake, the ocean, the entire planet, and finally the galaxy and the universe beyond. She almost never stayed awake past the waterfall, but for the first time in her life, she heard the entire journey.

She couldn't sleep.

She couldn't relax.

She got out of bed and put on her robe, intending to raid the kitchen again, when her phone finally made the familiar donking bamboo sound. She frantically unlocked the screen.

[U mad?]

Laura speedily texted back an emoji of a face with gritted teeth and then typed [Where r u?]

[Hotel. Checking in.]

[Where?] Laura waited for the three pulsing dots that indicated a reply was being crafted, but it failed to appear for a moment that went on too long. She sent a follow up. [Grams ok?]

A thumbs-up graphic appeared. [Tired.]

[Can we talk?]

[Later]

[Later 2night?]

[2mrw] was returned alongside a happy face with sunglasses, the sun, a rainbow, and a heart.

Laura was relieved, thrilled, and confused. She needed more. Like her father, she needed to know where they were, where they were going, how long they were going to be away, why Eve left, why she took Grams, how she thought she was going to get away with it, what about school, what about her mother, what about Liam, when was she going to text again, what, what, what, when, when, when, why, why, why . . .

Laura typed again. [Where r u going?]. She chomped on her thumbnail while she waited for the three dots to appear. They arrived and pulsed for a moment and then stopped. Laura swallowed a small piece of her nail and felt the scratch as it went down. At first she had assumed Eve was driving north and out of the state, but then it occurred to her she might go west—Eve was always talking about seeing Hollywood. *That bitch is going to LA!* Laura thought with mounting jealousy. *Without me!*

Laura also entertained her father's notion that Eve and her Grams might hop on a plane and end up on the other side of the world. Maybe they were at an airport hotel and scheduled to fly out in the morning. If they had passports, they could go anywhere while Laura was left behind in Deerfield Beach, buying her way through trig and biting her nails to the quick before they could replenish.

It wasn't fair.

She wondered why Eve was suddenly in charge and thought she could call all the shots. Laura didn't need permission to call her best friend! She pulled up the number, but then shut the screen down before making the call. Eve said it wasn't a good time, and Laura had to respect her wishes. It was possible she was helping Grams into the hotel room, and a phone call might be distracting, or even lethal, if Grams fell.

Laura was irritated that Eve hadn't called her before we left town. She would have been happy to join us. With the two of them driving, we would certainly get wherever Eve wanted to go faster, plus Laura would have been an enormous help with Grams—or they could have returned Grams to The Deerwood and gone on alone. If Eve had a desperately urgent need to go somewhere, why didn't she share it? Laura couldn't figure out why Eve had picked her grandmother over her. She was hurt, but she trusted Eve enough to know there was probably a solid reason for all the mystery and urgency and drama. Laura loved drama.

Laura considered calling Liam to pick her up and drive out to meet us. She had no idea where to go and we were already a day ahead, but she could also fly somewhere or take a train. There had to be *some way* that she could get into our exclusive club. She decided Eve needed her, even if Eve didn't know it, and Laura started formulating her own plan. Screw school and screw her parents; saving her best friend and her grandmother was far more important. She began to picture our cinematic rendezvous at some little country diner in the middle of nowhere. Laura and Eve would share a big slice of lemon meringue pie, and Grams would insist she was full but pick at the crust. Then we'd all continue to Wherever, taking turns behind the wheel and listening to the soundtrack of an old John Hughes movie . . .

But nothing would happen if Eve ignored her.

The three dots appeared again. And then [Will need ur help] arrived, followed by a heart, folded hands, and then another heart. She was in! She sent a thumbs-up response, but it was too mild a response for how she felt, so she added: [Love u E] and a unicorn.

A moment later, a single, large emoji of two interlocking links arrived, and Laura knew exactly what she had to do next.

TUESDAY

Chapter 9

Eve woke up. She glanced sideways, looking for her phone, but instead she found an unfamiliar clock radio by her bed. She blinked a few times, trying to focus. She could make out the six, but the other numbers were blurry. She rubbed her eyes, releasing crust from the corners. She swallowed and found a hardness in her throat. Why was she so dry? She looked again at the unfamiliar clock, unable to identify its origin, and accurately read the time as 8:56. She'd overslept nearly two and a half hours! She was *so late* for school! Why didn't her mother wake her? The alarm?

She leaned over and realized she was in a double bed, and the wall by her extra pillow had disappeared. And she wasn't wearing her long, soft nightshirt. The clock was different and the time was different and the bed was different and the clothes were different. The light was different and even the air was different because Eve didn't wake up in Florida, for the first time in her life. As her thoughts became clear, she lazily rolled over and giggled to herself. *I'm not going to school today!* The hotel room remained dark with only a sliver of white light clinging to the sharp edges of its opaque curtains, and what managed to break through formed a hot, thin triangle on the ceiling. A shadow passed—a chambermaid. Eve wondered about the life of these unknowable creatures who reset the rooms of vanished people. The hotel guests were ghosts on the road who moved in and out of reusable spaces, leaving muddled sheets and pubic hairs on the shower floors. But the dawn tide of the service industry erased the overnight residues of this ephemeral humanity, resetting the great and transient wave, one tiny bar of soap at a time. The shadow passed again, and Eve followed the lingering white line down as she cleared away the last of her mental fuzziness. Her gaze finally landed on the other double bed in the room.

Muriel was gone.

With olympic power, Eve tore off her sheets and leaped to the window to pull back the curtains. Blazing morning light flooded the arid room. I remained outside the window exactly where she'd parked me, ready to take on whatever was next. Eve looked back at the other double bed, hoping the fresh illumination would magically cause her companion to materialize, but instead she found a tidily made and fully empty bed. Eve slipped on her old clothes and found my keys in her pants pocket. She raced to the door, but stopped before opening it when the pressure on her bladder signaled. Panic won the contest as she ignored her bodily needs and opened the door to reveal a mostly empty parking lot glazed with heavy morning humidity. She spotted a maid's cart twenty doors down, and in a few broad strides, she reached it and poked her head into the opened room. The maid was startled but alone—the people in the room had checked out. Eve asked the maid if she had seen Muriel, and the maid said "No" before reaching to restock the toilet paper while humming something familiar.

Eve was both disoriented and rattled, caught in a loop of fear, desperation, and a need to pee that furthered the fear, desperation, and urgency of the situation. She finally flew back to the room and relieved herself hastily before resuming her anguished search along the exterior corridors of the Comfort Inn on Edenfield Drive. She stepped back from the hotel and took in the totality of the structure in one sweeping view. No Muriel. She raced to the other side of the second building and scanned again. The only other sign of life was a second humming maid by another empty room. Eve entered the courtyard between the two buildings where a turquoise, bean-shaped pool offered a respite for dusty travelers and their children. An older, portly man with a hairy belly and a sun-scorched scalp was sunning himself on a deck chair with his legs spread wide, his skimpy blue thong revealing more than Eve wanted to see. She cautiously approached and asked if he had seen Muriel. He didn't speak English, which somehow allowed Eve to excuse his apparel while she struggled to avoid looking at his groin. She was amazed the foreigner didn't seem to feel any shame or embarrassment about his body, and she secretly hoped he had some aloe to soothe his blazing head.

Eve contemplated her next move. Muriel was gone, but was she lost? The bed was made. Did she always make her bed? Was she cogent? Eve had to assume Muriel was thinking clearly enough, or she would have been audibly upset to find Eve in the other bed in a strange room when she woke up. Eve slowed her steps and tried to imagine what Muriel might want if she got up early but didn't have my keys. *Food?* But she wasn't in the lobby enjoying the free breakfast, so something else? *What? And where?* Eve suddenly remembered that Muriel fell asleep topless. A bare-chested grandmother running amok would certainly prompt a call to the police, and Eve had to consider the possibility that they were already headed to the hotel to arrest the heedless teenaged out-of-state quasi-caregiver. Eve returned to the room carrying this deeper panic and popped her sweaty card in the door. The electronic lock beeped twice, granting access.

"There you are!" Muriel greeted her brightly. "I figured you'd be hungry when you finally got up." The small table by the window was set with orange juice, four apples, and two toasted bagels with cream cheese already smeared on. Muriel was trying to stuff an ice cube into a bottle of water, but it was too big to fit. "Well, this isn't working." She smiled. "We'll pick up something cold when we fill up."

Eve was flabbergasted.

"You look flushed," Muriel continued. "Did you have a nice run?"

Eve closed the door behind her and sat down. She put her head down between her knees with her eyes closed, sourcing oxygen.

"Looks like you overdid it. It is pretty warm out." Muriel went to the bathroom and doused a washcloth with cool water. She squeezed it out and placed it gently on Eve's neck. It felt wonderful.

"I wasn't running—I was looking for you," Eve said. "You disappeared."

"I could say the same for you! I stepped out to get your bagel, and when I came back, the drapes were open and you were all but gone!"

"Because I was out looking for you."

"Oh, that's funny. We must have missed each other by a few seconds. Have some breakfast."

Eve poked her bagel and then blurted, "Muriel, you can't do that! You can't just leave, okay? You have to wake me up or leave a note! I thought you might be walking back to Florida on the side of the highway or something!" Eve's crinkled face was hot and wet.

Muriel sat down across from her and extended her hands, indicating for Eve to take them. She was calm. Patient. It took a long moment, but Eve, confused and piqued, finally reached out. Muriel's flesh wasn't papery and her bones weren't sharp like other elderly patrons in the salon; her hands were warm and dry and resembled an overripe peach with their delicate wrinkles and scattered brown flecks. Her nails were trimmed and clean and had a luminous clear lacquer. They were beautiful, comforting hands.

"I have to confess something to you, Eve. Something important."

Eve shifted in her chair to correct her posture.

"I'm sure you know I haven't been myself for a long time," Muriel said, her blue eyes glowing. "A very long time."

Eve listened as Muriel drew a long breath.

"When my Ira died they dug a deep hole in the ground for him. Everyone could see it, that emptiness. It was so big, a real cut in the landscape. Then we put him in there and they filled it up again. They planted grass and flowers and eventually laid the stone, and that was that. The hole was gone, but I could still see it. I could still see it because I had a matching pit in my heart . . . one that couldn't be filled."

They both swallowed.

"I made a lot of mistakes after Ira died. I was out of sorts for a long time. When you lose someone like that, your mind stops seeing through your eyes and runs everything through the pain. I couldn't see clearly after Ira died. I couldn't even think."

Eve nodded, remembering her father.

"And then Lem----" A tear fell. "He tried to fix it. To fix me. But Lem is not a patient man. He didn't have the time for my healing process, he just had to solve it—like a math problem—and being Lem, he skipped ahead to the solution in the back of the book without doing the work."

Muriel thought she saw a tear fall from Eve's face, but it was actually sweat. Eve's heart was still pounding from her frantic search.

"Lemmy thought he found the answer and he put me in *that place*. He said it was for the best, but it wasn't the best, it was the *easiest*. For him. I needed real help, but not like that. There were so many other possibilities for my recovery. I just needed . . . time . . . to find my own earth and grass and flowers to replenish the hollow, but Lem decided the only way was to fill it up with medicine."

"Medicine?" Eve asked.

"For the Alzheimer's."

Eve took this in. "You have Alzheimer's?"

"Lem thinks so. And the doctors."

"But you . . . don't?"

Muriel looked at Eve squarely and said, "I don't know. How *would* I know? That's why we have to talk about this. I was forgetting things and acting, how did they put it?—'out of character'—and then they did lots of tests and put together their data, but . . . I don't *really* know and I don't think they really know, either, but then they put me on that pill anyway. It's supposed to slow the disease down, but it slowed everything. It even slowed the clocks until a day was like a year, and soon all those years melted into each other like some big, muddy river. No, not a river—it didn't move or nourish—it was more like . . . a bog. That pill sent me to an endless, dreary, sleepwalking bog."

"That sounds awful," Eve whispered.

Muriel tightened her grip. "But when I woke up this morning, something was different. I felt like I could *think* for the first time in ages. I've only skipped one dose, maybe two, but I also----" she stopped.

"What?" Eve asked.

"This morning when I woke up—Eve, I wasn't sad." Muriel dropped her head down from the weight of the guilt, but then she pulled it right back up and said, "Some part of that hole got filled in yesterday. The woman who left Florida with you is not the same woman sitting on this chair. When I took my shower this morning, the mirror fogged, and when I wiped it away, I could see myself clearly. I haven't been able to wipe that fog for years. It was so strange, but I actually said, 'Hello there, Muriel!!'"

"That's awesome!" Eve laughed.

"It *is* awesome!" Muriel agreed. "But I'm worried because I don't know if it's going to last. I feel aware of being aware right now, and I really want this feeling to stay, but I'm pretty sure I won't know when it's gone. I don't think I'll know when I'm not myself."

Muriel's grip on Eve's hands tightened even more.

"So I guess this is my confession, a warning and an apology all wrapped into one for whatever I may put you through when the other me, that foggy-boggy Muriel, comes back. Maybe she won't. I don't know. I don't know anything about this terrible medicine or how it works. Right now I feel like I'm going to be okay, but if I get stuck again and don't know I'm stuck, I want you to know I'm sorry. I'm apologizing premur . . . permittish----"

"Preemptively?"

"I really don't want to scare you," Muriel assured her.

"Well, you scared me when you disappeared," Eve asserted.

"I was hungry and I didn't want to wake you! You need your sleep if we're doing a lot of driving today."

"Yeah, okay," Eve accepted.

"I'm sorry again." Muriel smiled. "I'm sorry I scared you."

Muriel squeezed Eve's hands once more and finally let them go, feeling satisfied with their talk. Eve was unsure what she had gained beyond an open apology for whatever might happen if and when Muriel wasn't herself, which could happen at any moment, but she felt a little better, too. At least Muriel was in the room again and she was wearing a proper shirt. Eve's pulse slowly returned to normal. She took a bite of her hotel bagel and found it to be surprisingly delicious.

After breakfast, Eve decided it was time to sort through and rearrange their belongings. She moved a few bags into the hotel room and spread the contents across the bed while Muriel half-watched with her other eye on a *Jeopardy* rerun. On her third trip to my trunk, Eve discovered a box of ice cream that Lucy had failed to bring upstairs. It had melted overnight and leaked out of the carton and through a small hole in the grocery bag, infusing a fatty stream of creamy sugar into my fabric. It was only the second discernable mess that had marred my interior in my entire forty-three years.

Eve maintained an upbeat attitude as she retrieved some wet towels and set about cleaning up the gloop. I could tell she was feeling very grown up—only a day before, that kind of sticky mess might have overwhelmed her and sparked a tirade of self-deprecation and angst. She would have lashed out at her mother and begrudged the chore, but something in Eve had also shifted. Spilled ice cream was a trivial problem; it was nothing like potentially misplacing her best friend's incoherent, topless grandmother at a freeway motel in southern Georgia.

When she successfully resolved the mess, Eve checked her phone and revisited Liam's images with the luminaria spelling out *"HOME?"* She had first seen it when we arrived at the hotel, and she was struck by his unexpected romanticism. She felt sorry she had missed the glowing yard in real life, but she also couldn't wrap her mind around any of it. Two days earlier her entire world had revolved around his potential proposal, but now it felt like all that trepidation and anxiety belonged to an entirely different person, much like what Muriel described. Eve started to reply to Liam, canceled it, started again, and canceled it again. She didn't know. She couldn't know.

Maybe later.

She put the phone away and refocused on packing. Muriel sat in the chair by the table and deftly peeled one of the red apples with a plastic knife, as if she'd done it a thousand times. "I don't remember the year, but I was with Ira, so it must have been a while ago," Muriel began. "We were in Atlanta, I think, for a wedding, and then we spent a few days in Savannah. Oh, you should see Savannah! It's one of the most beautiful cities in the South. There are all these square parks with grand old houses around them, and there's a waterfront area with little shops and galleries. The Spanish moss drips off those ancient trees like nothing you've ever seen."

"That sounds amazing," Eve said while folding her shirts. "Where is it?"

"On the coast, but I'm not sure how far up it is. Grace would know."

"Grace?"

"What?"

"You said 'Grace.'"

"No I didn't, I asked if we're near the ocean," Muriel said flatly.

"Umm . . ." Eve looked at her, puzzled, and then said, "We'll get some maps."

Muriel stood up abruptly, left the apple and went over to the far side of her bed where she pulled out a stack of maps from the night table drawer. "Maps!" She tossed the pile over to Eve, who had to reposition her fallen jaw with the back of her wrist.

"How did—where—?"

"The gas station across the street. You said we needed them. Maps and, umm, well. Adult pullups."

Eve was shocked.

"I'm not sure why I put them in the drawer, though." Muriel scratched her temple. "That was stupid. We almost forgot them."

Eve looked at all the state maps threaded by I-95 from Florida to New York, a map of the entire country, and a map detailing the northeastern states and Canadian provinces. Eve studied the Georgia map and found Savannah. It was only a short hop off the highway and a couple of hours north.

"We could probably get to Savannah by lunch," Eve said. "Should we?"

A Cheshire-cat grin enveloped Muriel's entire face.

"Oh, that reminds me," Eve blurted. "Did you brush your teeth this morning? We had some trouble with that last night."

"Yes. I used the . . . the . . ."

Eve prompted, "The toothbrush?"

"I know 'toothbrush'!" Muriel snapped. "I was going to say the . . ."

Eve waited while Muriel searched for the mystery word, an invisible nuisance that remained out of reach, like a gnat circling her head. Muriel scrunched her face and covered her ears, as if more words might leak out and float away if she didn't physically hold them in place.

"The . . ."

"It doesn't matter. Toothbrush was the impor----"

"Magenta! The magenta toothbrush. Oh thank heavens I remembered it; I love magenta." They both relaxed and Muriel repeated, "The magenta toothbrush. Magenta. Magenta . . ."

"That's the new one," Eve interrupted.

"I wasn't going to use yours."

"I would have survived it," Eve lied.

"Oh! I just remembered where we ate!" Muriel bellowed, reaching for the hotel pen and pad to write it down. Eve feared that saying "where?" might cause Muriel's thoughts to scramble, so she stayed silent. She still couldn't believe they had all the maps they needed or that Muriel had managed to get to the gas station and back again with breakfast during her morning escapade. She was spooked by Muriel's behavior, but she was also happy to have the printed maps and a lucid associate. She was worried that even with Muriel's supposed clarity, she was still forgetting words, and she knew Muriel said the name 'Grace', despite the protest. Perhaps Muriel's apology was preemptive, or maybe it was right on time.

Eve finished up and took a quick shower while Muriel tidied the breakfast table and made Eve's bed out of habit, not knowing what else to do. They checked out, and we crossed the street to refuel. Eve went inside to pay with cash.

"That's yer granny?" the attendant asked, pointing through the window. He was tall and lanky and his front teeth were brown. He was chewing a wad of tobacco, and he occasionally spat into a small glass jar that looked like it was half-filled with motor oil.

"Yeah. Hey, thanks for the maps. Did she pay you?"

"Yeah, she paid," he said. "But you should prob'ly watch her a little closer, miss."

"I know," Eve said, stuffing the gas receipt into her pocket. "She let me sleep in. I didn't know she came over here before breakfast."

"Before breakfast? She's here at three a.m.," he said.

Eve froze.

"See, I work nights—ten to seven, most days, but I'm covering Larry, so I'm here through lunch, which ain't my favorite, but it's good overtime, ya know? Anyways, yer granny comes in here 'bout three this morning to get her maps and all."

"I can't----" were all the words Eve had for him.

"Yep. And she's all wrapped up in bedsheets and barefoot when she comes in." He leaned in and whispered, "and I don't think she was wearin' no brar, neither." Eve went white. The clerk spat in the jar and continued. "Looked like a purty good toga party, 'cept she ain't no college chick!" He laughed hard, prompting a series of painfully deep coughs. He held his lungs in place with his black-stained hands, leaving a small smear of grease on his gray undershirt.

He steadied himself. "So she comes up ter me and says, 'We need maps and diapers' and I says, 'Okay, where's you headin' and how old's the baby, and where's yer clothes at, ma'am?' and she tells me yer sleepin' and she didn't wanner wake you with the lights and she couldn't find her pants and that don't matter right now 'cause it's just you and me anyways and I'm right over der across the street and we need maps for tomarraw and diapers for herself right now.'"

Eve didn't know if the accent he was using to relay the story was entirely his own or if Muriel also took on an accent when she was in Southern company.

"So I gives her a bunch of maps of the East Coast 'cause that's what most people like her want, and some of the underwear she needs 'cause we always keep that for emergencies, and she hands me forty, which more than covers it all, and she tells me ter keep the change. Then she waddles on back to yer hotel holding that sheet 'tween her legs with one hand and the rest with the other."

"Holy shit," Eve said. The story was outrageous, but she was equally miffed with herself for failing to notice that Muriel had changed into something fresh. Eve had forgotten all about it.

"That's right and you said it," he replied, and spat.

"I can't believe she did that," Eve cried out. "I chained the door inside and everything. What am I supposed to do, push the bed in front of the door? Holy shitfuck!!"

"*Hey*, now," he said sharply. "Keep it together."

"Sorry. I'm sorry . . ." Her eyes scanned the floor, but she didn't see the red and white tiles because images of Muriel wandering around in a bedsheet flooded her field of view. It took a few moments before she calmed herself sufficiently and stopped muttering "sorry." She looked the cashier in the eyes. "Thanks for telling me."

"You betcha, Junebug."

Eve cringed, and then she blurted, "Hey----" The man put down his spit jar and looked at her through warm green eyes. He looked haggard, but also trusting and relentlessly familiar. She could easily imagine him all cleaned up, without the grease lining his fingernails. She pictured him clean shaven, driving a convertible to a fine restaurant while a sexy model in the passenger seat blew kisses to the wind, instead of pulling double shifts at a highway gas station to support his chewing-tobacco habit.

"Miss?"

"You didn't call the hotel . . . or the police?"

He looked at her again and his expression shifted. Eve saw a blazing uncertainty cross his brow. She had underestimated both his intelligence and her own capacity for stupidity. She wished she could take it back.

"Is there a problem?" he asked, unblinking, with no accent.

She stammered, "No, no . . . I was thinking it must have been weird for you to see her in the middle of the night like that, but maybe . . . it wasn't . . . ?"

She laughed nervously. He just stared at her.

She continued rambling, "Anyway, if you had, um, called someone, I would have appreciated it. Like, for sure, if I'd known . . . if you had . . . I mean if she was lost . . ."

"She didn't seem lost," he said. "She seemed pretty okay to me, excepting her toga clothes." He leaned in, shifting back into his accent. "Look, all sorts come outta dat hotel at all hours, but most of 'em are just wannin' rubbers, not diapers. And we're happy to oblige." He stepped back and dismissed Eve with a wave of his hand before she could get herself in any deeper. He spat another glorious brown wad straight into the filthy jar. It made a plopping sound. "Good luck to ya!"

"Okay, thanks," Eve called back before sprinting over to Muriel and me. She turned the ignition and I purred for her. Muriel watched intently while another customer filled his tank with the pump next to theirs. Eve wanted to tell Muriel she knew all about her naughty after-hours map run, but she held her tongue.

"I know that man," Muriel said, continuing to stare out the window.

"You bought maps from him this morning," Eve hedged.

"The movie star pretending to be a cashier? No, not him. This guy, here. I know him."

Eve flipped her head around to find the clerk, but he was gone. He was *so* familiar . . . Then she turned back around and saw the bald sunbather from the pool filling his tank on the other side of the pump. He was wearing white shorts and a flower-print shirt held together with two buttons that barely contained his familiar hairy paunch. "Oh, that guy," Eve said dismissively.

"I know him." Muriel insisted. "I think we were lovers once."

"Muriel!" Eve blurted and blushed.

"He wears blue underwear. How else would I know that?"

"Seriously?"

"And it's small. The underwear, I mean. Not the rest."

"Oh my god." Eve's mortification prompted a shuddering giggle.

Muriel shrugged. Eve put on her seatbelt and asked Muriel to do the same. Eve started to pull away when Muriel lowered her window. "Goodbye, my love!" Muriel shouted.

The man with the sunburned head and little blue thong blew them both a kiss.

***

About two hours later, we departed the main highway and took I-16 toward Savannah's historic district. Following a friendly interaction with a local, we took a circuitous tour through Pulaski, Chatham, Madison, and Monterey Squares. We marveled at these magnificent urban parks with their classic old-money ambiance and ancient oaks, sycamores, magnolias, and pecans. I remembered driving through Savannah many years before, and it remained as magical as Muriel had described to Eve, who never encountered such a powerful grace in a constructed landscape. I could feel Eve envying the people who lived in this ornate town. She assumed they all possessed wit, charm, and closets brimming with fine clothing. She felt self-conscious and decided to pull a better shirt from the trunk when we finally arrived at Mrs. Wilkes Dining Room on West Jones Street.

"The parking angels are with us!" Muriel said, full of authority as we slid into a spot less than a block from the front door. "They want us to have a wonderful time so we'll return. Seriously, that's how it works," Muriel said in response to Eve's smirking.

They joined the line of people waiting to eat, and Eve dismissed her inclination to change when she saw that most of them were also wearing jeans and T-shirts. "We're right on time," Muriel remarked as they were cordially ushered in and seated at a broad wooden table with rounded corners, set for ten people. Eve reflexively equated the communal tables with church functions and was quickly swathed in a cold anxiety.

"Is this place . . . religious?" she asked quietly.

"What? Heavens no!" Muriel roared.

"What happened?" someone across the table asked.

"Oh, she asked me if this was a church!" Muriel laughed again.

"Church of fried chicken!" someone else said, and everyone chuckled. Eve was embarrassed, but she didn't fight it.

"Your first visit to Savannah?" the woman to her right asked politely.

"Is it that obvious?" Eve responded shyly.

"Well, don't you worry, doll, you're in the right place. This is the best food in town and that's all there is to it," the woman replied. "So where y'all from?"

"Florida."

"Oh sure, we see lots of people from Florida. Which part, Jax? Gainesville?"

"Deerfield Beach," Eve said, instantly regretting the casual disclosure of a key element that could threaten their anonymity.

"But that's downaways near Boca!" the woman cried out.

"Quite a hike!" another woman said before whispering something to her friend. Even though Eve couldn't hear it, seeing them talk drew even more air out of Eve's lungs. Then the first woman returned her attention to Eve and said, "You're here for SCAD?"

Eve surveyed the other guests at their table. They were all listening intently, and she felt sixteen eyes upon her, plus a few from the next table over. She continued to hold her breath and turned to Muriel, silently pleading for a sensible resolution.

"Eve takes beautiful photographs," Muriel replied. Eve was flattered by the compliment, but she hated that Muriel used her real name. Now everyone in the restaurant knew she was Eve from Deerfield Beach. "But we'll see," Muriel went on. "It's on her list and she's on theirs."

"Where else are you looking?" someone asked.

"RISD, CalArts, Pratt, Yale, and Skidmore" came tumbling off Muriel's lips. Eve was astonished with her facile and specific recall. Eve only recognized three of those schools herself, and she still had no idea what SCAD was.

"See?" the woman next to her relayed to her friend on the other side of the table. She mouthed the word "money," but the friend replied, loudly and for Eve's benefit, "You must be very talented."

"She's remarkable." Muriel winked.

"I like photography," Eve said, following Muriel's cue, and everyone nodded and said, "Ah . . ." as if that explained everything there was to know.

"SCAD has a great program," someone else added.

"I thought Chicago ranked higher than SCAD."

"SCAD wasn't even in the top twenty last year."

"What's your source?" someone else countered.

"*US News*."

"Oh, but that's not for photography."

"Yeah, it was architecture, I think."

"And interior design, isn't that right, Ralphie?"

"Or maybe film?" Ralphie replied. "But I don't know about photography."

"It's a great school for everything," someone new said. "Trust me, my nephew looked everywhere and it was his second choice."

"Where did he end up?"

"Yale."

The woman on Eve's right laughed to her friend, "Hey, do you think we can get all these rich college folks to pay for our lunch?" Muriel found that amusing, and she accented the mock-plea with her own little snort.

"SCAD had the best photography program in the country until everything went digital. They were pioneers with Photoshop and Mamiya cameras, but then everyone said if you weren't in a darkroom with physical film, you weren't making *real* photos."

"I remember that! It was in *The Tribune*!"

"Such bullshit," added Ralphie, who quickly apologized for the expletive, though no one was bothered.

"The article says, 'their move to digital equipment eliminated the complex human refinement necessary for capturing the expression of light on a subject.'" He was reading from his phone.

"What does that mean?"

"I think they're saying the act of taking a photograph is how you see and capture your subject with the camera and then work with the image in the darkroom, but turning it all over to autofocus and computers to fix the exposures and contrast means it's beyond human control, and only humans can make art."

"But that's crazy! A digital camera is still a camera and you still need a good eye and a concept and . . . and you still need *human vision*. Isn't that right, Eve?"

They all turned to her again, and she squeaked out, "Yeah."

"And *that's* where SCAD has always excelled!" someone proclaimed, and a few people nodded.

"You can do so much more with Photoshop in your toolbox. I think all those bells and whistles can really help the students enhance and refine their artistic points of view."

More nods.

"And SCAD started early. Their graduates have digital skills that are light-years ahead of everyone else."

"Well, I don't think *that's* true."

"Yes, it is."

"Okay."

They continued to quibble and debate as a woman fluttered around the table, pouring tall glasses of sweet iced tea with lemon. Eve drank her nerves and got a refill before the woman had fully circled the table. All these strangers were talking about her supposed college career, but she only said she liked photography because Muriel said it first. She was terrified someone was going to ask to see her work. Eve's phone was filled with pictures, but none of them were particularly artistic or worthy of a college portfolio. Liam's text of his luminaria was better than anything she took. She wondered if SCAD had a theater program.

"It's so nice you get to take your college tours with your grandma," someone said.

"My mom's dead," Eve replied, a little too quickly, and everyone fell silent. A piece of silverware fell to the floor on the far side of the room with a loud clatter and someone ran out of the kitchen to replace it.

Eve sipped her iced tea and looked down. Muriel felt like she should say something, but what? Everyone wanted to know the story behind the talented ingenue, but no one wanted to be That Person who pries into a family tragedy. The conversation stuttered and shuffled until it found its footing in local politics, and Eve and Muriel were happy to stay out of it.

Within minutes the food began to arrive. Enormous platters of authentic Southern cooking circulated and a bevy of flying spoons dispersed generous portions to the hungry herd. Eve eagerly took a sampling of whatever passed in front of her, and she helped Muriel load up, too. Fried chicken, meatloaf, and a peppery beef stew were the staple proteins, but Muriel warned Eve not to put too much on the plate or there wouldn't be room for the rest. Soon the veggies made a pass: collard greens, snap beans, butter beans, and black-eyed peas, each with its own distinctive seasoning. There were two kinds of rice with gravy, chunky potato salad, creamy macaroni and melted white cheese, sweet candied yams, and an outrageous looking plate of pickled beets with a red so alive it took Eve a moment to realize it was a root vegetable and not a bowl of beating hearts. A tangy okra and tomato salad capped off the meal. The platters eventually came to a rest as everybody dug in, and within seconds the political talk was replaced with "ummms" and "ohhhs."

"What do you think?" Muriel asked Eve.

"Amazing," Eve said, delighted. "It's weird that Florida is south of Georgia but this place feels far more Southern and authentic." Eve took a bite of the macaroni.

"I'd never thought of that," Muriel replied. "But I'm happy to know that some things in the world haven't changed." Her expression grew distant and Eve saw her posture shift slightly into a slump. "If they had food like this in the . . . the place . . . then we wouldn't . . . if they had . . ."

"Are you okay?"

"Hmm? Oh. How're the peas?" She shifted again.

"Do you . . . need a bathroom?" Eve whispered.

"No, I'm fine. Enjoy your lunch."

Eve kept an eye on Muriel as her fork danced across the piles on her plate, by turns marrying elements or enforcing a strict partition. The pickled beets converted whatever they touched, so she ate them first to eliminate future contaminations; potato salad mixed nicely with the collard greens; her mac and cheese demanded to remain pure. Muriel delicately picked at a few odd items, but most of her plate remained full of uneaten delicacies.

"What's wrong?" Eve murmured directly into Muriel's ear.

"I don't taste things the way I used to," Muriel said with a sigh. "It all looks delicious, but sort of tastes the same."

"Try the beets."

Muriel tried them and a small grin tugged at the corners of her barn-red mouth. As the grin grew wider her shoulders followed, and soon she was fully upright again. She ate the rest of the beets and asked for more from the bowl across the table. Then she scarfed down about half of what remained on her plate. There were more calories in one meal than she typically ate in three days, but she couldn't stop. Moments after everyone finished and the plates were swiftly cleared, fresh bowls of sweet banana pudding tantalized the diners.

"You've got to be kidding," Eve blurted, and everyone laughed.

"Looks like you'll be facing the freshman fifteen before you even get to campus!" the woman next to Eve squealed, and everyone laughed again.

"Is Mrs. Wilkes on the meal plan?" another person quipped. More laughter. Again, Eve didn't get the jokes, but she smiled politely. The savory banana-cream concoction was delectable, and she knew these animated strangers meant no harm.

The meal ended and Eve paid from her stash. She was thrilled by the experience, the portions, and the craft, and she squeezed Muriel's hand with a silent "thank you" for the unforgettable Savannah excursion.

Without Muriel's guidance, we would have stopped at a service station or driven through a fast-food chain instead of dining at a culinary jewel in a treasured city.

The other diners wished them good luck as Eve and Muriel lumbered toward me with their slightly increased girth. Before they climbed into my cabin, Muriel faced Eve squarely on the sidewalk and held Eve's shoulders with her fingertips.

"Is your mother really dead?"

"No. I'm not sure why I said that, but I told you about her last night? Remember?"

Muriel gave a noncommittal "oh right," and I knew she was covering for a lapse; at that moment she didn't recall anything they had discussed at the gas station north of Singer Island. She continued to hold Eve as her eyes tracked a curtain of Spanish moss swaying a few inches above their heads. "Are you running away?" Muriel asked.

Eve shuffled under Muriel's persistent grip.

"Um, it's more like I'm running *toward* something?" Eve corrected.

"I see," Muriel said sympathetically. Her eyes pulsed with a radioactive intensity and she didn't blink. Under this unwavering stare, Eve suddenly thought about Laura, who generally gave Eve about as much focus as a ping-pong ball in a windstorm. She thought about her mother, who only seemed interested in transportation issues, house supplies, and all things Jesus. Liam didn't really know her, and maybe never would. The drama club was enjoyable, but the performers had the strongest bonds, not the people like Eve who literally worked in and on the backgrounds.

She had no one else but Muriel.

Muriel, who cared about her tender thoughts. Muriel, who didn't judge. Muriel, who stood there on the curb with her palms holding Eve's shoulders and her steady eyes propping up the rest, ready to listen. They'd had one luscious meal following a highly peculiar day, but already Eve knew she had found a rare friend who listened. The difference in their ages meant nothing as Eve quickly convinced herself they might even be soulmates. Eve realized she was crying. She stepped forward and hugged Muriel, tight.

But Eve didn't fully answer Muriel's question, and her tears prompted her new confidant to believe that Eve's mother was, in fact, the abusive catalyst for their excursion. Muriel wondered if it was about ignorance and neglect, or if there was something more. Something physical. Or even sexual. Muriel didn't recall seeing any marks on Eve's body when she had stepped out of the shower, but it was clear something major had recently occurred. Something terrible had driven Eve away from her home. Muriel looked for more details. Eve's teeth were in good shape and her clothes weren't tattered—but there was a pervasive darkness surrounding the young girl, like an aura of coal. Muriel knew she couldn't help Eve if she didn't know what happened. She had to know. To help her. Within the closed boundary of their hug, Muriel whispered cautiously and supportively into Eve's ear, "Did she . . . touch you?"

"What?"

"Did she put her fingers in your vagina?"

"No!!" Eve bleated as she stepped back to release herself from the mooring.

"It's okay, you can talk to me. You're safe now." Eve's temperament quickly turned to frost as she closed her overshirt and clasped her arms across her chest. "Tell me," Muriel implored. "You know you can trust me. What did your mother do to you?"

"Oh my god, nothing! Nothing . . . *like that!*"

Eve was grossly perplexed by Muriel's assumption of sexual malfeasance, and she searched her words to discover what had led to such an insidious, erroneous conclusion. As the older woman stared at her, she also felt like she was being accused of something, but she couldn't decipher what that might be.

"I told you everything last night: my mother sucks and she's a liar, but it's only, like, *emotional* bullshit. She's not a pedophile!!" Muriel's face softened while Eve's continued to shape itself into something sharper and more angular. "I mean, really?" Eve started to pace. "Really?! Do you really think I'm *that fucked up?*"

Muriel didn't flinch. She simply watched, hoping Eve would let it all out.

"Okay, look," Eve finally said. "When my mother isn't trying to indoctrinate me, she pretty much forgets that I exist, and after Dad—whatever—after Dad, she fell in with a bunch of freaks from her church and it's . . . it's too much. She's just too much."

Muriel nodded.

"There are crosses everywhere, and she can't go five minutes without saying Jesus this or Jesus that, and she's got these stupid Bible quotes taped up on all the walls. They're like, *everywhere*, like even in the bathroom so I'll get a lesson when I'm taking a shit. I used to flush them, but then she'd pin those fuckers right back up again. I can't escape it!"

Muriel blinked again, but didn't move.

"And you know something? You would think with Jesus as her BFF that she wouldn't be a bold-faced liar, but she's such a hypocrite! And now I know it. The truth. I know who she is and I know *exactly* what's going on and *that's* why we're driving north." Eve dropped her arms to her hips, forming crisp triangles with her elbows. "So no, my mother never stuck her fingers anywhere. If anything, it's the opposite," Eve choked out. "She doesn't even hug me anymore. She's, like, not even a real person. I mean . . . god!! *GOD!!* And God? What is *that?* I work hard at my job and I get good grades and stay out of trouble. I'm a good person! A *really* good person, if you look around and compare, but she thinks I'm a mini-Satan because I like doing plays and piercing my ears and I hate wearing skirts and I won't sit in the fucking living room and pray with her ten hours a day!"

"And the stripe," Muriel pointed out.

"What?"

"She probably thinks Jesus wouldn't approve of your hair." Muriel smirked.

Eve laughed a little, but she felt like she was sinking. At the gas station she had been elusive and mostly spoke about what she had found on the internet—this was the first time she had fully verbalized her situation to anyone, and the words felt as heavy as the exorbitant amount of food in her gut. She mentally kicked herself for gobbling a second helping of the banana pudding. And a third scoop of the mac and cheese.

Eve stepped back and leaned against me. My stability helped her catch her breath. She placed one hand over her heart and the other against her belly in an attempt to calm herself. She contemplated vomiting to release the tension, but she didn't want to insult Mrs. Wilkes or sully Savannah. Muriel looked around to see if anyone would notice if Eve left her lunch on the beautiful, pink-brick sidewalk, but the street remained quiet as Eve slowly regained her composure.

After a few moments Muriel decided it was safe to speak again. She chose an eloquent, scholarly tone that I used to hear back in the day when she and Ira would quibble.

"I was afraid for you, that's all. I thought . . . maybe . . . Well, you know what I thought. I'm pretty sure you're my responsibility now, so I'm going to protect you. Maybe I got confused when you told the table she was dead, but it sounds like, in some ways, that might be a little true?"

Eve looked up from the sidewalk and into the swirling sea of Muriel's eyes.

"I get it, kid. I had a difficult mother, too."

Somehow it had never occurred to Eve that other people, especially older people, could also have tough mothers. Especially Muriel, who seemed to have everything. Eve immediately wondered if Muriel had advanced the notion of a violation that she herself had experienced as a young girl. In the disturbance of that idea, Eve felt a sudden mix of compassion for Muriel and shame over her own outburst. She hated that she couldn't control herself, that she was so easily provoked.

Muriel continued, "I mean it when I say you can trust me—you know that, right? Eve, for heaven's sake, you saved me from that place! You *saved* me! I'm finally starting to feel like a real person again—a person who drove all the way to Georgia to eat a big lunch!"

Eve remained propped against me. She was feeling better. Her lunch would stay down.

A moment later, Muriel said quietly, "Would it be all right if I asked you something?"

Eve nodded.

"Will you . . . let me hug you again? I don't get a lot of hugs, either."

Eve opened her arms and Muriel stepped in to mend the circle. They banded each other with understanding and the mutual need to be needed. This time, within the hug, Muriel whispered, "And I think your hair is very pretty." Eve, feeling somewhat embarrassed, was relieved to find the only witness was the Spanish moss floating delicately above them.

"We should go," Eve said as they released the hug. She opened my door. "Can I ask you something?"

"You may."

"Can we put the top down?"

"No."

Eve was a little stunned by the blunt response as she helped Muriel inside. When she was settled behind the wheel, I could feel her inner peace, but I also felt her body battling the effects of too many carbohydrates and an excess of caffeinated sweet tea. I also sensed her urgency to continue: it was already early afternoon, and our delicious detour had cost us many precious hours. We took off and found the Piggly Wiggly on Augusta Road for cold water and an extra package of incontinence briefs once Muriel finally located her brand.

Eve and Muriel felt connected in a new way, and it revitalized their sense of purpose. The purity of the afternoon light illuminated them with a positive energy, and they basked in the glow. It had been ages since either of them felt truly happy, and recognizing their happiness made them happy all over again—they were prone to spontaneous giggling for the rest of the afternoon. We headed over the iconic Talmadge Memorial Bridge, topped off my fuel in Hardeeville, and before long we were once again cruising north on I-95. Eve noticed that the gas receipt read South Carolina, and she felt a slight pang that she'd missed the welcome sign to yet another new state, but she wouldn't allow such trivialities to tarnish her mood.

***

As we traveled on through Dorchester County, I felt Muriel's mind begin to drift. The repetitive pattern of trees lining the side of the road blurred into a tranquilizing horizontal plane, a smear of lustrous green, while her saturated digestive system summoned all the energy it could find. She felt heavy and dull and awash in the smudgy landscape.

I weigh a little over five thousand pounds and I'm supported by substantial tires, but even with my four-link drive suspension system, coil springs, automatic transmission control, and steel torsion bars, I still produce a strong vibration when I'm pushed. Eve liked to maintain our speed at seventy-two miles per hour, and I couldn't help but hum, adding to Muriel's sedation. She sank deep into her seat with her head propped gently against the seatbelt, fostering the perfect environment for mental levitation. As Muriel's mind floated up and away, she entered into the echoes of Grace's firsthand explorations in India . . .

***

I woke up alone in a mosquito-proof tent on top of my bed, bathed in a soft pink light. I specifically remembered closing the wooden shutters before going to sleep, but something had opened them—perhaps the night breeze, but it could have been a trained monkey searching for my wallet—such things happen here. I felt refreshed, and I quickly assessed that my sparse but important materials were safe inside the tent with me and my passport and money remained secure in the secret sleeve I had sewn into the underside of my traveling pillowcase. I decided to scrub away the lingering remnants of my fatigue with a hot shower. Then I would find a good chai wallah and caffeinate, and then I would explore. I read through the guidebooks on the train from Madras, but the description of this town seemed inadequate: *Thiruvannamalai is a quaint village of nearly 400,000 people at the base of Mount Arunachala in Tamil Nadu.* It went on to chronicle the bevy of ashrams located in and around the city, but the directory only listed two hotels and one restaurant. There was a small map showing the post office, the train station, three cafés, and two banks. For a city the approximate size of Atlanta, I figured there had to be more.

But first I wanted to enjoy the pink light that had stirred me from my sleep before the expected chaos of the streets resumed. In that quiet stillness, the rosy beam and its hollow purple shadows penetrated my netted enclave, and I followed the edge of my arms as the light defined them. The soft blond hair on my forearms, rarely visible in broad daylight, was silhouetted in a slanting glow that was already evolving into a brighter, crispier orange. The warmth penetrated my skin. I stretched fully and felt the nylon fabric of the tent edges with my toes. Bringing the tent had been a smart decision: it was lightweight and only took a minute to set up, and I had dipped it in a permethrin solution before I left so I could sleep with some confidence that I wouldn't be eaten alive by South Asian bugs during the night. I set the tent on top of my hotel beds and used my own clean sheets inside it. Sometimes the air was a bit stifling, but most of my accommodations had robust fans (if the power stayed on) or windows that opened to an ocean or mountain breeze. I awoke one morning in Mamallapuram, a coastal town on the Bay of Bengal, and found a dozen dead mosquitoes and a flailing spider the size of a golf ball (!!) on the mesh outside my tent. The last bits of human flesh they'd sampled in their short, parasitic lives belonged to someone else, and I was spared their infections by a few microns of poisonous synthetic thread.

I was safe.

I continued to roll and stretch in the sunbeam like a lazy dog on a well-worn couch. The train ride to Thiruvannamalai was uniquely uncomfortable—they still use narrow-gauge rails in many parts of the country, and the trains that run these tracks are not the super-sleepers that connect the major cities. It reminded me of the toy trains in seasonal amusement parks, on a slightly larger scale. The seats were slatted planks of wood nailed to the walls at ninety-degree angles, with no cushions. The bathroom was a hole in the pee-soaked floor of a small closet with no sink. The train also didn't seem to have any shock absorbers. I was crowded into a section with eleven other women, and no one could stand or extend her limbs without poking someone. The five-hour ride was confining and jolting, but now I was alone in my large tent. I could hear my joints pop and crackle as I elongated my neck, curved my back, raised my shoulders, and extended my legs. Eventually, the light from the window lost its early tenderness and assumed a piercing harshness, revealing more of the three-dollar room outside my protective pyramid.

The walls were painted a hospital mint-green that failed to coordinate with the orange-red tiles on the floor. It was impossible to ascertain the temperature visually, so I unzipped my tent and took a tentative step with flexed bare feet, anticipating an early morning chill. I was pleasantly surprised to find the tiles held a durable warmth, and they were also dutifully scrubbed. I stepped into the bathroom and opened a new bottle of water. Following my near-death skirmish with food poisoning and subsequent supercharged antibiotic treatments in a Madras clinic, I felt relatively indestructible—but there was still no sense taking a chance with the tap water in a remote, underdeveloped village that barely made it onto the popular maps.

I brushed my teeth and rinsed with the bottled water. I spat into the sink and turned on the tap to wash everything away, and a second later, my bare feet were saturated with the expectorant. The sink was merely a basin screwed to the wall with a drain that was unconnected to, well, anything. I ran more water and followed the angled stream of my minty spit as it made its way across the floor into a multipurpose bathroom hollow that serviced the toilet, sink, and shower where it met the wall. With the light coming through the broad slit, I could see that the tiles were stained—whatever was washed or flushed or expelled in that room quickly flowed down the exterior wall and into a public ditch on the backside of the hotel. I marked my discovery with a choice expletive and put *find better lodging* at the top of my explorations list, followed by *maybe six dollars?*

The owner of the hotel knocked on the door a few minutes after I finished cleaning my feet, and I assumed he either heard the water running or saw the cascade of aqua spit and my toilet flushings drop into the back alley. He offered me two buckets of hot water for my shower, which I happily accepted and promptly used when they arrived twenty minutes later. I was not only accustomed to bucket showers—I actually enjoyed them. First, I dipped my wash towel in the steaming water and fully wet my body and hair. Then I lathered with my liquid soap and extra dips into the water. My fingers slid across my deeply tanned skin and in and out of all my crevasses until I was a slippery, sloppy mess with millions of tiny bubbles migrating toward the floor, collecting dirt and filth and dried sweat en route. The cooler air met with my heated, soapy skin and formed goose bumps, which provided more friction for the washcloth. I'm not saying every bucket shower was an erotic experience, but I will admit that sometimes my slippery fingers forgot to clean and preferred to explore, and the feeling of a hot bucket of water cascading over your naked flesh when you're so ... open ... well. Well, well. As my trip progressed, sometimes just looking at a bucket of water might ignite a deep arousal, but nothing of the sort occurred at that particular cheap hotel; the toothpaste between my toes had stripped away any and all precursors to self-romance.

    I finished bathing, then ran my cloth under the cold tap water one more time and pressed it against my forehead, feeling the icy water snake behind my ears, then down my back and legs and ankles. I patted myself dry and put on a button-down shirt over a clean T-shirt. My traveling khakis were deliciously warmed from their accidental placement in the morning sunlight, and in no time I felt squeaky and fresh and ready to go. I re-zipped the tent walls into place and left the room, fully primed to explore the remote mountain town.

    I found my desired chai less than two minutes from the hotel. I savored its milky spice and quickly realized I was hungry—I'd skipped one or two true meals on my travel day, relying on ginger candies and lychee cookies for sustenance. I walked past a resting bull by the high walls of the Arunachaleshwar Temple grounds, and then I found a café with potato, spinach, and paneer *dosas*. I pulled apart the crispy shell and used it to pinch the hot, cheesy filling, admiring the complex flavors derived from only three primary ingredients. I was so focused on my meal I hardly noticed the unceasing racket emanating from hundreds of honking cars, trucks, motorcycles, and three-wheeled *tuk-tuks* claiming their space amongst the people and animals on the narrow, polluted road.

    An Indian man at the next table asked me if he could show me around the city. By reflex I said "No," and he returned to his newspaper, which was spread in sections across the large table. I studied him while I continued to eat. His perfect mustache bridged clean-shaven cheeks, and a stark-white scalp line neatly divided his thick, freshly cut, slate-colored hair. He wore a light-gray tailored suit, and his Nehru-collared dress shirt was buttoned to the top. He read with his fingers, which moved rapidly across the pages, unperturbed by the weight of his gold rings. He looked more educated than many of the guides I'd encountered before—the ones who seemed to know a lot about a little, typically their family's silk shops or carpet stores, and not much else. I looked through the open café door and saw the elegant anomaly of a modern, full-sized car parked amongst the typical kerosene-powered rickshaws. It looked new and seemed to magically repel the street dust.

"Is that yours?" I asked cautiously, pointing to the street. His fingers stopped moving, and it was his turn to assess me. I was happy to be washed and wearing fresh clothes as the gray eyes that matched his suit, encased in pencil-mark wrinkles, moved across me and lingered on my hands. I don't wear any jewelry, not even a watch, and especially not a ring.

"Yes, the car is mine," he finally admitted, lifting his head.

"Are you a politician?"

He laughed at this, revealing a large space between his front teeth. The warmth of his broken smile melted the ice, and he explained that the car belonged to his business and he used it to check on his properties and prospects. He was waiting for a colleague to join him the next day to assess some land for development, and then they would return to his home in Pondicherry together. He wasn't looking for money so much as something to do, and he enjoyed playing a tour guide for, as he put it, "the good travelers."

I looked around the café to make sure we weren't the only ones there. I spoke in a loud and clear voice so that if I went missing, someone might remember the vibrant blonde woman who enjoyed her breakfast *dosa*. There was no one to corroborate his story, but very few people had cars in remote India at the time, and even fewer had *nice* cars. Still, I didn't know whether I was lucky to find him or a complete moron for even considering his tour. I required more information.

"So where would you take me?" I asked. The idea of spending the day in a comfortable car with a wealthy dilettante guide was appealing. I'd hoofed it through so much of India; perhaps it was time to be kind to my feet and let my blisters heal. He stretched his hands across his flat newspapers, smoothing them with a quiet rustle, and asked if I knew anything about Thiruvannamalai. I mentioned the ashrams from the guidebooks and admitted I knew of little else.

"You are fortunate," he began, his voice sounding like smooth caramel flowing over little pebbles. "You have come to one of the most powerful spiritual places in all of India. We are now sitting on the base of the divine Mount Arunachala, Shiva's physical manifestation of the Temple of Fire. This is one of the places where the five elements of the earth were created.

It is the holiest of all places and you are a very lucky person to be here. There are many sights to see, and many important yogis and gurus call this land their home. Thousands of tourists come for the full-moon festivals, and once a year, hundreds of thousands join together for Karthikai Deepam, our festival of light and fire."

"Really? When?"

"Three months ago. You missed it." He followed this with the culturally ubiquitous head-wobble. I learned that this gesture can mean *yes*, or *I agree*, or *I understand*, or is sometimes the polite way of saying *no*. This time I took it to mean "oops".

"Well, shit," I blurted, and I instantly regretted being coarse.

He raised an eyebrow, then smiled again. "You are sarcastic. It is a very good form of humor, but I imagine it does not always work for you in the way that you intend. That is something you can work on here. This is a good place for you to be at this particular time in your journey. All the spirits of the world are focused here, and they want to help you become your true and very best self."

I felt like this stranger knew me intimately, and all my reasons for coming to India, but who was he to surmise I could be aloof and caustic and then forgive me for it? He knew I was desperate for a deeper understanding of myself, but wasn't everyone with my skin tone and dress who found themselves in the remote temple towns of India? He didn't seem dangerous, but wasn't that a danger in and of itself? I felt compelled to touch his arm, as if that might protect me from the possibility of harm, but I restrained myself.

He continued, "I would take you to Unnamulai Amman Temple, Annamaliyar Sannidhi, Arunachaleshwar Temple, Murugan Temple----" His beautiful, songlike lilt clinked like wind chimes on a breezy summer porch. I had no idea what he was saying, and I was surprised there were so many temples as he proceeded. "----Kamatchi Amman Temple, Abirami Thirumana Mandapam, the Kamarajar Statue----"

"Can I meet a guru?" I interrupted. I explained that I was happy to see all the important sites, but I knew I would eventually tire of them. I was hoping to experience some sort of spiritual interaction with a living master while I was here in the Shiva Zone.

"Yes, I can take you to a guru. I will take you anywhere you wish to go."

"Okay, but you have to let me pay you." The soft bags of flesh under his eyes tightened again. "Otherwise I'd be taking advantage of you," I explained, "and then you might . . . you might think you can take advantage of me." I narrowed my own eyes as I said this.

"You think I will try to make you my girlfriend?"

"I don't know. A little. Yes."

"You are very honest. This is another good quality."

"Thanks?" I stuttered. I knew what I was thinking, but I had no idea what was in his mind. Maybe he enjoyed bucket showers a little too much, too.

"Sixty rupees," he said automatically, twisting the gold ring on his wedding finger. "And a tip at the end of the day if you are satisfied with my tour."

"A monetary tip," I declared. "I'm serious. I don't want any misunderstandings here."

"Of course!" he laughed again. "You Americans . . . you are always so ready to be hurt by the world. Why is that?"

I didn't answer him. I knew being cautious was my own personal trait, part of being a woman and maybe part of being American—but it was also human nature for anyone traveling alone in foreign lands who was about to venture into a stranger's car for the day. I mentally calculated his rate in my currency. It was a splurge, but I weighed it against spending the day in polluting rickshaws going from place to place on my own, and the guidebook was so thin that exploring would be difficult without an adviser. I looked across the room and saw an older Indian man with wiry white corkscrews for hair looking at me. He appeared to be invested in our conversation. He winked at me and gave me a thumbs-up.

"I'm Katran," said my new guide. "Katran Prasad Balakrishnan."

"Call me Grace," I said as I pressed my hands together and gave a perfunctory bow. He did the same, but his head stayed down longer as he offered a small prayer on my behalf. He lifted his head and revealed the gap between his teeth in yet another broad smile.

I finished my breakfast and paid the bill while he continued to read his papers. Then he escorted me to his car and opened the back door. I insisted on sitting in the front seat, but he said that was not possible. I was seconds away from calling off the tour when a thin young man in an ironed button-down shirt ran up to me with an ice-cold Coke in a glass bottle. He apologized to Katran in Tamil for his delay, but Katran shook it off with a wave and introduced me to Paloo, his driver. I got into the back seat, and Katran sat in the front seat himself, to navigate. Having the entire back to myself alleviated my fears—I could always jump out if I had to. A friend later told me the seating arrangement alleviated Katran's innate concerns of being spotted in the back of his own car with a white woman.

Katran faced backward most of the time as he explained everything to me in great detail. First, we drove around the city for about thirty minutes so I could get a feel for it. Parts of it were ancient, with crazy streets that didn't always connect, stone buildings, mud buildings, steel buildings, concrete buildings, wires and pipes sticking every which way, animals, people, dust, dirt, colors, flags, signs, and a thousand smells that ranged from sewage to sandalwood in varying proportions depending on our speed. It was overwhelming and quintessentially India, but I did manage to pick out a few good-looking hotels along the way that might have sinks connected to actual pipes.

I asked if we could drive around the mountain itself, and Katran obliged. We toured the ancient hill on timeworn roads that ringed a path traversed by millions of annual pilgrims. Katran told me that once a year at the culmination of a ten-day festival, they light a cauldron of ghee at the summit. Ghee is a clarified butter, and the cauldron apparently holds about three tons of it. I was astonished by the concept and looked to the top of the mountain, hoping to see a river of butter flowing down its sides. When we fully circumnavigated the mount, Katran brought me to the Ramanashram, the home of Bhagavan Sri Ramana Maharshi, the preeminent guru of Thiruvannamalai. Katran was excited and spoke so quickly I barely understood what he was saying beyond the intermittent repetitions of the word "Ramana."

The ashram looked like a quaint country compound, with stone-and-plaster buildings set on a shimmering grassy slope. My eye was immediately drawn to the peacocks perched on the roof of an open-air building. Beneath it, a group of women were gathered in a circle of bright saris. They talked and waved their hands emphatically as they attempted to convince each other of their particular point of view, or so I assumed. Another lawn stretched to another set of buildings that appeared to be newer accommodations. I asked Katran if reservations were required, and he said he would check. Then he invited me to see the temple, and I readily obliged. I was swept into a beautiful sanctuary with white and gray marble floors and a fantastic abundance of fresh flowers and prominent crystals on the dais. I saw a small trench cut into the stone, encircling the back quarter of the room. Clear water flowed through it and around the pulpit area to separate it spiritually, like a divine castle with a holy moat. The atmosphere was simple, tranquil, and even with its incredibly ornate carvings, it felt refined. Despite it being a bright day, the interior light was suffused with pink, much like my tent early that morning. Noting my immediate affection for this temple, Katran indicated he would wait outside for me and that there was no need to rush.

I walked clockwise around the altar with dozens of other people for about fifteen minutes, and then I decided to meditate. I had practiced my meditations throughout my trip, and I was eager to see what would come of it in this special place. It took some time before I was finally able to relax by concentrating on my breathing. At first I was distracted by the chanting and the perfumed air from all the potent flowers and burning incense, but soon I managed to find some control as I settled into my familiar, clear-minded vacancy. I pictured myself alone in a movie theater, watching a silent film that only projected white light. Before long, the rectangle expanded to fill my mind, and it overtook my ears and breath as well. I was enveloped and became a part of the light itself. Physically I was planted on the floor with my legs crossed over each other, but in my mind I was rising through a stream of peace and joy, propelled by solitude and luminescence. In this nothingness I remained conscious of the rhythm of my breath (the vibration of my soul?), and I began to see the shape of a door in the distance. The door moved closer to me, or I toward it. This floating rectangle was vertical, and it blocked the light until it opened and I was able to fly right through it . . . to another door, which also opened as I arrived. The doors continued to come to me and open as I flew through their jambs, my movement effortless and uninhibited. Soon

I realized there were Sanskrit words carved on them. I don't know Sanskrit, but I felt like I understood the meaning of each door as I passed through. Finally I came to the last door. It was made of gold. It slowed down as I approached it, my nose practically touching the precious metal, until my field of vision merged with the glowing gold and angular Sanskrit texts melted into it.

That's when I felt a presence standing behind me, and I somehow knew it was Sri Ramana Maharshi. This was his ashram. I felt self-conscious and a little nervous, knowing he was the big guy on campus, but he calmly told me to continue my breathing. Then he told me the meaning of the script on the golden door.

"I am love," he said.

"You are love." I repeated.

My back was to him, but I could feel his grin as he placed his hands above my shoulders, without touching me, and symbolically cupped my head. He repeated, "I am love."

I understood my error. I repeated, "*I* am love."

"I am love."

"I am love," I said again. "I am love. I am love. I am love."

The door in my mind's eye flew open, and I was back in the white, flying away from Sri Ramana, singing "I am love!" over and over in my mind until I gently returned into myself, and into reality, on the floor of the serene meditation hall. I slowly turned my head to see if he was still standing behind me, but he wasn't there. I collected myself for a while, savoring the energy flooding my body. Finally I returned to Katran, who was waiting patiently by the car with Paloo. He was reading another newspaper, which was spread out across the hood and held in place with small rocks. It was in a different language than the first one.

"You are glowing," he said. "You have made a happy connection."

"That was . . ." I uttered quietly, trying to find words but feeling wary that speaking might spoil my current state. After a moment I whispered, "Where would I find Mister Sri Ramana? He spoke to me while I was meditating and I want to thank him for the lesson."

Katran looked at me like I was joking, but then quickly understood that I was not. He asked me to follow him. He took me back into the ashram compound to a little building that was exceptionally well kept, with a door so shiny it might have been painted that morning. Katran asked me to look inside the window. I peered through the glass and saw a study with a bed off to the side. There was a desk and books and pens, a silver water jug, and a stopped clock.

"What is this?" I asked.

"This is the guru's room," Katran replied.

"So we'll wait for him here?"

Katran released a small sort of cluck and then said, "The guru's room has been perfectly preserved from the very moment he ascended."

It took a moment for that to sink in. "He died?" I asked.

"Death is a clumsy description, but, yes, the guru left his physical body to become one with the universe. He was enlightened, and now he continues to bestow his blessings on devotees who seek his knowledge and worship here. And this morning it seems he gave his blessings to you."

My rational mind tried to comprehend what Katran was saying. I knew it was all true as my meditation continued to resonate, my limbs vibrating with the energy I'd received. Katran had promised me I would meet a guru, and he had delivered. I'd met a great guru. I'd met a great guru and been given a personal blessing. It didn't even matter that he had died.

"He ascended on April fourteenth," Katran continued. "In 1950."

We returned to the car and Katran pulled his papers together. He carefully placed the rocks back on the side of the road instead of tossing them randomly. I was consumed with respect for Katran, the ashram, the car, and Paloo. I respected the sky and the mountain and even my own consciousness. I didn't know I had the capacity for so much positivity and respect. I was also very, very thirsty.

Paloo stayed with the vehicle while Katran and I crossed the busy road to find refreshment at Om Restaurant. It was a strange time of day and we were the only ones there, so the owners kept the lights and fans turned off. We sat by a large window overlooking the ashram. A family of goats wandered up the road, rummaging through garbage piles looking for food. I decided I was more than thirsty, and I ordered a creamy coconut and vegetable korma that hid its spiciness until the end. Katran ate a chickpea dish I hadn't heard of.

Together we devoured two orders of garlic naan and a pitcher of lemonade made with fresh lemons, hand-pressed sugar cane, and bottled water for the American.

"What's next?" I asked.

"You're still hungry? They have good *kachori* here," he replied.

"No, I mean what's next on the tour?"

"Would you like to meet a swami?"

"Absolutely," I said, not knowing the difference between a swami and a guru.

Katran paused for a moment. He looked concerned.

"But you're not too tired?" he asked.

"Not at all... should I be?"

"A good meditation can give a person much insight, happiness, and peace, but it can also take a lot from you as well. You should be careful with your limited energies today."

"What do you mean?" asked my Western mind. *My meditation took something from me?* I felt more alive that morning than I'd felt in years.

"You are the caterpillar that turns into the butterfly. Until now you've been living your life with a hundred feet marching around, consuming, and going about your business. But something made you stop—something within yourself decided you should be wrapped in a protective shell. You disconnected from the world and went into the cave of your own making. You've been living in that cave for a long time, slowly evolving and transforming, but deep within your own isolation."

While he spoke he took the napkin from his lap and spread it out evenly on the table. He took a rough, beige rock from his pocket and centered it on the napkin. He wrapped the napkin around the rock repeatedly until it was a wadded ball on the table.

"And now you've come to India to break free of that cave. You are knowing that this is the time to move out and find another space—another space on your soul's journey."

He started to open the napkin and unwrap the rock.

"You received *ashirvaad* today. This is a blessing, a profound blessing from a very powerful and loving guru. You were open to the experience. You opened your heart and mind, and today you broke free from yourself, from the ego you have always known yourself to be. Today is your new birthday, and you were given a gift that you will take with you as you move into your new directions."

Katran unwrapped the rock. Where the rough, beige lump had been, I discovered a shiny black stone with a flat, cut bottom. *How did he do that?*

"Do you know what this is?" Katran asked me.

"I know it's a good trick!" I said.

He smiled. "This is a lingam. A lingam has many meanings, but primarily it is the symbol of Shiva. It is Shiva."

"Shiva is the blue warrior, right? Ganesh is the elephant and Hanuman is the monkey. Or is Krishna the blue one?"

"I am sometimes wondering what they teach in American schools." His eyes gleamed. "Shiva is not always blue, but, yes, sometimes he is depicted in that way. Shiva is the god of creation and destruction, reproduction and dissolution. Shiva manifests truth. He is the god of the cosmic dance. He is the lord of all beasts. The lingam is a representation of Shiva's male creative energy."

"I see," I said, detecting that this little rock did, indeed, have a strong phallic quality.

"The lingam often sits within Shakti's symbol of female creative energy, the yoni."

"The yoni," I responded.

"Yes." He took a breath. He knew he was going too fast for me. I was in a restaurant in India with a man I'd only known a few hours. Already I'd been given wisdom from a guru who died years ago, and now we were talking about lingams and yonis. It was almost too much, yet he was compelled to tell me more. "The lingam has another attribute," he resumed. "Shiva's Lingam also represents the beginning-less and endless Stambha pillar. It symbolizes the infinite nature of Shiva."

He picked up the lingam and held it in his palms. He turned it over a few times. "This lingam is very special. A guru gave it to me a long time ago. He manifested it specifically for me at a time when I very much needed it, but he also said I was required to give it to someone new when it was their time to receive it."

I sensed what was coming. "Oh, don't----"

He placed his Shiva Lingam in my hand and closed my fingers over it.

"You are no longer in your cave. You are no longer a caterpillar. It is plainly visible that you are flying free now. I saw it when you emerged from the temple. You had the translucent glow of a butterfly's wings, and now the world is going to open up to you as you learn to ascend to your new heights. You will take this with you to remind you that all things are possible, all things can happen, all things have happened, and all things will happen. Even though you are here, in this restaurant, looking at me like I am a little crazy through your bright eyes, you now know that you are also an important part of the infinite. You weren't sure until this morning, but now you know it in your heart. You can feel it. You can feel it in your wings."

Everything he said was true. I kept my hand closed over the lingam. It was warm and smooth and fit perfectly in the crevice of my hand between my palm and my fingers. It also felt like an extension of myself, in a way. A few tears slid down my cheeks.

"So we can go and meet the swami, if you wish, but I have to make sure you are still feeling capable. Exiting your cave is a lot for one day. We are all infinite beings, of course, but the vehicles of our bodies require both fuel and rest to stay viable."

"I think the naan and korma did it for me," I said. Then the feeling of ultimate respect hit me again. "Thank you, Katran. Thank you for the lingam."

He sighed with a little sadness. "The lingam is now yours," he said. "Until you decide it should go on to someone else. Happy new birthday." We paid for our lunches and went back to the car.

The trip to meet the swami took a little under an hour. The road was mostly unpaved, and Paloo drove quickly, generating a curling wake of dust. As I looked to the side, the repetitive pattern of trees lining the side of the road blurred into a tranquilizing horizontal plane, a smear of lustrous green that was somehow familiar.

The sun was high, and I realized it was only a little after one o'clock on my first full day there, but it felt like I'd been in Thiruvannamalai for weeks, or years. Katran told me a little about the man I was about to meet. His name was Vellaiyanantha Swami, but people also knew him as Karrumarapatti Swami, Karrumarapatti being the village where we were headed (Katran wrote down all of these names so I could relay them correctly). The swami was born in 1925.

He never had his own guru, but apparently he had an enlightened experience when he was a small child that led others to follow him in search of their own connection to the divine. He had a wife and three children. He never cut his hair and only cut his nails every few decades. Legend has it that he sat in the same chair for twenty-five years, and in that time no one ever saw him eat or drink. He spent up to eighteen hours a day in meditation, but he always welcomed visitors to his home. Katran told me the swami liked to touch people's heads, and not to be nervous.

We arrived at a simple, ranch-style house; its outer walls looked like the peeled skin of an old carrot. It had a low-pitched metal roof with rusty sediment nestled in the grooves. Two dogs chased us with wagging tails as we pulled in. I petted them unreservedly, despite their matted fur and the flies circling their heads like electrons around an atom. Katran indicated I should head straight in through the front door; there was no need to knock. He would remain by the car with the dogs, who vigorously licked Paloo's knees and ankles, waiting for the treats they knew were in his pocket.

I approached the weather-stained house. *If I were in Miami or Los Angeles or any other American city, I wouldn't be doing this,* I thought. I reminded myself that, despite my profound meditation, I was still in a foreign land being led around by two men I didn't really know. I had allowed myself to be taken out of the major city and into a dusty, dirty neighborhood miles away from anyone, and failed to leave a note with my plans or whereabouts. I didn't even know my whereabouts. If trouble appeared, I wouldn't even know which way to run. I breathed out and clutched my lingam. *I am love,* I reminded myself. And while I considered that I was supremely stupid for getting myself into this situation, I also knew I was somehow protected on my first day as a butterfly.

There was no turning back.

I removed my shoes and walked through the door into the house.

Two plump Indian women in striking vermilion saris jumped up excitedly to greet me. I exhaled my relief as they brought me into their modest living space.

"I am here to meet the swami," I said.

"Of course," one replied with a perfect British accent.

"There's really no other reason to visit Karrumarapatti, is there?" She seemed very happy to see me. She put her hands on my shoulders and spun me around to face the swami.

He was right there!

He raised his hands, beckoning me to come closer, and I obliged. I saw a fragile older man with ashen skin and deep-set black eyes that floated in a bog of crinkly flesh. His bristled white hair looped up around his head in a big bun and then traveled down below his back, wrapped around his waist, fell to the floor, and curled up in a ball at his feet. Katran had mentioned that the swami never cut his hair, but the mental picture I'd conjured paled against the actual sight of a man who had *never* cut his hair in his *entire* life. What struck me more, however, were his fingernails. When he summoned me over to him by flinging his wrist, I thought he was holding some sort of toy. I couldn't comprehend that the distorted objects he held were actually his nails, sprouting like *mafalde* noodles from the ends of his fingers. His thumbnail curved back on itself in a perfect large arc, but the remainders spiraled down like twisting keratin stalactites. A flash of memory from the *Guinness Book of Records* reminded me that when fingernails grew to such lengths, the nerves can extend into them as well, making it impossible to cut them without a surgical procedure or a lot of pain. But maybe he didn't experience pain.

I went over to him and bowed at his feet. He patted my head and spoke in a mumbled, scratchy voice that I couldn't understand.

"Swami would like to know if you have any lemons," the first woman said.

Lemons? He wants LEMONS? I suddenly recalled from the guidebook that it was customary to bring some sort of offering when going to meet a guru or a swami. But lemons? Why would I have lemons?

Then I remembered that I did have small lemons in my carrying bag! It seemed utterly impossible that he wanted lemons and I actually had them. When I was in the town of Pondicherry a week before, I had found a small convenience store called Churchgate that was stocked with rare American items like Oreos and M&M's. I went every day and bought my bottled water there, as well as other sundries and snacks. Every time I checked out, the cashier gave me a lemon. I assumed it was for the water, but I'm not partial to lemons in my water without an abundance of sugar, so I kept them in my bag and basically forgot about them.

In front of the swami, I took them out and discovered they were perfectly ripe. I extended the requested lemons, and the second woman took them from my hands and brought them into another part of the house. Swami spoke again. I was amazed someone understood him—to me his voice sounded like rumbling gravel mixed with consonants.

The first woman translated. "Swami says thank you for the lemons. He is taking away the lemons, so he is taking away the bitterness from your life." I could only smile, wishing I'd known it was that easy all along. I looked into his eyes. He spoke again, and then she said, "Swami would like to know why you have come to see him."

"Oh, please tell the swami, or is it just Swami? Tell him I was invited here by my friend, Katran, and I'm here because . . . I guess because I'm curious?" I stopped to think about why I wanted to be there. It wasn't clear. "I've always wanted to meet a living guru or a swami to . . . maybe . . . feel his power . . . ? Does that make any sense?"

I watched the swami's face as she translated, and he nodded his understanding. He spoke a very short sentence and put his head down.

The second woman said, "He says okay and please come over here." I stood up and, led by the second woman, faced him and took about ten steps backward. I asked if I should kneel again and she said, no, that wasn't necessary. I looked at Swami and he raised his head and his hands so I could see his pale-brown palms. He made a gentle pushing motion toward me and put his hands in his lap, near the end of his knees to accommodate his nails, palms up. He looked at me and I looked at him.

It is extremely difficult to describe what happened next. Essentially, he got very, very, very small . . . and then very, very, very large. See, first the swami seemed to shrink as he got smaller and smaller in my view, as if I were moving backward and far away. But my feet were fixed and I stayed put while he just . . . shrank. The whole room shrank. Everything dissolved into a tiny little space in my vision, like it was all being sucked down a drain the size of a pinhole. The walls stretched deep into that space, and everything I could possibly see or hear went with them. This lasted for a few minutes, and then it all rebounded back. With a quiet velocity, the room returned to its original size and state, but then it kept going, in reverse, as if I were moving closer and closer to him. The swami grew larger and larger. I continued to look in his eyes, and they mushroomed while I watched until all I could see was his face directly in front of my own, as large as a house. His wrinkles became a landscape of dry riverbeds, and his eyes glistened like wet boulders beneath the thick and snowy forest of his furry eyebrows. I was fully enveloped in his visage and felt lost amongst the brown puddled freckles on his cheeks, the cratered pores in his nose, and the deep crevasses crossing his mulberry-colored lips. And then, with the same elasticity as before, all the dots in the room reconnected to their normal size. My breathing was slow. Steady. I felt warm. Light. This whole "beaming of his energy" lasted a few minutes. I was calm but also thrilled by the experience, as if I'd gone around a long loop on a slow roller coaster. The swami spoke again and the first woman translated.

"Swami says you are very connected to the idea that you are human." I thought that made sense as she continued, "and the human is too often guided by only five senses. These five senses are important, but they are not the totality of your perception. In fact, the five senses can become barriers, like large walls, to the understanding of True Consciousness. The human can be very limited by these inputs and unable to go beyond them. The human also thinks he is the only one who holds his own perceptions. He thinks that what he sees can only be seen by him, and in his own unique and singular way. This is a mistake."

I wasn't sure if I was being coached or reproached as she continued to translate the rolling, mellifluous language. "The human mind thinks there is a difference between human and nonhuman matter. This is another mistake. The human mind and nonhuman matter do not contradict each other because each exists in reality, just as it is, and that reality is all-encompassing and reaches to all minds in all forms. You think you are the only one with your singular thoughts, *but all thoughts are all of the thoughts of the universe.* You think a human is different from a dog or a river or a tree, or even a car, but everything shares the same elemental materials: all the planets, the stars, the buildings, the rocks, the animals, the oceans, and everything within these things and everything made and unmade by these things. It would be a mistake to insist that your limited and subjective consciousness is a full comprehension of the objective world."

At that moment, the swami turned his hand over, and in his palm he held an orange stone. It wasn't there before, and he had no sleeves or materials to hide it. It simply wasn't there, and then it was. He gestured to me and placed the stone in my palm. It didn't feel like a rock. It felt very much alive.

"Your scientists have a name for this type of stone. They call it chabazite. They will tell you its properties, its elements, its uses, and its price. They will not tell you where it has been, what it has experienced, or how it vibrates with the songs of the universe. They will not tell you of its dreams or its memories of the comets that brought it here, but if you consider that there is more than what you see, more than what you taste or touch or hear or smell, there may be more to this little stone than all of history and humanity combined. This entirety is not impossible."

I looked at my little gift, the chabazite, and cupped it to my heart. The swami laughed and smiled, and I shared that smile and laugh with him, feeling lighter and lighter as he spoke. Then more words tumbled from his mouth, and I looked to the woman for the meaning.

"Swami would like to know if you have one million rupees," she said, as naturally as he asked for the lemons.

"Umm, what?" I replied.

"Swami wants to build a great ashram here, a temple to goodness and holiness and a testament to his enlightenment. He asks all of his guests if they can help. One day there will be someone who can, and today he is asking if that person is you."

"Please tell him that I don't have that kind of money. One million rupees? That's more than I'll probably earn in my whole life!"

"It's more than most people will make in one thousand lifetimes," the second woman softly hissed.

The first woman shot her a harsh glance. "We came from England to be with Swami about ten years ago. We used to see vast sums of money in our own land, but here it is not the case. Please do not be offended; it is a common question. Swami has a vision of his temple but he does not have the resources to build it. People seek him and he seeks them as well. This is all okay."

I reached into my bag and found some money.

"Maybe this will help?"

"Of course, and thank you," she said, folding it and putting it in a box by the wall without looking at it. "Swami thanks you."

I looked over at Swami and he was nodding. I felt good. He summoned me one more time with his calcified tendrils, and I returned eagerly to his feet with my head bowed. I lifted my head, and he dipped his fingers into a bowl of ash and drew a line with the back of his knuckle from the top of my forehead down my brow. Then he patted me on the head again, and I knew it was time to go. I thanked him again, and I thanked the women, who nodded and smiled. There was a lot of smiling that day.

I exited and found Katran asleep in the front seat of the car. Paloo was standing on a red metal chair in a nearby field, petting a cow. Somehow this seemed normal. The dogs ran back over to me and licked my legs. I knocked on the window, and Katran bolted upright as Paloo made his way over to us.

"Heyyy," he said wearily.

"Power nap?" I asked.

"What do you mean?"

"You fell asleep for a few minutes while I was in there. In America we call that a power nap."

He looked at his watch.

"You are so cute!" I said to the dogs. I stroked their ears for a moment before I opened the car and hopped into my seat. I put on my seatbelt and looked forward, energized for whatever was next. "Should we visit that temple with the painted elephant?"

"I fell asleep for a few minutes!" he laughed, facing the windshield. Something was off. Something was different. He looked darker, like he was losing light. As I continued to assess his strangeness, I quickly realized that the landscape itself was also darker. And softer. And a little pink. Paloo opened the door, started the car, and turned on the headlights.

"What's going on?" I asked cautiously.

"It is already after sunset, butterfly," Katran smiled. "You have been flying for many, many hours now. We can see the elephants tomorrow morning, but for today my tour is complete."

I clutched the lingam and my orange stone, one in each hand, as we drove away. The small side road was filled with divots, and in the darkening purple night it was difficult to see them. We bumped and bumped along until—

***

Muriel woke up, startled by something. "Where are we?"

"I'm not sure," Eve replied. "Hold on, there's a sign—we've got about fifty miles to Florence."

"That's all? I thought I was asleep for hours," Muriel said groggily.

"Just a power nap," Eve said, enjoying herself. Her window was cracked and her hair flew wildly to the side. "Hey, what's that?" she indicated.

"What?"

"In your hand?"

Muriel unfolded her fingers and revealed the shiny black stone in her palm. The bottom was flat and the texture was smooth.

"It's from Katran," she said. "He gave it to Grace." She didn't remember unwrapping the lingam from its tissue-paper casing inside the interior zippered pocket of her purse. Muriel looked down at her feet, where the purse remained closed.

Muriel clutched the lingam. Grace was everything.

Chapter 10

Earlier in the day, while Eve frantically scoured the hotel searching for Muriel, Cindy Worth combed through her closet with a nearly equal fervor. She finally decided on leggings with white and purple swirls and a lightweight, extra-long, sweater-type black garment that ended near her knees. It couldn't be definitively categorized as a shirt or a dress, and it wasn't particularly attractive on her top-heavy frame, but it was expensive, and she had dangling amethyst earrings to match its purple ruffled collar. Once dressed, she dabbed more purple on her eyelids, clasped her Chanel sunglasses and a book, and headed to The Deerwood to scream at the management and await Muriel's return. She also intended to connect with Judith and track down Lucy. It was going to be a busy day. Laura and Christian had begrudgingly gone to school after their reasoned arguments failed, and Cindy had held Lem to the same standard by sending him off to the bank. "You can worry from there," she said, and Lem quietly tied his tie and slipped on his painful shoes.

Cindy was in a good mood, owing some of it to Lem for his particularly satisfying performance the night before. He was unusually aggressive when he was stressed out, and she made a mental note to provoke him the next time such needs arose. More than she enjoyed Lem, however, she was enjoying the month of October. The winter tourists were still away, presumably distracted by the autumn colors up north, and the summer vacationers took their sunburns and left. With the kids back in school, the only people on her roads were shoppers and museum-goers, random errand-runners, and the mobile elderly shuffling to their houses of worship, exercise classes, bridge games, or the beach. There was typically a midday migration through the restaurants, but other than that (and the normal business-fueled rush hours), the roads were wide open. Cindy took advantage by speeding, weaving, and running questionably yellow lights for no reason other than the fact that she could.

She pulled into The Deerwood's visitor parking area when a text arrived from Lem. [Lucy's gone.]

"What do you mean gone?" Cindy replied through the car's Bluetooth speaker as she remained buckled in her seat.

[She's in Jamaica.]

"Siri, call Lem."

Lem answered. "She says she drove home, threw some clothes in a bag, and took a cab to the airport. The only flight out of West Palm went to Charlotte and then Miami to connect her to Kingston, and then she had a three-hour ride to the other side of the island."

"That's insane."

"She would have gone straight to Miami, but she didn't want to leave her car for who knows how long, at nine bucks a day, and Uber was surging and ridiculous. She also said her phone died and her charger was in the checked luggage. She just got our messages a few minutes ago."

"You told her what's going on?"

"Yep."

"And?"

"And she's freaking out!" Lem said gleefully. "She says she asked Eve to park the car and bring Mom upstairs and that was all, no big deal."

"No big deal, my ass."

"Yep. So now she's in some remote part of Jamaica and I told her she can fucking stay there."

"You didn't! Lem!!"

"You want her watching Mom after this?"

Abandoning Muriel mid-shift and then traveling sixteen hours to another country without so much as a note was certainly grounds for dismissal, but Lucy wasn't any run-of-the-mill employee. Cindy and Lem had interviewed nineteen candidates from a pool of over two hundred applicants, and Lucy had earned her place and then further secured it through her reliability, care, and bright personality.

"We'll talk about it," Cindy replied. A heart attack was a highly unusual circumstance, and Cindy didn't want to go through the tedious process of hiring and training and trusting someone new. Muriel loved Lucy, and that also meant something to Cindy. Lucy was practically family. "What did she say about Albi?"

"I don't know, I didn't ask." Lem didn't want to admit that he didn't know who Albi was.

"Typical," Cindy replied, although she would never admit she had no idea who Albi was, either. Maybe Lucy wasn't really *family*, per se.

"That's not our problem," he added.

"True." Cindy unbuckled her seatbelt. "I just got here. I thought I'd check on things."

"Where, The Deerwood? Don't."

"What do you mean, 'don't'?"

"I mean don't call them and don't go in there."

After a pause, Cindy said, "Lem, they do know she's gone . . . right?"

"Ahh . . . no." Lem explained the situation to Cindy in his own roundabout way: he had instructed Vivette to keep it quiet for the time being because he feared The Deerwood might expel Muriel for leaving the property without notice—they frowned upon any upset to their procedures. There were other managed care facilities in the area, but it could take months to find a good fit. It could even ruin the holidays. He thought it was best to wait, and Cindy reluctantly agreed, knowing full well it put Vivette's job in jeopardy, too, for covering up Muriel's absence. She suddenly felt conspicuous in the open parking lot as her primary concern shifted back to herself: she was dressed for the day and didn't want to waste her primping efforts by staying at home. Cindy remembered her thwarted shoe purchase for the Southern Florida Bankers Convention and considered returning to the mall. She didn't care if it was inappropriate to go shopping during a family crisis, but her watch indicated that the mall wasn't open yet.

"Do you have Judith's number?" she asked.

"Why?"

"Because I want to call her. Do you have it?"

"Hold on, I just had that screen up."

"Why?"

"I don't know."

He texted his wife the number and then changed the subject to his sore toe while Cindy studied her face in the visor mirror, admiring her clear complexion. She noticed a small bead of sweat forming and turned up the air while he continued to whine.

"You're an adult, take an aspirin. I gotta go," she said, abruptly switching him off to focus on her new plan for the day: Judith.

Although their children were best friends, Cindy and Judith barely knew each other, and the night before, Judith had seemed even more enigmatic and morose than she had remembered, and also kind of rude. It was odd, and Cindy didn't like having a gap in her social sphere. Judith was closed off like a dangerous mine, but Cindy knew there were hidden gems deep within that would require great skills to extract. She was up for the job of getting inside Judith's mindset to discover who she was, how she lived, and why Eve took off. Cindy also felt a strong compulsion to shake some life back into the poor woman, whom she assumed had no friends. Judith was a walking corpse in need of Cindy's beneficent hospitality— Cindy planned to stir some much-needed color into that gray base.

The answer was lunch. Sometimes Cindy enjoyed a midweek meal with Lem, but his lunch hour never left enough time for cocktails, and his current intensity might crush the mine of Judith's psyche before Cindy could extract the valuables. She had to go it alone. After a few rounds of gentle coaxing, Judith reluctantly agreed to meet her, following an ardent promise that Cindy would control her swearing and Lem wouldn't suddenly show up. Once the lunch date was solidified, Cindy called Lem.

"She knows something," he said. "Or she did something. They had a fight about something—find out everything you can."

"That's the plan," Cindy agreed.

"She isn't normal. She should be totally freaking out like we are." Then he choked up a little and said, "They didn't come back last night. I really thought they would, ya know? Where the hell do you think they are? She's gonna ruin that car."

Cindy hung up again before he started to cry.

***

Cindy drove to the mall and stayed in the parking lot, blasting the air conditioning like the dozens of other early risers. She scrolled through the news on her phone and ended up in a wormhole of entertainment gossip until the doors finally opened and she leisurely bought her shoes. A bit later she drove up South Military Trail and picked up Judith at Flora's HandyCrafty. Her new possible friend was waiting outside. She wore a conspicuous lemon-colored button-down shirt, tucked deep into dark khakis and held tight above her hips with a braided belt. A heavy-looking cross, different from the one she wore the night before, took up much of the space between her cotton-ball breasts, which Cindy pitied; they weren't the robust cantaloupes that she hauled around. With her immaculate white sneakers, Judith resembled the undeveloped nerds Cindy had verbally abused in high school. Cindy hoped Judith's work smock covered most of her ensemble, including the cross that screamed its constant presence.

Cindy unlocked the door, and Judith approached but didn't get in.

"Shall we?" Cindy smiled cheerfully, lowering the passenger window.

"I have to ask you something," said Judith.

"What's up?"

"Are we going Dutch on this?"

"No, it's on me." Cindy continued her smile, but it suddenly felt forced.

Judith hesitated. Then she added, "Does that mean I'm allowed to eat whatever I want, or are you going to get mad if I pick something you don't want to pay for?"

Had this woman never been treated to a lunch date? Cindy couldn't care less about what Judith ordered because it failed to enter Cindy's mind that Judith, or anyone, lived on a strict budget. She didn't comprehend that Eve worked at The Deerwood's salon to afford her own living expenses while her mother toiled at a strip-mall craft store to meet their monthly bills.

"You can eat whatever you want. Even kosher," Cindy said with a chuckle.

"I'm not Jewish," Judith pronounced.

"I know. It was a jo—never mind."

"And I want to go to Charley's Crab."

"Wow, that's specific."

"Is it okay?"

"Sure, but I think Charley's closed a few years ago."

"Oh no!" Judith suddenly wailed with profound distress. "They closed? That's terrible! What happened?" Cindy was taken by surprise. This upset her? *This?*

"No, I mean the restaurant is still there, but it's called Two Joes now. No, wait, not Joe. It's Two Georges. Two Georges at the Cove, that's it."

"Is it still good?"

"Yeah, it's good."

"And we can go there?"

Moments like this made Cindy feel like she was the only adult in the world, and she started to doubt her resolve to spend time with Judith—just as she was climbing into the car.

Soon they arrived at Two Georges at the Cove, formerly known as the Cove Restaurant, Charley's Crab, and long before that, the Captain. Colloquially, it was simply known as the Marina, and the menu had remained consistent through its multiple incarnations, rendering the name practically irrelevant. Floridian open-air restaurants on the waterfront are susceptible to weather and water issues, but they also have the most sought-after ambiance and views. The building had suffered hurricanes and floods, and it had been sold, rebuilt, renovated, and resold over the years, but it always provided a casual fine-dining experience, which meant a couple could wear shorts and flip-flops while they dropped over a hundred dollars on their lunch.

Judith felt out of place, but Cindy was perfectly comfortable. Eating in good restaurants with friends and family was a normal part of her life, but Judith cooked nearly every meal, except for the occasional delivered pizza with Eve or the food at church events. The ladies were ushered to a table directly on the water, and for the first time, Cindy witnessed Judith's smile, indicating her approval of the view. Judith had a beautiful smile, when she showed it, and remarkably good teeth.

"Can I get you some drinks?" asked the server, a sunny young woman with freckles and a mountain of orange hair pulled tight into a bun.

"Tap water, please," said Judith.

"Get what you like," offered Cindy. "I'll have a Pink Lemonade Chiller."

After a beat, Judith succumbed to the invitation. "Two please," she chimed.

"Two for you or two for the table?" The server winked.

"The table," Judith replied sternly, dismissing the attempt at humor.

"Are you sure?" asked Cindy, sensing that Judith was completely unaware of the contents of her selection. Was Judith so desperate to please her she was willing to compromise herself? Or was it a compromise? Some religions sanctioned peyote, for Christ's sake—Cindy suddenly felt odd for even thinking about the term *Christ's sake* in Judith's presence. Judith was beginning to have an effect on her.

You said I could get whatever I want was the clear message on Judith's face, and Cindy backed off.

The server set off to retrieve the drinks, and Judith studied the menu. Cindy knew before they arrived she would have the broiled sea scallops. She always had the broiled sea scallops and she could probably eat ten orders without being pressed. The only time she avoided it was when she thought Lem might make love to her later and she didn't want the garlic to interfere. When she felt him giving off that vibe, she ordered sea bass with lemon butter, or the coconut shrimp salad. Lem knew when she made those selections that they were going to have a romantic evening, and he would rush through his meal and skip dessert.

"I think I'll have the coconut shrimp salad," Judith said.

Cindy smiled secretly to herself and said, "Good choice."

When the drinks arrived, Judith examined the tall glass and was faced with a conundrum. She had made a stink that she was not to be criticized, but clearly the Pink Lemonade Chiller was not what she'd expected: her drink was slushy and obviously expensive, and when she sipped it, the Stoli Citros, sour mix, and grenadine were a sudden and unwelcome surprise. For the first time in nearly a decade, Judith was consuming alcohol that wasn't a part of a sacrament. If she had ordered a regular lemonade and received an alcoholic drink on an outing with anyone other than Cindy, she would have sent it back. But the two of them had clearly established that Judith wasn't paying, and she wanted to be a gracious guest who didn't embarrass her host by sending back the first item she ordered.

Normally Judith felt confident in the regular domains of her life, but Cindy Worth, much like Lem, made her feel scattered and judged, tested and weak. Judith reasoned that maybe there was a higher purpose to their meeting, something that might override her conviction to abstain. Cindy was reaching out, and it was Judith's obligation as a good Christian to at least meet her halfway. They were, after all, in a crisis together. Judith wrestled with her identity and ultimately decided that one drink was forgivable. She wasn't an alcoholic, after all, and it was a deliberate choice that came from a place of strength. She wasn't driving, and she could have a drink in the middle of the day as someone's guest if she wanted to. She had gotten someone to cover at work for a few hours, and ultimately, she felt God would understand. Hopefully. She took another sip, then snapped the rubber band on her wrist under the table as she swallowed.

Cindy watched Judith intently from the moment the drink was placed in front of her, through her first and then her second sip. She was fascinated. It was obvious that Judith hadn't known about the alcohol, but Cindy was surprised Judith didn't send it back to get the virgin version. She assumed Judith was afraid of offending their server.

They sipped their drinks quietly and looked out at the water and the passing boats. They ordered their meals, and then it was finally time to talk.

"Lem thinks you know where they're heading," Cindy said. She wanted Judith to know her primary objective for their lunch. She expected the truth and wasn't willing to play any games.

"Maybe Disney World?"

"Seriously?"

"We took Eve there as a little kid. Richard got the tickets at work and they were only good for one day, and it was so far we didn't stay for the fireworks. She didn't complain, but a good Christian mother knows when her child is disappointed." Judith took another sip of her Pink Lemonade Chiller. The icy beverage sent a pleasant alcoholic warmth to her belly and continued to disrupt the magnetic pull of her moral compass. She stopped snapping the rubber band and allowed herself to relax.

Cindy took some long sips herself and debated ordering an extra shot after hearing the words "a good Christian mother." While looking at shoes and thinking about their impending lunch, Cindy had felt some guilt over never connecting with Judith. She told herself that the opportunity had never surfaced, but the truth was Judith was religious, so Cindy had sublimated any notions of becoming friends with her to avoid the inevitable conflicts. Cindy believed that organized religions manifested bigotry and hatred through their followers' presumptuous versions of history and their own righteousness. By their very nature, religions created barriers to a harmonious coexistence with people outside the faith. Most religions also obliterated the unique and personal nature of spirituality. Religion was both a hindrance and a distraction to one's true inner peace and quest for enlightenment. Religions relied on identifying God as an external presence in order to maintain control, rather than an internal connection to the universe and everything in it, including its wonderfully varied peoples.

Cindy was afraid of impeding on Laura and Eve's friendship by expressing her opinions, so she had left the subject—and Judith—entirely alone. But in that process, she realized, she'd also failed to consider that Eve probably needed a different kind of mother figure in her life.

"If they went there and stayed for the fireworks, wouldn't they be home by now?"

Judith shrugged. "Maybe they stayed another day to see them again? I hear they're incredible."

"Or maybe they went somewhere else altogether." Judith shrugged again, and Cindy decided to change course. "So tell me about Eve's dad. Laura said he died from a heart attack when she was little? That must've been . . . I can't even imagine."

Judith coughed and took another sip. As she put down the glass, Cindy watched her bite her upper lip with her bottom teeth and touch her cross with both hands.

"I'm sorry," Cindy prompted. "I was only hoping we could . . . you know. Talk."

"I . . . I'm not sure."

Cindy raised her eyebrows.

"I don't know if I can trust you," Judith blurted, and then she immediately added, "I mean . . . to understand. To really understand."

Judith hedged some more, amplifying Cindy's curiosity and signaling that the story of Eve's dad was something bigger than she'd thought. Something juicy, perhaps. Cindy wanted to convince Judith that she was there for her, not only as an equally concerned parent, but as a confidant and a friend. To achieve that end, she decided to reveal something about herself first, something deeply personal. "Maybe I should start. When I was a kid, I was, well, I was actually pretty chubby, and there was a girl in my class, Stephanie Brenner, who was really mean to me. So one day I took a fork----"

"He was gay," Judith interrupted.

It was the first time Judith had told anyone the truth about Richard. Ever. She immediately put her head down so it was level with the edge of the table. She stared at the floor, unable to comprehend why she'd told Cindy, of all people, the sacred secret that even Eve didn't know.

"Are you okay?" Cindy asked, unsure if she should look under the table and feeling rather bemused that her lunch pal's face was suddenly parallel to the floor.

Judith fixated on her clean white shoes. Why couldn't life be like her shoes, so tidy and comfortable and capable of absorbing all the shocks? She raised her head a little and the two women's eyes met. Cindy's were shining emeralds, while Judith's looked like pelted mud after a hard rain.

"I can't believe I said that."

She took another sip, and it was Cindy's turn to shrug.

"Richard's . . . gay." Judith reaffirmed, delicately.

"So you said."

"I married a homosexual. I mean, I didn't know at the time—when I married him."

"Of course not."

"Because he didn't look like one."

"Um, no?" Cindy said cautiously, fearing where Judith's thought was headed.

"No, not at all! Richard was NOT one of those thong-wearing, parade-going, flag-waving, leather-and-chains Key West rainbow people you see everywhere. What do they call them? Bears? Otters? Twinkies?"

"I'm not sure," Cindy said, not willing to admit to Judith that she knew every descriptor and term. "But I don't think they *all look*----'

"Can you believe I did that? I married a gay? I married someone who wanted to lie with other men. He wanted to . . ." she whispered. "He wanted to give another man a blow job."

"I get it," Cindy said, hoping Judith might return her gaze to the floor, but instead she raised her neck even higher, allowing more oxygen into her lean throat.

"And anal sex!!" Judith boomed. Cindy immediately blurted a laugh at equal volume in a feeble attempt to mask the words before they landed on the other diners. Judith's eyes wildly scanned the room and found a dozen pairs of eyes staring back. They both felt embarrassed for each other; Cindy laughed again, and Judith snapped the band on her wrist and contracted into her chair like a threatened turtle. They both reached for their drinks and sipped. Cindy decided she was having fun. She relished talking about sex and looked forward to the day when her daughter would feel comfortable enough to discuss her own experiences.

Cindy didn't care too much about their decorum in the bustling open-air restaurant, but Judith, who never discussed sex with anyone, felt grossly exposed and deeply self-conscious. Yet, thanks to the drink, she pointed her finger at Cindy and continued: "You know, he was a wonderful lover. Have you ever heard of that? A homosexual being a good lover to a woman? Is that even possible? I mean—if he hated it so much, why was he so good at it? He was attentive, *attentive* if you know what I mean," she cooed.

"I do know what you mean, but I don't know the answer. Maybe he was bi?"

"No, that's not even a thing, and his being wonderful made everything worse. Our intimacy was a lie. Even after all this time, I still can't wrap my head around it."

"Then maybe there's a simple answer? Maybe he loved you?"

Judith shot Cindy a look like she'd punched a puppy.

"I found his magazines. That's what started it."

"Oh?"

"They were wrapped in a brown paper bag under a pile of old T-shirts he never wore. You wouldn't believe the pictures. All those men doing unspeakable things to each other—how could anyone be turned on by that?"

Cindy decided to listen and keep her enjoyment of homoerotica to herself. She loved the gorgeous male bodies, hairy or smooth, muscled and clean with all their bubble butts and bulges.

"And they were all from the same month. Maybe he got a bulk discount." Judith snorted. Cindy laughed, too, wondering if Judith still had the stack and if she might be able to see them one day. "And he wanted—oh, I shouldn't talk about this."

"Let it out."

Judith coughed. "I was collecting his sweaters for the dry cleaners and then I found *that smut*, but I didn't do anything about it for a while. I didn't really know what to do, you know? I remember thinking—no, *deciding*, that they were a gag gift for a buddy or he was holding them for someone in his office and forgot about them. Something stupid like that. I just couldn't picture or even imagine Richard buying them. Or, um . . . using them. And where did he get them? What if someone saw? I tried to put it out of my mind, but then we were in bed a few nights later and he started kissing my ears and stroking my back. I was so relieved because that's when I knew the pornography wasn't really his and I could finally relax. But somehow in the dark he lubricated his own—I'm not going to say it in a restaurant—and then he grabbed my hand and tried to put my finger *in there*, and I screamed at him and told him I wasn't one of his magazine playthings."

"Uh oh."

"And then we had this really weird fight. I think at one point I even apologized for having breasts? Oh, and then he asked if he could bring another man into our bed and we could enjoy him together. *Enjoy him together*, he said, like we were going to share some Chinese takeout. I told him 'No way.'"

"Good for you, standing your ground."

"Not really. Richard said if he couldn't be his true self anymore, then it was over. He wanted what he wanted and it wasn't me, which I couldn't understand because he was kissing my ear ten minutes ago! Then it dawned on me that all those magazines? They were nearly a year old, which meant he'd been thinking about it for a long time. That made it even more confusing because I thought we were good. We were really good! At least once a week!"

"That's a lot of hetero sex for a guy who doesn't like vaginas."

Judith recoiled at the word, but she accepted the remark because it was true. She took another sip and then resumed. "So then Richard told me he had a friend, but the meaning of that didn't really register right away because I was thinking how great it was that he had someone else he could talk to about his problem. I was literally that naïve. Finally, he explained he wanted to have sex with his friend and I was, like, nooo . . . but he also said he couldn't do that to me. He said he wouldn't betray me."

"So he was faithful," Cindy added.

"And deeply confused," Judith said. "Or maybe just a coward? Definitely he felt trapped. And then he got sad. Like, deeply sad—I could literally see the light draining from his eyes. He was stuck in this self-made gay prison in his head, and somehow I became the warden. He couldn't have sex with his friend or fake his happiness with me anymore. My gay husband's *principles* wouldn't allow him to cheat, or to be with his wife. What do you think of that?"

Cindy couldn't think of anything to say, but her face seemed to provide the solidarity Judith sought.

"He slept on the couch that night, but I actually wanted him to stay in bed with me. I still wanted to be with him. I wanted his warm breath on my neck, and he had this way of spooning my feet, which I loved. I remember lying there, staring at our ceiling, trying to figure him out. That's pretty much when I decided he wasn't gay."

Cindy cocked her head like a dog trying to comprehend an unfathomable instruction.

"My brain wouldn't accept it," Judith explained. "It literally would not allow me to understand. I decided my husband was a healthy heterosexual with a funky kink that he wanted to explore, and it was my duty to be a supportive wife and help him out. We had a daughter together—a life—and I was willing to, you know, work with him. I wasn't really open to it, but I realized I wanted to be. I had to be. I loved him and I was sure he loved me, and Eve, of course. I couldn't understand why sex, that kind of sex, was so important to him—it's only sex, it's not everything—but I wanted him to be happy. So when he got home from work the next day, I told him I was sorry I got so upset, but I was caught off-guard. I told him I was willing to try. I wanted to be a good wife and a generous lover who was open to his desires."

"That's . . . incredibly liberal. What did he say?"

"He said he spent that night on the couch rethinking his life, and then he didn't go to work. He went to the beach and looked at the water for ten hours. He didn't even eat. He said he couldn't live a lie anymore, and I begged him not to throw away our marriage over a sexual *complication*. I'm simplifying here—we actually talked for hours, and at some point I finally submitted to the idea that I was going to have to give him his backwards sex."

"I think you mean backdoor?"

"Whatever..." Judith replied. "He wanted it. He wanted to be..."

"... penetrated," Cindy finished, transfixed. She *loved* that the Pink Lemonade Chillers were having this effect.

"I was terrified, but frankly, I was also a little relieved it wasn't me. I had no concept of the mechanics, but as I was trying to wrap my head around it, he was already dropping tears. And that's when he did it."

"What?"

"He came out. Like, *out* out. Richard said he knew he was gay when he was twelve, but he never told anyone or acted on it in his entire life because he never thought it was possible until he finally found a man—a specific man—and he still didn't act on it yet, but he really wanted to. He wanted to be with this guy. This *friend*."

"His boyfriend."

Judith scowled. "He said it could never be real with me, and if he was forced to stay with me he would actually die. Like, *die* die. He'd throw himself in front of a truck on the freeway."

Cindy gulped. She felt deeply sorry for Richard. And Judith. And Eve, who probably regretted choosing Judith over Richard after they split. Or maybe she didn't choose? Maybe that was how he really died: suicide on the interstate, covered up as a heart attack?

Judith took another long sip. "So now I'm in our marital bed where we conceived our beautiful daughter, and I'm thinking about how I'm going to screw my husband with a plastic—you know, or a warm cucumber or whatever'll make him happy enough to stay with me, and he's telling me he's gay and always has been, and he's desperately in love with some random man that I've never even heard of and he's going to kill himself if I don't let him go."

"Ouch."

"Yeah."

Cindy and Judith both sighed. Cindy wondered how Judith could be letting all of this out—supposedly for the first time—without even coming close to producing a single tear. Most of this information was being dispensed like a news report.

"And then he left."

"You let him go."

Judith's voice cracked as she said, "Not really, but he didn't ask me again."

Cindy absorbed this for a moment. "What did Eve say when you told her?"

"I didn't tell her. Why would I? Isn't it enough that he's dead?"

"And you never met the other guy?"

"No."

"Not even at the funeral?" Judith stared at her, and Cindy slowly surmised that she hadn't attended. "Oh Judith, that must have been so awful. I'm sorry you had to go through all that."

"Thank you."

They both took another long sip. They were nearing the bottom of their glasses.

Cindy said, "It's so tragic. For all of you. And how long was it after he left? I mean, when he died?"

Judith didn't expound further, and they sat in silence for nearly a full minute while the reality of the story, the space between the words, and Judith's deliberate nonanswer to the last question began to coagulate in Cindy's mind. Finally, Cindy cautiously uttered, "Judith, *is he dead?*"

"Probably. You know they all have AIDS."

Cindy felt like a passenger in the back of a plane as it was blown apart, watching the disaster unfold before her with the sudden knowledge that the sky itself was about to fall. She had achieved her goal of cracking Judith's shell and now had to come to terms with the slimy animal she'd found living inside. *Convincing Eve that her father was dead instead of gay? This horribly bigoted perspective? Wasn't all of that one big stinking pile of sin?*

Cindy was utterly disgusted, but she forced a smile and kept her outrage in check. She needed Judith to believe she was on her side if it would help them locate Eve and Muriel. Finally, she admitted, "It sounds like you tried your best in a crummy situation. You can't be expected to make a marriage work if your husband isn't straight, and I suppose you were protecting Eve."

Judith thought about that. She *did* try. After Richard's abrupt departure, Eve asked about her daddy nearly a million times. Judith couldn't bear her daughter's questions, or her own. Would he ever come back? What should she do? What did it mean? Was it her fault? Did she try hard enough? The questions went on and on, swirling like a tornado around her psyche, tossing her thoughts and splintering her ability to function. She was shredded and exhausted.

Richard left his old T-shirts behind, along with signed divorce papers, nearly all of their money, and the deed to the house in her name. When Eve innocently asked again if Santa would bring her daddy back for Christmas, Judith blurted out, "No, your daddy's dead."

Eve couldn't comprehend it, and Judith responded with a hug that nearly crushed the small girl. "He was broken, baby. Your daddy was . . . he had a bad . . . heart." It was one hard, terrifying moment, and she instantly felt both horrible—and released. She opened the hug, Eve burst into tears, and they grieved together.

Once they were past the initial trauma, his imagined death became their mutual truth. Eve stopped giving the mail carrier unaddressed letters. She stopped searching the aisles at the grocery store. She avoided the electronics store at the mall where Richard had enjoyed exploring new gadgets. The storm was over, and Judith worked on clearing the debris. With his "death," she stopped her own little voice that told her things might work out some day. Their marriage was over because death did them part, and death was more tangible, more manageable, than truth. Judith kept her married name and assumed life as a widow.

"I think at one point after he left, I offered Richard a deal in my own head: he could sleep with as many men as he wanted, even his special friend, so long as I was his only woman." Judith laughed tenuously, then the laugh trailed off. "Stupid, but I didn't want to lose my family."

"Hey, you didn't know. And it sounds like he didn't really know either."

"When I asked him what we were doing for the last decade he said, 'making a long mistake.'" She exhaled slowly through her even teeth. "He said he wished we were never in the same dorm and that there were times when he couldn't believe his own thoughts. I thought he meant about being gay, but he was talking about leaving his family or suicide. I had no idea we were so far apart. It's like we were on two totally different airplanes heading in opposite directions that still somehow crashed."

Cindy still felt like she was falling, but she reached for a parachute. "Judith, he's probably still living somewhere with that other man—did you ever find out who he was or where they went?"

Judith barreled on. "Richard left, my parents are dead, and now Eve is gone, too. I guess it runs in the family. Get it? Runs? *Ha.* They all run. Oh gosh, maybe it's me? Must be . . . Did you know I was trying to get her a car? I mean, imagine if I actually did? Then I'd be out a husband, a daughter, *and* a Hyundai!" Judith's laughter came in loud, weird pulses, like a stuttering ignition. Her brain was soaked in sugar and alcohol, and the server finally remembered to bring them a basket of bread when she delivered their meals.

They ate together, watching boats scoot up and down the waterway and listening to the gentle slap of wake water against the building. The sun was high and the temperature was rising, but they were shielded by a high canvas roof. Slow-spinning ceiling fans maintained a comfortable breeze and the women began to physically relax. Cindy ordered another round of drinks. Judith protested slightly, but she took the glass from the server's tray and started sipping before it was placed on the table.

Cindy pressed on, "Richard was also religious?"

"Him?" Judith laughed, "No way."

"Oh? I thought maybe he was having a crisis of faith," Cindy suggested.

"N-n-n-n-no no no, that's wrong. We had a Christmas tree for Eve and ate jelly beans on Easter, but I didn't let Christ into my heart until after Richard was gone. I wasn't religious back then and he was never religious, and now he's burning in Hell."

Cindy skipped over the last part, and said, "You weren't always . . ."

Judith put her fork and knife on the table with a deliberate clank.

"Devout?" Cindy clarified.

"You think religious people are stupid," Judith huffed, lowering her eyebrows. "I almost have a master's degree."

Cindy paused. She didn't think Judith was unintelligent, but she was obviously broken by her trauma. Cindy had another manifesto about vulnerability and brainwashing on the tip of her tongue, but instead she steered her boat toward a different port. "I don't think you're stupid and I didn't mean to give you that impression. I have a lot of religious friends," she lied. "I guess what I'm asking is—did you wake up one day and just . . . find Jesus?"

"You know, it was actually something pretty close to that." Judith took another bite and chewed deliberately, savoring the creamy coconut before continuing. "Maybe a year after Richard left—I think Eve was seven or eight?—I was driving the carpool. I dropped the kids off and headed to work when I suddenly felt compelled to drive in a completely different direction. I have no idea why, but it was a really strong feeling and I went with it for no reason. Before long, I was driving in the middle of nowhere and the radio station changed all by itself."

"Really?"

"I guess it can happen if you cross into another zone or something? I don't know. I replay that morning over and over, and the radio found a new channel all on its own. There was a woman talking about how her husband left her and she was saddled with all these kids and bills and she didn't know what she was going to do. Then Christ entered her life and suddenly all of her problems started getting fixed, one by one. She got a better job, and soon she could afford a good nanny who eventually became her best friend and helped her regain her self-esteem and work through the divorce. The woman eventually married another man, who also found Jesus after his wife died, and he had children, too, about the same age. It was this long train of good fortune."

"Isn't that the plot of *The Brady Bunch*?"

"Ha!" Judith exploded with an expansive laugh, the alcohol disabling her typical sensitivity. "So that story was going on and I was listening and thinking about my life, and then I turned a corner and realized I had no idea where I was. I was driving and listening and I got totally lost. Have you ever done that? I was lucky I wasn't in an accident because I honestly don't remember driving around at all, but then I stopped the car to get my bearings and I saw it."

"What?"

"The church. It was this beautiful white building on a gorgeous green lawn that stretched on forever. I always thought places like that were intimidating, but this one was so clean and welcoming. It was happy, and I could feel its energy inviting me. It literally lifted me up, and my face floated to the sky where I saw a big sign, way up on a steel pole, and I read it and cried because the message felt like it was written just for me."

"What did it say?"

"Jesus is your valentine from God."

Cindy bit the inside of her lip. She couldn't believe this was Judith's big epiphany. It seemed so obvious that Judith had been devastated; she was searching for meaning in her failed marriage, she was overwhelmed raising Eve on her own, and she was questioning her identity, her ability to love, her sense of dignity, and even her own sexual powers. But to turn it all over to Jesus because of a church marquee on a detour? To Cindy it seemed like Judith had experienced a mental breakdown, and even after a decade of Jesus, she didn't seem remotely restored. Cindy believed in therapy over faith because the persuasion to heal was grounded in the self, not a collective and blinding mythology. Cindy believed Judith had exchanged her existence in reality for the comforts of an influential fairy tale. It was a powerful force, but none of it was real.

Judith looked across the table at her new confidant and felt accomplished. Cindy was finally seeing her as an intelligent, strong, and practical woman; a quality decision-maker; a paragon for both womankind and positive, faith-based spirituality. Judith hoped Cindy might one day find those same attributes within herself, in her noble heart. Maybe Cindy would start coming to church.

"I let Jesus in," Judith beamed, "and my life got better, just like that woman on the radio. And it continues to get better every day because I am always in love."

"With Jesus."

"Yes! Yes!! I'm so glad you understand!!" Judith reached to clasp Cindy's hands across the table, but it was a little too far, and Cindy didn't extend her hand. Instead, she pulled back.

"Hey, well that's . . . something," Cindy managed to say.

"Yes. It really is."

"And how does Eve feel about it?"

Judith's enthusiasm deflated a notch, and Cindy noticed a tremble in her upper lip. "There are a lot of influences on her right now. I think it's harder to be a teenager now than it was for us. I do what I can, but she's always on her phone, and she isn't spending time with the best people."

"Like my daughter?" Cindy crinkled her long, thin eyebrows.

"No, no, Laura's fine. I wish you'd let her go to church with me sometime, but no, not Laura. It's more about this new boy and that drama club."

"What boy?"

"Liam something?"

"Oh, Liam's a sweetheart! He's friends with my son. Eve could do a lot worse."

Judith was mildly relieved by the vouch, but she also didn't know anything about Cindy's son and wondered whether he was as boisterous as his mother, or conniving like Lem.

"And what's wrong with the drama club?" Cindy asked. "Did you see *Hairspray*? That Jackson kid was terrific."

"The boy playing the mom? Our tax dollars at work . . ." Reading Cindy's face, Judith continued, "I didn't see it, but I heard about it after church. Listen, okay, I'm *not* prejudiced. I'm really not. I mean, even though Richard obliterated our family with his perversion, I don't judge him because that's God's job, not mine. I mean, it's really a shame that he gave up the eternal bliss of Heaven for a sordid life on Earth, but I still don't think he's a bad man. Bad choices can be forgiven. Heaven's gates are gold, and gold is a pliable material if . . . well . . . I guess a lot would have to happen before he could pass. Repenting might not cover it."

Judith's volume rose and fell as her speech gained and lost momentum. Cindy recognized the signs of a wistful drunk.

But Judith pictured herself in a bucolic scene of radiant clouds and trumpets, sporting feathery wings on her back, with Eve and maybe Liam by her side and the earth far below populated by thousands of their glowing, righteous descendants. Meanwhile, beneath the earth's crust, Richard and his "friend" slowly dissolved in a sludge that seeped into the hot fires of the planet's core, where they were destined to burn for eternity in a dirty churn of compression and excrement.

Judith's distant gaze slowly returned to Cindy. "There are a lot of homosexuals in drama, that's all I'm saying. It attracts them. Something to do with all that showing off."

Cindy held herself together and wondered if she could smack Judith over the low banister into the oily waterway below and make it look like an accident.

"Eve put that ridiculous color in her hair because of them," Judith added.

"I think it's cool," Cindy protested.

"Those drama gays said the same thing, and they brought her to that kiosk in the mall where she got those terrible piercings. Those holes won't go away, you know. No . . . Eve is very impressionable. Maybe that's to be expected, but right now she does the opposite of everything I ask just to get a rise out of me. I bet if I walked in and said I *wasn't* going to church anymore, she'd start going just to contradict me."

"She's rebelling. That's normal. But it has nothing to do with the drama club."

"She's a very angry girl, Cindy. She left a note on my dresser calling me a liar—and I literally *can't* lie! Living in the Truth is my whole being!"

Cindy didn't respond. Richard probably wasn't dead.

"Eve found an old picture of her father in my room and that kind of set her off," Judith reluctantly admitted.

"Do you think she also found his address?" Cindy said, leaning in.

"I don't see how, he never told me where he was going."

"Really?"

Judith shook her head.

"Do you think maybe she tried to contact him some other way?" Cindy asked. "Or maybe he reached out to her?"

"Impossible. We moved when I lost the house, about two years later, and he never wrote. He also quit his job, and his emails bounced back. He deleted his Facebook. His dad had a real heart attack when Richard was in grade school, and his mom died from lung cancer right after we married. Never even smoked. He didn't have any siblings or relatives I know about. I looked for him once, but he must have changed his name. That was a pretty bad night." She paused, caught in the bear-trap of the memory. Then she pried it open and said, "It's easy for me to say he's dead because, really, he's long gone and out of our lives, and Eve never knew otherwise." She lifted her chin to Cindy, a quiet demand that the secret be kept.

Cindy thought for a moment. "Is there a gravestone?"

"Cremation. I got some unclaimed ashes from the dog pound and we cast them in the inlet at Deerfield Island Park."

Cindy blanched. It kept getting worse, and she feared she was losing her ability to hide her revulsion. "So . . . so maybe she thinks it's her fault he died? Kids blame themselves for everything."

"Huh," Judith said. It was a new thought that had never occurred to her.

"Or maybe she just misses having a father."

Judith pictured Eve and Richard playing together on the floor of the family room. They had a special game where Eve would simulate a grenade with her tiny fist and throw it in slow motion against his chest.

Then she'd pull it back quickly and squeal "Baboom!" while he shook and danced. They played Baboom! nearly every night when he got home from work, and then he would tickle her until she'd giggle herself into the hiccups. Judith would watch them with a tinge of jealousy. She didn't have a Baboom! connection with either of them.

Cindy and Judith's plates were cleared and they decided against dessert. Cindy paid the bill without looking at it and dismissed Judith's appreciation with a wave. Cindy decided Judith was conniving, infuriating, and homophobic, but beneath her pulverized psyche and trauma-induced notions, there was a smart woman in there who might be worth knowing if she would only allow herself to return to the real world.

Cindy failed to recognize that Judith enjoyed living through her spiritual lens, and from Judith's perspective, Cindy's penchant for the drama club and youth culture were deeply problematic. Still, both women thought that maybe, somehow, there might be a way for them to unite for the sake of Eve and Laura's friendship. At least until their daughters graduated.

"Richard used to bring me here," Judith divulged. "We loved Charley's Crab. I've driven by a thousand times and always wanted to come back."

"And?"

"And now he's dead and they changed the name and life goes on."

Chapter 11

As we traversed the Carolinas, Muriel looked at the youthful girl commanding their journey and wondered precisely what Eve thought of the old lady to her right. Muriel knew it didn't take long to cross the chasm between their ages. She looked at Eve's bare arms, so white and pure and plush, and then at her own. She followed the rapids of her raised blueberry-colored veins as they navigated around her freckles, folds, and slow-to-heal bruises, terminating at her tightly hinged wrists and slender fingers. She could feel music pulsing from her pinkies to her thumbs as her heart pumped a distant beat through the tingling extremities. Her feet united in the rhythm with light taps and side-to-side kicks. She looked at her hands, her fingers, her rings. She knew they were hers, simply because they were attached, but they were so often unfamiliar. Her nails were trimmed and painted, but she didn't know who had taken the scissors and the file to them or who had used the little pink tissues to collect the scraps. Muriel remembered when her arms used to look like Eve's, tautly upholstered, fresh and unblemished, firmly encasing her strength.

She also remembered that she used to play the piano. I felt Muriel's mind as she searched back to the day when her father returned from New York in a rented truck instead of on the train. The truck's back doors opened, revealing bundles of blankets tied together with thick yellow ropes, surrounding a mysterious object. It took four large men to carry the beast inside, and Muriel held her breath as they untied the preserving bandages and released the cords. When the last man carried the last scrap away, a shiny ebony virgin stood nobly on three intricately carved legs, occupying the corner between the floor-to-ceiling windows that overlooked the gardens. Muriel cautiously approached. She finally exhaled when she realized this was no beast—this was a delicate soul who would command beauty and omnipotence in her new home. They both remained silent.

A short, stocky man with purple suspenders and a folded handkerchief pressed into his shirt pocket slid past her, cheered on with a slight pat on the back from her father. He entered the sacred corner, a new sanctuary, and shared in Muriel's awe and reverence. Then he floated across the floor to the new being's side. He stroked her, lifted her lid, and slid the bar into a brass divot to expose her interior mechanics. Her copper wires gleamed, and the metallic light brightened the deeper wrinkles on the short man's face. Muriel's mother and brothers joined the revelation of these two new strangers, and they all held their breath with a frenetic anticipation as the little man slid out the bench, sat, and made an adjustment. Suddenly, he didn't seem quite so short. They leaned in, afraid to move their feet lest the wondrous moment they knew was coming be ruined by a squeaking shoe. The man lifted the protective casing and showed us her teeth, black and white, polished and perfect, ready to sing, or bite. He lifted his hand dramatically . . . such suspense! *Enough already! Play something! Play everything! Make her sing and cry and shout! Make her buzz! Elate us!!*

He came down hard and brilliantly on the keys, flying in a fury of scales and notes, his hands a blur, the emotion crisp. Melodies rose as arpeggios plummeted. The brass pedals imbued his precise tantrum with a controlled softness. The house stopped her settling creaks and the other furniture in the front rooms held itself in silence, allowing the newcomers to take center stage. The small man played large, and everyone was moved. They continued to absorb the vibrations when he stopped abruptly, spun around, and stared directly at Muriel. She was more startled by the sudden death of the music than by his intense gaze, but his warm eyes drew her in, and she yielded. She sat on the padded bench as he curved her fingers into small domes. He played a note, and she played the same note in a higher octave, not yet knowing what an octave was but already recognizing the repetition of black keys floating like thin islands on a sea of even white planks.

Ever appreciative of good organization, Muriel flourished in her practice regimen. Scales yielded to simple tunes, and before long she learned how the printed notes on paper corresponded to the keys. A mere decade later, Muriel G. Kelley performed a thirty-page Shostakovich piano concerto in a statewide competition, completely from memory. She came in third out of 180 competitors and wore the bronze medal around her neck for a week.

Her teacher's name was Mr. Clifton, and he was also delivered in the truck with the piano, fresh from a little box of his own in the Chelsea neighborhood of New York City. When the moving crew finished their task, Mr. Clifton's began. He sought a change from city living, and Muriel's father had a compelling proposition: Mr. Clifton was charged with changing everyone's perceptions of earth, time, and space . . . through music. And so he did. Through the piano he taught the Kelley children about romance, history, and revolutions. He instilled confidence, broke it down, and bestowed it again and again until Muriel and her siblings learned to claim it for themselves, note by note, performance after performance. Mr.

Clifton always had a handkerchief at the ready to wipe the keys before and after anyone played. He had a wide variety of colorful suspenders, but in Muriel's memory, they were always purple.

Mr. Clifton was not only their new piano teacher, but he was also the new boarder who rented the spare room and private bath beyond the kitchen. The quarters had been built for the maids in earlier days, but it was more interesting and elegantly art-minded to have a live-in musician in cultured Saratoga Springs. Free lessons for the Kelley children were exchanged in lieu of cash, and four nights a week, he earned for himself by teaching a dozen others how to play on the Kelleys' grand piano. Muriel eventually learned it was actually Mr. Clifton's piano, and he'd used it to teach in Manhattan for over twenty years—their vestal heroine wasn't a virgin at all! Mr. Clifton gave Mrs. Kelley a portion of the money he collected from his lessons for food and heating oil. Muriel thought it was an unnecessary and unreasonably generous gesture.

For Muriel and her siblings, it felt natural to have an artist living in the house, and Mr. Clifton felt more like an elder cousin residing in their back room. He joined in many of the family occasions, and his demeanor was always pleasant and grateful. It was a stark and welcome contrast to Mrs. Kelley's erratic moods. No one remembered discussing the idea ahead of time, but Mr. Kelley made all the decisions in the household and beyond, and they were unconditionally accepted. In today's world it would likely raise eyebrows, but to the Kelley family in 1943, the situation was as normal as their twice-weekly deliveries of milk. Mr. Clifton moved into their lives when Muriel was a child, but despite his authority in the music room, she never regarded him as a third parent. He wasn't their disciplinarian or a mediator for sibling disputes. He was the strict and kindly master who taught her fingers how to invoke their innate magical qualities and produce musical delights.

Muriel shifted and adjusted her seatbelt as her reminiscence about Mr. Clifton continued. She knew she was coming to The Memory—some memories can burn in the mind's eye and linger like the pulsing afterimage of an accidental glance at the sun. It was a particularly snowy Christmas when Muriel was about ten years old, and the Kelley children had finished opening their presents. They ate a few too many cookies and the excitement triggered a surge of energy that Mrs. Kelley couldn't abide, so the rabble was sent to the yard to add to their significant collection of snow angels. Muriel ran to her room to find her snow pants and extra warm socks. Her mother flitted through the living room, riding her drug of the day and dreamily collecting shiny wads of torn gift-wrap, which she casually stuffed behind various chairs and couch cushions and threaded beneath the piano's shorter treble strings.

"If you lose something, go backwards through your day," she said in a singsong voice when Muriel complained she couldn't find her mittens.

"I did that already."

"If you lose something, go room by room and focus on the color of the item," her mother added. Muriel returned to her bedroom to identify everything that was red: a comb, a sweater, a heart-shaped pillow. That little spot of dried blood on her doorframe was also considered, even though it had long turned to brown. No mittens. She went into her parents' room. No mittens. She went into the dining room. Nothing. By that time, the others were heading into the neighborhood to continue their snow-molding for the neighbors. She had to catch up! She looked everywhere, but her mittens were gone for good! Muriel thought of Mr. Clifton's room—perhaps he had them by mistake? She bolted through the house and curled her hand into a little fist to knock on the door, but it was unlatched and opened about an inch. She peered through the gap and saw something red reflected in the mirror on the other side.

Mr. Clifton and Muriel's father were on the bed, sitting next to each other, kissing. Her fist fell limp by her side as she tried to understand what she was seeing. The flash of red was Mr. Clifton's long underwear. It was unbuttoned at the chest and pulled off to the side of his naked waist, where her father's hand moved rapidly. They both seemed to be panting. Muriel couldn't comprehend the action, yet she understood everything. She knew whatever she was witnessing was off-limits and adult and foreign and dangerous and wrong for a child to see, but it was also exciting because her father and Mr. Clifton seemed so playful and intent. Connected. She wanted to know *exactly* what they were doing. Her father stopped kissing Mr. Clifton's lips, and he slowly moved down the side of his neck, and then across his chest, and then further down. Muriel felt a coldness behind her as her mother's feet flanked her own. She turned, and her mother put a finger on her lips and let a slight "hush" escape. Mrs. Kelley clasped the doorknob and silently pulled it shut.

"Leave Mr. Clifton alone," she said, pulling Muriel into the kitchen.

"I was looking for my mittens."

"Mr. Clifton isn't interested in your mittens."

"I was just looking."

"Mr. Clifton isn't interested in your mittens," she said again. She didn't emphasize any of the words the second time, as if a phonograph had skipped. "And they are the color . . ."

"Red."

"And you looked in the front hall for everything red?"

"Not yet. I thought—I'll look in the front hall."

"Yes."

And there they were: Muriel's red mittens were neatly tucked inside her boots, the next item on her list of things to find so she could endure the sunny cold. Muriel looked through the cut-glass front door and found her hyperactive siblings reorganizing the snow on Mr. Hammond's lawn.

"Mother?"

"Yes?"

Muriel wanted to tell her that her father was in Mr. Clifton's bedroom in case she was looking for him, but as she looked into Mrs. Kelley's dilated eyes, she understood that her mother already knew. Muriel felt a deep and unfamiliar instinct to keep the knowledge of her father's secret from everyone, including her father himself. She didn't fully understand the secret she was keeping, but she knew fathers were only supposed to kiss their wives, and maybe their mothers and children, but never with their tongues and only on a cheek, a forehead, or the back of a hand. At the same time, she knew her father was happy. The household was always tense until Mr. Clifton arrived with his piano, and her father's joy then became more important than anything else. Muriel also loved Mr. Clifton and couldn't imagine him ever leaving. Plus, she was right in the middle of learning a complicated piece by Strauss, and she would never play it properly without his guidance. Mr. Clifton and Mrs. Kelley never seemed to clash or exchange hard words, despite her antics, and already a few years had passed since he started renting the back room.

Well, sort of renting.

"Yes?" her mother prompted again, pulling a length of gift-wrapping ribbon out of her pocket. She wrapped it around her forefinger until the tip of the digit turned purple.

"I forgot what I was going to say."

"How sillly! Go on, angel, go make angels, my little aaannngel. Merrry Chrrristmas." Her speech sounded as if her tongue was stuck inside a melting caramel. Muriel went outside reluctantly, but the cold wind was refreshing and it temporarily wiped her discovery away. She focused on finding a fresh patch of snow, crossed the street, and located the perfect plot near an evergreen tree. She flopped backward and spread her arms and legs as wide as possible, up and down, sweeping and stroking, flattening the dry snow. Then the tricky part: getting up without ruining the angel. She curled her legs under her knees carefully, then sprang up and jumped out of the silhouette as far as her small legs would allow. She turned back to survey her work. It was perfect. Muriel Kelley was a superior angel-maker. *I should get a trophy*, she thought. She looked back at her house across the street, hoping her mother would see what she made and admire her talented daughter. She squinted through the snowy glare with a red-mittened hand over her eyes. She could see through the tall windows of the house. She could see the piano in the living room, the lid open, the keys patiently waiting for the next song. She could see their spectacular Christmas tree, bursting with lights and ornaments and strings of colored popcorn. She could see her mother still in the kitchen, sitting by the window in the eating nook. Her mother continued to pull the ribbon tight around her strangling finger, her gaze affixed to the closed door of Mr. Clifton's room.

***

Three hundred miles later, the smooth road brought us to the city of Dunn in North Carolina, where we all agreed we should stop and rest. Despite the passing hours, Eve and Muriel were still feeling the lingering effects of their Savannah feast. They opted for a few sprigs of lettuce with a smattering of accouterments in the smallest possible food containers from the Food Lion salad bar. As they picked their way through the cherry tomatoes and garbanzo beans, they communicated more through simple gestures than words, like longtime companions with their own shorthand. Compared with the tribulations of our departure, it was a relatively easy second day for all of us. Personally, I relished the somewhat cooler temperatures as we worked our way north, but I'm not sure Eve and Muriel noticed the shift. Their minds were preoccupied with more significant concerns.

When Muriel was at The Deerwood, she had lived in a perpetual battle against her situation, her son, and her wits. Lucy and Vivette gently redirected Muriel's non sequiturs and rambling projections back to The Present and The Now. *What is today? Who is this person? Do you know who the president is, Muriel? Come back to us, Muriel.* She perceived their benign steering as continual admonishment and rebuke. With every answer judged, every step corrected, and every decision predetermined, her intellect felt swallowed. The medication also hindered her ability to enjoy any of her varied realms: the past was a dark and grainy film, the present was an intolerable beige, and the future was a black hole beyond the mist.

Out on the highway, as she broke free of the burdensome drug, the haze began to lift and the hole began to shrink. Muriel soon discovered she could not only locate specific memories, but she was also free to enjoy them. She recaptured the simple pleasures of thinking about Grace's travels, her childhood, and Ira. To be robbed of his physical presence was a torment, but lacking access to her memories of him was a more penetrating anguish.

Muriel came back to herself a little more with every hour that passed and every mile we crossed. As she remembered her life, she talked about it; another deeply missed pleasure, recaptured. And dear Eve, so stressed and downtrodden at the beginning of our journey—she spent most of our second day smiling and reacting to Muriel's stories. Grace was so brilliant and brave! Muriel played piano! And Mr. Kelley and Mr. Clifton!!

Muriel loved looking at Eve's face, especially when Muriel made her smile. Her youthful teeth were as white as fresh snow and straight in her head, not crowding out the bottom or spreading on the sides, not punctuated with metal or irreparably stained by decades of tea and berries. Muriel wanted to keep Eve's smile going forever, a bracing wall of light against the darkness. She didn't want to tell her that the chemical grip of the medicine was waning, but she still felt the presence of it like a snap-jawed pit bull that could bite at any time, unprovoked and unrelenting. She didn't want to solicit undue concern, become a burden, or interrupt our trip in any way, but there were moments on that second day when Muriel's mind froze like an overworked computer and threw her back into that dark attic, locked behind a knobless door. There were also a few piercing moments when Muriel's mind was clear, but her extremities felt like fire.

Not long after their simple dinner, I was parked neatly between the lines outside their window at the Comfort Inn off Exit 72. I cooled and settled my fluids while the ladies flipped on the television and prepared themselves for a solid rest. Muriel fell asleep effortlessly, and within minutes she was dreaming about her beaches.

Cape Cod. A hot day in July hosting the grandchildren. Outside their cedar-shingled cabin, the children populated their impressive sandcastle with a collection of bewildered sand crabs. A blue plastic tray of melted-chocolate pita sandwiches propped up on a wire rack, inches above the sand. A garden hose on a nearby railing with fresh water to clear their sandy fingers. Muriel walked toward the water as the larger waves dropped into froth.

Florida. Ira joined her walk as they became the first witnesses to a magenta sunrise. They held hands as the sun climbed above the horizon and touched the nearest cloud.

The Arabian Sea. The sun reversed direction, pulling oranges and pinks into the calm, reflective water as it lapped against Grace's henna-decorated feet. Her clear-polished nails mimicked the pinkish-white sand. Smells of burning sage and buttery cooked fish rose into a cinnamon sky.

In these rolling dreams, Muriel was soothed by the gentle rush of familiar waves. She looked content as Eve climbed into the other bed, flipped off the light, and watched an hour of nothing on the television before sleep finally took over.

I was tired, too. For many years, I'd spent most of my time alone in underground parking garages, waiting to be of service. Once or twice a week I got to enjoy my roads, but those first two days with Eve and Muriel were strenuous and, I must admit, I was out of practice. There were a few times when I thought I might overheat simply to get a break, but I didn't want to upset my companions, so I did my best to keep it all in check. They didn't notice that it took me longer to calm my ticking once we were finally stopped, but my oil pressure was steady, my fluids were full, and my engine was immaculate. I was always cared for by my service agents, and no expense in my maintenance regimen was ever questioned or skipped. I was created to provide reliable transport, and I would never fail my friends.

Despite my fatigue, I don't sleep and I don't dream. Since nothing of significance occurred as Eve and Muriel settled into sleep, this feels like the perfect opportunity to tell you about Muriel's youngest, the inimitable Sandra Levine. I may ramble a little with Sandra's story, but please bear with me—you'll need to know this information for later.

***

Ever since she was a little girl, Sandra looked forward to the mail. The idea that anonymous strangers were entrusted to carry important materials across the globe and directly to her door never lost its sublime appeal. Even as a grown woman with five children, the youngest already a freshman in high school, she still believed there was a small magic involved when she heard the clang of the metal lid on her front-porch mailbox. Kubrick barked wildly whenever new people climbed the broad steps leading to their door, but he let the mail delivery woman pass with only a cocked, semi-interested ear. She could be trusted because she was part of the established routine, or possibly because she was already bounding down the steps and moving on to the next house before his Labrador instincts could identify a threat. Or perhaps Kubrick knew Sandra gave her a bottle of wine every Christmas, and also on her birthday. Who else knows their mail carrier's birthday? It was a neighborly gesture that signified a small friendship, and Kubrick never barked at Sandra's friends.

Sandra still received Netflix DVDs in the mail. She enjoyed the small labor involved with opening the envelope and setting aside time to watch, as she termed it, "a real, physical movie." Streaming entertainment didn't give her the same experience because it lacked the weight of the obligation to return the product quickly and intact, in consideration of the next person who might enjoy it. Streaming shows were also chopped up for bathroom breaks, popcorn refills, or phone calls, but movies on DVD were sacred and were never paused. There was no logical rationale; it's just how things were in Sandra's house. As Sandra flipped through the mail, she saw the red envelope and hoped it was the next Jennifer Jason Leigh film on her list. She felt a kinship with Jennifer and sometimes wondered if they could be friends in real life.

Sandra was also expecting a check from Pete Caldwell, her favorite ex-husband. Pete's checks appeared like clockwork at the end of the first week of every month. Sometimes there were extra checks for birthdays or holidays or when she needed a new refrigerator, but this time it was the standard check that Sandra was accustomed to—the same check she'd received every month for nearly eighteen years.

Sandra was a wealthy woman, even by the standards of affluent Saratoga Springs. The cost of her accidental pregnancies was significant, yet it was chump change for Pete Caldwell, who over the course of two decades had amassed a spectacular fortune through his savvy in venture capital investments and real estate. Sandra sent him a thank-you note, again enacting the power of the United States Postal Service, every single time a check arrived. It was a quality Muriel had instilled, even though the checks were mandated in their amicable divorce settlement and not technically gifts worthy of a response. Pete's personal assistant was the only one who saw Sandra's notes, and he filed them away seasonally in the catacombs of Pete's generally irrelevant papers that the company stored in an off-site facility in Yonkers.

The mail finally arrived, and Kubrick lifted an ear while continuing his nap. Sandra sorted through the offers for new roofs and siding, solicitations from cruises and insurance agents, pizza coupons and charity requests, until she located the expected red envelope with her Jennifer movie and the privacy-lined security-sealed envelope with Pete's check. Sandra put the entire stack aside and opened the envelope with the money. After verifying the amount, she put it in her wallet where it kept company with six twenties, a slate of paid-off credit cards, her health insurance card, a license bearing a photo taken one week after a terrific haircut, and the 1976 two-dollar bill her father gave her on her tenth birthday. She had hidden the special green note in her bottom dresser drawer under the summer T-shirts and rediscovered it when she was packing for college. Delighted that it had survived, she'd folded it perfectly in half and slipped it into a secret slot in her wallet. It was a good luck charm and a symbolic reminder that not every dollar need be spent. Occasionally, Sandra shuffled things around and found it again. She would smile and think of her dad and wonder how many other people in the world kept a secret two-dollar bill tucked away.

Sandra was financially flush, but her personal time was always in the red as she attended to the constant needs of her vivacious and numerous children. For twenty years, her energies had been spent preparing and cleaning up after thousands of nutritious meals and doing loads of laundry. She had also worn out three cars shuffling everyone to and from activities.

It was during her eldest's ninth birthday party when Sandra discovered a clump of birthday cake was trapped in her thick hair. Food in her hair wasn't terribly unusual, and the chocolate sponge was camouflaged in her brown mane, but when she saw how the white frosting exactly matched the salt-white strands by her forehead, she required a nerve-correcting hit of marijuana and a quick trip to the store to find a dye that could restore her appearance to the age that she felt. Once the dye was obtained, she'd happily strolled the store, enjoying the bright colors of the cereal boxes, the mellow tunes, and a moment of peace away from her children while her parents watched them. Then she'd turned the corner and found a handsome stranger bothering the butcher.

Micah was a beautiful man: thin but not wiry and muscular but not excessively, with a full head of dark shaggy locks that were lengthy but not unkempt. His perfect facial hair was thick, tidy, and soft. The first time he smiled at Sandra, she felt an instant need to kiss him, but conversational foreplay seemed socially requisite, so he accompanied her to the car and they lingered before accepting one another's tacit invitation. The kiss was so warm, comfortable, and familiar that they were both genuinely surprised. Micah would later describe it as a homecoming that tasted like birthday cake.

Nine months later, Sandra birthed Sam.

She wrestled for months with the conundrum of legally committing to Micah Levine and potentially losing her income stream from Pete Caldwell. Micah was undoubtedly the (third) love of her life, but he was a freelance graphic designer, a musician, a poet, and a league bowler whose annual income hovered near the national poverty line. When she met him, she failed to notice that he purchased his kosher chicken with food stamps or that they had sex in a fifteen-year-old Honda with rusted bumpers and a door that didn't match. But Sandra decided that their connection was too great and too pure, and Micah was worth the potential loss of Pete's funding. She sped to Manhattan to cautiously tell Pete she had once again found love.

Pete took her out for an expensive dinner and they talked about their daughters. Nancy and Abby regularly sent him drawings, and he forbade his assistant from filing them in Yonkers, preferring the office in his apartment instead. Even the deformed papier-mâché bunnies and glittery macaroni art found a shelf. The girls visited him occasionally and knew conceptually that he was their father, but they didn't have a practical sense of what that meant because Sandra was the only parent in their true home. In many ways, they loved Pete like a year-round Santa Claus, but without the requirements of making a list, baking him cookies, or waiting in line for his affection.

Sandra had rehearsed a speech to try to sell Pete on Micah, but Pete interrupted her two minutes in. His daughters deserved to be raised by two compatible parents who loved each other and also lived in the same home. He felt Sandra's passion and knew Micah wasn't a fling. Pete wasn't bothered when Micah quickly came to serve as Nancy and Abby's father in an emotional sense, as well. Pete had wealth, but he had learned through significant trials that domestic bliss couldn't be purchased. One of Pete's finer attributes was his ironic self-awareness of his own emotional limitations, so after conditionally agreeing to assess Micah for himself, he quickly assuaged Sandra's fears.

"I'm not going to stop the checks, Sandy. Marry Micah and have a dozen babies with him if you want, our girls are our girls and Russ and Jamie will always be my little men, too."

"Are you for real?" she choked out, her eyes glistening.

"They can call him Dad if they want to, but I'm still going to take care of them. And you. I made that promise and I'm a man of my word."

"You're actually insane, you know that?"

"My parents think I'm an idiot."

"But then you bought them a house!"

"Yeah, I bought them a house. And a condo at the beach."

"Well, those idiots should know that you'll always be our children's father!" she cried. "I promise."

"I know. Whatever. Dessert?"

Pete and Sandra clinked crystal, and she spent the night in a guest room down the hall while he Zoomed with an underwear model in Prague. A day later, Micah took the train down and shook hands with Pete, who seemed mildly bewildered by his own instantaneous affection for Micah. The day after that, Micah officially moved in.

Sandra was lucky, and she knew it, and she took responsibility for her good fortune by providing her household with unlimited and unconditional love, nutritious organic food, and the best in orthodontia. She worshiped her zealous and attentive mate, who in turn doted on and adored all the children in equal measure. Life was nearly perfect, with money in the bank and a pervasive happiness, but for reasons that tended toward emotions over finance, the clan of seven had continued to live in Sandra's first apartment.

Going back a little further: Sandra was nineteen when she dropped out of college to attend to her first pregnancy. She had moved into Saratoga's less impressive west side with Craig Shift, her first husband and the biological father to Russell and soon after, Jamison. Muriel and Ira were consistently dismayed by Sandra's choices at the time, but they allowed her the latitude to live her own life without too much interference. Craig worked at a local printing press and made decent money, but he drank the bulk of it in Saratoga's numerous downtown bars. Their apartment was spacious, with its three bedrooms and two baths, but Craig sublet the back half to a sketchy friend from work who quietly dealt drugs off the rear porch. Craig and his buddy worked the third-shift hours together and often returned to the apartment in the early afternoon to sleep. Sandra took their young boys to the park, the library, or anywhere she could to avoid them. She also generally avoided her parents, who lived on Saratoga's east side, one mile over and a thousand lifestyles away.

Despite his boisterous conduct, shady side hustles, and open-door bathroom habits, Craig was somehow a sufficient husband and caring father. He never drank at home, and he slept elsewhere when he'd exceeded his limits; he was ever-considerate, even in a stupor, of his small children and overburdened wife. He also prioritized a date night with Sandra every month and served up a reliable babysitter for the boys, a generous meal out, and a clean room at a local motel. Sandra always expected the wayward roommate to end up in jail, but her world splintered when the cuffs were put on Craig instead. One windy and portentous night, a drug deal gone awry resulted in gunfire that struck an innocent passerby in the throat as he crossed the street to visit his ailing wife in the hospital. The man died instantly, and the wife dropped dead of a heart attack when she heard the news. Craig had stolen both the drugs *and* the unregistered gun. Then, they found pornographic Polaroids of slightly underage girls tucked under his car seat *and* he attempted to pay off a friend with a personal check. He even wrote *Alibi* in the subject line. Craig was drunk and high and mysteriously naked when they finally tracked him down, across state lines, in Vermont. It took time to apprehend him because he climbed to the top of a cell tower and proceeded to urinate on the police.

Needless to say, Craig never returned to the apartment. He was sent over a hundred miles away to a federal correctional institution in Otisville, New York. Two weeks later, he was raped by his cellmate, and four days after that he was transferred to Safford, Arizona. Back in Saratoga, the druggie roommate disappeared, and Sandra was left to fend for herself and their toddlers. Muriel once asked Sandra what she ever saw in Craig. Sandra said he knew how to cook, he shaved his face every day, and he never hit her— not even once. Muriel wondered to her close friends how she had failed to imbue her daughter with any standards. At the same time, she and Ira helped Sandra pay the rent, and they babysat the boys while Sandra looked for work. Sandra was further humbled when she was told she was wholly unqualified for either of the newly vacant jobs at the printing press.

With $600 remaining in her checking account, Sandra purchased a plane ticket and flew to Arizona to beg Craig for help, hoping he might have at least one noncriminal friend, a lead on a job, or a secret stash of cash. And she missed him. But Craig was broke and broken and had nothing to offer but the divorce that Muriel and Ira happily paid for. Sandra was crushed, but she refused to let it affect her optimism. She still had two bubbly and resilient boys, a parental safety net, and an unexpected upgrade to first class on her delayed flight home, where she was fatefully seated next to Pete Caldwell.

Pete had never met anyone like Sandra. He was tiring of the superficial Park Avenue women with their immaculate blond coiffes and red-soled shoes. Despite her tough situation, which she unabashedly relayed, Sandra's smile was genuine and untrained. She had an infectious joy, a lively sense of humor, and a keen mind. She extended an attractive warmth he severely lacked in his monied granite-and-glass world.

It was a good flight. They drank and laughed and connected and, somewhere over Terre Haute, Nancy was conceived in the first-class lavatory. Sandra's luck had already changed, though it wouldn't be evident for about six weeks.

Pete married Sandra one month before Nancy was born, and the whole family moved into his new apartment in Tribeca. It was a four-bedroom, five-bath, modernized prewar penthouse duplex on Greenwich Street with spectacular Hudson views from the private rooftop garden. It was expansive and renovated completely to Pete's museum-like taste. Thinking of the children, Sandra decided to cozy it up with brightly colored throws, oversized soft-yarn pillows, and beanbag chairs. She taped moons and stars cut from glow-in-the-dark felt to the bedroom ceilings and repainted accent walls with colors like Happy Sky, Dusty Rose, and Celery. Pete found her aesthetic alienating and, in combination with the increasing clutter of self-replicating toys, it prompted him to take numerous and relatively unnecessary business trips.

A long year went by before Abby, their second daughter together (and Sandra's fourth child), was born. In theory, Pete loved his family and the tender comforts they provided, but he felt burdened by their relentless vibrancy. He was out of touch with his subdued core. The girl babies were loud and smelly, and the young boys attacked him gleefully when all he wanted to do was drink a fine wine and watch some HBO. He longed for his sophisticated friends and the events, galas, and theater outings of his former life. He missed playing tennis and abhorred the expansion of his waistline. Attending to his perpetually pregnant wife and their brood became an unsavory chore, and his inability to condescend to Sandra for her shabby-chic taste was another quiet friction that whittled him down. It reached the point that even when he was in town, he would often rent a hotel suite instead of going home.

Sandra felt isolated. Even with her added flourishes, the dream apartment remained adamantly Pete's: a castle of polished slate and exposed brick with rules upon rules detailing the prohibited activities for each area. The dining room table was not for coloring. The Kasthall rug was not for board games with sharp pieces, or science projects. The living room was not for pillow fights or blanket forts or spontaneous dance parties—or any loudness in general. Children were not permitted to touch the refrigerator or play with the trash compactor or go to the roof deck unsupervised. No one was allowed to leave any portion of any bathroom wet.

Despite the space, Sandra and the children didn't fit. She also didn't have any friends in the city, nor the time or wherewithal to meet anyone. Even with the help of a full-time nanny, she felt cloistered by the inconvenience of her lovely children. Pete rarely scheduled date nights, and he never considered taking her to a show. They spent more time enjoying phone sex while he was in Europe than holding each other in their own bed because he was unapologetically terrified of any future pregnancies.

They didn't argue much, and to their credit neither cheated, but they each felt the other's despair, thick and oppressive like a muggy July. And it hurt. One day, Pete finally admitted that he had continued to maintain the empty apartment in Saratoga Springs as a backup plan, and after three difficult years, Sandra and the children moved back without him. Her life was infinitely easier in the North, where she was a pleasant walk from her parents and a few steps away from ever-helpful friends. It was also better for the children, with its beautiful parks bursting with color, spritzing fountains, and fleets of ducks waiting to be fed and chased. Pete continued to pay her rent, and he hired a local nanny to help. He was utterly thankful that Sandra and most of her deplorable stuff had found a comfortable existence upstate—it was a short private flight away, and he had more patience for the kids in smaller doses. Pete remained exceedingly aware that the eldest was entering the first grade, and Sandra had birthed three additional babies in only five years. It was tremendous work, so when Pete visited his wife and kids, he considered it a business trip and expensed it.

They continued to trust each other and extend good will, but their upstanding intentions naturally waned with the distance. Sandra needed a consistent partner to help her raise their tiny army, and she deserved someone who took an active interest in their shared life. It didn't take long for Pete to classify their marriage as a failed business venture and close the books. His family remained a viable asset that didn't belong in storage, so he drafted papers and signed a legal promise that he would continue to care. Sandra's name came off the digital intercom in Tribeca, and she continued to live in the apartment in Saratoga Springs for nearly a decade.

There, anyone could use a crayon on any surface, build a fort in any room, leave the bathroom soggy, and dance until they dropped under the glow-in-the-dark stars.

Craig was gone and Pete had relented, but when Micah was introduced to Muriel, she was smitten. Muriel found him to be handsome, intelligent, clearly invested in the kids, and calm. *The perfect man for Sandy!* she thought. With the birth of Sam, Muriel had five grandchildren less than a mile away to spoil, plus Laura and Christian down in Florida. Muriel was resigned to the idea that Sandra might never learn to close her legs, but she continued to push the dream that her daughter would eventually finish college. When Sandra finally revealed the amount of Pete's monthly checks, Muriel capitulated: "Your French Lit degree wasn't going to do much, anyhow." It was then that she taught her adult daughter how to create a budget, the value of good credit, and, crucially, how to save and invest.

Time passed, and eventually Muriel and Ira decided that splitting the year between New York and Florida was becoming inconvenient. They abdicated their proud title as snowbirds and announced the permanent move to Singer Island. Sandra asked if she could give up her apartment and rent the family home, which continued to showcase Mr. Clifton's piano by the garden windows decades after his passing. The children deserved their own rooms, and they definitely needed more bathrooms. Muriel and Ira were delighted by the idea—they had delayed their move by at least three seasons because of the horrifying prospect of selling the house to strangers. They'd originally considered offering it to Sandra and Pete when she moved back to town, but Ira feared Pete had children in other places who might one day stake a claim on the house if Pete was also on the deed and died prematurely. They liked Pete, but it also didn't feel right when they sensed the imminent divorce. Muriel and Ira always weighed their financial and personal decisions against a high bar of keen intuition.

Sandra was given the key, but no rent was to be paid. Instead, she became responsible for the upkeep and taxes, and the deed would remain in Muriel and Ira's names until their deaths. Lem objected. He felt like his parents had given Sandra a house for free while he had to work so hard for his own. He didn't want to hurt his sister by raising a stink, but Cindy was outraged and prodded Lem to do just that. Cindy believed Sandra was a little too adept at playing the victim with her convicted-felon ex-husband and her personal choice to have so many kids. She reminded everyone that Sandra was a millionaire's divorcée and that Micah worked as a full-time freelancer and set his own rates. They should be paying *someone* some form of rent.

Lem endured his wife's jealousies, but another decade passed before Ira was dead and he gained access to Muriel's finances. Lem didn't want to risk losing the equity in the house to pay for Muriel's long-term care, and he decided it was best to remove it from her list of assets. He convinced Sandra and used his unlimited power of attorney for Muriel to officially sign over the deed to his sister in exchange for half of the market value, which Sandra secured through a loan from Pete. Lem was entitled to his share of the proceeds of the house in the original will, but he wanted the money immediately to pay off his own house. He also wanted equilibrium: Sandra would have a mortgage while he lived debt-free for a change. And he wouldn't have to wait until Muriel was dead.

Pete continued to send Sandra monthly support checks, and Sandra wrote loan checks back to him when they cleared. A few months after Muriel moved into The Deerwood, Sandra and Pete learned that Lem had pocketed the entire sale of the Singer Island condo as well, under the guise that it would be used in a trust to pay for Muriel's care. Sandra felt she was entitled to half of the beachfront property, too, even though Muriel's revised will was curiously devoid of this provision. Pete offered to front the money for a lawyer to secure her fair share. Against his advice, Sandra chose to honor her father's wishes that families should never fight over money. Pete didn't like that. He wanted Sandra to use his money for their children, not to pay for Lem and Cindy's cruises and whims. So Pete forgave his loan to Sandra to spite Lem, and also to extract himself from any possible financial connection to his ex-brother-in-law. Sandra was flabbergasted, but she happily accepted his generosity. She didn't know that Pete earned about $3 million in the first quarter of that year alone, and he considered the payoff as both an investment in everyone's future and a loss on the books for the tax benefits.

***

On the same Tuesday evening, when Eve was helping Muriel pick out a salad dressing at the Food Lion in North Carolina, the phone rang in Saratoga Springs. The sound startled Sam, Sandra's fifth child (and only child with Micah), who was concentrating on a math problem at the kitchen counter. Sam enjoyed algebra more than he thought he would, but his disdain for biology surprised everyone, especially considering he placed second in the junior high science fair the previous spring.

"Mom! Phone!" he yelled. He was the only child left in the house, and he asserted his newfound authority by shouting more than was actually necessary.

"Hello?" she said, but she forgot to hit the Talk button first, and the phone belted a second ring directly in her ear. "Shit!" she cried out, and Sam giggled. She missed the flip-phones that answered a call when they were opened. She believed new technologies were actually making everything in life a little more difficult. She pressed Talk and tried again, speaking in a whisper for no apparent reason.

"Hello?"

"Sis?"

"Hey!"

"Hi."

Lem and Sandra talked about once a month and emailed jokes and photos with more frequency. They both waited for the other to speak next because typically Sandra called Lem and started, but this time it was Lem who initiated the call.

"You go," they both finally said at the same time, followed by the mutually repressed urge to yell "Jinx!"

"Sammy's failing biology," she started.

"Mom!" he called from the counter, aghast.

"He already tanked the first two tests and it's only October."

"I'm not!" he hollered at her. Then he repeated, "I'm not" to himself, quietly.

"How bad is it?"

"Sammy? What'd you get on the last one, fifty-three?"

"Fifty-two," he muttered. "But it was rigged."

"He says it was rigged." She smiled.

"Oh yeah? The Biology Mafia's been screwin' with my nephew?" Lem said, attempting the braggadocio of Tony Soprano while sounding more like a cartoon cat.

"*Gabagool!*" Sandra laughed. "Hey, Uncle Lem wants to know how they rigged your test, Sammy." He shrugged, muttered something about bell curves, collected his stuff, and ran off to his room. She heard the door slam in the distance.

"He says hi," she lied.

"Yeah," Lem replied. He knew the sound of a door slamming all too well, though in his house it was typically Cindy and not the kids.

"Teenagers," she sighed.

"Sure," he replied.

"Last one, though. And thank god he's a boy."

"C'mon, Nancy and Abby were easy."

"If easy means messy and making fun of my clothes and criticizing my hair for a decade, then sure. I think I raised some very critical children." She sighed again.

"They love you and you know it. You're a perfect mom."

"Well, Kubrick loves me, don't you, baby?" She gave the dog a chicken cookie, and he trotted off to another room with his prize. She continued, "Boys are easy, but they jerk-off *all the time*. Micah finally told Sam to use tissues instead of his socks, so that stopped the athlete's foot, and his hamper doesn't smell like a marina anymore."

"Ew."

"But now I have to tell Micah to tell Sammy to flush the fucking tissues instead of shoving them under his mattress. I mean really . . ."

Lem remembered his own experience of being a teenager. He told his sister that Christian's door had been locked for four years straight, eliciting another laugh. He liked making her laugh.

"So . . . what are you up to?" she asked.

Lem was silent for a long moment.

"Lem?"

"Yeah, I'm here. Um . . ." She knew immediately that something was wrong, and she sucked in her breath, not wanting to find out. The last time she'd heard a silence followed by that particular tone in his voice, she had learned a moment later that their father was dead.

"Is it Mom?" she whispered.

"Okay, so something happened." Then, quickly, "But don't freak out—everything's gonna be okay."

Sandra sat down and covered her mouth.

"Did she fall?"

"Oh no, no, no . . . nothing like that."

"Stroke?"

"No, she's----"

"So it's cancer."

"No, she's—wait, what?" he said, distracted.

"Spit it out!" Sandra pleaded.

"I'm trying, San! Okay. So Mom's, uh . . . Mom's missing."

It didn't compute. Falling or dying made sense, but missing? From an elder-care home with constant supervision?

"What do you mean, where is she? Did you call Lucy?"

"Lucy's in Jamaica. She took off when Albi had a heart attack. That's kinda what started this."

"Who's Albi?"

Lem breathed heavily into the phone, filling Sandra's ear. He wanted to tell the story without scaring her. "Okay, do you know Laura's friend Eve?"

"No."

"Okay, well Laura has this friend, Eve----"

"Is she the one with all the piercings and the cool boots?"

"Uh, yeah, that's her. You met her last spring, hanging out by the pool. Anyway, Eve works in the salon at Mom's place and she went in to get her check."

"Lem, where's Mom? Why are you telling me about Eve and what's-his-face—Albi?"

"Just *listen* for a minute," he growled. "So apparently Eve took Mom out."

"Took her out where? How?"

"Well, they drove off together and we're not really sure where they are."

"After school?" Sandra said, checking her watch.

"Yeah, after Eve got her check yesterday----"

"—Wait, yesterday? And you're telling me *now?* Shit, Lem! She's my mother too!"

"I know, I know. I meant to call you last night but we were talking with Judith and trying to figure it out and then Cindy and I got into a fight and----"

"Who's Judith?"

"Eve's Mom."

"And she doesn't know where they are either?"

"No."

"Well, what about Laura?"

"No."

"I thought they were best friends?"

"Yeah, they are. Or maybe not? I don't know, I can't keep up. Anyway, Cindy and I really got into it and then it was too late to call you."

"It's never too late when it's about Mom, okay? Do you hear me? I don't care if it's three-fucking-thirty in the morning, you have to tell me what's going on."

"I know, I know. You're right."

Sandra's heart was pounding. "And this morning? They didn't come back? And you didn't call the whole day? Dammit, Lem, I'm already starting dinner for Christ's sake!"

"No, I know, I know. Hey, I meant to call last night, like I said, but it was rough and today was all over the place at work and I couldn't even get five minutes and----"

"You went to the fucking bank?"

"Some of us still have to work, Sandra."

She didn't appreciate the dig but held her tongue. She didn't want to revisit his You-Live-On-Easy-Street trope until she knew what was happening on Muriel Avenue.

"So what did the police say?"

"We didn't go to the police. Not yet."

"Oh *come on!!* Okay, I'm booking a flight----"

"No, *please* stay put! Please stay there—that's partly why I'm calling.

We think, um, *I* think there may be a chance they're driving north and they could come to you. To the house."

"From Florida? That's crazy! Was there a note or something?"

"No, but Mom texted and—

"Mom texted?"

"Ugh . . . I don't know, San. I just feel like they might be driving north. I don't know why. We don't really know anything, actually, but it's possible and I wanted to let you know. Mom's been talking a lot lately about going home."

"You mean Singer Island home or *here* home?" She also silently considered that Muriel might have meant the proverbial Home, somewhere on the other side of life with Ira and the rest.

"I don't know."

Sandra took a moment to process everything and accidentally put one of Kubrick's chicken cookies in her mouth. "So, if they went somewhere specific, like California, would you still be calling me?"

"C'mon, it was just some bad timing, and I'm calling now."

She bit down and quickly spit the cookie out, revolted, noting it tasted nothing like chicken.

"Okay, well, thanks for the call, bro. I guess I'll make up the beds in case they stop by."

"Don't be pissed. I know I should have called you right away."

"Or emailed. Or texted. FaceTime. Skype. Zoom. WhatsApp, Facebook, smoke signals, a telegram?!"

"Okaaay, I said I was sorry!" he cried, exasperated.

The word "sorry" hadn't actually fallen from his lips until that moment, but Sandra calmed down. She took a swig of sparkling water and swished away the gritty taste in her mouth. "And why didn't you call the police? What's that shit about?"

"We have to wait twenty-four hours."

"Aren't we past that?"

Lem cleared his throat, "Almost, yeah. We're waiting for Judith."

"Why?"

"I think she's more worried about Eve getting some sort of a record than actually going missing. Laura said Eve's a really good student and Judith doesn't want this to screw up her chances with college. She also read an article that said an Amber Alert takes it to another level and could even make it dangerous because any random idiot could try to catch them. I'm not sure about that. Maybe she just watched *Thelma & Louise* or something. Whadda *you* think?" Before Sandra could answer, Lem continued, "And yeah, Mom texted us last night and said they were fine. 'We need a break,' she said, so . . . ah . . . anyway, they'll probably be back tonight.

They'll be back tonight."

He stopped rambling.

"So they're *not* coming here." It was a statement more than a question, and he didn't respond. "Lem, this is ridiculous."

"Yeah, Cindy thinks so, too. She had lunch with Judith and said the woman's kinda off the rails. She thinks they went to Disney."

"Bullshit."

"Why bullshit?"

"If you were sixteen, would you drag grandma there? Put her on Space Mountain? No way."

"Shit."

Micah came in from the garage carrying white paper bags with red menus stapled to the cuffs. Sandra forgot they had decided on Chinese and was relieved that she had failed to start dinner.

"Crab rangoons?" she asked him.

"What?" Lem said.

"Yeah babe, of course," Micah replied. He put the bags down and kissed her lips. She held up a finger to stall him. He raised his eyebrows and opened his eyes wide, trying to read her mind. Fifteen hundred miles away, Lem continued to pace, carefully avoiding putting pressure on his bad toe.

She returned her attention to the conversation. "Did you say Mom texted? When did you get her a phone?"

"I didn't, it was Eve's phone, but Laura said it sounded like Mom was writing to us."

"How? She never even used a typewriter."

He didn't answer.

"All right." Sandra exhaled. "So what's *your* plan?"

"I dunno. I guess we don't really have a plan, which is why I didn't call you, but then I thought you should know what's going on in case they call----"

"Or show up on the doorstep. Got it. Okay. Jesus Christ, thanks."

"But please don't call the police," he added. "We'll take care of that here, if it comes to it."

"You know something, Lem? Somehow you always make the wrong thing sound right. I'm pretty sure that's your superpower."

Lem didn't want to digest that nugget, and he quickly replied, "Lemme know if you hear anything, okay?"

"Yep. I promise *I will call you* if they show up," she said, wondering what Eve looked like. She only remembered the pierced ears, the hair, and the boots and had no recollection of her face. Was she an Elle or a Dakota Fanning, or an Evan Rachel Wood? Kristen Stewart? Sandra went through the cast of *Glee, Euphoria, Thirteen Reasons Why*, and all the teen vampire movies she could think of. Images of her own daughters came into the mix and were quickly discarded. Ultimately, she fixated on the image of a young Jennifer Jason Leigh in *Fast Times at Ridgemont High*. That seemed to work.

"Lem?"

"Yeah?"

Sandra wasn't ready to hang up. She had once made a pact with her brother that they would avoid all talk of weather because talking about the weather was stupid and cliché. The allowable caveat was if there happened to be a tornado or hurricane in either of their neighborhoods, or something equally exceptional. "Any tornadoes out there?" she prompted, hoping he would stay on the line.

"Nope."

"All right. Okay. Love you."

"Enjoy the crab rangoons."

They were both about to hang up when Sandra remembered something. She shouted into the phone, "Lem!!"

Lem continued to hold the phone next to his ear, knowing every conversation with Sandra had an epilogue, but he didn't know she would scream its arrival. He yelled back, "What?!" as they both switched their phones to the other side of their heads. Later that night, they would both wonder why they had minor earaches.

"Sorry, sorry. Hey, does Mom have her medicine?"

Lem started pacing again while shifting the pressure to the side of his foot and away from his toe. "I don't think so."

"She was pretty messed up without it. She said her feet were burning."

"Before she went on it, yeah," he replied, wishing he could forget.

"And she'd go on and on about India and Grace and all that stuff..."

"What're you getting at?"

"Oh, I'm just thinking if she's not taking her meds and starts to go a little crazy again, then maybe we can use that, somehow? We can warn her."

"Warn Mom?"

"No, warn Eve! Keep up! You said the text came from Eve's phone, so send a text back to Eve and tell her if Mom starts talking about Grace or her feet being on fire, then something's really wrong, like *medically* wrong. That should get her home. Or at least on the phone."

Lem loved when his little sister was smart, but it also made him jealous. She was always thinking a few steps ahead and with an imaginative flair. She saw things he couldn't. Sandra could go into any art museum and find a thousand magical stories where all he saw were boring paintings of dead people and boats. "Wow," he muttered.

"Doncha think?"

"Well, hopefully they're on their way back and we won't have to deal with that, but yeah."

"I'll call Doctor Parker to see if going off Halzoron is gonna mess her up," Sandra offered, "but send Eve that text. Or, better yet, have Laura send it."

"I'll call him," Lem said quickly, but then he was silent. After a beat he added, "You know, there might be a problem with this."

"What?"

"Well, if Mom's really the one who texted us, then maybe she's using the phone while Eve drives. What'll Mom do if she sees a text from us warning Eve about Grace? It could set her off. When we upped her dosage she blamed me for Grace disappearing and then she started digging her nails into the couch or . . . remember her forehead?"

Neither of them knew what to say next. Micah unpacked the food, set the table, summoned Sam, and tidied up the rest of the kitchen while he waited to hear about the drama. Sandra stared out the kitchen window and watched the evening light fade. Micah moved behind her and wrapped his arms around her waist.

Sandra said to Lem, "Mom once told me that Grace was deeply in love with a magical tree. Did you get that one? I think it was before she moved out, when things were—anyway, she said she wanted to spend all of her time hugging it."

"Hugging a magical tree? No, I get to hear about Grace being sick and pooping in a hole under the stairs in front of a crowd of strangers. Yaw."

"She really shouldn't be on a road trip," Sandra whined.

"No kidding."

Perhaps it was the nervous tension, but they both started to laugh while silently agreeing that nothing was funny.

WEDNESDAY

Chapter 12

Muriel's beach dreams ended.

She wriggled in a circle, around and around in the same direction, unable to find comfort within the Comfort Inn's thick pillows. Her earlobes chafed against the smothering marshmallow that seemed resolved to separate her head from her neck. The temperature dropped, and Eve turned on the heat in the middle of the night. Within a few hours, Muriel's throat and sinuses were assailed by the aridity while the hard cotton sheets absorbed whatever cushioning fluid remained in her sweaty flesh. The ridges of her fingerprints felt like corduroy. As she dried out, her mind conjured images of the Sahara, Arizona, and Mars. She finally discarded the pillow and tried resting her head on the mattress. Solid concrete was likely more pliant. She considered a towel wrapped in a soft T-shirt—but it was too dark and too late to locate such disparate objects.

Hunger was fueling her unrest. Eve and Muriel had overcompensated for their enormous Georgian lunch by pecking at bird-sized portions of salad for dinner, unaware that their expanded stomachs would require additional contents before resuming normal operations. The emptiness cranked within her, increasing her discomfort, while the warm air, brick-cloth pillow, and starched sheets conjoined into a clotted knot of distress that traveled through her extremities like lightning. She got out of bed and drank some highly chlorinated, lukewarm tap water from a plastic-wrapped cup. She woke up again an hour later to oblige her stimulated bladder. She ate a little toothpaste, thinking the peppermint would quell her appetite. And then she just felt sick.

At precisely three o'clock in the morning, Muriel's exhausted body finally relented. She entered an uneasy slumber with the back of her head nudged deep in a well of gathered crevices, the result of twisting beneath the asparagus-colored comforter. Her back was to Eve, who mewed quietly in the other bed, enjoying pleasant dreams of gently falling leaves. Eve had left the bathroom door cracked with the light on to facilitate any nighttime necessities, and in the fluorescent sliver, a painting of a country cottage glowed green on the wall facing Muriel. Muriel teetered beneath the surface of sleep while her eyes remained partially open. This was not unusual for her, and autonomic tears lubricated the slits as warm air continued to circulate. As her consciousness meandered, her optic nerves steadily received the image of the cottage.

Muriel decided to explore it.

She floated from the bed to the wall and then inside the painting's frame to the road, past the cow, and up the porch steps. The liquid brush strokes retreated, and the scene fleshed itself out authentically as she approached. She admired the stained-wood door imbued with brass fixtures, the floor-to-ceiling windows, and the light-blue wicker furniture set for sweet lemonade and conversation. As she looked around, she discovered the tidy summer cottage was only a small piece of the facade—this was a large country farmhouse with outbuildings and a pond and a tire swing secured beneath an ancient cottonwood that was releasing its annual fluff. Muriel smelled the earthiness of fresh-cut grass. Then a clear whiff of bacon instilled high hopes that breakfast was ready, but the windows of the homestead failed to convert themselves from paint to glass, and the interior of the house remained obscured. Muriel heard a horse pulling a cart off in the distance, and somewhere nearby, a dog gave chase. She turned her attention to the fields and saw a tractor slipping over a hill. "Rush hour on the farm," she chuckled.

The bacon scent returned with something sweet beneath its high, crispy notes—possibly syrup or freshly peeled fruit. Muriel turned back to the house and was delighted to find that the windows were clear glass and the front door was wide open. She stepped inside and marveled at a surprisingly grand, curving staircase with at least forty steps. It looked like it was imported from a European hotel, and she half-expected to see Marilyn Monroe descending in a red gown. Instead of walking up all those steps, Muriel decided to float. She discarded her body's density and her feet lifted, gently rising from one step to another, barely touching the tread with her tiptoes as she ascended, her fingers gliding along a mahogany banister that felt like wood wrapped in silk.

Bits of cotton continued to float by.

As she neared the top of the stairs, she heard the horse and the cart and the dog and the tractor off in the distance. She also heard Cindy and Lem arguing in the kitchen. She glanced over her shoulder, expecting to see the graceful spiral below her, but instead she saw the fields. She turned to discover she was floating up the path again and being pulled toward the cottage with its glossy white steps, stained-wood door, brass fixtures, and blue wicker furniture. The brush strokes of the windows were thickly gray. She smelled the grass again, and the bacon and—strawberries?—but they were quickly overtaken by an influx of manure wafting off the fields.

She stopped floating. She had reached the limits of her weightlessness and knew the law of proportions required her to experience the crush of gravity. All the cotton fell to the ground, hard, and blanketed the lawn like thick spider webs. She couldn't move, trapped in their glue. She reached the porch steps but didn't have the strength to climb them. Her legs were lead and her feet were anchored.

Muriel wept.

She was stuck somewhere between the imagined cottage and an uncomfortable bed in a North Carolina hotel. She wiped her tears with the back of her hands and saw they were full and pink with the nails painted robin's-egg blue. The ruddy spots and carpal compressions were gone, and she felt dexterous and restored. She heard the music vibrating in her fingers. She wondered if the rest of her body was also young, and she reached inside her coat, and inside the coat beneath it, and inside the coat beneath that one until she found a #11 Cotillion White pocket mirror with IRA1 engraved on the case. She snapped it open, and a beam of sunlight reflected directly into her eyes. She tried to change her angle, but the beam caught her again. She forgot about the extra gravity as she tried to spin around to find her reflection, but the distracting sun remained because her feet couldn't move. She decided to spin anyway, twisting her legs like a corkscrew. She spun and spun herself into a thin stalk of licorice.

She stopped spinning when she saw the horse was only two inches away, with no cart and no driver. He shimmered with the fine mocha paint that was used to depict him, and Muriel thought it an amusing paradox that he was brushed into existence using horse hairs that might have been his own. They studied and admired each other. So strong. So young and smooth. Fluid. She reached out to touch him and he brayed with a fiery burst of energy, flinging himself up the steps in a hearty gallop and disappearing through the open door of the house.

The manure smell was powerful in his wake.

She lifted her hands to her nose to block the odor, and discovered a familiar tune was stuck in her fingers; the sound was leaking out from under her nails. She flipped one nail back like the roof of a convertible, and the music grew louder. Someone was chanting in India and it was coming out here, through her extremities, on the other side of the earth.

Om Anandamayi Chaitanyamayi Satyamayi Parame.

It was Grace, somewhere, experiencing bliss and truth and divine consciousness. Muriel breathed in solidarity as she locked her fingers into each other to send the sound into her wrists, her arms, and throughout her body. At some point she became untwisted and decided to go back into the house. This time she wouldn't levitate. It was levitating that got her into trouble.

She stepped inside the house once again, and the same amazing staircase welcomed her. She walked halfway up, like a normal person in a normal body. No tricks. She wore a summer dress made of the same fabric as the cushions on the wicker furniture. She looked back over her shoulder and saw the porch beyond the doors, the road beyond the porch, and the tractor crossing the field in the distance. Everything was as it should be. Everything outside was bright and colorful, not quite paint and not quite real. The cotton continued to float.

Muriel turned back to the stairs and looked up again.

Her mother.

Her mother stood in a white nightgown that flowed in a robust wind that Muriel didn't feel. She looked exactly like her old photographs: tall, soft, and colorless. She smiled at Muriel, beaming radiance and sunshine from her eyes. Muriel perceived her mother's golden health and took more steps toward her, up the staircase, but her mother drifted backward in equal time, keeping their distance intact. Muriel thought she was nearing the top, but the staircase added more steps as she used them up. It took hours before she finally reached the landing.

"Grace," her mother said.

Muriel's mother flew toward her with outstretched arms and a draping embrace, her gauzy nightgown sleeves forming expansive wings, but she didn't stop. She flew right into Muriel and evaporated through her. Muriel could feel her mother's love twinkling like glitter in her veins in the explosion of their mingling atoms. Her mother smelled like bacon and manure.

Muriel opened her dry eyes as she coughed herself awake. She felt something like cotton stuck in the back of her throat. Her heart was pounding and her neck was stiff. Her bladder was full again, and she quickly made her way to the bathroom. A few moments later, she returned to the bed and sat on the edge. In the slip of light she studied the painting of the cottage. It looked familiar but she couldn't place it. She glanced at the clock and snorted; it was twenty past three.

Eve continued to sleep, breathing softly, her head buried between two pillow mounds and a pile of unruly hair. She also caught a dry tickle and gave a tiny cough, no louder than a click on a cell phone. To Muriel it sounded like a gunshot.

"Oh!!" she cried out. "Wake up, you!! Wake up! Wake up! Wake up!!" Muriel prodded Eve with strong and coiled fingers.

Eve mumbled something and then followed it with a more intelligible, "What's going on?"

"What are you doing?" Muriel bleated.

"I'm . . . sleeping?"

"No. No-n-n-no. Wake up, you!!"

Eve sat up.

"Why are you sleeping *in my house?*"

"What?"

"What are you doing here?! Get out!!"

Eve turned on the light by the bed, and it shattered the darkness with a pale mustard glow that had both women cowering. Muriel continued panting a stream of words. "Who are you who let you in what are you doing this is my house get out who are you----"

"Hey! It's me, it's Eve! It's *ME!*" Eve threw her hair back and showed her face to Muriel. Muriel stared at her, blank and terrified. "We're in a hotel, remember? We're taking a trip? I'm Eve! Remember?"

"What trip?" Muriel inquired dubiously.

Eve shook her head, then ran her fingers through her hair and pulled it back again.

"What trip?! Where's Ira? *No.* I need to talk to Ira."

"Hey, hey hey hey," Eve soothed. "It's okay, Muriel, you had a bad dream is all. Everything's okay. Everything's fine. Let's go back to sleep. Let's go back to sleep." Eve leaned back, hoping to show Muriel how easy it was to relax. Muriel watched and sighed, but she didn't move. "Everything's fine. Let's get some sleep," Eve reiterated, yawning.

"Mmm . . ."

"It was just a dream. You'll feel better if you lie down again. I promise."

"No."

Muriel got up and opened the drawer to the bedside table. She found the Bible, lovingly placed by the Gideons, and threw it violently across the room. It bounced off the window shade with a loud plop.

"Muriel!!"

"No!!" Muriel cried out again. She pulled the drawer the rest of the way and dropped it to the floor, barely missing her own toes. She tore the comforter off the bed and started pulling at the sheets while Eve got up and tried to figure out if it was safer to try to stop Muriel or smarter to flee. Muriel stripped the bed, revealing her diaper, and it was suddenly clear that Muriel had released her bowels and then removed it in her sleep, the smell entering her dream. A fresh stain snaked from the center of the bed to the edge, and Eve realized Muriel's legs were also soiled as the stench hit her. She winced. Muriel spat on the stain and started rubbing it with her fingers before Eve could stop her.

"Ira?!" Muriel called as she spun around and focused on the closet. She tried to pull the hangers down, but they were attached to the rod so they couldn't be stolen. She found the iron and threw it across the room onto her sullied bed, narrowly missing Eve's shoulder. Eve flew back into the corner of the room, grabbing a pillow on the way, and curled into a tight ball behind it to protect herself as Muriel moved to the drawers in the bureau under the television.

"Muriel—stop!"

"Where's Ira?!" Muriel repeated, again and again, as she pulled each drawer onto the floor. "He should be home by now!" She returned to the nightstand and looked at the phone.

"Don't touch that! Your hands are----"

Muriel picked up the receiver.

"Front desk," said a tinny, tired voice on the other side.

"Ira, is that you?"

"No ma'am, this is the front desk. How may I----"

Muriel slammed the phone down on the cradle five times with such force the reverberating rings could be heard outside the room. Had there been more people in the hotel a complaint would have been made, but Muriel and Eve were isolated by at least a half-dozen empty rooms on either side and across the hall. When Muriel approached their luggage, Eve summoned the courage to protect her belongings from those sullied fingers. She successfully crossed Muriel's line of vision and distracted her.

"Stop it!" Eve said sharply. Muriel reached out and Eve caught her by the wrists.

"Where's Ira?" Muriel bawled, exasperated.

"He's dead!" Eve returned, and Muriel suddenly froze like a crazed squirrel before an oncoming car, paralyzed with indecision and fear.

"Ohhh . . ."

Eve's breathing intensified. She had never seen someone go crazy before, except in the movies where they ended up shot or stabbed or punched.

"Ohhh . . ." Muriel continued as Eve loosened her grip and gently sat her down on the soiled bed. Muriel was utterly forlorn. Her tirade subsided, but Eve remained cautious.

"Hey . . ." Eve said. She let go of Muriel and took a gentle step backward, crossing her arms. She didn't know what to do or say—her father would know how to handle something like this. Eve remembered how he held her shoulders when she was upset. He would stand there with those warm, firm clamps until her miseries dissolved. Muriel rolled her head around in a long, slow motion. Then she started scratching at her temple.

"Don't . . . well, okay . . ." Eve soothed. She wanted to slap Muriel's polluted hands away from her face, and she moved toward her again, but slowly, like a lion tamer nearing the cage with meat in hand. "Everything's okay. You're okay." Eve breathed through her mouth as the fecal stench permeated the room. She reluctantly returned Muriel's hands to her lap by the wrists, again. She was firm, but not aggressive. Muriel provided no resistance and then collapsed her head against Eve's chest and sobbed. Keeping one hand on Muriel's wrists, Eve sat beside her in an awkward pose, avoiding the crap-smeared legs. She wrapped her other arm around her while Muriel quivered and sobbed. Her body was hot. Eve continued to whisper, "You're okay . . . everything is fine . . ." She wondered if that was true.

Muriel calmed and eventually faced Eve, meeting her warm eyes.

"I saw her," Muriel said.

"Who?"

"My mother."

"It was just a dream," Eve reassured her. "I think you had a bad dream."

"No, it wasn't bad. It was wonderful."

Eve lifted her brow, opening her eyes wide.

"She was beautiful." Another series of quiet little bursts and sobs ensued. "But Ira wasn't there. He was supposed to be there. Or here. He has to be somewhere. He can't be . . . nowhere. I need to find him. I need my----" Muriel lifted her hands to wipe her face before Eve could stop her, and at once she snapped into full cognizance and understood the manure wasn't in her dream. "Oh!! Oh god. Oh god. Oh god." She turned her head to the side, as far away from Eve as she could manage.

"Yeahhh . . . let's take care of that," Eve replied.

Eve helped Muriel take a perfunctory but effective shower. She felt strangely at peace as she helped Muriel wash. The filth moved effortlessly down the drain, and Eve wasn't bothered in the slightest as she held the older woman's naked body under the warm spray and silently chastised her own immaturity over seeing Muriel's breasts only a day before.

She called the front desk for a fresh set of sheets and disinfectants. She didn't provide an explanation, and the hotel clerk didn't ask for one. Eve wiped down the phone, the iron, and all the drawers as she reset the room. She sprayed the Bible and wondered if her mother approved of the Gideons' version, and if a Bible was still pure if it was touched by someone's shit. A faceless, nameless maid would do it all again in a few hours and would never know about the mess or her efforts, unless the same maid was also responsible for loading the washing machines. Muriel was already snoring before Eve put the last drawer in place and turned off the light.

It was nearly four.

The adrenaline dissipated, but Eve remained wide awake, agitated. It didn't make any sense that Muriel was looking for her husband in the hotel drawers. And why had she thrown an iron at her? Who throws a tantrum after a *good* dream? Eve slid into a gully of overwhelm lined with pangs of remorse. Muriel's mother must have been even more confusing and damaging than her own, and the idea that Eve might be affected by her own mother's harms, even seventy years down the road, was depressing. The whole scene was crazy. Muriel was crazy. And Eve thought maybe she was crazy, too, for even attempting our journey. In normal life, she would be in her own bed in her own room. She would have spent the evening working on the sets for the play or studying for a quiz while half-watching Netflix with Laura. Or maybe she would have been with Liam, kissing and touching. Or more. Instead, she was in an ugly hotel room that smelled like lilac-scented Lysol, miles from anything familiar, facing an uncertain future that probably included some form of youth prison or community service.

And there was no one to blame but herself.

Eve opened her phone and sent a message to Laura who, despite the early hour, replied less than ten seconds later.

***

It was about a decade earlier when Ira Daniel Worth collapsed during a rigorous game of tennis. One moment he was up forty–love in the third-set battle against David Sperling, then he'd overheated and collapsed into a pile of tan flesh leaking a steady flow of saliva, sweat, and blood on the hard macadam. His body fell awkwardly on his elbow—it broke backward and a bone protruded—and the back of his head crushed like an eggshell and rested perfectly flat against the ground. His eyes stayed open, staring into the hot sun. He felt none of it.

Ira and Sperling (they always called him Sperling) had refused to wait out the lengthy reservation lists at their condos, so they'd opted for the public courts a few miles away. After Ira collapsed, Sperling didn't want to wait for an ambulance to arrive, either. The emergency mandated immediate transport to the hospital in a readily accessible vehicle—it was the first discernible mess in my interior and the only time I ever saw blood.

Sperling steered me like a maniac up the Old Dixie Highway to the hospital. He slammed his bloodstained sneakers on my pedals with no attempt at nuance. He ran three red lights and nearly hit a pregnant woman, who stepped back to the curb with inches to spare. I was literally in the hands of a heroic lunatic and I couldn't bear it, so I shifted my focus to Ira. His swelling brain was about to stop his heart and lungs, but for most of the short journey, his thoughts remained clear as he exited our world.

He knew he was dying. The impact had pinched the spinal column and provided near-complete paralysis. This, and the shock, eradicated all physical pain. He couldn't speak or move. He wasn't afraid, but his mind screamed with remorse for leaving his life without an apology for Muriel. Ira was nine years older than she, but he had taken tremendous care of himself to ensure his longevity for her sake. All that tennis and swimming, all those long walks, the healthy diet, the meditation and self-awareness, the deliberate intention to make life enjoyable, to laugh, to connect, to explore . . . he'd fully expected to reach a healthy century and felt cheated out of his last twenty years. As he comprehended his fatal situation, I could feel his astonishment and anger, his love for Muriel, his family and close friends, and his monumental sadness.

All I could do was hold him firmly on my leather while he bled on a pile of towels, and assuage his fears. Muriel wouldn't be alone. I would do everything in my power to stay with her, to guide her, to listen, and to comfort her. I think he appreciated that. Maybe it helped. I really liked Ira; he was a true gentleman. When he exhaled his final shallow breath, I was relieved my windows were shut tight so I could hold onto it as long as possible.

Ira and Muriel had swapped cars that morning because my brakes were squeaking and Ira always took care of such matters. He was supposed to drop me off after tennis, and then Sperling was going to drive him home. Muriel took their other car, a soulless blue BMW with tinted windows and stark black rims. Lem had found it in a police auction for less than half the market value. Either it was uncommunicative or I don't understand German, but I suspect that car likely had blood on its seats, too.

While Ira and I experienced his departure, Muriel shopped across town for fresh-squeezed organic grapefruit juice. She always assumed she would know if her husband died—that she would somehow feel a psychic chill, a whisper in the air, a quietude in her soul. Instead, she felt annoyed because she couldn't find the coupon for her brand. The magic slip of paper didn't make it from the kitchen counter into her purse, and it nagged at her like a pulled hangnail. She paid full price for the juice, scowling at the register, and continued her errands. She stopped at the sporting goods store to get more tennis balls, hit the dry cleaners to retrieve her preferred yellow suit for the symphony, and returned home to Singer Island for lunch.

There was a message on the machine, but the telemarketers would have to wait while Muriel put together a salad and sipped her beverage. Nothing important was happening anywhere. The kids were fine, the grandkids were fine, her friends were fine, and Ira was playing tennis. According to the news, the world was going to hell, but that world seemed very far away from the good life that Muriel and Ira enjoyed together on the sixteenth floor.

They had enough money, and some to spare. They supported animal shelters, children's hospitals, and cultural causes like the orchestra and the ballet. They were members of the United States Tennis Association so they could get better tickets to big events. Sometimes they participated in disaster relief efforts or brought canned goods to the local food pantries. Mostly they did what they could for society by voting and recycling; the rest was for the politicians, the nonprofits, and the police to wrangle and solve.

Muriel found the errant coupon and tucked it back inside her purse for a future visit. Then she paid two bills, flipped through a home-decorating magazine, and fell asleep for thirty minutes. She awoke and took a swim, warmed up in the hot tub under the shady pavilion, and then strolled along the beach, hoping to find her husband. Ira liked to dip himself in the ocean after tennis to cool off. When Sperling drove, Ira often went to his friend's condo five buildings down, swam there, and then walked home along the beach to join Muriel for dinner. Sometimes he would stay at Sperling's to shower and dress, and then he'd call Muriel over for a splendid evening of fish and cards. As she passed the third building, she wondered if this was going to be another one of those frequent spontaneous nights. She would wear her new green top with the coral starfish on the collar. After the fourth building, she turned around, feeling revitalized, and went home to await his call.

Time passed and Ira didn't return, but Muriel assumed he just fell asleep on Sperling's couch, another frequent occurrence. Sometimes Ira woke up before dawn to walk on the beach, but in recent months, Muriel had noticed that he often added a second nap to his afternoons. The tennis was good for him, but she worried when he pushed himself. He was seventy-seven years old, after all, but his competitive nature mandated a tie-breaking third set even if he was limping after two.

The answering machine continued to blink, and Muriel chastised herself for failing to check it earlier. There were five messages, and she assumed they were all from Ira calling with the evening's plans.

"Mom, it's Lem. Call me when you get this."

Beep.

"Mom? Mom . . .? Call me." It was Sandra. She sounded out of breath.

Beep.

The third message was a hang-up.

Beep.

"Mrs. Worth, this is Annette Crofts at St. Andrews Memorial Hospital. Please call me when you get this message, my number is 239-1686, extension 4120."

Beep.

"Mom, where are you? I'm coming over."

Beep.

The apartment intercom rang as she finished deleting the last message. She didn't write down the one from Ms. Crofts. She buzzed Lem up and spent a small eternity staring blankly at the corner of the vestibule until his elevator finally reached her floor. She opened the door and looked into his wild blue eyes and knew in a flash that Ira was dead. He wasn't hurt somewhere—he had actually died. The whisper had finally arrived.

She didn't ask for details, knowing they would overtake her soon enough, like floodwaters rising after an upstream storm. She was surprised that she didn't feel a break in their connection, even when she knew he was gone. She quietly scolded her soul for its inability to notice. In her heart they were still together, Muriel and Ira Worth, one month shy of forty-five years, with the anniversary dinner plans already set.

As her body numbed, her mind raced. She didn't know how to process the news, which she still had yet to hear. Her mouth felt dry and her tongue zipped across her teeth. She tasted grapefruit juice, but that was from hours ago. Hours—when Ira was still alive? Should she return the new tennis balls? Cancel the anniversary party? Take his name off the magazine subscriptions? Lem reached out to hold her, and she let him.

"Dad passed out on the courts this morning and hit his head when he fell. Sperling said it happened faster than he could blink. They rushed him to the hospital but it was too----"

"This morning?"

"Around ten."

"What time is it now?"

"A little after four."

She clutched his back. Over six hours and she didn't know anything about it! She cursed herself for being in a good mood all day. She tried to maintain her grip, but Lem felt larger than normal. She could barely reach around him or hold on to him—he was sweaty and slippery, like an oil-slicked whale. She tried to swallow, but her throat felt like the revealed flesh beneath a freshly ripped scab.

"Where the hell were you?" she croaked.

Lem exhaled, tears slipping down his face.

"I called a number of times and I left you messages, but you didn't answer. I was supposed to drive all over? Where were *you*? Down on the beach? You really need a cell phone. We'll get you one of those new ones with the tracking, so we can find you if there's an emergency. We can connect it with a special program on the computer. Cindy has the Razr, but LG makes one with a full keyboard that flips out----"

Cell phones. He was talking about cell phones.

He read her mind and stopped. Then he whined, "Sandy said she called, too. And the hospital called. Everyone called, like, a thousand times, but we couldn't tell you on the machine."

"How did you find out?"

"Sperling called the bank when he couldn't get a hold of you, and I met him at the hospital."

"Did you see Daddy?"

She felt Lem tremble and she quickly absorbed his shudder. She felt his wet cheek against the top of her head. He emitted a soft, long, draining moan. This was how he cried, with his mouth shut and the sound leaking out from somewhere below his throat. She couldn't move. Her mind tried to recap her entire day. Where *was she* at ten? Did Ira kiss her when he left the house before he went out to play tennis and die? What did he look like in the morning? Which shirt did he wear? She tried to remember if she saw him leave; she tried to picture him going out the door. He must have been wearing white. He almost always wore white, but sometimes light blue or yellow, too. Did they make love, or was that the day before? Yellow socks. He wore yellow socks. Where was she at ten? Did he die right away? What was she doing when he died? Was she on the phone? Or making the bed and smoothing the wrinkles and pummeling the pillows? Was she eating? She was always eating. Maybe she ate too much. She liked granola. Someone said granola wasn't healthy, but she ate a lot of it and she seemed to be doing just fine. She was running out of granola. In fact, she did run out, so she went to the store. The grocery store. She went to the grocery store. At ten? She got granola and blueberries and grapefruit juice. Organic. Healthy. But she couldn't find the coupon. *Was all of that at ten?*

Her body convulsed.

Lem whimpered. "We have to go to the morgue. We have to make plans."

Lem and Muriel propped each other up in the doorway. He didn't want to go in, and she didn't want to leave. They procrastinated over their new reality.

***

About two weeks later, everyone gathered.

"My father was the kind of guy who stopped whatever he was doing to help you out. He was really smart, and he had a great sense of humor. He had a thousand stories and you've probably heard them all at least twice, but somehow he made them feel new. He also had this great ability to make you feel special and important. If you were feeling down or upset about something, he always said exactly the right thing to make it better." Lem cleared his throat. "He . . . he would know what to say here to make us all feel better. He would know."

It was an exquisite day in early autumn, the kind of day when employees lied to their bosses about a sniffle and then absconded for the lakes, trails, and frozen-custard stands sprinkled throughout the Adirondacks. Such perfect weather was somewhat rare in upstate New York, and Lem wished he could enjoy it instead of sweating in his black suit, eulogizing his father. Greenridge Cemetery was especially green that day, but Lem knew that in a few short weeks it would be nothing but bare trees and frost.

He continued, "Dad was passionate about three things: family and friends, the law, and his loving wife, Muriel."

"That's four things, Lem," called one of Ira's former colleagues. A few chuckles reverberated until people remembered where they were.

Lem looked up from his paper. "Hey, no, that's okay. It's totally okay to laugh. Dad loved to laugh. He—ugh, he'd probably be mad at us for being sad here, you know? And for having a funeral on such a nice day when we should all be at the lake." A few more titters escaped. "He wouldn't want, ahhh, wouldn't want us to be—hah, sad."

Muriel took his arm in hers. He continued, through tears and numerous choked pauses, clinging to his notes.

"Dad's life wasn't always easy. He was born a twin, but there were complications. He made it through fine, but his sister had brain damage, and he said he always felt an irrational guilt about that. It was during the Depression and they didn't have the resources to help her like today, but they did the best they could. They were teenagers when she died, and Dad used to tell me that even though it was really hard and maybe he had to grow up faster than other kids, he couldn't imagine his life being any different. Those early years gave him an incredible sense of empathy and a tireless work ethic. He had a great curiosity and a strong desire to do everything in life that she couldn't—it was kind of like he had to live one life for both of them. He traveled for a while, and when it came time to start a career, he said he didn't care what he did, so long as it helped people.

"Everyone said he should run for office, but Dad believed that politics could turn friends into enemies and enemies into friends, so he chose to stick with the law. He said there was great honor in the profession, and he was always held in high regard throughout his long career. And he got me out of a few speeding tickets, too."

Lem earned a few more laughs. He looked up and saw someone yawning, so he folded up the speech and spoke from his heart.

"Yeah, speeding tickets . . . So, uh . . . Dad also loved a good lawyer joke, and, uh, well here goes: A man walks into a bar with an alligator on a leash and says, 'Does this bar serve lawyers?' and the bartender says, 'Yes, of course we do,' and the man says, 'Great, I'd like a beer please, and I'll take a lawyer for my alligator.'" After an awkward pause, a few people managed to laugh (mostly the lawyers). Muriel tightened her grip.

"Mom and my family . . . we're truly appreciative of how many of you are here today. Dad told me once that he was on the fence about retiring to Florida because he didn't want to lose touch, but many of you visited there and welcomed them into your homes up here, and he said the distance made it even more special. He also said that even though he could look at the ocean every day and he would never have to buy another shovel, Saratoga would always be home."

Lem looked at the coffin, which was suspended over a deep rectangular hole.

"I, uh, and I felt really lucky when they moved to Florida because we got—we . . . we got to see them—all the time," he whimpered.

Laura cried out with a loud sob. She was seven years old at the time, and it was her first funeral. All the grandchildren were there, even four-year-old Sam, but they all sniffled while she wept with vigor. Cindy tended to her while Lem continued.

"Dad also said his greatest achievement in his life was marrying Mom. It would have been forty-five years next week, and they never spent a single night apart. Their love, respect, and care for each other set a pretty high bar for the rest of us."

Muriel knew Lem's words were well-meaning, but his speech made her feel like she was dead, too. And without Ira, perhaps she was.

"Dad gave us so much. Those summers in Cape Cod, the ski trips, the funny stories . . . all the good times. And Dad was a hugger, too. Whooo, we're all gonna miss those hugs."

Lem's face turned red and his throat constricted as he imagined a future devoid of his father's impressive squeezes. The fluids in his nose traveled backward and thickened. He couldn't conform his voice to his final sentiments. "I lovvve you, Daaad. We all—we're really, ugh, we're gonna . . ."

Everyone waited patiently for the last word: "miiissshhhyewww . . ."

Cindy ran over and handed him a lavender-scented handkerchief. He sank into it, and Muriel let go of his arm. She didn't dare attempt to speak. Her grief was so embedded in her body that her muscles nearly forgot their purpose, refusing to stretch or bend. People even commented on her statuesque appearance. She stood like a steel column through seven more speeches from grandchildren, colleagues, and friends. She felt fully connected to everyone and yet entirely alone, rooted beside the coffin. She waited patiently for them to drop it in the ground so she could walk away and finally collapse, in private.

She couldn't believe her Ira was in that box.

Throughout the proceedings, the obvious images flashed through her mind: weddings, vacations, and birthdays, but the more obscure moments seemed to burn brighter and linger longer. She thought of when they went to a popular movie and the only available seats were in the front row. Rather than strain their necks, they looked into each other's eyes, locked hands, and listened as if it were a radio play. Once, she shaved Ira's back hair to form a smooth and hairless heart without telling him, but she also knew that he knew. After Lem's agonizing birth, she was deathly afraid to be intimate again, but Ira was so patient and tender that when they finally merged, she experienced a half-dozen rolling orgasms before Baby Lem began his morning cries. And on every anniversary, Ira gave her roses to match the number—the arrangement for forty-four was too heavy for her to carry, but of course he was there to help.

She also remembered their troubles: disagreeing on the best discipline for a naughty child, missing the last flight home from Japan because she took ten extra minutes to buy a plate, the three weeks of her pneumonia followed by four weeks of his, the day the dog died, the day the next dog died, everything they went through with Sandra and her husbands, every injury or surgery or lost key or wallet or jacket, Lem's car accident, the lump in Cindy's breast . . .

Everything had seemed so consequential in those moments.

Everything became trivial at Ira's graveside.

When Dave Sperling began to speak, Muriel coughed up a little acid. As he rambled about tennis, her rocky muscles contracted and she feared her bones might snap. In her rational mind, Sperling was a true friend—it was good of him to come up from Florida and talk about Ira's passion for the game—but in her emotional mind, it was all Sperling's fault.

"That's enough," she hissed as he prated about a famous match point, but a breeze caught her words and took them away with a flurry of golden leaves. Muriel followed the leaves as they floated past the black outfits and weeping mourners, past the stoic oaks and maples, and beyond the empty southern plots near the far fence. Then a squirrel caught her gaze as he sprinted across a patch of flat gravestones. He narrowly avoided a woman who stood apart and alone, watching from a distance, wrapped in an obsidian shawl.

It was Grace.

Muriel rubbed her eyes.

Grace? How . . . ?

Muriel desperately wanted to break away from the group and run to her, to breathe her in and hold on to her. Forever. Ira would understand. He, of all people, appreciated Grace's wanderlust and knew firsthand how she lived life on her own terms, in a world of her own making where she was never judged and had no obligations. But there she was, obliged to be with them, to say goodbye. Grace remained stark, radiant, and alone on the far side of the field of buried death.

Sperling began a new paragraph about Ira's skillful backhand. It was a gross distraction and Muriel swept her gaze to the group of mourners. Lem was with the crowd again, holding Laura and Christian under each heavy arm. Cindy cried and even allowed it to affect her makeup. Muriel didn't want to be there; she wanted to be with Grace. She wanted to run across the lawn with her arms opened wide. Her pulse was frantic and her nose began to drip. Lem saw her demeanor shift as she indicated for him to look to the edge of the far trees. He didn't understand her jerky movements, and she did it again, fingers pointing, completely disregarding Sperling's overwrought summation.

Lem turned his head, along with a dozen others, but everyone failed to see.

Grace was also gone, compounding Muriel's crushing sadness.

***

Muriel looked dolefully out the window at the farms of North Carolina in the early, honey-colored sunlight. She hadn't slept well the night before, and she awoke with a small headache. She found a damp towel hanging on the back of the hotel chair, but she didn't remember either of them taking a shower. Plus, Muriel would never hang a towel on a chair—it could stain the wood. The room held a saturated cleaning smell, and there was a pile of bundled sheets wrapped in plastic outside the door. She wondered how she'd slept through the maid service, but that still didn't explain the towel. Muriel felt off. And strangely sad. And supremely hungry.

Eventually, she turned her gaze from the distant silos to Eve, who looked so very much like Laura with her shining smile and post-braces teeth. They both had small noses. They both had delicate brown eyebrows. If Eve didn't put color in her hair, they could pass as sisters, except Eve was three inches taller and Laura had a bigger chest. Laura's eyes were a rich brown, like a chocolaty dessert, while Eve's seemed to vacillate between hazel, gray, and green depending on her mood. At the moment, they shone like peridot gemstones set in rings of gold.

"So Grace didn't even talk to you?" Eve asked, first looking at Muriel and then checking the blind spot behind her companion as we changed lanes.

"What?" Muriel asked.

"At the funeral."

Muriel didn't know she was talking about Ira's funeral.

"Um, no," Muriel replied, reluctantly. "She . . . was gone."

"That's shitty."

"It's—hey, can we eat?"

"Really? You're still hungry?"

Eve was worried. She had thought sleeping in a little would restore Muriel after her predawn tirade, but when Eve finally roused, shortly before ten, Muriel was already sitting in the chair on the far side of the room, fully dressed and watching her.

"Where are we?" Muriel had asked, scanning the room.

"North Carolina," Eve said, rubbing her eyes.

"Am I kidnapped?" The question had been parsed with a childlike matter-of-factness, like a four-year-old wondering why bricks are red or what snails eat.

"What?" Eve laughed, "Of course not!"

"Is this about money?"

Muriel didn't seem despondent or upset, merely curious. It was a disconcerting way for Eve to wake up, but at least this time Muriel was still in the room.

"No, you're not kidnapped and we have plenty of money. Don't you remember? We're taking a special trip?"

"Right, right, right," Muriel said, nodding her head. "We're on a trip. A trip. A trip." She tapped her temple to stuff the information inside, and they both hoped it would stick. Then she looked at Eve and asked the other question ubiquitous among four-year-olds: "Why?"

"We talked about this." Eve said patiently with a sigh. "My mother and your son are both liars, and now we know the truth so we're driving to—you don't remember any of this? Think for a second. I know you know the rest." She was tired of saying "remember?" and searched for another way to say the same thing.

"I know you know the rest," Muriel mimicked, unsure, trying to please.

"At the gas station after the condo? And yesterday in the car?"

Muriel's face remained blank.

"Maybe you should sleep a little more. We don't have to check out for a while."

"I think I'm hungry?" Muriel said, unsure of her own disposition.

Eve realized she was ravenous, too, as she headed toward the bathroom. "We'll get some breakfast in the lobby. Gimme a sec." She returned a few moments later and picked through her things to find some fresh clothes.

"Am I kidnapped?" Muriel asked.

Eve exhaled through her mouth. "Nope, we're taking a trip."

"Do we need money?"

"No, we're all set."

"Okay. You'll let me know."

Eve had correctly sensed that we were heading into another long day. She wasn't sure when, why, or how Muriel got the kidnapping nugget stuck in her craw, but Eve was worried it might create trouble if Muriel talked to anyone at the hotel, a restaurant, a rest stop, a gas station . . . Kidnapping was a serious crime, but it didn't really match the situation. Eve wasn't asking for a ransom, and I can attest Muriel was never threatened or in any physical or even emotional danger (it could be debated whether going off her drugs was detrimental or beneficial). They were simply traveling together, and Muriel was the consenting adult companion who had told Eve to drive away in the first place, and in her own vehicle.

But Muriel's memory lapses and outburst were significant. Her medicine, or lack thereof, was clearly affecting her brain chemistry, and we still had a ways to go. Eve couldn't fill her prescription from the road without disclosing our location, and we were going to have to work through it. Somehow. Eve made a quick mental list of alternate conversation topics in the hopes she could U-turn Muriel's focus quickly if needed.

Muriel had watched Eve wriggle into fresh underwear and a pair of jeans. Eve was normally shy when she changed, and she opted for Laura's bathroom and a closed door to put on her swimsuits, but ever since the towel dropped in front of the prayer group, it seemed unnecessary to relocate for a quick change—especially in front of the woman she had bathed in the middle of the night. Eve put a light zippered sweatshirt over a red T-shirt that proclaimed *Ironic T-Shirts Suck*.

"Am I kidnapped?" Muriel asked again.

"Hey, so here's a question: what's it like to get old?"

"You think I'm old?" Muriel laughed, raising her voice. Eve shrugged with a coy smile, and Muriel said, "*I'm* not old, but *if* I were, I would probably say it's not as bad as you might think."

Eve was surprised. She had always thought all old people were miserable. At least, no one at The Deerwood seemed happy. Even in the painting studio, the dance classes, or while doing chair yoga, they wore broad scowls and complained endlessly about their sore bodies and bad relatives.

Muriel sensed her answer was a little too simplistic, and she continued, "You really wanna know what it's like?" Eve nodded.

"Okay, here it is: the difference between aging and actually being an old person is when you cross that invisible line from participant to spectator. You never even knew the line existed, but once you cross it, no matter what age you really are, I think it's nearly impossible to go back."

Eve tried to comprehend what Muriel meant. She didn't feel like much of a participant, either. Her mother, school demands, and work schedule dominated her choices, and even in drama she stayed far behind the proscenium to build the sets.

"When Ira was alive, I never felt old. Never once, and neither did he." She swallowed. "Because we were in it together, every single day." Eve watched Muriel's face as a thousand thoughts ignited, but then Muriel's lips quivered to form a strangely squinched expression, half smile, half frown. "I have to tell you, just saying his name . . . between us, I'm a little mad at that man right now," she whispered to Eve.

"You're mad at . . . Ira?"

"He left me!"

"He didn't *leave* you, Muriel. He died."

"Without my goddam permission!!" Muriel sniffled.

Eve leaned in and gave her a big hug that also served to lift Muriel out of the chair. It was precisely the physical and emotional support that Muriel needed in that moment, and her sharp angst quickly dulled. They walked to the lobby, where they drank some juice and ate bananas while Eve also prepared a batch of toasted bagels and cream cheese for the road.

Soon we had resumed our drive and Muriel, probing her abilities to talk about Ira, had begun to cautiously relay her memories of his death and the funeral. She had never discussed those lost weeks with anyone—not even me. For years I had wanted to tell her about Ira's last moments, how he was madly in love with her and infinitely apologetic, but even though I can easily absorb the lives of my passengers, the transfer doesn't always go the other way. They have to be open to it, and something in Muriel shut down when Ira died. She stopped listening beyond the scope of normal hearing and relegated her life to the tactile. Time, ideas, and other intangibles became unimportant, or simply too painful.

She finally got to the part of the funeral when she saw Grace, and then she didn't.

"That's shitty," Eve said, seeking solidarity with Muriel. Muriel disagreed with the assessment, though she couldn't expect Eve to understand why. Muriel quickly opted to change the subject with a distraction of her own.

"Hey, can we eat?"

"Really? You're still hungry?"

Eve reached over the seat and felt for a bag of snacks in the back while keeping her eyes on the road. "I think we have a few tangerines in there, and some granola bars."

Muriel peeled the fruit and took her time with each juicy wedge. She was used to filling the hours by extending the smallest of tasks, and she was also used to mundane repetitions. We had traveled over eight hundred miles by that point. The landscape was conforming to a pattern of broad farms and fields that gave way to suburbs and shopping malls, then a town or city with taller buildings, then more suburbs, and then back to the farms. For Muriel it held a sameness, but for Eve, each locale seemed unique and limitless in its possibilities. Even the billboards told a fresh story as they filled the emptier spaces with promises of newer homes, better cars, or a stronger relationship with God—or fireworks, if you dared to cross the border between the Carolinas.

A truck flew by, triggering a road trip game that Muriel and Ira had liked to play during their decade of semiannual drives from north to south and back again. The idea was to imagine the contents of the eighteen-wheelers based on their license plates, but you weren't allowed to use agricultural products. There could be electronics from California, car parts from Michigan, or whiskey from Tennessee, and so on. Muriel explained the game, but Eve interrupted her as we passed a massive distribution complex with endless bays feeding farrows of trucks. Everything was available everywhere, Eve explained, and three clicks on the phone brought it right to your door in a day. *All* of the trucks could *all* have iPhones and steering wheels and booze, and they didn't make electronics in California—they only designed them there—and almost everything was made in China anyway, and wasn't whiskey really a subset of agriculture? Muriel was disappointed: Eve had ruined the game, and another quaint element from the past was eroded. She began to wonder if, perhaps, she had become old.

Another truck zipped past us. It had Texas plates.

"Nothing but oil," Muriel said, hoping for the game's resurrection. "Are we in Texas?"

"Nowhere near it. We're getting close to Virginia, I think."

"Textiles."

Eve blinked rapidly. Muriel's game made her feel incompetent, and she tossed out another topic from her queue: "Hey, I was wondering something . . . you don't have to answer, but what's it like to have Alzheimer's?" Muriel thought they were talking about trucks and manufacturing, and Eve's little non sequiturs were jarring. She couldn't tell if she'd had another memory lapse, and she quickly checked herself to see if she was dressed properly. "Do you get headaches?" Eve added. "Does it . . . hurt?"

"Oh, no. It's nothing like that," Muriel said with a sigh, a little unsure of where to begin. "Lem says I repeat myself, but I don't think that's always true. I think the little shit likes to play mind games with me."

She seemed pissed, and Eve regretted choosing a provoking topic. She considered switching to old movies or something less riling, but she had seen so many people in the salon struggling, and she genuinely wanted to know what it was like from their side. Who better to explain it?

"Have *you* noticed anything?" Muriel prompted.

"Um . . . sometimes," Eve said—an understatement.

"Oh no. I'm sorry."

"It's not like you can help it."

Muriel shrugged.

"And you seemed pretty okay for most of yesterday. Sorta."

"What happened yesterday?" Muriel twitched.

Eve didn't know what to say.

"I also forget that I forget," Muriel sighed. "And then I forget that, too." She wanted to laugh at how silly that sounded, but her comedy didn't have an audience.

Then Eve said, "You know, sometimes I'll be standing by my locker and thinking about a TV show and I won't remember the name of the actor. Like, I'll see his face and I know the whole story and who the guy is dating in real life and all that, but his name, *the name itself*, is a big blank, and I have to look it up on my phone. And then I'm like, oh right, stupid. Do you think maybe it's kinda like that?"

It took a moment for Muriel to review Eve's story. Then she said, "Maybe, but I don't remember that I'm trying to remember the actor's name. The whole thing goes blank, and there's no phone to sort it out, and even if there were, I wouldn't know how to use it, or what I'm looking for in the first place."

Eve couldn't imagine a life without the phone telling her what was what.

"But it's more like this," Muriel said, painting with a different brush: "When you drive, you don't really think about the steps. Everything is automatic. You move your foot and watch the road and steer, but you can also talk and eat a bagel and do all these different activities. I can't do any of that anymore. Nothing is natural. There are too many steps and I forget the order, and when I think about the pedals, I forget to steer, or if someone's talking, I forget where we're going!"

Eve listened intently. "Right, okay, but *eventually* the actor comes to me. Like, if I don't look it up, and then I'll be brushing my teeth at night and suddenly I'm all, hey! It's Jude Law! Does your stuff, like, *ever* come back?"

"I don't know," Muriel sighed. "What's Jude's Law?"

Before Eve could think about crafting a response, Muriel turned her body and sat sideways to face her directly. I felt her take a deep breath as if she were preparing to swim a long lap underwater. "Okay, sweetheart, here it is, this is exactly what it's like. Imagine if everything you've ever done and every memory of your life was an individual grain of sand."

"Okay."

Muriel paused for a long beat and exhaled. She wasn't going to get through it all in one breath. "No, wait, not sand. That's not it. Forget the sand."

Eve continued to drive while Muriel searched for a better expression of her idea. It was there, floating in front of her near a sticky web, patiently waiting for the slightest breeze to catch her thought. About three miles later, she nabbed it.

"Imagine if everything you've ever done and every experience you've ever had was written down on a card, like the ones you find in a library book. You tie your shoe or kiss your husband or spank your kid or bake a cake—and it all gets recorded and filed. Your brain holds the biggest diary in the entire world, and it's all about you, in endless rows of organized, immaculate cabinets. For most of your life, this mini-universe is available to you, and for the most part you can pick out any cards you want, whenever you want them. It's beautiful.

"Then let's say you find yourself in front of a fresh strawberry. You've been here before because you have this magnificent Strawberry Reference Archive—this *knowing* about strawberries from the past. It's so detailed you can almost taste the new one before you bite down. You remember your tongue exploring the texture of the seedling grooves, that rush of saliva hitting the roof of your mouth while your cheeks pucker from the tart flavor. As you chew, your new strawberry moment gets recorded on its own card and filed with the others, but it's also merged and forever linked with your third birthday when you ate a strawberry for the first time, and the thousands of strawberries since. With me so far?

"Throughout your life you're filing and sorting and cataloging and retrieving, making links and cross-references, without even knowing you're doing it! All your cards are chugging and buzzing and everything is fine until . . . Alzheimer's—let's call him Ali—steps in.

"Ali wasn't invited, and he doesn't have permission to be in your head, but there he is anyway. Did he spawn from a toxin? Pollution? Radiation or aluminum? Will eating fish or turmeric keep him away? No one knows for sure, but if your parents met him, then you probably will, too—maybe because you built your own mental cabinets with their blueprints. I don't know. All I do know is once Ali shows up, there's nothing you can do because now you've got a terrorist in your brain."

We hit a small piece of rubber from a blown tire and it made a loud bang as it bounced against my undercarriage. Eve gripped the wheel a little tighter, and Muriel went on.

"Ali lurks in your cards, armed with his Plaques and Tangles. Everyone knows about this. The Plaques are a treacherous, pasty tar. They jam your file drawers and make the cards stick together so you can't read them. Sometimes you can copy the damaged cards and secret them to another location, but Ali knows when you're doing this, and he only allows these droplets of occasional mercy so you can convince yourself you're really fine. It's part of his game.

"Then he uses the Tangles, like Rapunzel on the worst hair day ever, to reshape the corridors of your wonderful library. Now you've got these jumbled twists and scratchy, frizzy knots to navigate, so you think you're in the strawberry aisle and you're about to eat some delicious fruit, but the Tangles have misled you to the chocolate cards, or a Charlie Chaplin movie, or that time you got seasick on the cruise. The new strawberry tastes wrong, it might make you sick, and sometimes you start laughing and have no idea why."

Eve glanced at Muriel, and then her eyes returned to the road.

"But all these Plaques and Tangles? They're not even the worst of it. Even with that, there are times when I'm feeling totally secure in my mind and all my lovely life-cards feel neatly organized and available. Ali is around, and maybe a few paths are twisted and some of the drawers are a little sludgy, but I'm getting by and finding new ways to get to my cards, with lots of sleep and healthy foods and my medicine. I'm feeling good enough and in control enough—and that's when Ali turns on the Fan."

Eve dropped my window a notch to let in some fresh air. Her hair went wild.

"Yes! Just like that! But this fan is major, like that storm on Jupiter raging for a thousand years. When Ali turns on the Fan, *all* of the cabinets open at once, and *all* of the cards are shaken into space, flying at crazy speeds, smashing into each other, shredding in the blades, and moving wherever the tripping winds take them. I'm completely obliterated!"

Eve shut the window.

"I'm about to eat my strawberry when everything turns to mayhem. I can feel my father braiding my hair and I think we're in Prague and then I see Lucy down the hall riding a camel. It's like some crazy dream, but it's also completely real. I smell dead skunks and I think the floor is covered in soggy brown cornflakes. A card zips by with pumpkin spice coffee, and another with gasoline, and when I bite into my strawberry, I can't reconcile any of it. I have no idea what I'm eating or why I'm thinking about Anne Bancroft or smelling wet leather sandals or if today is the day they'll find my mother's frozen body in the woods. None of my thoughts have disappeared or become inaccessible—this isn't Plaques or Tangles anymore—instead they're *all there* and I can't control any of them or stop the whirl. All I can do is accept the chaos and take each card as it comes, one by one by one by one . . . until it ends. When Ali finally turns off the Fan, the strawberry is gone and everything in my mind is on the floor. People look at me as if I've left the planet. And maybe I did."

Muriel gave Eve time to let all of that sink in.

"But, you know what? In a weird way, the Fan may actually be a bit of a gift. I like to think it gives me the opportunity to reexperience my whole life! From one random flash to another, I can taste everything, see everything, and feel everything. It's like those miniscule dots in a Seurat painting, each with its own precious color, and it all comes together to form the whole of what I am, and in that great and horrible moment, I can see it all . . ." Muriel reconsidered her comparison. ". . . except everything is out of order, and the unpleasant memories are mixed up in there, too. I guess my life isn't entirely like that picture of a pretty park."

She continued. "Anyway, that is why it can take me a week to write a simple birthday card, and that's what it's like to have Alzheimer's. All of the scientists are working on the Plaques and Tangles, but no one seems to give a fat fig about the Fan. I don't think Ali has ever turned it on during a brain scan, and no one's ever asked me to describe it."

Eve was quiet for a long moment. Muriel watched her. It was a lot to process. A few more miles passed.

"So every memory is a grain of sand?" Eve asked. "Or it's *not* sand? So then what? What happens to the sand?"

I heard everything Muriel thought she said out loud, but Eve doesn't share my abilities. From her perspective, Muriel had entered another frozen lapse. Muriel turned to look out the side window. She saw pieces of a deer smeared along the shoulder.

"Sometimes my joints ache and my feet and hands feel like they're on fire. Or I can't feel them at all. And I get dizzy from time to time. And hot. And cold."

"Oh god, that's from Alzheimer's?"

"I don't know."

Chapter 13

After a quick lunch, we were nearing Petersburg when Eve noticed a new, acrid smell. Apparently, we encountered a long series of malodorous effluvia throughout our travels on I-95, but since smell is a sense that I don't possess, I could only enjoy Muriel and Eve's banter as they attempted to identify the various possible origins.

"Skunk."

"Really?"

"Absolutely."

"No, that's not a skunk. It smells more . . . dead."

"Dead skunk, then."

"If you say so."

Some hours later: "Diesel."

"Burning rubber?"

"Could be an old car burning oil."

I shuddered at the thought of that.

And even later: "Garbage dump must be nearby."

"Ewww."

"Or maybe it's fertilizer. They're spraying the tomorrows."

"You mean tomatoes?" Eve corrected.

"Tomatoes," Muriel confirmed.

"I didn't know they grew tomatoes in Virginia. The ones at the store are usually from Mexico," Eve stated.

"Why Mexico? That seems foolish. Why would they go all the way to Mexico when Virginia is right here?"

"I don't know, but Mom always has me check. She doesn't trust any Mexican food because she got sick in Cancun, like, twenty years ago, and the organic tomatoes are usually from Canada anyway. It's hard to find good local tomatoes unless you grow them yourself. Did you know they pick conventional tomatoes before they're ripe, and then they spray them with carbon to make them turn red? Isn't that weird?"

"That's terrible!" Muriel cried out.

"They also add these crushed seeds from South American trees to make up all the colors for cheese and butter. It's all fake."

"No!"

"And some food coloring is actually made out of tiny bug shells and skeletons! Seriously! The bugs eat red berries and then they crush them up, and it takes a million dead bugs to make a little bit of red food color for cranberry juice and strawberry yogurt and candy. And the green and blue colors are made in labs, and they've been linked to cancer."

"How do you know all this?" Muriel marveled. She always considered herself a relatively healthy eater, but she had no idea even her yogurt might be corrupted.

"Oh, my mother thinks the devil is working through the food industry to make human beings stupid and sick, so we're easier to control. I don't know if it's *actually the devil*, but she still makes a good point. We get most of our food from the farmers' markets."

"I remember farmers' markets! We used to go all the time." Muriel smiled. "The food was fresh and my friends were always there." She sighed and cautiously added, "Your mother may be right about this."

Eve wished she could disagree, but devil or not (and the garbage she'd consumed at the gas station notwithstanding), she avoided nearly ninety percent of the items in the grocery store. Eve and Muriel savored their newfound foodie connection until the persistent smell reclaimed their attention.

"Tobacco!" Muriel blurted. "I meant tobacco, not tomatoes! I think we're smelling fertilizer for the tobacco fields. I *know* they grow that here."

"It could also be all the cows," Eve said. "Virginia produces a lot of meat. Everyone thinks of Texas and Oklahoma, but it's big here, too. The meat industry took over tobacco, something like twenty to one, a while ago, if you include all the chickens."

"How on earth do you know that?" Muriel widened her eyes to their limits.

"It was on *Millionaire* once when I was home sick. The guy got it wrong and lost two hundred thousand dollars or something. He also thought Virginia was mostly tobacco."

"But you remembered it? Well, I'll be, Miss Smarty Pants!"

"I thought it was weird, so I looked it up." Eve shrugged. "Virginia also grows more soybeans than tobacco."

"I think you know too much about this," Muriel jabbed.

"I know, but I can't help myself. I get curious. Laura says I'm a dork."

"She calls you a dork?"

"She doesn't mean it."

"Well, I think you're remarkable."

"Thanks," Eve said sheepishly.

"But I'm getting a little tired of hearing facts about Virginia, you dork."

There was a split second where Eve wasn't sure if she'd been insulted, but then they both laughed at Muriel's affection and independently imagined how different their trip would have been if Laura were in my back seat.

Muriel closed her eyes and rested for a bit while Eve and I drove on. She was concerned she might slip into a fugue and express her jealousy. When she was young, Muriel knew everything about everything, too. She was sharp and filled with ideas and color. She couldn't pinpoint the moment her pink mind had started to gray, but she figured it aligned with the color shifts of her hair, her teeth, and her toenails. All her vibrant tones drained away as the decades wore on, replaced with pallid yellows and oatmeal beiges.

Perhaps another hour passed when another smell emerged, quite different from the odors of crops or cars or animals. It was familiar to Eve, but she couldn't place it at first. Was it body odor? They'd both showered and put on deodorant and clean clothes, so it seemed unlikely. Muriel never seemed to have that tired, sweaty ripeness that some of the patrons of the salon cast about, that fetid tang that managed to overcome even the strongest of hair products and nail lacquers. Eve wondered if she had become used to Muriel's scent or if my fragrant, aged-leather seats masked everything. To Eve, Muriel generally smelled nice, like pastel flowers. And wealth.

But there was *that smell*, familiar and alarming, yet unrecognized. Eve lowered her window, and fresh, warm air rushed through us, taking the stench with it. It didn't originate in the fields. Eve scanned the shoulder of the road. It wasn't an animal. She closed the window and the smell returned, more ferocious than before. Eve looked over at Muriel and discovered the growing stain spreading around her companion's crotch.

"Oh Jesus, Muriel!"

Muriel snapped awake.

"You pissed yourself!" Eve cried out.

Muriel looked down and realized that she had, indeed, had yet another accident. "Oh no," she said, with unusual calm. "That's not good."

"I thought you were wearing the diaper!" Eve wailed.

"Calm down, Cindy."

"'I'm not Cindy!" Eve bellowed.

"Well—okay, umm . . ." Muriel pleaded.

"Oh god, you . . . are you *still* peeing? Stop it! Ugh!"

Muriel looked at her crotch again with rational disappointment and said, "You've never had an accident?"

"Maybe as a little girl but—but you're a grown woman!!"

"No, I'm an *old* woman. We already established that, so stop yelling at me."

But Eve couldn't help herself, and she continued to rant.

"Cindy, please stop----"

"Oh my god, it's everywhere! Why couldn't you . . . oh god, we're totally fucked!"

"Cindy, watch your mou----"

"I'm not fucking Cindy!!" Eve shrieked, and Muriel began to cry. She opened the glove compartment and found a napkin inside, dabbed her eyes with it, and futilely rubbed at her slacks. She knew Eve wasn't Cindy, but Cindy was the only name she could remember.

Eve wanted to stop yelling, but she couldn't find the spigot to turn it off. Her anger gushed, and she didn't realize her foot was pressing hard against my pedal, forcing me to inch upwards of eighty-five miles an hour. Everything was fine and wonderful, but then, with a flip of the switch, Muriel took a nap and pissed herself and started calling her Cindy. She didn't go to the bathroom when we stopped for gas—she insisted she didn't need to.

"You're not wearing the diaper," Eve reiterated forcefully.

"No," Muriel whispered.

"Why not?!"

"I don't know." The voice Muriel used, small and quiet, came from seven decades earlier, when she had apologized to Mr. Clifton for spilling milk on his piano.

"Fuck!!" Eve shouted again. "FUCK!!!" She banged her hands against me and I released a few honks. They were not in solidarity. I wasn't happy about Muriel's acidic liquid running down my crevasses and saturating my hand-stitching, but I also didn't approve of Eve's hostility, or our current speed.

Eve opened all of my windows. "It stinks!!"

Ninety-three miles per hour.

Muriel cried quietly to the side with her face to the open window. Her lips trembled and she exhaled little moans while her tears formed and dropped sideways, captured by the whipping wind. She rubbed her eyes with the napkin she found in her hands, forgetting she had already used it to wipe at the growing puddle. The sting and stench were simultaneous, and Muriel cried out in horror, prompting Eve to scream another round of expletives, inducing even more tears from both of them. The smell was wrenching and tannic and the napkin flew out the window, happy to be released from the scene.

Muriel felt terrible. Lucy took her to the bathroom with regular frequency, and she rarely wore extra padding during the day in her apartment.

She put on extra protection when they were going to be out of the house for a few hours and at night, but even then, she rarely wet herself because she only slept in three-hour clips.

When we reached ninety-seven miles per hour, I couldn't stand it anymore. I let out a high whine, and Eve immediately responded. She was disgusted with Muriel, but she was more repulsed by her own behavior. She knew Muriel hadn't deliberately peed to torture her, and she recognized it was likely her own fault for not attending to Muriel properly, though it remained unclear what she could have done to prevent it. We had been together for two nights and two full days, and Eve thought she was learning and adapting well. She thought she had everything under control. She'd watched Muriel go fuzzy, take a nap, and then rise without confusion. There had been so many moments of clarity and insight that Eve had difficulty comprehending how Muriel's mind could so quickly vaporize into the repeated nothingness, or how her bladder could so willingly follow.

The puddle was an angry yellow against my immaculate white leather. Eve finally pulled over, and the sound generated by the rumble strips on the shoulder overpowered her continuing cussing.

She flew from her seat and popped my trunk. She opened the bags and furiously rummaged until she felt what she was looking for. She opened Muriel's door and held out her hands.

"I'm not mad, I promise. Please come out and let me take care of this." Muriel saw an enraged barbarian at her window, threatening violence. She didn't budge. Eve thought she was speaking gently, but in reality, her tone was closer to what Muriel perceived.

"It's okaaay," Eve cajoled. "I'm sorry, okay? I didn't mean to get upset."

Muriel's mind downshifted into first gear, and then it parked. She could no longer hear what Eve was saying because she was floating backward in time. Sandra was a little girl and had pooped her pants at a neighborhood picnic in the state park. Sandra was squeezing her legs and dancing and pleading for someone to take her to the bathroom, but everyone was distracted by potato salad, light beer, and shirtless volleyball.

When Sandra finally let her bowels go, Muriel was mortified. She scooped up her child and brought her straight to the restroom, stripped her naked, tossed her soiled clothes in the sink, poured in as much pink soap as she could flick out of the dispenser, and scrubbed the stains. Hard. Sandra stood there bawling, terrified, embarrassed, and bruised where her leg had banged against the bathroom door. A moment later, she was also plopped into the adjacent sink and scrubbed even cleaner than her spotless undies. Muriel didn't utter a word. When she was done, she wrung out the clothes, asked her daughter if there was any more poop on its way, and then re-dressed her. The whole process took less than five minutes. Within half an hour, the afternoon sun fully dried both the garments and evaporated the hard feelings, and Sandra was restored to her perch on the tree stump, blowing bubbles with her friends.

Muriel felt one of those bubbles land on her arm. She looked to her right. Eve was tapping her, prompting her to get out, but she was still afraid of the maniac. She was safe within my confines, despite the smell and the dampness in her crotch that was spreading around her buttocks. She couldn't imagine what Eve might do to her. Muriel was too old to get scrubbed in a campground sink.

"Pleeease, Muriel . . ." Eve continued to beg. After a protracted minute, Muriel finally recognized that we had stopped. She had no idea how long she had been sitting in her own wet, but the pieces slowly came together as she listened to Eve's words, which were softer now and could even be described as kind. Eve wasn't a lunatic; she was trying to help. She'd kept a towel from one of the hotels and it was already in use, soaking up murky urine before it reached my carpets. Muriel didn't even know she was standing until warm air pushed against her from a passing truck.

Whoosh.

The towel was saturated and Eve was disgusted, but she fought to appear calm. She threw the towel into the nearby ditch and returned to the trunk to rummage. Finally, she procured an adult diaper and a pair of gray sweatpants.

"Put these on."

"Where?"

"Here."

"Oh, I don't think so."

"You can't wear your wet pants in the car—you'll ruin the seats."

"I'm not going to strip down to nothing on the side of the road!"

Eve pictured Muriel roaming the streets of Kingsland in a bedsheet two nights prior.

"Just . . . just go in front of the car door. Nobody will see. The door will block the view and I'll block from the other side."

Muriel didn't move.

"You have a better idea?"

Muriel couldn't think of a better idea and she didn't want to stay on the side of the road until she was dry. There were no rest areas nearby, and an endless barbed-wire fence stretched across the length of all the nearby fields, preventing any access to modesty. "Fine," she muttered. She went to the front of the car and placed the clean sweatpants on the hood. She took off her shoes, being careful not to step on anything sharp. She proceeded to take off her sodden pants and underwear.

At that moment, an eighteen-wheeler whizzed by, blaring an obnoxious horn. Muriel was only a foot away from my hood and the car door, but the truck had a clear view of her white buttocks as she bent over to remove her garments.

"You shut the hell up!" Eve yelled at the truck, her voice obliterated by the slipstream before reaching human ears.

"Do you still have that towel? I want to wipe up a little." Muriel spoke with her head down low, not looking at Eve. The soaked towel wasn't an option, and Eve returned to the trunk to find something else. She found one of her mother's shirts bearing an image of Jesus with the words *Our Lord in Heaven* in a crescent of calligraphy. Muriel used it to fully wipe her genitals dry.

Another truck bleated.

"Um, let's get your sweats on," Eve urged.

"So he got a show, big deal," Muriel snorted. She decided to be amused instead of unnerved, and I heard her thinking, *One moment you're drinking grape soda and sharing stories about your husband, and then you're on the side of a highway cleaning your crotch with Jesus on a T-shirt.* Muriel pulled herself together and returned to the scene of the crime. I was dry to the touch, but the odor remained prevalent.

"We'll stop at the next exit and get some cleaning wipes," Eve said, closing my door after Muriel was secure. She held Muriel's fine linen pants, with the underwear still inside, by a tiny belt loop with her quivering fingertips. She was surprised by their urine-laden weight, as if Muriel had expelled a full coffeepot of fluid into the fabric. Eve didn't know what to do. She wanted to wash them as soon as possible, but she didn't want to stop for laundry. Everything was already taking too long. She also didn't want to put the corrupted items back in the trunk, where the polluting stench might infect their other clothing, but the tag on the pants read *Saks Fifth Avenue* and she wasn't keen on throwing away something of such quality. Finally she made a choice: Eve pretended to put everything back, but she tossed the saturated pants and undies on the ground beneath my trunk, figuring Muriel would never know. Eve waited until there was a broad clearing in the traffic flow, and then we rumbled back onto the highway and quickly resumed a comfortable speed.

"Kicked 'em under the car, did ya?" Muriel asked, looking at my passenger's mirror. "G'bye pants!" She giggled, and Eve frowned.

We drove in silence to the next exit. Eve parked at a grocery store, lowered the windows, took the keys, and left Muriel in the lot while she fetched antibacterial cleaning cloths and a package of cashews. She reached into her backpack to pay with cash from the FloridaTrust envelope. She found one hundred dollars. She quickly flipped through the other pockets of her bag in a panic, but it was clear that the only money in her possession was a tiny grouping of five $20 bills. She broke a twenty and returned to the car with the wipes and nuts.

"Muriel, where's the money?" she asked, glaring.

Muriel looked at Eve and saw her crossed arms, tight face, and tapping foot. The barbarian was back.

"What?" Muriel replied quietly.

"The money. Where is it?"

"You need my credit card?"

"No, we're not using credit cards. Where's the cash?"

"Oh, I don't have any cash," Muriel said. She looked down, found her purse by her leg, and lifted it onto her lap. Eve grabbed it from her and opened it.

"Hey!"

Eve ignored her and started going through it. Makeup, a small sewing kit, a package of stamps, a sombrero magnet from South of the Border, an old letter, and her Louis Vuitton wallet. She opened the wallet. The credit cards remained, the photos of the grandkids remained, and the section for cash contained a five-dollar bill and three ones.

"Oh god," Eve said.

"Give it," Muriel said, waving her hands toward herself.

"Muriel, this isn't funny. I need to know where you put the money."

"What money?" Muriel asked with another prompting motion. Eve handed the purse back and Muriel found the eight dollars. "Is this it?" she asked, holding the bills up in a fan.

Eve turned around and cried out. She spun around again.

"No! No, that's not it! We had over three thousand dollars!"

"We did?"

"Yesss," Eve hissed.

"Where did we get that kind of money?"

Eve threw the bag of cleaner and nuts on my back seat and brought her face right next to Muriel's inside the passenger window. Her expression was taut and she spoke slowly and with extreme precision: "We went to the bank and I took out my life savings in cash. We spent about three hundred dollars so far and the rest was in the envelope."

"The envelope," Muriel repeated.

Eve pulled out the white envelope with *FloridaTrust* printed on the side. She showed Muriel what remained.

"That's not enough?"

"No, it's not enough. There was a lot more in here," Eve growled, her voice entering its lowest possible register. She left the side of the car and opened the trunk. For the next ten minutes, she carefully and methodically went through every inch of their belongings in all the nooks and crannies of my cargo hold. Satisfied the wad of money wasn't in there, she made her way to the driver's side and pulled up the seat. She scoured the floor and the back, and she was quickly reminded by the odor that we were in this parking lot to clean up Muriel's spill. Muriel was working on the glove compartment.

"Is it in there?"

Muriel shook her head.

"I have to check under your seat. Can you get out?"

Muriel obliged, and Eve visually scoured the remainder of my interior to no avail. She moved over to the passenger seat and checked the contents of the glove box herself. It was then that she had a thought . . .

"Muriel, you didn't put the money in your pockets, did you?"

Muriel checked her pockets. "These aren't my pants."

"No, in your real pants. The blue ones."

"The blue ones?"

"The ones you just pissed in?"

"Oh." She looked down and didn't respond. She put her hands in the pockets of the sweat pants again. She'd never worn sweatpants before, and she found them to be exceedingly comfortable.

"Is it possible you took the money and put it in your blue pants?"

"My blue pants?" Then, after a moment of consideration, "money goes in the purse," said the woman who had once put her laundry detergent in the refrigerator next to the eggs.

"But are you sure?"

Muriel scrunched her face. She wasn't sure of anything.

A wave of fatigue crashed over Eve. She tried to remember the sequence of events involving their money that day. After buying another quick lunch and grape soda, she'd grabbed forty dollars from the envelope and gone inside the gas station to prepay for fuel. All the money was there when she did that only a few hours earlier. So where was it now? She reached into her pocket, and the remaining change from their lunch was still there. She looked under her seat again and found nothing. She checked her bag and the envelope again. She checked Muriel's purse again. She was caught in an unceasing loop of checking and rechecking and re-rechecking, with the faint hope that the money might magically reappear on her fourth or fifth or maybe her tenth try.

Muriel continued to stand in the parking lot, checking and rechecking her two soft pockets.

Eve watched her and finally understood what had happened: Eve had left the envelope behind when she paid for the gas. She left it in her bag, with Muriel. Muriel saw the tight stack of bills and must have thought it was dangerous to leave the cash in a visible, vulnerable place—anyone could walk off with the bag, after all. Muriel had erroneously assumed that Eve kept a good amount of money with her in her pockets, so she instinctively grabbed what she thought was the rest and stuffed it in her own pockets, as well.

And then Muriel forgot about it.

Before Muriel had her accident, her wrist grazed her pants. She felt the padded wad and mistakenly assumed it was a diaper. Feeling secure, she allowed herself to drift into the nap.

Eve had been squeamish about touching Muriel's soaked pants, had barely looked at them, and never considered venturing into the dripping-wet pockets. She never felt the cash, and had assumed the extra weight of the pants was due to the liquid and not their stash.

Eve returned to the trunk and checked the pockets of Muriel's other pants, but she only found a few wadded tissues and an unwrapped hard candy. She looked out toward the highway. They had to go back. The pants could still be there.

Before she allowed Muriel to get back in the car, Eve took ten seconds to wipe down my seats. The stench disappeared, and I was unscathed. Eve silently cheered the small victory as we returned to the highway and headed south. We traveled a few miles to the next exit, scooted over the bridge, and resumed traveling north, slowly, in the right-hand lane. Eve scanned the side of the road for our corrupted, folded fortune. She figured it would be simple to spot the flash of blue near the rumble strips, but she couldn't locate the treasure. A few minutes later, we were back at the first exit for Petersburg again. She exited, and we repeated the entire loop.

"You look to the right and I'll look to the left this time," Eve said, thinking the wind might have blown their bounty across the road.

"Okay," Muriel responded. "I'm looking."

Eve drove even slower the second time. Nothing.

"Oh god."

"Try again."

"Oh god."

Muriel wanted to put her hand on Eve's shoulder, but she feared Eve might bite it off and spit it out the window.

We took a third lap and went one exit further. Eve drove on the shoulder of the highway the entire time, at a low speed with the hazards on. The rumble strips chewed on my tires and I shook, but Eve ignored my distress while she scanned the landscape like a science fiction cyborg, dividing the world into a grid and identifying every object within the squares. The road was immaculate. Where other parts of our journey had presented us with tossed cups and plastic bags, dead rabbits and other flattened creatures, torn tires, occasional bumpers, and even a few piles of shattered glass, this stretch held nothing but a paltry collection of cigarette butts and one banana peel, still yellow and unspotted. Eve considered that the powerful winds generated by passing trucks could have blown their articles up against the fence, but it was also clean. The pants were gone, the money was gone, and all of Eve's hopes quickly followed.

Before exiting again, Eve noticed a blue sign with a simplistic graphic of a colonial building floating over bold white letters:

>*Highway Maintained by*
>*Petersburg Chamber of Commerce*
>*Drive Safely*

The sign was a tombstone and its words an epitaph. In the few moments following Eve's littering, she imagined that one of Petersburg's chamber members had been traveling I-95 and discovered our debris. Taking it upon himself to retrieve it, he scorned the loser who had dropped her soiled trousers on the street, only to be rewarded with a magnificent cash bounty for his efforts. A couple thousand dollars goes a long way toward cleaning the urine off one's hands. Eve imagined the guy telling his friends about it at a dinner party furnished with filet mignon and lobsters purchased with his karmic reward.

Or maybe a chamber member resembling her mother had discovered the foul treat. She would use the story as an example of God's benevolence and educate others on their civic duty to remove objects from the road with frequency and care. Maybe she would donate the money to her church to fund an operation called Clean Pants from Heaven that clothed the poor.

It was also possible that a trucker or any random wanderer had simply stopped and grabbed the slacks. *Hey, free pants! What the . . . pee? But then what's this . . . ? Cash!!*

Eve miserably entertained these thoughts instead of confronting our newest and biggest problem: we didn't have any money. We had enough gas and could buy a little more to get up the road, but then what?

Eve pulled off the exit and returned to the parking lot by the grocery store. Her anger toward Muriel had been replaced by a tired agony. It was all too confusing. *Why did Muriel do that?* Eve wanted to talk to Laura. And Liam. She even considered a conversation with her mother. She tried to pretend that—maybe, somehow, perhaps—the money wasn't in those blue pants after all. She looked around, and I could feel her wondering if she should try to tear me apart and search again. And then again, and then again.

"Muriel?"

"Yes?"

"I think we're in trouble."

"Oh no." Muriel checked her purse and showed Eve the eight dollars. Eve shook her head and Muriel put the purse away.

"Where are we?" Muriel asked, looking around.

"We're in Petersburg, maybe five hours from New York." Eve slowly released what felt like a gallon of air, and Muriel watched her deflate. "I thought we could stay there tonight, but the Caddy won't make it with what we've got left."

I liked when she called me that. And when she patted my dashboard.

Suddenly Muriel turned her head and gave Eve her full attention. "New York City?"

Eve nodded.

Muriel responded excitedly, "What time is our flight?"

Eve ignored her. "And even if someone gave us some gas money we won't have a place to stay, and if we use your cards they'll find us."

"Then we'll stay with Petersburg," Muriel said with a strange air of satisfaction, as if all our problems were solved.

Eve considered the idea, but it didn't make sense to finally escape from Florida, only to be stranded in Virginia. Virginia was not the destination. Everything was falling apart in Virginia, and Eve boorishly decided she hated the place, even with its spectacular green hills and perfect blue sky. Assuming Lem had already canceled the credit cards, it suddenly dawned on Eve that without the magic envelope, we couldn't go home, either. Someone was going to have to come up from Florida to retrieve us. *Without funding, it's impossible to do anything*, she realized. We were trapped. Paralyzed. Virginia was a bust. Everything was a bust. Eve couldn't imagine how she had been so irresponsible with the money and failed to realize just how important that little envelope was. *Where was it?*

"He's got a great place," Muriel continued.

"What?" Eve focused on her babbling companion.

"Petersburg."

"What about it?"

"We can stay with Petersburg."

"We don't even have enough cash for a hotel."

"That's why I'm saying we'll stay with Petersburg," Muriel emphasized.

"I don't want to stay here!"

"Neither do I!" Muriel's voice was also rising. "So drive to the city and we'll stay with Petersburg!" Muriel tapped her forehead forcefully, suddenly realizing her error. "Shoot! Not, not—I hate . . ." She tapped again with mild violence and then looked directly at Eve. "I mean—Peter. We'll stay with *Peter!*"

Eve and Muriel were equally exasperated that a simple lost syllable could so easily decimate a concept. Eve spoke slowly, "Who's Peter?"

"Sandra's ex-husband Peter lives in New York."

"And you know him?"

"Yes."

"And you know how to find him?"

Muriel's enthusiasm waned. "Well, I've been to his apartment," she said meekly.

Eve knew her stats on New York City: there were nearly two and a half million apartments, and hundreds of thousands of them changed hands every year. "Do you know Peter's last name?" she asked, casting a thin line into the murky water.

Muriel struggled. She knew it started with a *C* or a *K*, but probably a *C*. "Camden. No, that's not it. Cali. Calding. Cully . . ."

Eve sat still while Muriel continued to generate words that started with the letter *C*. Afraid to move, speak, distract, or even cry, she focused intently through my windshield on a steady stream of shoppers. Some were there to grab a quick prepared meal, and others were loading up their carts to feed their families for a week. Every stranger had a personal story and a unique set of bonds, like the spouses choosing the right fish for their dinner party or the bored children who suddenly ignited when they hit the cereal aisle. Eve realized most of the people in the store were probably strangers to each other; even the face of Eve's friendly cashier was already lost to her.

Eve also started to realize that she rarely paid attention to anyone beyond her immediate purview. She never took the time to really think about anyone else. She viewed life through the small end of a paper-towel tube, but while facing that one insignificant store for only a few minutes in contemplative silence, something broadened, and she began to see people the way I see them. She saw the unceasing magnitude of their needs. She saw their unlimited capacity for story. She felt the chaos of their intersecting objectives, and in that new mindset, she was suddenly overwhelmed. The store had but a few dozen people and New York City had eight million more, including one guy whose name was Peter *C*-something.

"Catcher . . . Calder . . . Concord . . ."

Eve slid the key back in my ignition. We drove out of the parking lot and continued north without a plan.

***

Lem continued to work, seeking solace in the routine of managing accounts, qualifying loans, and replacing the pens in the ATM vestibule. Monday was Shock, Tuesday was Trauma, but now it was Wednesday, the day when Muriel and Eve would certainly come home. And if not, then tonight, after work, he was going to take charge. He was done with Judith infringing on his jurisdiction—it was time for him to alert the authorities and post "Muriel Worth and Eve Harvick" on every highway sign and milk carton in the country.

Lem was typically even-tempered, and he prided himself on the good rapport he shared with his staff. "Good mornings" were always returned in kind, but for two days he had wanted to scream, "Do you have *any idea* what's going on?" and shout, "How would you feel if someone stole *your* mother?!" His inability to confide in his coworkers, whom he mistakenly considered his friends, added black olives of stress to Lem's seven-layer dip of anguish.

And his toe was killing him, too.

He sat in his office and elevated his foot, balancing it on the edge of the desk with his heel to reduce the pressure. He pressed the *I'm Feeling Lucky* button on his browser and took an impromptu point-of-view roller coaster ride, found a recipe for empanadas, and discovered a website featuring Brazilian baby monkeys. He wanted to smile at their cuteness, but nothing could distract from his angst.

Lem was seven years old the first time he went to sleepaway camp in the Adirondacks. During his first night, he was vividly alert and unable to sleep amidst the screeching crickets and burping frogs. He spent hours tracing the metal mesh pattern of the bunk above his bed, illuminated by the central flagpole's eternal, buzzing light, which strobed with a whirl of mountain insects longing for daylight's warmth. Camp was nothing like home, where his real bed and a bevy of stuffed animals suffered without him. He telepathically apologized to each one of them and cried quietly into his elbow. Lem missed his mommy.

Sitting at the bank four and half decades later, he missed her again with a similar physicality. His abdomen and lungs were tight, and his throat felt constricted, even after he loosened his tie. But there were also new aches in strange places, like the tops of his ears. And, of course, his infernal toe repeatedly stabbed him every time he shifted or flexed his foot.

"Mr. Worth?"

He scrambled to restore order to his stretched limbs, and he minimized the baby monkeys on his screen. "Hi Danielle, what's up?"

"Mr. Denton is asking for information about his wife's private account." She looked over her shoulder at the service area and whispered, "He thinks she's having an affair."

Danielle attracted drama, even at a boring, mauve-colored bank.

"You can't give him access unless he becomes an authorized user with her consent," Lem said at full volume. "In writing."

"I know, and I told him that, but he's . . . very upset."

"It is *illegal* for you to tell him *anything* about her personal accounts. No balance, no transactions or deposits, nothing. It doesn't matter if they're married. This isn't 1950, Danielle." Lem's eyes blazed with power. "Maybe you need me to tell him?"

"No, no. I already explained all that, but he's *really* upset," she reinforced.

"I'll come out." Lem lifted himself and winced.

She held her hand out like a crossing guard. "No, Mr. Worth. I'll take care of it. It's fine. I'm sorry I bothered you."

"No bother. Let me know if I'm needed," Lem reassured her, resettling himself.

She left, and Lem clicked on the security camera access to verify that Mr. Denton didn't look like the kind of person who might bring an automatic weapon into the bank. Anything was possible. He knew Danielle had come to him so Mr. Denton would believe the verdict was coming from a higher-up. People thought tellers were stupid, or worse, malleable. Mr. Denton left the bank, but the only thing he shot was a grinding look at Lem through the glass.

The discussion triggered a new thought in Lem's mind: the accounts! If the police could use Muriel's financial movements to locate her, then Lem could do that, too! His heart raced while his mind trumpeted a thunderous *duh!* He audibly cursed Judith and switched from the baby monkeys to the mainstay banking program. He shot into Muriel's account histories.

And there it was.

Muriel had withdrawn cash from two separate accounts at his very own branch. Lem went into Eve's account, relishing his authority, and saw her personal withdrawal. The timestamps between the transactions were within minutes of each other. *Mom must have been right there in the parking lot!* his mind howled. He remembered his brief encounter with Eve. *That little bitch!* Lem scanned all of the accounts and saw nothing unusual before or after the withdrawals. There were no purchases or transfers to friends in other places, and nothing indicated that Eve or Muriel had stockpiled a reserve of cash beforehand. Lem quickly calculated the sums they had withdrawn and deduced they could be anywhere. They even had enough to fly to another country. He was surprised his mother knew her PIN, but he decided to ignore the inconvenience of her complicity, opting instead to presume Eve's dastardly coercion.

Lem's adrenaline rush met with his partially digested lunch and triggered an immediate need for the restroom. He stood up, and the pain once again pierced his toe. "Dammit!" he yelped as he limped across the lobby and offered a small pretending-to-be-normal wave to the tellers. While he relieved himself, more thoughts swept across his mind: Eve's full cashing out of her account was troubling. It could indicate she wasn't planning to return. His forehead squeezed and creased.

There was nothing he could do about his sweaty armpits, but as he washed up, he drew a cold paper towel across the back of his neck and splashed his face. He felt like piano wires were holding his brow taut. He looked in the mirror.

This was a tired man, a man with sixty extra pounds hanging over his belt and a few more pulling on his jowls. Despite living in Florida, this man was very pale. Lem looked at his eyes. They were the same, but the surrounding flesh had become a gray areola stamped vigorously in the corners by a baby crow. He also saw other marks, deep in the flesh, that resembled disintegrating concrete. He saw flaccid bulges and laden droops. *How did this happen?* He focused more deeply into the mirror, pupil to pupil. *But you're still a kid. You still have the dreams of a child.*

He generally felt young, even with two nearly grown kids of his own. *No, Mr. Worth, you are fifty-one years old and you are fat and unhealthy and this is exactly what that looks like.* Lem couldn't remember when the man in the mirror had swallowed what he remembered himself to be. He couldn't remember the physical benchmarks between twenty and thirty, or even forty. He grabbed his gut and chastised its imperceptible expansion, forgetting the thousands of pizzas, cookies, shakes, burritos and beers he forced it to absorb. The belly was a wellspring and marker of his aging and stasis and he wanted it gone, but with his bad toe, he literally couldn't stand the pain of exercising. Lem felt his bicep. The once hard parmesan was now ricotta. In college, he had a physique as lean and chiseled as the plastic army men he played with as a child, but now he resembled the fat walrus plushie he clutched in his childhood bed.

He returned to his face again and studied the unsightly bumps, cratered pores, and sunspot freckles. Stray hairs sprouted like wild grasses from his ears; white stalactites poked from the caves of his nostrils. He used to pluck between his eyebrows and now saw that the broad lawn growing there was overdue for a mowing. He wondered how his wife could stand him. He saw a man his mother would never invite to a dinner party.

Lem returned to his office and clicked from Eve's accounts back to Muriel's. He was about to expand the screen of baby monkeys, but something caught his eye. Something was different. He blinked and clicked refresh and verified he was looking at the right account as he scrolled down. His self-deprecating bathroom break had lasted less than ten minutes, and in that time, Muriel Worth had four new pending charges from Target, Qdoba Mexican Grill, BP Eastern Petrol Corporation, and the

Baltimore County Savings Bank of Rossville, Maryland, 21236. The last entry was a significant withdrawal.

Lem picked up the phone and dialed the police.

***

We were through most of the Baltimore traffic when Muriel and Eve decided to make one last attempt at securing supplies. Eve popped the credit card into the bank lobby's ATM, fully expecting it to suck up the card, drop the iron gate, sound the siren, and send her to prison. Instead it prompted a PIN, and moments later she gleefully returned with a fresh stack of twenties and some new pens. They topped off my fuel (which I was doing my best to sip), then hit up the store for one more box of adult briefs (uncontained liquids would never touch my interior again), a few more pairs of sweatpants (Muriel now loved them), and enough caffeinated drinks to last the remainder of the journey. Eve also bought two pillows, anticipating a long night under my protection if they couldn't find some guy named Peter in New York City.

They stopped for some fast food and Muriel ate very little, but Eve overindulged. The Tex-Mex quelled her hunger, but combined with the stress of the day, the long ride, or possibly the combination of sour cream and soda, a rest area quickly became necessary. Muriel had already used the restaurant restroom while Eve scarfed down her quesadilla, and she insisted she was fine despite Eve's counter-insistence. Eve's need was too urgent to quibble over, so she left Muriel with me, but without the keys or money.

"Stay." Eve winked, and Muriel crossed her heart.

As Eve's slender silhouette disappeared into the facilities, Muriel sat still—her *modus operandi* post-Ira. No one who saw her sitting there, motionless as marble, could imagine the swirling parade of colorful thoughts flying through her mind. I felt them darting about like manic circus performers competing for her attention.

In Muriel's mind, Eve was a tightrope walker at risk of a perilous fall. She had to get to the other side. There was no turning back. Lem was there, too, uncaged and circling, loose in their new wild with his rapid pulse and dark heart. He was capable of anything, and their heads were in his jaws, ready to be snapped and consumed. Or maybe he was the trapeze artist, a thousand miles away on the other side of the chasm, waiting to capture and bind Muriel to him with his ferocious grip. But she knew he was really the ringmaster, in charge of every element and waiting to collect the entirety of her fortune at the gate. He ran the show and was surrounded by clowns like Cindy who seemed innocuous while they amused themselves, but who were also capable of terrifying tricks.

Muriel closed her eyes. The circus wasn't real. In real life, people don't explode out of cannons and animals don't dance. In real life, Lem was at the bank, attempting to put on a brave face while he grappled with her absence. Muriel wondered if it was Thursday. Every Thursday, Lem entered her room with a greasy pizza that he ate by himself while she berated him for taking away her life. Why did he visit her and endure her tirades? To show his love? To assuage his guilt? To provide care like the good son he professed himself to be?

For a moment Muriel felt Lem's pain, and she began to wonder if maybe, perhaps, in some small corner of the circus tent, it was possible that he wasn't really her enemy. She had enjoyed many years of accumulating, and downsizing was a natural counterpart to that, later in life. There was no getting around the fact that one day Muriel would die, and "coffins don't have pockets," as her mother used to say. Things had to go. Lots of things. Such a task required outsourcing and muscle, and Lem had stepped up, albeit as an unhired manager—but if not Lem, who else? A stranger? The government? Ira was gone, and Sandra was busy with her own life up north. Maybe, perhaps, in another small corner of the tent, Lem was the best option.

But Lem also lied. Muriel couldn't imagine that her resistance to change had been so great that his astonishing levels of deceit had been necessary to circumvent it. He'd fabricated a grim scenario involving a broken seawall and scared her into believing she had to leave her condo before it collapsed into the ocean. When she wondered why her neighbors stayed, Lem had explained that the higher floors had priority in case the elevators failed. He had an answer, a lie, for everything. She had scurried to The Deerwood, and Lucy had been so kind to help her unpack and sort her things, but many of her possessions were missing, sent to a mysterious storage locker until her apartment was fixed.

One day, Lem told her the seawall had, in fact, failed. The building had been demolished. She would have to wait until they built a new one, but because of the slippery land, it could take years, maybe a decade. In a strange twist of fate, her storage facility also succumbed ... to a sinkhole. Lem even manufactured some tears when he laid that whopper down—he was a true master at his craft. And supposedly the news channels were paid off to keep both incidents hushed, or she was watching the wrong channels at the wrong times. Everything was implausible, but through the gaslighting and deflections, he'd convinced her that she was a survivor and that she could relax in the safety of The Deerwood because it was inland. Everything she really needed in her life was spared, including me, her precious car. She was lucky and she should be thankful. When she asked about her neighbors, Lem assured her they'd all managed to move out in time, and he promised to collect their new addresses when work calmed down a little. But by that time she was on the medication; time slowed and the days repeated themselves until she no longer remembered to ask.

Lies.

All of it.

Singer Island was fine and everything was in its place. Frank was ever-attentive at his post. When Eve and Muriel had walked out of the lobby, arm in arm, she'd glanced over her shoulder at the tennis court. Ira once hit a miraculously hard ball that got stuck near the top of the high chain-link fence and continued to weather a decade of ocean-charged storms without budging. There it remained—it was only Muriel's world that had crumbled and scattered, blown away by the words from Lem's lips and the ink in his pen.

Cindy came for a visit once, sporting one of Muriel's "lost" and favorite bracelets, the one with the Mexican opals. That's when Muriel decided she'd had enough. This was her tent! This was her show! *She* was the ringmaster of her own life and mind! Maybe she wasn't the fresh potato chip she used to be, but that didn't automatically render her a moldy crumb at the bottom of the bag. She may have lost her husband, her home, her friends, her property, and maybe even a few brain cells along the way, but Muriel was still here, and Muriel was still Muriel.

The only way from the bottom is up, and Muriel suddenly opened her eyes and bolted upright to physically embody this idea. There was *always* more to learn, more to do, and more to enjoy. Eve was at the very beginning of her self-empowered life, and Muriel could be, too. She still had potential. She still had power. And because Lem had begrudgingly capitulated, *Muriel still had her car!!*

I was cheering at this point, so proud of my dear friend's long-overdue epiphany, and I wish I could have honked my own horn or flipped my lights on and off. Eve had left her phone charging through my cigarette lighter, and maybe my 1976 hardware isn't exactly calibrated for the sensitive nuances of new technology, but in that moment, perhaps by chance, the screen turned on and caught Muriel's attention. Muriel opened the phone to reveal a long exchange of messages with Laura.

As Muriel read the thread backward, she smiled at her discovery. Laura was doing what she could to help, and she could be trusted. Channeling her newfound re-empowerment, Muriel decided to call her granddaughter to see if she was in touch with her cousins and happened to know Peter's whereabouts in New York. And his last name.

Muriel shook her head rapidly from side to side, stimulating the blood flow so she could remain fully engaged. She knew Lem might be there, on the ledge of his trapeze platform, hovering and waiting for the magic moment when he could swoop in and capture her. But he was only part of the act, and Muriel was in control. He couldn't catch her if she was even a little bit . . . slippery. If Lem wormed his way in and took control of the conversation, then Muriel would talk to him the same way he talked to her.

She would lie.

***

Lem, Cindy, Judith, and Laura sat in the Worths' broad living room, directly across from officers Ron Carroll and Steve McNichols. Cindy had insisted the men enjoy the comforts of her rotating leather club chairs, but neither officer liked the swiveling—it triggered their trained inclinations to contain excessive movement. Still, they sat politely, if a little nervously, with pens and notepads in hand.

Officer Carroll was in his fourth month on the job and looked like a teenager dressed for Halloween. To appear more aggressive and mature, he shaved his head and maintained a bushy mustache, but it only added to the costume effect. Laura thought she recognized him from their high school, and Cindy noted with a pang of silent guilt that he was the first black man to visit her house. She shifted her attention to Officer McNichols, who reminded her of an older Steve McQueen, "the King of Cool," with his furrowed brow, thick wavy hair, and a chest that looked like it could double as a battering ram. She wondered whether he was hairy or smooth and if he'd ever appeared shirtless in a fundraising calendar. Lem was instantly jealous of Officer McNichols, with his extra height, herculean build, and defined jawline. He expected that Officer McNichols had perfect toes, too.

Judith had no thoughts about the uniformed men; instead, she stared at the floor through the glass coffee table. She failed to speak beyond her initial "no, thank you" when Cindy offered her a drink. Cindy caught her small smile, but it flattened when Lem pointed his finger at Judith and said, "Two days ago her daughter stole the family car and took off with my mother."

"That's not exactly true," Judith amended. "That's your version of it."

"Let's start at the beginning. Where did this happen?" asked one of the officers.

"At The Deerwood. That's where my mother lives and where Eve works after school."

"Okay, what are their names?"

"Eve Harvick," Judith replied. "H-A-R-V-I-C-K."

"And your mother?"

"Muriel Worth," Lem responded.

"And you are?"

It took a few minutes before everyone was fully introduced and the relationships were established and recorded.

"All right, let's go back. You said Eve stole the car two days ago? Do you know what time?"

"She didn't steal it," Judith corrected. "They both left together."

"All right, everyone will have a chance to talk, but first we need to know what time the vehicle left the property."

Lem and Cindy looked at each other. Then they looked at Laura.

"Don't ask me," Laura said.

"Somewhere between three and four thirty," Lem said.

"And you tried calling them?"

"They didn't answer at first, but later they sent a text."

Laura scrolled through her phone and told the officers that Muriel and Eve said they were fine, they were taking a drive, and not to call the police.

"She said don't call the police?"

Laura shrugged and flipped the phone screen to them. Officer McNichols scribbled something in the margin.

"And what's the vehicle?"

"It's a white '76 Cadillac Eldorado convertible. The roof is also white and she never takes it down. The license plate is I-R-A-1. Ira's my Dad."

The officers looked at each other.

"That's quite a car."

"It's a classic."

"Is your dad also at The Deerwood?"

"No, he died, but the car was always Mom's."

"So it's registered to her, but the license plate has his name?"

"Yeah, it was kind of a thing between them. She won the car a long time ago, but he said he was the lucky one because he won *her*, or something like that, so she put it on the plate as 'Ira won' but she used the number one because I-R-A-W-O-N is a place in Nigeria, I think she said, so I-R-A-number one."

Laura hated the way her dad stumbled through one of her favorite romantic stories about her grandparents.

"Does your mother still drive?"

"Oh god no!" Cindy chimed in. "Lucy takes her out in the car, usually once or twice a week."

"And Lucy is . . .?"

"Her daytime caregiver. She's been with Muriel ever since Lem put her in The Deerwood."

"*I* didn't *put* her there. *We* moved her there *together*," Lem whispered to Cindy. Then, to the officers, "No, my mother doesn't drive anymore."

"Okay, so we'll assume Eve is doing the driving."

"I was going to get Eve a car of her own, but I couldn't afford it," Judith added.

Lem said "not exactly" with the same cadence Judith used earlier, accompanied with a sneer. Judith didn't feel it was appropriate to register a response.

"Eve's a great driver," Laura added.

"I thought she didn't have a car," Lem huffed.

"Christian let her drive a few times."

"Who's Christian?" asked an officer.

"Hold up—we've talked about this, young lady," Lem cut in. "You know we're not insured for other drivers."

Laura shrank a little and said, "but sometimes she *has to* drive."

Lem stared at her.

"Because . . ." Laura glanced at the officers and then glared right back at her father, but he couldn't read her. Cindy leaned over and whispered in his ear, "Because sometimes Christian and Laura drink at parties, Lem." Lem sat up straight and cleared his throat while Cindy continued for the officers, "Christian is my son, and my children aren't allowed to use the phone when they drive, so sometimes Eve takes over, isn't that right?" Laura beamed at her mother. The officers had stopped taking notes.

Officer Carroll finally spoke. "You said this happened two days ago. Why didn't you call us then?" Everyone looked to Judith, who continued to look at the floor.

"After we got the text, we *all* decided to wait for them to come back on their own," Cindy said. "They said they were fine, and we didn't think it made sense to use up your valuable resources if they went to the beach."

"Two days ago," Officer Carroll said. It wasn't a question.

Cindy blinked.

"For the record, I was against it. I thought that plan sucked," Lem chided. "And I called you when I found out they're in Baltimore, and that's a lot fucking further than Deerfield Beach!"

"How do you know they're in Baltimore?"

"There were new charges on her cards. It just happened."

The officers looked at each other and wrote some more.

"They're not in Baltimore." Laura laughed.

Judith looked up, and Cindy said, "You know something? What do you know?"

"Nothing."

"Then what are you saying?" Cindy demanded.

"Where are they?" Officer Carroll asked, even less gently.

Laura tensed, her shoulders creeping forward more than usual, but she spoke naturally and with her usual quick rhythm. "I don't know, but c'mon, *Baltimore?*"

Laura's assertion was dismissed.

"Ma'am?" Officer McNichols started. "Mrs.----" he flipped through his notes, "Harvick? Do you know where they are?"

"No, not really."

"Is it no, or not really?"

"It's no," she clarified.

A loud voice suddenly crackled unintelligibly on the officers' radios. They listened, one of them shook his head at the other, and they resumed their questioning.

"So basically, Mrs. Worth and your daughter—Muriel and Eve—are on a road trip without your permission, and there's reason to believe they may be somewhere in Maryland. Is that correct so far?"

"No," Lem said, "It's not a road trip, it's an abduction. Eve *took* my mother. She stole the car and took money from her account. Basically, she kidnapped her!"

"Has she asked for a ransom? Has anyone asked you for money or any other material goods or services in exchange for a resolution?"

"What are you—on their side? No, there's no ransom yet, but don't think there won't be!" Lem clasped his hands together and pointed the fleshy wedge at the officers to emphasize his position: "Mom didn't pack any bags, not even her underwear, and Lucy said Eve took her when no one was looking."

"Lucy the caregiver?"

"Yes, Lucy Abendana. A-B-E-N-D-A-N-A."

"Got it. And where can we find her?"

"She's in Jamaica taking care of Albi. That's kind of what started this whole fucking thing," said Lem.

"And who's Albi?"

No one answered.

Finally Cindy broke the silence by offering the policemen a drink.

"No thank you, ma'am," Officer McNichols said for both of them before Officer Carroll had a chance to request an iced tea.

"Eve stole the car and kidnapped my mother," Lem restated, the record scratch returning him to his repeating groove.

"Was your mother . . . was Muriel already in the car when Eve started driving?"

Lem said "Yes," Cindy and Judith said "No," and Laura said "I dunno" simultaneously. The officers put down their pens.

"Lucy left my mother alone in the car and that's when Eve took her."

"Dammit, Lem," Cindy said.

"What?!"

"Don't throw Lucy under the bus!"

Lem glared at Judith while he spoke sideways to his wife: "I don't know what's going on with you and your new friend, Cin, but neither of you seem to get that her daughter committed a bunch of *serious* crimes here. My mother, the money, the car . . . skipping school?"

"Oh for god's sake, it's a silly road trip!" Cindy rose while Judith swallowed her objection at the use of His name. "And after all she's done for us, you want *Lucy* to lose her license?"

"Maybe she won't leave old women alone in their cars anymore!" Lem shot back.

Judith interjected, "Maybe Eve did the Christian thing and went out to check on her, and then maybe Muriel asked her to go for a drive? What if Muriel started this . . .?" She trailed off.

The officers looked at Judith and encouraged her to continue with her story, but she lifted her shoulders, indicating she didn't have anything else to add. Officer Carroll swiveled to face Lem and Cindy. "Is that possible? Could your mother have asked Eve to drive her somewhere?"

"No!!" Lem shouted. "You think a seventy-seven-year-old woman with Alzheimer's is going to ask some punk teenager to take her out on the town? And go where? To get a tattoo?"

"Maybe she offered her some money?" Judith added.

Lem seethed.

Office Carroll said, "All right, it's obvious we don't know exactly what happened, but it doesn't sound like any of you believe there was a struggle involved. It seems more like—like what you said—like they decided to take a trip together."

"But they're *missing!*" Lem continued to shout. "They're *gone!*"

"We're going to check out this Baltimore lead and----"

"They're gone and nobody cares!! Fucking assholes!!"

"Mr. Worth, calm down now!" Officer McNichols stood, and his imposing frame filled the oversized room. Officer Carroll stopped swiveling his chair, Lem stopped grumbling, and the neighbor's dog stopped barking. Officer McNichols resumed speaking, with his hands on his hips and one foot forward in a power stance.

"We're going to see what we can do about locating your mother and your daughter. We'll hold the possibility that this *may* be an abduction until we get more information, but my gut tells me it's, how did you put it? 'A silly road trip.' The negligence on the part of your caregiver will be noted in the report, but with the extenuating circumstances, that's really a matter between you and Ms. Abendana and her agency."

"I meant they're the assholes for driving off, not you guys," Lem murmured.

Officer McNichols nodded and continued, "You need to keep yourselves calm while we figure this out. It's good you called us, and we're here to help."

"Keep ourselves calm? Jesus Christ," Lem muttered.

"*He'll* take care of them," Judith answered Lem with assurance, and she didn't mean Officer McNichols.

"We'll need to speak with Ms. Abendana," Officer McNichols continued. "And Mrs. Worth's case manager at The Deerwood."

"Oh, so . . ." Cindy stammered, "We, uh . . . we haven't exactly told The Deerwood yet." She coughed. Then she beamed at them with a rehearsed smile.

The officers looked at each other and jotted down another note on their respective pads. "The Deerwood doesn't know she's missing? For two days? Who made that decision?" Officer McNichols asked, perplexed.

"It was . . . I think it was mutual, wasn't it?" Cindy asked the room.

Judith nodded yes and Lem shook his head no. Laura abstained.

"I don't understand—do they think she's still in her room?"

"Well, Vivette knows," Cindy explained.

"Who's Vivette?"

"She's on the night staff for The Deerwood."

Officer McNichols sat down again and slowly reviewed his notes. Everyone watched as his mind turned with the pages. Finally he cleared his throat and said, "Okay. Okay." Then he took another long pause and flipped another page back and forth three times. "Okay. As I see it, we don't know if Eve took Muriel, if Muriel took Eve, or if no one really 'took' anyone. They're both presumably somewhere in Maryland, maybe, with the big fancy car, and no one wants The Deerwood to know what's going on because Lucy might lose her job even though you personally employ her. Is all of that correct?"

The group nodded.

Officer McNichols had learned after thirty years on the job that the more information people withheld about an injustice, the more likely they were to be involved in the making of that injustice. The Worth–Harvick Story had holes. He recorded all the conflicting information and used the margins for his theories and impressions. There was a knotted truth mixed in there, but his gut told him the whole incident would resolve itself when the missing ladies returned on their own.

But Officer Carroll was a newly minted product of a generation that expected immediate answers and instantaneous results. "Has *anyone* heard from them since that first text?" he probed.

"No."

"Nope."

"Nuh-uh."

Cindy watched her daughter carefully. Cindy knew how to tap into the mindset of fiercely protective teenaged girlfriends, and she correctly assumed her manipulative daughter had been in touch with Eve the entire time. She remained unconvinced that Laura didn't know anything about Baltimore.

"Give me your phone," she said to Laura.

"Why?"

"Give me your phone, I want to look at it."

Laura didn't move.

"You're hiding something."

"I'm not!"

"Then give it." Cindy held out her palm. Laura unlocked her phone and started pressing on the screen. "Don't do that—give it here, now!" Cindy snapped.

"I'm unlocking it, hold on!"

"I *see* what you're doing!"

"I pressed the wrong code because you're stressing!" Laura cried out.

Cindy snapped at her again, and Laura palmed her the phone with a light slapping sound. Cindy looked at the highly organized screen, every app grouping tightly contained within an alphabetized descriptive folder on the home screen. It was exactly like her phone and the antithesis of Lem's and Christian's, with their disjointed messes of page after unruly page of discombobulated colors. For a moment, she was secretly proud.

Cindy pressed on the Messages app, searched for Eve's name, and found the infamous text from two days prior. There was nothing after that. Cindy scowled. She opened Laura's email app and looked there, too. Nothing. She also flipped through WhatsApp and Instagram and Facebook.

"Anything?" asked Lem.

"No."

"Let me see it."

"I went through it all," Cindy said.

"This is an invasion of my privacy!" Laura said to Officer Carroll.

"You're a minor," he replied flatly, but with a sprinkle of sympathy in his eyes.

Lem held out his palm and Cindy relinquished the phone. Lem looked at the tidy home screen. Bewildered by its structure and logic, he gave up trying to find anything. He turned to the police officers and said, "I think a missing persons whatever-you-call-it has to happen right now. It's been well over twenty-four hours since anyone's seen them, and I'm telling you my mother is in real danger, and *until I hear from her myself----*"

Now I know it sounds impossible, and I've questioned myself over the timing and veracity of what occurred next, but Laura's phone buzzed while Lem was holding it, as if he had employed some actual magic. The caller ID showed a picture of Eve smiling as the phone belted a tune that only Laura and young Officer Carroll recognized.

Lem gasped and nearly dropped the phone twice while trying to answer it with his thick, shaking hands. Before he could start yelling at Eve, he heard the thin, stern voice he longed for.

"Laura? It's your Grams. Laura? Are you there?"

"Mom?" Lem's voice cracked.

There was a pause. The officers looked at each other.

"Lemmy? Is that you?"

"Yeah, Mom, it's me, Lem. I'm on Laura's phone."

"Oh, isn't that funny, I'm on Eve's phone! It's like *we're* the teenagers! Hello, kid."

Officer Carroll motioned for Lem to put the phone on speaker, and he quickly obliged. Some crackling accompanied the broadcast audio, but Muriel was clear enough to be understood.

Muriel continued, "How's everybody doing?"

"Are you kidding me, Mom? We're freaking out and the police are here!"

Both officers cringed when he said that, rebuking themselves for failing to advise Lem to keep their presence a secret.

"The police? Why? What happened? Is Laura okay? Is it Christian?" Muriel sounded genuinely worried.

"We're fine, Grams," Laura called out. "They're just worried about you!"

"Oh! Laura, sweetheart! Hi honey!"

"Hi Grams!"

"Lemmy, why are the police there? Did someone have a fall?"

"Uh, hello ma'am. This is Officer Ron Carroll of the Broward County Sheriff's Office, Deerfield Beach District. I'm here with Officer McNichols and some members of your family. Mrs. Worth, I need to ask you—are you okay?"

"Me? Oh sure, I'm fine. How are you today?"

"I'm fine, ma'am, thank you for asking. Mrs. Worth, we were called here to investigate your recent disappearance."

"My disappearance? I didn't disappear, I'm right here."

"Right, and Mrs. Worth, can you tell me exactly where you are?"

There was another long pause, and Lem bounced his head up and down like a monkey who won a banana. "Here it comes," he muttered.

"We're at the beach," she finally relayed.

"Okay, Mrs. Worth and----"

"You can call me Muriel."

"Okay, Muriel, thank you. Muriel, do you think you can be more specific for me? Do you know which beach?"

"I'm not sure. Hold on, there's a sign."

"Okay, but please don't leave the phone, Muriel."

"Okay mister, um . . . I think I forgot your name."

"Officer Ron Carroll. You can call me Ron."

"Hi Ron. Ron, I don't like to walk and talk at the same time or I can't do either very well. Especially on the sand."

"I understand, Muriel. I'm going to have you walk to that sign in just a moment, but first I need to know something important."

"Yes?"

"Muriel, is Eve Harvick with you?"

"Eve? Of course Eve's here. Who do you think is doing all the driving?"

"Muriel, can you please put Eve on the phone for me?"

"No."

"Did you say 'no'?"

"I did. Eve's taking a swim right now, but I'll have her call you when she's done."

"Oh, I see. Okay. Please have her do that."

"Yes, of course. I'd like to speak with Lem now."

Officer McNichols made a motion with his hands that only Officer Carroll seemed to understand. Then he continued, "Yes, Muriel, I'll put your son back on, but first I want to ask you a question that may sound a little delicate."

"Oh?"

"Please listen to me very carefully: we were told you might have been abducted and are currently being held against your will. Because of this report, I have to believe that even if you tell me you are fine right now, you may not be. So I'm going to give you a code word that you can repeat to me if you are in some sort of trouble. Okay? Do you understand what I'm saying?"

"I think so."

"The code word is 'Thankful.' Muriel, if you are in any sort of trouble, please use the word 'Thankful' in a sentence for me right now, and then I will know that we need to respond right away. Muriel, do you need to use the word 'Thankful' at this time?"

Muriel was silent.

"Muriel?"

More silence. Laura, Cindy, and Judith inched toward the edges of their seats. "Mrs. Worth? Are you there?"

"Yes?"

"Do you need to use the code word?"

"Oh, no. Of course not." Everyone relaxed. "I was trying to think of a sentence *without* that word, and I think I got a little confused if I was supposed to say it or not say it." Muriel laughed. "We're fine, officer. I promise. No codes are needed. Now please put Lem on the line."

"Hi Mom, I'm here."

"Lemmy, why did you call the police?"

Lem coughed and tried to clear the thick paste from his throat, but he was unsuccessful. His voice traveled through it with a quantitative rasp. "Because Eve abducted you and you've been gone for two days already. What was I supposed----"

"Eve didn't abduct me, don't be ridiculous." Muriel emphasized every consonant and the words clicked like a dropped box of tacks. "Did Cindy put you up to this?"

"I'm right here, Muriel," Cindy called out.

"Oh, hi Cindy. Didn't know you were there."

"I'm always here," Cindy said, rolling her eyes. Judith cracked a smile. "Are you and Eve having a nice trip?" Cindy continued.

"Yes, thaaank—I mean—yes, everything is fine," she said, stumbling to avoid the code word.

"Mrs. Worth? Hello? This is Judith Harvick, I'm Eve's mother."

The phone crackled, but Muriel didn't say anything.

"Hello?"

"Hello, Judith," she said, and everyone sensed her apprehension.

"Mrs. Worth, how is Eve? I'm very worried about her."

The officers looked at each other and nodded their heads in silent agreement that if there was actually some sort of trouble or malfeasance, then this is where they would find out.

Muriel hesitated.

"Mrs. Worth?"

"I have to tell you something about your daughter, but I'm not entirely sure you're prepared to hear it," Muriel said.

Judith held her cross to her chest, and her heart thumped beneath it. "Please tell me."

"Okay." Muriel drew in her breath. "Judith, your daughter is the most incredible and wonderful human being. She's truly a remarkable young woman, and you have a lot to be proud of. She knows so much and cares so deeply, and she's an absolutely excellent driver! I can't imagine a better driver. We'll call you later so you can talk when she's done swimming. I don't want to ruin her swim. She really wanted to get in the water again before the sunset."

"Mom, where are you?" Lem asked.

"What?"

"Where are you?" he demanded.

"Oh! I forgot all about the sign! Hold on."

In the ensuing silence, Laura watched her dad. He was shaking. She couldn't understand why he wasn't happy, or at least relieved. He was talking to Grams just like he wanted, and she sounded great. Greater than great, actually, for the first time in years. Laura didn't notice at first that she and her mother were holding hands, but she continued to hold on when Muriel returned to the phone.

"Okay, let's see. Oh right, it's Miami Beach, of course. You know, I don't think I've been here in thirty years. I don't recognize any of it."

"You're only an hour away?!" cried Lem, but Officer McNichols signaled for him to pipe down quickly.

"Miami Beach?" asked Officer Carroll.

"Yes, that's what the sign says."

"Muriel, can you confirm that you're *not* in Baltimore?"

"What? Why on earth would I be there?"

"Ma'am, your credit card showed new charges in Baltimore about an hour ago."

"Oh . . ." There was another strange pause, and then, "I lost the money and we couldn't find it, but I guess someone else did. And I was so worried! You can fix that, right Lem? At the bank? Eve! They found the money in *Baltimore* of all places! Oh, she can't hear me now because she's swimming."

Lem leaned over to the officers and whispered, "She's lying."

"How do you know?"

"Because I'm her son. If she really lost her credit card, she'd be screaming about someone from the Middle East getting on a plane with her identity."

"Muriel? This is Officer Steve McNichols speaking. May I ask you just a few more questions?"

"Okay, what is it now?" she clipped through the cell phone.

"Muriel, nobody here seems to know anything about you and Eve planning this trip together. Can you tell me anything about that?"

"Well, see, that's because it wasn't exactly planned."

"See?" Lem said.

"We both decided we needed to get away for a little while. Everyone needs a vacation now and then, Lemmy."

"We can take you on a vacation any time you want, Mom. All you have to do is ask. You don't have to run away."

"Oh listen to you with your running and hiding like the child who broke the cookie jar?! Nobody *ran away*, Lem. And don't take this the wrong way, son, but I don't want to take a vacation with you. Sometimes a person needs to *get away*. I hope you can understand that."

Lem looked over at the officers. His eyes were wet and pleading.

The officers shrugged.

"Thank you, Muriel. Please have Eve call us when she's done swimming. I'm going to text the number to your phone."

"Oh, okay. I'll tell her."

"Mom?"

"Yes, Lem?"

"Mom, I'm coming to get you. I'll be there in an hour."

There was one last, long pause. No one moved. The ticking of the kitchen clock was audible from two rooms away.

"Now you listen to me, Lemuel David Worth: NO. We're doing fine and we'll be home soon enough, so *shut it down* or I'll tell Eve to drive us somewhere else. I told you we needed a *break*, and *we* will decide when that break is over, so if you try to . . . to . . ."

"To what!?" Lem cried as all the blood in his body moved north of his thick neck.

"Lemmy! Oh dear god, Lemmy, if you *fuck this up* for us, then I'll be very upset and I will never forgive you! Ever!! You hear me, young man? You're going to send your mother to her grave completely pissed off!" Then she shifted gears faster than even I could imagine. "Okay, it was nice talking to everybody. Tell Laura and Christian I love them, I'm hanging up."

"Mom!"

Muriel hung up, and the officers grabbed their hats and notepads.

"Wait, you're leaving? Are we going to Miami? Shouldn't we wait for Eve's call?"

The officers looked at each other and silently determined who would talk. Officer Carroll spoke. "Mr. Worth, you called us here to investigate an abduction and to file a missing persons report, but your mother isn't missing. She said so herself—she's down at the beach with this woman's daughter, and as far as I can tell, the only real issues here are between you and Lucy, and Eve missing some school."

"She is missing school," Judith acknowledged. This was the first time she'd even considered it. "I should call the school."

"Ah, yes, ma'am. You should do that and maybe have Laura here pick up her assignments."

"But . . . but she's sick!" Lem wailed. "You can't take her word for anything!"

"Mr. Worth, there are five other people in this room who heard that phone call, and we gave your mom the chance to let us know if she was in trouble."

"She sounded like a pretty happy lady to me," Officer McNichols said, nodding in agreement.

"But she's *not* happy! That's proof right there that she's in danger! My mother is a miserable person! She's got *Alzheimer's*!" Lem cried.

"Really? She seemed pretty together as far as I could tell. How far along is she?"

"Stage three," Lem replied.

"All right." The officers looked at each other for silent clarification, neither wanting to admit their shared ignorance of the stages. Based on Muriel's side of the conversation, they both assumed it was out of ten, and three didn't seem like a crisis. Their walkie-talkies dispensed another string of nonsensical static that they somehow understood as instructions requiring immediate attention.

"This is crazy!" Lem continued.

"Sir, most people in a managed care situation are unhappy. Cut your mother some slack! Let her have a trip! It's obvious she's being taken care of and she's having a good time. Let her watch the sunset, and then she'll come home."

"But what about the charges in Baltimore?" Lem couldn't relent. The facts swirling around him indicated that Muriel and Eve were safely enjoying nearby Miami, but he felt like he was walking on the top of an oily labyrinth and might slip off into a crevice at any moment. Muriel's call didn't *feel* right, and therefore it *couldn't* be true. They weren't at the beach, and he knew it. They were in Baltimore, or somewhere near it, heading north. Somewhere.

"Cancel the cards and send me the info. We can run a trace, but it's likely whoever took them already got what they needed and tossed them in the dumpster somewhere. Eleven million people had their cards stolen last year. The fraud department at her bank will credit the charges if you report it immediately. We can also provide you with a consumer protection number if you need help with that."

"I run the fucking bank."

"Okay, I think we're done here. Good luck with your mom. Call us if you need us."

"Thank you, officers. Have a nice night," Cindy said cheerfully, closing the front door behind them. For once, there was a situation that was entirely beyond her control, and she felt blissfully free of any responsibility. It wasn't her battle, her drama, or even her problem, when she thought about it. It wasn't her mother or her kid, and she could sit back and watch the show. She empathized with Lem, of course, but Judith's inane calm and her faith in a well-intentioned outcome seemed to placate Cindy as well. For a split second she feared that some of Judith's devout religious energies were rubbing off on her, so she uttered an unnecessary expletive and quickly felt restored. She ventured into the kitchen to continue her work on the lasagna, and Judith followed, surprising them both.

Lem watched them go. Cindy was more interested in layering noodles with Judith than attending to his mood, so he went out on the patio, hoping the tall whiskey he brought with him would do its work quickly. As he watched the undulating turquoise reflection from their pool, Lem quickly succumbed to the comforts of their long chaise with its soft green pillows.

Through the kitchen window, Cindy could see he was sliding toward the unconscious when he wrapped his right arm over his face. She was relieved. She returned her focus to Judith, who silently added more piles of shredded cheese to their dinner.

While Lem drifted and the mothers cooked, Laura retrieved her phone and moved to the corner of the room so she could secretly message Eve. About a year earlier, they had decided to create fake LinkedIn profiles where Laura was a blond, high-powered realtor in Montana and Eve owned a string of Waffle House restaurants in the Southwest. They posted bogus success stories about their imagined clientele and periodically augmented their résumés with bizarre skills, like speaking Lithuanian. They also enjoyed endorsing strangers for abilities such as Baby Blessings, Basketry, or Quality Hydration. They had great fun with it for a while, until they grew bored, but Eve reminded Laura they could secretly message each other through the platform when she sent the interlocking links emoji late on Monday night. Their communication method was also parent-proof: when Laura had pretended to unlock her phone earlier, she had quickly deleted the app before Cindy could spy. When it finally reloaded, she signed in and dashed a message to Eve that her dad was canceling the credit cards.

Laura knew Eve wasn't swimming in Miami because Eve only swam in chlorinated pools. Eve was afraid of sharks and needles and would never go in the ocean. She wouldn't even consider getting in a lake after they saw a movie about a girl who cut her leg on a rock and got an infection that required an amputation. While Laura remained jealous of her friend, mostly because Eve didn't have to deal with trigonometry, she was relieved to hear her Grams sounding so happy. Eve was obviously taking good care of her. Her mother's suspicions were on point, but Laura was allied with her best friend and her grandmother.

Never the parents.

Laura was astonished, however, that the police officers, handsome as they were, were so dense. For one thing, a thief couldn't take cash off a stolen card without a PIN, and this whole Miami Beach ruse was hilarious—it took seven seconds for Laura to look up the beaches near Baltimore and discover that Maryland's Miami Beach Park was only twenty miles from downtown. She smiled. So maybe that wasn't a total lie, but Grams walking in the sand while Eve swam toward the sunset? Laura was pretty sure the sun set on the *west* coast, and she never heard the crash of a single wave.

***

"Feeling better?"

"Yeah. Sorry about that," Eve said, a little embarrassed about the time it had taken her to set things straight. The bathroom at the rest stop was gross, and she felt like she was dragging its reek with her, but Muriel either didn't notice or didn't care. A look of disbelief crossed Eve's face when Muriel offered her the phone. Eve checked the screen and found multiple messages from Laura.

"It's been making that sound ever since I hung up," Muriel said. "I think you're getting some messages."

"Wait, what? You called someone?"

"I told Lem to leave us alone."

Eve wasn't sure how to react. She opted for panic and fear.

"What?! On *my* phone? How? Oh my god—you didn't tell them where we are, did you? Ohhh no . . ."

"I wanted to talk to Laura but Lem was there, so I told him we were at the beach, and I'm pretty sure he believed me because he threatened to drive over and get us. Then I told him to *eff* off." Muriel chuckled, and Eve felt a low heat rise up her back while a simultaneous chill moved down. She thought it might be possible to expel steam from her ears like a cartoon character.

"I . . . you . . . I . . ." she stammered. She was so tired of yelling at Muriel. "This----"

"Now don't get upset."

"Don't get upset?"

"The police were very kind."

"The police?!"

"Oh, you have to call them. I think they texted you their number. I told them you were swimming, but they want to speak with----"

Eve got out. She slammed my door and stormed back toward the restroom, desperate to escape the horror of Muriel's revelations. She made it halfway when her vomit hit the pavement. It was, in fact, some bad sour cream.

"Oh dear," Muriel said, as she watched her companion literally lose it.

Chapter 14

While Richard and Judith were married, she rarely drank. The night he left, she'd downed vodka shots in his preferred crystal tumblers and chased them with the chilled champagne they were saving for their anniversary. The next morning, she'd awoken at the foot of her bed, naked and trapped in a damp ball of sheets and sticky wedding photographs. She discovered a splay of vomit, mostly broccoli shards, on Richard's untouched pillow, and a complementary dry crust on her left foot. She felt like she was wearing a tight hat that wouldn't come off and her stomach was in a bad neighborhood. The remaining half-bottle of vodka sat defiantly on her nightstand, overlooking the smashed glass on the floor below. Judith had quickly decided becoming an alcoholic wasn't for her, and as the rest of the firewater flowed into the sewer lines, she resolved to never drink again. Meeting Christ a few months later had solidified that vow.

Then she had lunch with Cindy Worth.

Judith surmised that showing up drunk to work in a store filled with scissors and hot glue guns was a greater sin than calling in with an emergency excuse, so four minutes after Cindy dropped her at the craft store, an Uber took her the rest of the way home. Debating the public reason, she had opted to complain of the headache she knew was looming—not entirely a lie. Judith was a valued employee and was duly released with the manager's concern.

She sobered up at home, alone, again begrudging Eve for being the only resident of their house who could operate the coffee maker without generating a hot brown river that flowed across the countertop. Judith quickly weighed the reduction in her paycheck from the lost afternoon hours against the expense Cindy had incurred for the coconut shrimp and the unwanted (yet highly enjoyed) beverages. It was a wash. Cindy snapped the rubber band on her wrist for getting drunk. It broke, and she couldn't be bothered to find another.

Judith looked around her house, which was rarely occupied in the midday hours during the week. This was a happy house, she thought as sunlight streamed through a skylight and illuminated her employee-discounted craft-store picture frames with their pleasant Bible scenes: Isaac spared from death at the hands of his father. Moses leading the Israelites through the Red Sea. All the animals standing proudly with their ark under the rainbow. Survivors. All of them. And Judith had survived Richard's exit, too.

Judith liked that her house didn't sprawl like Cindy's, and there was plenty of room for two in her comfortable abode. The couch, a Craigslist find, was plush, and her surfaces were clean and maintained, even without the luxury of a housekeeper. In her life with Richard, they had lived in a four-bedroom, four-bath house with large front and back yards, a formal living room, a separate family room, an additional playroom for Eve and her friends, a home gym, and a library/office where Richard kept the crystal tumblers on his built-in bookcases. There was always work to do, even with expensive weekly help. Downsizing to the townhouse had meant a quarter of the space to manage, with two bedrooms, two baths, and an open living/dining area adjacent to the dated but serviceable kitchen. All the windows were on the near and far walls, and they could occasionally hear the neighbors to their sides, but the HOA mowed the small lawn, there were no toys to put away, and fewer surfaces to dust. It took ten minutes to vacuum.

Judith unlatched her belt, exalting in the release. Still feeling a bit of a buzz from the second Lemonade Chiller, she absentmindedly stripped down and rummaged through her closet for her favorite sweatpants. She couldn't find them, but another pair sufficed. She scrolled through her tops in search of her good sweatshirt, envisioning another quiet evening under a warm-light reading lamp with a soft cotton throw and the Good Book. The sweatshirt was also missing.

Judith knocked on Eve's door before entering, knowing there was no reason yet still feeling obliged. She couldn't remember when she was last in her daughter's room alone, and she studied Eve's walls, feeling the vague guilt of her trespass, as if Eve were a new roommate who'd stepped out for a quick jog. She recognized the poster of Taylor Swift, but Billie Eilish, Ed Sheeran, and Ariana Grande were strangers. Eve's Broadway poster for *Hamilton* was next to the high school bulletin for *Hairspray*, signed by the entire cast and crew. Judith was surprised by the number of travel photos Eve had tacked to her walls: San Francisco, New York City, Japanese gardens, European villages, seaside cliffs, and mountaintop castles, all downloaded from the internet and vividly printed on glossy stock. Eve's desk was neat, her bed was made, and her closet was organized—it slowly occurred to Judith that there wasn't much left in it. She opened Eve's dresser and discovered the top two drawers were empty. Eve had also taken the photo of her father on the beach.

But all of that was Tuesday.

On Wednesday, Judith awoke clear-headed. She messed up the coffee, cleaned it up, and proceeded through another normal day until she got the late-afternoon call from Lemuel Worth to meet the police at his house in half an hour—Muriel and Eve were somewhere near Baltimore. Two hours later, she was inexplicably making a thick lasagna with Cindy.

"I wish we had a pool. Eve's such a good swimmer, but there's too much chlorine at the high school. She lost her cap once and in one afternoon the water turned her hair green," Judith complained.

"Did anyone notice?" Cindy laughed. She never knew which of her quips would be considered insulting, but she saw a slight smile disrupt the flatness of Judith's face. It was safe to continue. "All the kids in Florida are good swimmers."

Judith agreed.

"You know you're welcome to go for a dip here anytime you like."

"No thanks," Judith said automatically, crossing her arms over her chest. "I wouldn't want to impose."

"Impose?" Cindy's eyes gleamed. "What do I care if you swim? You can even go now—Lem's sister left a suit that might fit you. It's clean."

Judith shook her head again, but Cindy's cavalier offer sparked an insight: Judith was social with her church friends, but only at church-sponsored events. She was never invited to private dinners, birthday parties, or even an afternoon coffee, and her work friends were equally non-solicitous. Judith was surrounded by people, but perpetually alone. She was never invited to swim in a pool. Her phone chimed, signaling it was time to leave for the new Wednesday prayer group, but she found herself rooted to the spot beside the granite counter. She was utterly perplexed by her desire to continue talking with the loud woman who usually provoked her, but she couldn't help being drawn to her. Cindy was the only person who seemed to truly notice her.

Judith's fingers reached out to snap a fresh rubber band for abandoning the group, but she didn't pull. Instead, she extended her arms wide and said, "You have a very pretty house. I had a pretty house once. In Cypress Head."

"That's in Parkland?"

Judith nodded, and Cindy was impressed.

"With Richard."

"Ah," Cindy sighed. Seeking to change the subject, she said, "How was your hangover this morning? Took me three Advils to shake it."

"I was fine. I don't take drugs."

"Advil's not a *drug*."

Judith shook her head.

"Oh wow. So you're one of those."

Judith stared at her and Cindy stared back, neither wanting to be the first to avert her eyes and lose the upper hand.

"So what do you do when you get sick?" Cindy probed.

"Rest and get better. The Lord does heal, you know. It's one of His powers."

"And what about Eve?"

"She doesn't get sick," Judith said, surprised at the realization. The last time she remembered Eve having so much as a sniffle was far in the past, and Richard had taken care of her. Judith recalled his tenderness when little Eve was down. He stayed with her all night until her fever broke, dabbing her shiny forehead with a cool cloth. If he saw her twisting with a bad dream, he'd sing quietly and stroke her arms until it passed.

"Eve had strep last summer," Cindy stated. "She didn't go to the beach with us because she was contagious."

"I don't think so."

"I'm sure of it," Cindy replied. "I gave her penicillin from our Mexican stash because she said your insurance was in flux."

"You gave my child medicine without calling me?"

"She said she spoke to you, and like I said, we were practically out the door for Key Largo. Don't you remember? Her voice was scratchy for two weeks."

Judith shook her head vigorously. None of that made any sense. "It must have been one of Laura's other friends," she insisted.

"It was----"

"It wasn't Eve." Judith was adamant, and she crossed the room to retrieve a bottle of water from the fridge. Cindy backed off. Eve went to Cindy when she was sick and not her own mother, and now Judith knew, even if she didn't accept it. What else didn't she know?

"I think it's dangerous to turn your back on modern medicine," Cindy said. "When's the last time you had a mammogram or a colonoscopy?"

Judith frowned. "I'm healthy. I eat well, I exercise and I don't smoke or take drugs or drink—except for yesterday. And that was a mistake."

"A fun mistake, I hope?"

"My body is one of God's many temples and we take care of it together. If I get sick one day and can't recover, then that would be His Will."

"But you *could* recover if you filled a prescription," Cindy bleated. "Why would God create scientists and give them the ability to make medicines if He didn't want any of it to exist? Isn't human progress a part of His Plan?"

"No, that's Satan meddling with our natural lives. God also didn't create pollution—it's one of Satan's byproducts because we try to go faster and farther than our legs will take us."

"But you drive."

"I still have to live in the modern world, but some lines shouldn't be crossed. Humans shouldn't interfere with biology, and medicine stops everything that's natural. They invented all of these drugs to help overweight people who can't process their insulin, but all the drugs do is trick the body into handling insulin spikes that shouldn't be there in the first place. The *real* solution is to stop eating deep-fried powdered donuts dipped in chocolate!"

Cindy tried to follow the logic while Judith continued, "The medicines are really the problem. They make us think we can do anything with our bodies and get away with it. If I drink too much and get a headache, then I'm meant to get a headache from drinking too much. But if I take a pill for it, then I'm telling myself it's okay to drink too much, and it's not. It's all connected to the same faith and belief that if I'm meant to be okay, I'll be okay."

"Okay, I get the headache thing, but diabetes or cancer? That's just stupid," Cindy replied. "Even strep is a big deal—it can spread to your heart and kill you! I think we're lucky we can knock it out with antibiotics. What if Eve died?" Judith returned to her preferred action of shaking her head as Cindy continued, "I also believe in a higher power, you know. I have no doubt there's a universal energy that's bigger than all of us and we're all tapped into it. I think it's great you believe in something beyond yourself, but I don't think taking Tylenol when you have a headache makes anyone less worthy in God's eyes."

"You don't speak for God," Judith rebuked.

"And neither do you."

The women acknowledged their impasse by putting dinner in the oven and proceeding to the island to prepare a stack of veggies for the salad.

"What about Band-Aids?"

"Wounds will heal without them."

"And leave a scar."

"Scars are God's reminders."

Judith was surprised by her own tranquility. She felt unusually self-possessed and relished how she didn't need to raise her voice or blood pressure to get her point across. When Eve challenged her, they typically ended their altercations in separate rooms behind slammed doors, with Eve turning up her headphones so loud the music was audible in the hallway.

Talking with Cindy was different.

Judith's unchangeably erect posture made it difficult for Cindy to tell if the woman was upset, but then she caught a glimpse of a delicate smile tiptoeing around Judith's lips. She allowed Judith to continue her work with the tomato knife, and to talk.

"Cindy, why are you so threatened by my relationship with Jesus Christ? Is it possible you're unsatisfied with *your* life in some way and you're projecting that onto me?"

Cindy's life was wonderful and she appreciated her good fortune. She didn't have to work, and she didn't lack material things, nor friends. Her family was close and generally loving, and her pool didn't break down like the Kirklanders' next door. Muriel was a drag, but nearly everyone she knew had a cranky parent facing a dotage tinged with more rust than gold. It took one second for Cindy to reply.

"No, my problem is not your spirituality. Believe it or not, I'm happy you're happy, for whatever that's worth. My problem is . . ."

"What."

"Can I be frank?"

"Yes."

They both put their knives and vegetables down. Cindy chose her words carefully. "Judith, your religion can affect other people in some very negative ways, and you seem to be completely clueless about that."

"I don't see how—"

"That's my point—you don't see. You don't see that you're not one person who happily found God; you're an instrument for a very powerful religious organization that has mandates for other people and how they should live *their* lives. It's one thing to have your own personal relationship with God, but it's quite another when your group believes it *speaks for God*. You judge and preach and even legislate against anyone who is different, and yes, that's a big fat problem for me."

"But I don't do that. We're all God's creatures and I'm not hurting anyone."

"Your religion persecutes gay people for something they can't control, for being exactly who they are."

Judith looked around to make sure Laura wasn't in the room before whispering, "Look, my husband—my *ex-husband*—chose his own path. If anything, I want to protect him. I don't *want* Richard and all the others like him to go to Hell."

"Just the fact that you think they will *is* the judgment I'm talking about! *You've* decided he's going to Hell!"

"No, Cindy. God makes those decisions. I'm not judging or deciding; I'm only a witness to His actions. You're the one who refuses to look at things the way they are. It's like you want me to tell little children it's okay to jump off a diving board headfirst into a pool with no water, and I'm not going to do that."

Cindy mashed her lips, and her head rocked from left to right, preventing the words behind her true thoughts from escaping. She recalibrated and said, "Okay, okay, Heaven and Hell or whatever—that's after we die. Let's talk about being alive. Do you think Richard should be allowed to marry?"

"He was married."

"I mean to a man."

"Are you kidding?"

"No, I'm dead serious. Should Richard be allowed to marry his boyfriend if they're in love and they've committed their lives to each other?"

"That's ridiculous."

"Why?"

"Because they're men! What kind of a marriage is that? I don't even understand the question—why would they *want* that?!"

"For the same reasons you did. Because they're in love and they want to build a life and raise a family and have all the rights and benefits that you had when you were together."

"But they . . . *can't.*"

"Why?"

"Because it's wrong. The Lord said so, many times. Look at Leviticus and Corinthians."

"The Bible is only a book, Judith. It's not God."

"You know, ignorant people always say that as some sort of defense. 'It's just a book.' And, what? God is 'just an author'? We've got Judy Blume, Stephen King, and, and . . . GOD?" Judith's nostrils flared.

Cindy didn't flinch. "Personally, I think God is in *all* of the authors and painters and, well, everyone, but no, I don't think God sat down one day with his quill and wrote an instruction manual for humanity called the Bible. I think it's pretty obvious that people wrote and rewrote these books over hundreds of years to make sense of their world and to craft some order out of the chaos. The Bible is a collection of political stories that may have been *inspired* by a godly force, but I see it as a complicated series of opinions that have been endlessly edited, and a lot of them contradict each other and don't even make sense in today's world. It's mythology and fairy tales. You know, I also don't believe there was an old woman who lived in a shoe with a ton of annoying children, either."

Judith laughed. Hard. It came out like a disembodied voice in a horror movie, and it even frightened Cindy a touch. "HA-Ha-ha-haa, HA-Ha-ha-haa, oh wow, Cindy. I'm sorry, but you are so wrong!"

"I'm wrong?"

"Oh gosh, when I think about what you're saying, it makes me really sad because you seem like a smart woman. No one sat down with a pen and said, 'What should I write about today? A poem about olive trees or Samantha's vacation to Crete or—oh, I know! I'm going to write *the Bible* and I'll give God all the credit so everyone will take it seriously! This is a great idea and I'm such a fantastic writer no one will even question it! So let's see . . . how should I start . . . in the beginning, um . . . darkness . . . and then some light . . .' I mean think about it, Cindy, that's just crazy. The Bible is *obviously* the word of God."

"Have you read Robin Lane Fox? Or Tony Bushby?"

"You've never heard of a politician manipulating the truth to serve his own agenda?"

"You mean . . . like the Bible?" Cindy said, and Judith dug her hands into her hips so hard that later she would discover brown bruises. "I don't think we're going to convince each other of anything," Cindy finally relented, her voice low.

"I don't understand why you're so invested in disproving what I believe," Judith said plainly.

"Because I think you're a smart woman, too, and I'm frightened when you characterize your opinions as indisputable facts. I'm frightened to live in a country that's so heavily influenced by a group of people who find fuel for their engines in some very narrow fears."

"What fears?"

"Well, you're afraid your ex-husband could marry another man and find happiness there."

"I'm not afraid of that. My heart aches for the children brought up in these perverted and godless houses because they never had a choice, but I'm not afraid of it. There's always hope for all of their souls."

"You said you're afraid of the drama club, too."

"If they did plays like *Godspell* or even *Fiddler on the Roof*, I might feel differently, but *Hairspray*? Boys playing girls? All that overt sexuality? It's too racy for children." Judith shook her head, and Cindy decided it was time to change the subject.

"So . . . so you said something about Eve dating Liam. That's pretty exciting, doncha think?"

"I don't know. I don't know him."

"Do you think they're having sex yet?"

"You! I don't—this isn't!" Judith choked.

Cindy realized she was leaning across the kitchen counter. She took a deliberate step back and relaxed her posture. "Hey, I'm sure they're being smart. You gave her The Talk, right?"

"We talked about boys," Judith said sullenly. "I thought Eve was too young to hear it, but I was worried she might get bad information, so yes, we talked." Raising her eyebrows, Cindy prodded Judith for more details. Judith coughed and said, "I told her to wait, that boys her age had a lot of growing up to do first, and her job was to concentrate on her schoolwork."

"Judith, that's not The Talk."

"She's way too young," Judith protested.

"She's sixteen," Cindy countered. "These girls need to know as much as we can teach them about sex so they're prepared when it finally happens. Sixteen isn't young, it's practically too late! God knows what they're seeing on the internet."

"See, once again—it *doesn't* actually *have* to happen, and the more you tell them about it, the more it becomes okay when it's really not okay. It's like beer."

Cindy shook her head. "Beer?"

"You can't show children pictures of beer and say here's what it tastes like and here's how it makes you feel, but you're not allowed to drink it! It's all those commercials and movies that make them want to drink it even more. But if you don't bring it up or shove it in their faces, then you won't have to worry."

"Oh, c'mon! Of course, they're going to drink beer and have sex! They're teenagers! All we can do as parents is be brutally honest with them about the responsibility that goes with it!"

Judith shrugged.

"Otherwise *we're* the irresponsible ones," Cindy added. "You're worried about Eve getting bad information, and then you basically gave her *no* information. How do you suppose that'll work out?"

Judith's arms folded into tight horizontal lines with her elbows as sharp endpoints. "This is why kids need Jesus in their lives," she countered. "A positive role model who will help them navigate these sinful temptations."

"If Eve believes in Jesus, she won't drink or have sex?"

"It's more than that. It's taking Jesus's teachings and His love into your heart and practicing His wisdom to live a decent life. It's going to classes and feeding the hungry and trusting your spiritual leaders with your problems. It's a full package, and I live my life as an example for my daughter."

"So Eve is a better person because you're religious?"

"Yes."

"But we're not religious at all and Laura's still a virgin, and as far as I can tell, she never stole a car."

Judith's tranquil air was finally overtaken by Cindy's turbulence. Her routine was upset and her logic dislodged. She felt numb and uncertain. She couldn't understand why Cindy didn't seem to care if her children were drinking and having sex, or how Cindy managed to twist around her every thought. Judith had chosen a world where no one challenged her beliefs, yet she was attracted to something she couldn't understand in Cindy's freewheeling sphere. Judith was vexed. Judith looked out the window at Lem, snoring on the chaise where Cindy's kids probably had sex when she wasn't home. Judith had been invited to swim in a pool where they probably had orgies every weekend. Maybe it was Cindy who lived in the dark. Maybe Laura was enjoying rampant intercourse with Liam every night.

Maybe that's why Eve took off.

"I need your restroom," she said with some urgency as she bolted down the hall to find relief.

***

"Are you a virgin?" Muriel asked politely.

My engine revved as Eve unconsciously pressed her foot to the floor and her chest tightened, bracing for the pending crash of conversation. A little over half an hour passed following Muriel's talk with the police, and Eve had chosen silence. She purchased a ginger ale to settle her stomach, and her sips, swirls, and swallows were the only sounds emanating from the driver's seat. Muriel's hands rested neatly in her lap as she watched the road, alert and thinking.

"Are you?" she repeated.

In the young night on the shadowed road, it was impossible for Muriel to differentiate Eve's coloring, but they both felt her blush.

What the hell? Eve thought. She was still flabbergasted that her partner in crime had secreted a conversation with The Enemy, and now she was expected to have a sex talk with her best friend's grandmother?

Eve first learned about sex from a video in sixth grade health class that detailed reproductive anatomy and showcased a live birth. She was so freaked out from the sight of that fuzzy coconut head emerging from the bleeding, pooping orifices of the screaming, crying mommy that she slept anxiously for months and then wept bitterly when her periods finally started. She didn't want to think about the new powers of her own body. Then Laura started menstruating, too, and their nearly simultaneous cycles became a consistently shared experience that further bonded them.

But Laura seemed far more casual about the horrors of childbirth.

"They say you forget the pain. Like, your body makes chemicals so you'll bond with the baby, and it's like this magic potion on your brain, or something."

"Bullshit."

They watched more birthing videos on the internet together, which led to snippets of pornography so they could learn more about the pre-process. Without the benefit of full-length porn subscriptions, however, they were only provided previews, highlights, and endlessly shocking kinks.

It appeared that sex started when a woman pulled down a man's pants (she was almost always naked already), and after a minute of sucking and admiring, there was a quick dissolve to another crazed minute of animalistic pounding. It looked ugly and weird, and the pubescent teens quickly came to believe that sex ended when the man grunted and Elmer's glue flew from his penis onto a woman's face in slow motion, set to bad music. They never saw a video with foreplay, post-play, pillow talk, or even a mediocre expression of love. Most couples (or groups) didn't even kiss, and the whole experience took less time than microwaving a burrito. They also saw a lot of penises, and none of them seemed smaller than a root beer bottle. Eve was traumatized.

Two years later, Judith had made her attempt at sexual education. She came home from work one evening and found Eve under the reading lamp with *The Great Gatsby*.

"Hey, kiddo."

"Hi."

"Whatcha reading?"

Eve flipped the cover over.

"Any good?"

"Sure."

Judith picked at her nails, making a clicking sound.

"Eve, do you know about boys?"

Boys?

"Is there anyone special in your life, honey?"

Honey?!

"No," Eve said, wondering what Daisy Buchanan would say.

"Huh. Um, listen," Judith continued, "I've been thinking a lot about this, and when you do find a boy, he's probably going to want to do things with you, but you, well, you know you don't have to. I mean, actually, you shouldn't because there are diseases and even with cond—with protection—you can get things, and, and, and I'm sure you know about babies and how all that works, right? And, Eve, Eve? I'm saying stay away. If a boy wants to do . . . that stuff . . . if he wants to, you can tell him no—you should tell him no. Tell him no, and later, when you're married, when you get married, then it's fine. Sex is for married people. That's what the Lord says: you have to really know someone before you—before. I promise you're not missing anything, so don't waste your time worrying about it now because it'll happen, I promise. When you're married. If you want to go on a date, I'm—I guess that's okay, but um . . . just keep your head on straight and focus on other things, like reading your books. Reading is good. Is that a good book? I remember reading it but I don't remember the details. Okay." Judith didn't look at Eve once during her broken monologue. Eve thought her mother had either memorized a script that was missing some pages, or maybe she was having a small stroke.

Judith touched Eve's shoulder and then left the room with her flushed face. Eve returned to *Gatsby*. She read the same paragraph six times and then called Laura to laugh about what happened. She wished she had taken a video.

"Eve?" Muriel said a third time from the passenger seat.

"Yeah," Eve replied, breaking her silence. "I'm still a virgin."

"Do you have a boyfriend?" Eve was thinking about her answer when Muriel amended, "Or a girlfriend?"

Eve looked at Muriel. Muriel looked back at Eve. The question seemed innocuous, but it threw her off. "You think I'm gay?" she said quietly.

"I have no idea. Are you?"

"I don't think so."

"I don't think I am either," Muriel confided, "although the thought did cross my mind once."

"Really?"

"Oh, sure. There was this stupid-hot summer, the kind where the A/C can't even keep up, and my friend Fran came over for an iced-tea visit on the porch. She was so funny, my Fran; she skipped the porch and marched straight into the kitchen and took my dish towel, the one with the little red cows, and soaked it in cold water from the sink. Then she opened the freezer door and draped the dripping towel right over her face and stood there, ahhing, as a cloud of icy mist swirled around her. Now I don't know if it was the afternoon light or the rum I added to our tea, but Frannie's shirt was damp and she wasn't wearing a bra, and well, with the cold there, she started poking through it. I thought her breasts looked amazing, and don't ask me why, but I felt like I had to touch them. I just had to."

Oh. My. God. Eve thought to herself as she forced me to accelerate.

"And she let me."

This isn't happening. She pushed my pedal to the floor.

"But that's as far as it got, a little squeeze over her shirt. When I dared to pinch her left nipple, she pulled back and laughed. She rinsed the towel and hung it over the faucet to dry and we carried on like normal for thirty-five years until she died."

"So nothing really happened," Eve said, finally realizing our speed and letting me naturally slow down as we returned to my preferred right lane.

"But then . . . it might have been that Christmas, or maybe the next one," Muriel continued, "when I leaned in to kiss Fran on the cheek, you know, as a hello at a party, and she turned and held my face and kissed me, deeply, the way the French do. She tasted like a maraschino cherry, and I definitely felt that kiss in more places than just my mouth." Muriel winked.

Please. Stop. Please. Stop.

"But I don't think kissing a girlfriend makes you a lesbian. I told Ira about it, and we talked it through and we're both pretty sure I'm not. But I'll never forget that kiss."

"Huh," Eve said. There was nothing else to say.

"I know the world is a different place now and you've probably seen a lot more action at sixteen than I can even imagine, but my old-lady-advice is stay a virgin until you're in love, Eve. Don't give it away because you're curious."

"But I am curious."

"I know it. I was too. But wait for love. It will only feel right to share your body with someone when there's love and trust on both sides."

"But what if I don't fall in love?"

"That's not gonna happen!" Muriel clapped her hands once, definitively.

Eve felt encouraged, yet wary. "What if I love someone and he doesn't love me back?"

"Well then, he's stupid. Try to pick someone who isn't stupid."

Eve smiled, but she didn't know if she could put off having sex until there was mutual love in her life, as per the recommendation. Part of her wanted to get it over with so she could think about other things. More than half of her classmates had already done it, and it seemed to be one of only four topics of conversation, the others being terrible parents, boring teachers, and the next party. Even Laura couldn't shut up about her own self-imposed deadline, the junior prom.

Muriel continued, "It's better to masturbate."

"Muriel!!" Eve screamed.

"What? You don't masturbate? Or you don't like the word masturbate?"

"Stop saying mastur—stop saying that!" Eve cried out.

"Eve, look outside the windshield. Every single car on this road has a person in it who masturbates on a regular basis."

"Oh my god!"

"Oh, Eve . . . you can't be afraid of things that are normal and human."

"I'm not afraid, it's . . . you. You talking about----"

"I know, it's embarrassing. Well, that's human, too, I suppose."

Muriel saw the rosy red of Eve's cheeks as the headlights of opposing cars flashed across them. Eve thought for a microsecond that she preferred her mother's stumblings to all of this blunt truth, but despite her mortification, she did have more questions—questions even the internet couldn't seem to answer without inundating her screen with unnecessary images of pulsating flesh.

"Can I . . . ask you something?" Eve reluctantly said.

"Anything," Muriel said, quickly and utterly engaged. She was excited. Finally, there was something interesting to talk about.

"When did you . . . when was your first——"

"I was twenty-two."

"Really?"

"I know you're thinking that's pretty late, but it wasn't the same then as it is now. Well, okay, maybe it was the same, but in a different way. Most of my friends were married by twenty-two, and some already had a few kids, but I needed to explore the world before I was ready to settle down. Maybe I was a bit of an old maid, but that was the right time for me."

"So you waited until you got married?"

"No, but I knew I was going to marry Ira, so for me that made it okay. Ira was always my one and only."

Eve took that in. Most of the kids her age who were having sex had already been with multiple partners. Being with only one person for an entire lifetime seemed both ludicrous and unfeasible.

"So did you, like, know anything?" Eve asked.

"Not really. My brothers spread it around that they'd pretty much kill anyone who touched me, and that kept most of the boys away. I did kiss a handful of handsome men in college, though."

"But you never slept with them." Eve imagined earning a bachelor's degree but remaining devoid of the fundamental knowledge that everyone else seemed to have. It seemed highly unrealistic.

"Good girls weren't supposed to know anything until our husbands taught us, and I was a good girl, so I waited. I didn't wait all the way, but it was close enough. My mother said I should 'relax and let him do his thing,' so that's what I did. Mother also said kissing was her favorite part, and on that we agreed. My mother was . . . well, Mom and Dad were . . ." Muriel trailed off as her eyes followed the light of a remote cabin on a distant hill. Muriel slowed, nearly mid-sentence, like a wind-up toy at the end of its spring. Eve brought her back by asking if she was scared that first night.

"I was petrified!" Muriel proclaimed, her coil rewound. "But Ira made it a beautiful night for me. He was very patient and gentle and he talked to me about what was happening—that made a big difference. Not all men are like that. Like I said, you have to find someone who loves you and makes the experience about you. Especially the first time. That's very important."

"Did it—hurt?"

"Oh . . . I don't know if hurt is the right word."

"So it didn't?"

"No, it did, but it's not like smashing your thumb or slipping on the ice. It's different. Deeper. It was a bit like ripping a Band-Aid, I suppose, or popping a Band-Aid, if that's a thing? Or maybe like catching yourself on a hot iron so fast that it's practically over the moment it happens. I felt the throbbing for a while, and a little achy, but it wasn't debilitating. It doesn't feel like anything else I can describe, probably because it was also very emotional. I can replay that night like an old movie and remember every line, but there's also a sweet glaze over it that makes the whole thing shiny and kind of—unspecific. Anyway, the second time it hurt less, and by the third time it didn't hurt at all."

Eve wanted to know more. She was fully over the fact that her sexual teachings were coming from a woman who was born before the end of the Second World War. For Muriel, it was equally strange that Eve was born after 9/11, which to her still felt like a current event.

"Did you . . . um . . ."

"You want to know about orgasms."

This was where Eve's internet research had failed her. She saw naked women moaning and making crazy faces like they were in pain, but supposedly they were experiencing otherworldly pleasures. The men had visibly gooey orgasms and they grunted a lot, but the women would go on and on and on—sometimes even squealing like hungry pigs. How could that be something everyone was supposed to want? She also heard that most of them were acting. How was she supposed to know what was real? A girl in gym claimed she had an orgasm. She explained how her whole body contracted and she felt every nerve, but it didn't sound enjoyable. It sounded stressful. And once an orgasm started, how did it stop? And was there really a special button in her body that she could just . . . press? Eve had so many questions.

"Did you have one that night?"

"The first night? No. Ira did, of course. You know until he got into his fifties he could turn around and have another one almost twenty minutes later. Sometimes on vacation, he'd go three or even four times a night—boy, those were the days. I was jealous because he was always so *happy* afterwards. I enjoyed being with him, but there was nothing like that for me until I was finally able to relax, and that didn't happen until after Lem was born."

"Really? Why?"

"I think I was very self-conscious for the first few years. I didn't know anything about real intimacy when we started, or how the body and the mind talk to each other. The first time I put Ira's penis in my mouth, I scraped him with my teeth and he flew backwards off the bed."

Eve laughed.

"Oh no, it was terrible! He even cried! But until that moment, I didn't know anything about how his body worked or what felt good to him, or why."

Eve never imagined a boy might *not* like a blowjob. She wondered if her mouth was big enough. She harbored a new worry that one day she might injure Liam. Or someone else. Or anyone and everyone who got too close.

"I was also deathly afraid that if I got too excited, I might pee, so I held back. I liked the way Ira smelled, and since we're being frank, the way he tasted, but I didn't think my own parts could possibly be appealing to him. Even though I opened myself up to him, somehow I remained closed, if that makes any sense. I used to keep my arms to my sides so he couldn't smell my armpits, and I used to wake up early and brush my teeth in case he wanted me in the morning. I was afraid of my own body, like I was the only one on the planet who wasn't allowed to fart. It took a long time until we felt equally comfortable with each other."

Eve was entirely *un*comfortable learning the details of Muriel's sex life, yet somehow she needed to know more. Muriel's memory seemed flawless, and Eve wondered if it was the stimulating subject matter or the lack of medication. Eve noticed Muriel also rubbed her hands and feet more than before, and when she nodded off, she emitted strange and guttural moans. Muriel always said she felt fine, but Eve was suspicious.

"After Lem was born—this was back in '69—I was afraid to have sex for a long time. The pain of passing that lump through my vagina was simply too much, and the idea of putting anything up there again was very upsetting. Ira was a saint, but after another season passed, he said enough was enough and it was time. I remember he made margaritas before we climbed into bed, and it was probably a triple pour. Now I'm not advocating for drunken sex, but that night I realized how much my body missed him. My arms were high above my head and he was fully engaged in every inch of me, armpits and all."

"Whoa."

"Yeah, whoa!" Muriel said breathlessly, "and then he took me doggie style."

"Oh my god," Eve repeated, like before, only this time it was followed with a giggle.

"I know." Muriel giggled back. "Maybe I'm being too graphic."

"No, that's okay." More blushing, from both of them.

"For some reason, that angle made it work for me."

Eve remembered a particular video clip where the man and the woman were in no less than ten configurations. Some of them required muscles normal people probably don't have, and others looked silly, but Eve wondered why one position might be better than another if the same parts were going into the same places. Was it possible even sex could get boring if the view was always the same?

"My first orgasm was a little frightening because I didn't know what was happening. It was the first time I ever got to a point where I couldn't take it anymore, but in a good way, and I wouldn't let Ira stop for anything."

"But what did it *feel* like?" Eve urged.

"What did it feel, what did it feel . . . I suppose it felt like I was filling a bag with a bunch of slippery little warm marbles and it was already full, but then I got even more marbles and I had to put those somewhere, so the bag got bigger. And bigger. And warmer. And then more marbles and more expansion and on and on. Soon the bag was so big the seams started stretching, but those marbles kept on coming, and I kept on stuffing them in, more and more and more . . . and then the whole damned thing exploded, and there were zillions of little spectacular hot marbles flying around everywhere, rolling over every atom of my body. Maybe it felt something like that."

Eve gripped my steering wheel, trying to imagine.

"There aren't really words, I guess, and maybe that's the point—it's a physical thing that has to be experienced firsthand. While everything was rolling through my body, I also felt like I was floating, like I was everywhere and nowhere at the same time. It was confusing and fantastic and I couldn't catch my breath or stop trembling, and then all those marbles came back together and exploded again, and it felt like I was riding these big waves that kept crashing into the shoreline and then pulling me back to the sea, but it wasn't a struggle, it was a pleasure. It was pure.

"When I finally opened my eyes, Ira was looking into me as if he'd seen a golden vision. And I felt him, every part of him, everywhere, like we shared the same beating heart."

Fresh tears overflowed from the wells of Muriel's eyelids. A small stream followed the creased banks of her cheeks and fell from the escarpment of her long chin. She found a fast-food napkin in my glovebox to collect it.

Eve took it in and tried to picture herself in a similar situation with Liam. She saw most of his body at swim meets, and his broad shoulders and toned muscles were certainly attractive, but suddenly he seemed very much like a teenaged boy and not a real man. Was he capable of merging with her? Could he give her marbles and share a heartbeat? Could he lead her through those crashing waves? Was Liam an Ira?

"Do you think guys feel the same thing?"

"Maybe the marbles, but they don't get the ocean. Ira usually gave six or seven good pumps before he was spent. And men can wipe it up and go to sleep, but for me the feelings lasted—not with the same intensity, mind you, but I felt the warmth deep inside for hours, like a long summer sunset. Maybe that's the glow some people talk about?"

The internet never showed what those porn women looked like the next day, and that girl in gym class who liked to brag usually just looked sweaty.

"I don't know if I can do that . . . to myself."

Muriel put her hand on Eve's shoulder. "You can and you should, but it might take you a while to learn how. Until you feel it the first time, you don't really know what you're trying to feel, so it can be a little difficult. But trust me, with patience, a bathtub of warm soapy water, and maybe a good toy, you can get there."

"I don't want to rip my hymen."

"That's true, but you may have already. Many active young women lose it long before they start having sex. I say start slowly and don't do anything that hurts."

"Did you touch, umm . . . before you were married, did you . . . ?"

"I could make myself feel a little tingly, but no. Not until Ira got me there the first time."

Eve sighed. "I guess I need an Ira."

Muriel sighed, too. One of the bigger adjustments to her post-Ira life was the disquieting lack of sex. There were only a handful of widowed men at The Deerwood who weren't sickly *and* retained their libidos, but the competition of more than twenty neglected women for each of them seemed perverse. It was even harder to find a listening ear, and even if she did, perhaps at the salon, Muriel found she couldn't express her thoughts cogently under the weight of her pills. She returned her attention to Eve, whose mind was swirling.

"So do you have a boyfriend? Maybe somebody at school?"

"I'm not sure. I thought I did, but probably not."

"I don't understand."

"I really like this guy and everyone said he was going to ask me out, but then he didn't and then he sorta did, but now we're here and—I dunno. It's confusing."

Muriel nodded.

"I kinda wish he was—I mean, like—so he's a senior and that's pretty cool, but that kind of gives it an expiration date, if you know what I mean."

"You don't want to get attached."

"Yeah. But maybe I already am? See? I don't even know! You said I should wait for love and that sounds great and all, but how do you know if it's really love or, like----"

"Lust."

Eve nodded.

Muriel said, "So do what we talked about and wait until you're in college to find someone."

"But that's, like, two years away, and I don't want to lose Liam if there's a chance there, you know? Like, maybe it's better to have a great year with him even if we both know it's going to end anyway? At least then there's no pressure."

"Huh. That's not how I would go about it, but as I said, your world is different. The one thing I do know for certain is we don't know the future. You might stay together even when he's in college. Or you might go to the same college. Or you might find you don't really like him all that much anyway, even a month from now. Anything can happen." Muriel's smile reached her friend and soothed her.

"That's true. But there is one other problem."

"What's that?"

"Liam is in Florida, and in about two hours, we're going to be in New York."

Chapter 15

Eve was barely eight years old on the tenth anniversary of 9/11. Judith did her best to filter and downplay the tragedy of that day for as long as she could, but the sheer volume of internet videos, television reports, and print media replaying the destruction made it impossible for anyone to remain ignorant. Relieved parents happily signed approval letters delegating the task of explaining 9/11 to the schools, and Eve's third-grade teacher provided a succinct and sanitized explanation for her young and innocent audience.

"Ten years ago today, there were some bad people who didn't believe in freedom. They were very angry, and they steered the airplanes into some of our favorite buildings. Remember when Chelsea and Alison spent the whole morning building the block tower, and then Chad knocked it down at recess? In a much bigger way, it was something like that."

"Did people die?"

"Yes, and we are very sad about that."

"Are we going to die?"

"No. This was a crazy tragedy that only happened once, and it was a long time before any of you were born. It also happened very far away in New York—remember our maps? Remember the funny state that looks like a triangle with a little tail?"

Two-thirds of the class nodded. One raised her hand.

"My mommy said people were going to burn on fire so they jumped off the buildings."

"Okay, Amanda, that's enough. The only thing you need to know about this important day is that we are all very, very lucky to be Americans and—class? What do Americans believe in?"

"Freeeddoommm."

"That's right, very good. In a few minutes, Principal Martinez is going to make an announcement, and the whole school is going to be very quiet for one full minute to show our respect. Chad Engleson, I have my eye on you."

As they grew older, Eve and her generation became freshly minted secondhand witnesses to the horror, with the internet providing repeating details from every possible angle. Unlike the Holocaust and other distant, black-and-white catastrophes, 9/11 remained a current event that felt sickeningly new every time YouTube showed the airplanes merging with steel and glass and unaware workers. Eve and her friends decided the lucky ones were the people on the planes and those directly in their paths; they were instantaneously pulverized, while thousands of others succumbed to the impossible choices of burn, jump, or hope (as young Amanda had aptly described). Most of those trying to escape were crushed, and the next-level horror was reserved for the firefighters and police who ran into the buildings to help but didn't stand a chance against the collapse. The day was flattened into a premature night, and panicked hordes fled the blackened, noxious discharge. The cancerous effluvium produced in those ten endless seconds continued to claim lungs and lives for decades. It was wholly unfathomable and profoundly unbelievable. But it happened. It wasn't a movie.

Eve often thought of the children of the victims, and she claimed a silent solidarity with them. She remembered how the aroma of her father's morning coffee had merged with her own cereal-sweetened milk-breath in their routine kiss before he departed for work. Like those other children, she'd had no idea her last moment with him would be The Last. But those hapless kids could at least point to the day, curse the enemy, visit the site to lay a wreath, and weep in the arms of America. Eve mourned alone, not knowing the exact circumstances, or even the precise day, of her father's demise. She harbored a unique jealousy for children who had lost loved ones on 9/11, for the simple fact that they had the videos. It never occurred to her that most of them wished they didn't.

For Eve and her young Floridian friends, the disasters of September 11th made New York City a frightening place. In earlier years, Laura augmented these perceptions by eagerly describing the downsides of her visits: there were millions of foreign people who didn't even speak English, and all the taxi drivers smelled like curry, oregano, or onions, and also sweat and smoke. People peed on the buildings, and the garbage piles were taller than the cars. She also kept a log of all the rats she saw scampering in the subways. After each and every bullet point, Eve and her friends all said, "Ewww!"

But Deerfield Beach had blue skies and lush palms. They had the beach and their grassy yards and the best weather. They were obviously in the very best place to live, and without skyscrapers, they all felt safe.

Everything changed when *Gossip Girl* hit Netflix. The sutured wounds of the city healed, and it became a new and fantastic playground for wealthy, immature teenagers who knew about fashion, parties, and sex. This vibrant conceit was furthered in their minds through streaming binges of *Sex and the City* and *Friends*. Manhattan became the dreamy

Place To Be, and the tweens of Deerfield Beach plummeted into despair over their geographic inadequacy. They found fault with the monotonous topography, lack of culture, and a climate that rebuffed any need for stylish outerwear. They wished for subways instead of depending on parents for transit. Only a lucky few, like Laura, could "Christmas in New York." She showed everyone her *Lion King* tickets and returned with selfies from the High Line, a belt from Barneys, and personalized M&M's made right in Times Square.

Eve had come to regard the Big Apple as a confusing and intimidating, yet accessible and oddly intimate, world capital. For her, the metropolis was always edged with intrigue and possibility, and in Eve's mind, everyone in New York had to be smart, sophisticated, accomplished, or lunatic. Or all four. Without seeing it for herself, though, she had no idea what she could expect, and her anxiety swelled as the atmosphere above the approaching skyline grew brighter.

As we moved toward the glow, Muriel remembered how much she missed New York. For most of her life, Muriel and Ira had never gone more than a few months without a trip to see a show, explore some museums and galleries, eat a great dinner, or visit with cultured friends. At first, they alleviated the psychological discomfort of becoming permanent residents of Florida by promising to return to the city at least twice a year. However, it didn't take long for them to realize that the inconvenience of the journey often outweighed its benefits. They soon opted for nonstop flights to Albany when it was time to visit Sandra and the grandchildren, flying past all the wondrous mayhem at twenty thousand feet.

As a younger woman, Muriel thought nothing of ambling from the Met to MoMA, a beautiful thirty-block walk down Fifth Avenue over historic stony sidewalks. After she had children, the subway became a convenient and economical choice. When the children were grown, she found taxis more comfortable, and as a senior citizen, she discovered that visiting two museums in one afternoon was dishearteningly exhausting and there was no longer a need to traverse the city at such lengths.

Over time, their fabulous city friends and guest-room gatekeepers retired to the Costa Del Sol, the Côte d'Azur, and Tucson. Hotel and breakfast expenses were suddenly added to the mix, and even with their considerable resources, the Worths had trouble reconciling the experiences with the price tags. So they replaced Central Park with the beach, Carnegie Hall and Broadway theaters with West Palm's Kravis Center. They made new local friends for socializing, but Singer Island was never an adequate substitute for Manhattan.

Muriel yearned for New York City, where history and modernization worked in tandem, akin to different-sized wheels on a bicycle. In her mind, she could pedal past towering skyscrapers standing alongside old-world churches, or vintage pizza shops huddled beneath giant digital screens. Everything was gleaming and new or rich with centuries of stories—or miraculously both, like Pete Caldwell's Tribeca address.

As we drew closer, the interstate splintered and merged. Its corkscrew ramps and tendril-like lanes extended into bridges, underpasses, toll plazas, and service areas. Everything flowed with its own logic, like a mermaid's hair in water. Motorcycles zigged and sports cars zagged as Eve clutched my wheel in the ten-and-two position, keeping us steady in our lane. At one point, Muriel told her it was okay to blink. She also reminded Eve that she still needed to call the police.

We pulled into the Joyce Kilmer Service Area off I-95 in East Brunswick, and Eve tried to rehearse the impending scene without the benefit of a script. She knew she would endure the consequences of this singular conversation for the rest of her life; it was a scarier notion than anything she imagined she'd find in New York City.

As sweat formed along Eve's hairline, Muriel carefully reexplained what she told the police for the fourth time, but her story mutated with each telling: someone stole their money, or it was lost, or it was lost and then stolen, or found, and whoever stole or found their money used it near Baltimore, but they weren't in Baltimore because they were in Miami, but the police didn't know about the second Miami except that the cards were used near there, near Baltimore, but someone else used the cards, not them, because they were in Florida at the beach without the money and they didn't use the money in the other Miami, near Baltimore, which the police didn't know about at all. I knew exactly what happened, and I couldn't follow it either.

While still trying to grasp Muriel's slippery version of events, Eve reluctantly pressed on the number that arrived by text.

"Carroll."

"Hello? I'm calling for, um . . ." She looked to Muriel for reassurance and received a wink with a nod. Muriel's rolling wrist also sprouted a thumbs-up. "This is Eve."

"Eve Harvick, hello." She could hear the officer return his feet to the floor as he swiveled to find his notepad. Pages shuffled. A pen clicked. "How are you doing?"

"I'm fine. You asked me to call?" Her voice was laced with a softness that belied her chunky eye makeup and chiseled nerves.

"Yes, I'm glad you did." She heard him snapping his fingers, then his young and somewhat familiar voice echoed as he sent her to speakerphone. "So where are you?"

"Miami Beach."

"Uh huh, and what time is it there?"

"What? Um . . ." She glanced at her phone. "It's almost eight."

"In Miami."

"Yeah."

"Okay." He didn't say anything for a long moment. Eve wasn't sure if she was supposed to say anything, either, and soon she wondered if the pause was purposely manufactured to keep her on edge. Then he said, "Eve, you know why we asked you to call?"

"I guess so."

"Okay, so why do you think?"

"Because we're not home yet."

"Your mom and the----" he checked his notes, "----the Worths are very worried about you and----" he checked again, "----you and Muriel."

"Yeah."

"They called us over to file a missing persons report because they're so worried."

"But we already told them we're fine."

"I know, they said you sent a text."

"Yeah."

"And you told them you were taking a little vacation?"

"Yeah."

"In the middle of the week and without anyone's permission."

She didn't say anything, and it was Officer Carroll's turn to wait out a disconcerting pause. Eve didn't want to add any more information to his notebook. Agreeing with whatever he said felt like the best tactic to get through the interrogation. She pictured the gun in his unsnapped holster, ready to shoot through the phone if she took a misstep. Finally, he broke the silence: "Muriel's still with you?"

"Yeah."

"And she's doing okay?"

"Yeah."

Eve scratched her leg even though it didn't itch to fill yet another empty moment.

"Okay then, that's all I needed to hear. Get your ass back home, apologize to the Worths, and give your mom a hug. She's your mom and she deserves your respect."

Eve wanted to scream, "Oh really? Do you know what she did? Is your mother a liar? Is your mother a two-faced nutjob who can't even make a fucking cup of coffee?"

Eve muttered, "Okay."

"You have my number, but listen—I don't wanna get any more calls from your family. Get home now and have a good night."

Eve knew it was impossible to follow both instructions.

"Okay. Bye."

She had worked herself into shreds over nothing. There was no fallout, and all the tensions leading up to the call—her stomach pain, headache, and nail-chewing torment—were self-imposed. She looked over at Muriel, who gave a strange shrug. Eve misinterpreted the gesture to mean that Muriel's earlier conversation with the officers had required serious nuance and mind-bending machinations compared to Eve's little bland exchange. Then Muriel said, "Who was that?" and Eve understood the shrug for what it was.

"Everything's fine," Eve replied.

"Who was that?"

"The police."

"Oh right, the police. What did they say?"

"It's fine. Everything is fine."

Muriel didn't believe her until Eve exhaled and Muriel saw the relief it provided. The LinkedIn app buzzed, and Eve gave it her attention while Muriel breathed deeply, too, hoping to stymie the insecurities rising in her like the endless bubbles in fresh seltzer. She quickly rolled down my window for some clarifying air and was silently smacked by a metallic tang riding shotgun with the early night. New Jersey's Garden State moniker was an accurate descriptor for the ninety lush miles post-Wilmington, but the remaining distance harbored fuel-storage tanks and refineries, diesel-run shipping yards, and other heavy industry. I ached to get to the Holland Tunnel quickly and unblemished, ever fearful of marring my #11 Cotillion White shell in the pollution.

I wondered if I was experiencing the equivalent of human worry. I knew negotiating New York's dense streets would be tricky—I'm nearly nineteen feet from tip to toe, almost a man's length longer and a foot wider than contemporary cars. Eve managed me expertly in the squares of Savannah, but the pace there had been leisurely. How would she cope with the fast and twisting turns and maniac motorists on the dynamic route to Tribeca? Her GPS would never keep up, and one wrong turn could send us to Brooklyn. Or Staten Island. Or into a bodega. It was daunting, but there was nothing I could do but stay the course and attempt to summon a parking angel for our imminent arrival.

**

Lem woke up to an apneic choke of silence that broke his rhythmic snoring. In the split-second dream before his heavy breathing resumed, he saw himself asleep in the chaise, as he was, but at the bottom of the pool instead of beside it on the deck. The immaculate landscaping and hazy night sky were replaced by a haloed ring of creamy blue pool walls that rose to a taut rectangular sheet of black nothingness six feet above his head. It was a coffin's view from a new grave, in negative. There was no air, and to obtain it, he would have to surface past the light walls and into the dark void. He reached up and grabbed at nothing, the water slipping through his grasp, taking him nowhere. Confusion, then annoyance, then panic.

And then he was back, patently alert. He put his hand to his chest and felt the thick muscle of his heart bouncing against his ribs in its focused effort to send blood to the borders of his unwieldy frame. As the panic subsided and confusion converted itself into certainty, his pupils narrowed and focused. The annoyance remained.

His mother was lying.

Eve was a juvenile delinquent.

The police were worthless.

Earlier, while Lem surrendered to his alcohol-soaked nap, Christian finally arrived home from swim practice. The rest of the family ate without disturbing Lem, and when Judith departed, Cindy put half of the remaining lasagna on a plate in the microwave and the rest in a Pyrex for his Thursday lunch. Then she floated noiselessly to the pool area in her bare feet and sat on a low, polished stone table beside him. She smiled at Lem, her man, her lug with his arm draped over his face. She contemplated joining him outside for the rest of the warm night when she realized he was still wearing his shoes. She gently removed them and was startled by the deep-brown, blood-soaked tip of his sock. She stripped it off, revealing the serious mess of his problematic toe.

Cindy used the outdoor entrance to their bedroom and returned to Lem with her supplies. She gently washed his feet and then scraped about one third of the center of his nail plate away using the edge of a small scissor, properly following the advice of the doctor and relieving the pressure of the arch. Once the nail lifted, she was able to cut the dagger off a corner that undoubtedly caused most of his pain. She treated the toe with a topical antiseptic and then a dab of an antibiotic ointment before wrapping it in an aloe-infused bandage. She deftly slid his slacks off and placed a light cotton throw over his plump, blond legs. He never stirred. She kissed his thigh and whispered, "Have a little faith," before heading back inside, deciding against an outdoor sleep in favor of reading snugly in bed after a little TV.

Lem had no idea what time it was when he revived. The house was mostly dark except for a sprinkling of night-lights, but the timed pool lights were still on. The blanket dropped to the ground unnoticed as he ambled toward the kitchen door in his white briefs and unbuttoned work shirt. There was a perceptible lilt in his gait from the residuum of whiskey. After a quick shuffling, a faithful cabinet yielded his desired Advils, and he chased four of them with tap water gulped directly from the faucet. He experienced a fleeting vertigo when he restored himself after leaning over the sink, and after standing for a long moment, looking out the window at nothing, he finally noticed he wasn't in pain.

Lem knew it was impossible to feel so normal in such a short amount of time, even with the numbing action of his drinks. He brought his naked legs over to the light of the kitchen vent hood and lifted the sore subject, like a crane moving a felled tree, up to the counter. His toe was wrapped, nearly professionally, and it felt defect-free.

When? How?

He smiled at the thought of Cindy, his woman, his boon companion, no doubt already in bed with a reading light, sleeping with a thick book resting squarely on her breasts. Lem brought his heavy foot back to earth and pressed a little, testing it. Nothing. No throb. No blood. No affliction.

She had done it. She'd fixed him.

Everything was as it should be.

Judith was finally on board.

The police were on the case.

Eve and his mother would return and life would go back to normal, the whole event a silly blip he looked forward to looking back on, perhaps to be revived one day as an amusing anecdote at a dinner party: *remember that time when Eve and Mom took the car?*

Lem smelled the remnants of dinner and found his share in the microwave. He wolfed it down without reheating it and then walked confidently through the house, familiar with the dark and guided by a bar of pink light between Laura's bedroom carpet and the bottom of her door.

"You still up?" He knocked quietly, not wanting to shake a fist at his sudden good mood. She opened the door, and a small vertical crack of light entered the hall. She was wearing her normal bed wear, a colorful T-shirt that dropped to her knees, and her hair was captured at the apex of her forehead by a scrunchie, giving an expensive cleanser time with her complexion.

"Hi Daddy."

"It's late. You should----"

"I'm almost done," she said, indicating her face. "I had a lot of homework."

"Sure," he extended in an affable tone.

Laura looked over her shoulder at something in her room and then opened her door a little more, just barely enough to slide past him. She closed it behind her, scurried into the bathroom across the hall, and closed that door, too.

"Goodnight," he called, knowing she probably couldn't hear him over the sound of the sink filling up. He lingered for a moment, half-expecting a reply. Lem looked down the hall to see if there was a light coming from his room, too, but it was dark; Cindy had given up.

Lem didn't consciously acknowledge the soft music coming from Laura's computer behind her closed door until it was interrupted by a beep and a dip in the volume. A moment later, the volume returned to normal, and a moment after that, it happened again, the beep and the dip. He turned the handle and opened the door enough to see that she had been sitting on her bed to do her work.

Something twitched in his mind: Laura always did her homework at her desk and read her books in the papasan chair by the window. He remembered her fervor about an article proclaiming that the use of any electronics before bedtime was destructive, and a person would never sleep well if they used their bed for *anything* other than sleeping. The three nonvirgins in the household held their tongues about other uses for a bed, but they mostly agreed, and Laura, being Laura, remained diligent about her self-imposed rules. Always.

The computer was on her bed.

It beeped a third time, with another dip in the volume.

Lem looked over his shoulder at the bathroom's unwavering stream of light, as constant as the sound of the faucet. He looked back at Laura's bed, where the computer rested on a second pillow across from her own, its screen turned slightly away from the door. What was she listening to? What was she watching in the middle of the night? What kind of assigned homework could possibly make her change her zealous rules? And what was making her computer beep like that?

He ventured in.

***

As anticipated, the drive on the I-95 corridor became increasingly white-knuckled as the City sucked us in. The space to maneuver decreased even as the road added lanes to accommodate the burgeoning traffic. Muriel remarked that there were a lot of cars but it was normal, and we were fortunate to arrive after rush hour. Eve couldn't imagine the road being any more filled than it already was, with eight lanes pulsing in both directions. She followed the signs for the Holland Tunnel, awestruck that every exit seemed to have sub-exits and each one led to at least ten new places. She knew the island of Manhattan had millions of people living on it, but she was unprepared for the density outside the city limits. She had pictured the glassy skyscrapers flanked by wide rivers skirting tranquil suburbs and farms. She hadn't expected to see other massive cities a full hour before the main attraction.

An airplane landed parallel with us at adjacent Newark Airport as we followed the signs leading from I-95 to I-78. It was the first time in Eve's young life that she had been on a new interstate highway (we took the county routes in and out of Savannah). She thought I-78 felt different, a slinky cat instead of the sturdy dog of I-95, as it stretched over the sudden blackness of Newark Bay and wrapped itself around Liberty State Park. When a cluster of skyscrapers emerged, she assumed we were in New York, only to learn from her sprightly companion that it was actually Jersey City, a multi-pronged city seeded in part by its proximity to Manhattan, but with somewhat more reasonable real estate.

I-78 ceased to be a highway, and soon we were crawling on 12th Street. There were traffic lights on every corner, and over a dozen gas stations vied for our business. Eve couldn't imagine why there were so many stations in one place, and Muriel explained at our third stoplight interruption that gas was cheaper in New Jersey, plus they pumped it for you. We pulled over to partake in the savings and service before joining the steady queue into the Holland Tunnel.

Muriel and Eve were given a choice of nine gates to pay for the toll. They were prepared with cash, but they quickly learned that those without an electronic tag were now billed by mail after a strobe light captured the license plate. Eve sucked in her breath and wondered how long it would take for the system to generate a bill based on my registration records and deliver our time-stamped location to the desk of Lemuel Worth. She was further daunted when the nine lanes merged into two in less than five hundred feet, but she zippered with the best of them and held on for dear life as we charged through the mile-long tunnel ninety-seven feet beneath the Hudson River. Muriel pointed at the tiled wall delineating the border of New Jersey and New York as we passed, but Eve couldn't avert her eyes from the steadfast taillights of the black sedan in front of us. She feared any collision beneath the river would be disastrous, as if the ceramic tiles themselves were holding back water, instead of two feet of steel and concrete carved out of solid bedrock. She didn't want to be the reason everyone got wet.

Soon the road ascended and snaked around St. John's Park, offering five exits that led to different parts of the city. Eve never saw the park as we followed the first spoke and abruptly stopped at the jagged corners of Hudson and Laight.

Eve wanted to look up at the towering buildings and wished again that Muriel would relax her stance on *never* opening my roof. What was the point of having such a splendid convertible if we never got to experience the open-air freedom my creators intended? Feeling constrained, she twisted her head out the window to see what was above. There were no stars—they were scraped off by the tall buildings and organized like refrigerator magnets on the columned behemoths that filled every conceivable inch between the roads. Everything was shining and alive.

The light turned green. Two blocks later we turned left on Greenwich Street, and six blocks later we arrived. It was almost too easy. My work with the parking angels was rewarded as we found a generous, legal space directly out front. Muriel said it was rare and a good omen. Eve was too jaded to believe in omens and too young to appreciate the luck. In later years, she would spend hours circling the blocks, sometimes desperate to the point of convulsion, and she would look back and admonish her naivete and nonchalance over our simple glide into that first perfect spot. It was a lovely introduction to New York City.

Eve grabbed a few small items and locked me up, pulling on my doors a few times to ensure I was secure. She looked around to assess the neighborhood, but she lacked the context to know if this was a good area. The buildings were a mix of spartan-new and ornate-old; some had skeletal fire escapes, while others held robust balconies; some stretched themselves with tall, skinny windows, while others displayed massive arches with ornate cut glass. Modern or historic, every inch of each facade was unique. Eve was in awe.

She saw the Freedom Tower with its ninety-four floors soaring a few blocks away. She wondered if the debris from the World Trade Center had reached this far, or if the people in these buildings had felt that heat. She wondered if Pete Caldwell was in the city that day, or if he knew people who perished. When her gaze returned to street level, she found a sophisticated scene of stores and restaurants that captivated her and helped to expunge her darker thoughts. Eve imagined she could live her whole life on this one extraordinary block and still fail to appreciate it fully.

I watched from a distance as they approached the building, found the entry buttons, and inputted the code. A moment later, a man's voice said, "Come on up, top floor," and a buzzer rang. Muriel grabbed the door before the buzzer stopped and bounded in with a juvenile energy. The elevator button was already illuminated when they stepped inside.

"Did you press it?" Eve asked.

"You don't have to. The elevator is connected to the buzzer, and he owns the whole floor."

"Are you serious?" Eve's eyes started out wide and continued to expand when the elevator arrived and the steel doors parted, revealing Pete Caldwell's modern, warm, and colossal apartment. Pete stood in front of a smooth concrete entry table backlit in blue light and replete with blooming orchids. His arms were extended.

"Muriel."

She rushed in.

"Oh Peter, Peter! Oh, it's so good to see you again. I never thought . . . I wasn't sure . . ." She couldn't let go. Eve stepped inside cautiously, as if her sneakers might crush the hardwood. She placed her bags on the ground as if they were filled with grenades about to slip their pins. Laura's house was amazing, but this . . . this was beyond. She felt like her unkempt presence might disrupt its soaring grandeur. Pete looked over Muriel's shoulder while she continued to hug him. He nodded at Eve.

"So you're my niece's friend."

"Hi." She wasn't sure if she should step forward, or possibly curtsy.

Muriel's mind and body continued to swirl in the details of their warm reunion as she remembered his athletic build, freshly shaved jawline, neat hair, and light vetiver scent. Pete extended his right hand to Eve while still holding Muriel with the left.

"Pete Caldwell. It's nice to meet you."

***

The tour was brief, not for lack of square footage but because the open-concept rooms melded into each other. The bedrooms and baths were the exception, and they were numerous but similar. Within fifteen minutes, Eve and Muriel were settled in. They mutually decided to sleep in the same guest room, despite having options, so Eve could attend to Muriel if necessary. Eve changed into a pair of clean black shorts and found a gray T-shirt that somehow matched the decor. At Pete's insistence, all shoes stayed off in his home, but the floors were warm, even in the sealskin-gray-tiled bathrooms.

Pete offered them dinner, but with the late hour and Eve's recent sour cream incident, they opted for light tea and delectables from La Maison du Macaron on West 23rd, which were already displayed on a lacquered steel serving tray. Pete poured a glass of red wine for himself, and they convened on the angular living-room sofa, a piece of art unto itself, composed of seventeen feet of soft suede floating on thin steel pins.

Eve sipped her chamomile with honey and calmed her turbulent stomach with a cinnamon macaron. It seemed like everything was designed to calm her nerves and unknot her neck. She turned her head and studied their welcoming host.

He appeared to be the exact opposite of Lem in nearly every way. Where Lem was uncooked pizza dough, Pete was a trim and delectable biscuit. Lem was losing his hair, but Pete had a thick and tidy mane streaked with ash in the blond. They both had a few wrinkles, but Lem's were drawn with a Conté crayon across his flaccid flesh, while Pete's were whisper thin and elegantly connected, like the invisible fishing line in a magician's trick.

Lem redeemed nearly all his uncomely features with his incomparable blue eyes, and Pete, once again, held opposite; his eyes were jet-black vacuums that seemed to pull the rest of his face inward. It was easy to believe in the kindness of Lem's nonthreatening gaze, but looking into Pete's eyes, people often felt inconsequential and wondered whether they were being seen or mechanically scanned by an alien device. It was an unfortunate twist that Lem's eyes belied his sinister guile and his conniving notions. Like the juice of a Venus flytrap, his gaze was sweetly alluring, but one could easily be captured and desiccated under his control. Pete used his eyes to see new routes around old problems, and he'd made his fortune through his keen perception. It took a moment, but like most who made his acquaintance and despite the vortex of his eyes, Eve decided instantly that she loved Pete.

As she continued to sip her elegant tea and indulge in a second confection, Eve had the surreal feeling of having slipped inside a magazine spread. There was a long, slim fire in a granite niche that Pete sparked with the flip of a hidden switch, and his books and magazines seemed to be chosen for their colors, as they coordinated with the concrete and the glass coffee table and the bespoke steel lamps. Pete also matched the space with his relaxed black jeans and a long-sleeved gray polo. He wore it untucked, and the unbuttoned neck revealed a grassy tuft of blond hair. Everything about him seemed effortlessly comfortable and intensely masculine. Even his manicured nails.

"Are you still traveling the world?" Muriel asked.

"I should ask the same of you," Pete replied with a wink. Muriel looked to Eve and encouraged her to speak with a little nudge.

"We're, umm. I'm not, like . . . what?" She suddenly felt excruciatingly self-conscious.

Pete always wanted his guests to feel relaxed and couldn't find enough material in Eve's stammering to formulate a response, so he returned to Muriel and said, "Actually, your timing is perfect. I was in Amsterdam on Monday, and I'm leaving this Friday for three weeks, mostly Singapore and Bangkok. If we can tidy the paperwork, then Kuala Lumpur in November, but it's not set."

"That's very impressive, Peter. You know I'm very proud of you."

"Ha, well, that's nice to hear. If you knew the gritty details you might not be so impressed, but it's not a bad life."

"Don't sell yourself short! You do very important work."

He laughed, taking another sip of wine. "Well, thank you. It's nice you think so. Let's hope the banks continue to think so, too."

"What *do* you do?" Eve interrupted.

"I'm a consultant for a multinational conglomeration of banks that use my company to identify and secure overseas development investment opportunities, typically in the technology and urban planning sectors, but not exclusively."

"What does that mean?"

"Well," he said, slowing down, "we basically decide what projects should get funding approval, but it's a little more complicated than that because we also work with government regulators to affect the fundamental policies relating to our core abilities to authorize international loans for our investors."

"So you're sort of a politician?"

"Please god, never!! Haha, no, I'm just a businessman who does business things."

"In Asia."

"Lately, but also in Europe and a little in South America, though it's getting trickier there."

Eve looked around the room and discerned that most of the paintings, photographs, and sculptures were foreign. She'd never seen so many Buddhas and other wood, stone, metal, and ceramic deities in one place, yet nothing felt cluttered.

"Do you, like, speak a lot of languages?"

"Mostly Spanish and some French. I can understand enough Italian not to embarrass myself, but I've been told my German is horrendous and I shouldn't even try." He laughed, taking another sip. "We hire local translators for Asia, but most of my counterparts there also speak English."

Eve pictured Mrs. Lanza twirling around her classroom at the beginning of the week. It seemed a fascinating, distant, and mostly irrelevant memory.

"Did you go to college?" she asked.

Pete laughed again, "Four years at Stanford, MBA from Wharton."

"Wow."

"He's no dummy," Muriel chimed in.

"Trust me, I'm no brain surgeon, either. Really, anyone can do what I do, but you need the credentials and a good track record before anyone will believe you can do it." He paused, remembering the emotional space of being sixteen, like Eve, and then silently thanking his parents for expecting the best of him. "But I gotta tell ya, I watch the kids at the coffee shop and the way they handle their customers and make those complicated drinks. They're pretty smart and highly conversational—they should be making a hell of a lot more money. Or maybe I should be making a hell of a lot less!" Another laugh and another sip.

"You know you're better than some coffee girl," Muriel said. Eve gasped at the slight to all baristas—it was a job she'd failed to get after ten applications, and a clear step up from her brainless tasks in the salon. "Millions of people can make coffee, but only a few people on the whole planet can do what Peter does," she explained.

Pete shrugged, a small smile playing at the corner of his lips. It was a gesture he used with some frequency to downplay his own accomplishments when others brought them up.

"I'm right," Muriel finished, crossing her arms and sitting back on the couch.

"Okay. Is my side of the interview over?" Pete asked Eve.

"What?"

"Do you have any more questions, or is it my turn?"

Pete Caldwell winked again, and Eve's crush on Liam flitted into the ether. In a flash, she retreated to the paper doll cutouts of her childhood and pictured Pete's sublime figurine in the three-piece suit, the scuba suit, the swimsuit, the pink tuxedo . . . he looked great in everything.

"Sure," she said.

"So what the hell are you doing here?" he said, putting the wine down. His polished black eyes drilled into Eve's, abruptly converting their color from a bright green into a dark pewter.

Eve sipped her tea and considered her answer carefully. She couldn't remember who brought up the idea of finding Pete—was it Laura or Muriel? She trusted them both, but what if Pete was a Venus flytrap like Mr. Worth? They were enjoying his sticky treats and feeling completely relaxed, but he was still pretty much a stranger to her. It might mean nothing for him to rat them out, and then—Police cars! Juvenile Hall! Eve couldn't calculate whether it was worse to tell the truth and suffer the consequences, or lie to someone who seemed to be helping her finish her quest. And what if she lied and still got caught? Would it worsen the outcome? Eve turned to Muriel for guidance, knowing "we're in Miami" wasn't going to work when they were sitting in the living room of a Greenwich Street penthouse.

Muriel studied Eve, absorbing the quandary.

"We went to the beach," Muriel said.

Pete studied them both intently.

"But then we kept on driving," Eve added. No lies so far, if you counted Singer Island as the beach.

"Is this like a *Bonnie and Clyde* thing? Are you in some sort of trouble?"

"No," Eve said, definitively.

"It was Laura who told me you were coming, not Lem. Can I assume he doesn't know you're here?"

"That's correct," said Muriel.

"So what's your game plan? What's next?" Pete asked.

"We're going home," Muriel replied. Eve looked at her quizzically.

"You mean back to Florida?"

Muriel raised a condescending eyebrow to the brilliant international-investment-banking magnate for asking her such a stupid question, but it was Eve who surprised them both with her firm response: "I'm never going back to Florida."

"Really?" Muriel asked. She had always assumed that Eve would return home. Within a week, she was supposed to be back with Laura, building sets for the next school play, and discovering the wonders of Liam. Muriel also figured Eve would find a way to work things out with her mother.

Eve equally assumed Muriel would return to The Deerwood, and she was completely unaware that Muriel had decided otherwise.

Pete bounced his gaze between the two of them. It was clear that whatever plans they each had, they had yet to share them with each other. He quickly recognized it wasn't in his best interest to know anything, and he didn't have the time or countenance to be a witness. He was simply a layover on their journey, and he decided to act accordingly.

"Where's your car, Eve?"

"It's on the street."

"Oh, don't do that. You'll have to move it at seven, and you could both use a good night's sleep. Go down to Chambers, take a right, and put it in the Central. Tell Vincent you're my guest and I'll cover it. Wait—never mind, I'll go with you. Let me get a coat."

He moved to the closet, but Eve stayed on the couch.

"You should get one, too," he called.

"My sweatshirt's in the trunk."

He found a sheepskin-lined leather bomber jacket and tossed it to her. The label read *Burberry*. Eve gasped. "It's October," he said, "and this isn't Florida. Do you have some jeans? It's too cold for shorts. Check the dresser—you're about the same size as Nancy." He winked at her and then disappeared into his study to fetch his wallet and keys.

Eve sat on the floor of the foyer to put on her shoes. "Will you be okay for a few minutes?" she asked Muriel.

"What do you mean you're never going back to Florida? Where are you going?"

"Where are *you* going?" Eve returned.

"I thought . . . I *thought* you were driving me home."

"I can't go back there."

Muriel shot Eve the same look she'd issued to Pete.

"No, Eve. Home. My home."

"The condo? You don't live there anymore. Remember?"

Muriel was incensed. Of course she remembered. She remembered everything, even when she couldn't express it. "No, I mean *home* home. My real home in Saratoga Springs."

"What!?"

Pete returned wearing a cashmere scarf loosely draped over a tailored black leather jacket. The smell of the jacket was similar to my seats, and Eve began to wonder if being rich meant you were constantly enveloped in leather. Pete put on his matching leather driving gloves, reconfirming her new opinion.

"No jeans?"

"I have some in the car." Eve turned to Muriel. "We'll talk about this later, okay?"

"Okay. But I want to go home, and you said you'd take me."

Eve acknowledged her whining and knew that Muriel was nearly done for the day. She asked Pete for a few minutes so she could bring Muriel to the guest room and help her settle for bed. "I want to go home," Muriel repeated, walking down the long hallway.

"I know, but . . . I'm not sure if you *can*," Eve said.

"Of course we can."

"But it's not the *plan*," Eve pleaded.

"I want to go home!"

They reached the bedroom, and Eve brought Muriel to their adjacent private bathroom where she had already unpacked the toiletry kit. She handed Muriel's toothbrush to her and said, "Listen, don't worry, I promise we'll figure it out."

Muriel looked into Eve's eyes and was contented.

A few moments later, Eve traipsed back down the hall and popped into the waiting elevator with Pete. As they descended, she realized she was almost an inch taller than he was. Somehow, in his apartment, he loomed larger than life, but once he left his dominion, he appeared to be a normal and accessible guy. She liked the way he spoke about his job as if anyone could do it. Even her. She wanted an apartment like his, one day. Even a few floors down and a quarter the size would suffice.

"How long have you known Laura?" he asked.

"Since first grade, so pretty much forever."

"Have you met my daughters? Nancy and Abby?"

"I kinda remember when they came down for spring break? But I don't think I put together who they were."

"They're a few years older than you guys. They didn't want to stay at Cindy and Lem's, so I put them in a hotel on the water. Cindy was pretty insulted, but they did go to the house a few times."

"Yeah, I kinda remember that. Christian was doing backflips off the diving board to impress them."

"Cindy has this idea that all of the cousins should be closer, but Lem doesn't seem to care either way."

"Huh. I like Mrs. Worth. I think she comes on kind of strong to a lot of people, but she's nice to me, anyway."

Pete raised his eyebrows. "I think you're the very first person I've met to say Cindy's 'nice'! I married Sandy over twenty years ago—that's how long I've known them."

Eve laughed out loud a little.

"I heard when Cindy was a fat little kid, she stabbed her schoolmate in the face with a fork."

Eve's eyes expanded.

"She spent four months in a psych ward for kids, or something like that."

Eve's mouth dropped open.

"But maybe you're not supposed to know that."

They arrived in the lobby, and Pete saw me glistening through the front door glass, reflecting the colorful neon signs of the restaurant next door.

"Holy shit, you brought the Caddy!?" Pete ran toward me, propelled by an unseen wind. "You fucking brought the Caddy to New York City! Holy shit, you are *one crazy fucking teenager!*" He ran to me and circled me twice, his fingers and palms freed from the gloves, caressing my shell. "I seriously can't believe you brought this car. I only saw her on the road, like, maybe twice? They *never* drove her more than a few miles. And you're just a kid! I figured you swiped your dad's Honda from the garage or something, but oh my god, Eve! What were you thinking?" He bent down to look at the blue and red decals striping my hood. He skirted along my length a third time, checking for marks and dents. "I can't believe—she kept it all this time? How did she get Lem to let her—ohhh . . . wait—ohhhshit, is this Lem's car now? Did you swipe *Lem's* car? But with . . . Muriel . . . ?"

He stopped.

"Eve, what's really going on?"

Eve crossed her arms over her chest. Pete continued to inspect me while keeping an unwavering eye on her. She was terrified he'd find a gash or a scratch or bird feces marring my hood.

From the first moment he touched me, I felt Pete's entire life. I could see his apartment, his thoughts, his memories with Sandra. He traveled endlessly to keep the idea of returning home precious, but after a few days in his apartment, the walls would close in around him. He was surrounded by people, even people who loved him, and he could have whatever material items he wanted, but Pete was profoundly alone.

He finished another round and returned to Eve. He stood inches from her face. She could feel the heat coming off him. Even his breath smelled luxurious, like red wine and dark chocolate.

"Eve, this is serious. You've got to be in some big fucking trouble if you drove all the way up here in Muriel Worth's Cadillac. Are you in big fucking trouble?"

"I don't know," she said. Then she added, "maybe." She didn't intend to be reticent because he seemed genuinely concerned, but her diluted answer provoked even more worry on his part. Eve quickly ascertained that Pete could only assume she was running away from something major. He must be thinking she *had* to be pregnant or abused by a relative or dating a heroin dealer. She *had* to take the car for some reason, but there was no explanation that made any practical sense. There were plenty of cars in Florida. Why this one? She probably had lots of friends, too. Why Muriel?

Up until that moment, Eve had figured she was probably in *some* trouble, but she didn't think of it as "big fucking trouble" until Pete repeated it over and over. She couldn't explain that she *had* to leave because her mother was annoying.

And her mother was a liar.

And she'd learned on Monday morning that her dead father was still alive.

Pete peered into her. He enjoyed being a host and perhaps even a friend, but he loathed the rare creep of paternal feelings, even with his own kids. If one of them absconded with one of his cars, however, and *his* mother, he would have found that child and had her ankle-cuffed to the kitchen table for a year. He had to know what had made Eve run and whether he could throw money at the problem, not to help her so much as to distance his conscience from the knowing, much in the same manner he'd helped Sandra extract her finances from Lem's.

"Listen, I'm not going to turn you in or anything, but you have to tell me what's going on. Other than a few random holiday cards, I haven't seen or heard from my ex-mother-in-law for almost a decade, and now she's sleeping in my guest room while her teenage friend is driving around the streets of New York in her hundred-thousand-dollar Caddy. Something's seriously messed up here."

Eve looked at me. Until that moment, she was unaware of my monetary value. She knew I was an immaculate classic, but she'd never calculated that it would take over thirteen years of full-time floor sweeping to afford me, at my current price, and only if she saved every single cent. In thirteen years, she'd be thirty.

"Are you serious?" she gulped. She meant my price tag, but Pete thought she was referring to his earlier statement.

"I won't turn you in," he reiterated.

Eve paused for a beat, then caught up with the conversational disconnect. She put her cobalt-painted fingernail between her teeth and bit down. She finally replied, "Yeah, I think I'm kinda screwed."

"I'm working under the assumption that no one knows you're in New York? Only Laura?"

"We told them we're in Miami."

"Lem and Cindy?"

"And my mother. And the police."

"You talked to the police?"

Eve divulged the key points of the previous three days, partly because she wanted Pete to like her—*maybe he needs an intern?*—but mostly because somewhere in the back of her mind it dawned on her that the more Pete knew, the more power she had to pivot the narrative: a sixteen-year-old from Florida magically appears in Tribeca in a kerjillion-dollar collectible automobile? Surely the wealthy business magnate had *something* to do with it, especially if she was staying with him and they indulged in expensive macaroons and wine by a warm October fire . . .

But Pete, being Pete, was attuned to her strategy.

"You're ballsy. I get why Laura likes you."

"I'm not trying to be. I just . . . I had to get out of there."

Pete sympathized with her desperation.

"I still can't believe I'm actually standing next to this car! Goddamn!" he exclaimed. He realized he was in our story now and all he could do was help.

"You should drive," she said, tossing him the keys. The parking lot was only a block away, but it took us twenty-five minutes to get there because Pete wanted to loop me around the entire financial district. Twice.

***

Eve returned to the penthouse lugging a garbage bag stuffed with warmer autumn clothing, but it was the weight of the long day that pulled her down. Pete insisted they bring in their belongings, and he hauled in a second bag of equal bulk. He dimmed the lights when they entered the bedroom, careful not to disturb Muriel, who was already snoring gently on the far side of the bed by the windows. The tidy lump of her body was wrapped in a fetal position around a second pillow and resembled an oversized marshmallow under the milk-white sheets.

Pete wished Eve a good night and opened himself wide for a hug. Captured in his faultless arms, she understood why Muriel had lingered in their earlier embrace. There was something about Pete and his benignity, his sturdiness, and his status in the world that awakened the submerged vulnerabilities of others. It was also the first time in ten years that a father, anyone's father, had hugged her. Pete stood firm, a cashmere-covered column, as Eve shuddered against his shoulder, and cried.

He rubbed her back, aiding the release, and then called off the moment with a few light taps. He again wished her a good night as he disappeared down the hall.

Eve prepared herself for bed. She went to the private bathroom and instinctively touched Muriel's toothbrush to ensure it was wet before using her own. She returned to the bed and gently lifted the cover, barely considering Muriel's naked back while checking for a diaper. *Good girl*, Eve thought, while also applauding her own maturity as a caregiver.

Eve slipped into her side of the bed after shutting off the light, awestruck by the contradictions of the fine organic bamboo sheets in the way they draped her with weight and warmth while remaining crisp, but also soft. Muriel stopped snoring and shifted. The entire wall on Muriel's side was composed of nine-foot windows masked with thick, combed-silk curtains layered over sheer draperies. The moon floated along an ornamental parapet across the street and pierced a slit between the drapes like a flashlight in a cave. It was so bright! Eve stared directly at it and then she looked up at the ceiling and followed the afterimages against the glossy paint as the circle shifted from orange to magenta to deep brown. She closed her eyes, and it continued to mutate through greens and blues on black. She moved her eyes beneath the lids back and forth, and the remnants of the moon's glow followed.

Despite her exhaustion, she couldn't sleep. She rolled again toward the windows, facing Muriel, and opened her eyes. Muriel was awake and looking directly at her with blue eyes shining in the moonlit room. Eve was too tired to be startled. They studied each other in silence. The singular, bluish light amplified Muriel's wrinkles as her skin sagged and settled a touch against the pillow. Eve's features were held together by her youth, symmetrical and firm. Muriel found the same shining moon floating on Eve's corneas.

Such a light in this girl. Such vitality. Such a future.

Muriel never imagined in her wildest dreams that she would ever leave The Deerwood, travel to New York, or see Pete Caldwell again. She resisted her disease and its gray fate, but every day it chiseled a little more, a little too much, as it turned the magnificent sculpture that was her life into a pile of scrap and dust.

But then this girl on the other side of the bed, this girl with the wild stripe in her hair and ears trimmed with sparkling shrapnel, this girl who jumped into her car and pressed hard on the gas . . . Muriel thanked Eve with a soundless smile that stretched across the blue-white distance of the soft bed, across the chasm in their ages and experience, across the traumas of their lying, nescient families.

People have their dreams and people have their realities. It's rare when the two intersect, and rarer still when two people can experience dreams and reality simultaneously with someone they love.

Eve smiled back, and they both closed their eyes for the night.

THURSDAY

Chapter 16

It was late morning when we turned a few lazy corners and steadily climbed up a meandering hill. I felt a remarkable kinship with the opulent houses lining the road—powerful constructions of old brick and thick stone. They possessed a weatherproofed resiliency and stoically mocked the long, wet winters year after year. Balancing their hard defiance were graceful proportions and elegant details that showcased generations of meticulous care. At long last, we pulled over.

"This is it," Eve said.

She looked around, marrying the immediate view of the house with the online version she had memorized. The pixels had failed to convey the resolute stateliness of the neighborhood and its expansive properties, with houses set like weighty jewels in a velvet case of perfect lawns. Her laptop had failed to capture the magical quality of the light as shimmering golden leaves lent their radiance to the early afternoon. The computer had further neglected to display the detailed fingers of a purple-leaf grapevine as it crawled skyward and broached the perimeter of a ten-foot window capped with an impressive hemispherical arch. Eve followed the vine's scarlet twists and was startled to see a man standing in front of his chocolate-brown curtains, peering down the driveway at the long and mysterious car.

"C'mon," Eve said, catching her breath as she traipsed around my hood to help Muriel. The perfectly flat flagstones made for an effortless upward journey from the street, but the women slowed considerably as they approached. Eve's nerves matched the scale of the oversized wooden front door. She clutched Muriel's arm, perhaps a little too hard, and Muriel felt the electric vibration of her courage through their sweaters.

"Breathe," Muriel said, standing back as Eve rang the bell. A two-tone gong reverberated through a storm door, the heavy wood behind it, and the stone walls of the suburban mini-château.

"*J'arrive!*"

The first door opened. At first they could only see the foyer with a grand curving staircase that flowed between black iron rails. It wrapped around a stone fireplace where tiny pewter dog figurines begged, played, and slept on their polished mahogany mantle. The entry exuded style, warmth, and history. The man from the front window casually reemerged from behind the door and into the light.

"Est-ce que je peux vous aider?" he said. Eve didn't speak and he tried again. "May I help you?"

The man looked the part of a professor. His brownish hair was parted neatly on the side, and he maintained a decent crop of it. The fur on his face was martially contained; nary a strand escaped to his neck, nose, or ears. He looked young. He looked handsome, but not aggressively so. He looked exactly like the photograph Eve had discovered in her mother's bedroom, as if it had been snapped the day before.

"Hi Daddy," she said.

From the street, I could sense his face fall and then rise and then fall again—as if stretching his upper cheeks was the only way to comprehend this apparition.

"Eve—?"

He scrutinized her teenaged face, untangling the Gordian knot of missing time. He studied her—probing, piercing, scanning, identifying. She had uttered foreign words, and yet he recognized them from this strange girl whose eyes matched his own.

"I found you," Eve whispered. "I found you."

She saw the recognition blasting through his synapses, connecting the vision to his brain, then his heart, and then his arms. Eve's father threw back the second door and scooped her up, spinning on the front porch with a velocity that nearly generated its own wind.

"Eve! Oh my god, my sweet girl, my sweet little Eeeve!" he cried as they spun, his body collapsing and pulling her in, as if the space between them could be halved and then repeatedly halved again until they were molecularly impossible to separate.

She reached her arms up as he held her and she touched his face, that warm familiar beard, gold spreading to the tips from the oblique sunlight; the forgotten space, a staple's width, between his front teeth; the slight bank of his once-broken nose, always steering left.

"Ma vie est enfin terminée!" he cried. *"Mes rêves sont tous devenus réalité!"*

They stopped spinning and he let her go. He looked her up and down again, gauging, assessing, and realizing all over again that she was there, his daughter, his beautiful, long-lost, courageous, brilliant daughter who found him—found him after all this time and distance and bewilderment and pain.

"Hi Daddy," she whispered again.

He pulled her in again.

But he pulled too hard, mistakenly calibrating for her former weight as a six-year-old. She flew into his slender body and they stumbled toward the edge of the porch, the back of his heels unable to support the movement of two fully grown humans in motion. It was almost comical until they reached the precipice, Eve wavering frenetically while she sought a railing or a column to halt the poor maneuver. She could see the basement-level driveway carved into the hill beneath the house. It approached indignantly as their launch continued, and she realized they weren't going to stop, and there was nothing protecting them from the imminent twelve-foot drop. Eve felt her father succumb to gravity a moment before she did, the split difference between the front and back seats of a roller coaster edging over its principal bluff.

They were falling. She could see his face in the foreground and his terror expanding as the pavement in the background rose to meet them. She looked to the side, searching for Muriel or a ledge or one of those ancient vines to cling to, but instead she saw the North Tower of the World Trade Center burning. She looked back at her dad as she rode their fall and clutched his maroon sweater vest, the distance interminable but rapidly disintegrating as his head seemed to shrink and the pavement expanded, expanded, expanded—

Eve woke up with both hands clenched and throbbing and pinned beneath her heaving chest against the guest room mattress, her open mouth screaming into the impact that never occurred.

"Eve! It's okay, sweetheart! It's okay . . ."

A hand against her back. Warm. Familiar.

"It was just a dream. Just a bad dream. You're here. You're safe. There there, now. There there . . ."

The soothing voice. Intimate. Compassionate.

Eve came back into herself and slowly extracted her numb hands. Her breathing was shallow and tight, and even in Pete's large guest room, everything felt compressed. Muriel continued to stroke her back. "Just a dream, Eve. It was just a nasty dream."

***

Hours later, the sun replaced the moon with a hot orange light that slowly meandered up the bed until it found Eve's pillow. She reluctantly woke up again. The dream was so fresh she thought she could still smell her father's coffee. She wondered if he was, in fact, somehow in their room, and she opened her eyes hoping to find the maroon-sweatered man leaning in to kiss her forehead. But the room was empty and the bathroom door was closed, and as she roused, she came to understand that Pete was brewing a fresh pot of coffee in the distant kitchen. She rolled back over, her eyes focusing on a corner of the pillowcase but seeing the dream instead. The house. The vines. Her father's look of joy at their reunion, and then terror.

Muriel exited the bathroom. She was showered, and dressed in a motley ensemble of green sweatpants, a red silk shirt, and a lavender knit cardigan.

"I'm not sure." Eve laughed, answering Muriel's visual request for an assessment of her appearance. "Maybe a different sweater. And the other pants—the black ones. And let's change your shirt."

Muriel began to undress, and Eve bounded off the bed to find the garbage bags containing their belongings. Instead, she discovered two identical hard-shell suitcases by the door and a third one, already opened, on the upholstered bench at the foot of their bed. Muriel's (Judith's) clean clothes were folded neatly, and her worn articles were sealed in a zippered plastic bag to the side. In the other suitcases, Eve's items had received the same treatment.

"What is this?" Eve said, looking up.

"Peter must be jet-lagged," Muriel said. "Probably got up at three a.m. and gave himself a project."

"He found luggage at three a.m.?"

Muriel grinned. "This is New York."

Eve helped Muriel find some better clothing options, careful to avoid items that too strongly evoked the presence of her mother. Once these were selected, she said, "I'm gonna take a shower, but you don't have to wait for me."

Muriel leaned in, like her father in the dream, and kissed the top of Eve's head before turning around to re-dress herself. Eve headed toward the bathroom, but she turned halfway and said, "Hey, can I ask you something?"

"Anything," Muriel replied.

"If it's nice out, can we put the top down today?"

"No."

Muriel didn't have anything else to add, so Eve continued to the bathroom, which was twice the size of her own in Florida and magically stocked with her favorite coconut shampoo. *Nice touch, Laura,* she thought. Twenty minutes later, she sauntered down Pete's hallway with straight, wet hair and a cheerful demeanor, her dream washed down the shower drain with the grit of the previous day. She moved past geometric oil paintings by important artists, passed the warm door to the apartment's electronics cabinet, and glanced at a built-in glass showcase housing Pete's collection of Hindu gods and other spiritual figurines. His expansive castle was already beginning to feel intimate and homey.

Eve rounded the corner into the kitchen and saw Muriel sitting perfectly erect on a barstool at the end of the lengthy stone island. She held a steaming cup of coffee, and her face was contorted into an angular pinch that Eve had never seen. Pete was next to her, his face equally sallow. They looked at her with a daunting caution, as if hoping she wouldn't notice the horror they themselves couldn't unsee. She felt instantly discombobulated, and she reached for the island to stabilize herself. Pete looked beyond her right shoulder, and Eve turned to follow his gaze.

It was Lem.

***

He was eating a powdered doughnut rather sloppily, its dandruff settling on his ink-blue sweater when he exhaled in between bites. As he chewed those soft buttery chunks, he managed to keep most of the sugar on the surface of his upper lip and front teeth. It accumulated rapidly, forming a paste.

"Lem, you're making a mess," Muriel said. "Get a plate."

Lem looked to Pete, who reluctantly got up to retrieve one, not wanting the mess but also hesitant to accommodate Lem in any manner. The cleaning woman was coming in two hours and she would clean up after Lem, but Pete decided to play a proper host for Muriel and produced a dish for her messy adult son.

Eve remained frozen next to the open archway to the kitchen.

"You want a doughnut?" Lem asked her. She anticipated the harsh rasp of a bounty hunter, but his voice seemed light, as if sweetened by his breakfast. She couldn't answer. She couldn't understand whether he was really there, or whether she was back in the clutches of yet another ultra-realistic nightmare. She looked to Muriel, who slowly pushed the box of doughnuts forward. Pete, having done his duty, remained by the sink. "Coffee?" Lem offered.

Eve looked at him with curious apprehension, like a gentle cow meeting an affable executioner a few seconds before the slaughter. His eyes, like his mother's, were an entrancing blue, but where Muriel's shone with welcome, Lem's were impenetrable. She knew he must be furious with her, but was he? She expected castigation, not an invitation to share in a pleasant breakfast. Could a man who treated his own mother so horribly really be tempered by a doughnut?

And how did Lem get there? And when? Who betrayed them? What did he want? Or, rather, how did he plan to detain them and *what was he going to do?* She wanted to turn around and reverse the entire morning—away from this scene, down the long hall, past the art and the sculptures and the hum of the electronics cabinet, back into the shower, and finally back into the sunny bed where she could bury herself deep beneath the warm sheets. She thought maybe she could reverse everything all the way back to late Sunday night when she'd finally found her father on the computer—but she also didn't want to go back that far.

"So the schmuck got a raise anyway! Can you believe that? I swear it's the incompetent dumbfucks who win at every turn," Lem expelled to Pete, the wholly disinterested businessman he desperately wished to impress. "I'm telling you, it's not what you know, it's who you're screwing and----"

"Uh huh . . ." Pete said flatly, still watching Eve.

Muriel watched her, too, trying to figure out how best to intervene, but the sight of Lem in Pete's kitchen had also paralyzed her. It had been less than a week, but somehow he looked fatter and even more unpleasant than usual. She held her mug two inches off the counter with both hands, fearful that putting it down might signal her compliance with his wishes, whatever they might be.

Eve tried again to come up with something to say.

Nothing.

There's a moment in every game when the winner knows he's won and the loser knows she's lost, but the loser doesn't want to admit defeat and the winner wants to savor the moment of palpable torture for the vanquished. Muriel and Eve had the advantages of age and youth, beauty and smarts, strong allies and the overriding asset of their hunger for self-improvement, yet somehow Lem—with all of his shortcomings—had won. He turned back to his mother and took a second doughnut from the box, a chocolate-covered old-fashioned that crumbled under the pressure of his chunky grip.

As he pecked at the pieces, he turned back to Eve and said, "Pete told me you took excellent care of the car."

And your mother! Eve wanted to shout while continuing her stunned silence.

"I also told your mom that when you're done being grounded, we can help you find a car you can afford."

Did he think he was being nice?

"In about thirty years!! Bro!" he snorted, seeking a high five from his ex-brother-in-law. Pete left him hanging to attend to Muriel, who remained frozen like the subject of a Grant Wood painting.

"Are you okay?" Pete whispered to Muriel, gently helping her return her beverage to the countertop. When it landed, she started shaking, having lost the comfort of that singular focus.

"Did you know?" she asked Pete. She studied Lem, that strange creature whom she remembered loving more than anything before he'd managed to turn all her gold into grime.

"He just showed up," Pete said, "kind of like you. He must've found out you were here and took the six o'clock from West Palm."

"I can hear you," Lem said, the chocolate from the second doughnut sticking to his bottom lip, oddly repelled by the silky powder that still clung to the top. "I got the five-fifty from Miami. Been up since three, actually." He poured himself another coffee to swish out the sugary remnants stuck in his back teeth. Pete assumed it was his second or third cup of the young day. It was his fifth.

"How did he find us?" Muriel asked Pete.

"Ha, well, that is the big question, isn't it, Mom?" Lem said. It was like an audition for a James Bond villain, and Eve smirked at his overacting. In that moment, Lem existed both in the foreground and deep in the background as her mind splintered between her hard reality and the ramifications of her next move: escape or surrender.

"Laura and this one had quite a little conversation going," he said, while actively wringing his hands. *All he needs is a white cat to stroke and he'll get the job*, Eve thought. "You were pretty clever, too, Mom, throwing us off with that call from Miami."

"Miami?" Muriel asked, not remembering. She hadn't been to Miami in over a decade. Her enveloping glaze triggered him. Lem started fishing around the burly coat he'd plopped on the counter when he arrived. He had dismissed Pete's desire to hang it, and Pete's chagrin was renewed as he watched Lem's metal buttons and a steely zipper bounce along his slick marble.

"That reminds me, Mom. I have your pills." The coat pocket yielded a small orange bottle with her name on it. He uncapped it and presented her with two capsules.

Muriel looked at his palm. There was a dab of chocolate on one side, a dusting of powder near the thumb, and the two purple-and-white pills in the sweaty center.

"Take them."

Like a puppet with unseen strings, Muriel felt compelled to extend her hand as Lem flipped his palm and placed the dangerous pellets on her papery flesh.

"Take them," he said again.

Something passed between Muriel and Eve. Something unseen by Pete and Lem, but keenly felt by all of them.

"She doesn't need them," Eve blurted.

"She speaks!" Lem said, still looking into Muriel's eyes. "Now shut the fuck up."

"Hey!" Pete said. "Don't talk to her like that in my house, *bro*."

"You know what? I think the police will be happy to know Muriel and

Eve are finally safe, don't you, Pete? Safe here, in New York City, *in your cozy little penthouse?* Harboring fugitives—pretty sure that's a felony, guy."

"What, did you look that up?"

Lem cocked his head in a silent admission that yes, he had looked it up.

"A fugitive has to commit a crime, Lem. What's the crime here? Visiting a relative?"

"Oh . . . I dunno . . . Kidnapping? Abduction? Auto theft? Credit card fraud? Take your pick."

"You're ridiculous."

"I don't care if it all gets thrown out, and maybe you won't get five years for helping them, but I can't imagine the publicity will do you any good. You know, with your important business associates, I mean."

Pete glared at him through his black irises. Lem's steely eyes met them and held.

"I'll say whatever the fuck I want." He flipped from Pete to Muriel so quickly it took a moment for the rest of his large head to catch up. "Take the pills, Mom."

Muriel brought the pills closer to her face and continued to peer at them. They stayed huddled in her palm like tiny animals suddenly released from the zoo with no idea where to go.

"No!" Eve yelled. In one swift motion she ran over to Muriel, took the pills from her trembling hand, and finished her journey at the stainless-steel sink. She flicked her wrist and ran the water down the drain.

Pete smiled. Muriel exhaled.

"Pack your shit, we're leaving in five!!" Lem hollered.

Eve faced him with her back to the sink, one foot on the floor and the other flat on the cabinet door, her hands positioned against the counter for leverage. She was about to leap. She was about to throw her body against Lem's and knock him to the pavement, reliving the fall from her dream. She was about to grab the box of doughnuts on the way and smother him to death with the remaining jelly, coconut cream, and cinnamon twist. Lem wasn't going to stop her. Lem wasn't going to show up out of nowhere and threaten her, her new best friend, or her possible future boss.

She was going to win.

But she couldn't move. Her body was rigid. She felt her adrenalized strength coursing through her, but she also felt fragile, as if the slightest breeze from a distant whisper might cause her to crumble into a million shattered pieces. She stayed there, heart pounding, clinging to the counter by the sink as Muriel and Pete turned their heads to the other side of the kitchen in time to see Lem's face resume its normal, dull color.

"Five minutes," he said again, irrationally calm. "Where's the can?"

"You know where it is. You've been here a dozen times."

Lem ambled down the long hall to find it. When they heard the door close, Eve finally released her grip.

"I'm sorry," she said to Pete and Muriel. "I'm so, so sorry." She ran down the hall to her room and closed the door. She didn't want Pete to see her cry again.

***

Lem provided the details of his plan: while they packed, Pete would fetch the car from the garage and wait for them; then they'd go down the elevator together, load up in one shot, and Lem would drive them away from Pete's safe harbor.

"I don't want to go back to Florida," Muriel complained. "We just got here."

"We're not going to Florida, Mom. Not yet."

"No?"

"Don't you want to see Sandy?"

Muriel was surprised. "Really?"

"Hey, I'm not the bad guy here! It's only three hours, so yeah, we're going to Saratoga and we'll all fly home from there."

The women finished collecting their things under Lem's soldierly supervision, but there wasn't much to pack thanks to Pete's preemptive efforts with their new luggage. Eve and Muriel's moods were yin to yang; Eve succumbed to the encircling darkness, while Muriel threw back the tall drapes to let the sunshine she felt inside explode into the room. Sandra had visited Florida earlier in the year, but Micah and Sam had stayed behind. Soon they'd all be together in the same place at the same time, and without Cindy. It was wonderful.

"Grace, I'm going home!" Muriel said in a singsong voice.

Lem sighed, "Go to the bathroom, Mom. I don't want to stop more than we have to."

A few moments later, they rolled their sleek suitcases to the foyer and summoned the elevator. It arrived carrying Pete, who stepped back into his apartment.

"What the hell, Pete?" Lem cried. "You were supposed to get the car!"

"It's down there," he said, handing Lem the keys.

"You just left it on the street?!"

"Yep."

"Oh fuck you, Pete. C'mon, ladies!" Lem held the elevator door with his back against the jamb while Eve rolled in the suitcases. Pete whispered something into Muriel's ear, and she turned around and hugged him.

"You know I love you," she said. "Good luck in Singapore tomorrow."

Their eyes met and lingered.

"Take good care now," he replied, finally releasing her. Muriel joined Eve in the elevator, and Lem moved away from the stopped door.

"Eve? Can I get a goodbye?" Pete beckoned.

The doors began to close and Eve deftly escaped, her lithe form moving past Lem like a vapor. The door sensor caught her movement and held for a moment, but it succeeded in sealing its cargo before Lem could find the button to hold it in place—partly because Muriel took a deliberate step to the left to shield the controls. The elevator was already a few feet below the penthouse before Lem finally stabbed the button, but without Pete's approval code, it didn't light. The elevator deposited Lem and Muriel in the lobby and forbade them from returning.

"I didn't get a chance to talk to you," Pete said hurriedly to Eve from his secured and personal top-floor lobby. "We only have a minute, but you need to know I didn't do this. Lem texted me after he landed and he was already in the cab. Laura's on your side, but I'm thinking maybe Cindy got her phone?" As he spoke to Eve, he simultaneously crafted and sent a text to Lem informing him she would be right down. Eve was mesmerized by his multitasking. "Anyway, I'm sorry I can't help you out of this."

After a beat, she replied, "No, you did help. You helped a lot."

He dismissed it with a shrug and continued, "Listen, I gotta tell you, that was a really brave thing you did with those pills back there. Has Muriel been off them all week?"

"I'm not sure about Monday morning, but yeah, since then."

"Look, I know she's not a hundred percent----"

Eve nodded in agreement.

"----but I don't think it's Alzheimer's."

The words passed through Eve's ears, but her brain failed to translate the sounds into a concept she could comprehend. She thought he'd said Muriel didn't have Alzheimer's, but it felt as misguided as if he'd said Muriel didn't have feet. Of course she had Alzheimer's.

Didn't she?

Eve wondered if he knew his simple sentence had the power to entirely change Muriel's predicament. It felt like he had dropped a boulder into a wading pool.

"My mom had it," he continued. "And two uncles, three grandparents, and my oldest cousin. I know this disease, and I give a lot of money to fight it. The point is, Muriel isn't really acting like any of them."

A white dot of hope at the center of Eve's jet-black yin expanded.

"For one thing, she didn't repeat once," he said.

"Repeat?"

"You know, like a record stuck in a groove? 'What's in that bag?'

'Lunch.' 'Oh.' Two minutes later, 'What's in that bag?' 'That's our lunch, Mom.' 'Oh right, our lunch.' And then a minute later, 'What's in that bag?' and so on until you finally put the damned bag back in the fridge."

"Yeah, she doesn't do that, but she mixes stuff up and forgets things all the time. And she can be pretty random. She also falls asleep in the middle of sentences and she . . . she pees herself." Eve stopped, but Pete nodded his clear comprehension of everything we had been through.

"I'm not saying there isn't something wrong, but Alzheimer's is a pretty specific condition. I think it's highly unlikely someone who is both stage three *and* going through a week like yours could possibly remember that her distant sorta-relative is flying to Singapore tomorrow. Heck, *I* almost forgot."

He pulled his phone out of his pocket and wrote a text to Sandra while continuing the conversation with Eve.

"So, what is it?" she asked. "You don't think that . . . Lem, like—like he made it up?"

"I wouldn't put it past him. He's not a good guy, Eve," Pete replied. "He really did a number on poor Muriel. I should've stayed in touch." Eve peered into his inkwell eyes and thought she saw something resembling remorse. Then his phone buzzed, and he blinked a few times to clear his vulnerability. He glanced at the text, hoping for Sandra's reply, but the disgust on his face clearly showed that Lem was growing impatient.

"Go to Saratoga and take care of her, but when you get back home, *promise me* you'll stay away from Lem."

It was another boulder in the shallow pool. How could Eve be friends with Laura if she had to avoid Lem, and without Laura's house, where could she go to escape her mother? Eve also thought about her job at The Deerwood: how would she see Muriel if she got fired and Lem banned her from the visitor list? She had already announced she would never return to Florida, but that dream was freshly pulverized, and, paradoxically, Eve yearned to return to the much-needed segments of her familiar life down there.

The adult human brain processes information through the prefrontal cortex. It quickly generates an awareness of pragmatic outcomes. But teenagers process information through the amygdala, a small, emotional almond buried deep within the brain's intricate folds. Pete watched as Eve's young mind stretched itself, as her rash actions began to align with the hard-nosed ramifications of her choices, as her brain began to manifest a brand-new concept: consequences. Pete watched dolefully as biology quickly remapped her young mind.

He held her shoulders in his palms, steadying her and subtly apologizing for adding more stress to her situation. "It's okay," he said. "Everything's going to be okay. Look, don't worry about Lem. Focus on Muriel. She needs you more than ever. When you get to Saratoga, talk to Sandy and Micah and tell them everything you told me about Muriel. I'll give them a call, too. Sandy and Micah are good people. We can trust them."

We. He used the word "we." Eve didn't want to leave.

"And you can call or text me whenever you want," he said, dropping one hand to fold a small wad of cash and his business card into hers. Then he pulled her in and hugged her again, doing his best to absorb her spiking anxiety. The elevator arrived. The door opened, and Pete gently pushed Eve inside with his trademark wink as he pressed the button for the lobby.

Down below, Muriel and I patiently waited in the sunny trapezoids reflecting off the windows across the street. She sat in the front passenger's seat. A grotesque view of Lem's squashed, khaki-wrapped buttocks filled the glass of my driver's side window as he leaned against my door. His head shifted repeatedly from his phone to the entry of Pete's building, like a dog waiting for someone to finally throw a stick.

Eve appeared at the far end of the lobby, a ghost behind tinted glass reluctantly reentering our world. Like a trained chauffeur, Lem opened my side and aggressively pushed her seat—now his seat—forward. Muriel looked away from the subtle violence as I prepared myself to receive Eve, to support her, to protect her from within. She hesitated, then finally stepped to the sidewalk. She looked terrified, her head low, shoulders high, arms crossed. She clutched her own hard biceps.

As she neared, Lem grinned: the hunter collecting his prey. I remember my outrage and dismay when he corralled her into the back seat, but Eve was probably lucky he didn't strap her to my hood. I was accustomed to Eve and Muriel's mode of entry as they gently maneuvered themselves with consideration into their seats, but Lem plummeted and plonked like a sack of hard potatoes, slammed my door, and jammed the keys into the ignition, abrading the metal with the edge of his ungoverned key.

"Take it easy!" Muriel scowled.

He adjusted the mirrors and snapped the seatbelt and repositioned the seat, all with the same sharpness as his labored breathing. Then he ceased all movement as if someone had pressed pause on the remote. Muriel paused too, unsure and wary. Eve assumed he was charting the route in his mind, as she often did before starting me up.

Lem flapped his hand backward over the seat like a pancake attached to hairy sausages. His calloused thumb was inches from Eve's face, and nearly the same shade as my leather.

"Phone."

In the two short years since Eve got her phone, it had become an inseparable appendage, as critical to her being as clothing, food, and shelter. She had 132 apps and used more than a third of them weekly, perhaps a dozen daily, and at least two nearly every waking hour. She used her phone to monitor her physical location in time and space and to stay current with popular culture. She accessed her bank balance, obtained weather warnings, and practiced her Spanish. Eve watched videos of baby animals, travel adventures, and teen-centric comedians; she stored recipes, kept track of her periods, and swiped a color wheel to change her bedroom lights from pink to orange to blue. She used it to listen to music. She used it to shop for earrings. She used it to order burritos.

But mostly she used it to communicate with Laura.

"Now." Lem flexed his hand, and she heard two knuckles crack.

"I won't use it," she said.

"I know," he replied, his hand firmly stationed. "We're not going until you hand it over."

Eve looked to Muriel as Muriel studied Lem. She had lived with this man for eighteen years, from diapers to diploma, and a near-daily relationship with him had spanned the three decades beyond. Yet here he was, two feet away and sharing a bench, a complete stranger. It wasn't Muriel's memory that disappeared in that moment; it was her understanding of the man she knew to be Lemuel Worth. Despite all that he had done to her, flipping her life and the rest of it, Muriel had wanted to believe that somehow, in some incomprehensible way, he might have performed his deceits for her own good.

But now here he was, smelling like tired deodorant and black coffee, antagonizing a young and defenseless woman. Her friend. In that precise moment, Lem ceased to be Muriel's Lem, and any lingering respect she may have preserved in the smallest chamber of her heart was annihilated. It was *her* car and it was *their choice* to leave. Muriel wondered if Lem knew that by taking Eve's phone, he also risked losing a mother.

"Stop it, Lem. Leave her alone."

"Phone," he said again, continuing to look forward while his arm bent back.

"It's dead," Eve said. "I forgot to charge it."

"Phone."

"That's her private property," Muriel insisted.

"Ha, you're funny," he said. "Property." He stroked my steering wheel and tapped it with his left hand. His right hand remained on the back of the seat, upside down, held firmly in the hardening cement of his resolve.

Eve looked at Muriel again, but she knew there was nothing to be done. She looked at his hand with its grotty sheen of sweat, crevassed lines, and the faint discoloration of a long-dissolved wart. Lingering chocolate stained the canyon walls between his ring and pinky fingers.

Eve wondered what would happen if she bit him. She could picture his terrorized surprise as her teeth sliced through the fleshy tips, splintering the nails and cutting through bone, popping the ends off like champagne corks on New Year's Eve with a bubbly splay of blood. If she bit him, he couldn't drive. If she bit him, she could still escape and find her father.

She thought about taking hold of his wretched paw and bending it further, pulling it down along the back side of the seat until the wrist snapped. Or she could take off an earring and stab the meaty center of his palm with its post.

Anything to make it go away.

Anything to keep her phone.

But Eve knew none of that would happen. She couldn't hurt him, as much as she wanted to, and he was going to win yet another round. She was trapped in my back seat, and she decided to proceed with the inevitable to, at the very least, shorten the remaining length of the painful day. She reached into her pocket and made sure her phone was locked before placing it delicately on his palm.

"Please don't hurt it," she said.

His hand snapped around it like a sprung bear trap. She experienced a split second of horror as his fingers grazed her own, his chewed nails and slimy hagfish fingertips spreading an unseen residue on her as she pulled away. He may have said "Thanks," but none of us heard it—our focus remained squarely on Eve and her contaminated hand, which she held in a hang-drop position like a puppy who'd just stepped on a sharp rock for the first time.

With Eve's second life stowed securely in his coat pocket, Lem clutched the keys, threw his right foot against the floor, and backed up halfway, sending excessive fuel into my engine as he turned the ignition, inciting me to holler.

Lem had never known how to properly drive me, but to be fair he wasn't given much opportunity, as Muriel was understandably loath to lend her keys. He spent most of his driving years with newer, computerized cars that processed his intentions when he pressed his foot to the floor, so without practice or nuance, Lem charged forth, lurching with the gas, shorting the brakes, and providing my headrests with fresh purpose. Eve was positioned squarely behind Lem's sizable head, and, already ailing from her tensions, she found both the view and his staccato maneuvers nauseating. She held the edge of my seat with one hand and the back of her neck with the other while her stomach wobbled at the intersections. She was additionally annoyed that her experience of New York was being truncated, and now, even the view of the beautiful buildings was cropped by his mass.

There were only a dozen or so lights before we launched up the elevated West Side Highway, nimbly fingered the harp strings of the George Washington Bridge, and snaked the rock cliff edges of the Palisades. Eventually, we joined a steady stream of migrating leaf-peepers, paying annual homage to Mother Nature's palette in the form of oohs and aahs and camera clicks.

New York's vertically structured view abruptly returned to rambling forests, and Eve was understandably perplexed by the evolving scale of the city. At night, the artificial lights illuminated the entire seaboard and elongated its borders—it took hours to drive in. But in the daylight, the whole of Manhattan glistened like a crystal shard on the silk of its rivers and, once crossed, nineteen million people wondrously disappeared. The trees overtook my rear window and retained their stance for the duration of the trip.

Eve eventually returned her gaze to the front, and she traversed the horizontal folds in Lem's neck up to the corona of his remaining salted hair. She finally landed squarely on his soul-sucking eyes in the rearview mirror. He was watching her.

"I get it," he said.

"Get what?" Muriel replied.

"Not you, Mom. I was telling Eve, 'I get it.'"

"Get what?" Muriel said again, protectively. She wanted to know what he thought he "got" about Eve, but Lem erroneously assumed she was repeating herself in precisely the same manner that Pete had described. He already had Eve's phone, but Muriel's words now retriggered his earlier resolve.

"You have to take your pills, Mom."

"No thank you."

"It's not a request."

She huffed.

"Mom, you're not yourself," Lem said.

"I think I'm exactly myself and you wouldn't know the difference," she erupted.

"But you're not!" He grunted. "I can't make you see it, but trust me, you're not *you* and you just don't see."

Eve continued to wonder what Lem "got" about her, but she correctly assumed anything she said would be used against her in his personal court, and possibly a real one. She took Pete's advice to avoid Lem, even while seated a short distance behind his bald spot.

He returned his eyes to her via the mirror. "I get it," he repeated, followed quickly with "I met your mom. A few times, actually. She's a lot."

Eve bit her lip softly and looked away.

"She was trying to get you a car, you know," he said, luring her back to his clipped reflection in the mirror. His neck and head didn't move when he talked, and she couldn't see his mouth, but there was no escaping his disembodied voice. "We approved her for a loan, but she wouldn't sign the paperwork. I keep wondering if you knew that—if that's why you picked this car instead."

Was this narcissism? Lem thought Eve chose to drive me to get some sort of revenge? On him? Because her mother wouldn't sign for a loan?

"I did this," Muriel interjected. "I asked Eve to drive me home."

"No, you were *already* home, Mom. You were confused about that and Eve took advantage of you. She took advantage of both of us."

Muriel wanted to correct him, to shout at him, to spank her naughty child and send him to the corner, but instead she matched Eve's tactic of pressing her upper teeth against her lower lip and saying nothing more. She gave Eve an *I tried* look, and Eve returned it with yet another *There's nothing we can do.*

"But man, your mom," Lem laughed. "All that Jesus bullshit? And Cin told me about your dad and how you thought he was dead all this time when really he's just a faggot."

Shut up!! Eve screamed in her head. *Shut up Shut up Shut up!!*

"Lem!!" Muriel commanded, "You're a damned bully! Apologize this second!!"

"What, me to *her?* I don't think so."

"Oh Eve . . ." Muriel extended her hand across the border to the back seat. Eve clutched it with one hand and wiped her eyes with the other. Lem might have stolen information about her dad from Laura, but that didn't necessarily mean that Judith knew he was alive and well. Or where he was. *Or did she?* Eve struggled through her tears to sort out who knew what or when, but ultimately, she decided, none of it mattered anyway.

They were all liars.

Nothing mattered anymore.

"I'm okay," Eve whispered, collecting herself while Muriel continued to hold her hand and wrist, tenderly soothing Eve's bruised emotions with small, supportive strokes. "You should take your pills," Eve added quietly.

Muriel released her sharply, as if pricked by a rose's thorn.

"Thatta girl," Lem smiled. "Now you're playing ball."

Muriel was scandalized, more by Eve's clashing betrayal than Lem's vindication. She searched for absent words, failing to vocalize her shock.

"They're in the other pocket." He continued conversing with Eve through the mirror. "Give her two."

Eve unbuckled and leaned forward over the center of my banquette to fetch the coat. She reassembled its form, pulling an inside-out sleeve back to normal, and found the pills resting in their tangerine tomb on a bed of unused tissues and crumpled cinnamon gum foils. She pulled out a handful of the familiar capsules and handed two to Muriel.

With a wink.

"Don't even try it," Lem said.

Eve stopped cold.

"The phone stays with me," he affirmed.

Lem failed to see Eve and Muriel's relief as a zooming red Porsche drew his attention to the left-hand lane. Retrieving the phone was not the intention. Eve didn't need a single app to accomplish her newly formed plan.

Chapter 17

For the next one hundred miles, my passengers were enchanted by our route through the Catskills as it flaunted a leafy display of fleeting golds, citrines, and rubies. Eve was completely unprepared for the North's autumnal dramatics, and she became the one who quietly repeated, "Look at that, look at that, look at that."

Muriel pretended to take the pills with an unpracticed yet skillful legerdemain, then continued her performance for Lem by simulating the ensuing fatigue. However, the stream of constant colors, my unremitting highway vibrations, and her overuse of fake yawns ultimately triggered an authentic weariness. She shifted her gaze and witnessed a cluster of trees across a broad clearing, caught by a sudden gust. She followed the captured leaves as the wind dispersed them. Chimneys, water towers, and pockets of sky strobed through the denuded branches. Muriel wondered about all the towns unvisited, people unknown, and animals unseen beyond the abdicating forest.

Slips of lives on other roads.

Her eyelids dropped as we sped on, and the falling colors were gracefully smeared into a hazy, wheaten-colored paste. Within her desaturated focus, the neurons of Muriel's unmedicated mind began to scamper. Another "Look at that!" echoed off her eardrums unheard, for she had already tuned in to her preferred internal channel, broadcasting another correspondence from Grace.

***

Some people travel to India with a one-way ticket. They upend their lives in search of new meaning as they dedicate themselves to learning and service under the careful guidance of a guru. Other people traverse the country sampling its spiritual offerings and return home wrapped in colorful shawls, with carved deities in their bags and their minds stocked with new and compelling ideas. Some people go for business and later regale their Western cohorts with tales of chaos, poverty, and filth to defend their ethnocentric sensibilities. Still others spend vast amounts on luxurious tours and are whisked through sanitized hotels and catered meals; plopped before proven marble-carvers, rug-makers, and silk merchants; and spirited in tight, protected bundles through the world-renowned sites. Some go to India to live a simpler life, easily affording their necessities and appreciating the luxuries of a slower pace and reduced responsibilities. Some people are called. Some people seek adventure. Some go to sit on a beach for a week or ride a painted elephant.

And then there are those, like me, who don't consciously know why we ventured into India at all.

One month ago I was standing on the Quaibrücke Bridge, where Switzerland's Zürichsee drains into the Limmat, when a bank of swans floated out from under me. Two of them broke away from the group and swam in opposite directions, dropped their heads simultaneously, found equal-sized opalescent fish, and then rejoined the rest in synchrony. That's when I realized everything on my post-college European expedition had been a little too perfect. I'd had enough of the green grass, blue water, gray castles, purple mountains, and extraordinary churches with rose-windows using up the rest of the colors in the crayon box. Even the fluffy white clouds mimicked the balanced arc of the swans' elegant backs, as if a fussy artist had assembled the scene from a technicolor catalog of faultless elements. Like a worker in a chocolate factory who ate too much of the product in their first week and then never ate it again, I felt like my experience of Europe had been too neat, too designed; it was immaculate and historic and irreconcilably delicious.

I got tired of consuming its magnificence.

I had nothing to contribute.

I walked bitterly to the main station, possibly the only visitor to ever display a bad mood while snacking on hazelnut *Frisch Schoggi*. I was scheduled for the train to Milan and then Venice, but I impulsively chose the opposite track. Fifteen minutes later I was at the airport, in front of a clicking and flickering billboard of options. As hundreds of white letters churned out gate codes and boarding times on the copper background, I discarded the European options and gave more serious thought to the wilder destinations: Buenos Aires, Hong Kong, Tel Aviv, Cairo, Shanghai...

To my right, an Indian family appeared, dressed in vivid fabrics. The hues of their garments radiated, as if dyed by light instead of pigments. The man checked his watch and then spoke through a bushy black mustache: "We have two hours—let's get one more buttery croissant and some coffees." As they shuffled toward the airport bakery, I unpacked the concept of visiting a foreign land where they also spoke my language. I weighed the reduced hotel and food expenses against the cost of changing my itinerary—and then happily followed their colors to Bombay.

This was better. My first impressions of India were probably typical: it was humid, smelly, loud, overwhelming, unexpected, disturbing, and fantastic. Everyone met me with kindness and sunny, broad smiles, and despite the apparent challenges of sanitation, mobility, and a population density more than thirty times greater than America's, I got the impression that people seemed generally happy, or at the very least, content.

After a week of rampant sightseeing, I took a leisurely train through Rajasthan on the recommendation of a woman looping through India in the opposite direction. After short bursts in many cities, I found a friendly group to share a private car into the mineral-rich and conflict-laden state of Bihar. On paper, the drive from Benares was supposed to take six hours, but paper can't predict a herd of tall camels in the road with their unexpected forest of red hairy legs eclipsing the view. Maps don't tell you your driver will stop ten times to service his betel-leaf addiction, then offer you his wife's homemade sandwiches by turning his body completely around in his seat while the vehicle continues forward in an increasingly veering line.

When a journey begins at dawn, one expects to arrive somewhere in the early afternoon with time to shower and stretch before dinner. But as we watched the sun disappear and another two hours vanish, my fellow travelers and I believed we'd either collectively misunderstood our maps—or one euphorically stoned driver with choppy, stained teeth and delicious chickpea masala snacks was kidnapping five Westerners for a tidy ransom. You could smell our mounting fears as we surreptitiously placed our passports and cash in the torn fabric sleeve of the old roof and mentally summoned a bubble of golden light from the good side of Oz to encapsulate us with protection. Knuckles were white as back-seat hands held onto each other and we thought of our families, our friends, and our mistakes.

And then we arrived.

As with all things in India, our expectations were diverted, our sense of reason challenged, our comfort and security questioned—but we successfully emerged from our self-conjured drama fully intact, with only the emotional scathing we had put upon ourselves.

We were safe in Bodh Gaya, the small village where Buddha sat under a tree for seven weeks and attained enlightenment, nearly twenty-five centuries ago. I'm not sure if it was the golden bubble refusing to pop or the electric energy of our harrowing journey searching for its grounding, but I felt something in the temperate air, a serene vibration that cradled me to sleep.

The next morning, I was lured by a repetitive chant toward Emperor Ashoka's eighteen-story Mahabodhi Temple, an ancient linchpin marking this holy place. In a field to one side of the intricately carved tower sat no less than five thousand Tibetan monks in saffron robes, their sweet and unified chorus directed at a tree.

The Bodhi Tree.

I came to learn it wasn't the original tree that had provided comfort and shade to Siddhartha Guatama Buddha himself, but a direct descendant of the descendants that now shared the soil and power of its divine lineage.

I positioned myself with my back against a low wall to admire the morning light as it folded itself into the undulating orange sea of devout men. A few friendly dogs came to sit with me. One put his paw on my knee, but he didn't beg for food. He faced the tree with the monks. *Yes, we're both here and we're both seeing this and hearing this and yes, it is amazing*, said his gentle paw.

I closed my eyes and focused on aligning my breath with the pulsing air in passive meditation. Maybe half an hour went by. I gathered my awareness and opened my eyes to find myself flanked by two excited women. One appeared to be in her sixties, and she writhed and twisted and felt dangerously close to jumping out of her skin with an adoration I couldn't comprehend. I felt a little jealous of her engaged enthusiasm, but also wary of her apparent craziness. The other woman's slight frame was wrapped in a jade-green sari with golden trim. She rocked on her shoeless tiptoes and craned her slender neck with anticipation. I stood and followed her gaze, and that's when I saw the man.

He was surrounded by four other men, presumably for protection, and I came to realize I was in a line of hundreds of people who were eager to be in his presence. None of us were Tibetan monks in saffron robes and none of us were chanting. We were tourists or fans or devotees of this guru, swami, holy man (I still don't know). I remained in the line, curious.

He stopped to press his palm against someone's head. When he released her, she bounced back and held out a note for him. He took it without looking and handed it gently to one of the four men by his side. I saw that the writhing woman and the toe-rocking woman on either side of me also had notes for him. It seemed nearly everyone had a note. I wished I had a note.

I could sense his serenity from ten feet away as he slowly approached, his flawless skin resembling driftwood—soft in appearance yet exuding a perceivable strength beneath. The bindi on his forehead was a perfect scarlet circle. His eyes looked like carob chips floating in milk. His hair held the shine of being washed in organic flower oils under crystalline waterfalls. His ivory robe flowed, untarnished by the dust or grit of travel. As he drew closer, I felt scruffier than the wild dog who sat with me.

Soon there were only three people between us. Then two. One. He stopped moving and looked at me. Deeply. I wanted to say "hello!" but even a pleasant greeting seemed like it would be an affront to his gentle presence. Again, I wished for a scrap of paper, even if it was blank. He was a few inches from me, and the unique vibration I had felt in the hotel room returned. Was this a manufactured adoration? His physicality seemed entwined with something spiritual, an energy I find difficult to describe.

The man placed his cupped hand on my forehead.

"Blessings," he said.

He could have said anything to me, but he said "Blessings." He probably said it to millions of people, but when he touched me with that word I felt as though an important transaction had taken place. He moved on, but I could still feel his palm against my forehead. In a few seconds, I was part of a wedged crowd dispersing in his wake.

Blessings. Where was I?

Blessings. Was that real?

Blessings. I felt a little dizzy.

I resumed my seat at the base of the wall. The crowd disappeared. The monks never stopped their chant and the world looked entirely the same as it had before; the sun was only slightly higher in the sky. The dog jumped off the low wall from above and sidled up, returning his paw to my knee.

"You've come all this way. Do you want to see the tree?"

I thought the dog was talking! My mind was still processing the scene, and it took me a moment to realize one of my travel mates from the car ride had found me. He looked refreshed, with his wet hair and clean-shaven face. He wore khakis and a button-down shirt that closely resembled mine, possibly sourced from the same travel gear shop in Jaipur where we first met. We traveled together when it was convenient, with no itinerary or obligations. In one month, we had parted four times, yet somehow relinked. Once we found each other on opposite street corners in a remote part of busy Agra, nowhere near the Taj Mahal or the Red Fort. It seemed wholly inexplicable, yet also entirely normal.

"I don't want to disturb them," I said, indicating the monks.

"They're chanting for world peace," he said, sliding down the wall to share my view. "This is day three and they have seven more to go. As a group, they never take a break."

The dog got up and padded away in search of another non-conversant knee.

"You have----"

"What?"

"Just a little . . ." I wiped a lingering dollop of shaving cream off the back of his ear.

We watched the sun climb higher, enjoying the chant and the chance to rest.

"Thanks," he said, perhaps five minutes later. Time had slowed.

"Did you see that guy?" I asked. "That guru, or whatever he was?"

"Where?"

"Right here."

"Really? When?"

"A few minutes ago. You didn't see him?"

He looked around. "What did he look like?"

"I don't know. Like a guru, I guess, but not old. Maybe he wasn't a guru. I don't know."

"Huh."

Another five minutes passed.

"He was literally walking away when you showed up," I said, perplexed. "There was a whole crowd!"

"You mean the monks?"

"No, not them, people like us. Tourists or whatever. Everyone was lined up and he walked down the line and . . ."

He raised his eyebrows and looked into my eyes.

". . . it was interesting," I said.

He shrugged. "So, do you wanna see the tree? We can't touch it, but we can get closer."

We crossed the field to a smooth, marble pavilion. A high stone fence, intricately carved and with gates made of gold, surrounded a solidly crafted berm that held the tree. It looked like an ancient, elevated crib with a mattress of soft soil. Thousands of ribbons and prayer flags were loosely tied to the pampered trunk and lower branches. Whenever a leaf would fall, a monk would rush to it and sweep it into what looked like a golden dustpan.

To describe the Bodhi Tree as merely a tree belies its significance. This was a *being*—a living entity unlike anything I've ever seen. To start, there's the scale: the center of the tree consists of a massive trunk with a wider circumference than a large American car. As the column extends over sixty feet into the air, it splits and divides to support scores of branches that resemble horizontal trunks themselves. Thousands more branches project from those beams, and everything is unified under a canopy of decorous green. It takes up the space of a baseball diamond.

All from a single seed.

People were spread around the pavilion beneath its universe-hugging arms. Some meditated while others enjoyed the cool shade. We walked slowly until we found a suitable place to sit. Once again, I closed my eyes and listened to the endless chant and the whispered squawks of passionate tourists as they blended with the sounds of morning birds and the whisking of precious leaves into the pan.

I was cross-legged with my hands on my knees, palms facing up, and in my mind's eye I entered through the golden gates to touch the tree. I approached hesitantly, feeling the trespass even within my own psyche. I tentatively reached out, enjoying the warm flutter of air against my fingertips as I emulated the tree's long arms. The space between us slowly dissolved as I crossed without momentum; I sometimes think I stayed in place while the tree moved closer to me.

I placed my right hand on the trunk, and the entire world became silent.

It was unusually cool on the bark, like a stone beneath a river, and the texture approximated the leathery flesh of an elephant's trunk. When my left hand joined my right, I felt a pulse that was so slow I was certain it wasn't my own. I could feel the individual molecules of energy keeping the tree alive, a life force that brought slow nourishment up from the earth and out into the air, and from the sun back down, deep into the soil.

I took one more step and pressed my forehead against the tree, framing it between my hands. It was then, in that darkness, in that quiet, in the mind's eye of my mind's eye, that I finally understood why I was in India.

I was there to see the fabric of the universe.

If you're anything like I was before this moment, then you're probably listening to this and scoffing. She touched a tree in India and thought she saw God! How arrogant! She was dehydrated. Deluded. Desperate. A whack-job ready for the rubber room.

If only that were true.

If only you were right.

When I pressed my forehead against the tree, we melded. I felt the energy of its ancient life, and I saw my true self merging with that power. I saw the person I know myself to be, living in this body and doing all the things this body does, as a vast system of complicated, interlocking, interchangeable forces with the unified purpose of guiding and propelling me through my own particular and singular life. I could see myself within the vehicle that I call "Me" and, for a moment, as we touched, I could open the door and step outside of that vehicle.

I saw my own life as one piece of a larger, more connected life, a frantic push of accelerating moments. I saw clearly how all the paths intersect, how dreams and subconsciousness correlate, and how all that swirling matter, including what I claimed as my own, was actually shared. I saw how all of life moves through those slow branches to commune with the trunk and roots and leaves, how it perpetuates new growth and constantly drops whatever is no longer necessary for eventual redistribution. The tree did that. We all do that. The universe does that.

I touched my spirit to the Bodhi Tree and we amalgamated.

I understood, clearly, how everything works.

How it has always operated.

How everything is one.

How everything is everything.

All from a single source.

Eventually, I pulled back. I felt myself leave that infinite space and squeeze myself back into this body, this familiar mind and intuition that feels so much like me, this borrowed costume I will one day give back.

In my reinhabited self, I couldn't contain what I had experienced. I wept in the cool shade of the pavilion with five thousand monks in saffron robes chanting in my direction. The dog had returned, and my squeaky-clean human friend remained at my other side.

Eventually we moved on together from Bodh Gaya, on from India, on from that irresponsible time of important freedom. But I continue to carry the weight of my realizations, and they are magnificent. And light.

In this time and in this place, I am Me. I share experiences and express opinions. Sometimes I am bold and sometimes I am humbled. My body eats and excretes, bathes and sleeps, maneuvers through space and surrenders to time. I scratch my mosquito bites, get wet in the rain, and sometimes, I wear lipstick. I require money. I explore and I communicate. I vote for reason and I sustain hope for future generations. I will likely exist for a few more decades, acquiring, giving away, consuming, wondering, solving, and making important connections with other living entities. If all goes well.

I am also the Me who stayed in India with her third eye inhabiting the universe through the portal of an endless tree. I watch my own actions, typically with amusement, knowing the true play of light and energy, the twists and vibrations of manifestation, the show behind the show. I know what will happen beyond my death, what happened before my birth, and the sacred privilege of inhabiting an eternal soul.

Our eyes comprehend a physical spectrum of light that illuminates the world. There are also wavelengths beyond our optical capabilities, and they are no less real. I live in this rainbowed day-to-day of our shared reality, but I also live in the unified light beyond the sensory, in the space that isn't space, in the endlessness of the infinite.

Blessings.

***

Eve watched Muriel's head from the back seat as it bobbled to her chest, quickly caught itself, and slid two more times before finding the secure chasm between my headrest and the door.

"Blurrsssnnng..." Muriel murmured in her nebulous nap.

Eve shifted from the left seat to the middle to expand her view and escape Lem's notice, but he shifted my rearview mirror and continued to check on her, irrationally fearful she might somehow slip out onto the highway without his knowing. She put her palm on her pocket every few minutes and was consistently reminded of Lem's violation, her phone-addiction withdrawal enhancing the agitation. When she was behind the wheel, she could go for hours without caring, but the utter uselessness of simply sitting without a book or a screen was painful. She almost wished for homework simply to have a task to pass the time. She was stripped down to the foundations of her bare thoughts. Thinking was distressing.

Did her mother know that she knew her father was alive? Now that Lem was here, Eve wondered if her mother might have texted. She reached for the phone again, her fingers once again pressing on her thigh instead of the thin, glassy brick.

"Ugh."

"Problem?" Lem was disturbingly quick to ask.

Eve ignored him and looked back at Muriel, who was sleeping soundly and spewing random incoherent words, something about a tree. She had watched Muriel fake the pill-taking, but she wasn't sure of her success until Muriel pushed the little devils through the bottom of my seat on the far-right side. When Eve moved into the center, she plucked them from the floor. She touched her fingers to the outside of her other pocket and felt them again, grouped with the few she'd managed to squirrel away at Pete's while pretending to wash them down the drain. So that was something.

But what did her mother know? Did her mother still talk to her father, or did she really think he was dead? Did her father know she was coming?

Another reach for the phone was met with another blast of disappointment.

Eve looked out the window at a small blizzard of sideways leaves blowing across the road, beautiful discards whose purpose was fulfilled. Did her father travel these roads when he left? Did he see these same trees throwing away their vital foliage? Those leaves worked so hard to provide sustenance. They nourished and decorated the trees and even added movement to their stationary lives. And yet the trees dropped them, their most precious assets, surrendering their darlings to an unpitying wind.

She wondered how he could throw her away.

**

Ten years earlier, Richard Harvick sat in his packed Toyota Camry and gripped the steering wheel. If he let go and turned the ignition, the car would start, the garage door would open, and he would drive away. Or, he could turn the ignition and start the car, but keep the garage door closed and asphyxiate. He could also go back inside the house and resume his existing life, but then what?

When he let go of the steering wheel, his hands would make the choice.

He couldn't let go.

For the hundredth time, he considered his options.

He couldn't stay married to Judith. He deserved to be with Michael and they couldn't waste any more time. He respected Judith, occasionally adored her, mildly cherished her, but never entirely enjoyed her company. He was tired of accommodating her moods, her acute neediness, and the burden of being ever-responsible for her happiness.

He enjoyed the physical activity of sex enough to continue to engage in it with her, but through the repetitive years, he'd gradually abandoned any sentimental connection to the act. It eventually became so rote he almost felt he could substitute a warm cantaloupe for his wife. One time he'd rolled off to sleep with a wet trail of semen lacing her thigh, and she had complained that she'd been "mildly raped" because he hadn't attended to her completion. He tried to focus on her, but he couldn't muster a sustainable enthusiasm—lovemaking with Judith had become a repetitive house chore with an appreciated ending, like a cold beer after mowing the lawn. Judith needed him, but he only needed the release.

And then he found the letter.

Someone in his office complex had a crush on someone else and had written, explicitly, what he wanted to do about it. The subject and the object were both men, and the description of the action was detailed and raunchy. Richard read it. Twice. His erection was so profound that he carried his sport coat in front of him like a seventh grader and then masturbated in the privacy of the executive washroom. Twice.

The letter wasn't intended for him—it was mistakenly placed in his workplace mailbox—and there were no names, only *You* and *I* and *We* and an illegible squiggle at the bottom. The building contained more than eight hundred employees in sixteen offices that served countless clients. Richard found it remarkable that one silly piece of misfiled paper could find him and so quickly and unsubtly change his life.

Richard grew up in a time and place without gay references. No one in his high school was forthcoming about the subject; there were no prominent celebrities or gay-themed movies at the AMC, no gay family members or friends (that he knew of), and no internet. He and his friends found only devoutly heterosexual *Playboys* and *Penthouses* to steal from their fathers' bottom drawers, and even the lesbian spreads they contained were photographed for the benefit of straight males with limited sexual imaginations. Richard followed the expected path, lost his virginity in college to a precocious sorority girl, met Judith two years later, liked her enough, and married her after graduation. He never consciously considered he might not be straight. Not consciously.

In his dreams he sometimes encountered men, often behind a veil of mist or in dark water with the light of a shooting star defining the edges. His tongue would probe the fur of a muscular chest until it found a nipple; his hands would slide across the familiar hard genitalia that matched his own. But he always woke up before he saw another man's face or tasted his breath, before the exploration became a daytime longing or his deeply buried desires could hope to manifest.

The handwritten scrawl in the anonymous letter wasn't merely descriptive and provocative, it was emotive. It was penned by someone who knew his way around words as much as the body he desired, and it not-so-quietly pushed Richard's overcast dreams into the daylight of a world that he realized had changed. Being gay was suddenly permissible. There were prominent celebrities, a local politician, someone he knew in college. There was the internet. He slowly ventured into online chat rooms, hoping to find the men contained within that letter, but the emotional male bonding he reluctantly came to crave felt cheapened when he had to type *oooh* and *yeeeaaah* with his left hand while achieving a climax with his right. JeremyBear92 was only another version of inconsequential, lightly microwaved fruit.

And Judith continued to require him. Respect and obligation were strong forces, but eventually, he reached a breaking point when he finally found a new love. The right love. An equal love, and neither of them could wait.

Michael.

The garage light clicked off automatically. The garage window hid behind an opaque curtain, and Richard sat in near darkness while the Florida sun blazed on the other side of the wall. Everything he might need for his next life was packed into the car.

Everything except his daughter.

Eve was the only reason he clung to the wheel like a lifebuoy ring. As an engineer, he dealt with forces and their interplay, but he couldn't balance the equation of leaving his family in despair versus staying in perpetual self-torment. He couldn't solve the mathematics of his emotional purgatory.

After the letter and before he met Michael, suicide was rapidly becoming a viable option. A quiet checkout seemed the simplest way to avoid the admonishment for coloring outside the lines. He had even drawn up a few plans, but as he wrestled between a lethal volume of pills and booze, an oceanic drowning, or "accidentally" falling down the thirty-story elevator shaft on the A1A project, he came to realize he genuinely liked himself and the idea of his life sans Judith. He was only fatally depressed within the cloaked sexuality of their marriage. People who are sixty-eight percent happy don't kill themselves, he reasoned, after calculating how much of his life was related to Judith on a minute-to-minute basis.

But the untenable thirty-two percent was also too large.

He needed Michael. And Michael needed him.

But Eve.

He clutched the steering wheel even harder. If it wasn't leather-wrapped steel, it would have shattered. His temples throbbed. His heart stormed.

Richard and Judith had witnessed a few divorces in their circles, and they were greatly impacted when people they cared about ripped their lives in half. Estates, social standings, mutual friends, and the children were all irreparably torn, but meticulous Richard had found the best solution: there would be no fights and no reason to punish anyone. It was his choice to leave, so Judith would get the house with ninety percent of the mortgage paid off, a car with no loans and the insurance paid up, significant money in the bank, and a handful of high-limit credit cards he ordered in her name. He sold his substantial trading card collection, his Rolex, two important paintings, and his deceased mother's jewelry and put it all into a trust account for Eve's college.

Richard was slithering away with the black Japanese dishware he picked up in Kyoto (they couldn't be microwaved, so Judith didn't use them), a few photos, his computer and his clothes, the cufflinks his grandfather gave him, and his electric shaver. He was taking the older of the two cars and some emergency cash. He left the signed divorce papers with a letter begging Judith not to contest it. The lawyers would get more than she would gain if she went after him for child support or alimony, he explained, and he no longer had an income or a home. *Sign the papers and then go about the task of hating me forever,* he wrote at the bottom of a legal pad. The long yellow paper resembled the scintillating correspondence that had shaken him permanently awake nearly a year prior.

Judith would be fine.

But Eve.

Eve would be confused, but she was young. Almost seven. Richard tried to remember when he was seven. Who were his friends? Who were his teachers? No one came to mind. It would take time, but Eve would get over him. Kids were remarkable in their ability to move on—far more resilient than their adult counterparts. Judith was a good mother. She would take care of Eve. There was plenty of money, and they were strong. Judith would be free to get on with her life, and Eve would . . . Eve . . . would be okay.

Everything was set. He gave them everything he had to give and more. The only thing he had left for himself was his own future with Michael, and it was time for that to start. All Richard had to do was let go of the wheel and turn on the car. Open the garage. Turn the key. Spark the fucking ignition.

But Eve.

He was going to miss her seventh birthday.

He couldn't stay.

He couldn't leave.

They had to leave.

Michael had said, "You don't have to do it like this. You can still be her dad. You can come back and visit her whenever you want, take her to Disney for her birthday."

"It'll torture everyone if I come and go—especially Judith. No, I have to rip off the Band-Aid. I know it'll hurt, but the wound will heal and the scars will fade. Judith is still young; she'll find someone else to marry, and Eve will get a new dad, a better dad, and they'll forget this ever happened. They'll forget *I* ever happened."

"Liar."

"I know," Richard cried, "but we can't put them through . . . us. We can't do that to them, Michael. It wouldn't be fair."

"You know this isn't better."

"It's fifty-one to forty-nine percent. I ran the math."

Michael laughed quietly, through tears.

"Okay, maybe it's the other way around, but I'm putting you first. I'm putting *us* first. For now. Let's get settled and then we'll figure it out," Richard reasoned. "We'll figure it out, and then maybe one day . . . they'll understand."

"They'll never understand, but one day they might forgive you. Or maybe it's the other way around."

Richard Harvick sat in his packed Toyota Camry, gripping the steering wheel. He finally let go. His raw hands found the key and turned it. The garage door opened slowly, letting in the light.

***

As we passed the exits for Woodstock and Saugerties, I shifted my attention to Lem. For over an hour he tried to understand how he had become the bad guy. *He* didn't steal the car. *He* didn't skip school and drag someone across the country. *He* was the one who was put out, lied to, stepped on, and forced to deal with a conniving daughter, dismissive police, and an unsupportive wife. *He* was the one who had to use up his saved personal days to collect the absconders. *He* had to leave the house at three in the morning and shell out the dough for a middle seat on a last-minute fare. *He* was the one who suffered through the taxi's toxic Coronado Cherry scent in the Holland Tunnel during rush hour. *He* had to listen to goddamned Saint Pete, with his perfect body mass index and his wine-club life, tell him that medicating *his* sick mother was somehow wrong. *He* had to endure a morning with all of them in Pete's sleazy, blonde-trapping, private-elevatored fuckhouse. *He* had to deal with the hair-sweeping, white-trash drama punk in the back seat and her lunatic, Christ-obsessed mother in Florida. *He* was the good guy, saving the day and restoring order! *He* was the sweet panacea to their whole out-of-control train-wreck, he thought.

Lem's toe throbbed.

My cruise control worked flawlessly, but Lem failed to locate the switch because it wasn't on the steering wheel where he expected it to be. If something wasn't where Lem wanted it, then it wasn't there at all. He purchased new milk whenever Cindy blindly returned the carton from its labeled door holster to the unruly wilds of the upper shelf. He ranted when she parked her car in his spot, the closer stall, even if she had a mass of groceries to unload. He couldn't sleep in an unmade bed, he griped if the shower head shifted, and he protested any alterations to his regularly scheduled television programming. He should have enjoyed the consistency of his foot against my gas pedal, but like an old dam forming small cracks from the pressure of the lake it created, the constant force against his brittle toenail—still wrapped from Cindy's care—made the second hour of our drive a fresh agony.

He was being stabbed in slow motion, but neither of his passengers could be trusted to drive. I watched his mind generate a thunderhead of anger and resentment threaded with the sharp lightning of his pain. I feared the acid rain of his determination to return Muriel and Eve to their respective prisons. The storm intensified as Lem thought about returning to Saratoga Springs, even for a short visit, because every change there was marked and compared against a memory—and memories only served to empower Lem's most unyielding nemesis: Time.

When Time was under his control, it provided the illusion of consistency: Monday through Friday, nine to five; Saturdays ten to one; Sundays and holidays off, along with one week in winter and two more in summer. But Time slowly cut through his life without regard, much like the lazy Colorado River gouging the Grand Canyon out of a serene prairie. He would paddle down and look back, only to realize it had already taken his athleticism, his vibrancy, and most of his hair. Time stole his darling babies and replaced them with unappreciative teens. It blended all of the seasons into a slurry, where it was always time to put up the Christmas lights, even when they had just come down.

He hated that his mother accepted Time for what it was; she never seemed bothered by its relentless dedication to erosion. In fact, when the doctor had explained how her new medication would dramatically slow the effects of her Alzheimer's, she had challenged the notion.

"Why would I want to do that?" she asked, her eyes blazing. "You want me to stick around for ten years so you can drain my bank accounts? So the children get to watch me disappear in slow motion? No thank you. Give me the other ones," she said.

"The other ones?"

"The pills that make it go faster. Surely, if you can slow the disease down, you can also speed it up?"

"I don't understand----"

"I know you don't, and that's the problem right there. You took an oath to save lives and to—what is it? Do no harm? But how are you defining *harm* in my situation? How is keeping me around to go through a horrible decade of disease *not* a gross and senseless form of harm? You haven't figured that out yet, have you, doctor?"

"Mom, they're doing lots of research. They're gonna find a cure," Lem had tried to persuade her.

"Oh please, what, in twenty years? You want to keep me catatonic with your magic medicines, just in case I . . . what? Grow a new brain?! And you think I've lost *my* mind? Wake up, Lem, I'm just a math problem to these people. X is how long it will take me to die and Y is how many pills they can sell me until Z hits the fan. Shame on you both. I already lost my Ira and now you . . . you want me to suffer even longer? Slow it down? Jesus Christ, you are vicious animals."

"Don't you want to be here for your grandchildren?" implored the doctor, trading roles with Lem. "Think of the birthdays and holidays? And maybe one day . . . weddings?"

"Give the pills to someone else," she said, tightly folding her arms. "It's too late for me."

Lem and the doctor discussed it privately. Muriel was obviously depressed and potentially exhibiting signs of early-stage Alzheimer's. The pills would help with both, and once she was on the medication, she would likely forget that she didn't want them in the first place. It was the medically responsible thing to do, and she was lucky because she could afford them. She was lucky they existed at all.

After Muriel was diagnosed, Lem had obtained a prescription and secreted the pills into her extensive vitamin regimen. Then finally, with a swift move into The Deerwood, he had pushed the shapeless dough of his mother's life into a tidy square pan. He was in control of Time once again, and all was as it should be because *he* was the good guy who took care of her. She had nothing to worry about anymore, thanks to him. *He* deserved a gold star.

Lem looked at his mother on the other side of my seat and a million miles away. She was asleep and quietly mumbling. She could hate him all she wanted, but Lem knew he had saved her from herself.

It was a few weeks after the funeral when Lem and Cindy had finally gone to Singer Island to check on Muriel. She was increasingly despondent in their daily phone calls. She seemed muddy and quick to ignite over innocuous queries, and then she missed Laura's birthday. No gift. No call. Unprecedented. A day later, the building phoned Lem about an overdue maintenance check. They told him her mail was piling up and reiterated it was against the rules for her to hang her laundry on the balcony, page 38, section 9.

When they arrived unannounced, Muriel was asleep by the pool and warmly cocooned in a soft towel on a shaded lounge chair. They left her there, undisturbed, and rode the elevator sixteen floors while sorting her junk mail from the overdue bills.

"What's with all the forks?!" Cindy called out as they walked into the apartment.

"Leave it alone," Lem said, though he was equally unnerved by the sight of forty-two forks spread across the entryway carpet, tines up.

They ventured further.

Dozens of people had sent flowers when Ira died. The flowers were all dead, and some were crunchy, while others had gone gooey. The rest of

Muriel's treasured house plants were suffocating in glass vases filled with orange juice. Everything stank.

They found oven mitts in the oven and cereal boxes in the fridge.

The dishes were piled high, and the kitchen smelled like unwashed tuna cans and burnt cheese.

Cindy zeroed in on the laundry room. The washer was stuffed with dryer sheets and fresh rolls of toilet paper, but fortunately everything was dry. When Cindy opened the dryer, she found stockings and bras and a soiled pair of pants, an expensive wool sweater, a recipe book for vegetables, something that might have been an eggplant, and a partially melted plastic bath mat. Everything was caked together in a broken ball encrusted with blue-gray laundry powder clumps. It resembled a poorly executed science fair model of planet earth after a nuclear disaster.

After the sound of her shriek dissipated, Cindy donned thick rubber gloves (found between the couch cushions) and successfully extracted the smelly orb. Then she visited one of the bathrooms and shrieked again.

"What now?!"

"She didn't flush!"

"So flush it, for god's sake!"

"I think it's . . . like . . . a week's worth."

They assumed Muriel had stopped flushing her toilets altogether, another undeniable sign.

In the bedroom Cindy searched Muriel's drawers.

"She only has four pairs of underwear?"

It was disturbing behavior, and the evidence compelled them to believe that their dear Muriel was no longer in her right mind. They nitpicked her other gaffes and lapses: missing the key plot points in movies, repeatedly questioning how the fish should be prepared, the time when she forgot where she parked at the mall. They staggered through the apartment, carefully avoiding errant objects, and talked each other into the conclusion that Ira had probably covered for her more than they realized, and now that he was gone, she was clearly unfit to live on her own.

What they failed to comprehend was that many of the ill-fitting pieces of their self-imagined puzzle actually fused quite neatly into an entirely different picture.

Ira's death was also the end of their dinner parties, so Muriel was organizing her lifelong collection of antique forks to sell them. The foyer provided space, a strong light, and good contrast for the photographs against the black carpet. She was afraid to use the dining room table for fear she might scratch the glass, and the forks were only in the foyer on the afternoon that Lem and Cindy arrived.

Muriel lived alone and flushed her toilets when there was a need, but not every single time when she wasn't expecting company. It had only been a day, not a week.

Muriel didn't notice the various smells because she always kept her balcony doors wide open in the temperate late fall. She only shut out the breezes when she left the apartment, like when she ran down to swim and nap by the pool.

Lem and Cindy didn't know that most of Muriel's underwear remained in the unopened suitcase from her trip to bury Ira, nor did they know she typically went without underwear at home, opting for her cozy robe in the mornings and bathing suits most afternoons. Underwear was requisite for shopping and social events, and neither was occurring often, post-Ira.

Muriel's habit was to drop the bottom third of a glass of water into her plants, but she was drinking more juice than water because she kept forgetting to pick up a new filter at the store. The topping-off routine, a habit for over forty years, didn't fully adjust.

She knew the kitchen was a mess, but she was overwhelmed, and it made her sad to be in there, cooking for herself. One holiday season, many years prior, she had casually mentioned she needed better oven mitts and three friends had sent them her way. Her kitchen in Florida was a quarter the size of Saratoga, and when she ran out of space, she stored the extra mitts in the oven, trading them for the food when she cooked and returning them when it cooled. It was a system. And the granola cereal found a shelf in the fridge because she worried its organic berries might turn moldy in her neglected pantry.

The bereavement flowers became a daily reminder of her catastrophic loss. She couldn't bear to look at them, but she also couldn't fathom the wasteful cruelty of discarding such thoughtful gifts. So they sat and withered and died and rotted with their scripted cards attached to their stems.

After a short hiatus following the funeral, Muriel's weekly maid appeared. But instead of cleaning, Lurlene consoled, and Lurlene's style of sympathy was to share her own experiences. Muriel couldn't abide the fourth hour of hearing about Lurlene's father's cancer, Lurlene's mother's diabetes, Lurlene's uncle's cirrhosis, the sister's stroke, the brother's fall from the roof, and so on. She paid Lurlene double and told her gently that her services were no longer required. Without Lurlene's detailed weekly sprucing, the condo quickly corroded in the sea air and fell into a crusty depression of its own.

And also for forty years, Muriel had used a top-loading washer and front-loading dryer. She often joked with Ira about their confusing, new-fangled machines with the fabric-type labels suggesting Cotton, Denim, or Wool instead of Hot or Cold. There was no setting for bath mats. It also didn't help that both machines were front-loading and looked nearly identical, making it extra difficult for her to identify their specific purposes. Muriel also didn't do much laundry after Ira's death because bathing suits were deemed "self-cleaning," and the rest didn't seem very important. The toilet paper, eggplant, and book remain a mystery, but Muriel would be the first to admit she was sleep-deprived, anxious, and depressed—she was floating through those early days after Ira's death, and her typical, fastidious self was operating at about ten percent capacity. She made mistakes and could use some help, but she was still a far cry from the madwoman headbanger that Lem and Cindy had hastily assessed. When they walked in and saw the forks, it was already too much.

Muriel and Ira's guest room doubled as their home office, and Lem cautiously approached the neat row of imposing built-in filing cabinets opposite the queen bed where Muriel had taken to sleeping. While Cindy collected the towels and dead plants from the balcony, Lem opened the drawers to assess what he assumed would be further disarray.

The Worths had kept every scrap of paper that had any sort of number on it, going back to the beginning of their union. It was a prodigious lot, but it was also magnificently organized.

"Bless you, Dad," Lem said, entirely unaware it was Muriel's labors he admired. Ira brought in the paychecks, but it was Muriel who researched investments and diligently saved their earnings. She kept meticulous records of receipts, balanced the checkbook, and monitored the stock market. Over the span of many decades, her consistent and careful efforts resulted in their financial security and significant wealth.

"I found her gold watch with the little diamond!" Cindy wailed. "It was in the freezer!" Muriel had learned from the television that she was supposed to keep her jewelry in a frozen-dinner package to thwart would-be thieves. She had yet to get to the store to purchase a decoy Lean Cuisine, but the watch had gone in preemptively.

Lem opened another drawer, and his fingers danced along the data. Medical papers. Travel papers. A folder thick with pre-purchased, unwritten birthday cards. One had a picture of a monkey blowing out candles; another had a nude model with a cupcake over his crotch. Lem mentally scanned the family tree and tried to identify the potential recipients.

Legal papers.

Insurance papers.

Automobile papers.

The will.

Lem read through their most important document three times, checked the date, and checked the files for revisions. It was the latest version, and it revealed that upon Ira and Muriel's deaths, the house in Saratoga and the condo in Florida were to be sold and the combined proceeds split amongst the children. Certain charities were designated to receive a small percentage of the estate, and the rest—the entire investment portfolio, art, jewelry, bank accounts, and the like—were to be split evenly amongst the children *and the grandchildren*. Aside from the properties, Lem would stand to inherit the same as Laura and Christian and each of Sandra's numerous rug rats. His sister's multi-fathered collection of genetically variegated kids would inherit the same amount as his own fully legitimate two. In his mind, his sister was being rewarded for breeding, and it was coming out of his personal share at a grossly disproportionate six to three. Sandra's clan would collectively get double.

The will lacked any consideration for his relationship with his parents. *He* was the one who took care of them when they moved to Florida. *He* was the one who called his mom every day to make sure she was okay. *He* was the one who arranged everything for Ira's funeral. *He* was the advocate who would stand by Muriel until the day she died. And he was supposed to receive the exact same inheritance as Sandra's latest baby, a pooping blob that Muriel would never even come to know?

Lem realized he was sweating. Muriel kept her thermostat at seventy-nine degrees (because her doors were typically open), but even with the steady breeze, it was a particularly humid afternoon and Lem's armpits were soaked. He scowled when he wiped his brow and caught a whiff of his souring scent. His hands were sticky from the fine layer of damp dust coating the surfaces, and his fingerprints were filling in with the grunge, making them smooth. When he rubbed his palms together, they squeaked.

Lem began to wonder what he could do, legally, to protect what he felt was his rightful share of the family's fortune. He was already Muriel's health care proxy, but he had limited powers of attorney. With his dad gone, he needed more. In fact, he probably needed full authority over Muriel's finances to design a proper plan for her estate, but was it too late? Muriel had to be clear enough to convince a witness that she knew what she was doing, but fuzzy enough not to recognize that he was taking control. Like Lem, Muriel had a thing about control.

It dawned on him that he didn't know the full value of the assets in question, so he opened another drawer. Bank statements. Lem mentally added up the high numbers while simultaneously calculating his diminutive percentage. He held a sheet of paper as he wiped a bit of sweat off his forehead and gave himself a thin-but-deep paper cut along the top of his eyebrow. "Shit!" he cried out as his salty sweat dripped into the stinging wound. He wondered if the cut would show. He flexed his eyebrows, recoiling further from the slicing pain. He couldn't think—and he needed to think.

He opened the top drawer of another cabinet.

Investments.

There were many, many folders in that drawer and all of them were thick. Lem knew his parents were comfortable, but as he perused, his mind continued to add up the numbers. Astonishing numbers. Numbers in folders that he was supposed to share equally with his own children, who already owed everything they had to him. Numbers to be further whittled away by the undeserving children of his sister's ex-con husband, the children of her stupidly wealthy second husband (who would take care of them himself), and the gurgling baby of the lazy third. And how many *more* times was Sandy going to stuff her uterus with his money before their mother was dead? Or start adopting? Her baby addiction was costly—to him.

Lem was dazed by the combination of the heat, the disorderly apartment, the grief of losing his father, the slice on his head, the papers in his hand, the big numbers in the thick folders, and the overwhelming sense of what had to happen to make everything right. It was all incredibly important, and it was all just plain incredible. He felt like he was peering over the ledge of a bungee jump and he couldn't be sure the cord was attached properly. He quickly and deliberately sat down, seeking stability from the floor. A bead of sweat traveled along the diagonal, bloody line on his forehead and fell, leaving a crimson circle on Muriel's white carpet. He focused on it absently to calm himself.

"I don't see a toothbrush!" Cindy called from a distant room. "Better call a dentist, pronto!"

Lem knew his mother never neglected her teeth and probably kept the toothbrush in her purse, but he didn't respond; the inputs to his brain were mostly shut off as the information contained within his skull swirled. Numbers. Accounts. Percentages. Legalese. A new Action Plan began to materialize as the red stain browned. He returned to the cabinet and pulled more papers, more numbers, more details. As Lem stroked the thin gash on his brow with his smooth and filthy thumb, he began to harbor two empowering certitudes: his mother had money, and *he* was the good guy.

Chapter 18

Sandra was beyond excited about our imminent arrival, and she channeled her enthusiasm into what needed to be done. Pete called her the moment we left, and before they even hung up, she was making sure the guest beds were made, towels were fresh, and toilet papers were restocked, with the edges folded over into little triangles. She put new soaps in the bathrooms and dusted, swept, vacuumed, and mopped. She even straightened all the picture frames on the stairwell. She remembered when the house had been filled with kids and she hadn't had time to breathe—for years there was rarely an hour when she wasn't collecting clothing from a hamper or returning it to drawers, but she had always loved the busywork of being a mom and caring for the family home. For Sandra, it was the difference between the energized fun of battling the wave-breaking surf versus burning up with boredom on the stagnant sands.

Four of her children were already grown up and living elsewhere, and the last, Sam, was nearing self-sufficiency. Micah was often busy with his graphics projects, and through more error than trial, she had learned that as much as he appreciated her backrubs and midday affections, he required, and even deserved, some time and space of his own. Sandra helped out with part-time retail work and volunteer stints when friends requested it, but she didn't want to commit to anything full-time or the least bit routine. The house was supremely organized, and sometimes she woke up wondering how she was going to fill her day, but she always found a project. Now, with family coming, she had too much to do, and she was blissfully in the zone.

It was shortly after noon when she fluffed the last pillow and took a shower. Dinner would take some time, but we were still a full hour away and it was far too early to start. Sam wouldn't be home until after three, and Micah's office door was closed with his pilfered *Do Not Disturb* hotel placard hanging from the knob. She smiled when he did that and wondered if he was really working, or if he was watching porn or playing video games or napping. He told her he sometimes hung the sign when he wanted to meditate, but she always knew what her husband was up to by the color of his mood when he emerged.

Kubrick watched Sandra towel off with canine indifference, and he flopped his head to the floor while she dressed in jeans and a warm sweater. She faced the dressing-table mirror, unable to decide whether makeup was warranted and, if so, to what extent. Lem wouldn't care or notice, and her mother would likely make a critical comment either way. However, Sandra chose a subdued base, a natural lip color, and a hint of eyeshadow in the hopes that Eve would see her as both casual and hip. She pulled her hair back with a wide headband and allowed it to cascade freely to the center of her back. Then she pulled that off and recaptured her mane in a ponytail while Kubrick began to snore. Then she chose two earring studs that matched her sweater, returned her hair to the headband, and chose another pair of earrings with small silver loops.

Sandra fretted under the erroneous belief that Eve would report her findings back to Laura, who would then share them with Cindy. She could sense her sister-in-law's desire for a report on gray hair and wrinkles so she could feel young and superior. Sandra exhaled, blinked rapidly, and then reapproached her reflection for a final assessment: the gray was less prominent when it was pulled behind her head, and her eyes could use a little liner, but not too much. The wrinkles were there, but not defining, and there was nothing else she could do in the given timespan. Kubrick jumped awake and farted when he sensed Sandra's unspoken decision to take him for an impromptu walk. She finished all her tasks and attempted to quell her needling anticipation.

It was a beautiful October day, a little crisp on the nose, but still warm enough to go without gloves. Sandra went into the back hall and retrieved the leash and collar. Kubrick was stuck to her side from the moment she left the bedroom, his thick tail wagging in sync with his wet tongue. "You wanna walk?" she sang. "Walkie walkie?" He danced. "Let's go, big boy!" She opened the back door and he bounded out, his prison walls erased. He ran straight to the oak tree, marked it, and looked back at her impatiently for a directional cue.

"I'm here, I'm here," she called, heading toward the corner with the leash and collar in her pocket. Kubrick ran to her side and heeled perfectly. He sat at every street corner and never ventured into the road without a human by his side. His leash was only a courtesy for strangers; Sandra would snap it on quickly if it became necessary, but that action was rare.

They walked a few blocks down and several blocks over, then made their way back in a lengthy, leisurely loop. They passed the gates to the cemetery where Ira was laid to rest. She had been reprimanded sharply on more than one occasion for ignoring the *No Dogs Allowed* sign, and this time she waved, whispered "Hi, Dad," and continued without going in. She allowed Kubrick to mark his favorite hydrants and the blue mailbox, but he was forbidden from exploring other people's landscaping. He kept an even pace with Sandra, who voiced her appreciation for the ravishing autumn leaves. His ears perked up each time, as if her observations might mean something to a dog who can't see the color red.

They rounded the last corner, and Kubrick barked. Sandra reflexively put on the collar, and he barked again. She looked at him and woofed her own censorious "No!" He whined and sat down for a half second before standing again to emit a long groan. She looked up, expecting to see another dog or a squirrel, but instead, a long, white classic Cadillac convertible was pulling into her driveway.

We had finally arrived.

"Mom!!" she called out, and Kubrick took off, barely touching the crispy, yellowing grass as he flew across the neighbors' yards to greet us.

Micah appeared on the porch and whistled twice. If Kubrick controlled his own destiny, he would have pounced with vigorous joy and scratched my doors to reach my recoiling passengers, but instead, under Micah's authority, he tottered gently past us without a second glance and headed straight into the house. Sandra and Micah moved in tandem to the passenger door. She tugged on the handle and released the door a crack, and he continued the pull until my side was wide open. In the flash of their mutual touches, I instantly caught up with everything in their lives.

They helped Muriel out of the car and released the seat for Eve.

I found it telling that they both hugged Muriel and Eve before Lem, although it could be argued that the passenger door was closer, plus Lem took an extra moment to dangle his sore foot over the driveway to relieve some of the pressure before he had to stand.

Muriel pressed against their bodies, and they held her long enough for their heartbeats to synchronize. Eve was equally enfolded after she extracted herself from my back seat. The four of them stood in a huddle next to me, sharing their mutual relief and the joy of reunion while I ticked quietly in the background and cooled. Eve was expecting another reprimand instead of their welcoming embrace, and she was overcome by the solicitude.

Lem finally approached. His "Hey Sis!" splintered the mass in four directions, like an ax reaching the square center of a dry log. Sandra circled back toward him while the others retreated in the direction of the house. She gave her brother a perfunctory hug, holding his upper arms and keeping a clear inch between them instead of wrapping herself around him in her typical style.

"You made it," she said flatly.

"You can't be pissed at me for bringing them here," Lem said, feeling her shift from warm to cool.

"They were coming anyway," she said, "You didn't have to----"

"What?"

"I dunno, *inject* yourself? Pete called and said----"

"Jesus, I'm sick of that guy."

Sandra pulled away and examined his face. Her brother looked like he had aged a decade in the year since she last saw him, and her anger waned in the face of his alarming appearance. She wondered if he was sick, beyond the stress of the wild week. She had also lost sleep worrying about Muriel, but when they'd arrived in New York and Pete had vouched for Eve, Sandra finally slept a recuperative nine hours. She would have flown to Mars to find Sam or the other children if they went missing, so she understood his angst, but, being Sandra, her indignation quickly melted when she realized she was actually glad to see her brother. She leaned in to give him the full hug he was expecting when she accidentally stepped on his swollen toe.

Lem collapsed to the pavement as a throbbing wall of razor-edged heat rose from his foot in a dark wave and pelted him like heated sand. He couldn't breathe. He couldn't see. He couldn't hear his own wailing as he writhed on the flat driveway and clutched at his shoe, struggling to pull it off and release himself from the digging hot-iron tines.

"Oh my god!" Sandra cried out, confused by the reaction to her innocent misstep. "I'm so sorry!"

His arms continued to flap at the shoe as if he were a trapped bird until he managed to unlace it enough to pop it off. The sock went with it, and Sandra and Lem both held their breath when they saw the black blood-and-pus-soaked bandage clinging to his foot like a burnt marshmallow at the end of a stick.

"Jesus, what happened to you?" Sandy cried out, throwing herself down toward his foot and staring with an intensity that failed to help.

"It's been . . . bothering . . . me," he managed between gasps for air. "It's a little ingrown."

"That's not ingrown, Lem, it's infected. Your doctor did a piss-poor job of wrapping it," she said upon further inspection.

"No doctor . . . Cindy." The sharpness of the pain began to subside as the chilled air enveloped his naked foot. "I think. Last night."

"And you haven't changed the bandage since yesterday? Oh god, Lem. C'mon."

Micah ran outside when he heard Lem screaming, and together they helped him stand.

"Hey, Lem."

"Hey, number three," Lem said, offering his usual joke. Micah was unamused, but he took over helping Lem limp and stagger up the stairs and into the house. Micah planted him horizontally on the couch in the family room with a towel-wrapped pillow to elevate the foot. Sandra handed him a bag of frozen peas, also wrapped in cloth.

"We have to get this bandage off and see what's going on," she said.

"Pass."

"Lem, don't fuck around. This is serious."

"I'm fine." He leaned forward and gently lowered the peas to his foot. The instant the bag brushed the bandage, another wave of hot, sharp-edged pain screamed up and through his leg. He dropped the bag of peas on the floor and leaned back against the couch, sucking in his breath. "Maybe get me a drink?"

Eve and Muriel stayed in the kitchen while Sandra and Micah tended to Lem. They sat at the oak table by the window and looked at each other, neither knowing what to say. They had finally arrived, but neither knew for how long, or what it meant that Lem had arrived, too.

"What's up with his toe?" Eve finally asked.

"It's his nails," Muriel replied. "Something about the shape of his feet, potatoes instead of pears. He says he cuts them right, but they still grow sideways and dig in. He also has pills for the fungus, but he doesn't take them. Gives him diarrhea."

"Gross."

"He tells me about it almost every Thursday," Muriel mused. "I hate pizza night."

"Hey, today's Thursday!" Eve said, brightening with the realization.

"Must be why we're talking about Lemmy's toes!" Muriel snickered. Eve reached over and gave Muriel's hand a squeeze, enjoying the fact that Muriel didn't have to crinkle her forehead like crepe paper to find her words. There was a quantifiable difference in Muriel after only three days off her meds.

Micah came in, reintroduced himself to Eve a little more formally, kissed Muriel on the top of her head, and then fetched Lem's beer. A moment later Sandra came into the kitchen, too.

"Are you going to join us?" she asked.

Muriel and Eve remained parked. Neither wanted to be anywhere near Lem.

"Look," Sandra pleaded, "I know he kinda busted your butts, but can you blame him? He's just trying to look out for you the only way he knows how."

Muriel and Eve each looked to see if the other was buying what Sandra was selling as she continued, "Can we please all sit in the other room together as a family?"

"Can I have my phone?" Eve asked.

"Where is it?"

"Mr. Worth took it. I want to call my mom and let her know we're here."

Sandra pivoted and quickly returned to the other room, scowling.

"What the hell did I do?" Lem said under the weight of her frown. He was genuinely astonished that everyone was continuing to be so hostile. No one ever appreciated his efforts.

"You took her phone?"

"Why are you on their side? You're not sixteen, San. You're the adult."

"Hey!" Micah interjected, but Lem found him easy to ignore.

"We were just as worried as you!" Sandra cried out, but then she took a breath and said with a summoned calm, "but now everybody's here and they're safe . . ."

Lem lowered his chin and eyebrows, concentrating.

"Look, I know it was a shit week, Lem, but it's over. They're here and everything's fine, so stop being an asshole and give Eve back her phone."

"Is it?" Lem challenged.

"What?"

"Is it *fine?* Is it *over?* You think everything is suddenly hunky-dory because the Caddy's in the driveway and everyone's all chatty in the kitchen?"

"Mom wanted to come home," Sandra muttered.

"Mom doesn't know her ass from her elbow," he retorted.

"We talk all the time, and she's not as bad as you make her out to be. In fact, she may not even----" Sandra closed her lips tight and sealed the remainder of her thought, remembering Pete's request to get a fresh assessment of Muriel's cognition without Lem's influence.

"What?" Lem pried. "What?!"

"She's not as bad as you think and . . . and she . . . she asked me to help her come home," Sandra said, finding a workaround.

"We didn't know how to talk to you about it," Micah expounded as he wrapped his long arms around his wife. He knew she couldn't stand confrontations of any sort, especially with her brother. He was surprised Lem and Sandra had started in on each other so quickly—I was still warm in the driveway, and Kubrick was barely into his post-walk bone.

"Singer Island," Lem said. *"That's* home. She wants to go back to the condo, but we all know she can't live on her own anymore. That's why we sold it! Jesus, we've been through all this!"

"I think she means *home* home. Here."

Lem scoffed and took a swig from the cold beer in his tall glass. "Well, that's awesome," he said, but neither Sandra nor Micah knew if he was sarcastically referring to Muriel's desire to return to Saratoga Springs, or if he was sincerely enjoying his beer.

***

The afternoon sun moved quickly over the grand pink Georgian house as Sandra made toasted sandwiches for everyone, accommodating for every preference of meat, cheese, and type of bread. Micah joined Muriel and Eve at the kitchen table while Sandra sat with Lem in the family room. He said he was feeling light-headed after polishing off the sandwich with a second beer, and he quickly fell asleep with his exposed foot elevated and the bag of peas thawing on the floor. He slept on his coat, continuing to block access to Eve's phone. Sandra returned to the kitchen and apologetically offered to call Judith herself, but Eve had programmed the digits once and never found a reason to learn them. Plus, Eve reasoned, Judith could have called Sandra through Cindy if she really wanted an update, so maybe it didn't even matter. Eve really wanted the phone to talk to Laura more than her mom, anyway, but that could wait, too.

Eve washed her hands at the sink and admired the ancient maple that gently smothered the backyard with its barn-red leaves. She looked around the stately kitchen, triple the size of her own, and asked for a tour of the grand old house.

Muriel took her through, and they cautiously avoided Lem's snoring in the family room to take a perfunctory peek at the underused formal dining room and its handy butler's pantry. Then they crossed a wide foyer at the mouth of a large central staircase and landed in a sophisticated living room with tall windows, thick moldings, and incongruously modern furniture that somehow worked. Eve was in awe. Everything was perfect. It all smelled like old books and looked like a movie set for a drama that she imagined took place in England.

Muriel recognized the architecture, but the rooms looked both smaller and larger than she remembered, and her shifting perceptions were disconcerting. She could see herself as a child, tracing her fingers along the carved-marble fireplace figurines, and later as an adult, dusting them when company was set to arrive. But who was the company and where had they gone? The fireplace figures neither moved nor aged, and their motionless eyes didn't recognize the old woman who stood before them as the former child who had been so intrigued.

Muriel turned her back on them, shut her own eyes, and listened to the room. She heard the resounding echoes of family life. She heard the graduation toasts and wedding announcements that took place beneath the chandelier; all the silly plays, concerts, and dance recitals the children performed by the far wall; and even her own piano skills expanding through diligent practice. But when Muriel opened her eyes, all she could hear was the silence of Ira's absence.

Mr. Clifton's piano had grown roots where it was originally planted and continued to stand stoically on its brawny legs, overlooking the side yard. *Such a fine antique*, Muriel thought with admiration as she slowly realized they were essentially the same age. She opened the fallboard and slid her fingers along the top of the ivory keys, expecting to find dust that wasn't there. She pressed a chord gently. The piano responded clearly and in tune.

Muriel sat on the bench and adjusted it to her height, but then stopped herself.

Not yet.

Both Eve and Muriel pictured the cheerless piano in The Deerwood's lobby, caged behind avocado-colored velvet ropes. It felt very far away, in a place where no one could bring it to life.

Sandra came in behind them and set down a clattering tray of teacups and spoons.

"Grace *is* coming back, you know." When Muriel said this, Sandra looked into her mother's piercing blue eyes and saw the ocean reaching somewhere beyond Sandra's comprehension.

"What's that, Mom?" Sandra said quietly, laying out the coasters.

"I think she wants to call your sister," Eve offered to Sandra.

Sandra winced and said, "Come help me with the tea." They walked out together, leaving Muriel at the piano bench. Muriel flitted her fingers across the tops of the keys without playing.

"She talked about Grace with you?" Sandra asked. "What did she tell you?" Her eyes were skittish, and Eve noticed a small section where she had missed with her eyeliner. Eve thought it made sense that Sandra was reticent about Grace; she and Lem must have felt equally abandoned when she left to explore the world, but Grace had shown up at the funeral, so Eve knew she wasn't entirely written off.

"I can call her if things are weird with you guys," Eve offered again. "She doesn't know me, so she probably won't hang up."

"We're not calling Grace," Sandra said, suddenly holding Eve's arm.

"I think India's only eight or nine hours ahead----"

"No, that's not it----"

"We can use my WhatsApp if you can get my phone back from Mr. Worth."

Sandra continued her hold, and then pressed firmly. "You *really* don't know, do you?"

Eve stopped talking. Sandra brought her to the kitchen table and sat her down, finally releasing her arm and then brushing the spot apologetically to soothe it. Sandra dropped her head, and a clump of hair fell over the headband. She removed it and shook everything free. Eve saw lengthy streaks of white darting about like lightning until Sandra lifted her head again, tucked her bangs behind her ears, and attempted a forced smile. Eve read Sandra's face and suddenly realized the problem.

"Oh," Eve said quietly. "She doesn't remember."

"What's going on?" Lem interjected, suddenly appearing in the doorway.

Eve stiffened, and Sandra jumped up and went to him. She clutched his arm in the same manner as Eve's and brought him to a seat at the table.

"Easy, easy!" he said, stumbling across the room on one foot while using Sandra as a crutch. He propped his sore foot up on an empty chair. Eve and Lem were about the same distance from each other as they had been during our drive, but this time they faced each other and he filled her frame of vision.

"I was about to tell her about Grace. Mom just said she's coming back," Sandra said.

"Ha!" he started to laugh. "God almighty, I can't even take a stupid nap without you finding a way to mess her up." He was talking to Eve, but Sandra assumed he meant her.

"No, I was just explaining," Sandra asserted, "and Eve's only trying to help."

"I'm so sorry," Eve whispered. "I had no idea Grace was dead."

Lem and Sandra looked at her with blank expressions. Eve put her head down, feeling their loss, sharing it. After three days of listening to stories about Grace, she felt like she knew her intimately, and she loved her. Grace was a dynamic, incredible person. Eve had always longed for a sibling, but she couldn't imagine the pain of having one and then losing her. Muriel made her seem so alive—it was almost incomprehensible to think she was gone.

Lem burst into loud laughter. It escaped from his lungs in bursts, like the smoke from a chugging, coal-powered train. Eve lifted her head and saw Sandra shaking her head. "Tell her already!" Lem continued laughing. "Tell her the truth about our dear mother and her precious Grace!"

Eve bit down on her lower lip, but she kept her posture straight and her eyes wide open as she came to realize that maybe Grace wasn't dead after all. Maybe she was in a religious cult somewhere? Maybe she was in prison? Or maybe she ran away and had a bunch of kids and never talked to any of them ever again?

"Grace is Mom," Sandra said flatly.

Eve heard her, but she didn't understand what that meant. Lem could see the utter lack of comprehension, and it reminded him of the look most teenagers had when they were presented with a house chore or a curfew.

"Mom is Grace," he said, reversing the sentence to clarify. Eve's face remained expressionless and frozen, like someone in a photograph from the turn of the previous century.

"Our mother's full name is Muriel Grace Worth," Lem continued.

"Muriel *Grace* Worth," Sandra emphasized.

Eve considered everything Muriel had told her about Grace. The ashrams, the butterfly, the pink light in her hotel, the tree, the blessings, becoming one with the universe . . . and she came to realize Muriel had never once said that Grace was her daughter. Somehow, Eve had drawn that conclusion, even though it was never actually spoken aloud.

But it didn't make sense. How was Grace writing about her experiences and sending them to Muriel if Muriel was actually Grace? And why did Muriel think she could call Grace on Sandra's phone? Or . . . did she? Eve began to grasp that she was filling in Muriel's blanks and drawing her own rapid conclusions that weren't there. *She* was the one who was making things up! But was she? What about the other people? Were any of them real? Katran? The swami who didn't eat? Grace's travel companion in Bodh Gaya?

"I don't under----"

"I know," Lem laughed. "It's a mindfuck."

"Lem, shut up," Sandra said. "Listen, Eve. I know it's a lot to take in, but the stories are probably real. Or at least Mom thinks they are. But Grace isn't----"

"Your sister." Eve said, confirming. "Or dead."

"That's right. It's always been just the two of us: Lem and me. Mom went to Europe after college and then, I don't know, somehow she took a wrong flight and ended up in India, which is kind of a good thing," she looked over at Lem and smiled, "because that's where she met our dad."

"You mean the guy?" Eve interrupted.

"She told you about him?" Sandra asked.

"She said she met some guy and they weren't, like, boyfriend or girlfriend or anything, but they kept running into each other."

"Yeah, well, that's Dad. They came back from India together and got married pretty soon after and . . . the rest is the rest."

Sandra's smile was infectious and Eve caught it, but only because she was comically embarrassed for having failed to determine the narrator's identity after listening to her stories for three full days. "But why call herself Grace?" Eve probed. "Like she's someone else?"

"It's that fucking disease," Lem said, his laughter cutting off abruptly. "Mom's totally dissociated—she doesn't even know her own memories anymore. She *needs* The Deerwood, Sandy. I don't care if you're bored."

"I think she wanted to be someone else for a while," Sandra said, ignoring him. "Grandma's suicide did a real number on Mom, and I think she needed a sort of reset button. Plus, you know, it was the sixties. Everyone was reinventing themselves."

Eve took that in.

"Somehow, I think she's back in the same mindset—losing Dad. Being Grace again, or just connecting to those old feelings is how she can . . . escape. Or cope."

Lem slammed his hands on the table.

"No!" he boomed. "No no NO!!" As his breath gusted over Eve, she expected to smell beer or old coffee, but instead there was a surprising tinge of something metallic, like nail polish. Lem stood up and hobbled his way to the bathroom for the fourth time in two hours, muttering, "She's just crazy. Why can't anyone see she's a crazy old lady?"

Sandra said quietly, "Anyway, now you know." She shrugged and called out, "We're coming, Mom!" Sandra grabbed the teapot and Eve followed her back to Muriel in the pink light of the late afternoon.

***

A bit later, Lem tried and failed to continue his nap, so he staggered into the living room and positioned himself in a contemporary wingback chair. He heaved his unclad foot onto the matching padded ottoman as a rogue chocolate chip from Sandra's latest batch of homemade cookies tumbled down his chest and landed on the bunny hill of his abdomen. His thick fingers found it around the same time Muriel decided to leave the piano bench.

She had only sat there and didn't play, but her wrists were beginning to throb, and her hands felt hot for no clear reason. When Lem entered the room, she felt a sudden need to protect Eve, and she sat between Eve and Sandra on the couch. The three of them resembled a collection of silent dolls, warily watching the mordacious child in the corner and praying they wouldn't get picked for play.

Lem started with Sandra.

"After we fly back tomorrow, you'll take the car to Boxley's and have it cleaned and detailed. I already called them, and they'll assess if there are any damages to the paint or chrome. Hagerty's is working out the diminished value from all the extra miles, and then we'll figure out if we would have made more money selling it in Florida instead of----" He coughed and squinted. "----here."

He tossed her aside and turned to Muriel.

"I don't know where your head's at, Mom, but you could have stopped all of this. Now you've just made everything harder for yourself—and Eve. When we get home, I think we have no choice but to move you into the Rose Garden Wing and ramp up your care."

He didn't wait for a reply before he fixed his attention on Eve.

"As for you, we'll figure out the car stuff and the money you stole from Mom, and also my flight and my missed work and, well, everything. Even the doughnuts. To the penny. We'll draft a promissory note and a payment schedule. I don't know if I can get you back into the salon, but you'll need to grab more work hours somewhere, so I think you can say goodbye to your little drama club."

Eve clenched her fists in her lap and locked her jaw.

"You won't have time to hang out with Laura anymore, either."

Sandra shook her head in disbelief as Lem continued, "Mom was off her meds for nearly three days and her withdrawal wasn't tapered. There could be—there probably *is*—irreparable damage. We'll see how it goes, but we may be talking about criminal and civil lawsuits, too, for your negligence."

Eve looked at Muriel, wondering if that was true, but Lem didn't want the dolls to interact with each other, so he snapped his fingers to seize Eve's attention.

"Do you even know what you did or the harm you've caused? You stole a hundred-thousand-dollar vehicle and a very sick, elderly woman. You took money off her credit cards and you lied to the police and your own mother. You lied to your best friend, who happens to be my daughter, and you lied to *me*."

Eve desperately wanted to leave the room. There were six bedrooms upstairs to hide in and Lem could barely walk, but she also knew she couldn't avoid him. Her knuckles were turning white and her jaw began to ache. She fought her tears as they formed and willed them to stay put. She didn't want to give Lem the satisfaction of affecting her, but he saw the glassy sheen thickening and decided to push further.

"Who the fuck do you think you are, anyway? I was always on your side! I got you a job and a bank account, and I was helping you establish a good credit score. I was even fighting for you to get a goddamn car! You ate our food and drank our soda and slept in our beds. You swam in our pool and wiped your wet sorry butt with our towels! We trusted you, and you betrayed us, you little bitch!"

"That's enough!" Sandra cried out. Muriel instinctively reached her arm forward and across Eve, as parents do for their children when the car is about to crash.

"You're an asshole!" he hissed. He was ready to unleash another verbal barrage, but then his phone rang. He tried to tame his vocal cords when he saw it was Cindy, and he half-managed a chunky, "Helll—oo?!"

Eve cried.

She cried without crumpling over herself or putting her arms in front of her face. Years of frustration and a new torrent of fear surged down her cheeks, and she let it all go without moving, without making a sound.

She cried at her reversal of fortune and the shattered dream of seeing her father.

She cried as she pictured her pathetic mother, alone in her gloomy bedroom surrounded by old religious artifacts instead of living, nurturing friends. Maybe her mom *was* worried. Maybe she *did* care.

She cried over Laura. And maybe Liam. And definitely for Muriel Grace Worth.

But mostly, Eve cried as she began to realize that she may have, in fact, actually hurt all these people. Throughout our long drive, she'd deeply believed she was helping Muriel as much as herself, but Lem's harsh words and the revelation about Grace forced a necessary reevaluation. The worst feature of Lem's tirade was the disturbing knowledge that he may have been right all along: Muriel wasn't well. Maybe it wasn't Alzheimer's, but something was definitely off-kilter in her mindscape. Muriel never seemed lucid for more than an hour, with or without the pills, and it was true that she couldn't care for herself. It appeared she couldn't even remember her own life properly—somehow, she had convinced Eve that she had another daughter.

Eve looked to Muriel, who lowered her arm and stared past Lem and the piano and the walls, the blue in her eyes dropping to low tide. The euphoria of her homecoming was wearing off. She couldn't physically sustain the pleasure of even pretending to play her piano. How long before she started to piss herself again? Or got lost in her own neighborhood? Or burned the house down trying to make a pot of cinnamon tea?

"Eve?"

It was Cindy, on Lem's speakerphone. Lem placed it near the plate of cookies as he grabbed one coated with chopped walnuts.

"Yeah?" Eve sobbed, finally rubbing her arm against her cheeks.

"Eve, listen to me. I know everyone is upset, but I also want you to know we're *very* relieved that you and Grams are okay. Lem and I will have a long conversation with Sandy and your mom about the next steps, but I don't want you to worry about that right now, okay?"

Cindy's voice was calm. Rational. Lem spoke as if he had charred meat in his throat, but Cindy's tone was a creamy foie gras.

"You're not mad at me?" Eve sniffled.

Cindy thought about it for a moment. "No, I don't think I am. At least not the way Lem is. I guess I'm . . . disappointed, but I know you, Eve, and I think I understand what happened here. I don't think you're a bad person or anything, and Lem doesn't think so eith----"

"Yes I do!!" he hollered toward the coffee table.

"Don't listen to him," Cindy said in a placating tone.

"But he wants to have me arrested!" Eve pleaded.

"No one is arresting anyone," Cindy assured.

"Yes we are!" he shouted with conviction.

"Shut up, Lem!" Cindy bellowed through the tiny speaker.

"She's just a kid, Lem, cut it out!" Sandra echoed. Eve tried to gulp away the knot that had formed in her throat, but she couldn't seem to pull her neck in far enough.

"Eve?" It was Cindy again.

"Yeah?" she managed to choke out.

"Eve, I need to know if Laura helped you do this. Lem found your conversations about Uncle Pete, but I mean . . . initially? Was this something you girls planned together?"

"No," Eve said, forceful and assured.

"Okay."

"Muriel and I never had a plan, and Laura didn't know anything."

"I want to believe you," Cindy said while Lem squawked, "But she's a liar! You *know* she lies. She told the cops they were in *Miami!*"

"I swear I didn't plan any of this----"

"----we did go to Miami," Muriel interrupted. "We watched the sunset."

"That's enough, Mom," Lem said.

"Could you take me off speaker and give the phone to Sandy, please?"

Lem tried to lean over to grab the phone, but his stomach got in the way, and his whole foot throbbed when he stretched over his extended leg. Eve handed it to Sandra, who took it to the foyer. Feeling awkward after his failed attempt to capture the phone, Lem decided to make the most of it and snatched yet another cookie. He leaned back, chewing, and then put his wrist to his forehead. His foot was killing him and he felt hot and light-headed. He blamed the tea.

Eve tried to listen to Sandra and Cindy's conversation as her future was being decided, but beyond the immediate range of Sandra's left ear, most of Cindy's high-pitched chatter seemed to reach an aural spectrum that only dogs could hear. Kubrick, unable to stand it, retreated to a distant bedroom on the second floor. At one point, Sandra and Eve locked eyes. Eve was hoping for some sort of wink or nod, but then Sandra looked away.

Sandra asked Cindy if Lucy was planning to return from Jamaica to take care of Muriel again. "She's fired!" Lem called out, but it was apparent from Sandra's expression that Cindy felt otherwise.

"And Albi? Did you ever find out who that is?" Sandra asked into the phone.

"Albi is Lucy's twin," said Muriel, perfectly alert.

Everyone was silent.

"He's twelve minutes older than Lucy and he drives a cab," Muriel continued. "He has a big scar on his cheek and he likes to tell tourists he was stabbed in the face defending a passenger, but really he ran into a tree branch as a kid. He's a character."

Only Eve was grinning. On Monday Muriel had no idea who Albi was, and by Thursday she remembered his life story. How could Lem not see that even with her deficits, Muriel was so much better now that she was off the medicine and in her real home?

Wow?! mouthed Sandra as she shrugged shoulders with Lem. Then, the mostly one-sided banter continued for nearly eight minutes as Cindy flexed and took charge, as expected. Eve watched Sandra appear to melt under Cindy's formidable heat; she slowly slid down the living room archway and scrunched in a near-fetal position on the floor. Eve had seen Laura and Christian dissolve under similar radiation, and even Lem had been known to surrender to Cindy's flaming glare.

The longer Cindy and Sandra talked, the more Eve came to realize she lacked advocacy. Pete had done his best, but she was still cut off from both Laura and her own mother. Sandra and Micah had no real reason to defend her, and Muriel was equally vulnerable.

There was only her father.

Eve could almost feel his warm pulse when they locked hands in her dream, the slight crunch before the softness of his product-laden hair, the sand behind his knees when she'd held onto him as a child at the edge of the frothy ocean.

Her father was so close.

***

Samuel Levine came home from school later on, following a rigorous soccer practice. He plopped his backpack, jacket, and shoes next to the kitchen island, swallowed fresh-squeezed orange juice from the glass pitcher, and grabbed a homemade granola bar from the breadbox before tearing upstairs to his room. Kubrick matched every step, with four fast legs to Sam's two.

"Sammy?" Micah called from the downstairs office. It was Mr. Clifton's former quarters, and it was situated past the back door that Sam had once again failed to close. "Sam?!"

Sam rushed down the back staircase two at a time and slipped on the last step, crashing into the banister with a bang. Kubrick narrowly avoided a similar outcome by digging his claws into the wood.

"Slow down, boys!" Micah scolded, meeting them in the kitchen.

"Whatever," Sam muttered, rubbing his arm. "Whassup?"

Micah pointed, and Sam begrudgingly slid to the back door on his socks and shut it firmly. It was a fairly common routine, only this time Kubrick nearly got his nose caught thinking he was going for another walk.

"Sorry, buddy," Sam said, providing Kubrick with a conciliatory rubdown.

"Did you hurt yourself?" Micah asked.

"No."

"Maybe don't run around in your socks?"

"Whatev—okay."

Sam slid back to the stairs. He was about to fire his teenaged jet-propulsion pack and launch back to his room when he stopped like an animated character with his nose sniffing skyward toward an invisible aroma cloud. "Hey, did Mom make cookies?"

Micah replied, "Yeah. Your Grams and Laura's friend got here with Uncle Lem a few hours ago. Mom said she texted you."

"Are there any left?"

"Do you think maybe you should go say 'Hi' first?" Micah shrugged and waited for Sam's priorities to properly assemble.

"Are there cookies or not?" Sam asked in a pleading voice.

Micah pointed toward the counter, where a covered Pyrex with Sandra's second batch was still moderately warm. As Sam took a bite, Micah continued, "Since you're obviously so invested in your family, you may also care to know that Mom took Uncle Lem to the hospital." Sam continued to eat the cookie while the rest of his face registered interest in the news. "He's got some sort of infection in his toe."

"Ew."

"Yeah. I saw it. It's gross." They both grinned, sharing a mutual fascination for pretty much anything body-related, especially wounds and scars.

"Did Eve and Grams go with them?" Sam asked. He still had half a cookie left but was already reaching for another.

"No, Grams is resting in Abby's room, and Eve's up in Nancy's." Micah said this while responding to the attempted cookie-grab with a light slap as he replaced the cover. "They're both pretty beat, but Grams looks better than I've seen her in a long time." The last time Micah was in Florida, he'd shared with Sandra that he didn't think her mother was very long for this world. At the time, she had sadly agreed.

"I like Eve," Sam said. "We hung out at Uncle Lem's last time we were there. She can hold her breath underwater longer than anyone, and she's super smart."

Micah said he also remembered her and made an uncharacteristic remark about her colored hair and piercings. Sam knew how lucky he was to have the coolest dad in the world, but sometimes, every now and then, even Awesome Micah said something that made him seem like an old man. Sam's mission as a young teenager was to keep Micah on track by calling out every out-of-touch platitude, cliché, or lame dad joke.

"No, Dad. Wrong."

Micah accepted the admonishment and said, "Here, this came today. It's from your cousin." He handed Sam a medium-sized box from the kitchen island. "What'd she send you?"

"Just some books." Micah raised his thick eyebrows and Sam explained, "We were texting about our reading assignments, and she's got everything I need for Mrs. Griggs, so she sent them."

"That was nice of her."

"Yeah. And they're already highlighted!"

"Maybe don't tell me that," Micah said. "Highlight your own books."

"Whatever," he muttered again, followed by a modest "sorry" for his lapse in respect. He didn't mean to be short with his dad, whom he loved and adored, but sometimes he wanted to get his mail and a snack without the obligatory after-school conversation.

Micah followed up with "Why'd she overnight them?"

Sam sighed. The conversation had already gone on too long. "I'm supposed to be halfway through the first one already. That's how the whole thing got started."

Micah accepted the response but felt compelled to add, "We have books here, you know. And there's this big building only four blocks away—it's filled with free books whenever you want. I think they call it the library."

"It's five blocks!" Sam retorted as he took his package to the stairs.

"Hold up, smartass." Sam provided his father with another look of impatience that Micah deftly vanquished with his next sentence: "The Caddy's in the garage if you're done ruining your dinner."

"Dad!" Sam dropped the package on the bottom step and ran over to thump Micah's arm with a fake punch as he continued his spin around the kitchen island to retrieve his shoes. He slid the last three feet and crashed into a stool. As he crouched to put on his shoes, Kubrick licked a lingering cookie crumb off his chin. Then Micah and Sam headed through the breezeway to the semi-detached garage where I welcomed their touch and admiration.

Eve awoke from her nap the first time Sam hit the banister. She listened to Sam and Micah's exchange from the edge of the back stairs, and their simple father–child conversation brought her to tears. Again. She couldn't stand how her emotions were completely out of whack from Lem's castigations, her fears for Muriel, and the general question mark over her own future. She felt as beat as Micah described, and suddenly and surprisingly, jealous. Why couldn't she have a mother who made cookies? Why couldn't she have a father who was interested in scabs and cars and whatever she was reading?

Sam and Micah didn't realize how precious their small exchange was, but Eve knew. She desperately wanted to join them, but she feared her presence would pollute their purity. Lem believed she was toxic, and Eve was on the cusp of agreeing with him. She returned to Nancy's room to await a more communal time to reappear.

Nancy Caldwell-Worth was Pete and Sandra's first daughter. She was four years older than Eve and was currently spending her junior year of college in Italy. Abby, one year younger than Nancy, and Jamison, one year older, were also away at different universities. Russell, the eldest, was finishing graduate school and was already engaged. As the children moved out, Micah and Sandra had made a joint decision to keep all their bedrooms intact. The idea of altering them while the kids were in college seemed both premature and disrespectful, since most of them returned for holidays and events. Plus, as Sandra repeatedly dreamed aloud, "Why convert them when grandchildren are only a few years away?"

Micah did rearrange Russell's old room to accommodate a treadmill, however, and soon a weight set and yoga area followed. He used the room every day as a fixture of his morning routine. Shortly thereafter, on the other side of the hall, Sandra had swapped out Jamison's queen-sized bed for a twin and removed his reading nook to create a much-needed craft corner and a separate gift-wrapping station. Despite their parents' pledge to maintain the bedrooms, every time the older boys returned home, they discovered that a few more items from their childhood had been lovingly packed away in plastic bins and stored under the sharp-nailed eaves of the attic. Since the girls were a little younger, their rooms were still left alone.

Nancy would describe her room as pink, but unlike Laura's ballet-slipper-colored walls in Florida, Eve thought it was closer to a chalky plum. The curtains were lace, and a thick bedspread sprouted dark-green floral accents that matched the pillows. It was sweetly posh, and Eve was particularly drawn to Nancy's posters: a herd of stylized unicorns, a movie poster for *Wild at Heart,* and a series of *New Yorker* cartoons, all framed and behind glass. Nancy also had a small piece of art in an exquisitely carved frame over her bed. It depicted a woman spreading sheets across a clothesline with a farm in the background. Eve couldn't make out the signature, but it was numbered X/XV, and Eve correctly assumed it was both important and expensive. Nancy already had an heirloom.

Eve sat on the puffy queen-sized bed and tried to ascertain what kind of a girl Nancy was based on her decor. There were a few googly-eyed stickers stuck to her desk. There were postcards from numerous European countries taped to her full-length dressing mirror. There was a fuzzy array of stuffed animals crowding the upper shelves of her bookcase and scores of dog-eared books filling out the rest. It was definitely the room of someone with intelligence, someone popular and with a great sense of humor, someone who probably had good skin.

On Nancy's dresser, Eve discovered a high-contrast black-and-white photo in a brass frame. It took a few moments to recognize the young and unwrinkled subjects as Muriel and Ira, especially since she'd never seen him before. They were on a vacation, somewhere tropical, and the handsome couple emanated a comforting joy.

As her eyes moved around the thick moldings and brass doorknobs of Nancy's room for the tenth time, Eve compared it to her own cheaply constructed home with its almond-hued kitchen floor tiles, popcorn ceilings, and bifold closet doors. She had a big window, but her room didn't feel sunny like Nancy's. Eve chose her photos and effects and made the space her own, but the room itself was decidedly generic. Even if she painted it the exact same color as Nancy's, it would still lack character. If she moved out and someone else moved in, the room wouldn't know the difference, whereas Nancy Caldwell-Worth's bedroom was unique in the world.

Eve stretched out on the foreign bed and further tried to imagine Nancy's life. Nancy's family tree had a few knots: Pete was her biological father, but she had mostly been raised by Sandra and Micah. Pete was wealthy and wonderful, but he didn't want to live with his own children.

That must have been hard.

But Nancy also had a second incredible bedroom in New York City where she could stay whenever she wanted. Did she use it? Pete was smiling with Nancy in silver frames in both locales, so they probably got along. Everyone got along with Pete Caldwell.

Micah wasn't her biological father, but even if he only had a quarter of the affection for Nancy that he showed towards Sam, the girl was drenched in paternal gold. And Sandra seemed to be the kind of supermother who made all the kids with normal mothers jealous. The Worth children must have heard "I wish I had your parents" a thousand times a week, like a practiced mantra. Nancy had three amazing parents, while Eve was left with barely half a mom.

Eve rolled over on her stomach and pressed her face deep into the pillow, stopping her breath. Knowing that Micah and Sam were still with me in the garage, she clenched her fists again and screamed. The people in this house were actually *loving*. This house oozed with their pervading affection for one another.

She screamed again.

Eve pictured the people in this house waking up with a song in their hearts and little birds dressing them on the patio while giggling squirrels slid buttery pancakes down the rainbows for them to share.

Another release.

In this house, "Have a nice day" always came with the unspoken subtext *because I love you* and *you are special and important to me* and *I truly hope you have the kind of wonderful day that a wonderful son or wonderful daughter like you deserves.*

It took a few minutes for Eve to calm down, and she finally rolled over on her back when oxygen became imperative. She stared at the cut-glass light fixture and the glow-in-the-dark stars carefully affixed to Nancy's ceiling in the shape of her astrological sign. Nancy had an exquisite life in this house, and she was continuing to live it in Italy, where she would likely meet a gorgeous European man with an accent and scads of money and a mustache. Together they would forge an unfailing union and replicate their own blissful childhoods with their perfect and lucky Worth family descendants.

But Eve was the horrible person who had abandoned her best friend, ignored the only boy who ever liked her, and screwed over the one sincere adult who actually gave a damn and tried to help her. Lem was mild and good natured up until Monday; it was always Cindy whom everybody feared. If Lem was a monster, then it was probably Eve's fault.

All of it was Eve's fault.

But then Eve remembered Muriel's exuberance when she learned she was returning to New York. Muriel was in a prison, and Lem was both the judge and jailer until Eve set her free! Muriel seemed utterly restored in those therapeutic hugs with Pete and Sandra and Micah. Lem couldn't appreciate the ecstatic bliss that emanated from his mother when we pulled into the driveway, but Eve felt it, and I felt it, too. That was also Eve's doing.

Micah knocked on the door, gently pushing it open.

"Hey, I think this is yours," he said, smiling as he handed Eve her phone.

"Ohmigod, how did you—?"

"It was in the glove compartment. Lem must have stashed it there when you arrived."

Eve was speechless as thirty new curse words for Lem circled her lips.

"Yeah, I know." Micah paused. "You should call your mom."

He disappeared, and Sam slid into his place, a young and precocious version of his father with startlingly similar mannerisms.

"Hey, Sammy!" Eve said, excitedly extending her arms. He glided like a speed skater into her hug, and she was instantly engulfed in the fresh deodorant he had liberally applied for her benefit.

"You actually drove it all the way from Florida?" he said, utterly impressed.

"Yeah."

He released her and held out his fist. She bumped it, accepting his props.

"I heard Uncle Lem's pretty pissed at you," he added, raising his eyebrows in the corners in an expression that looked exactly like Micah's.

"Yeah, I guess so."

They looked at each other until he cocked his head and said, "He'll get over it. I've got homework, see you at dinner, c'mon Kubee!" He ran down the hall and slid the last six feet to his room with a panting Kubrick closely in tow.

Eve propped herself against the headboard on five of Nancy's pillows. She sent a quick text to Laura explaining how Lem stole her phone and he was going to sue her for millions of dollars. Laura replied a second later that she would never in a billion years allow that to happen.

They exchanged a few more lines, and then Eve said she had to call her mother. Laura sent a string of emojis: love, fear, prayer hands, and meditation. Eve responded with the screaming cat, steak knife, and bomb emojis, and her message received a heart comment that quickly changed to a *haha* and then an exclamation point. *Nancy may have everything,* Eve thought, *but Laura's only her cousin, and she's MY best friend.*

Eve switched out of texting and over to the phone function. Her index finger hovered above the screen until she finally allowed gravity to take control, triggering the call. Judith picked up immediately, but she didn't talk. Instead, she and Eve listened to each other listening as they silently prepared for the duel, a salty thickness forming in both of their throats.

"Hi Mom." Eve finally broke, her voice wavering in its effort to calmly deliver the two short syllables.

"Did the ark make it safely through the storm?" was Judith's response.

"Huh?"

"Are you done wandering the desert for forty years? Are you in the Promised Land?" Judith followed with a shallow laugh, but Eve couldn't tell if she was joking, and she couldn't fabricate an answer. She shifted the pillows a few times and then kicked three of them off the bed. There was no getting comfortable.

"Mom?"

"Eve."

Neither spoke for another ten seconds. Then Judith continued, "Cindy gave me Sandra's number, but I figured you should be the one to call first."

"Why?"

"So I know you actually want to talk to me," Judith said in a whimper.

Eve could hear her mother pacing on the hard kitchen tiles in her house slippers with the cork soles, which meant she hadn't showered and had skipped work.

"What else did Mrs. Worth say?" Eve asked.

"Well . . . we both think you should all drive back here together because I don't know how you're ever going to repay them if there are three more last-minute plane tickets on the bill, but Lemuel's adamant about not putting any more miles on the car or risking another long drive. I guess we're still trying to iron it out."

"Oh."

"But the most important thing is the ark is safe."

"Please stop saying that, Mom. It's stupid."

"No, sweetie, *you're the ark*. I don't mean the car, I mean you."

Sweetie?

They each stared at the walls in front of them. Eve wondered why her mother couldn't speak like a normal human being until Judith finally asked the question she longed to hear: "But you're okay?"

"I'm fine." Eve relaxed a touch. "Maybe a little tired."

"You drove quite a ways."

"It wasn't hard. It was just . . . long."

"I know it. Would you believe I once did that drive straight through in one day?" Judith said.

"Really?"

"Twenty-six hours in one shot. It was the spring break before I met your father, and a bunch of us piled into a cheap little Nissan and took turns driving all the way from Syracuse to Disney and then Fort Lauderdale."

"You never told me that."

"You never asked."

It was exactly the type of statement that drove Eve up the wall. How was she supposed to know to ask? Why did she always have to come up with esoteric questions and play conversational darts with her mother? *Hey Mom, did you ever pile into a car with a bunch of college friends and drive to Florida for spring break in one day? Hey Mom, did you know last Sunday night I found out that Dad was gay and he isn't really dead?*

"Mom?" she said.

"Yes?"

"Mr. Worth said he's gonna to turn me over to the police when we get back and he's gonna sue me because Muriel didn't get her medicine."

Judith was silent and her clog-clicking stopped.

"Mom?"

"Eve, I don't really have any power here."

"But you have to help me! You're my mother!"

"Yes, but you took *his* mother, and he's obviously very upset about it. Instead of going to work today, he had to fly to New York and figure out how to get everyone back home," Judith replied.

"How can you be on his side? Muriel doesn't even wanna go back!" Eve argued.

"That's not her decision."

"Why?" asked the daughter.

"It's complicated," said the mother.

Eve collected all the pillows and placed them against the headboard with the sleeping pillows in the back, the king-sized ones up front, and the colorful accent pillow set tidily in the center. She had to keep her hands busy so she wouldn't punch the wall. While she arranged, she argued. "It isn't complicated, Mom. None of this is complicated. Muriel's an adult, and it should be her decision. That's, like, the whole point of being grown up!"

"I think you're too young to understand," Judith offered.

"I'm almost eighteen!"

"Hardly!" Judith laughed.

"Well, it's closer than you think." Eve slung these words at Judith, who abruptly discarded her laughter when they hit her and she realized it was true. She conceded and searched for a better answer. Muriel had to go back to Florida, even if it was against her will because . . . because . . . Even as Judith spoke, she knew her answer wouldn't satisfy her self-proclaimed nearly adult daughter.

"She can't make the decision for herself because she's sick, Eve. She has Alzheimer's, and she needs to be in a place where people can take care of her."

"People can take care of her here," Eve said.

"No, not just any people—the right people. As I said, it's complicated."

"But it doesn't have to be. The only reason Muriel is in Florida is because Mr. Worth wants her there for his own convenience. And it's costing her, like, everything."

Judith didn't have an answer, and Eve knew that in some miniscule and miraculous way, she'd managed to send her message-in-a-bottle across the great divide, and surprisingly, it had been received. Sensing a tenuous bridge, Eve decided to test its tensile strength.

"Mom, are you mad at me?" she probed.

Judith said, perhaps a little too quickly: "Matthew 7:1, 'Judge not, that ye be not judged.'"

"I don't know what that means! *Are you mad at me?*"

"It means I don't know, Eve!!" Judith was rattled, and she snapped the fresh rubber band on her wrist for raising her voice. Then, with a sudden calm that surprised them both, she said, "I don't think mad is the right word. Maybe I don't know what I am."

Eve considered this and said, "Well, whatever it is, I'm sorry."

"I know you are," Judith replied. Then she added, "And I know you didn't do this because of me."

Eve's response was lodged deep in her throat, but she wasn't sure if she should keep it there. If she allowed it to rise, the little progress they'd made might be negated. She looked at herself in the full-length mirror and was struck by the strong young woman looking back. Even with all the pressure, stress, worry, and tears, her reflection carried a powerful disposition, and it urged her to find out whether she could be completely honest with her mother. She sat on the bed, steadied herself, and practiced the next five words in her mind. Five little words that might save their fragile relationship—or possibly end it.

"That's not really true, Mom," she said in a crisp staccato.

Judith clenched her teeth, hands, and rectum simultaneously. She realized she had paced up the stairs and into the doorway of Eve's room, where she was blankly staring at Eve's bed, her desk, her pictures on the walls, her half-empty closet.

"I . . ."

"But I *am* sorry for scaring you," Eve added.

Scared was the correct word. Judith wasn't angry; she was terrified. Judith knew that once college arrived, their daily difficulties would settle back like the dust following a truck down a dirt road, but she had never imagined that Eve would *entirely* leave her. Physically, perhaps, as all children should, but not emotionally. Not like this, without even a note for the person who had sacrificed her entire life to care for her.

And loved her.

Judith never imagined she would come home one day to find that her exquisite, invaluable Eve was gone—in exactly the same manner as her husband.

Eve heard her mother's breathing accelerate.

"She could stay here with Sandra," Eve whispered.

"That's not the answer," Judith whispered back.

"Sandra's not as good as Lem?"

"I'm not saying that, but Muriel has to go back to The Deerwood. She can't live in a normal house anymore."

"Even with full-time care?"

"No."

"Why?"

"Because."

Parents often use a why/because exchange to protect their child from an inability to understand consequences, but Judith had improperly invoked it to shut the conversation down. Her belief that Eve was oblivious to cause and effect had only been reinforced when we drove out of The Deerwood parking lot. But Judith had failed to consider that for three full days on the road, Eve had pretty much done nothing but think. And grow.

"Because . . ." Eve repeated, astonished. "Fine. Then maybe we'll keep driving."

"Oh god in heaven, stop it!" Judith crossed herself. "*Please* stop! You're a fully grown adult now? Here's an adult truth: You can't fix your problems by changing the geography. You can't run away from me because you think I'm a bad mother any more than Muriel can run away from her disease. You're both stuck with it, the same way I got stuck with your father's problems and Cindy and Lem got stuck with a party-boy son. Sometimes people just get stuck with things, and there's no fixing it by driving yourself halfway to the moon. It doesn't work like that, Eve. Trust me, I know."

Eve let the phone settle next to her ear on the pillow as the words circled the nucleus of her brain like manic electrons.

"But you find a way." Judith quieted and then continued, "You find a way to live with it and you find a way through. You pick yourself up and go through the motions until maybe one day you wake up and realize you have your problems, but you can also have faith. Faith gives you the strength to get out of bed. Faith is the warm blanket of protection for those cold nights when you really think you're done for. You can lose everything, Eve, but you'll always be fine if you hold onto your faith."

Eve listened to the sermon. For years their conversations were like vinyl records with Judith's tracks of lectures on Side A and Eve's well-worn rebellions on Side B, and it was impossible for either of them to listen to the other when they were playing their own sides. But this time, something felt different as Eve tuned in and began to understand something fundamental about her mother.

"You know it isn't fair," Eve quietly whined. As the words slipped out, she felt juvenile and wondered how her mother had the power to strip a decade off her vocabulary.

"I know it isn't, and we'll talk about it when you're home. But for now we have to focus on what's best for Muriel."

"But that's what I'm doing. That's why she *can't* go back to Florida. She *hates* it there, Mom, and she's *so much better* here."

"Eve, I hear you, but it's only been a few hours, and everyone's excited, and, like I said, I don't have any power in this. All we can do is let the Worths know how you feel."

"They won't listen."

"Do you think—Eve, maybe it's possible that Lem knows more about this than you? Maybe? Part of being an adult is finding a way to work with the other adults in the room, even if you don't agree with them. Being an adult means trusting the other adults who know better."

"I trust Muriel," Eve said as she hung up.

***

Muriel awoke from her nap in Abby's room, adjacent to Nancy's on the western elbow of the second floor. Her bed was against their shared wall, and she could hear Eve talking to her mother. Muriel felt relief. It was time.

As she stretched and yawned, the early afternoon scene in the living room returned to disturb her. Muriel and Eve had managed to enjoy the tea and cookies for less than five minutes before everyone decided it was time to turn around and go back to Florida! Who treats their guests like that, inviting them in and then kicking them out? She thought she and Ira had raised their children better. When Cindy and Sandra started talking about flight schedules, Muriel decided she'd had enough. She patted Eve on the thigh and asked her for help to get settled.

As they climbed the stairs (were there always so many stairs?), Muriel studied the photographs on the wall. The older ones remained in place—class photos, anniversaries, and the four original Worths on various vacations—but they only claimed a quarter of the wall space. The rest was filled with Sandra's clan and their newer milestones and undertakings. Eventually, these would also be replaced by yet another group making their way through schools and life, marking their many adventures in the world. Muriel didn't fret; she was comforted by the continuum and felt the privilege of witnessing the passage. *Everyone has a time and place,* she thought. *Everyone gets a turn.*

After the nap, Muriel took a few minutes in Nancy and Abby's turquoise-tiled bath before the familiar floorboard creaks carried her down the long hall to the double doors at the far end. She advanced into the primary bedroom, and her eyes immediately led her to the fireplace. She remembered the blustery winter nights spent with Ira, safe in their naked warmth by the flickering marigold flames. She remembered the pewter clock on the mantel, its unfaltering tick injurious to an agitated sleep, but also, far more often, a diligently soothing sound.

Again, the scale seemed askew. Were the windows always so far apart? Was the bathroom door always taller than the closets? The furniture was newish and probably expensive, but, like the walls, it was subject to Sandra's penchant for ice cream colors, and it looked cheap despite the quality. Muriel remembered how she and Ira had painted and decorated the space, all those years ago. Whipped-butter and pecan-wood tones came to mind.

Eve was angry with her mother, and the sharper crests of their conversation traveled down the hall. They were battling to salvage their relationship, but both seemed to lack the requisite stockpiles of esteem and respect. Muriel believed all that was required to soften a thorny relationship was the parent's admittance of understanding for their grown child and the child's acceptance of the parent's limitations. It was easy in concept, yet it was nearly impossible in practice. She knew her theory would never apply to Lem.

It was possible that Eve's deliberate distancing from her mother was the healthier choice, though Muriel felt she was still too young for such a bold decision. The world was moving faster and there were more resources to support out-of-the-box moves, but sixteen in any era was early to fully break away. Muriel hoped Eve and Judith would find a way to stay united.

Muriel thought about her own mother. When this was Elizabeth Kelley's room, it held a richly carved four-poster canopy bed and matching mahogany pieces with brass handles. Her mother's moody palette also tended toward mossy greens and smoky Wisteria. Muriel's father slept down the hall, citing his preference for early nights and mornings, plus her mother often had headaches and required lengthy afternoon naps. As a small child, Muriel would occasionally join her in the darkened room for those naps; her mother was always kinder when she was drowsy.

"Hello, snow angel," her mother would whisper, even in summer. With the opaque shades drawn, she would curl around her small daughter like a baby's fist around a thumb. Muriel rarely slept when they were together. Instead, she watched the dust falling through the narrow beam of light and listened as the sound of her mother's slow heartbeat collided with the pings and pops of her noisy stomach, a side effect of Elizabeth's many medications.

In the February after Muriel left home for college, Elizabeth Kelley wandered into the Saratoga State Park forest in her nightgown and, aided by an avalanche of sleeping pills and alcohol, succumbed to hypothermia. Two days later, she was found under a dusting of fresh snow. In her bloodless hands, she clutched a blown-glass Christmas ornament of a snow angel; the glass had cracked and it was frozen to her flesh.

Muriel sat on the chaise between the windows on the far side of the large bedroom. She was now nearly double the age of her mother when she died. She looked out the window at the maple tree, which was halfway through its annual shedding. Winter was on its way. Muriel had moved to Florida to avoid it, but now she was back, and she desperately craved a holiday season with frosty windows and tall candles and brothy, root-vegetable soups. The season in Upstate New York was cold and dark and could span as many as five months from the first frost to the final muddy melt. There were a handful of illusory warm days where everyone celebrated the sunshine and assumed the worst was over, only to be snookered by another series of smothering snows. It all served the purpose of making springtime infinitely sweeter.

But perhaps seasonless Florida was better—at least there she felt the sunshine every day, and she couldn't imagine being apart from Laura and Christian for months at a time. It was definitely a better environment for me: with the leaves and ice and snow and salt and rain, there were probably less than forty days a year I could be allowed to run on the tougher roads of the North.

But Lem and Cindy were also in Florida, with their greasy Pizza Night and endless jibber jabber about his bank and her shopping and everyone's various ailments. Florida had been wonderful with Ira, a vacation that failed to end, until he died and her condo was gone and there was no longer a place to grow tomatoes or orchids—or friendships.

Florida was also a big problem for Eve. Muriel suddenly couldn't remember specifically why, but she knew that wherever they were, they needed to be together.

"Muriel?"

Muriel pulled her eyes away from the glowing tree and slowly adjusted to the figure framed by the bedroom door. Even in silhouette, she could see from his posture that her dear husband had finally arrived. Ira looked exactly like he did when they lived in this house together, all those years ago. It made her feel comparatively old.

"Sweetheart," she replied with a warmth that flooded the room.

"Welcome home," he said, his voice soft, his arms outstretched. They walked to each other, kissed quickly, and then held on to each other in a tightly anchored hug. She recognized the relaxed plaid shirt she gave him for his birthday. How funny that he should wear it now, what with all the choices he had from other celestial planes. She figured he chose it so she'd be sure to recognize him, and the shirt even smelled as she remembered: an unobtrusive and masculine pine. She put her hands on his face. His cheeks had a slightly soapy aroma and he seemed a little thin, but she wasn't going to make an issue of it. She was going to hold him and be held by him and leave it at that. For Muriel, the entire drive was worth that singular moment—Ira never visited her at The Deerwood, she reasoned, because he had never been there in the first place, plus all of the rooms and most of the residents looked the same. At The Deerwood, she was difficult to find.

"I've missed you so much," she cried, sliding her hands up and down his arms. She wanted to tell him everything about Eve and Eve's mother and lunch in Savannah and losing all their money and Pete's beautiful apartment and Lem—but she knew he already knew. She pulled back, shifted focus, and looked into his patient eyes.

"I need your opinion on something," Muriel said.

"Anything," Ira replied, laughing a little as he recounted the thousands of times their conversations had started with those words.

"I don't know if I'm supposed to be here," she sighed.

"But you are here. The question is: will you stay?"

"Of course I *want* to stay—this is my home! Our home." She exhaled.

"So stay," Ira replied. Everything was always so simple in his presence.

"What about winter? You hate the winter, and you know I can't shovel anymore or drive on the ice. How will I get to the store? If I could sit in front of the fireplace with a warm cup of tea, I'd be perfectly happy, but you know I have my responsibilities," she said.

"You don't have to shovel or shop if you don't want to—we can easily take care of all those things," he offered.

Muriel again considered her two potential lives: Saratoga was home, but Eve and Laura were in Florida. It seemed impossible to have both.

"I'll have to go back," Muriel said, her eyes swirling.

"It isn't Eve's job to take care of you," Ira said gently. "She can be a great friend, but she still has her own life to live."

Muriel sucked in her breath and whispered, "Lucy and Vivette are in Florida, too, and they know how I get. Oh, I can't stand that I'm a burden to everybody!"

He burst into the weirdly high, giddy laugh that she loved. "You're talking like we're throwing you away! This is still *your life*, and you deserve to live it wherever you want."

Again, so simple. Muriel tapped on his chest. "You were always such a good man." The tapping slowed as she continued, "but my problems are . . ." The word floated in front of her, but it was slightly beyond her reach.

"Permanent?" he said, watching her wavering eyes.

"Yes. No. The other one. Superous?"

"Serious? Your problems are serious?"

Muriel realized she was hunching her shoulders and scanning the floor for the fallen words. She straightened herself and spoke proudly, "Yes, my serious is very . . . I mean my problems are . . . I'm more . . ."

Ira pulled her in and held her again, whispering in her ear, "You don't have to worry. Everything will be fine. We can help you here just as easily as there."

And that was enough for Muriel. She clung to him, moored to his familiar essence as she buried her face in his plaid chest. "We've been traveling for days," she reflected. "I was Grace again. So free."

He continued to hold her, rocking a little, almost the beginning of a slow dance as the pewter clock provided a steady beat. The morning after their wedding, Muriel and Ira had awakened in a bright room, entangled in white sheets. Resting peacefully in the bed, they had gazed into each other's eyes, sharing the profound sense of their deeper, marital connection. They recalled the heartfelt vows they had exchanged and knew with unwavering certainty that their love would only grow stronger.

Ira had reached over, found her hand, and clasped her fingers, forming interlocking rows like slender pink bricks. Then he pulled himself on top of her and wrapped himself around her body. At first she tensed, wondering if this was another round of lovemaking, but soon she relaxed and held him, too. They stayed like that for an infinite length of time and allowed their souls to meld. *Plants need water and animals need food, but humans need love to survive*, she remembered thinking, conjoined in the white light of their shared consciousness.

And now she was finally back in his eternal arms, repossessing that love.

They released each other's hold, but their hands remained clasped like that very first day, and every day after for the next half-century. He returned her to the chaise to watch the maple stretching its long shadows into the dusk. He finally let go, bent down and kissed her cheek, and then suggested she join the family for dinner in a bit. He left the room and disappeared down the long hall.

"How is she?" asked Sandra.

"She'll be down soon," Micah replied as he rolled up the sleeves of his inherited plaid shirt and began to set the table.

FRIDAY

390 | The Limited Edition Bicentennial Cadillac Convertible Joy Ride

Chapter 19

"You've come this far."

Eve's reflection continued to advise her the following morning as she tossed her hair over her shoulder, grabbed her bag with her shoes on top, and slunk down the old back staircase in her socks. She mitigated the creaks by keeping her feet on the far ends of each step while propping herself against the banisters to reduce her weight. She imagined herself floating and managed to get to the main floor with minimal noise, but Kubrick heard her anyway and pawed against the inside of Sam's bedroom door. Eve heard his scratching and bolted from the kitchen through the breezeway, rapidly shutting the doors behind her with astonishing silence. She put on her shoes and slipped into the garage.

She had my key.

When Sandra took Lem to the hospital, she'd asked Micah to park me in her spot in the open garage. As a creature of habit, he hung the keys where he always hung all the car keys: on the hook by the fridge. Eve had noticed my famous Cadillac crown on the keychain, hanging there like bait on a hook, and it had taken a sincere effort to keep her gaze focused elsewhere throughout dinner. Fortunately, she had Sandra's homemade version of Pizza Night to keep her distracted. The first pie had goat cheese, fig, and a balsamic drizzle, and the second was a concoction of arugula, roasted peppers, and sausage. It was so delicious and special, and Eve carefully paced her intake with the others to avoid consuming it all.

After the family had their fill, Eve cleared the table without being asked. While loading the dishwasher, she remarked that the coffee maker was exactly like the one she had at home, and she offered to make some decaf to accompany Sandra's homemade apple cake. Sandra, Micah, Muriel, and even Sam were impressed by her helpful overtures. They stayed at the table with their bellies full and continued to express their concern about Lem while Eve slipped the contents of the four pills she'd pilfered from Muriel into the pot. She pretended to drink with Sandra and Micah, dumping most of it when she got up to add milk. She was secretly relieved when Muriel abstained and Sammy said, "Ew, coffee's gross."

Eve was gambling. She didn't know if the medicine would trigger the same fugues or drowsiness in her lively hosts. It could also have other terrible and unforeseen consequences. She didn't know how long it would take to kick in. She didn't know anything about the possible side effects, short or long term. She rationalized it was only a few pills, shared, and provided only once. Muriel had been on it for years and didn't die overnight.

At dinner, Sandra had announced that Lem's toe was acutely infected and required urgent treatment. Then she relayed they had discovered he was approaching a deadly blood sugar level due to his undiagnosed diabetes. Eve asked how long they expected him to stay in the hospital, and the answer was at least a day.

At least a day was enough.

It took a moment for Eve to adjust to the dim light in the garage. The morning remained dark, with only the faintest lavender slowly igniting the horizon. My long white hood reflected the pale light just enough for her to see her way around me. Eve opened my driver's side door, put her bag in the back, and faced her next great conundrum: start me up and then open the garage door, or open the garage door first? Which would make less noise? Which might trigger Kubrick to switch from pawing to actual barking?

Eve didn't want anyone to chase her down the street in their underwear. Or call the police. Or wake up at all. She wanted to get some real distance so that by the time the family meandered downstairs and realized she wasn't accepting their invitation for cereal, we would be gone. Long gone.

Eve needed me for a few more hours.

A few more miles.

One more little trip.

Garage first or car first? Eve sat on my front seat, shivering in the cold dry air, and assessed her options. The switch was on the wall next to the door. Would they hear the garage door inside the house? Was the breezeway enough of a buffer? Did the primary bedroom face the garage or the other side of the house? Were the windows new and soundproofed, or old and thin? She finally decided to open the garage door, put me in neutral, and roll us down to the street. I could be noisy with my engine reverberating inside a concrete garage, but starting up away from the house might allow us to drive off in relative silence. Potentially.

Eve let her door remain open as she slid the key in my ignition but didn't turn it. She scooted over to the passenger seat and opened the right-hand door, stepped outside, and hovered over the garage door button as she mentally practiced her impending gymnastics routine.

She pressed the white square button.

The garage door cracked the dawn's silence like a sudden summer thunderclap, and the cranking chain rumbled overhead like dragons bowling on the roof. Eve threw herself back inside my cabin and shut the passenger door, hoping the sound would be smothered by the ruckus above. When it finally stopped, Eve listened and reassessed. Kubrick wasn't barking. No one was on the street. A drowsy bird chirped briefly and then stopped.

Eve cautiously turned the key without sparking my ignition, and I began my singsong pinging to let her know my electrics were engaged and my driver's side door was still open. She asked me to be quiet as she slipped me into neutral. She pressed her left foot to the ground through the open door, released the brake, and pushed off. It was enough force, and we slowly rolled backward. After a second push, we were moving, and Eve shut the door as quietly as my metal molecules would allow. The driveway wasn't steep and we weren't going fast, but Eve turned her head around, faintly recalling a lesson from driver's education class.

Muriel was standing directly behind us.

"Jesus!!" Eve screamed, slamming extra pressure on my unpowered brakes with both feet to get me to stop, followed by an instinctive side step to crack my emergency brake pedal with her left foot. I was impressed with her intuitive mastery of my controls, but I couldn't help emitting a barely audible squeal from my tires that sounded to her like two trains colliding over a scrapyard. Muriel touched my rear bumper. She only had to extend herself one inch.

"I could have killed you!!" Eve scream-whispered.

Muriel's look was sharp and demanding as their eyes locked, both sets as deep and clear as the emerging dawn. Eve lowered her head, realizing Muriel didn't seem to care that she'd been nearly run over—for her, it would have been far worse to be left behind. Eve sniffled as an evaporating cloud carried her faint "I'm so sorry" through the cold to Muriel's reddened ears. The lawn held a glaze of frost, and a squirrel made a delicate crunching sound as he escaped our encounter through a pile of leaves.

"Okay." Muriel touched Eve's shoulders with both of her palms and steadied her. Then she walked around me and opened the passenger door. "Well, c'mon then," she crooned as she climbed inside. "Crank up the heat!"

It dawned on Eve that Muriel was fully dressed. It appeared she'd had time to brush her teeth and comb her hair as well.

Eve climbed inside my cabin. "I didn't think you'd----"

"This is my car," Muriel interrupted. "You don't go anywhere in my car alone. That's the rule." Eve smiled at the idea that *now* there were suddenly rules she needed to follow. They soaked in the moment until Muriel said, "Um, before the dog wakes everybody up?"

"Right!" Eve flew back to the garage, pressed the button, and exited out the side door. This time, the sound shook the birds awake in three nearby nests. They wailed with fright and hunger as Eve flung herself back into the driver's seat, released my emergency brake, looked back carefully, and rolled us silently into the street. She looked at Muriel. Muriel took her eyes away from the windshield and stared at Eve, transmitting a radiant energy and a profound lucidity.

"You know I'm at my best in the mornings," Muriel explained as Eve started me up. She turned on my lights, and we chased the few remaining stars down the street.

***

We were gliding majestically along pristine Lake George when the sun finally emerged above the trees and shooed away the lingering banks of mist. Muriel held her hand over my right mirror to prevent herself from being blinded and redirected her focus to the illuminated west. "It's peak!" she exclaimed, surveying the rolling mountains with their deciduous colors ablaze. "I didn't think we'd catch it up here, but you timed it perfectly!"

Eve accepted the compliment with a quick bow, as if she were Mother Nature herself. "I aim to please," she sang as the dazzling light reflected her hopeful mood. In a few hours, she would finally be with her father.

"And it just gets better," Muriel said. "The forest, the lakes . . ."

"You know these roads?"

"Like my own hands."

"Amazing," Eve said, referring to the clarity of both Muriel's mind and the view. The highway climbed to a relative summit, where we faced nearly a hundred miles of textured forest in one sprawling vista. The women audibly gasped, and Muriel felt ever thankful that she had managed to maintain sharp vision throughout her life. She relaxed and settled into the streaming kaleidoscope, light-years away from her bland room at The Deerwood with its ecru walls and carpets.

Eve surveyed the sensational panorama, and suddenly it occurred to her it was Friday. Her sense of time generally flowed like a quick river, with routine schoolwork, hair to sweep, rehearsals, events, and so on. People were always saying "Can you believe it's already [whatever]?" as the holidays approached and then passed like ports along the steady stream. Her freshman and sophomore years were cursory tributaries that were already nearly forgotten as she rafted through her junior year, rapidly approaching the downstream delta of college and the ocean of her life beyond.

She remembered being upstream on the Sunday following her naked rant in front of the prayer group. She'd hunkered with Laura to study for their next physics exam, armed with jelly beans, a YouTube playlist, and Laura's conversational distractions.

"You're still not talking to her?"

"No."

"She's your mom, E. You can't avoid her forever."

"We'll see. What'd you get on question eight? I think it's 31.42 degrees."

Physics was another subject Eve excelled in but didn't care about. She knew she wouldn't pursue it in the future, but she navigated those bends in the river knowing that consistent success would propel her toward a scholarship and far away from Florida. Eve was adept at navigating rougher waters, and she guided her paddles with the strength of her even diligence.

"No, wait, I divided instead of subtracting. Stupid," Eve berated herself.

"Huh," Laura said, trading out a licorice jellybean for a coconut. "Hey, I really think Liam's gonna ask you tomorrow."

And so the afternoon went, with Eve learning physics and Laura interrupting her to discuss the more interesting topics. Eve was used to it—they'd studied together for years. Eve wanted to be excited about her prospects with Liam, but she was also wary of the rapids; a boyfriend might cause her to lose her sense of direction, but maybe it was time to let someone else steer for a bit. Maybe it was time to enjoy the view.

Eve's wild look suggested a fearless nature, but it was preppy Laura who sought the turbulent rapids and waterfalls. Eve kept her bearings by staying near the shorelines, but Laura didn't much care where the river took her, so long as it was fun. After thoroughly canvassing the topic of Liam, Laura popped a tangerine bean into her mouth and proceeded to her next concern: "So, do you still have the picture?"

Eve put down the textbook, ate a peach-flavored nugget, and retrieved the photo of her young self with her father. Since her big fight with Judith, she now carried it in the inner pocket of her bag inside a second wallet. She slept with the bag behind her back, against the wall, and hid it in her closet when she left her room, fearing Judith might take the photo at any moment and hide it again, or possibly shred it.

"Oh my god you were so cute! And your dad was a babe!" Laura cooed. "So how long after this----?"

"I think he died a year later. I'm not really sure," Eve said, tracing the shape of his head with her finger.

"It's so weird you don't know," Laura probed.

Eve agreed, but whenever she asked for explicit information about her father's death, Judith would cry or move to another room to pout. Eventually, Eve had stopped asking—it wasn't worth triggering a mood—but the pang of not knowing any details worsened the loss and ultimately seeded deeper doubts. Eve's paternal grandparents had been killed in a tourist-helicopter crash in Hawaii long before she was born, and Judith's parents had died from successive heart attacks a few months apart, shortly after Eve turned three. There was no one left to fill in the gaps. There were no siblings, cousins, aunts, or uncles that she knew of, and if there were any family friends, they had also disappeared.

Everyone Judith and Eve knew in the present day had entered their lives after Richard, and Eve came to suspect that was a deliberate choice on her mother's part.

But as Eve grew, Judith's narrative, or lack thereof, slowly lost its shape. When Eve and Laura were twelve, their classmate Dina died from brain cancer. Cindy took them to the funeral together, because Judith had to work. After the burial, Laura asked to see where Eve's father was laid to rest. Eve was embarrassed. She had a hazy recollection of releasing his ashes into a gentle current, but she didn't know where, nor where they kept his urn. They combed through the cemetery's columbarium searching for his name until Cindy got bored and took them out for ice cream.

"Where are Dad's ashes?" Eve marched through the front door that evening.

"I don't want to talk about it," and Judith left the room.

"Did you ever find the urn?" Laura asked again, jolting Eve away from her memories.

"No."

"Isn't there an obituary? It would talk about the service and list his surviving family and stuff. Oh, and if it says 'died peacefully at home,' that usually means a heart attack or a drug overdose, unless the donations part lists a disease." Laura let a lemon jellybean loll on her tongue.

Eve had never seen an obituary.

"Oh my god, look it up, dummy!" Laura said, fetching her laptop.

They searched Google together and couldn't find one.

"That's weird," Laura said. "Maybe he died before the internet?" Eve reminded Laura that everything they knew about 9/11 was from 2001, and Laura screeched, "Then what the hell? He's gotta show up *somewhere*. And if he's in a jar----"

"An urn."

"----those are usually, like, on the fireplace or a bookshelf," Laura insisted.

"But we don't have a fireplace," Eve said.

Laura was fed up. "Your mother is such a bitch. He's *your* dad and you deserve to know what happened. E, it's your goddamn *right* to know."

Laura commandeered Eve's laptop and went through another extensive search while Eve returned to physics. At one point, Laura found a photo of a cemetery in Japan that contained over 150,000 graves on a tiny plot of land. The tombstones were inches apart and looked like stone dominoes ready to be tipped. "Good thing your dad isn't buried in this freakshow," Laura quipped.

"Maybe he is?" Eve retorted.

Laura resumed browsing and casually said, "There's still totally nothing. I think he's alive and he changed his name. Hey, maybe he's a spy! Or in witness protection?"

Eve put down her textbook and popped a cinnamon jellybean into her mouth. They talked about her dad endlessly—it was one of Laura's go-to topics when she wanted to avoid studying—but Eve was stunned and somewhat annoyed that they'd never considered this idea before. He couldn't possibly be alive—or could he? Where *was* the obituary?

"Physics?" Eve pleaded, trying to stay calm.

"Maybe he's only a few miles from here? Like, in the Keys? Or . . . or maybe he has a ranch in Utah and a whole second family? Oh my god, do you think he's a Mormon? You could have ten half brothers and sisters!" Laura was excited, conjuring how the drama might play out. "Your mom has to know something!" Laura decided she had to be there when Judith was finally caught in her lies. It would make an amazing TikTok. It would definitely go viral.

"He's dead," Eve moaned. "We Googled him a thousand times and nothing comes up because he obviously isn't doing anything anymore."

"If he's dead, it would show up *somewhere*," Laura said, typing in *Richard Harvick Utah* and getting nowhere.

"What'd you get for number nine?" Eve begged.

"C'mon, you're gonna study at home anyway—play with me!" Laura begged back. "Let's find your dad!"

"I'm only here so *you* don't fail, stupid," Eve said, finally relenting with a snicker. She grabbed a root beer pellet and threw it at Laura, who returned fire from the discarded stash of licorice beans. The friends settled down, and Eve slowly explained how to calculate the force of a boulder rolling down a hill. Laura was on a sugar high and complained that she'd rather perform brain surgery on herself with kitchen utensils than do another physics problem, but Eve was relieved that her friend had dropped the topic of her father.

Judith was at a church event when Eve got home later that evening. Eve tossed her books on the couch and got to work finding the obituary. She scoured every piece of paper she could find. She foraged through the office portion of their kitchen where her mother paid the bills, she hunted again in the forbidden underworld of her mother's closet, and she scavenged through the ignored file boxes they stored in the garage. She learned her mother had prescriptions for yeast infections and that she ate a weekly lunch alone at the Chinese buffet near her store. The electric bill was more than Eve had imagined, but the mortgage was far less than she'd expected based on her mother's monthly gripes.

There was no trace of her father. There were no family trees growing in the files, no legal papers with his signature, no obituary, and no secreted urns or bags of ashes stashed in other vessels. There was nothing.

Eve gave up searching and switched her focus back to Liam, who was real and alive and supposedly interested in her. She had less than twelve hours left until she'd see him, and she had to do some laundry and think about her look. Judith texted to say she was eating at the church event and there was food for Eve in the fridge. Eve returned a thumbs-up response, the minimum requirement for viable communication. She fed herself and cleaned the kitchen, reset the coffee maker for the following morning, and went to her room to finish re-reading *The Stranger*. Eve heard her mother come home late, and she turned the music down when Judith knocked lightly on her closed bedroom door.

"Can I come in?" Judith asked quietly.

Eve didn't reply.

"Maybe tomorrow we can talk?" Judith said through the door. "I'm sorry about the picture, Eve, but you know that's a very sore subject for me." Eve waited for Judith's shadow to move away from her room. The shadow hesitated, but a few moments later, it shifted and Eve heard Judith's bedroom door finally close.

Eve pulled out the photo again.

Her dad on the beach with Eve on his shoulders.

A bright, crisp, sunny, perfect photo of his smiling face.

His unique face.

"Idiot!" Eve huffed as she grabbed her phone. She took a picture of the photo and emailed it to herself. Then she opened the photo on her computer and cropped it close to his face. She opened Google and clicked on the Images tab; she clicked on the camera icon, uploaded the photo, and then held her breath as it transferred through the ether and became one of four trillion photos in their archives. In less than half a second, Google kindly returned nearly a thousand images of similar male faces taken from the same angle with the same lighting.

In the fourth row of visually similar images, three in from the right, Eve zeroed in on one face that seemed particularly similar to her photo. She clicked on it as her heart thumped. Her bangs fell over her face, as was their usual habit. She swiped them over her ear as Google located a Facebook page. She clicked the link and landed on a screen showing a man named Michael Charter. She clicked on Michael Charter's personal photos.

The man who looked exactly like her father was hanging out with Michael Charter on the beach, at a park, at a rooftop restaurant with a stunning view. The visually similar image she had clicked on was also there, mixed in with all the others, but the man she thought she knew wasn't tagged or labeled with a name. For the next twenty minutes, Eve scanned through hundreds of posts by Michael Charter. There was nothing specific to identify her father's doppelgänger, but through the images and captions, she learned two critical facts: Michael Charter lived in Montréal, and, perhaps more importantly, Michael Charter was dead.

Eve opened a new tab for Canada 411, the equivalent to America's white pages. Her fingers tripped over themselves; she had to make three corrections before she entered the data successfully and pressed the yellow Send button.

Michael Charter's address appeared. Eve copied it and, on a hunch, typed it back into the system as an advanced search for the reverse address. This time, the search revealed there was a property on Summit Crescent in Westmount that was home to two people: Michael and Rick Charter.

Eve's bangs fell again as she rapidly typed *Rick Charter Montréal* into Google, and in less time than it took for her to once again stash her hair behind her ear, she had over twelve million results. The top link was for Professor Rick Charter in the School of Urban Planning at McGill University. She clicked the link.

On a clean white screen bordered by the university's red marquee, Eve read the left-aligned Helvetica text, her green eyes wide. Rick Charter had an office in the Macdonald–Harrington Building. Eve saw the classes that he taught, the papers he'd published, and his professional affiliations. He had an email. He had a phone number. He had three degrees: an undergraduate from Syracuse and two more degrees from Florida.

The website showed another photo.

He was smiling.

The same small space between his teeth.

The slight turn of his nose.

Less than a week ago, the river of Eve's life had reached a dam. The water had stopped moving through the canyons and instead flooded Eve's consistent, student-minded trajectory. Less than a week ago, Eve had suddenly found herself adrift in an amorphous and uncharted lake; her normal life had stopped, and a cold basin of bewilderment and distrust had filled.

The computer screen was a white-hot flashbulb that she could neither look at nor tear her eyes away from. The image of her father strobed deep into her corneas. She closed her eyes for a second, and his negative afterimage continued to fill her vision. She opened her eyes again.

There he was. He was there.

Her father, pulsing in a million dots of light, and very much alive.

She returned to Michael Charter's Facebook photos. In some of the shots, her dad looked fatter than she remembered, but there was no question that this was the man who had gently combed her long hair and straightened out the tangles after her bath, the man who bandaged her childhood scrapes, the man who knew she liked strawberry ice cream and strawberry cereal but that real strawberries made her mouth pucker, so blueberries were preferred.

The man she'd been told was dead.

Mr. Richard Harvick was supposed to be buried or burned and dropped into the ocean or sent off into space, never to return. Accept it, get over it, move on, kid. Don't look at the picture on the screen; don't look at the proof he's alive. You believe everything you read on the internet? That guy may look a lot like your dad, but get real: how? How could it possibly be true? If he's alive, then that means he left you. He left you and your mom with no note and no trail. He left to do . . . what exactly? Enjoy the patisserie of Montréal with his boyfriend?

Her dad had a boyfriend?

Eve looked at the clock and was confused by its assertion that it was nearly midnight—practically Monday. It was too late to call Laura, plus she needed her friend's physical presence, not a voice on a phone. And Laura had to *swear* she wouldn't tell anybody—especially their mothers—until Eve had time to process.

Eve was in shock. Without changing her clothes, she pulled the covers all the way up and buried her head beneath her pillows. It was dark. Suffocating. For a moment she felt relief until her rapid pulse and a slight nausea invaded the safe space. She smelled her breath going stale as it accumulated in the limited air. She lifted the distant edge of her sheets with two fingers and felt the flow of fresh air. She became a bear cub in the back of a long cave, emerging from her first hibernation. She struggled unsteadily out toward the light, the blazing whiteness of the computer screen displaying the newfound details about her living father.

Nourishment.

Everything absent from her mother's story became obvious: there was no obituary or precious ceramic on the bookshelf because there was no death. She was deceived. She felt foolish and gullible. Empty. She felt she was being punished instead of rewarded for her diligent trust. She felt harmed. She wondered how much her mother knew and what had actually happened a decade ago. Did her mother ever meet Michael Charter? Did she know about Canada?

Her mother was a liar.

She prays a lot because she knows she's going to Hell, Eve thought. Her stomach hurt. Her heart hurt. She wanted to cry out. Scream. Throw. Tear.

But most of all, she wanted to see him.

She *had* to see him.

She returned to Facebook. Michael Charter was a handsome man with tan skin and sandy-brown hair. He had sideburns that defined his long cheeks, and the short goatee seemed perfect for his chin. His sweet smile was further perfected by an incredible set of teeth. He was skiing in one of the posted photos. *They* were skiing. Together. In matching outfits. She flipped back and studied Michael Charter's relationship status: Married.

Eve opened a new Facebook tab and searched for her father using his new identity, but nothing came up. She had to know more. She returned to the McGill webpage and read it again. And again. She clicked every available link and opened a screen to compose an email—but held herself back. What could she possibly say? He fled once . . . he could do it again.

Eve realized she was shaking. She expanded the structure of her bed-cave with her shoulders, knees, and more pillows. Then she brought the computer in with her to return to the world of Michael Charter. There was a posting with a photo of a waterfall flowing into the ocean. White script with deep shadows crossed the scene: *"For life and death are one, even as the river and the sea are one."—Khalil Gibran.* In a smaller pink font at the bottom: *Michael Charter 1980–2015.* There were 3,591 like, love, care, and sad responses; 358 shares; and 516 comments.

Eve read every one of them.

***

"Wake up!" Eve cried out. "We're at the border!!"

Muriel shot upright and automatically pulled down the visor to check herself in the mirror, a motion she performed countless times before any arrival. She saw an old woman reflected in the small flap and was trying to untwist the illusion when Eve flipped the visor back up with a frantic, "What do we do?!"

"We calm down," Muriel said, lowering the visor again to fix a smudge on her cheek she forgot was a freckle.

"What do I say? Do I tell them about my dad? I've never been to another country—will they ask why I'm not in school?" she said in a panic.

"Don't worry, Laura," Muriel assured her. "Everything is fine."

When we were traveling through Virginia, it had taken nearly an hour of confusion, followed by a long nap to straighten Muriel out when she'd called Eve by Laura's name. Eve needed Muriel to be sharp. The border crossing had to be smooth, and they needed a good story. In two minutes.

"I mean Eve," Muriel corrected herself.

They looked at each other.

"Whoops," she added.

Eve's lungs collapsed with a palliative puff, and she relaxed as much as the oversized tea she drank in Keeseville would allow—her mounting pressures were physical as much as mental. There were three lanes open to accept applicants for admission into Canada, and there were two cars ahead of us in each lane. Eve guided me behind a black SUV.

"Light traffic. It's a good time to cross," Muriel said, checking her watch. "We were stuck here for hours once during Jazz Fest."

Eve silently cursed the "good" timing and wished it were Jazz Fest again, whatever that was. She felt like a performer on opening night who had never bothered to read the script.

The SUV crawled ahead to the border agent. Eve opened my window, hoping to catch their conversation, but we were purposefully stopped too far out. She tried to see who was in the booth behind its tinted glass. She kept her foot pressed hard against my brakes while her mind raced at top speed. She had no idea what to do or say, and Muriel wasn't helping.

Suddenly, a border patrol officer seemed to step out of thin air, crossing directly in front of us on foot. To Eve, he looked ferocious with his official government uniform, a badge, and a gun. He gave us a double-take as he crossed the lane. We were used to people staring at us and even honking with their thumbs up to acknowledge my rare elegance, but Eve forgot I was something to look at, and she burped from her nerves and squeezed her legs together to contain herself.

The border control guard moved on and reached a squat building beyond the booths. He passed a group of young men being escorted by two officers into their beat-up minivan. He exchanged words with the other agents as the dejected clan drove through another gate and back into the United States. They were being returned. They had failed to cross. Eve wondered what they did or didn't do, what they said or didn't say. Her throat felt pinched. She knew she had to get a grip, and quickly, or the border agents might deny her access simply for being too high-strung for Canada.

"She's waving you forward," Muriel said loudly.

Eve stared at the booth and saw a woman's hands with bright red nails urging us along. We crept up, and Eve carefully put me in Park before daring to look at the agent in the booth.

"*Bonjour*," the woman said brightly. Her auburn hair was tied in a thick braid that dropped over her shoulder and partially obscured a name tag that read *Alice*. Alice had red lips to match her nails and couldn't have been older than twenty-five. Eve wondered why Alice was a border guard instead of a model, or if Mrs. Rubinow had a daughter in Canada who was also obsessed with the color red.

"*Où habitez-vous et quelle est votre nationalité?*" Her words were as smooth as melted chocolate as they poured through my open window.

Eve was dumbstruck.

"Where do you live and what is your citizenship?" Alice restated through her rhythmic French Canadian English.

"I'm from . . . we're . . ." Eve stammered, looking to Muriel for guidance. Muriel didn't think the question was overly complicated, but as she leaned over to answer, she saw the sheen of sweat on Eve's brow and thought she could hear Eve's heart thrashing beneath her ribs. Muriel stretched a little further until her eyes met with Alice's. She thought Alice was pretty, and also pretty young.

"*Bonjour?*" Alice said again as Muriel placed her hand on Eve's knee to steady her fretful companion.

"*Bonjour mademoiselle. Nous vivons en Floride, mais nous sommes partis de Saratoga Springs où vit ma fille. Ma petite-fille n'est jamais allée au Canada, alors j'ai pensé que nous prendrions quelques jours pour l'explorer,*" she said, indicating Eve.

She knows French? Muriel knows French?! Eve was flabbergasted as Alice and Muriel continued to converse.

"*Comme il est agréable. Êtes-vous ici pour le Festival du Nouveau Cinéma?*"

"*Est-ce que se passe maintenant?*"

"*Oui, bien sûr.*"

"*J'espère que nous pourrons encore obtenir des billets.*"

"*Je suis sûr que ce ne sera pas un problème.*"

Eve sat in the friendly crossfire of delicate, foreign words. She had no idea what Muriel was saying and hoped she wouldn't be asked for any form of corroboration beyond the word "*oui.*"

Then Alice said, "*Puis-je voir votre passeport, s'il vous plaît?*"

Eve quivered. She understood the word "passport." She reached for her bag, but Muriel stopped her.

"What are you doing?" Muriel whispered.

"I'm getting my license," Eve whispered back.

"She doesn't want your license, she wants your passport."

"I don't have----"

"Shttt . . . tut . . ." Muriel pressed her cold fingers to Eve's lips quickly before they vanished into her own leather purse. Muriel moved a few items to her lap, including her lingam from India, a comb, a compact, and a box of floss before she managed to procure a small envelope containing two crisp, dark-blue American passports. She handed them to Eve and silently urged her to give them to Alice, who flipped her braid to the other shoulder and waited patiently. The line behind us was now four vehicles deep.

"Um, here..." Eve said, extending her arm.

While Muriel returned the items to her bag, Alice took the passports and analyzed the data. Muriel looked like her picture, but Eve's was off. Alice studied it closely. She looked from the passport to the live version in front of her four times, back and forth and back and forth while Eve's bladder continued to swell.

"Your passport is going to expire soon, and you look like a little girl in the picture," Alice said.

"Oh?" Eve croaked.

"And your hair isn't purple in this photo," Alice continued. "For next time, please make sure your passport is more current, Laura."

Laura?!

"If you tie your hair back in the next photo, you can change the color whenever you like, but we will still see that your face belongs to you. *C'est bon?*"

"Okay."

"Okay," Alice repeated with a wink that Eve misunderstood to mean the interview was finally over—but then Alice continued, "And where will you be staying in Canada?"

"In a hotel?" Eve returned as Alice typed something into the computer.

"Which hotel?" Alice solicited with her eyes locked on her screen.

"The Holiday Inn?" Eve said, silently praying there were Holiday Inns in Canada.

"For how many nights?"

"Two?"

"Are you bringing any food into Canada?"

"Umm, just some snacks from the gas station?"

"Do you have any alcohol or drugs?"

"No." This was the first query Eve didn't answer in the form of a question.

"And how much money are you bringing?" Alice finally looked away from the screen and stared at Eve, who felt like any physics exam would have been easier than this horrible, complicated, never-ending interrogation.

"I have about four hundred dollars?" Eve mumbled, remembering the amount from the last ATM but forgetting the wad Pete had given her.

Alice typed the details into a keyboard, and for a moment, she looked like she was about to wrap things up. She held the passports in her hand and made a forward gesture, but then she looked at her computer screen, withdrew her hand, and paused. A little wrinkle appeared between her eyebrows.

"I would like to ask you one more question," Alice said flatly.

She knows! She knows I'm not Laura and she ran a trace on the license plate while we were sitting here, and Sandra and Lem and Cindy all called the police this morning, and now I have two countries who want to throw me in prison, and she knows everything she knows everything she knows everything—

"I would like to ask: what can you tell me about this beautiful car?"

Eve turned to Muriel in a panic. Alice didn't see the blood draining from Eve's complexion as it fled her howling mind because Muriel, once again, leaned across Eve and recaptured Alice's attention.

"It's a 1976 Cadillac," Muriel boasted as she reapplied a steady pressure to Eve's knee. "A limited edition of only two hundred, and I got the best one!"

"That's wonderful," Alice said, her voice sincere. "Your granddaughter must be an excellent driver for you to trust her with such a rare automobile."

"*Oui. Elle est très spéciale*," Muriel replied, patting Eve with both hands. Eve continued to look to the side for fear that if Alice saw her criminal face, she might be able to read her criminal mind.

"Hey?" whispered Muriel.

"What?" replied Eve.

"She's trying to hand you the passports."

Eve took the passports and muttered a quiet "Thank You" without looking directly at the pretty border guard who had the power to summon the entire Canadian army with a click of her manicured nails.

"Welcome to Canada! Please drive safely and have a nice visit!" Alice said, clicking the return key on her computer and resetting her braid for the next visitor.

Eve handed the passports back to Muriel and cautiously drove us through the raised gate. We stopped at three seemingly unnecessary stop signs and then continued on the same road, now renamed Autoroute 15 Nord.

We drove about twenty minutes in Eve's stunned silence until she found a restroom at the Flying J in Napierville. She lingered in the stall and tried to steady her quivering hands. Alice's terrifying inquisition was over and we'd made it into Canada, but for the first ten minutes Eve kept her eyes on the rearview mirror more than the road in front. She expected a squadron of security officers to arrive and escort us to the maximum-security prison in Plattsburgh.

It took five more minutes and more than a few splashes of cold water on her face before she was able to settle down. Eve reviewed herself in the mirror as she patted herself dry and remembered Muriel's anger over the last time she'd impersonated Laura in the FloridaTrust parking lot. Monday felt like a dream from another life.

Eve bought some Canadian Smarties and was surprised to find a creamier version of America's M&M's tucked inside the pastel box. She loved Canada! She climbed back into my driver's seat and offered Muriel some candy.

"All better?" Muriel asked, accepting a small handful.

"Much," Eve replied. "You sure you don't need----?"

"No, I'm fine." Eve gave her a questioning look. "I didn't have any tea," Muriel explained, but Eve's look persisted. "What?" Muriel put her fingers in her crotch and checked herself.

"You speak French!?" Eve laughed.

"Oh! *Oui!*" Muriel tittered as she relaxed her hands. "*Nous avons tous appris le français à l'école.* My mother was half-French, and I took lessons right through college. I also spent a summer in France and I had a good friend from Montréal, so I got to practice when we visited. I guess it's all still in there," she said, tapping her temple.

"That's awesome," Eve said, hoping she would one day be able to speak another language and tell someone she spent a summer in France. Eve pictured Mrs. Lanza spinning around and realized it was unlikely that fluency could ever be obtained through her insipid forty-five-minute class. Then Eve pictured Liam, truly in another country, sitting across the circled desks with his vacant gaze on her empty seat and a thick pen wedged between his even thicker lips. Was he thinking about her?

"It doesn't matter what languages you know, you can't go anywhere without a passport," Muriel said as she readjusted the contents of her purse. She seemed piqued that things weren't fitting as neatly as before.

"How----?"

"Sammy gave them to me," Muriel replied, sounding obvious.

"But----how?"

"Laura sent them to Sammy with the books," Muriel said.

"What books?"

"Sammy's school books."

Eve's face was blank as she tried to untangle their furtive plans. Once again, it seemed like there were plain answers to simple questions, yet she couldn't follow any of it. She wondered if Muriel experienced the same disorienting feeling, like walking down a long spiral staircase in the dark with no idea when your feet would meet the floor.

"Sammy said Laura couldn't get your passport without your mother being involved, so she took a chance and sent her own instead. She also sent mine because she knows my rule about not driving my car without me." Muriel sent a stern glance across the front seat as she spoke while Eve digested this information. "It makes more sense if we're related," Muriel went on, "if the passports have the same name."

"But why did Sammy give them to you? And when?" Eve was bewildered. Between withstanding Lem's verbal abuse and talking to her mom and eating Sandra's pizzas, between getting Muriel situated and exploring Nancy's room and enacting her secret plot to drug her hosts, Eve's arrival had been nothing but a chaotic blur. She had completely forgotten to ask Sam or Laura about her passport, yet somehow, remarkably, Muriel was on top of it.

"Ira came in after my nap----" Eve cocked her head and Muriel skipped ahead. "----and you were talking to your mother and I didn't want to interrupt, so I went to Sammy for a catch-up. He's grown so much, that one. He told me about the passports and said he and Laura were, how'd he put it? They're 'totally on our side.' Bless those little rascals."

Eve listened intently as the dark spiral stairs continued to unwind.

"I wanted them for myself because I know you, Eve. I know you didn't drive all the way up here just to bring me home. I had a feeling you'd try to go the rest of the way alone."

"I didn't mean to----"

"And I knew the border wouldn't let a sixteen-year-old with a child's photo on her passport and a mismatched license cross over alone in this fancy car. I didn't know if you could get through with your license, and if you showed them Laura's passport, that might've sparked real trouble. Plus, what if someone called in the license plate? A car can't be stolen if the owner is sitting inside it."

Eve was embarrassed. There were more spiraling stairs than she'd imagined, and Muriel, of all people, was helping her down.

"So I spent half the night watching the door to your room. I almost missed you slipping out, but thankfully the doggie made some noise."

Eve tried to hold it together.

"You brought me home, Eve. I think that's wonderful, but we both know *you're* not done."

Eve needed Muriel as much as Muriel needed her. She finally reached the bottom of the staircase and doubled over from stepping too hard on the unfamiliar ground. Her body lost its fight against gravity as she crumbled sideways onto Muriel's thigh, sobbing. She was so tired of crying, but once again she couldn't stop. One more cry. One more good, long cry, and then she'd be done.

"You're my family now," Muriel said, stroking Eve's hair. "Don't you know that? You're my family and this is what families do for each other. You haven't had a real family for a long time, but I think it's high time you did." She continued to soothe her crumpled companion with long, soft strokes. "My nightmare is finally over because you're so brave. You're *so* brave, Eve, but sometimes even the heroes need some help, and it's your turn. It's your turn to be happy. It's your *time* to be happy."

Muriel patted Eve firmly. "Okay?"

Eve looked up at Muriel. Everything was okay.

"So let's get out of here and go find your father."

Muriel's words would dance on Eve's heart for the rest of her life.

Chapter 20

The leaves were gone and only black skeletons remained, silhouetted against a thick, dull sky. The clouds lay heavy, like worn mattresses, impossible to move. All brightness absconded as summer lawns desaturated into wheat-toned carpets that bordered asphalt streets and gray stone houses. The drained luminescence surprised Eve; she had only seen pictures of Montréal online where it was always aglow with its luscious parks in summer, startling foliage in autumn, and periwinkle skies in the sharpest days of winter. She didn't know the sun failed to pierce the port city's thermal blanket nearly sixty days a year, including the day Eve would reunite with her father.

We crossed the implausibly long Champlain Bridge from Brossard, floating twelve stories above the brownish Saint Lawrence River and the grayish Île-des-Soeurs, until Rue Sherbrooke and Roslyn Avenue swept us up, and up, and up, into the Westmount neighborhood. There were only a handful of turns from the highway, and Eve navigated the route as if she'd been there a thousand times. Perhaps, in her mind, she had.

The homes exceeded her expectations. Modern steel-and-glass-walled visions sat alongside two-hundred-year-old brick Tudors and wooden Georgians and Colonials. The visual display was as symphonically adept in bringing together its disparate materials as a master composer uniting wind, strings, and brass. Eve was accustomed to her bland townhome community, the rambling brick ranches of Laura's neighborhood, and an occasional art deco flourish on her flat peninsula. Saratoga had already been a welcome surprise with its intricate dollhouse architecture, but the impressive estates of Westmount, set against the shimmering downtown skyscrapers perched boldly along the water's edge . . . it was a lot to take in, even without a blue sky. We drove slowly so we could see it all.

I felt right at home amongst the opulent homes, and I happily powered through our steep ascent until Eve pulled us to the side of the road.

"That's it," she said, pointing across the street.

"Very impressive," Muriel exclaimed. Eve knew Muriel had seen many expensive homes in her day and felt somehow compelled to take the observation as a compliment. Eve took a deep breath as we pulled into the driveway.

The memory of Eve's dream returned in vivid color, but the gloomy late morning didn't correlate. The purple-leaf grapevine had already passed into a graphite ash, and the rich chocolatey brown curtain that lined the ten-foot arched front window was closer to the color of dry rye bread. The house was impressive and resembled the images from the internet, but it felt closer to the street than Eve had realized, and the lush landscaping was already shriveling under frequent frosts. Still, they had arrived, and Eve lightly pinched Muriel's arm to ensure it was real and they were both awake.

"Rascal!" Muriel cackled as they opened my doors to the crisp air.

"Tu ne peux pas te garer ici!" came a voice from the street as they climbed out. "I'm sorry, but you can't park here, this is private property. You want to head back down to Sunnyside and then take Roslyn up the hill to Queen Mary Road. There's parking for Saint Joseph's over there," the man elaborated.

Eve recognized his voice before she turned to look. It was deep and completely devoid of the border guard's silky accent, instead employing a slightly southeastern American lilt. There was also a bit of gravel, as if the voice were approaching an elder's scholarly gravitas but had yet to fully evolve from middle age. Eve closed her eyes and listened, remembering. Then she turned to face the source of the voice as it continued to insist that she return to her seat, put the key in the ignition, and find another place to park.

He looked nothing like the dream, and barely like the photograph.

Rick Charter was returning home from a jog. He was drenched in sweat, his skin was rough and flushed, his eyes were hollow, and his beard was gone. Eve realized she had never seen his naked chin and had no idea he had a pronounced cleft. He seemed bigger in person and also smaller than the memory. Eve and Rick were now the same height.

"Hello? Will you please move it?" he said again, out of breath from his run and exasperated by their lack of acknowledgement. He took out his earphones and whisked off his black knit hat to wipe his sweaty neck. Eve drew in her breath at his sudden lack of hair. The sides remained full, with more salt than pepper, but the top had only a few strands straddling it like a tenuous rope bridge across a wet and shiny mound. Eve realized the photograph on the website must be old, or it was possible he wore a toupee. If it weren't for his voice, the turned nose, and the space between his teeth (which was sending unintended spittle in our direction), Eve would have been hard pressed to recognize him at all.

He continued to eye them suspiciously.

"I'm Muriel Worth," Muriel extended pragmatically.

"Do I know you?"

Muriel looked over at Eve and Rick followed her gaze. He saw a young woman, casually dressed and wearing an expensive leather jacket. She was laden with ear piercings and had a wild stripe of color in her hair. She smiled and lifted her eyebrows, urging him to recognize her. He instantly saw a brightness in her eyes and a familiar creative spirit, but he identified these qualities in the countless students he taught at the university.

"Oh no, were we scheduled for an interview?" he said as he started fiddling with his iPhone to locate the calendar. He was still panting from his run, and a sweaty ombre spread past the armpits of his McGill sweatshirt. He turned around and leaned against me. He casually placed his hand on my rear side panel for support—and that's when I knew everything there was to know about Rick Charter.

"We do the interviews at the school," he reprimanded, still looking down. "The new secretary shouldn't have given you this address."

"I'm not a student," Eve said quietly.

He had some trouble returning the phone to its jogging holster on his arm, but once he succeeded, he turned back to Muriel. "Oh, are you lost? Where are you trying to go?"

Eve had spent many nights picturing her dead father with golden, outstretched arms at the gates of Heaven, where words were unnecessary. Then she stopped believing in Heaven and tried to find him in other versions of an afterlife, including many misguided attempts to recognize his transmuted essence in reincarnated beings, like dogs that watched her intently, or babies at the mall. Then she finally learned he was alive, and she spent most of our long drive thinking about what he would say when he came to the door. When he instantly recognized her. It had never occurred to her that she might have to speak first.

Now we were in his driveway with ten years and sixteen hundred miles behind us, and he was dripping and bitching and seemed inconceivably clueless that his own daughter was standing in front of him. To be fair, he lacked context, but Eve needed him to recognize her on his own; needed to see the flash of his recall as the memories surged into view. She needed him to open his arms of his own accord so she could run into them, but it didn't feel like any of that would happen if she had to announce herself, like a student interviewee.

Muriel innately understood all of this and prompted him. "We drove here from Florida," she replied. "This is my car."

Rick turned his head back to Eve.

"I'm . . ." she stammered. Something about the way Muriel said "Florida" triggered the understanding that this young woman wasn't interested in attending his Urban Planning program. "I'm . . . I'm sorry. We'll go."

Eve opened the door as something inside her surrendered.

It didn't feel right. It wasn't the right time.

I wished I had the power to push everything I knew about Eve into his mind as he continued to press against me. I wished I could tell him what I knew and what she knew. It felt like the entire day had already passed, but in reality, we had only been standing in front of the sweaty man who had yet to find his breath for about forty seconds.

"Eve?" he choked.

Rick Charter stood in front of his teenage daughter, his mind both flooded and blank as he saw her again for the first time. He saw the beautiful, grown-up young woman who had left her mother and abandoned her friends and risked everything in her life to be there. Rick Charter looked into Eve Harvick's shining face, a ghost in the flesh, a remnant of a life long since discarded, as she stood across a vacuum of time, a mere arm's length away.

"I found you, daddy," Eve whispered.

He cried out as the emotions burst inward, the implosion stopping his heart, shutting his mind and freezing his legs to the ground—while simultaneously sending his arms and hands and fingers out, desperately out, to capture her.

She ran into them.

Eve didn't realize she was bouncing on her toes when she finally lifted off into her father's embrace with the force of her six-year-old self at the gateway to the Enchanted Castle. He wrapped himself around her with equal vigor, pretzeling around her torso and pulling her head, her dear and precious head, against his thumping chest—for about four seconds. She barely cogitated the wet rank odor from his run before something in Rick's mind swiveled and his engineering brain recalculated, recalibrated and released her. It was a barely noticeable push that sent her back, a little dazed, like the child who spins too fast and then has trouble relocating her own feet.

She didn't understand what was happening, any more than he did.

And then he threw up.

***

We all lost our sense of time as they reunited, the emotions of their torn relationship literally churning. The mess on the driveway showed something eggy and something pink, and Rick remained bent over like a scientist studying a pinned specimen, or perhaps like a man in prayer.

"Uggghh."

His body fought a second wave of nausea as his mind combatted the entire situation. Eve wasn't sure what to do next, but Muriel came to his aid. "Let's get you cleaned up," she said, arriving at his side and offering an arm.

He didn't take the arm, but he followed her suggestion. Instead of floating up the flagstone pathway toward the grand entry hall of Rick's mansion, the group descended his shadowed driveway to the underground garage, where he pressed in a code to gain entry. I watched as they moved past a silver SUV and the garage door swallowed them into darkness, and ultimately, I learned what happened inside when they eventually reemerged.

Rick shed his soiled sweatshirt and shoes in a modern basement bathroom that serviced the underground gym. He was unable to sort the flashes of his life with Eve as they pulsed through his mind. It was like a movie playing on ten screens at once, in fast forward and reverse, in slow motion and on pause. He lacked the resources to cross the chasm between years six and sixteen. He thought he might be sick again as he croaked a request to Muriel and Eve that they make themselves at home on the main floor while he collected himself with a quick shower. As he pulled off his soaked shirt, they quickly scooted away to find the kitchen, where Muriel located a kettle and Eve found the tea.

Forty minutes later, Rick Charter emerged, fully dressed in slacks, a button-down oxford, and a silk tie, and with a full head of hair, possibly real but not entirely his own. He was clean shaven, kempt, and ironed, and his bright eyes matched Eve's in their luminosity and hue. He looked more like her and less like the bedraggled man we'd met in the driveway. This version of Rick also seemed eminently calmer.

"Eve," he said, again holding out his arms.

She didn't run into them with quite the same vigor, and he held her more gently, acutely aware that his prior embrace emulated a clumsy mover gripping a falling piece of valuable furniture. But Eve enjoyed the second hug as much as the first, and she had time to absorb his honeyed scent before he released her and patted her shoulders. He stared at her for a sustained moment that felt completely natural to both of them.

Muriel noticed that even in the hug, his sport coat remained draped over the arm holding his briefcase. "I have to be at the school soon," he said, "but let's go into the living room for a moment." He pointed out the direction he wished his guests to go, like a butler. "And please, bring your drinks."

"I thought you could use some tea as well," Muriel offered, matching the tone of his discomforting formality. "Do you take sugar?"

"No, thank you," he said, rejecting the beverage entirely with a small backward wave. As they passed him, Muriel detected a thick floral scent, a little like apricots. It wasn't until later that she registered it as cognac.

"You said your name was Muriel?"

"Yes."

"And how do you know my daughter?"

"It's a long story," Muriel replied, clutching Eve's hand as they moved forward and noting Eve's smile when he said the word, "daughter."

Rick Charter was fastidious about his home, owing to a combination of his strict upbringing, his husband's influence, and living as a refined Canadian in Westmount. Muriel, knowing none of this, gave sole credit to his gay gene. She thought of her Florida art dealers and gay celebrities who shared tours of their estates on daytime television as she connected the harmonizing colors, cultivated knickknacks, and absence of dust in Rick's home with a homosexual lifestyle. Muriel failed to relay her adulation for his walnut cabinetry and black ceramic teaware in the kitchen, but she supplied more than a few compliments on his refined art pieces as they stepped down into a broad space overlooking his gardens, already impeccably serviced for the looming winter season. The house was arresting. Eve was in awe.

The women settled into the comfortable center of his bark-hued sofa. They faced him across a thick glass coffee table, which floated on bronzed steel legs that resembled toothpicks. Rick sat opposite them on his favorite mid-century recliner after setting his briefcase and coat on a matching leather ottoman. *More leather,* Eve noted. His posture was formal and erect, as if he endured the same turgor pressures as the exquisite orchid in his centerpiece.

"Those are coasters," he said. He pointed again, indicating a short stack of square slate mats backed with felt. Eve held on to her mug, fearing one clink of the ceramic might shatter this meticulous house, but Muriel put hers down and remarked, again, how lovely his taste.

Rick didn't hear her over his own chattering thoughts. He wished he'd skipped the jog and headed straight to the office to avoid this moment, but he also knew they would have tracked him down at the school, or camped out on the porch.

It was inevitable. She was there. On the couch.

Eve.

She looked at him looking at her. His expression had gone flat; a canvas without paint. He wasn't observing so much as absorbing. Over the years, he'd witnessed hundreds of young students transform into early adulthood, and he sometimes wondered how Eve's shape might have changed. Did she grow tall like his own father or stay short like Judith's mother? Did the delicious chubs of her baby cheeks remain, or were they ravaged by acne when her rubbery, block-shaped body lengthened into the natural curves of a woman? She looked nothing like he imagined, and yet exactly as she should. The more he looked, the more normal it seemed, and the stranger it all was.

"Eve told me your partner died. I'm very sorry for your loss," Muriel said, hoping a tactful engagement might begin with some sincere sympathy. Rick stayed in his studied posture, but something behind his eyes pulled inward. Eventually he said, "Husband."

"Beg your pardon?"

"He was my husband, not my partner. We got married ten years----"

He looked at Eve as he started to relay the timeline and was stopped by a pinprick of shame, or possibly diplomacy—Michael and Rick had married within a week of his divorce from Judith. They had shared their vows at a municipal office and held an effusive and elegant waterfront dinner for eighty guests the following spring. Rick remembered standing on the terrace at twilight, holding Michael's warm hand in his, both with new rings. In his mind's eye, Rick saw the long bridges spanning the St. Lawrence River, the iron sheets neatly separating his old life from the new.

"I apologize—your husband," Muriel corrected after his pause.

Rick crumpled like thin paper as his elbows met his knees and his palms stretched across his face. He stared at the floor. He knew Eve wanted to know his story, but he didn't know how to tell it. And he didn't *want* to tell it. "You know, I should have said yes to the tea," he said abruptly as he headed back to the kitchen. "Do you both want some more?"

"Sure?" Eve replied, controlling her voice while she sent Muriel a look of ardent vexation. *What's wrong with him? Isn't he happy to see me?*

Rick returned with the cup Muriel had prepared for him and topped theirs off from the teapot. "It's jasmine," he said. "Organic. Packed with antioxidants."

"It's great," Eve said, failing to sound nonchalant.

He carefully aligned four coasters together and placed the teapot on it. Then he picked up his mug and blew on his tea three times, took a micro-sip, and attentively placed it on a complementary side table. He closed his eyes, and Muriel saw him press his index fingers to his thumbs in a mudra figure she remembered from her own meditations. They watched as he slowly inhaled and exhaled, with his back straight and his feet flat on the floor. He breathed in slowly and deeply through his nose, and then the breath escaped his mouth in blasting harrumphs. Eve and Muriel didn't move. It was too weird, and Eve fought her nervous desire to laugh. After the third breath, Eve thought he was stalling, while Muriel maintained he was preparing. They were both right.

Finally, Rick opened his eyes and drew his shoulders back.

"How's your mom?" he said, recognizing Judith's face in Eve's stern eyebrows and high cheekbones. "I did love her, you know . . . or at least I felt about her the way I think love feels when you're young."

He was ready to speak, and Eve was prepared to receive every precious word.

"But we were too young," he barreled on. "I was only eighteen when we met. She lived in the dorm and we were friends. And then we were more than friends. And then . . . well . . . marriage seemed like the next logical step. At the time, it felt right. I suppose."

Muriel sipped her tea and returned it to the table with a bit of a clank, but Rick stayed focused on Eve. His story was for her, and everything else dissolved into the background.

"But you probably knew all that," he said.

"Not really," Eve said.

"Huh." He took another sip. "I always felt like something was off, like something was missing with me and your mom, but I didn't really know what it was until, well . . . until I did." His eyes moved up to the high ceiling where his memories floated like liberated balloons. As he spoke, he pulled them down for his daughter, one by one.

"This was Michael's aunt's house. He bought it from the family when she died. He didn't pay much for it, and it took a long time to fix it up." Rick could have spent the next three days talking about their house project, but he knew that wasn't why Eve was there, so he let go of the string and picked a more relevant balloon.

"Michael's company sent him down to work with us. We collaborated with people from all over the world who wanted to build in Florida. My firm kept a bank of small apartments, and Michael moved in. He was supposed to be there for four or five months."

Eve tried to picture it. She remembered her father's study in their former home, with its tall architecture books, thick rolls of drawings, and scale models. He used to hold her up and fly her over them for the bird's-eye view. She had no memory of his workspace at the company office.

Rick inhaled. "When Michael walked in and introduced himself, we shook hands. And that was it—that's when I knew."

"Knew what?" Eve asked.

"That he was my future. I know it doesn't make any sense, but that's exactly how I felt. It was a completely normal handshake, but I—we . . . we both felt this . . . connection. I don't think we even talked for the first minute. We just sorta stood there, shaking hands." He exhaled again. That particular balloon didn't come down easily, and he gauged Eve's reaction. She seemed open and interested, and it gave him the confidence to pull down the rest of the batch.

"But, uh, I didn't do anything about it. We were about two weeks into the project when he finally said something like 'Why don't you come over tonight and we'll order a pizza.' There was something about the way he said it, so I went over there and we ate pizza and we talked. We talked for a long time. It was comfortable and unpressured and I realized I was . . . happy. I went back the next night, and then the next. I told your mother we were coordinating with a Japanese firm and dealing with the time change. That gave me a few hours after work to hang out with him.

"I felt a little guilty about the lie, but I wasn't really doing anything wrong. All we did was talk and eat and laugh in those first few weeks. We laughed a lot, actually. I had a new friend, and for the first time, I was really excited about someone."

Eve swallowed audibly.

"I mean the second time—you were the first."

She swallowed again. Rick cleared his throat and took a deep sip of his rapidly cooling tea. "This was huge for me, having a male friend, a *gay* male friend who was, uh, interested in me. I felt like I was waking up."

"Was he also married?" Eve asked. "To a woman? When you . . . shook hands?"

"Oh gosh, I can see your mother has joined us," he replied. Eve didn't want to antagonize him, but she was trying to understand how one handshake had managed to change the trajectory of her life. He registered her grievance and explained, "Eve, Michael and I were both gay men long before we met each other, only I—I had never really put it together for myself."

This was an important puzzle piece. Maybe even a corner.

"Michael had girlfriends in high school and he started dating men in college. He came out to his whole family at the graduation dinner. He said his grandparents were instantly supportive, but it took a while for his parents to get there. Their problem was mostly about the boyfriend, because that guy was a bit of a drug addict and he was sometimes abusive. It took a few years until Michael found the strength to end it, and that's partly why he came to Florida. He needed a change."

"I like the grandparents," Muriel broke in. "They seem nice."

"They were nice," Rick recalled. "People are more accepting here."

The next balloon revealed that Michael was worried about Richard's inexperience, and he was very concerned about Richard's wife and little girl.

"He said I had to be comfortable with myself before we could be a couple, which was kind of a catch-22 because I needed him to show me how. I couldn't even go into an adult bookstore without feeling ashamed—and forget about the gay section. When I finally summoned the courage to do that—and even looked the sales clerk in the eye to collect my change— that felt like a small victory."

Eve imagined it felt similar to the first time she went bra shopping with her mother. She wondered if Liam ever bought condoms and if that also felt the same.

Rick continued, "I thought I was ready and I didn't want to waste any more time, but Michael was right: I had a lot to figure out. I watched some gay movies and read some articles and novels in secret, but I still felt like an outsider. I didn't feel like I was gay, or whatever I thought gay was, but at the same time, I was in love with this intelligent, handsome man, and we were building this wonderful and intimate friendship."

"That sounds difficult," Muriel said, sympathizing.

"Thank you, it was, but mostly because I didn't want anyone to get hurt."

"Really." Eve was blunt.

"Really," he replied. "I really, truly didn't want anyone to get hurt. Not me, not Michael, and especially not you."

"And not Mom."

"No, and not your mom, either," he said with a sigh. "But after a few months, we----" he cleared his throat again, "----we had a deadline for a presentation. It was getting late, and we were going over the renderings when we both stopped and kind of realized that we designed this pretty great structure together. Michael asked me what I liked most about the building process, and I said it was the moment when we flipped the master switch and the electricity coursed everywhere, all at once for the first time. I told him 'that's when a building becomes real.' Michael leaned in and put his hand on the back of my neck and said—I'll never forget it—he said, 'I think it's time we flipped that switch.'"

Rick shrugged to indicate that the rest of the story was obvious and he was out of balloons.

"Don't stop!" Eve cried out, gripping the edges of the couch. "So you fucked him? You fucked him in your office and it was so great the two of you packed up the Toyota and rode off into the sunset?!"

Rick thought he was telling a beautiful story, a story he had shared many times, and the responses were always propitious and supportive, never abrasive or inimical. Rick felt like a dog who had been sleeping peacefully in his crate, and Eve's outburst snapped him awake. Suddenly he was being pushed into these strangers' arms under the guise that they were somehow family? He didn't want to bite them, but why didn't they leave him alone? "No!!" he barked. "No, that's not what happened at all!"

Rick threw his hands up and stood, sputtering, and paced the length of the long room. His voice became a simmering geyser, and his flailing arms and heavy stomping signaled an imminent eruption. He went to the mirrored wet bar and poured an umber liquid into a crystal tulip tumbler. He swirled it twice and drank it all while keeping his glaring eyes on Eve.

Muriel took Eve's hand as she scanned the room for a potential weapon of defense, just in case the suddenly angry man broached their personal space. The crystal vase. The fireplace poker. The slate coasters had sharp corners.

Rick returned to his chair, breathing rapidly, but to Muriel his breaths sounded more like small yelps. He closed his eyes and tried to calm himself, but then he flew to the couch and fell to his knees, hard, right in front of Eve. He snatched her hands from Muriel and held them tight. His eyes were full and frenzied, like hard-boiled eggs rolling in a bubbling pot.

"You don't get it," he growled, three inches from her face, "Michael had *cancer*!!"

Explosion. Magma. Heat.

Searing ash rained down as Rick fell back backwards to the floor and expelled the air from his lungs.

"He tripped on the goddamned beach and twisted his ankle," Rick cried out. "When they prepped him for an X-ray, they found a black spot on the bottom of his foot, a melanoma that had already spread. Sometimes he felt achy and he had a cough, but we were working crazy hours and he said he wasn't used to the constant air conditioning. He left the hospital with an ankle brace and a life expectancy of maybe five years. Five years?! He was only *thirty*! So don't sit there and judge me when you don't know anything about it! You don't know!!"

As he spoke, he shuffled backward on the floor until his back found the support of a stoneware planter cradling a five-foot-tall dracaena. He pulled a crisp handkerchief from his pocket and dabbed his eyes. Eve had never known anyone to carry a handkerchief. Muriel saw it as a white flag, and she uncurled her small fists.

"You think I *wanted* to leave you?" he sniveled. "You think I *wanted* to blast my life apart and lose everything I ever worked for? Michael was in Florida for a few months, we fell in love, and then we found out he had cancer. He didn't know what the hell to do, and neither did I. That day—that was the worst fucking day of my life, because I knew. I knew I was going to lose everything to be with him—and then I'd lose him too. You can't imagine what that was like," Rick whimpered.

Muriel interrupted to ask for a tissue, and Rick snorted out a bizarre and embarrassed howl. He still didn't know who she was or why she was there. He stood up, carefully checked the plant, and left to retrieve a tissue box from the powder room off the foyer.

Eve and Muriel stared at each other in his absence, profoundly perplexed.

"Here ya go," he said as he returned to his chair and looked at Eve through softer, saturated eyes. She was moved by his display, but she didn't cry. His narrative was missing another crucial puzzle piece, and the picture wasn't yet assembled.

"But you didn't have to lose everything," she explained, modulating her voice to sound less belligerent. "I mean, I get you couldn't be with Mom anymore, but what about me?"

"Oh god, Eve, oh god, we tried to figure that out. If Michael could have stayed in Florida it would have changed everything, but with his health plan he had to come home right away to start his treatments. Plus, his family was here, and he needed them. We couldn't be married in the States at the time, but it was legal in Canada, so I had to move to take care of him as his spouse. We had to make all of these insane, life-altering decisions, and there wasn't any time. Everything happened so fast, and all we knew was we *had* to be together for whatever time Michael had left—*we* had left. It was that handshake. I'm telling you, it meant something."

It was an impulse decision. Eve could relate.

"We fought about you, Michael and I. All the time. We wanted you in our lives, but we had no idea how to do it. It killed me leaving you behind, but—oh god, Eve, it was no place for a young child. We had to cut out everything and focus on his treatments. It was too rough."

"No," Eve said.

His eyebrows pulled his face into a questioning squint.

"No!" Eve yelled at him. His volcanic heat transferred to her, and she burned with ignited fury. "You didn't have to cut me out! I wasn't the cancer!"

"That's not what I meant----"

"Because we could have helped him, Dad. With you. Mom's weird and unbearable, but she's not unkind. Michael would have loved us, but you wanted to keep him all for yourself. We could have read him stories and watched movies and made him laugh. You said I made everyone happy. You said my hugs were the best in the world. You said that!"

"You were only a child----"

"And he wasn't that sick, not right away, anyway. I saw his Facebook with you guys eating out and traveling. You went skiing! You *renovated!* He's dying so bad you can't be with your little girl but you're picking out bath tiles?! It's bullshit!"

"No, it wasn't like----"

"They don't have phones in Canada? Or email? They don't have airports up here?"

"We----"

"No," she continued to berate. "No!! You were fucking selfish! You didn't even try! *Why didn't you try?* How could you leave me alone with her? How could you do that? How could you make us all think you were dead?"

The echo of her rant bounced between the ceiling and the tall window, and then the area rug absorbed it into its thick wool pile. The sudden silence startled everyone.

"You thought I was dead?" Rick whispered. His face turned white. He slipped off the chair again and started another advance toward Eve on his knees, but he was stopped by her eyes, gray but hot, like cooling lava. He scooted back to the familiar planter on the hardwood beyond the edge of the carpet. At some point, his shirt became untucked, and his tie was loose.

"Our neighbors still call Mom 'The Widow.'"

"Oh, Evie . . . no . . . no, I never told Judy to say that, I swear. When you didn't write or call me back, I figured you guys were done with *me*." Then he admitted, "Maybe I didn't . . . maybe I didn't know what it would mean for a little girl to have two dads. I know we were screwed up by his illness, and we didn't want to drag you through it . . . the pain . . . you were this little . . . delicate. . ."

He pictured her third birthday when she'd fearlessly climbed up a chair in her pink Converse sneakers and stood on the edge to reach her frosted cake. She wore little black jeans and a white jersey with pink sleeves proclaiming her a *Wild Child*. Her hair was in a long braid that she lashed around like a whip. Eve was never delicate.

"I went away to protect you," he said, adjusting his words. "The math said you'd have a better life without our problems, so I left you and your mom with plenty of money and the house until we could figure something out. I left you with everything I had."

"Except you," Eve said.

He crumbled under the hot mass of her words. He tried to flee the burn by returning to his chair. Muriel wondered why he couldn't sit still. His mortification prevented him from looking at Eve, and he turned to Muriel above his clasped palms, hoping to find a modicum of her prior sympathy.

"Eve's mother is a Christian now," Muriel remarked.

"Oh?" he muttered, but he could tell from Eve's face that this was unfortunate news. He dropped his head and stared at the floor, hoping he might vomit another resolvable physical mess instead of suffering through more of this intangible agony.

"Pops and Gramma died after you left," Eve explained, pulling down a few memories of her own. "Then Mom lost her job and she wouldn't get out of bed. I was eating peanut butter out of the jar with my fingers because she wouldn't go to the store to get bread and all of the spoons were dirty. I wasn't tall enough to wash the dishes. I remember bringing my clothes into the bathtub with me when she stopped doing laundry, and I took home toilet paper from school. The house smelled like spoiled meat, and Mom didn't notice any of it."

"Oh god," Muriel gulped.

"So I don't know what you left for us, but it wasn't enough. She had to sell the house to pay off her credit cards, and then we moved into a shitty condo near Military Trail."

"No . . ." Rick gasped.

"And last year I got a job at Muriel's old-age home so I could buy some clothes and maybe go to the movies with my friends, but I'll never be able to pay for college."

He wondered if that's why she'd decided to find him. Was she asking him for money? Did she want to use him for the family rate at McGill?

"Jesus," he whispered.

"Oh right—*Him*. Well, I guess things got a little better when Mom joined the church. Someone got her the job at the craft store and she started taking care of the house again, but now everything is *Apostle* this or *Holy Ghost* that. I can't even put salt on my mashed potatoes without hearing some stupid comment about Lot's Wife. She won't watch regular TV anymore—she thinks even the baking contests are immoral. All she does is organize church fundraisers, underline her Bible, and pray. Oh, and judge everyone."

Muriel noticed Rick was looking at the wet bar.

"So I'm happy you met someone and had this great handshake or whatever, but the life you thought you left for us didn't happen."

His glass was still over there.

He shifted as if he might get up again, but Eve continued, and he couldn't seem to rise above her polemic. "Michael sounds amazing and I never even got to meet him. And this great love you had for him? You took that from me. From both of us, actually—if you didn't break Mom by totally abandoning her, then she could have, like, met someone. I could have had four awesome parents instead of this. . . fraction."

As her volcanic discharge continued to flow, Rick was consumed by his own agitated thoughts. Judith said he was dead? She lost all the money? Did she throw away his letters, or did she sell the house before she got them? He knew he should have called, or visited, but the five years he had with Michael went too fast, and the five years after. . . it was blurry. And now it was ten years later, and what could he possibly say?

The pain of the flowing heat was too much to bear and he needed another drink to cool it, but the large room felt uncrossable; the vitriol spewing from the couch was too ferocious. To survive this unnatural disaster, Rick's self-protective ego kicked in and filtered out the painful content, allowing a surprising wellspring of pride to form. This strong and courageous girl, his girl, held a great power that had been directly obtained through his wrongdoing. She would never have become this force of nature if not for him. The adversity he provided had *forged* her.

"You know what I did for my last ten birthdays?" she went on. "I blew out the candles and wished every time that I would die so I could see you again."

The Eve who sat in front of him moved into the background of his thoughts. In the foreground were his buildings and his house, his program at the university, and the life he built with Michael, but rising above these accomplishments was the presence of his brilliant daughter. Somehow, even his biggest blunder had created yet another outstanding success.

But only if he owned it.

Eve kept going. "There are lots of kids with two dads or two moms and nobody cares. You weren't afraid of what it might do to me—you were afraid of yourself. Talk about a self-loathing homophobic----"

"You're right," he interrupted.

The pressure in Eve's core slowly decreased, but she wasn't quite done. "----and now I have a boyfriend, maybe, I don't even know, and I need a father to, like, tell me if he's good for me or not because I obviously can't trust Mom's opinion and----"

"You're right," he said again. And then time seemed to stop and rewind.

It was only five hours earlier when Rick had awakened on his side of the bed, still unable to venture toward Michael's side without causing the morning to disintegrate. He made coffee in the still house and flipped through the news on his phone. He hated the days with afternoon classes—the days with empty mornings when his mind, uncluttered with distractions, instinctively returned him to grief. Even after five years, it was still as fresh as the roses he brought to Michael's grave every week.

He felt leaden and thought a run might do him good, so he put on his gear, cued up "Michael's Jogging Music" playlist on his headphones, and headed out. He ran over two miles through Summit Woods Park and all the way up Remembrance Road to the edge of Beaver Lake. He stretched against a bench at the water's edge and recovered.

He tried not to think about Michael as Michael's music continued to play.

Then he ran home.

And then he saw me.

And then he saw an elegant old woman.

And then he saw his daughter and learned that he had made a tremendous mess of her young life.

As time resumed and Rick returned to reality, he tried to look away from Eve. He had successfully looked away for years and even believed he could continue to look away forever, but she was simply too magnetic. She held his gaze as he finally faced her.

"You're right," he said again. "About everything."

Muriel put her hand on Eve's knee to steady her, and Eve dropped her own hands down to hold it there. Muriel's skin felt refreshingly cool against Eve's searing palms.

"And I'm sorry," he said, seeming to wither. As he claimed responsibility for the debris of his great earthquake and the subsequent tsunamis, everything Rick knew about himself flattened and washed away. His ego and filters, his walls and conceits, the stoicism that lined his core. The history he imagined for his daughter and his self-defined outlook dissolved into the first waves of his apologies.

"I'm sorry," he declared again.

It was never fifty-one to forty-nine percent. It was only a mistake.

"Eve . . . my little—my sweet girl . . . I am so sorry."

The angry man in the driveway and the indifferent man in the Windsor-knot tie were gone. In an oversized living room on Summit Crescent in Montréal, on a dark wood floor beneath the shade of an oversized plant, Eve Harvick found her real father, the man in the photo, a man no longer buried six feet beneath the earth's hard crust.

She went to him. She leaned across his back in a lateral hug. Her fair fell across them both as he shivered and cried beneath her embrace. Muriel left the room so they could be alone as the searing lava of their past finally reached the cold ocean.

**

When Muriel returned to the living room, she found the father and daughter sitting neatly together, connected at the kneecaps in the corner of the couch. After a disaster the debris is overwhelming, but in time the roads are cleared and wires and pipes are untangled. Eventually, with effort and care and resources, life resumes.

Muriel made herself comfortable in Rick's black leather chair and extended herself fully. After her feet were settled on the ottoman by his briefcase, she registered that Rick and Eve's relaxed postures contradicted their strained expressions.

Rick's alarm beeped.

"We can talk about this later. I *really* have to get to the school," he said, standing. "And your mother is probably wondering when you're picking her up."

Muriel and Eve exchanged a look.

"You left her at St. Joseph's, right? If she's as devout as you say it'll be tough to get her out of the room of crutches—it's too amazing."

"Mom doesn't know I'm here," Eve admitted.

"What?"

"She doesn't know anything about you."

It was his turn to exchange a look with Muriel, but her shrug bounced him back to Eve.

"I don't understand. How did you—?" His confusion settled into a look of fatherly disappointment, and Eve reveled in it as if she'd discovered a hidden treasure.

"We came up from Florida," Muriel offered again. Rick couldn't build in sandy soil, and he prompted them for firmer bedrock. Eve and Muriel quickly poured a basic foundation and concluded their report with the unpleasantries of Lem.

"Well, there's another big reason," he clucked. "You gotta straighten that out, kid."

"Another reason for what?" Muriel asked.

"And don't drag me into it," he added.

"Drag you into what?" Muriel continued.

"He won't let me stay here," Eve said, catching her up.

"Oh? You want to stay here? Why can't she stay here, Rick?" Muriel asked.

Rick felt choked by their swift talk, and he removed his tie. He sat down again and faced Eve to answer her, but in a way, he also answered himself when he said, "Because it's too late, Eve. Or maybe it's too soon?"

"I don't know what that means," Eve said. She looked to Muriel, who audibly repeated what he said, verbatim, from across the room.

"Too much has already happened," he explained to them both.

"But we can forget about all that," Eve said. "We can start over again. We can start now."

Rick sighed. He admired her optimism, but he didn't seem to be reaching her. He tried another approach: "Look, I can't have your mother back in my life, even if she's half of what you described." His eyes twitched. "I never thought she'd fall apart like that. I knew she'd be mad at me, but she was stronger than that. Especially with you around. She signed the divorce papers, you know. She knew what was happening. And I didn't deadbeat you—I did the math and paid everything you were both owed upfront, and then some."

"So whatever, things are different now," Eve asserted, brushing aside the financial aspects. "Mom's in Florida, but I'm here. I'm sitting right here."

Even without the tie, Rick still couldn't seem to get enough air. He unbuttoned his top button and stuck his finger in the neck of his undershirt to pull it loose. He cleared his throat. "I'm sorry your mother blew it, but that's not my fault and I can't be responsible for it. Not anymore. If I say yes to you, then I'm letting her back in and I . . . I can't . . . sort through all that wreckage."

"There's no wreckage," Eve claimed. "It's a clean slate for everyone."

"You think so? You just disappeared for a week in that crazy car, and then this Leonard guy had to fly across the country to find you."

"It's Lem," Muriel said.

"Lem? What is that, Welsh? Anyway, I don't think Lem or your mother or anyone with eyeballs will see this as a clean slate."

"It's Hebrew," Muriel cut in again. "Lemuel means 'devoted to God'. We're not Jewish—we took it from *Gulliver's Travels*. It was my late husband's favorite book, and we wanted Lem to think of life as an adventure and explore it with some gusto."

"Oh. Okay, thank you," Rick said flatly.

"This sucks!" Eve exclaimed.

"Excuse me?"

"It sucks! You *are* responsible, Dad. You know you steered the boat right into the iceberg on purpose, and Mom was the one who had to scramble for a lifeboat." Eve couldn't believe she was actually defending her mother. She felt something acidic rising in her throat.

"Well," he rebuked, "if everything is my fault, then it's going to be pretty hard for me to live with you, when you're making me feel guilty all the time, doncha think? I think so. I think I've been through enough already." Eve hated how he twisted her argument.

"But I *have* to live here so you can make it up to me to get rid of your guilt!" she retorted, twisting it right back. "It's the only way."

"Huh!" he laughed. When she was a child, he'd envisioned her future as a fairy princess, but now he easily foresaw a fruitful legal career.

Eve shook her head a few times and tried again. "Okay, let's say you're not responsible for anything. You were in an impossible situation and you did the best you could, right? Mom got everything she needed to make a good life, so it's not on you if she chose to sit in her own shit, right?"

He nodded reluctantly.

"If the problem is Mom, then you and I—*we're* both good!" Eve beamed.

"I don't think it works like that."

"If we can look at each other without feeling bad, doesn't that kinda . . . release you?"

"You're oversimplifying," was his response. Seeing Eve again was bewildering, and possibly wonderful, but taking her under his roof an hour after their reconciliation was preposterous. You can't build a tower without considering the infrastructure, the context, the site plan . . . There were so many issues to examine, including, for his part, the basic question of purpose. It required significant study and processing, but Eve had already grabbed the shovel and was digging without a blueprint. Or a permit.

"I really can't face her." Rick retreated to his primary argument, unaware that his voice was modulating upwards. "And I don't have to. If Judy decided I'm dead, then maybe we should . . . respect that. You can't just show up here and expect me to *rise again* for everyone's benefit, like, like . . . who's that Bible guy? Lazarus." He paused to think about his words. "Hey, what happened to him, anyway?"

"He moved to Cyprus and became a bishop," Eve replied, hating that she knew that. "But he also had a great second life." She couldn't believe her father thought he could stay dead to her, and his unwillingness to include her in his life was both disorienting and humiliating.

Rick shared an observation. "You know if I let you stay here, you'll be doing to your mother exactly what I did ten years ago, and last time it didn't work out so well for her."

"I said the same thing," Muriel said, "but Eve will be in college soon. I don't think you can really equate Eve leaving home a year and a half early with what you did, can you?"

Eve nodded at Muriel and smiled a small thanks.

"Please say yes. Dad."

"You just got here," he hedged. "Out of nowhere. I need time to think."

"You've had ten years," she said. He put his fingers back in his undershirt collar and stretched it again while pulling his neck to the left and the right with a little crackling sound. "Please let me live here. You have tons of room." While he had showered, Eve and Muriel had toured his four bedrooms and three more upstairs baths. She had already decided she liked the one in the corner with the windows on both walls overlooking the back garden.

"I can't just snatch you away from your mother and move you to Canada, Eve! There are legal issues and financial issues—there's *school*. I don't even know if there's a school bus in this neighborhood. You'll need a winter coat and boots and . . . and we can't do anything without talking to Judith, and I'm *not* going to do that. Not today. I'm sure she wants you to stay in Florida and at least finish out the year." He saw a chance at a compromise. "I'll tell you what. Finish up the year, and then maybe we'll see."

"But that's eight more months."

"Then you'll go back for eight months."

"How? How am I supposed to do that knowing you're here?" she whined. Rick remembered that tone from a decade prior when she'd wanted a pink bicycle, or maybe a pink dollhouse. Something pink. Something she didn't have. And he got it for her to avoid the tantrum. "Eight months is *forever*, Dad, and I can't even think about school! How can you send me back to Mom? She's crazy, Dad! Come on! We drove all this way, Dad, and I already have all my stuff. Dad----"

"FUCK, EVE, I'M NOT YOUR *DAD* ANYMORE!!"

No one expected an aftershock, and Muriel's hands flailed, knocking her black ceramic Japanese mug clean off the side table to the floor, where it shattered into thick, dorsal-fin-shaped shards. Rick was panting and no one moved. Muriel watched Eve and feared her reaction. Would more mugs fly? Were the orchids at risk?

But Eve remained utterly still. It has been reported that the eye of a hurricane is the most tranquil place on earth, and Eve's grousing terminated abruptly when Rick's words thrust her from her outrage into that motionless calm. Muriel watched as Eve stared into her father's blustery eyes and the spinning winds of his torment. In her low-pressure center, she was able to witness the gales without succumbing to them, and within the peace of that sundrenched circle, Eve discovered the solution that ended all storms.

Time.

Eve shaped her hand into a small fist. She slowly, very slowly, brought it to the center of her father's chest. Then she spread her fingers apart and lifted it gently away.

"Baboom," she whispered.

Rick was paralyzed.

"She's come all this way, Rick. Just think about it." Muriel said.

He remained captured by Eve's motion like a bug on a sticky web.

"Okay." He tried to breathe.

"Eve, he's going to think about it."

Eve returned her hand to her lap. Then she raised her eyebrows with expectation and said, "Can we at least stay the night?"

It was a reasonable request, but Rick only saw the spider who wanted to trap and wrap and consume. "No. No, that's not a good idea." Again Muriel watched Eve's face. If his answer surprised her, she didn't show it. "I have to think," he stammered. "You, you both, being here doesn't help. This equation is, your mother . . . please let me think. I need to think." He sputtered like a broken robot in an old science fiction movie that needed a good whack.

Eve wanted to forgive him. She was desperate to forgive him, but he had to allow her the chance. He had to let her in. For good. And he wasn't ready.

Muriel understood: he wasn't the same person Eve knew as a child. This version of Rick was broken by his grief over Michael, just as she was over Ira's abrupt departure. But Ira and Michael weren't coming back, and Eve was sitting right in front of him.

"What about tomorrow?" Eve asked. "Maybe we could come back for a little while?"

Rick said automatically, "I don't know. I have a full schedule."

"On a Saturday?"

He lowered his eyes to the floor. He couldn't move. Then his alarm beeped again. He remained adhered to the couch while Eve stood and helped Muriel out of the chair. They walked numbly up the steps and past the shattered mug to the kitchen, where Eve found a pad of paper and printed her email address, Instagram handle, and phone number. She added a heart at the bottom.

Rick stayed put in the living room, his eyes fixed on a distant spot he didn't see. Eve sucked in air through her lips and then exhaled. "Bye, Dad. I'll see ya." She exited with Muriel through the front door. They were both surprised to see a vast blue sky emerging.

Muriel and Eve touched my door handles, and I silently absorbed the entire scene. In the long gap while Rick cried in the shower, Muriel and Eve had poked around the house. Through their wanderings I recognized something rather peculiar: there were no photographs. There was plenty of fine art, but there were no people in the images, no picture frames going up the stairs or resting on desks and bureaus. There were no magnets pressing memories to the fridge, and I couldn't locate a photo album on display. Michael, the love of his life, was also nowhere to be found. None of his clothing or jewelry remained. There were no towels with his initials.

Judith and Rick were alike in their exacting and cruel approach to their losses. For some people, the residue of a life cut short, whether by death or other means, is simply too sticky to tolerate or too corrosive to abide.

"Shame on him," Muriel said to Eve as they buckled themselves up. "The least he could have done was buy you lunch."

"We'll find something," Eve said, feeling eminently serene.

Muriel looked at her with a surge of pride. Eve reminded her of Grace: so open, so willing to see beyond the immediate. Muriel felt the urge to say something profound. She wanted to mark the moment and thank her young friend for the unspoken reminder that the appearance of an end may, in fact, be the beginning.

"Eve?"

"Yeah?"

"Eve, I think we should put the top down."

Eve swept her bangs back in a flash and released my forward handles. Then she lightly pressed down on the third toggle to the left of my radio, and I instantly obliged. Ten seconds later, my roof canopy was neatly collapsed and tucked behind the rear seats as we sat in the driveway, fully exposed to an unpredictably temperate afternoon. The sun had won her battle against the clouds.

Muriel busied herself with the seatbelt and shuffled a few items into her purse so they wouldn't succumb to the forthcoming wind. She failed to see Rick standing behind his iron-framed living room window above the garage, but Eve watched as he rebuttoned his top buttons, retied his tie, and put on his jacket. Perhaps he was using his reflection, but his eyes never left Eve's. She smiled at him and gave a small wave. He gave a small wave back and then disappeared.

THANKSGIVING

432 | The Limited Edition Bicentennial Cadillac Convertible Joy Ride

Chapter 21

Lucy returned from Jamaica. Albi survived his heart attack, and other family members stepped in to support his recuperation so she could reclaim her job. From the beginning to the end, she was absent less than two weeks, and she was thus surprised to learn that Muriel had already vacated The Deerwood for Saratoga Springs. Without hesitation, Lucy readily accepted her position in the new locale. At first, Lucy fell prey to the common Floridian mistake of thinking someone said Sara*sota* instead of Sara*toga*, but after the coordinates were sorted and her innate apprehension for cold weather was subsumed by the prospects of earning her living working for someone she loved, she was all in. She rented a one-way U-Haul with a car trailer, and she purchased three thick sweaters and a coat on her way out of town.

Lucy took a similar route to Eve and Muriel's, but she bypassed New York City, fearing the spaghetti-like roads would conspire to direct her toward expensive tunnels and bridges whether she needed them or not. She accomplished her drive in only two days and one night to save money, and by the time she arrived, at the beginning of November, she was exhausted but happy. She credited forty podcasts, a stop at Mrs. Wilkes Dining Room, and half-priced Halloween candy for getting her through.

Once Lucy was decided, Sandra and Micah performed a great reshuffling in the house, switching out furniture and room purposes to accommodate everyone's new needs. Micah left Mr. Clifton's old room and claimed the rest of Russel's for his office so that Muriel could remain on the first floor with her own private bath. Lucy was offered the studio apartment above *my* garage on the other side of the breezeway. Sandra and Micah typically rented the studio in the summer season, but providing Lucy with private quarters and a useful kitchen and bath was deemed a better use. Micah outfitted Lucy and Muriel's rooms with a video intercom system in case there was an urgent late-night need, and they had windows that faced each other across the narrow end of the yard so Lucy could also visually keep tabs.

As a live-in caregiver, Lucy's hours became harder to define, but with rent and utilities off her mind and full use of the main house, she was able to comfortably coordinate Muriel's care with Sandra and Micah. It didn't take long for everyone to establish a mutually beneficial and financially workable routine. Lem was the only one who seemed unhappy with the arrangement, but not enough to justify the expense of The Deerwood for his mother now that she was a confirmed flight risk.

"What time are they supposed to land?" Micah asked again. He often lost track of everything beyond his computer screen when he was on a tight holiday deadline.

"About two hours, but traffic's gonna be murder," Sandra replied. She massaged his shoulders as he continued to work, ever-entranced by his skills. "You sure you don't want me to go?"

"We can both drive to the airport," he said, craning his neck for an upside-down kiss, "but only one of us can cook. Need anything from the store?"

"See if they have more heavy cream," she said, obliging him with a peck before heading for the back stairs to the kitchen. "Oh, and pick up some more pancake mix. And milk and eggs. And bacon."

"We can go out for breakfast." He grinned. "You've cooked enough."

"After tonight, no one should ever want to eat again, but----"

"Yeah?" he laughed.

"Get some cereal, too, but nothing too sugary. Granola. Get some strawberry granola." She laughed back.

"Eve prefers blueberry," he said.

"It doesn't matter if it's in cereal."

A bit later, Micah was ready to head out. He stopped by Sam's room first and asked him to get Eve and start a fire, and then they could help Sandra set the table. Sam shot down the hall with Kubrick on his heels and banged on Eve's door. "Dad wants us to start a fire!"

"Be right there," Eve called. "I'm on the phone."

"Is it Laura? They missed the flight?"

"No, it's George," she said.

"Ooo . . . Geooorrrge," he sang.

Sam heard her tell George that she had to get off the phone, and Kubrick barked when Eve opened the door to Nancy's former room. "Hi Kubee-baby!" she squealed, stroking the ends of his ears the way he preferred. "Did you get the wood yet?" Sam joined in the petting and shook his head, unsure whether she was talking to him or the dog. Eve slipped on her shoes, grabbed a coat from her closet, and gave Sam a gentle pat on the back. "Lead on!" she called.

Sam, Eve, and Kubrick launched out the back door behind the main stairs to a broad covered porch where Micah had previously stacked one full cord of seasoned oak on elevated rails. They each took a bundle in separate suede carriers and carefully maneuvered to the family room's large stone fireplace, where they neatly repacked their loads into the designated side shelves.

"Are they here already?" Lem yawned. He rubbed his eyes and tried to sit up in the rocker recliner, but it was a difficult undertaking from his near-horizontal position.

"Dad just went to get them," Sam replied, helping him upright as Kubrick sniffed around Lem's bandages. Sam handed the fallen remote back to his uncle, and Lem turned down the volume. "Who's winning?"

"Washington was ahead when I nodded off," Lem replied, knowing neither of them really cared.

"Do you want some water?" Eve asked.

"Oh, yeah, that would be nice," Lem replied before calling out, "San?! Is there any grapefruit seltzer?"

"I think so!" she hollered from the kitchen.

"Ice?" Eve asked.

"Yes, please." Eve retrieved the tartan wool blanket that had fallen to the floor when he sat up, and aired it out. They locked eyes as she folded it into eighths and brought the ottoman over so he could stay upright but keep his leg extended. She gently lifted his calf and placed the blanket underneath what remained of his ankle, with a thin fold overlapping the top, creating a warm envelope. His leg felt heavier than the large piles of wood they had carried, even with his right foot now gone.

"Is it a good day?" she asked.

"Last night was rough."

"You can have another pill in an hour," she said, but he declined, specifying that a painkiller addiction was the last thing anyone needed. "The doctor called when you were napping—you're officially cleared to fly home on Monday, so that's good news," she said encouragingly, and Lem's twinkling blue eyes agreed.

Sam came in with another bundle of wood. "You're supposed to be helping!" he groaned as Eve left to fetch Lem's seltzer.

Muriel, Lucy, Cindy, and Sandra were all in the kitchen with separate projects: smashing yams, coring apples, and pulling tarragon leaves off their stems.

"Smells amazing in here," Eve said.

"Five hundred dollars, two days, and four chefs!" Cindy boasted.

Eve gulped as she filled a glass with ice. "Lem's up."

"He's getting stronger," Muriel said to no one in particular, and they all silently agreed.

Cindy bit down as she searched her bowl for a misplaced apple stem. "It'll be nice to be home in our own bed. No offense, San."

"It's not so bad, is it?" Sandra asked, sounding worried. "We didn't want him to risk the stairs."

"No, no, it's fine," Cindy reassured her. "And it's better we're together, so I can nudge him to move around. I don't know how people stand that crappy rehab center. Visitors are only allowed three hours a day? What's that about?" Eve considered that it was about the same amount of time she'd spent with her mother on a daily basis when she lived at home. Three hours could sometimes be too much.

Muriel shifted from the tarragon to the parsley and thought about the people left behind in The Deerwood, where time held virtually no meaning between the sporadic visitors. Three hours there meant everything.

"I was thinking," Cindy continued, "maybe you should leave the piano in the family room? It was a bitch to move it, and I think it looks good against the bookcases."

"That'll leave a pretty big gap in the living room," Sandra thought aloud. "And the bed goes back on Tuesday."

"Maybe some large potted plants? There's great light by those windows."

"I don't think so," Muriel said, weighing in. "The piano hasn't moved an inch since the day Mr. Clifton brought her in. And no one lets me play in the family room when there's a game on."

"How old is the piano?" Eve asked.

"Never ask a lady her age." Muriel winked and the others laughed while Eve returned to Lem with his seltzer.

"Really?" Sam droned. He finished the third load of wood and was crumpling old newspapers to build the fire by himself. "Really?"

"Give her a break, Sammy," Lem said as he thanked Eve with a nod and took a sip. "Oh, that's good."

Lem had been in the hospital for a month, and Eve had visited every day. He went in thinking he'd get a painkiller and some Epsom salts, but he was instantly hooked up to vast machines with tubes going every which way while the surgeons drew dotted lines to determine what they could save. As much as Eve hated Lem at the time, she believed it was her fault that her best friend's father was in that bed. She said she walked the mile from her new high school to keep tabs on him for Laura, but Muriel and I both knew she made the walk in the hopes of attenuating her profuse guilt.

With Cindy's encouragement, Lem felt emotionally well enough one blustery afternoon to admit that he didn't blame Eve for his outcome. "You didn't make me eat the doughnuts," he said, "and I was chugging beer and eating whole pizzas before you were born." He indicated his swaddled appendage, or what remained of it, and said, "My diabetes and that nasty infection are not on you." Eve wondered how strong the drugs were when he said this, but she accepted it.

There were still financial matters to discuss, but I was fully assessed and deemed to be as perfect as ever, with nary a ding. Lem had ample time to consider Eve's remarkable care for me and his mother, and when Muriel relayed the details of what had transpired in Montréal, he softened. He knew he would have gone a lot further than Eve had if he suddenly learned his own father was magically alive. It took time to accept and adapt, but for Muriel's sake, and Laura's, and as part of her initial conditions to remain at Sandra and Micah's, Eve continued to provide a strong shoulder for Lem once he was discharged from the hospital. Still, even with Lem's quasi-pardon, Eve felt quasi-culpable. True to his nature, Lem took mild advantage by allowing her to make her amends one glass of cold seltzer at a time.

Sandra was right about the traffic. The thirty-minute ride to the airport ate up more than a full hour, and Micah's short trip to the store managed to gobble the rest. He pulled up to the baggage claim the moment everyone walked through the sliding doors. After quick hugs, he loaded the trunk like a professional taxi driver and pulled away from the mayhem at Arrivals before the song on the radio had a chance to change.

"How was the flight?"

"Crowded," Laura said.

"Fine," Christian said.

"We were blessed with exit row seats and no turbulence," Judith replied.

Judith asked how Lem was doing. Micah explained that the amputation and immediate recovery were only the beginning and that Laura and Christian should prepare themselves for a long haul. "Getting your dad healthy again isn't going to be easy, but he's already made a lot of progress. He hasn't had a beer or any sugar for almost six weeks."

"Really?" Laura asked. "*No* beer?"

"Nope, and Sandy's teaching your mom how to make his favorite foods without carbs. He really can't eat the way he used to. It could kill him."

"Death by pizza!" Christian hollered.

"Shut up!" Laura threw her elbow into his chest. "This isn't funny!"

"She's right," Micah said, "but he'll be okay. He already lost around ten pounds."

"Water weight," Judith said, sharing her newly acquired knowledge of diabetes and corrective diets for insulin resistance. She had been aware of the possible conversation topics and wanted to be preemptively informed.

"Uh, sure. We probably shouldn't be doing a big Thanksgiving, but I think there's a lot to be thankful for." He smiled at Judith to include her in his sentiment, and she returned a nervous smile of her own. She'd agreed to let Eve remain in Saratoga and become a part of Sandra and Micah's household on a let's-see-how-it-goes basis, but the decision had been made primarily through long conversations with Sandra while Micah stayed in the background. Judith was worried about the influence of his Judaism, but once she was in his presence, she felt an unexpected sense of calm mixed with relief. Eve was probably lucky to have him as a role model.

"So, what *are* we gonna eat tonight? Rice cakes and celery?"

Micah quickly assessed that Christian had a lot to learn. Later in the weekend, he found his nephew on the back porch, distressed to the point of tears upon witnessing Lem's bandage change and the sight of the alien wound. Micah held Christian, told him they would eventually craft a prosthetic, and reiterated that everyone should join Cindy in her resolve to bring Lem back to good health. "Maybe don't bring junk food into the house anymore," he suggested. This small moment was one of millions that made Micah everyone's favorite uncle, even if Pete was the wealthier one.

The sun sets remarkably early in late November, and as Micah pulled up to the house, their car lights illuminated my garage through the long row of divided glass panels. I watched as Eve leaped off the porch and seized Laura so tightly they both thought they heard a pop, but neither of them cared as they embraced each other with equal strength. The heat of their friendship was enough to melt the early snows as they rotated in the embrace, and each took turns pulling the other up on her tiptoes, giggling the whole time. Christian, Sam, and Micah grabbed the luggage while Cindy and Sandra came to the driveway and gave Judith a gentle, welcoming hug.

"Eve?"

"Laura?"

Eve and Laura separated and went to their respective mothers.

"Hey, baby," Cindy said, pulling her daughter close. "Judith said you guys made things easy on her, and I really appreciate that."

"No big deal," Laura tossed back. "She's actually a pretty good cook."

"Well, I think it's a big deal. You really stepped up, and don't think we didn't notice," Cindy said sternly before pulling her in for another hug.

Near the edge of the lawn, Eve and Judith also embraced. To an outsider it would have appeared formal, like the cordiality extended to the friend of a friend after a personal introduction, but for Judith the stiff hug was all-encompassing, and for Eve the familiar rigidity was curiously welcome. "So, this is the place?" Judith ventured, duly impressed with the glowing Victorian behind Eve's shoulder. She released their embrace and her hands instinctively found the cross on her chest.

"You're cold!" Eve said, misreading the gesture. "I know, it takes some getting used to. We'll go up in a second, but first I have to show you the car!" She offered her mother an elbow, and Judith looped her arm through it as they came to see me. With Judith's touch, I finally had the complete story.

A short while later, Judith stood in the kitchen and warmed herself to the concert of aromas emanating from every conceivable cooking source. The kitchen was three times the size of her own, and she correctly determined that there were enough ovens and burners to service a small restaurant. She had become accustomed to working in Cindy and Lem's large kitchen during her six-week stint as Laura and Christian's den mother, but the stark white kitchen in Florida lacked the warmth and history of Sandra's, with its dark-green granite, hand-painted ceramic vegetable tiles, and pressed tin ceiling. Judith remarked on the extravagant scale of the refrigerator, the freezer, and the wine cooler, all separate appliances. She talked as if she had drunk a shrinking potion in Wonderland, droning on about the oversized opulence while Eve bit the inside of her cheek to keep her own comments contained. Micah noticed Eve's discomfort and quickly dispatched Sam; Judith suddenly found herself swept up in the young man's version of a tour through the rest of the richly carved home.

"This used to be Nancy's room, but now it's Eve's 'cause Nancy's still in Europe. Laura's gonna bunk with her on the pullout. You'll sleep in Abby's room 'cause Aunt Cindy moved downstairs when Uncle Lem came home, and Abby and Robert are staying at her friend Amy's on the West Side," Sam explained to Judith, who only heard him buzzing like an active beehive. "Robert's her boyfriend," he explained, "and Russ and Natalie were going to stay at the Adelphi, but they jacked the rates, so Dad and I moved the treadmill to get the old bed back in his room. She's nice, but she dresses kinda weird."

Judith had no idea to whom he was referring. Sam was fourteen, but small for his age. From Judith's perspective, he radiated the energy of a ten-year-old who'd consumed three bowls of cereal washed down with candy.

"Mom cleared her shi—her stuff—out of Jamie's room this morning when he *finally* said he *is* coming. He was supposed to be in Connecticut with Travis, that's his boyfriend, but now the guys are coming here. Or Trevor? I forget. Anyway, Christian's on the air bed in my room with Kubrick, and you get Abby's room, like I said."

Judith didn't remember him saying that, but she took his visual cue and wandered down the hall, where she discovered a sweetly decorated light-blue room. The freshly made bed looked like a stage for the towel that was folded into the shape of a monkey, ready to perform. Her luggage was waiting for her on a special rack by the arched window.

"Eve and I did the towels," Sam said proudly as he slid over to Judith on his socks. "If you need more, they're in this closet." He quickly opened and shut the door. "And you guys can use the bathroom here. We put extra TP under the sinks, and Mom always has toothbrushes and stuff if you forgot."

"Did you say this was Cindy's room?" Judith asked, overwhelmed.

"It's Abby's room," he said more slowly, "but Aunt Cindy stayed here until Uncle Lem got out of the hospital, and now they're both in the living room, like I said." Judith looked confused. "We got one of those hospital beds on wheels, but it's double-sized for both of them," he explained. "There's a bathroom under the stairs down there, and Uncle Lem uses the shower in the back bath 'cause it has a seat for old people."

"That's the bathroom next to your grandma Muriel's room?"

Sam smirked. No one ever called her that.

"Yeah, Grams is in Dad's old office so she can be close to Lucy in the garage."

"Lucy sleeps in the garage?"

Sam thought there should be a TV program called *Adults Say the Dumbest Things*. He never understood why they couldn't seem to keep up with him. "*No*, she's in the *apartment above* the garage," he enunciated.

"So . . . how many people are coming for dinner?" Judith dared to ask.

"All of them!" Sam said again, walking away and shaking his head. He was done with Judith and the tour—he had to find Eve. She may have bailed on the firewood, but she wasn't going to get out of helping him set the table.

***

When large families get together for short periods, their conversations tend to follow predictable patterns, beginning with an accounting of their various endeavors and activities. If they work, they try to share the most interesting aspects about that work: Micah's new design partnership with a major medical firm, the remodel at Lem's bank, Judith's encounter with a B-list celebrity seeking purple glitter. If they don't have a traditional job, they discuss other contributions: Cindy's fundraising efforts for the annual breast cancer walk or Sandra's contributions to help the local bookstore stay alive. Family members still in school will attempt to find a key subject to highlight: Laura's winning essay on existentialism, Christian's second-place win at the swimming regionals, Eve's scenes with George in the upcoming play.

Once all the What We Do's are up to date, people will share the year's more enjoyable highlights: the trip to Greece, the concerts in the park, the anniversary party on the rooftop. This invariably leads to the darker moments: Mrs. Silver's diagnoses, the Mishkins' divorce, the death of Whiskers. To rebound from the subsequent disquieting pauses, drinks are refilled and fresh hors d'oeuvres are issued. As the freshly lubricated conversations rise again, deeper ideologies regarding money, politics, and health may be explored. Many have learned to steadfastly avoid these subjects, however, regardless of how many hot toddies they've consumed, in favor of recounting dynamic sporting events, sharing humorous online video links, or even going so far as to predict the weather. These benign topics will ensure the evening remains pleasant for the tireless hosts, whose honor is deserved.

Eventually, the convivial talk in a large and comfortable room warmed by a tended fire will migrate to an expansive, vintage mahogany table such as Micah and Sandra Levine's. Amidst the clanks and clacks and oohs and aahs of the arriving feast, the familial conference will likely splinter into more intimate groupings. These clusters, prearranged with great care, will gravitate toward more pressing and personal discussions: the fallout of someone's breakup; the hardships of children, or coworkers, or a new diet; and the obvious comparisons between cars, or phone plans, or cities.

It was in this latter, chummier vein that Sandra, finally seated and awaiting Micah's and Lucy's arrivals with the final two dishes, quietly confided to Judith, immediately to her left, that Muriel never had Alzheimer's at all.

"I don't understand!" Judith gasped. "I thought the people at The Deerwood were specialists—how'd they miss it?"

"That's what I'm saying!" Sandra excitedly relayed in a hushed tone while keeping an eye on her brother. Lem was seated on the other end of the long table with his leg elevated on a separate chair. He was deeply engaged with his nephews on the importance of cultivating an excellent credit score when Lucy placed the terrine of cranberry-pomegranate chutney directly in front of him. Lem continued talking numbers while internally wondering if Cindy would allow him to eat it.

Distanced from that dilemma, Sandra continued her discussion with Judith. "Lem was going to move her into the Rose Garden when they got back to Florida, but then Pete said your daughter----" she looked further down the table at Eve and was distracted by her sudden discovery: the magenta stripe in Eve's hair was gone.

"Pete is your ex in New York?" Judith confirmed, trying to keep up.

"Yeah. He was supposed to come tonight, but he had to go back to Singapore."

"Kuala Lumpur," Abby corrected. "They funded the Kemajuan Project."

"Really?" She loved that her daughter was informed, but she was more focused on Eve's absent stripe until she realized it was still there, buried within a braid to temper its dominance. Eve had also removed five of her upper-ear piercings. Sandra wondered if Eve did that to make Judith more comfortable or if she made the change for George, or to service her character in the play. "So then we ... wait, what were we talking about?"

"Alzheimer's," Judith prompted.

"Right! So Pete said we should have Mom tested again, and we finally got an appointment, and *then we found out*." Sandra whispered the tail of her sentence, again regretting that she'd introduced the taboo subject with Lem so close. She blamed her lack of filtering on the strong predinner cocktails, conveniently forgetting the midday bottles of white they had also consumed while they cooked.

"So it's not Alzheimer's," Judith said, encouraging her to continue.

"It's Lyme!" Sandra bellowed, penetrating all the conversations with her enthusiasm. The room went silent, excepting the clinks as napkin rings were emptied and glassware was filled in anticipation of the forthcoming feast.

"What's Lyme?" Lem asked from the opposite edge of the room.

"Um, it's ... um ...." Sandra faltered.

"In the turkey," Muriel cut in. "We stuffed it with your Grandma Elizabeth's famous citrus dressing: oranges, lemons, and a little lime zest. The fruit keeps it moist."

"Oh?" he said.

"Judith was asking," Sandra explained.

"We literally can't wait to eat it!" Lem said, and everyone laughed and resumed their talking, pushing words upon words into the stately space.

"Never put in lime," Muriel whispered to Lucy as she sat down beside her. "Only lemons and oranges. Lime will throw it off."

It was obvious to Judith that Muriel wasn't afflicted with Alzheimer's. At the craft store, she often watched caregivers spend hours helping their stricken loved ones choose crayons or beads for a simple creative project. Judith knew it was unlikely any of them could rattle off the ingredients of an old recipe, let alone skillfully cover for a drunken daughter's gaffe.

Judith had learned everything she could about diabetes, Alzheimer's, Cadillacs, and Saratoga Springs so she wouldn't embarrass her daughter, but she was unprepared to discuss the topic of Lyme disease. "I thought it affects the joints," she said, pushing the limits of her knowledge on the subject.

"That's what I thought, too, but apparently it can disrupt the entire nervous system, and it can cause memory loss and other problems also," Sandra whispered. "Mom was always complaining about her hands burning or hurting, but we thought it was arthritis or neuropathy from playing the piano for so many years." Sandra's eyes grew wet.

"You can't blame yourself. How could you know?" Judith responded reassuringly.

"We talked all the time!" Sandra looked at Lem. She wiped away the forming tears and her eyes narrowed. "I'm not blaming myself entirely. I trusted the diagnoses."

"And now you know, so you can----"

"Sorry about the delay, folks!" Micah burst in. "Someone put the cheese grater where it actually belongs—why would I look for it there?!" Micah placed the platter of parmesan-garlic green beans on its trivet and finally plugged the sole remaining gap on the table. Sandra stood next to him, and together they assessed their Norman Rockwell scene. She clinked a spoon against her glass to focus the attention she already commanded.

"Hi everyone. Hi. Hi. Okay, the food's all here!"

This was met with a hearty round of cheers, appreciations, exclamations of "we've never seen anything so delicious," and the like.

"Okay, we're gonna eat in just a minute, hold your horses," she laughed, "But first, you know . . . a few words." She took a deep breath and conjured what she could remember of the speech she had formulated while mashing the potatoes. "So I know we're a big family even without all of our esteemed guests, but I don't think we've ever had a Thanksgiving quite like this," Sandra began. "Some of your chairs are rented, so please don't eat too much and break them!!"

Everyone laughed.

"But seriously, Micah and I . . . we wanted to thank you all for taking a break from your busy lives to come to our table and celebrate the holiday. Geez, I feel like a commercial for the airlines: 'We know you have many choices out there, but we wanna thank you for choosing us!'" Another round of laughter intensified when the dimmed chandelier suddenly brightened for a quick moment, as they sometimes do in older homes. Muriel secretly believed it was people long since passed, signaling their attendance.

Sandra continued, "As most of you know, Thanksgiving has always been my favorite holiday----"

"Because of the pies!" Sam burst out.

"----*Yes*, because of the pies," she bantered, "but also because it's a day when we can all come together and we get a chance to . . . to really take a look at our lives and appreciate how full they are."

"Our lives or our bellies?" quipped Cindy, earning some snickers and chortles of her own.

"Because life can be hard," Sandra continued, her voice softening. "It seems we're always struggling with one thing or another, right? But if we aren't careful, we can get so wrapped up in our little battles that soon we'll start to think that *everything* is bad, like losing your foot." She pointed at Lem. "Or your health." She reached her right arm toward Muriel. "Or your family." She stretched her left toward Judith, who didn't know what expression to wear.

Squeaks could be heard as people shifted in their chairs under the sudden weight of their uneasiness. Eve and Laura tapped each other's legs under the table and widened their eyes in mutual trepidation and wonder.

"Now *don't*." Sandra held up a finger. "Don't get all upset, because this is *exactly* my point! Thanksgiving is a special day . . . it's so special when we can stop focusing on what we might have lost, and instead we get to come together and really celebrate what we all have."

"Pretty easy for you to say," Lem muttered.

"What?" Sandra asked innocently.

"Nothing."

"Not nothing—what did you say?"

"I said." Lem cleared his throat and projected his voice. "That's a pretty easy thing to say, for someone who has everything."

Cindy held Lem's arm as everyone turned their heads one hundred and eighty degrees to look at Sandra. They expected to find a defensive expression of hurt or shock, but instead she glowed along with the two dozen candles spread across her resplendent table. "Lemmy! Oh my sweet brother Lemmy Lems, *you* have everything too! That's what I'm saying, we all do. We all have everything that matters. Let me finish----"

"I think you are finished," he said, wishing he could get up quickly, fill a plate, and storm back to his living-room hospital bed. But the food was too far out of reach, so he summoned his napkin ring and banged it on the table. Eve looked around the room. No one seemed to be breathing.

"No." Sandra's voice cracked. "No, Lem, this is *my* table and *my* speech. I love you, but please shut up." Micah wrapped his arm around her waist in a show of support and sent a pleading head-cock across the room to Lem. Lem squeezed his jaw and extended his upturned palms, regranting the floor to Sandra.

"Mom grew up in this house," she said. "Did you all know that? She grew up here and had dozens of Thanksgivings as a daughter and a sister, and then she became a wife and a mom and had, what, at least another twenty?"

"More like fifty," Muriel said. "Or maybe a hundred and fifty."

This broke the tension.

"So Mom is finally with us again and I think that's just amazing." She blew a kiss to Muriel. "To Mom!"

They all raised their glasses and proclaimed, "To Mom!" or "To Grams!" or "To Muriel!" and they drank. Muriel was embarrassed, but she tactfully raised her glass and imparted an appreciative look to each and every one of them.

Lem reached for his fork.

"Hold on, I'm not done."

"The food's gonna get cold, Mom," Sam said.

"So I realized," Sandra continued, "that when we give our thanks and count our blessings, most of us take two fundamental things for granted, and I'm gonna *quickly* share those two things with you right now."

Lucy leaned forward, deeply interested.

"None of us live in the moment anymore. Most of the time we're in the future, filling up the calendar with events and plans, and at the same time, we also live in the past and compare everything we have with what came before, like when your foot was fine and when Dad was alive."

Cindy squeezed Lem's arm, silently urging him to contain his tongue, but Muriel fully agreed with Sandra and found no reason to squirm.

"So I think the best part about Thanksgiving is it forces us into the present where we can let that go. All of it. We don't have to worry about a future that we can't control, and we can forget about whatever was getting us down. We can come together and *put everything on pause* and simply allow this beautiful table and these wonderful people to provide for all of our needs in this one happy moment."

"She's so cool," Eve whispered to Laura.

"And the second thing, baby?" Micah prompted.

"It's love!" Sandra sang as she kissed his lips. "LOOOVE!! No matter how *bad* you think things are"—she directed this again toward Lem—"there is no one in this room, and I mean *no one*, who doesn't have an unlimited supply of the most important gift in the whole freaking world! Love! We all have it and we all give it and share it and I'm just . . . I'm just so thankful! And not only today, but every day, but also especially today. I love you all, and I'm thankful that I get to love each and every one of you. Even you, Travis! I know we just met a few hours ago, but I already love you because Jamie loves you—and I also really love that shirt!"

"It's Trevor," he said, blushing, and everyone laughed, including Lem.

Sandra squeezed Micah's hand, and he was happy to absorb her tender and benevolent power. Then she turned and said, "Judith, would you please say grace?"

Judith was stunned. She looked around as a room full of expectant eyes fell upon her, all of them twinkling in the candlelight. As the aromas from the vast spread continued to rise and swirl, as spices and juices commingled in the warmth, Judith realized that she was the last barrier to the banquet. With her scissors on the ribbon, she had to find the right words, and her mind scrambled for a blessing until her eyes met with Eve's. Instead of scowling at the prospect of a religious moment, Eve radiated contentment. Judith registered this and appreciated that Eve was truly home.

Sandra had talked about taking a moment and sharing love, and it triggered the memory of a reading from Thessalonians. "Dear Heavenly Father," Judith began. "Or the God or Lord of your choice," she respectfully amended before resuming her bow, "we pause to thank you for this meal and for all the blessings You give to us. We are so thankful for our lives and the love you've given to this family. *Our* family. Thank you, in the name of Your son, Jesus." She looked up and then appended, "and in the universal spirit of Love, we pray. Amen."

Amens reverberated until they were overtaken by Sandra cheering at the top of her lungs, "Now eat!! Eat it all before it gets cold!"

***

A few hours later, the satiated family dispersed. Lem and Cindy retreated to their converted bedroom, where he promptly swallowed the pain pills he had delayed to the far edge of his ability. He continued to experience an irreconcilable stabbing sensation in the toe that was no longer there. The doctors assured him the pain would eventually retreat through physical therapy, psychological counseling, possibly drugs, and definitely more time, but Lem was impatient. He wanted to skip across the hard years ahead and immediately embody his thin, healthy future self with the functioning prosthetic. He also wanted to return to his youth with his adult knowledge so he could bypass all the alcohol and fried-food platters and every goddamned cookie. He wanted to ban the lollipops at his bank and replace them with packages of raw nuts. He wanted birthdays worldwide to be celebrated with fresh fruit and steamed broccoli. He wanted all temptations vanquished, the middle aisles of grocery stores burned to the ground—and he wanted to be in a house that didn't smell like melted butter and cinnamon.

"You know how long we've been married?" Cindy asked, reading his mind and sensing his need for a distraction. She was lying next to him with her leg draped over his thigh as she gently stroked his oversized belly.

"Trick question?"

"Do you know?"

"Twenty-five years in June." He sighed. "The cruise ship has our deposit."

"And do you know how we made it twenty-five years?" she prompted. He struggled to see her round, shining face beneath the heavy makeup she had yet to remove; she had looked more human by the dim light of the candlelit tablescape.

"We stopped listening to your mother?" he offered.

"Day by day," she corrected, pinching him. "Most were good, but some were bad."

"Really bad," he said, his voice coming out in a quiet wail.

"But most were really good, and those days will come again. Trust me, in a few years, we'll look back on this as a blip," she said, trying to encourage him.

"A blip?"

"A blip."

"You promise?"

"I promise you good days are ahead, yes."

She kissed him and left a pink smudge on his lips as the medicine carried him smoothly into sleep.

***

On the other side of the house, Micah continued to wash each fragile dish by hand as Judith dried them and Sandra put them away. Lucy was given the rest of the night off, and she vanished into her apartment to call her family.

"It was Lyme," Sandra finally, and soberly, reiterated. "We think Mom got a tick bite at Dad's funeral. It was the only time she came up that year."

"Wouldn't she feel something like that?" Judith asked.

"No, the doctor said it was probably—what are they called?"

"Nymphs," Micah supplied.

"Nymphs, right. Baby ticks. They look like little poppy seeds, or even smaller, and it could have been along her hairline where she wouldn't even notice it. It doesn't take long to get infected, and it probably washed away when she got a shampoo," Sandra explained.

"Eve washed her hair at the salon! It seems she has a long history of rescuing your mother!" Judith remarked.

"Ha, well . . . Mom was still in the condo back then, but yeah . . . that would've been poetic." Sandra put down her plate so she could use her hands as she talked. "So here's the thing: after Dad died and Mom got the tick bite, she was—how did you put it?"

"Obliterated," Micah said.

"Yeah, obliterated. I mean, we were all in shock and feeling pretty raw, but there was no way any of us could have known she had Lyme. Even looking back now, it's impossible to separate what was grief and what was the disease, you know? She was exhausted and complaining of headaches and being achy, but the doctor said she was run down because she wasn't sleeping or eating right or going outside. She had a mild fever that came and went, but she wasn't congested, so he said give her Tylenol and orange juice and bring over healthy meals. That was his advice."

Micah snorted.

"After a few weeks of that, we could tell on the phone that she was getting worse. She couldn't seem to concentrate and she was losing some words. God, we were so worried, and I finally told Lem to get over there with his key and figure out what's going on. He said it was like a hurricane blew through the house."

"That's terrible," Judith said, remembering the odious state of her own home post-Richard and her lack of will to clear it.

They were getting backlogged, and at Micah's silent urging, Sandra quickly picked up a towel and continued to help with the drying. The shiny back of a dish caught the light and shared her distorted reflection. Sandra imagined that was how Muriel must have felt at the time: warped and unrecognizable, even to herself. "Lem sent her to a doctor he knew from the bank, and that guy told us she was in the beginning stages of Alzheimer's."

"But you said it wasn't Alzheimer's," Judith reminded her.

"I know, that's the thing: *Lem lied* so he could take control of her estate."

"What?"

"He's asleep, right?" Sandra whispered to Micah.

"I hear snoring," he said, joining them at the island with the faucet trickling onto a pan to muffle their conversation. He stood behind his wife and slowly kneaded her shoulders.

Sandra searched the far wall for a long moment, like a child in a school play who forgot her lines. The play was too complicated. There were too many words and she couldn't find the order, but the spotlight was on her and she had to say something.

"It's . . . messy. Like, I'm not entirely sure how he did it, or in what order, but we've pretty much figured out that Lem paid a lawyer to write an unlimited power of attorney for Mom. Wait, was that before he paid the doctor for the phony Alzheimer's diagnosis?"

Micah nodded.

"Right, because she had to be competent enough to sign the POA, but then totally incompetent so he could do the rest."

"I don't get it—why would your mother sign something like that?"

Sandra, once again, looked to Micah.

"We're not entirely sure," he said, "but we think Mom didn't know what she was signing. It was a few weeks after Ira died, and Lem might have told her it was a bill for the funeral expenses or a life insurance form. He could have said anything, really."

"Mom also told me she got Lucy a gas card and a library card, but we've never seen either. She might have signed the POA thinking it was for one of those." They all shook their heads at the shameful depths of Lem's deceits. "But then—and I remember this clearly—then Lem told me I had to buy out his share of this house."

"I don't understand. What does that have to do with the Alzheimer's?" Judith asked.

"Ugh, it was all Lem and his bull—his baloney," Sandra huffed. "He was trying to reorganize the estate because, well----"

"He was stealing it," Micah said, eyebrows raised. Judith gasped.

"My brother said my mother was incompetent, and he had the doctor's signature. He said she had to go into managed care and he found a good place."

"The Deerwood." Judith sighed.

"The Deerwood. He said he could float the payments until the condo sold and then reimburse himself, but if it took too long to sell we'd be sunk, so he asked if I would consider selling my half of the house to him because that's what the will said I was supposed to do eventually, anyway."

Micah cut in. "He said if we did it sooner rather than later, we'd save a couple hundred thousand dollars because real estate prices were only going to go up and Muriel could live another ten or fifteen years."

"With the disease she didn't have," Judith said, understanding.

Sandra nodded her agreement and Micah continued. "Plus, somehow he made the whole thing feel like it was your plan, San, and not his."

"I know. And he said it would be more complicated later because after she died there'd be inheritance tax problems and other stuff," Sandra added.

"I still think he made that part up."

"I know, honey, I know."

"Oh gosh," Judith responded, unable to find any other suitable words.

"Right," Sandra said, remembering she was telling the story to Judith. "So that's when I went to Pete for a loan, and then Lem moved Mom into The Deerwood, only he told her it was because her building needed repairs."

"What repairs?"

"There were no repairs. Remember when that condo collapsed near Miami? He kinda used that idea to get her to move, but he also wanted it in her mind that she could go back someday so she wouldn't feel depressed about being at The Deerwood. He wanted her to feel like it was temporary," Sandra lamented. "A temporary emergency."

"I think it was his version of compassion?" Micah ventured, but Judith tacitly agreed it was sinister, and the more she heard, the more she feared for Lem's soul.

"When I went down a week later to help Mom get settled, I told her I sold my half of the house to Lem just like she wanted, and she totally freaked out."

Judith wondered what that looked like. Did Muriel cry? Scream? Throw things?

"And then Lem came over about an hour later with a pizza. I remember we had to sop up all the grease with paper towels and we practically used the whole roll," Sandra said.

"I remember you telling me that. So gross," Micah scoffed.

"Anyway, Mom confronted Lem. She told him he did a nasty thing by making me buy half the house and she wanted him to fix it, but Lem said it was in Dad's will so it was going to happen eventually anyway. He said we needed the money so she could stay there, plus it saved me all this money over the long run, but Mom wasn't buying it. She asked him where all her money was. I had no idea how much money she had or didn't have, but somehow Lem knew everything."

"And then he lied again," Micah said, taking over. "Mom demanded to speak with her financial adviser, and Lem looked up the number and gave her the phone right away----"

"It's like he was expecting it----"

"----And whoever she talked to told her the market went down and she lost a significant amount of her investments. He said she was being diversified, but it was going to be a bit of a process to recoup what she lost. She was going to have to be patient while they worked it all out."

"I bet it was the lawyer," Sandra said.

"The lawyer who wrote the power of attorney?" Judith asked.

"We don't know. It wasn't Mom's regular guy—Lem fired him when he took over with the POA—but whoever she spoke to said he was part of the same firm. You have to remember that Mom was super-savvy about money, so whoever she talked to must have been pretty convincing."

"But she was also completely disoriented from the move and everything else," Micah added. "I think it was that trip when she started crying about the car, right, San?"

"The Cadillac?" Judith wondered aloud. "I was wondering how she was able to keep it if she had Alzheimer's or . . . whatever."

"Yeah, well . . ." Sandra exhaled. "That was the only concession my brother made. I think he figured he'd get the car eventually anyway, and sitting in it kept her calm. I mean, he'd just lied and told the poor woman that her condo was in jeopardy and her money was gone and her daughter had to buy the family home just to keep her going. Plus she was in a new place and she didn't have any friends and she was facing Alzheimer's, all without Dad . . ."

"He let her keep the car because he's a compassionate man," Micah said, sarcastically.

"He's an asshole!" Judith cried out. Sandra and Micah both took a step back as the words echoed through the kitchen. She put down a plate and snapped the rubber band on her wrist. "Please forgive me, I am so sorry." She tilted her red face down to the floor.

Sandra released a chuckle. "Don't be sorry, Judith! We've said the same thing at least a hundred times over this."

"A thousand," Micah said. "It's the only fact about Lem we can all confirm is true."

Judith continued the drying. "So then what? She loses everything and you're paying this big loan and . . . and Lem gets away with it?"

"Well, no," Sandra continued. "When Lem sold the condo in Florida, I was supposed to get half, but Lem said the money was going into a trust to pay for The Deerwood bills. So I called Pete to ask if that made sense, and he said I should sue my brother. Pete was even going to pay for it."

"Did you?"

It was Sandra's turn to put her head down, but Micah touched her chin and lifted it back up. "Your dad always said families should never fight over money," he reminded her in a whisper. "There's no shame in honoring that." Sandra wiped away a forming tear.

"No, I didn't sue him."

Judith wanted to hug Sandra, and it was a strange feeling. She also wanted to hold onto her cross, but she was drying a stack of plates that seemed thinner than her own fingernails and more valuable than all her kitchen materials combined. She gave Sandra a gentle and loving look instead.

"You know," Sandra said, receiving the warm vibe, "when Lem moved her into The Deerwood . . . we all thought it was on the up-and-up. We were so stupid." She allowed her tears to spill over.

"We were played," Micah corrected, "and it didn't help that Mom was in a trance from that fucking drug."

"Don't say fucking, Micah." Then to Judith, she said, "I'm sorry, we get upset."

Judith excused it. She admired their cohesion. She also felt vindicated by her decision not to pursue her car loan through Lem. *Rejection is God's protection,* she thought as she prodded them to continue.

"The drug was supposed to slow the disease, but it really slowed everything. Mom was basically, like . . ."

"Catatonic," Micah finished.

"And then there's the whole Grace thing . . ."

"I meant to ask about that," Judith cut in. "Eve told me, but I'm not sure I get it—was Grace a part of the Lyme?"

Micah snorted again as he handed over the last dish. How Muriel manifested Grace into her reality as an external persona was impossible to understand, but it renewed Micah's anger toward the scammy doctor who had convinced them all that the psychosis was a definitive symptom for a disease Muriel didn't have.

"We have no idea," Sandra answered, sidestepping her husband. "But when she didn't have her medicine on their trip, Mom started talking about her again. The thing is, and it's taken me a while to see this, Grace wasn't necessarily a bad thing. It was Lem who made me think of Grace as a warning sign that Mom was going crazy, but in reality, Mom was remembering herself at a special time in her life when she was really, really happy. Grace was her way of . . . healing."

Micah exhaled. The plates were done. The left side of the counter held a shimmering low tide of lingering wines and waters, and the island was capped with sullied platters, pots, pans, serving dishes, cutting boards, and the soft remains of homemade garlic butter in a ramekin. To Micah's right, a working silver mine's worth of cutlery awaited his attention, and their two dishwashers were already running with everything else that wasn't china or crystal.

Micah picked up the first glass while Sandra picked up the story. "Anyway, we finally got a confirmed diagnosis for Lyme and Mom was treated with intravenous antibiotics every day for a month. Lem was upstairs at the hospital, and Mom was downstairs, and I was running between the two of them, back and forth, every day!"

"But now that part's over and Lucy's taking her to CBT a few times a week," Micah added.

"What is that?" Judith asked as she switched to a fresh towel and started on the crystal with even more precise attention than she gave to the vulnerable plates.

"Cognitive behavioral therapy," Sandra explained. "They're teaching her some new skills and helping her----"

"Recalibrate," Micah finished as he took extra care to scrub a greasy swatch of thick lipstick off a glass.

"Is she still having problems?" Judith asked.

"She's getting better," Micah said. "In fact, last night she was telling me about the time a monkey tried to take her bag in India and she started the story by saying, 'back when I called myself Grace . . .' So that's something."

He looked to Sandra for confirmation. She elaborated: "Having undiagnosed Lyme disease for almost ten years was way too long, but in a sorta crappy twist, that nasty Alzheimer's drug *did* slow everything down, and one doctor said it might have even mitigated some of the potential damage. He'll probably write a paper on it."

"She's also much better now that she's settled in here, and it definitely helps that she's motivated. Have you seen her little pad?"

"I was wondering what that was."

"They encourage her to make lists and write down her thoughts," said Sandra. "It sorta pulls it from her mind and takes away the stress and anxiety of *having* to remember everything, which in turn makes it easier for her to remember. I don't really understand it, but Mom's sleeping well, and she even started doing her crosswords again!"

"Tell her about Monday," Micah prompted.

"Eve said that on Monday Mom gave, what was it, like *twenty* of the right questions on *Jeopardy*?" Sandra exclaimed. "I can't even do that on my best day."

"That's amazing!" Judith was careful to constrain her enthusiasm so her hands wouldn't inadvertently shatter the crystal. Then she continued in a whisper, "Does this mean you won't be needing Lucy much longer?"

"Oh no, we *need* Lucy. Mom can't drive anymore, and it's better if she has some help in the shower and stuff so she doesn't get hurt. Lucy's great with that. Mom's definitely getting stronger, but she's been through a lot and she's not . . . young. We'll probably rely on Lucy a lot more in the coming years, so this is a good time for everyone to settle and adjust."

"Eve's also a huge help," Micah said, "but she'll be going to college before too long."

Judith smiled, believing it was her own community-minded influence that served as inspiration for her daughter's magnanimous ways.

It was then that Sandra put away a few of the dried glasses and sat down on an island stool. She motioned for Judith to come over and sit as well.

"And that brings us to what we really need to talk about," Sandra said with a seriousness that caused the hairs on Judith's neck to begin a slow reach for the ceiling.

Judith's primary fear for the weekend was learning that Sandra and Micah wanted to send Eve back to Florida. It wasn't working out. Eve did something. She said something or stole something or broke something or she was a bad influence on Sam. After everything Judith had been through emotionally to accept that Eve was going to live in Saratoga Springs with this family, after everything she'd gone through physically and financially to make it possible, after everything she'd endured spiritually to put her trust in their atypical situation, it was over.

Judith instinctively clutched her cross.

Sandra half-whispered with a little rasp, "About two weeks ago, Pete's lawyers came up from the city with a specialist to have Mom's memory tested. The doctor is a certified expert, and they were able to declare her fully and legally competent again."

"Okay . . ." Judith said, not knowing what this had to do with Eve. The news didn't lessen her suspicion that she should have brought extra suitcases for all of Eve's new clothes. She wondered what they would do with all the winter stuff in Florida.

"Mom worked with Pete and his lawyers to revoke Lem's power of attorney and draft a new will," Sandra went on.

"Did she cut Lem out?" Judith asked, sensing something ugly was afoot while her mind remained focused on Eve's imminent return to Florida. Was it cheaper to rent a car or get another plane ticket considering all the extra bags? Judith would have to figure out how to reverse the school transcripts and reenroll Eve down south; she might lose a semester and require summer school from all the switching. Judith wondered if they would at least allow Eve to stay in Saratoga another month so she could perform in the play.

"No, Lem's still in it, but Mom also included Eve."

Judith concentrated on Sandra's lips. It sounded like Sandra said Muriel had included Eve in her will, but then why were they sending her back to Florida? Judith needed a replay—she wanted to see the actual words because they disappeared before she could comprehend them. As Judith continued to think the worst, she couldn't help but see, quite clearly, that Sandra and Micah were smiling wide. It took a beat before reality poked through the mud of her erroneous assumptions.

"Not . . . the car?" Judith ventured reluctantly.

"Oh no!" Sandra burst out. "Oh gosh, that would be like the worst ending of a bad novel!"

"Eve drove off into the sunset in her beautiful Cadillac convertible----" Micah laughed, writing with his finger in the air.

"----and she arrived at the stately college gates to begin her bold new future!?" Sandra finished off. After a few seconds they calmed down as Sandra said, "No, Mom wants us to sell the Caddy through the Auto Museum's annual auction and donate the money to her charities."

"*After* she dies," Micah specified, "and not one damn—*darned* day before!" He channeled Muriel's voice for this and elicited another spate of titters. They were excited.

I thought selling me in an auction was a fine plan, and I didn't protest. Whoever wanted me the most would get me next. I was created primarily to go forward, after all, and innumerable examples have demonstrated throughout history that nothing ever, ever stays the same.

Then Sandra grew serious again and clarified: "Judith, Mom included Eve in the will with an equal share. I don't know how much it'll end up being, but the point is . . ."

"Eve doesn't have to worry about her future." Micah beamed. "Mom's investments never went down—it was all part of Lem's lies. It's been growing for decades, and she's actually a very wealthy woman."

Judith gasped again as her eyes searched the room for something to hold on to. They were telling her that Eve's inheritance would be significant, but Judith continued to hold her cross as she anchored her expression on Sandra, then Micah, and then back again. "So she can stay?" she finally confirmed.

Sandra and Micah's faces twisted sideways.

"I thought . . ." Judith shrank.

Micah pulled his barstool around and sat in a small triangle with Sandra and Judith. He extended his hands, and Judith took them reluctantly. He gently explained, in the soothing tone that defined his being, "Of course she can stay, for as long as she likes, and Mom's going to pay for Eve's college through the estate. If Mom dies before Eve goes to school, the money will be there, but the plan is to loan Eve the money, without interest, and have it offset from Eve's eventual share."

Judith watched as the room leaned sideways, like a cruise ship caught in a squall. She understood why Micah had offered his hands, and she used them to stabilize herself.

"But . . . why?"

"When Eve and Mom returned from Montréal, we had a long talk," Sandra said as she took over holding Judith's hands. "A really long talk. We were so scared when they left that second time."

"I remember," Judith said.

"But after we shared our hurt, Eve apologized. She promised she had no reason to do anything like that again, and then she explained what happened up there. We spent hours at the table that night, talking it through. We wanted to know everything, and in the process, Eve told us all about the incredible work you do to feed people and give them clothes through your church. Especially considering your----"

"Limited resources," Micah supplied.

Judith blushed and took her hands back out of discomfort, but not offense.

"When Sammy joined us, he told us that Laura thinks Eve is the smartest person in her school," Sandra added, "but money for college is a big problem." Judith felt her profound sense of pride for Eve mixing with the shame of her insolvency. Then both emotions were trumped by the humming confusion of why Muriel, with so many descendants, would want to take anything from her own family to help out a stranger in such a significant way. A moderate gift seemed appropriate, maybe, but an equal share of her fortune?

"Because Mom really loves her," Sandra said, reading Judith's whirling mind. "Eve *saved* her. She believes in your daughter and wants to give her a fair chance in life."

"And Lem doesn't know . . ." Judith realized aloud as the water continued to trickle in the sink.

Sandra and Micah looked at each other, and he took over. "When Mom saw the will that Lem manufactured, she actually spit on it before she ripped it up. I've never seen her do anything crass like that. Ever."

"We didn't want to ruin Thanksgiving," Sandra put in, "and we want to get him safely back home on Monday. Then we'll let the chips fall where they may."

"So did she cut him out?"

"No," Sandra admitted reluctantly, indicating it had been seriously discussed. "Mom understands what he did, but she also feels bad about his foot and all that. I don't know, it's her choice. Hey, maybe she's, you know, like a saint?" Judith balked a little, knowing Muriel turning the other cheek was a far cry from the requirements for sainthood, but she didn't interrupt Sandra's flow. "Mom basically restored the original version she made with Dad, but with a new plan for the car and Eve. She doesn't own this house or the condo anymore, so that part's gone anyway. In the new will, Lem and Cindy and the two of us will all get the same as the grandchildren and Eve, in twelve equal shares."

"Lem's not going to be happy about that," Judith said. "It sounds like he was expecting half."

"Ha!" Sandra exclaimed. "In Lem's version of my mother's will, he took over ninety percent!"

Micah added, "Yeah, Sandy, but *you* got her watch and some jewelry!"

"Which goes to the girls. I only wear my earrings and your ring, mister."

Micah bent down and kissed her finger. Then he returned his attention to Judith. "Pete's lawyers reworked everything with Mom and his finance people. They moved all her money and investments out of Lem's bank, and he's not on any of her papers anymore. He won't be able to access a single penny."

"Lem already paid for his house and cars and lots of other things with her money, but now that's over. If he challenges any part of the new will, he'll lose," Sandra said quietly, "and then he'll also be on the hook for the cost of Pete's lawyers, and we'll counter-sue him for everything he already took."

"He won't challenge it," Micah assured his nervous wife.

Judith was caught between two new physical feelings that were diametrically opposed.

First, she felt heavy, as if chained by the disconcerting idea that Eve had been a major catalyst in restoring order to this family's financial drama. She also bore the weight of knowing that her daughter was making a life for herself at someone else's expense. She was further distressed that Eve may have inadvertently acquired an embittered, lifelong adversary in Lem. These notions were all beguiling, leaden, and uncomfortable.

At the same time, Judith felt like she was floating high above the kitchen on shimmering, gossamer wings.

They were both free.

For years, Judith had lived in constant fear of the harsh realities they would face after Eve's graduation. As Eve's peers went off to expensive colleges, she would likely remain at home to work at The Deerwood and hopefully take classes at the local community college. Judith was already ineffectual in her daughter's financial and emotional life, and Eve rejected her guidance toward a spiritual one—Judith knew they would never function as housemates once a high school diploma leveled the field. It was only with God's arms wrapped around her that Judith found the strength to continue in the face of their looming and ominous future.

Instead of using Eve's cross-country trip as a practice session for an empty nest, Judith had imagined her daughter was on a supervised school trip. She'd avoided Eve's bedroom, her bathroom, her designated kitchen cabinets, and her personal shelf in the fridge.

When Eve told her she wanted to stay in Saratoga Springs, the nest had lost some of its warmth, but Judith still believed Eve was merely flitting about on undeveloped wings and would eventually return, either by Sandra's request or after she graduated. Eve couldn't live in someone else's tree indefinitely, and Judith continued to avoid Eve's Floridian perch, fearing the repercussions if she so much as dared to make up her daughter's bed.

But suddenly, with the stroke of Muriel's pen, it became clear to Judith that Eve wasn't coming home, and with this knowledge, Judith donned her own pair of wings. Instead of feeling indigent, isolated, and useless as a parent, Judith's vision for her own life opened like a lotus to the morning sun. Like in a game of Chutes and Ladders, Eve's roll of the dice had put them on the magic square that brought them soaring past years of tumultuous struggles, right to the top!

Still seated on her stool, Judith was already picturing a more affordable apartment—something with one bedroom, a better kitchen, and possibly a view. She imagined shifting her work hours to her liking in the absence of Eve's school schedule, meals and weekend plans. Judith realized there was nothing holding her back from talking to the friendly beekeeper at the farmers' market, the one with the cross around his neck that shimmered like his honey. He had invited her for coffee, but entertaining such thoughts had seemed irresponsible—inconceivable—when she had a rebellious teen at home. But maybe now it was time to try his honey.

Something in one of the dishwashers made a clicking sound, pulling Judith out of her gleaming reverie and into a reality that, by contrast, felt like a dark night in winter. As she pictured Eve's contentment at the dinner table, the shine in those candlelit eyes, Judith understood that Eve was primarily happy because she was in a better place—a place without her mother. The day Richard left, Judith had decided her every action would be for Eve's benefit, but instead of prospering under her guidance, Eve took a stranger's car and drove thousands of miles away to find a better life.

Judith had failed.

Even with the Lord on her side.

It didn't make sense: Sandra and Micah didn't pray or hold any strong religious convictions. He had a Jewish family, but if she hadn't been told, she never would have known. And Sandra's godless loins had begotten five children from three different fathers, so why did the Lord provide these heathens with an abundance of love and well-adjusted, happy children in a beautiful house with two dishwashers?

Judith realized she was coveting. She snapped her rubber band, hard, and winced at its brutal sting.

She reminded herself that the example she had set through her devotion to God was part of the reason why Muriel wanted to help Eve in the first place. Judith's faith had infused Eve with a goodness that extended beyond herself and, miraculously, rewarded them both.

But why couldn't Eve extend that goodness to her? What was it about her that provoked such spite in the people she loved? Why couldn't Eve embrace her mother's choices with the same openness she afforded to all these strangers? After everything Judith did to provide *and survive*, why wasn't it enough? All the other mothers and daughters in the prayer group were friends—why couldn't Eve and Judith be friends, too?

Judith understood that God works in mysterious ways, but He seemed to nurture everyone at that Thanksgiving table, even that gay kid and his boyfriend, while He put forth caveats for her. Her happiness had a price tag, and this time the cost was her daughter.

Eve leaving home was inevitable, but Judith began to comprehend that when she headed back, she would have to face the fallout from Eve's premature evacuation. Alone. Judith had no idea what her life would look like in a year, but without Eve, it would be empty. She detested their fights and disruptions, but she knew she would long for them in the forthcoming solitude. Judith only sought peace and quietude within their companionship, and she didn't know how she would function without Eve's constant noise.

Eve would get money for college, but Judith felt she was the one who had earned it by plowing and tilling and planting and watering and praying over her only crop for sixteen long years. Sandra and Muriel and the rest of them would reap the benefits of Judith's toil in the form of Eve's mirth and success while Judith was left behind, a farmer in the distance with a fallow field.

Richard left her and Eve left her. Maybe Judith would see the beekeeper, but maybe not. Why should she bother if he might also someday leave? Judith wasn't sure how much more God would take from her, and she wasn't sure how much more she could withstand.

Sandra and Micah watched with growing concern as Judith's thoughts appeared to rise and fall like an injured bird struggling to get off the ground.

When Eve had relayed Judith's lie about Richard's death, they, as parents, had understood Judith's desire to protect her daughter. But they also took Eve's side and agreed, wholeheartedly, that what Judith did "was totally fucked up."

They watched as Judith closed her eyes and kissed her cross. It wasn't a simple peck; it was a full kiss, executed with deep emotion. They listened as Judith thanked Jesus for providing Eve with such an incredible gift. They comprehended again, with full clarity, why Eve had to leave.

Judith wiped away a tear, rolled her shoulders and reset her posture. She intended to use her normal voice and was a little surprised when it came out in a whisper: "Does Eve know?"

"No," Sandra said as Micah walked over to the sink and turned off the tap. "I talked to Mom about it, and we both think the news should come from you."

"You're a part of this family now," Micah offered, though he secretly wondered what that truly meant for all of them.

Judith didn't know how to respond.

She no longer knew what to feel.

"She won't start looking at colleges until spring, so there's no rush," Sandra said, knowing she would eventually tell Eve if Judith couldn't. Or wouldn't. "You know you'll always be her mom, no matter where she goes in life." Sandra cautiously pulled Judith in for what she hoped would be perceived as a sisterly hug.

Judith was hesitant at first, and then she allowed it.

***

Up the stairs and down the hall, Eve was telling Laura all about George and the scene in the play where they had to kiss. George had offered to practice with her so their connection would be believable, and Eve shyly admitted to Laura that she was willing to offer him a lot more than simulated kisses. Laura approved of George after she looked up his house on Zillow and scanned his social media. Once that process was completed, Eve cautiously asked Laura how things were going with Liam.

"I dunno, I think you were right. Homecoming was fun, but I feel like everything we do gets uploaded to my brother, you know? It's kinda creepy. And he's really not that smart. Plus, he's always asking about you—but that's pretty much all anyone talks about."

"Huh," Eve said with a shrug. Her fame as "the new girl" was fading, and it felt odd to think she was a celebrity in a place where she had deliberately kept herself in the background. She shifted back to Laura. "Hey, what about Noah McNeary? You said you really like him and he's not in that crowd."

"Yeah, he's sweet but he's only a sophomore!"

"Yeah."

Eve and Laura passed Muriel's black stone lingam back and forth as they picked apart other potential boyfriends. They shredded their boring teachers and lauded those who inspired them in their respective schools. Laura and Eve discovered how much they actually missed each other, even though they still talked or texted at least a few times a day.

"Did you figure out Christmas?" Laura asked.

"I'm still not sure," Eve said, swiping through the photos that Laura took of her to find a good headshot for the play's program. "They're going to Micah's parents for Hanukkah and want me to come."

"Oh," Laura said, expressing her disappointment. "Well, his parents are super-sweet, I love hanging out with them. Maybe you should go."

"Yeah, maybe. But Minneapolis is cold as shit, and I wanna get some stuff from my room if my mom hasn't donated it already."

"I can send your stuff," Laura offered reluctantly, knowing it would make Eve's absence all the more real. "Or maybe you can do both?"

"Maybe," Eve said, rubbing her fingers together to indicate that she didn't have a job anymore and flying around the country for the holidays wasn't exactly free. "Or maybe . . . Montréal."

Laura stared at her friend with blank uncertainty, and then Eve finally shared the cryptic text exchange her father had initiated. Laura felt even more conflicted between the need to protect Eve from further disappointments, versus crimping their possibility of a renewed connection. It was the first time she had no idea how to be supportive, and all she could provide was an elusive, "k."

Eve continued swiping through her photos. She felt a strange and sudden gust push through her when she landed on the image of Liam's luminaria spelling "*HOME?*" on their lawn, just a few months before. She suddenly pictured her mother there, all alone in the living room, standing in front of a pathetic tree with one lonely present waiting in a cardboard box from Amazon.

"I'll come back for Christmas," Eve decided, putting the phone down. It was Eve's job to decorate the tree, and she knew it would be nearly impossible to wait until spring break, or even summer, to see Laura again.

"You mean it?" Laura squealed. She handed the warm lingam back to Eve, who returned it to a small copper tray on her nightstand, next to the orange stone.

From my station in the garage, I could see the light shining from Eve's window. It seemed to emanate from the young women directly, without the need for fixtures or bulbs, and when Eve declared her holiday plans, the girls' shared jubilation added another hundred watts. After a quick internet search to find a spill-proof coffee maker for Judith, they returned to the more important business of determining exactly how provocatively Eve should dress to work on her scenes with George.

Dropping my view down, through the side window I could see a sliver of a man as he walked towards the house, and then away, and then slowly back again. He had arrived partway through the dinner but stayed in the car, a silver SUV with a license plate from Quebec.

Beyond the kitchen and the breezeway, I found the family room window seat framing a thin, pale woman with elegant white curls. She was dressed in a smartly cut, gingerbread-hued suit. A gold-stemmed pin with opal petals was affixed to the lapel. Even from across the yard, I could see her eyes, the color of the earth from space. They were buoyant, tender, and unassailable.

Muriel was in the family room listening to the muffled giggles and exclamations that drifted through the ceiling above her, the whispers from the kitchen, and Lem and Cindy's snoring on the other side of the house. She absorbed the abundant musicality of her lively home and celebrated the simple art of being there, once again, to feel it.

The other grandchildren and their friends, fiancés, and loves had all retired to their respective quarters, both in the large house and across town, but Kubrick stayed with her, lazing on his bed near the struggling embers of Sam's fire and dreaming of fallen table scraps.

When there were too many photographs for the stairwell to contain, long rows of encyclopedias had been cleared from the bookshelves to accommodate the overflowing memories. Muriel's gaze swept across the eclectic assortment of frames: Ira was there with his big-lobed ears and twinkling eyes, needing a haircut. Lem was there, in athlete form from his early college days, the time between then and now a quiet flash. Sandra was there, with her hair piled high and an eyeshadow color Muriel remembered mildly disliking. And Grace was there in khaki pants and a white shirt held tight by her backpack straps. She stood in front of a Ganesha temple made of marble and she held a small polished lingam in one palm and a stone in the other while Ira snapped the picture.

I watched as Muriel took these images into her mind before she turned and slid her fingers along the nearby piano's long, smooth edge and settled onto its black wood bench. Mr. Clifton had taught her about the pedals, beginning with the una corda on the left. "It shifts the action," he said, "so you're striking fewer strings. That calms everything down." Muriel's feet had barely reached the floor at the time, but she stretched to try it out while he thunderstruck the keys. "Isn't that nice?" he said in a hushed voice. "All you have to do is press a pedal to make the world a little softer."

The middle sostenuto pedal allowed the player to hold her note long after the key was lifted. "We can keep it there, that sound, vibrating in our ears for as long as we want," Mr. Clifton said brightly, "and then, when the time is right, we can set the note free!" He hit a key and Muriel pressed the pedal down. He lifted his hand, and the sound held, as if by magic, like a hummingbird's body floating on unseen wings. It didn't take long for her small foot to ache, and when she lifted herself up, the bird vanished.

"And what about that one?" The little girl pointed down and to the right with great enthusiasm, nearly unable to contain her excitement for what powers the final enchanted lever might possess.

"Ah! That one's my favorite!" Mr. Clifton grinned, and his words seemed to sparkle in the air like diamonds. "The sustaining pedal keeps everything going. It builds up your music like an airplane lifting off the ground—pressing on that pedal gives the piano some real gas!"

"Oh! It's like a car!"

"Yes! It's exactly like a car!"

More than seventy years later, Muriel once again found her posture in front of her instrument, her arms and wrists straight and parallel to the floor and her fingers curved into mounds that held an invisible ball of air. Her left foot was sturdy and flat on the floor, while the right stayed poised on its heel, floating and ready.

I missed her. I missed when she pressed her foot against me, increasing our momentum with the power of two hundred horses. As I watched her through those sheets of glass, I realized she had me, but she also had her piano. And her family. And Eve. Her fingers were in constant motion, connecting her to others, connecting her to life.

I have never touched another car. Not a bump, not a graze, not even the edge of my door colliding with another in a crowded parking lot.

Without their touch, I have no concept of the experience of other cars. I have no idea if they also hold a consciousness like mine. When Muriel and Ira would take me to car shows, or when I would find myself facing other vehicles on a two-lane road, I always looked into their headlights to see if they, too, were aware and attuned to the lives of their drivers. We are descendants of the horse in our purpose and conceit, after all, and certainly the horses of yesteryear knew their passengers as well?

I long to receive some semblance of their thoughts, some shared connection of our sacred spirit and our conviction to protect our passengers, but there is nothing. Still, when I consider we've been around since 1886 and there are over a billion and a half of us on the road today, it seems impossible that I would be the only one.

But perhaps I was the only one for Muriel.

Or because of Muriel.

In about a week, Micah will drain my fluids and prop my chassis on blocks, giving my weary wheels a long-deserved break. He'll disconnect my battery and I'll go into a suspended animation, a hibernation of sorts, where I'll return to a place I haven't seen in years, a place where I'll rest and eventually reemerge to whatever's next with a renewed wonder.

Muriel studied the piano keys, as familiar as my dashboard and Ira's face and the beaches of their past. She found eighty-eight choices leading to infinite possibilities. She extended her right hand over middle *C*. Then her hand mysteriously rose and continued up and beyond her left shoulder as she turned her head to the side. She was reaching for her seatbelt.

Muriel shook her head and laughed at herself. Another gaffe! Maybe she'd remember to write it down for the therapist, who continued to insist she resume the piano. It had been years, too many years, but she played from her heart as much as her mind, and she wasn't sure if she could do it anymore. She readjusted herself and again placed her right foot over the pedal.

She closed her eyes.

I am love, she inhaled, full and deep, the warm air expanding inside her like a broad road reaching the apex of a hill and opening to the view.

Blessings, she exhaled, clearing her mind and opening her bright eyes.

The doorbell rang.

"Eve, it's for you," she whispered, as she pressed the right pedal down to the floor, dropped her fingers to the keys, and began to play.

Acknowledgements

I am humbled by the consistent support and practical contributions that were provided to me during this undertaking.

THANK YOU to the Manhattanville College Workshops and RevitalWriters for getting me from A to B with practical feedback and unyielding optimism: Donna Miele, Maureen Amaturo, Stuart Nagar, Susan Pasquantonio, Martin Foncello, Catherine Moscatt, Kressel Housman, Jessica Hughes, and Stan Konwiser.

THANK YOU to all of the readers and contributors who encouraged its viability and sustained my momentum, with an extra nod to Jennifer Armstrong, Jim Gladstone, Amy Lotven, Chris Millis, Candice Rosen, Wendy Walker, and Nancy Zucchino.

THANK YOU to the indefatigable team at Journey Institute Press who discover, believe, work, shape, guide and inspire. My publishers Michael & Dafna Jenet, and editor Jessica Medberry at InkWhale Editorial LLC.

THANK YOU to the friends and family who consistently checked in. If I name everyone we'll be out of ink for the book itself, but your support is invaluable and you already know you are grafted to my soul.

How far does one extend gratitude? Do I thank the internet and the libraries for their resources? Do I thank the pandemic for giving me extra time at the finish line? Do I thank all of India for its teachings and blessings? Yes, yes and yes.

Most of all, I thank Jon Maximillian Galt, my loving husband, mentor, sounding board and punching bag. It would take another novel to describe his brilliant contributions, his relentless questions and opinions, his wellspring of ideas, and his profound ability to leave me alone with my thoughts to absorb and consider and reconsider. Anything is possible when Jon is on your side—even small miracles, like writing a novel.

ABOUT THE AUTHOR

Michael Jai Grant is an American fiction writer, filmmaker, and photographer. Born and raised in Denver, Colorado, he hails from a lineage of attorneys, teachers, and scientists who profoundly influenced his perception of justice and reason. He subtly interweaves semi-autobiographical elements into narratives of heightened significance. Michael pursued his education at Syracuse and Boston Universities, where he distinguished himself as an Eastman Kodak Scholar. An ardent traveler and a devoted friend to all dogs, he currently resides in North Stamford, Connecticut, with his husband, the artist Jon Galt.

Journey Institute Press

Journey Institute Press is a non-profit publishing house created by authors to flip the publishing model for new authors. Created with intention and purpose to provide the highest quality publishing resources available to authors whose stories might otherwise not be told.

JI Press focusses on women, bipoc, and lgbtq+ authors without regard to the genre of their work.

As a Publishing House, our goal is to create a supportive, nurturing, and encouraging environment that puts the author above the publisher in the publishing model.

Wordbinders Publishing is an Imprint of Journey Institute Press, a Division of 50 in 52 Journey, Inc.